Mike Ashley is a full-time writer, editor and researcher with almost a hundred books to his credit. He has compiled over fifty Mammoth books including *The Mammoth Book of Extreme SF*, *The Mammoth Book of Apocalyptic SF*, *The Mammoth Book of Mindblowing SF* and *The Mammoth Book of Locked Room Mysteries and Impossible Crimes*. He has also written a biography of Algernon Blackwood, *Starlight Man*. He lives in Kent with his wife and three cats and when he gets the time he likes to go for long walks.

Recent Mammoth titles

The Mammoth Book of Weird News
The Mammoth Book of Antarctic Journeys
The Mammoth Book of Muhammad Ali
The Mammoth Book of Best British Crime 9
The Mammoth Book of Conspiracies
The Mammoth Book of Lost Symbols
The Mammoth Book of Nebula Awards SF
The Mammoth Book of Body Horror
The Mammoth Book of Steampunk
The Mammoth Book of New CSI
The Mammoth Book of Gangs
The Mammoth Book of SF Wars
The Mammoth Book of One-Liners
The Mammoth Book of Ghost Romance
The Mammoth Book of Best New SF 25
The Mammoth Book of Jokes 2
The Mammoth Book of Horror 23
The Mammoth Book of Slasher Movies
The Mammoth Book of Street Art
The Mammoth Book of Ghost Stories by Women
The Mammoth Book of Best New Erotica 11
The Mammoth Book of Irish Humour
The Mammoth Book of Unexplained Phenomena
The Mammoth Book of Futuristic Romance
The Mammoth Book of Best British Crime 10
The Mammoth Book of Combat
The Mammoth Book of Quick & Dirty Erotica
The Mammoth Book of Dark Magic
The Mammoth Book of New Sudoku
The Mammoth Book of Zombies!

THE MAMMOTH BOOK OF
Time Travel SF

Edited by Mike Ashley

RUNNING PRESS
PHILADELPHIA · LONDON

Constable & Robinson Ltd.
55–56 Russell Square
London WC1B 4HP
www.constablerobinson.com

First published in the UK by Robinson,
an imprint of Constable & Robinson Ltd., 2013

A copy of the British Library Cataloguing in Publication
Data is available from the British Library

UK ISBN: 978-1-4721-0025-2 (paperback)
UK ISBN: 978-1-4721-0026-9 (ebook)

1 3 5 7 9 10 8 6 4 2

First published in the United States in 2013 by Running Press Book Publishers,
A Member of the Perseus Books Group

US ISBN: 978-0-7624-4939-2
US Library of Congress Control Number: 2012942539

9 8 7 6 5 4 3 2 1
Digit on the right indicates the number of this printing

Running Press Book Publishers
2300 Chestnut Street
Philadelphia, PA 19103-4371

Visit us on the web!
www.runningpress.com

Printed and bound by CPI Group (UK) Ltd, Croydon, CR0 4YY

INTRODUCTION: TIME AFTER TIME   vii
Mike Ashley

CAVEAT TIME TRAVELER   1
Gregory Benford

CENTURY TO STARBOARD   5
Liz Williams

WALK TO THE FULL MOON   18
Sean McMullen

THE TRUTH ABOUT WEENA   45
David J. Lake

THE WIND OVER THE WORLD   83
Steven Utley

SCREAM QUIETLY   117
Sheila Crosby

DARWIN'S SUITCASE   129
Elisabeth Malartre

TRY AND CHANGE THE PAST   143
Fritz Leiber

NEEDLE IN A TIMESTACK   151
Robert Silverberg

DEAR TOMORROW   170
Simon Clark

TIME GYPSY   198
Ellen Klages

THE CATCH   228
Kage Baker

REAL TIME   253
Lawrence Watt Evans

THE CHRONOLOGY PROTECTION CASE   258
Paul Levinson

WOMEN ON THE BRINK OF A CATACLYSM   282
Molly Brown

LEGIONS IN TIME   316
Michael Swanwick

COMING BACK   343
Damien Broderick

THE VERY SLOW TIME MACHINE   365
Ian Watson

AFTER-IMAGES   387
Malcolm Edwards

"IN THE BEGINNING, NOTHING LASTS . . ."   401
Mike Strahan

TRAVELLER'S REST   419
David I. Masson

TWEMBER   437
Steve Rasnic Tem

THE PUSHER   453
John Varley

PALELY LOITERING   470
Christopher Priest

RED LETTER DAY   515
Kristine Kathryn Rusch

ACKNOWLEDGEMENTS   533

INTRODUCTION: TIME AFTER TIME

Mike Ashley

We all travel through time but for most of us (there may possibly be exceptions) we move ahead a second, a minute, an hour at a time, day after day, month after month. We can't move any faster or slower, or go back in time, other than in our memories.

Yet that desire to somehow shift out of time and move ahead faster or backwards is surely in all of us. I suspect most of us have wished we could go back and relive an event, either because it was such a happy moment or, quite the reverse, a moment we wish we could change or eradicate completely.

But we can't go back and we can't speed up and move ahead of everyone else. We are trapped in our moment in time. And the fact that we are prisoners of time is what makes us all the more fascinated with breaking free.

This anthology contains twenty-five stories that consider all aspects of time. Many feature not just journeys into the past or the future, but the consequences of travelling in time. What happens if you try to change the past? Would it be possible and, if so, would it set up a series of alternate timelines each stemming from some modification? And if that happens, how would you ever get back to your original time?

The stories also consider the mystery of time itself. After all, what is time? We are all aware of it, especially if it seems to be rushing past or dragging, but do we really know what it is? And would meddling with time set off other consequences, maybe slow it down, or stop it all together, or even set it running backwards? Maybe we would become trapped in an endless loop of time running round and round, as in the film *Groundhog Day*.

Writers have been fascinated with time for centuries. It has been the subject of thousands of science-fiction and fantasy stories, novels and films, most famously with H. G. Wells's *The Time Machine* (1895), but even earlier than that. I shall mention some of the classic works of time travel throughout this book as I introduce each story. For this volume, however, I have concentrated on relatively recent stories, mostly from the last ten or twenty years, featuring some of the more unusual and original treatments of time and all its mysteries. There is one new story, by Simon Clark, written specially for this book. Most of the other stories have seldom been reprinted so should be new to many readers.

The stories cover all aspects of time and the consequences of any attempt to manipulate it so it is my hope that you will find stories that are not only diverse in their approach but also raise questions that are not easily answered and which will linger in your mind long after you have finished reading. And maybe that will bring you back to the subject and the stories time after time.

Mike Ashley

CAVEAT TIME TRAVELER

Gregory Benford

Gregory Benford is Professor of Plasma Physics and Astrophysics at the University of California, Irvine, as well as the internationally acclaimed writer of such science-fiction classics as In the Ocean of Night *(1976),* Across the Sea of Suns *(1984) and, of particular relevance here, the award-winning* Timescape *(1980). In that novel scientists in the near future attempt to send messages into the past to warn scientists of the ecological and political disasters to come.*

The following story, though, is a light aperitif to get us in the mood and prepare us for some of the problems likely to beset the unwary time traveller.

He was easy to spot – clothes from the 21st Century, a dazed look, eyes a bit rattled.

I didn't have to say anything. He blurted out, "Look, I'm from the past, a time traveler. But I get snapped back there in a few minutes."

"I know." They stood in a small street at the edge of the city, dusk creeping in. Distant, glazed towers gleamed in the sunset and pearly lights popped on down along the main road. Jaunters always chose to appear at dawn or dusk, where they might not be noticed, but could see a town. No point in transporting into a field somewhere, which could be any time at all, even the far past. Good thing he couldn't see the city rubble, too. Or realize this was how I made a living.

His mouth twisted in surprise. "You do? I thought I might be the first to come here. To this time."

I gave him a raised eyebrow. "No. There was another last week."

"Really? The professor said the other experiments failed. They couldn't prove they'd been into the future at all."

They always want to talk, though they'd learn more with their mouths closed.

He rattled on, "I have to take something back, to show I was here. Something—"

"How about this?" I pulled out a slim metal cylinder. "Apply it to your neck five times a day and it extracts cancer precursors. In your era, that will extend your average lifetime by several years."

His eyebrows shot up. "Wow! Sure—" He reached for it but I snatched it back.

"What do I get in exchange?" I said mildly.

That startled him. "What? I don't have anything you could use . . ." He searched his pockets in the old-fashioned wide-label jacket. "How about money?" A fistful of bills.

"I'm not a collector, and those are worthless now, inflated away in value."

The time jaunter blinked. "Look, this is one of the first attempts to jump forward and back. I don't have—"

"I know. We've seen jaunters from your era already. Enough to set up a barter system. That's why I had this cancer-canceller."

Confusion swarmed in his face. "Lady, I'm just a guinea pig here. A volunteer. They didn't give me—"

I pointed. "Your watch is a pleasant anachronism. I'll take that." I gave him the usual ceramic smile.

He sighed with relief. "Great—" but I kept the cylinder away from him.

"That's an opener offer, not the whole deal." A broader smile.

He glanced around, distracted by my outfit. I always wore it when the chron-senser networks said there was a jaunt about to happen. Their old dress styles were classic, so they weren't prepared for my peekaboo leggings, augmented breasts and perfectly symmetric face. The lipstick was outrageous for our time, but fit right into the notorious 21st Century kink.

He raised a flat ceramic thing and it whirred. Taking pictures, like the rest. They still hadn't learned, whenever this guy came from.

"Your pictures won't develop," I told him with a seemingly sympathetic smile.

"Huh? They gave me this—"

"You've heard of time paradoxes, yes? Space-time resolves those nicely. You can't take back knowledge that alters the past. All that gets erased automatically, a kind of information cleansing. Very convenient physics."

Startled, he glanced at his compact camera. "So . . . it'll be blank?"

"Yes," I said crisply. My left eye told me the chron-senser network was picking up an approaching closure. I leaned over and kissed him on the mouth. "Thanks! It's such a thrill to meet someone from the ancient times."

That shook him even more. Best to keep them off balance.

"So how do I get that cancer thing?" he said, eyes squinting with a canny cast.

"Let me have your clothes," I shot back.

"What? You want me . . . naked?"

"I can use them as antiques. That cancer stick is pretty expensive, so I'm giving you a good deal."

He nodded and started shucking off his coat, pants, shoes, wallet, coins, cash, set of keys. Reached for his shorts—

"Never mind the underwear."

"Oh." He handed me the bundle and I gave him the cancer stick. "Hey, thanks. I'll be back. We just wanted to see—"

Pop. He vanished. The cancer stick rattled on the ground. It was just a prop, of course. Cancer was even worse now.

They never caught on. Of course, they don't have much time. That made the fifth this month, from several different centuries.

Time was like a river, yes. Go with the flow; it's easy. Fight against the current and space-time strips you of everything you're carrying back – pictures, cancer stick, memories. He would show up not recalling a thing. Just like the thousands of others I had turned into a nifty little sideline.

The past never seemed to catch on. Still, they stimulated interest in those centuries where time jaunters kept hammering against the laws of physics, like demented moths around a light bulb.

I hefted the clothes and wallet. These were in decent condition, grade 0.8 at least. They should fetch a pretty price. Good; I needed to eat soon. Time paid off, after all. A sucker born every minute, and so many, many moments in the lost, rich past.

CENTURY TO STARBOARD

Liz Williams

The oldest concept in fiction dealing with time is that of being able to step outside of time and exist in a separate time frame. The idea became most closely associated with the world of faery and there are many children's tales, such as Ludwig Tieck's "The Elves" (1811), where children enter the world of faery for just a few hours or days and return to their own world to find that years or centuries have passed. The following story, redolent with a feeling of dislocation, uses a similar idea to take us way out of time.

Liz Williams is a British writer more closely associated with fantasy than science fiction, though her first novel, The Ghost Sister *(2001), skilfully blended fantasy imagery with a solid science-fiction setting involving settlers seeking to solve the mystery of what happened to a planet's original colonists. Williams is probably best known for her Detective Inspector Chen novels, which began with* Snake Agent *(2005), where her Singapore detective has to fight all manner of supernatural foe. The following story has previously appeared only on the internet and this is its first publication in print.*

Vittoria Pellini, Diary entry, 12 August 2008

Julio and I went down to the port today, to see the Ship for the first time. It's truly amazing – I had no idea how big it would be. The hull, if that's what you call it, must have been hundreds of feet up from the water, and I couldn't see the other end at all. Not surprising, since it's supposed to be a mile long, but even so . . .

We flew into Singapore from Rome this morning – Julio had to see some people, so we thought we'd combine his business, whatever that is, with a visit to the Ship. After all, in only a few months, it's going to be our home. Rome's so hot these days, with all these climate changes, and the villa in St Barthelemy's been simply *unliveable* in. So, as I said to Julio, it really does make sense to go and live on something that can move around all over the place. I know it's costing a few million, but it isn't as though we can't afford it – and there's the whole tax avoidance issue, of course. And if the brochure's anything to go by, the shopping will be *wonderful* – the latest seasons will be showing, and as I told him, I'll really be saving on all the airfares, because it costs so much to go to New York these days, now that they've brought in the flight restrictions. So the Ship definitely makes sense. Julio muttered something about people saying the same thing about the *Titanic*, but he just likes to grumble. It's his ulcer.

Diary entry, 14 November 2008

Back in Singapore again, and this time we've actually been on board. I'm just so thrilled. We've seen our apartment, and it's a dream, it really is. It's twice the size of our place in Monaco, and the furnishings are beautiful – exactly as I told the design consultant, and you know how hard it is for these people to get things right. It's high up, too – right on the uppermost deck, just as we wanted. There are gardens below, and swimming pools, and full satellite links so Julio can work. I can't wait, but I'll have to, because the Ship doesn't set out until May. That's nearly six months away, and I'm going to go crazy in Italy.

Diary entry, 3 May 2009

Our first night on the Ship – we're sailing tomorrow. Julio and I have been getting to know our new neighbours, the Seckers – really, really lovely people, even if they are Americans. But not ostentatious – old money, you see. Well, old money for the States, anyway. Originally from Seattle, but they got out before the quake (obviously!) and since then they've been living in Houston. Said it was horribly hot. Commiserated.

Diary entry, 4 May 2009

Sailed today. Just fabulous, seeing all those thousands of people lined up on the dock to see us off. I didn't even realize we were moving, and neither did Lydia Secker, though she says that she's always been as sick as a dog on every boat she's ever been on and she's told her husband that if the Ship starts making her throw up, she's going right back home to Houston, firestorms or no firestorms.

Diary entry, 16 August 2009

Can't believe it's been a year since we first saw the Ship. I was a tiny bit worried that I might get bored here, but what with all the travelling I've just been so busy. And there's the salon, and then the shops – and I'm learning Japanese! Made quite sure that Julio was listening when I told him this as I'm getting just a little tired of that "you're hardly an intellectual, darling" line of his.

We're out into the Pacific now. The sea looks just like my Versace silk camisole, but apparently we're expecting a storm later on. We've been through a typhoon already, off Manila. I thought I'd be terrified, but actually it was quite exciting, and we couldn't feel it at all – the Ship's big enough to ride out even huge hurricanes.

(*Later*) They were right. We're in the middle of the storm now, and I'm looking down on these enormous waves. Feels safe in here, though. It's very quiet – we're totally soundproofed. I just went out on deck – couldn't resist – and the funny thing is that it's quiet out there, too. I thought there'd be howling winds and everything, but it was really silent. I suppose we must be in the eye of the storm or something.

Diary entry, 17 August 2009

Storm's still raging outside. I got up this morning when the alarm went off, because I'd booked in for a facial with Sylvie, and even though it was half past ten it was dark as pitch outside. Julio's been up since eight, trying to get through to the Network, but he says it's down.

(*Later*) Went out on deck again a few minutes ago and I was wrong – it isn't entirely dark. There's a kind of pale green light along the horizon, like a neon strip. Maybe we're coming out of the storm.

Diary entry, 18 August 2009

Storm's finally over, thank God. Not that I was scared, exactly, but it was so weird, seeing that faint light and then nothing else. Now, the sea's calm as a pond again, lovely blue sky. Apparently we're not far off Honolulu now, so they're going to put into port later today. Ship's communications are still down.

(*Later*) Well, we're in Honolulu, but I think something's wrong. Lydia and I called the purser and asked if we could hire a cab to go into the city, but they're not letting anyone off the Ship. They won't say why. And we can see the city from the deck, but it doesn't look right. It looks almost as though part of it has been bombed. Some of the apartment blocks are like ruins and I can't help thinking of terrorists. There's been so much of that lately. Just horrible. I ran back inside and asked Julio if he could find out what was up, but the Network won't come on.

Diary entry, 19 August

Ship left Honolulu last night, when everyone was asleep. Woke to find that we were back out at sea, and still no computer. Julio went down to complain to the communications people, and I went with him. Asked what had happened in Honolulu, but they wouldn't tell us. Julio thinks they didn't actually know, but they must do, mustn't they? We think we've figured it out, though – it must have been a volcano. That's why the city looked such a mess, and why the storm lasted so long. Must have been ash. Bit worrying, though – do volcanoes affect the sea bed? And I was looking forward to Hawaii, too. The communications guy says we're heading up to Tokyo.

Julio went quiet in the elevator and I finally winkled it out of him – he's wondering how long we've got provisions for. Told him not to be totally ridiculous; the Ship's massive; we must have food for years. Julio said not so sure – the whole point about luxury accommodation like this is that the food's freshly flown in; we've seen the helicopter landing every day, and now it's not coming, for some reason. Never mind, I said, there's a helicopter on board, isn't there? And if that doesn't work we'll just have to catch lobsters. Anyway, I'm sure they've got stuff on ice.

Diary entry, 23 August

Never fully realized before now how dependent Julio's business is on the damn Network. The system's still down. Says he's losing millions by the day. He can't even check the stock market, because we haven't got television, either. Really is a bit of a bore. No one's got DTV, and we're running out of things to talk about. Thank God for disc-clips, but I've already watched most of it and have fallen back on old Audrey Hepburn movies.

Earlier, a whole bunch of us went down to talk to the Captain, but all he says is that we'll be in Tokyo later today and he'll answer our questions then.

(*Later*) Well, so much for Tokyo. We couldn't even dock. Half of it looks as though it's slid into the sea, just like poor old Seattle two years ago. Must have been an earthquake right across the Pacific. Julio thinks maybe some kind of giant tidal wave. When he said that, I had to sit down. Asked him why we didn't feel it – surely a wave that ruins half a city would affect even this big boat? But Julio didn't know, and neither do I. We ate in the restaurant tonight. Quality of entrees definitely gone downhill.

Diary entry, 25 August

Talk about insult to injury. Got the most awful cold. Had it for days; we've even had the doctor up here. Said it was just a cold, though. Julio says it comes from prancing about on deck in middle of monsoon. Probably right. We're sailing to Hong Kong, now. Wondered aloud to doctor if we couldn't put in somewhere a bit closer, but he says there aren't that many harbours deep enough to contain the Ship, and Hong Kong's the nearest.

(*Later*) It just gets worse and worse. Julio says he's been talking to the purser and there's another storm on the way. I'm sitting this one out in bed.

(*Later*) Storm has hit. Like the last one. Quiet, and with the light, like morning on the horizon, all the time.

Diary entry, 28 August

At last, Hong Kong. Pulled in very early in the morning – storm didn't last as long as one before. Made me feel better, though I've still got this horrible cold. Went out on deck with Julio. When we last went to HK, about ten years ago now, someone (think Angelo's sister) said when I next came back I wouldn't recognize it – constant rebuilding and renovation. Well, Angelo's sister certainly hit the nail on the head! I mean, HK always had huge tower blocks, but these ones are *colossal*, and they've built all these little transparent bridges between them, like shutes. Also they've moved the airport again – saw a huge plane coming in over other side of the Peak, and I'm sure the airport used to be out near Lantau.

As we were coming into port Lydia came marching up and said, "Vittoria, nothing is going to stop us going shopping!" Few people are brave enough to stand between Lydia and Miucci Belloni's shoes, and I read (*Vogue*, of course) that the RetroPrada's really good here, too, so I agreed. Anyway, though I love the Ship, it'll be good to get off it for a bit.

(*Later*) Well, we got into HK. And this is hard to write, because I don't understand what's happened, not really. Lydia and I had to force our way past the purser, but nothing can stop Lydia when she's hell-bent on shopping – she nearly knocked him into the dock. There were cabs waiting on the quay, and we got into one, but there was no driver. A voice kept asking us for our slots (what does that mean?), and eventually we just got out and walked. Took a long time, too, and it was so hot. Remember HK as muggy, but this was boiling. Could see cars going along the road and they were very quiet, and small – one person only. Cute. Finally broke a heel – my best lime Manolos – and I couldn't stop sneezing. People kept looking at me as though I was mad. Can't think why.

Then Lydia and I got lost. Ended up in some back alley somewhere, and all these people started staring at us. Lydia asked where the nearest metro was, because I was still sniffling. And they answered, but we couldn't understand them. Definitely speaking English, I think, and they were obviously trying to be helpful – anyway, we staggered about and eventually we came out on to the quay. I said we ought to go back, because by that time I was starting to worry that the Ship might leave without us. So we did. And by that time we were both really hot – it was just too much. I mean, Rome was a furnace, and Lydia's from Texas, for God's sake, but this was like nothing else. Just shows this climate thing is getting way out of hand.

As we were trudging back to the Ship, something flew over-head, like a great big wing. There were lights along both sides. After that we saw a lot of little, quick objects darting through the air, towards the Ship. And I couldn't help wondering – I know it sounds crazy – but things seemed so different here. I asked Lydia if she'd seen a place that sold newspapers, but there didn't seem to be anywhere at all.

Eventually we got back to the Ship. I've never been so glad to be anywhere in my whole life, even if the Captain did yell at us. I suppose he had a point. Anyway, I cried. Couldn't help it. My feet hurt so much, and I spent the rest of the day on the sofa. When I got up again, we'd already left port. But Julio said that there were lots of little boats around the Ship, and he'd never seen anything like them – it was as though they were flying just above the water. He'd seen the big thing, too – he said it looked like a *Time* report of a suborbital aeroplane he'd seen, but he hadn't known they'd actually built it. I suppose we were concen-trating on the Ship, and I'm not really interested in that kind of thing, anyway.

Diary entry, 18 September

More storms. We've been at sea for days. And Julio thinks they're rationing the food, because the choice in the big deli on Deck 3 is really terribly limited now. When we were a day out of HK, before the storms really hit, we saw more of the flying things, and we were all asked to stay inside our apartments. Julio thinks the Captain had some sort of warning. I finally got my head together and told Julio what I thought – that maybe, just maybe, we've gone through some kind of slip in time, like the Bermuda Triangle, only in the Pacific. I know other people sometimes say – just to be spiteful – that I'm maybe a little bit of a bimbo, and Julio tends to laugh at me sometimes. Affectionately, of course. But this time I really thought he'd laugh, and he didn't. He said other people were saying the same. I didn't feel so stupid, then. But what if we have? How will we know? I know there's been all the climate stuff, but the world you understand, that you were born in, is just – there, isn't it? You don't expect it to change, not really. Not when you're as rich as we are – I mean, Julio and I have always said that we're international citizens, we can live anywhere. And it seems that now, we are.

Diary entry, 19 September

Captain called everyone together this morning in the banqueting hall and told us that we were going back to Singapore. Finally admitted that our rations were running low. He didn't say what was going on. Said that the crew didn't exactly know, but they were working on it. I could see from his face, though, that he did know, or at least suspect. I know it's awful, but I am actually quite proud of myself for figuring things out even if I might be wrong, and I wanted to say so, ask the crew something about where, or when, we might be. But then I looked at the people around me, and they all looked scared, and worried. And thinner, though I suppose that's not a bad thing in most cases.

I thought, if I say something, the crew probably won't be able to do anything about it and anyway, people won't have any hope then, will they? They'll just be more afraid. So I didn't say anything.

I went out on to deck later, even though the captain had told us not to. I looked up at the sky, and it had changed. It was a deeper blue than I've ever seen it before, almost green, and the sun burned like a big star on the horizon. And I thought, perhaps the future isn't so bad after all. At least it's beautiful.

Diary entry, 24 September

I suppose in a way it's easier for women than for men. Not eating, that is. After all, I've always dieted. Well, you have to, don't you, and none of these new metabolic pills really seem to work properly – and I'm used to it, but men get so *grumpy*. The crew have taken one of the hydrofoil launches out, and started fishing. I don't even know what sort of fish you get here. Another day and we'll be back in Singapore.

Diary entry, 25 September

Came into harbour this morning, and it really is different. The whole city's changed. The tower blocks have all fallen down, and the jungle's grown over them, but there are new houses along the water's edge – they look as though they've been built from scraps and waste. But there were people lining up along the dock, just as there were when we left. I saw the crew go down the gangplank, and everyone crowded on the lower deck. I thought I'd avoid the mob, so I went around the other side of the deck. And a boat drew up – a long, thin boat with a girl in it.

 She climbed up the side of the Ship, quick as anything. I didn't stop to think. I grabbed her arm. "Listen," I said. "Please, can you tell me? What's the date?" She just stared. Her arm felt like wire in my fingers, and her face was thin, too, and all eaten away. It was horrible. I let her go. "The date!" I said, "Please?" She touched a little box on a thong around her throat, and spoke. I didn't understand the language – I don't speak Malaysian or whatever it is. But the box said, a moment afterwards, "What did you say?" So I repeated it, and she stared at me. "You are from the past, aren't you? The legends are true, about the spirit ship." "The past?" "It is 2863," the girl said, wonderingly. "There have been stories in these seas for nearly a thousand years, about the great boat, how it comes, and brings the storms with it, and disappears." I just gaped at her. I couldn't say anything at all. She clasped my hand. "Have you come with a cure?" "A cure? For what?" "For the sickness, the skin-rot." The box buzzed and hummed, distorting her voice. "My *voice* is very old," she said. "They don't make them any more." She tapped the box. I must have looked blank, because she went on impatiently, "Two hundred years ago, the world was without illness. Little machines had solved sickness. The blood-takers have told me this. Everyone was well; we were about to fly to the stars. But then a new plague came; no one knows how. It started in a great city in the north. Within twenty years, millions were dead, and the starships left with the refugees, the ones who could pay. People died in the streets, with blood coming from their noses. And this city fell down and was never properly built again."

I looked at her, helplessly. "I'm sorry," I said. "I haven't got a cure. I don't think I can help you. But there's a doctor on board. Perhaps he can do something." I led her down to the medical bay, but the doctor made me go back upstairs. I argued and argued, but he and the nurses pushed me out and locked the door. An hour after that, the Ship pulled out of port and the green city was left behind.

I didn't see the girl again. But when I saw that we were leaving, I went back down to the medical bay and demanded that the doctor tell me what was wrong with her. He said that he didn't really know, that it was a disease he'd never seen before, but when the computer analysed it, the closest match was just an ordinary cold, like the one I'd had in Hong Kong. I told the doctor what the girl had said, about a plague. "How could a cold kill so many people?" I asked. "If the virus had time to mutate, or if it was introduced to a group of people who had no immunity to it," he said. He sounded tired. "The Spanish settlers brought all sorts of things with them, when they reached the New World. Thousands of the Aztecs died from ordinary diseases – measles and the flu. After all, the cold virus is linked to some terrible diseases, like Ebola. It wouldn't take much for it to do serious damage, in the right circumstances." "Why wouldn't people have natural immunity to it?" I asked. But I knew the answer as soon as the words were out of my mouth, and so did he. I could see it in his face. It was because we were no longer in our own time, not where we belonged. We were lost, and wandering, and dangerous to those we moved among. I went slowly back upstairs. I felt suddenly, strangely old. When I looked out of the arching window of the apartment, I could see a line of light on the horizon, faint and green.

Diary entry, 29 October

I suppose it's stupid now to label these entries with the date, since we don't even know when we are anymore, but it makes me feel as though I've got something to hang on to. The last storm was a bad one, lasting for over a week. Julio and I didn't talk much, just shuffled between the banqueting hall and the apartment like two old people. We're going to have to start planning what to do, how we're going to live. The captain called us all together last night and finally admitted that we'd become time travellers – a sort of *Flying Dutchman*, luxury class. They don't know how it happened, and they don't think we'll be able to get back again. They've tried contacting a whole lot of places by radio, but if there's anyone out there with the technology to hear us, they don't seem to be listening.

We're going to have to decide whether we stay on the Ship, or put into port and take our chances in this new world. And if we stay, then we can no longer be the spoon-fed idle rich any more. We're going to have to sustain ourselves, somehow. We managed in Singapore by bartering – the crew exchanged luxury items like cutlery, along with basic medical supplies, for food. But the Ship isn't a limitless resource. The crew are talking about converting one of the garden decks into a place where we could grow food, and they've been fishing. So maybe we won't starve, but it won't be as comfortable as it used to be. I talked to a lot of people after the meeting, and they seem to want to stay. I think they're too scared of what might lie beyond the Ship. I know I am.

Diary entry, 3 January

The blisters on my hands hurt. I'm not used to gardening. We didn't have one in Rome, and at the villas there was always someone to plant seeds and prune flowers. But now I spend hours on the garden deck, patiently slipping seeds into soil.

After the last storm, we could see that the sky had changed again – a deeper, darker blue. The Ship put in at what used to be Manila, but there wasn't anything there, just green, wild islands. We've crossed the Pacific now, and are sailing down the coast of

California. The sea level's risen. San Francisco is a ruin. We've seen no people. The Ship stopped and some of the crew took the helicopter up. They have to be careful with fuel, but they said they got as far as Salt Lake City. There's no sign of anyone, just desert and scrub and forest. As though no one had ever been here.

Diary entry

Up near what was once Vancouver, we finally found someone – an old woman, living alone on an island. The Captain spoke to her, but he couldn't understand a word she said, and she couldn't understand him, either. But she showed him a news-sheet – just a slip of what looked like homemade paper. The language had changed, but they figured some of it out. It was very old. It said that most people in America were dead.

· We left some people there, including the Seckers. They said they knew the area, having lived in Seattle once, and they might as well stay. But some of us – a couple of hundred people – are remaining on the Ship. We told them we'd come back in a month or two, to see how they were getting on. No one mentioned the storms. I was tempted to stay with them, but Julio wants to stay on the boat. It's strange – he seems happier these days, and his ulcer's gone. The old woman gave me a lot of seeds: zucchini, peppers, tomato. I keep going down to the garden deck and looking at them, to see if they've come up yet.

I've given up trying to record the date. It doesn't seem important any more, and I've been too busy with the gardens to keep track, or even write very much. When we were up near Alaska, we hit another storm, and afterwards, we sailed back down the coast. Even the old woman's island was gone. There was no sign of anyone else, and the forests looked different – plants I didn't recognize, with odd lobes and spines. The sky has changed again, too, and that evening I looked up at the clear sky and I've never been very good with stars, but they seemed different, somehow.

Julio and I went ashore in the morning, and when we walked back to the Ship we could see what a wreck it looks. Its white sides are scored and scratched, and my vines have spilled over the edge of the deck. We're wondering how much longer we'll actually stay afloat.

The crew have been thinking the same thing. Tonight, they're calling together those of us who are still here, to decide whether we're to head back to California, and try to settle, or whether we go on.

I don't know how I feel, and I thought I would. It'll be a relief in a way, not to keep travelling. When we started our voyage, I thought it would be such fun, but I never dreamed we'd sail so far. But I looked up into the unfamiliar sky last night and I wondered how it would be if we just kept on, running the time storms, until we sailed right out of the world's time and off the edge. And I wondered, too, if we were perhaps the last people living on Earth; destroyers and regenerators, like my gardens that grow and green, and fade again into the dark.

WALK TO THE FULL MOON

Sean McMullen

*Almost as old as the concept of time dislocation is the idea of a
time-slip where somehow an individual may suddenly slip from
the present into the past or the future. Edgar Allan Poe suggested
this might be achieved by hypnotism, or mesmerism as it was
known in his day, in "A Tale of the Ragged Mountains" (1844).
More recently Octavia Butler used a psychic link to establish a
connection between her heroine and a distant ancestor in
Kindred (1979). The following story also considers how the
power of the mind might create the ability to shift through time.*

*Sean McMullen is an Australian writer and IT specialist
who has been selling science fiction and fantasy since 1986. He
is probably best known for his eccentric post-apocalyptic
Greatwinter series which revels in the imagery of steampunk.
The first two novels were revised and reissued as one book,* Souls
in the Great Machine *(1999). Time travel features in several of
McMullen's short stories, some of which have been collected in*
Call to the Edge *(1992) and* Walking to the Moon *(2007).*

Meat was bought at a high price by the Middle Pleistocene
hominids of the Iberian Peninsula. Large prey meant more
meat, yet large prey was very dangerous. The pressure to hunt
was unrelenting, for the hominids were almost entirely carnivo-
rous, but they lived well because their technology was the most
advanced in the world.

It is unusual for a linguist to be called for in a murder investigation, especially an undergraduate linguist. Had my uncle Arturo

not been in charge, and had I not been staying at his house at the time, I would not have become involved at all. He told me little as he escorted me into the Puerto Real clinic and took me to a meeting room.

On a monitor screen was a girl in a walled garden. Crouching in a corner, she had a fearful, hunted look about her. I could see that she wore a blanket, that her skin was olive-brown, and that her features were bold and heavy. Oddly enough, it took a while for me to notice the most remarkable about her: she had no forehead!

"Who – I mean *what* is she?" I exclaimed.

"That's what a lot of people want to know," replied my uncle. "I think she is a feral girl with a deformed head. She was found this morning, on a farm a few kilometers north of here."

"Has she said anything?" I asked, then added, "Can she talk?"

"Carlos, why do you think I called you? This is in a clinic where the staff are quite good at dealing with foreign tourists who don't speak Spanish, but his girl's language stopped them cold."

"So she does speak?"

"She seems to use words; that is why you are here. Before you ask, she is locked in the walled garden at the centre of the clinic because she can't stand being indoors. We need to communicate with her, but we also need discretion. Someone senior in the government is involved. DNA tests are being done."

I was about to commence my third year at university, studying linguistics. Being continually short of money, I would drive my wreck of a motor scooter down to Cadiz every summer, stay with my uncle, hire a board and go windsurfing. By now I owed Uncle Arturo for three such holidays, and this was the first favour he had asked in return. My mind worked quickly: love child of government minister, hit on the head, abandoned in the mountains, DNA tests being done to establish the parents' identity.

"There are better linguists than me," I said.

"But I know I can trust you. For now we need total discretion."

I shrugged. "Okay, what do I do?"

"She must be hungry. When a blackbird landed in the garden she caught it and ate it. Raw."

I swallowed. She sounded dangerous.

"Maybe you could help her build a fire, roast a joint of meat," my uncle suggested.

"Me?" I exclaimed. "Cook a roast? I've never even boiled an egg."

"Well then, time to learn," he laughed, without much mirth.

It turned out that I had three advantages over the clinic's staff and my uncle's police: long hair, a beard and a calf-length coat. It made me look somehow reassuring to the girl, but it was days before I realized why.

I entered the garden with a bundle of wood and a leg of lamb. The girl's eyes followed me warily. I stopped five metres from her and sat down. I put a hand on my chest and said, "Carlos." She did not reply. I shrugged, then began to pile twigs together in front of me. The girl watched. I reached into a pocket and took out a cigarette lighter, then flicked it alight. The girl gasped and shrank back against the wall. To her it probably looked as if the flame was coming out of my fist. I calmly lit the twigs, slipped the lighter back into my pocket, and piled larger sticks on to the fire.

My original plan had been to roast the meat, then gain the girl's trust by offering her some. I placed the leg in the flames – but almost immediately she scampered forward and snatched it out.

"Butt!" she snapped, leaving no doubt that the word meant something like *fool*.

I shrugged and sat back, then touched my chest again and said, "Carlos." This time she returned the gesture and said, "Els."

Els stoked the fire until a bed of coals was established. Only now did she put the joint between two stones, just above the coals. Fat began to trickle down and feed the flames. We shared a meal of roast lamb around sunset and by then I had collected about two dozen words on the Dictaphone in my pocket, mostly about fire, meat, and sticks. Els began to look uneasy again. I had made a fire, I had provided meat, and it was fairly obvious what she expected next.

I stood up, said "Carlos," then gestured to the gate and walked away. The perplexity on Els's face was almost comical as I watched the video replay a few minutes later.

"What have you learned so far?" asked my uncle as the debriefing began.

Two other people were present, and had been introduced as Dr Tormes and Marella. The woman was in her thirties and quite pretty, while Tormes was about ten years older.

"Firstly, Els trusts me a little," I pointed out.

"I thought she was supposed to accept you as another prisoner," said my uncle.

"She doesn't understand the idea of being a prisoner," I replied. "She calls me Carr. Loss is her word for fire. For her 'Carlos' seems to be 'Carr who makes fire'."

"So, you made a fire after introducing yourself as a firemaker," said Tormes.

"Yes. All her words are single syllable, and she has not spoken a sentence more than five words long. Intonation and context seem important in her language, though."

"You say language," said Uncle Arturo. "Is it a genuine language?"

"It depends what you mean by genuine. Any linguist could invent a primitive language, but Els has a fluency that would only come with years of use. Do we know *anything* about her?"

My uncle glanced to Tormes and Marella.

"Els is just a feral girl with a severely deformed skull," said Tormes. "Perhaps she was abandoned in the mountains while very young, and animals reared her."

"Animals could never have taught her such a language," I replied. "Animals don't have fire, either."

They glanced uncomfortably at each other, but volunteered no more information.

We let Els spend the night by herself, then at dawn the three orderlies were sent in to seize her. Moments later I entered the garden, loaded with more firewood and meat, and armed with a sharpened curtain rod. I made a show of driving off the orderlies after an extended bout of shouting, and fortunately Els did not seem to have any concept of acting. I was treated like a genuine hero as we settled down to another day together. While we talked Els began to make stone knives and scrapers out of the garden's ornamental pebbles. She even charred the end of my curtain rod in the fire and scraped it into a lethal-looking, fire-hardened point. Again I left her at sunset and went through a long debriefing with my uncle, Marella and Tormes.

"If Els was raised by wild sheep or rabbits, how did she learn to make stone tools and fire-hardened spear points?" I asked with undisguised sarcasm.

"We are as puzzled as you," replied Tormes calmly.

On the morning of the third day I returned with a newly slaughtered sheep. Els skinned and butchered it with great skill, using her newly made stone knives and scrapers. It was only now that Els actually approached me. Coming around to my side of the fire, she rubbed mutton fat through my hair, then pinned it back with seagull feathers. By now I had learned to say "Di," which seemed to cover both *thanks* and *sorry*. Over the next half hour, she made me understand that although I was skinny, she thought I was very brave to go hunting at night.

At the debriefing on the fifth day I had an audience of a dozen people, two of whom I recognized from the Department of Anthropology in the university in Madrid. It took only a minute to walk the tens of thousands of years from the garden to the committee room.

"I now have over a hundred words," I reported. "I can communicate with Els fairly well, and she has answered a few questions. She talks about a tribe. They call themselves the Rhuun, and they have *always* lived here."

"What?" exclaimed Tormes. "Impossible."

"I'm only telling you what Els said. They have a detailed calendar, and a counting system based on the number twenty."

"Ten fingers and ten toes," said Marella.

"Did she do your hair?" asked one of the new observers.

"Yes. Grooming seems to be a bonding ritual for the Rhuun, and possibly a precursor to sexual activity as well," I explained.

"So she made a pass at you," laughed my uncle. Nobody else laughed.

"She has been removed from her tribe for the first time in her life," I added.

"Then you are her new provider," said Tormes. "She may be feeling insecure because you are not mating with her."

This time a few snickers rippled around the table.

"Look, this was not in the job description," I said to my uncle, scowling.

"Besides, she might be disappointed," he replied, and this time everyone really did laugh.

"From now on you will return to her after a couple of hours each night, and pretend you were lucky with your hunting," Tormes hurriedly advised, seeing the expression on my face. "Just having you nearby at night should gain her trust."

"But seriously, stay on your own side of the fire," advised my uncle. "Technically she's is a ward of the state, and probably a minor."

When the meeting broke up Marella and Tormes invited me to join them for a coffee before I returned to Els. Wearing my long coat over jeans and a T-shirt, but with my hair still greased and pinned back with seagull feathers, I felt quite out of place. The café was over the road from the clinic, and was about as sterile. Most people think of Cadiz as a pretty little port with more history than some countries, but this was Puerto Real, the messy industrial fringe of the holiday city that visitors barely notice as they drive through. Whatever the setting, it was my first filtered coffee for many days and I was very grateful for it. I also ordered a large salad. A man named Garces joined us, but he said little at first.

"There's more to Els than you think," said Tormes after I ordered another cup.

"You underestimate me," I replied.

"What *do* you think?"

"Had they not been extinct for thirty thousand years, I'd say she was neanderthal. Even her stone tools look very like what I've seen in museums."

"Not neanderthal," said Marella.

"Sorry?"

"Els's tools are relatively primitive, more like those of the neanderthals' ancestor species, homo heidelbergensis," Tormes explained.

"I don't know much about paleo-anthropology," I said, although I knew that half a dozen species of hominids have lived in Spain over the past two million years.

"The heidelbergensians were around for six hundred thousand years," said Tormes, as if he was speaking for a television documentary. "They were the first hominids to use advanced technology like clothing, artificial shelters and probably language. There is a cave in the north called the Pit of Bones where they even ritually disposed of their dead. They lived in an ice-age environment that would have killed any hominid that did not use clothing. They were once the brightest people ever, and they had the most advanced technology on Earth for longer than homo sapiens has existed. Their cranial capacity actually overlapped with the modern human average, but they were also phenomenally strong."

I had by now noticed that Els could break branches that were way beyond my strength. Perhaps there was more to this than a hoax.

"You talk as if Els is a real cave girl," I said casually.

"She is," said Garces.

At this point a waiter arrived with my second coffee. I took a few sips while the waiter cleaned up and removed some cups and dishes. My mind was screaming that Garces was mad, yet he lacked the manic enthusiasm of genuine nutcases. He almost looked unhappy. The waiter left, skilfully balancing a pile of plates and cups on one arm.

"The girl's DNA is not human," Garces continued. "True, it has more in common with human DNA than that of an ape, but there are not enough base pairs in common with human DNA for her to interbreed with, say, yourself."

"Take that back!" I snapped, already near my limit with this onslaught of weirdness.

"Sorry, sorry," he said at once. "I have been rather unsettled by all this, and . . ." He scratched his head. "Look, what I have found is impossible, but I have done my tests in good faith. The base pair comparisons that I ran give Els's DNA more in common with that of neanderthals than homo sapiens, but examination of DNA mutation sites and rates suggests that she could be from the neanderthals' ancestral species."

"There was also semen found on a vaginal swab," said Tormes.

"Indeed!" said Garces. "Its DNA was of the same species. Els's husband, lover or whatever is another heidelbergensian. He is also a blood relative, from perhaps three generations back, but this is not unknown in small and isolated tribes."

There was silence as I sipped my coffee. Almost before I knew it, my cup was empty. I was expected to say something, apparently.

"Genetic engineering was around in the early 1990s, when Els would have been born," I suggested, seriously out of my depth and well aware of it.

"Balls," replied Garces wearily, as if he had heard the suggestion too many times over the past few days. "That's like saying that Nazi Germany put men in space, just because they had primitive rockets. Even today we can't engineer genetic changes on the scale found in the subject's DNA."

"Her name is Els," I insisted.

"Yes, yes, Els. Whatever her name, she—"

"She's the victim of some cruel genetic hoax!" I began angrily.

"Haven't you been listening?" Garces demanded, banging his fists on the table.

"Yes, and to get back to your analogy, the Nazis flew at least two types of manned rocket, and they drew up designs for manned spacecraft as well. I saw a documentary on television, the Nazis put rockets into space big enough to carry a man—"

"All right, all right, Nazis in space is a bad analogy," he conceded, waving his hands. "The point is that we have *never* had the skills to make the massive changes to human DNA that I have observed in, er, Els. Yes, we could fool about with bits and pieces of the genome and clone the occasional sheep in the 1990s, but not create a new race – or should I say re-create an old one."

"But Els is a fact," I insisted. "Genetics only proves—"

"This isn't *just* genetics!" said Garces sharply. "Els has stepped straight out of the Middle Pleistocene! She has practically no radioactive contaminants in her tissues from bomb nuclear tests or the Chernobyl fallout. Her levels of industrial contaminants like dioxin also suggest that she had been eating food grown in this century for only two weeks."

"I don't understand," I admitted.

"Els and her tribe are genuine," said Marella. "That girl in the clinic across the road is an ice-age hominid; she is *from* the ice age."

That was a conversation stopper, if ever there was one. For a time we sat staring at each other, saying nothing. The waiter returned. We all ordered more coffee.

"Are you willing to put that in a press release?" I asked once we were alone again.

"Young man, if I had been unfaithful to my husband I would not want it in a press release, whether it was true or not," interjected Marella, almost in a snarl. "Not unless it was a matter of life and death, anyway. Before we all go making fools of ourselves with public statements, we need to know Els's side of the story."

Tormes looked particularly uncomfortable, and Garces squirmed. Marella glared at me until I stared down at the table. She was clearly used to taking no nonsense from any man, whether plumber or prime minister.

"All their pelt cloaks are new sheepskin, and their scrapers are new," said Tormes. "Their spears have been cut from modern hawthorn stands."

"You mean you have evidence of a whole tribe?" I exclaimed.

Yet again there was silence. Tormes had said too much in the heat of the moment.

"I think we have said enough," suggested Marella coldly. "Carlos, what do you have to say about Els – as a linguist?"

I was annoyed but cautious. The body language displayed by Tormes and Garces suggested that they were treating Marella very carefully. Her face was familiar, in a way that a face glimpsed countless times on television might be.

"Five days is not enough for a truly informed assessment," I explained first. "Els's language is primitive yet highly functional. It's adequate to coordinate a hunting party, pass on tool-making skills, and so on. She actually has a word for 'ice', even though there is no naturally occurring ice in the area—"

"That's significant," exclaimed Marella. "She may remember an ice age. Did she talk about bright lights in the sky, or flying things? Strange men with god-like powers?"

"No. She has no concept of gods and spirits. She doesn't even have words to describe what she's seen here in Puerto Real over the past five days."

"We must teach her Spanish," said Marella.

"No!" cried Tormes firmly. "She is our only window on Middle Pleistocene culture; she must not be contaminated. She will be kept with you, Carlos, well away from the rest of us."

"My marriage and reputation are at stake!" exclaimed Marella.

"Marella, Els is bigger than—"

"And your position at the university is *certainly* at stake," Marella warned.

"What else do you have to tell us, Carlos?" asked Garces hurriedly.

"Well, nearly a third of Rhuun words are devoted to arithmetic, their calendar, the seasons and the passage of time. Els can understand and name numbers up to a hundred thousand, and she even understands the concept of zero."

"So?" asked Marella impatiently.

"Zero is a very advanced concept, it has only been around for a few centuries," I explained.

"On this world, anyway," said Marella. "The rest of you may be too frightened to talk about aliens, but *I* am not."

Within minutes I was back in the Middle Pleistocene, dumping another dead sheep beside the fire. I had been bringing in the firewood wrapped in blankets belonging to the clinic, and I now found Els had made a simple, tent-like shelter from them. The heidelbergensians had invented artificial shelters, Tormes had said. I fed a few branches into the fire, then lay down beside it, wrapped in a spare blanket. Looking up at the stars, I recalled that I had not slept in the open since a school camp five years ago. Although I did windsurfing and rode a scooter, I am not the outdoors type and I prefer to sleep under a roof.

I gave a start as a hand touched my shoulder. Els! She moved as silently as a cat on carpet. Settling beside me, she said

"Crrun." The word meant something like fellow hunter, tribesman, and family member all in one, but this time her intonation was softer, almost a purr. Perhaps the Rhuun also stretched it to cover sweetheart and lover.

Aware that a video camera was recording everything, I gestured to the space between me and the fire. Els lay down, staring anxiously at me. Perhaps she was terrified that I had not mated with her because I was planning to abandon her. Only a few metres away a dozen anthropologists were gathered around a video screen, and were probably laughing. Els began to draw up the hem of her cloak. I seized her hand hurriedly.

"Els, Carr, crrun," I assured her, then added that I was tired from a difficult hunt.

The words transformed her. Frightening and dangerous this place might be, yet a male had now declared crrun with her, whatever that really meant. I was also a good hunter, and I liked to talk. After staring up at the stars for a while and reciting something too fast for me to follow, she eventually pulled my arm over her, pressed my hand against her breast and went to sleep.

The next morning Els began to make me a cloak out of the sheepskins that had begun to accumulate. This was apparently the only form of Rhuun dress, but it was immensely practical and versatile. In an ice-age winter it would have also provided the wearer with a sort of mobile home as well as a sleeping bag. Instead of sewing the skins together, she pinned them with barbed and sharpened hawthorn twigs. I made a big show of being pleased with it.

Because Rhuun words were short, simple nouns and verbs, strung together with rudimentary grammar, we were able to communicate adequately after only days. Intonation was important too, but that was far harder to learn. My theory was that Rhuun words, which were generally guttural, had developed to blend in with the snorts, grunts and calls of the animals they hunted. The hunters might have stalked wild sheep under the cover of their pelt cloaks, smelling like sheep themselves and calling to each other with bleat-like words.

On the other hand, the mathematics of the Rhuun calendar was quite advanced for a nomadic, stone-age tribe. The Rhuun might have developed their own, simple language, then come in contact with members of a very advanced society and copied ideas like counting and calendars. Els had no grasp of nations, laws or even machines. To her all machines were animals. She knew nothing of tame animals, either. To her all animals were either prey or predators.

That evening Marella was not at the debriefing meeting. Most of the discussion revolved around the way Els fastened the sheepskins of my cloak together, and how this might have been the birth of clothing. Tormes approached me later, as I sat alone in the clinic's cafeteria.

"Eating another salad?" he asked.

"Els is more of a carnivore than we humans," I replied, "but *I* can't get by on meat alone."

"She seems to be taking a shine to you."

"I like her too. She has a strangely powerful charisma."

"And pleasantly firm boobs?"

"That too. I appear to be her mate, even without consummation."

"Would you consider staying with her, say for a trip to Madrid?"

"Madrid?"

"For her unveiling, so to speak. As her companion."

Appearing on television in a sheepskin cloak was not an appealing prospect,

"There are far better linguists than me," I pointed out.

"But she really trusts you. You would gain a lot of favour with some very powerful people. Some would even like you to screw her, to research Middle Pleistocene sexual practices."

I closed my eyes and took a deep breath.

"Look, this is grotesque!" I snapped. "Just who are you? Do you think you can—"

"I am a professor of anthropology, Carlos, and I recognize what Els represents. A genuine archaic hominid, straight out of the Pleistocene."

I shook my head.

"Apart from Els herself we have no other evidence."

"We do have other evidence, Carlos; we just don't understand it. Last year I made a strange find, in what had once been the bed of a shallow lake. It was a collection of stone scrapers, knives and hand-axes."

"So?"

"So similar sites have been found since then. It's as if a tribe of heidelbergensians just dropped everything they were carrying and vanished."

"They probably dropped everything and ran when something frightened them," I said. "A bear, maybe."

"Possibly, but that's not the point. The site I found was seven thousand years old, four *times* more recent than the last neanderthal and a quarter of a million years later than homo heidelbergensis was around."

Reality began to waver before my eyes. I was sitting in a table in a clinic, wearing a Middle Pliocene hairstyle, eating a salad, and engaged to a heidelbergensian girl.

"There are some odd folk tales told in this area," Tormes continued. "Huge monkeys with spears, enormously strong wild men who kill cattle, that sort of thing."

"Are you serious?" I exclaimed. "A lost tribe of cave men in southern Spain? This is not even a wilderness area. There's little to hunt, apart from . . . well, okay, quite a lot of sheep and cattle."

"I said we have evidence, not an explanation."

I munched the last of my salad.

"I must get back to Els," I said as I stood up.

"Marella and I are – were – having an affair," Tormes suddenly but unashamedly confessed. "We were on a field trip, looking for excavation sites. When we found Els . . . well, our cover was compromised. Marella's husband is a minister in the government, and the government cannot afford scandals in the current political climate."

So there was no love child, but there *was* a sex scandal.

"Where do I fit in?" I asked.

"Els is to be made public. Very public."

"She will be terrified."

"You can make it easier for her by remaining her translator

and companion. There will be a lot of money and fame in it for you as well. You need only do one questionable thing."

"And that is?"

"Pretend to be Marella."

I agreed. The story was very simple, and the most important part was already on videotape. I had supposedly contacted Tormes about doing voluntary field work at a site called the Field of Devils, just north of Cadiz. We met had six days earlier at the farm of a man named Ramoz, and I had been videoing for two hours when Els had first appeared.

"We are about to watch the most important part of the video that Marella shot," said Tormes as we sat with Marella and Uncle Arturo in the darkened committee room. "A version has been made without the soundtrack. We shall say that you were inexperienced with the camera and disconnected the microphone."

"Why?" I asked.

"Because *my* voice can be heard," said Marella icily.

The screen lit up, showing scrubby pasture and hills. It was fertile, windswept country and a bull was visible, grazing in the long grass. Suddenly Marella zoomed in on a group of people dressed in cloaks and carrying spears. They were stalking the bull. The scene might have been straight out of the Pleistocene had the bull not been wearing a yellow plastic ear tag.

The hunters worked as a team, and there were three men and a girl. We watched as they stripped off their cloaks, then approached the bull naked. Their hair was drawn back and pinned with feathers. The men positioned themselves in long grass and crouched down. The girl collected some stones, then cautiously approached the bull. She flung a stone, which went wide. The bull ignored her. She hit it with her next stone. It looked up, then returned to cropping the grass. The next stone struck the bull just above the eye. It charged. The girl dropped her other stones and ran for the ambush site. The bull slowed, snorted, and then returned to its grazing.

"They're re-enacting a stone-age hunt," came Marella's voice.

"Why bother recording it?" replied Professor Tormes, disgust plain in his voice. "They're doing so much wrong, I don't know whether to laugh or cry."

"But it's a lot of fun," Marella said as she panned back to take in the overall scene. "They must be actors, practising for a documentary."

"Maybe. Their consistency people can't be there, or they'd be screaming about the bull's plastic eartag."

"There are no camera crews yet, they must be practising."

"Well as a re-creation of neanderthal hunting it has more holes than a block of Swiss cheese. I mean look at the girl trying to goad the bull into chasing her by throwing stones. It's all wrong."

"Why?"

"Neanderthals didn't have projectile weapons."

"But even monkeys throw stones."

"Bah, that's just behaviour learned from watching us humans," scoffed Tormes. "Real neanderthals would drive the bull to the hidden hunters, not let themselves be chased. As for the spears! Neanderthal spears had stone tips; those are just pikes with fire-hardened points."

I turned to glance across at Tormes. He was squirming in his seat.

"I presume that they cleared this with the man who owns this land – and the bull," said his voice from the speakers.

"Well, yes. Ramoz is a bit excitable," Marella agreed. "We should go down and warn them."

"Not with that bull running loose and no fences to stop it."

The bull looked up warily as the girl approached again, armed with another a handful of rocks. She shouted and waved. The bull stared at her. She flung a rock, hitting it squarely on the nose. The bull bawled angrily and charged, and this time it did not break off the chase as the girl fled. Although she was fast and had a good start, the bull closed the gap between them quickly as she ran for the ambush site.

"Well now what?" Tormes's voice asked. "They can't kill the bull—"

Even as he spoke, the naked three men erupted out of the grass and drove their spears into the flanks of the bull as it charged past them. Far from defeated by the initial attack, the animal turned on the hunters. Now two boys who had been hiding nearby ran up with fresh spears, and the leader worried at the bull's face with his spear while the other two men attacked its flanks and hind legs. After suffering perhaps a dozen spear wounds the bull's hind legs gave way, and then the end came quickly.

"I don't believe this!" Tormes exclaimed. "That bull is part of a prize breeding herd."

"Was," said Marella.

We could now hear the tones of a cellphone as Tormes punched in the number for the police operations centre. He described what had happened, there was a pause, then he reported to Marella that there were no re-enactment groups or documentary crews in the area. On the screen, a hunter jumped on to the bull's carcase and waved a spear high in triumph.

"The police said there's a military helicopter in the area, and they're diverting it to these GPS coordinates. That group is definitely illegal."

"So Ramoz does not know that one of his stud bulls is the star of a documentary on neanderthal hunting?" Marella asked.

"Apparently not. The police said to stay out of sight until they arrive."

"I'd better stay out of sight even after they arrive," said Marella.

"Yes, your husband might not react sympathetically."

"Pity. My tape could make the television news: the last neanderthals, arrested for poaching and taken away in a helicopter."

"Your tape must vanish without trace, preferably into a fire."

With the bull dead, several women, girls and children arrived at the kill. The hunters put their cloaks back on and sat down to rest. Using what appeared to be stone knives and scrapers the group began to butcher the carcase. They were efficient and skilled, and it might have even made a convincing picture had it not been for a woman with the cigar and the bull's bright yellow eartag. The children started gathering wood, and presently the smoker used her cigar to start a fire. They began to roast cuts of the bull.

"I later found the cigar; it turned out to be a roll of leaves and grass used for starting fires," Tormes explained to me.

"Els has told me she is a 'hunt boy', even though she's a girl," I explained. "Apparently boys began their apprenticeships as hunters by being decoys who lure dangerous game back to the tribe's ambush."

"That makes sense," said Tormes. "There were several children in the tribe, but the only teenagers were girls."

"Like in all societies, women could become honorary males in times of sufficient need," added Marella.

From the speakers I could now hear the sound of an engine. The tribe suddenly grew fearful and huddled together. The engine stopped.

"The police?" asked Marella's voice. "Already?"

"No, they were sending a military helicopter," explained Tormes. "Wait a minute! Someone might have called Ramoz to double check if he knows about those fools."

There was a distant gunshot. The camera swept giddily up to the top of a ridge, where a figure was waving a gun and shouting.

"Ramoz," said Tormes.

The farmer worked the pump action of his shotgun then fired into the air again. The camera swept back down to the carcase, but there was now nobody visible. Marella tracked Ramoz as he came running down, his shotgun held high. He reached the kill site, dropped his gun, waved his hands at the carcase, then at the fire, then at the sky. Finally he fell to his knees, clutching at his hair.

"He looks upset," commented Marella.

"I hope those idiots stay hidden," said Tormes's voice quietly.

"Real risk of a homicide here," agreed Marella. "Stay low. If he spots us he might think we were involved."

"If he kills someone *we* certainly will be involved. I can see the headlines now: MINISTER'S WIFE AND LOVER WITNESS MURDER. Stay silent. I'm calling the police again." There were more cellphone tones. "Cadiz, Tormes again. We have a dangerous situation. The farmer has arrived, armed with a shotgun. Yes, he's really distraught. No, he's hugging the head of the dead bull. The hunters have fled, but—"

At the edge of the screen the decoy girl stood up and waved her arms. She was again naked. Ramoz snatched up his gun and shouted something incoherent. The girl presented her buttocks to him. This was too much for the farmer. He levelled the gun and fired. The girl went down.

"Cadiz, we have a fatality!" Tormes cried.

Ramoz ran through the grass to where to girl had fallen. Suddenly spear-wielding hunters boiled out of their cover and lunged at him. The shotgun boomed one more time, then there were screams. The men stood over the fallen Ramoz, and their spears seemed to rise and fall for a very long time. The women and children arrived and gathered around the girl's body, wailing.

"Cadiz, we have two down now, both presumed dead."

Now there was the sound of another engine and the whirr of rotor blades, just as Ramoz's head was lifted high on a spear point. The field of the camera suddenly gyrated crazily.

"Cadiz, tell the pilot to home on the plume of smoke from the campfire," Tormes called above the sound of Marella retching. "No, that's just the sound of my assistant being sick."

Marella had dropped the camera, and the screen just showed out-of-focus grass. The video was stopped, and my uncle stood up.

"Nothing more of interest was recorded by Marella's camera," he explained. "The helicopter landed, and the crew found the mutilated body of Ramoz lying beside a naked girl. Luckily for her, the shot missed, but she hit her head on a rock as she stumbled and was knocked unconscious. There was no sign of the tribesmen who killed Ramoz."

"I left the field at once, and drove back to Cadiz unseen," said Marella. "The trouble is that dozens of people have now heard replays of the phone call where you can hear me vomiting and José talking about his assistant."

"I was taken out on the helicopter," said Tormes. "Carlos, we can say that you panicked about being left alone with the killers still loose, so you fled the scene."

"Two guards were left there, but they were wearing camo gear and were not easy to see," said Marella.

"It is a lie, but no harm is being done," said Uncle Arturo.

I nodded, but said nothing. In a year or two he would suddenly be given some very significant promotion. It was the way of the world.

"Everything that the Rhuun used or wore during the videotape we have just seen was just dumped," said Tormes. "They stripped naked and fled."

"Presumably wearing jeans and T-shirts," said my uncle.

He started the tape again, and a scatter of stone axes, spears, scrapers, and pelt cloaks appeared on the screen, marked off by police cones and crime-scene tape. The scene switched to an archaeological dig, showing a very similar scatter of stone tools.

"This has happened before, here," concluded Tormes.

"What has?" I asked.

"I am open to suggestions," said Tormes.

The video ended with footage of Els waking up in the clinic, and of three burly orderlies having a great deal of trouble restraining her. The heidelbergensian girl was at least twice as strong as a modern man. She could win an Olympic medal for weightlifting, I thought, but would she be banned for not being human enough? The others now left, and I sat watching replays of the extraordinary video to fix the story in my mind. As my uncle had said, it was a lie without victims. I made a necklace of paperclips as I watched. Presently Marella came back.

"I have come for the tape," she announced. "Seen enough?"

"I have a good memory," I replied. "It's in the job description for a linguist."

She folded her arms beneath her breasts and strutted around the table, looking down at me haughtily. I knew what she was going to say.

"I should have had the credit for that video," she said.

"That credit comes with a very high price tag," I replied.

"True, but I have lived in my husband's shadow for too long. Being part of this discovery will bring me fame, and I *will* be part of it. The story will be that I came to the clinic with a head-ache, saw Els being restrained, and was told by staff that she was just a badly deformed girl. I noticed that she had a very strange language, so I contacted some experts at a university."

"Better than nothing," I said.

Suddenly Marella sat on my lap, put her hands behind my head and stared at me intently. There was neither affection nor lust in her expression, but in mine there was probably alarm. She jammed her lips against mine, then pushed her tongue between my teeth. After some moments she pointedly bit my lip, then stood up and walked back around the table again, her arms again folded.

"I can do anything to you, Carlos, remember that."

Els was strong, Marella was powerful. I had not taken Marella sufficiently seriously, but, like Els, I had never met anyone like her. She removed the cassette from the video player.

"Try to cross me, try to rob me of my role in this discovery and I shall produce this, the original tape, sound and all. Remember that."

She left. Like Samson, she was both powerful and vindictive enough to destroy everyone concerned with Els, including herself. Power is a product of our civilization, but one can have it without strength. Suddenly I felt a lot closer to Els.

I got no sleep that night, which was taken up with learning my role as Tormes's supposed volunteer, and learning my lines. A press release about Els had been prepared and distributed by Marella, who was very good at publicity and knew all the right contacts. Just before dawn I looked through a clinic window, and was immediately caught by the beams of half a dozen spotlights. Security guards and police were already holding a line on the clinic's lawns. Tormes came up behind me.

"There is to be a press conference on the lawns," he said. "The Cadiz authorities want a share of Els before she is taken away."

"Professor, the very idea of a press conference is a quarter million years in her future!" I exclaimed. "What do they expect?"

"You can translate."

"No I *can't*. I can barely communicate—"

"Well try! Els is a star. Already we're getting offers for movie contracts and marketing deals."

"Marketing? For what? Stone axes? Or maybe hide cloaks?"

"Carlos, use your imagination: *She came a quarter of a million years for Moon Mist fragrances* has been suggested—"

"Tell me you're joking!" I cried. "I can't permit this."

"You have no choice. You signed a sworn statement that you were my volunteer assistant, and that you shot the video of Els's tribe killing Ramoz and his bull. Now get her ready to be a media star."

"How?" I demanded. "She could – she *will* – get violent."

"So? Good television."

A pinpoint of hate blazed up within me. He was powerful, but he had no strength. He could hurt Els, and I was her only defence. I could hear the distant crowd like the rumble of an approaching thunderstorm as I stepped back into the walled garden. Els called to me, then ran up and took my hands. She pressed them firmly against her breasts. I managed a smile. This was a obviously a bonding gesture, meant to remind me of the pleasures of staying with her. She was strong, yet powerless . . . and had neither strength nor power. I presented my necklace of paperclips to her, but was not surprised that she was more perplexed than delighted. She had no concept of ornamentation at all. Her hairpin feathers were functional; they merely kept hair out of the way during the hunt. I put the necklace around her neck. She scratched her head.

"Har ese," I said, lacking any words for lucky or charm. *Good hunt.* To my surprise Els suddenly smiled broadly.

"Di," she replied, then added "Carr iyk har."

A couple more questions revealed that although har meant "good" and ese meant "fight or hunt", when said together and quickly they meant "luck in hunting or fighting". So, the Rhuun had a concept of good and bad fortune, yet there were many other things for which Els had no words. Metal, wheel, god and press conference were all unknown concepts for her. I heard the approach of the helicopter that was to whisk us away to Madrid. There was certainly no heidelbergensian word for that. The sound made Els fearful, but I held her hand.

"Els, Carr rak," I explained. *Els and Carr are going to flee.* She immediately brightened at the prospect. "Hos," I added. *Follow* and pointed to the door.

"Thuk ong," she said fearfully. Death cave. To her the interior of the clinic as a dangerous cave.

I tried to explain that she was about to see frightening things, but that they would not hurt.

"Carr lan?" she asked.

Lan meant both help and protect.

"Carr lan," I replied, but I knew that I had a problem.

In the Middle Pleistocene, anything that was frightening was dangerous too. The idea of fear for a thrill did not exist. The idea of a thrill did not exist, either. To be frightened was to be in mortal danger. In the distance I could hear the sounds of sirens and an increasingly large crowd. Els was like some huge cat, a dangerous predator who was stronger and more of a carnivore than I, but for all that she was curiously vulnerable.

She followed me into the clinic's interior, holding my arm tightly and cowering against me. The lights had been dimmed and the corridors cleared. We walked briskly. Someone must have told the waiting crowd to be silent, but we could still hear the helicopter's engine. Els kept warning me about cave bears. We walked out through the front doors into daylight – and the waiting crowd roared.

Els panicked and tried to drag me back inside, but the doors had already been closed and locked behind us. Microphone booms, cameras, flashing lights, the helicopter, guards and police with batons, more people than Els had ever seen in her life, even a press helicopter approaching over the rooftops. Els tried to drag me across the lawn. I tried to stop her but she was too strong. Guards broke ranks to block her path and journalists surged through the breach in the line.

"Carr! Tek orr brii!" she shouted.

I dodged around in front of her, pulled my hand free from Els and tried to wave the approaching mob back. There was a loud pop and Els ceased to exist. I turned to see her cloak collapsed on the grass, along with her wooden hair pins scattered, an ankle beacon-circlet, and a necklace of paperclips.

That turned out to be the beginning of a very long day. Garces, Tormes, and Uncle Arturo were near-hysterical, predictably enough. The police already had the area sealed off, but it did them no good. Els had simply been snatched into thin air. Several dozen video cameras had caught the disappearance and although the angles were different, the event remained the same. In one frame Els was there, in the next she was gone and her cloak and hair feathers were falling.

Of all people directly involved, Marella alone was willingly giving interviews. Aliens had snatched Els away, she declared in triumph. Her abduction had been caught on camera. Aliens had brought her to twenty-first century Spain, then snatched away again. To Marella's astonishment, her theory was given no more credence than several others. A public survey favoured a secret invisibility weapon being tested by the Americans, followed by a conspiracy by our own government, a divine vision, alien abduction, publicity for a new movie, and a student stunt.

For the rest of the week forensic teams studied the area in microscopic detail, scientists scanned the area for any trace of radiation, and the lawns became a place of pilgrimage for psychics, religious sects, and UFO experts. I viewed the videos hundreds of times, but there was nothing to learn from it. In one frame Els was in mid-stride; in the next she was gone and her cloak was being blown inwards by air rushing to fill the vacuum where her body had been. Astronomers scoured the skies, observers on the space station scanned near-Earth space on every frequency that their equipment could monitor, and warplanes were almost continuously in the skies over Cadiz, but nothing was found.

A full two weeks later I was going through the folder of papers and statements that I had been given in those last hours before Els had vanished. There was a copy of the absurd marketing proposal for some perfume that Tormes had told me about. *She came a quarter of a million years for Moon Mist fragrances* – and then I had it!

"Carr! Tek orr brii!" she had called to me. *Carr. Walk to the full moon.*

The Rhuun could walk through time. Els had been telling me that she was going to *walk through time to the next full moon.*

For a long time I barely moved a muscle, but I thought a great deal. There was massive development at the rear of Els's brain. Why? For control of movement? For control of some subtle fabric in time itself? Step through time and escape your enemies. Escape famine, reach a time of plenty in the future. Why follow herds of wild cattle when you can wait for them to return by travelling through time? They skipped the long glacial epochs, they visited only warmer periods. The worst of the Saale and Weischel glaciations must have been no more than a series of walks through tens of thousands of years for them. If the hunting was bad, they walked a few decades. If there was too much competition from neanderthal or human tribes, they walked to when they have left or died out.

They visited the Spain of the neanderthals, saw the coming of humans, and saw the neanderthals vanish. *That* might well have made them wary of humans. Three thousand years ago they might even have seen the Phoenicians build western Europe's first port city where Cadiz now stands, then watched as the Iberian Peninsula became part of the Roman Empire. With the development of farms came more trusting, placid cattle and sheep, although there were also farmers to guard them. However, all that the Rhuun had to do was walk a century or so into the future whenever farmers appeared with spears, swords and crossbows. Perhaps Ramoz's shotgun was their first experience of a firearm, so they thought it would not be hard to defend their kill.

Homo sapiens evolved intelligence and had believed it to be the ultimate evolutionary advantage, but there are others. Mobility, for example. Birds can escape predators and find food by travelling through the third dimension. Homo rhuunis can do that by travelling into the fourth. Perhaps human brains are not suited to time walking, just as our hands and arms are better at making machines than flapping like wings. Could a time-walking machine be built? Would Els be vivisected by those wanting to find out?

What to do, how to do it? I felt a curiously strong bond with Els. I had a duty to protect her, and I owed no loyalty to Tormes, Marella or even my uncle. I was already outside the law, yet in a way that gave me a strangely powerful resolve. I had nothing to lose.

Nineteen days after Els vanished I was ready, waiting in a car beside the clinic's lawns. A borrowed police car. My uncle was at home, fast asleep thanks to a couple of his own sleeping tablets in his coffee. His uniform was a rather baggy fit, but I had no choice. Every so often I started the engine, keeping it warm. On the lawns, a dozen or so UFO seekers loitered about with video cameras, mingling with the religious pilgrims, souvenir sellers, security guards, and tourists. People always returned after an alien abduction, so the popular wisdom went, and so those who followed Marella's theory were ready. All but myself were concentrating on the skies, where the full moon was high.

There was a loud pop, and Els was suddenly standing naked on the lawn. Before the echoes of her arrival had died away I set the car's lights flashing, then scrambled out and sprinted across the lawn calling, "Els! Els! Carr lan! Carr lan!"

She turned to me. Everyone else merely turned their cameras on us, not willing to interfere with the police.

"Els, hos Carr!" I cried as I took her by the arm. She did not want to approach the police car with its flashing lights. "Els, Carr lan!" I shouted, not sure if my intonation meant *help* or *protect*. She put a hand over her eyes and let me lead her.

Els had never been in a car before, and she curled up on the seat with her hands over her face. I pulled away from the clinic, turned a corner, and switched off the flashing lights. Two blocks further on, I transferred us to a hire car, and after twenty minutes we were clear of Puerto Real and in open country. Using Ramoz's name I had located his farm in the municipal records, and by asking the locals in the area I had confirmed that the Field of Devils was indeed on the dead farmer's land. It was a fifty-minute drive from the clinic. I had practised the trip several times.

All along Els had just needed help to return to the Field of Devils, help to move through space to where she could walk through time and rejoin her tribe in our future . . . or had she stayed because of affection for me? Whatever the case, she had only resorted to time-walking in sheer terror, when the journalists and camera crews had charged.

My mind was racing as I drove. Glancing down, I could see Els by the gleam of the dashboard lights. In a strange sense, I longed to call Tormes on my cellphone, to tell him what had really happened in the Middle Pleistocene. The heidelbergensians had spawned *two* new species, not just the neanderthals. With the Saale Glacial's ice sheets approaching, the neanderthals went down the tried and true path of increased intelligence, improved toolmaking skills, and a stockier build to cope with the growing cold. Homo rhunnis evolved mobility in the fourth dimension instead. This instantly removed the trait from the gene pool – at least in normal time. Humanity had evolved later, but continued down the same path as the neanderthals.

In the distance I could see a helicopter's searchlight. It was hovering where we were heading: the Field of Devils. I turned off the headlights, slowed, and drove on by moonlight, but the car had already been noticed. The light in the sky approached – then passed by. The pilot was heading for where he had last seen my lights. It gave us perhaps another two minutes. Els could easily escape through time and rejoin her tribe. I would be caught, but what could they do to me?

We were only half a mile from the Field of Devils when the helicopter's searchlight caught the car. I braked hard, opened the door and pulled Els out after me.

"Els, tek var es bel!" I cried in Rhuun as we stood in the downwash of the rotor blades, imploring her to time walk two thousand midsummers away.

"Carr, Els kek!" she pleaded, grasping my arm.

Kek was new to me, but this was no time to be improving my grasp of Rhuun. The helicopter was descending, an amplified voice was telling me to drop my weapons and raise my hands.

"Els, tek var es bel!" I shouted again.

Els stepped out of the twenty-first century.

To me it had all been so obvious. The Rhuun could travel forward in time but take nothing with them. Their skin cloaks and tents, their stone scrapers, axes and knives, and their wooden spears and pins, everything was left behind when the time-walked. Only the person time-walking could pass into the future. What I had forgotten were the babies visible on Marella's video. If babies had could be carried through time, so could adults.

The brightness of the helicopter's spotlight vanished, replaced by the half-light of dawn. I was standing naked, in long grass, with Els still holding my hand. The air was chilly, but there was no wind. Els whistled, and awaited a reply. None came. The rolling hills were luridly green, and dotted with dusky sheep and cattle. It was an arcadia for Pleistocene hunters, but it was not the Pleistocene.

In the distance, great snow-capped towers loomed. The air was clear and pure, and there was silence such as I had never experienced. There was a series of distant pops, like a string of fireworks exploding, and the rest of the Rhuun appeared a few hundred metres away. Els whistled, then waved. Another tribe materialized, then another. Some sort of temporal meeting place, I guessed. Even at a distance, the towers looked derelict, and there should not have been snow in southern Spain. Els was unconcerned. There was game to hunt and nobody to defend it, so nothing else mattered. Taking my hand again, she began to lead me toward the other Rhuun.

In the years since our arrival I have concluded that humanity has ceased to exist, possibly wiped out by a genetically targeted plague, destroyed by a doomsday weapon . . . victims of their ingenuity. I have become a great shaman, inventing a primitive type of writing, the bow, the bone flute, the tallow lamp, and even cave painting, but when I die I shall end nature's experiment with high intelligence – once known as humanity. Sheer intelligence has not proved to be a good survival trait in the long run, and through their fantastic mobility the Rhuun have inherited the Earth.

THE TRUTH ABOUT WEENA

David J. Lake

The idea of having a machine transport you through time had first appeared in a short story, "The Clock That Went Backward" (1881) by Edward Page Mitchell, the editor of the New York Sun. *The use of a clock is perhaps an obvious symbol and was used to considerable effect in the children's novel,* Tom's Midnight Garden *(1958) by Philippa Pearce. The Spanish playwright Enrique Gaspar depicted a machine that was able to move backward in time in* El Anacronópete *(1887), a novella only recently made available in English as* The Time Ship *(2012), which is more a satire on human progress. The man who brought the time machine firmly into literature and who popularized the concept of time travel was, of course, H. G. Wells with* The Time Machine, *published in its final form in 1895. Wells's purpose was to use the story to consider the effects of the changes in nineteenth-century society on the evolution of humans, which he achieved with considerable impact. "A book of remarkable power and imagination," said the* Saturday Review.

The following is as much a treatise on the original Time Machine *as it is a continuation of the story. It provides a valuable analysis of the nature of time travel and raises questions and paradoxes that we shall encounter throughout the rest of this book. David J. Lake is a British writer and academic, born in India, but long resident in Australia, though he was educated in England and studied alongside Wells's grandson, Martin, at Cambridge University. Lake has written a separate novel based on* The Time Machine, The Man Who Loved Morlocks *(1981), but following a course in science fiction that Lake taught at Queensland University in 1990 he began to reconsider Wells's work and produced a novel which he subsequently distilled into the following story, which also introduces us to the concept of alternate time tracks.*

1

"The Time Traveller (for so it will be convenient to speak of him) was expounding a recondite matter to us."

That was how I began my famous story of the Time Machine; the foundation of my success as an author – and of much else beside. That story figured largely, around 1900, in the movement of Household Socialism, and all that *that* led to. The tale was laughed at, praised, used in serious social and political argument – yet by most people was treated as nothing but a fiction. Well, in its hitherto published form it *was* partly fiction, because at the time – 1895 – I could not write the full truth. The full truth was even more fantastic than the fiction – too fantastic, surely, to be believed; or if believed, too disturbing to received notions of Time. And besides, there were living people to protect: in particular, one young person who was very dear to us.

It was agreed, therefore, among our small group that I must abbreviate the ending, and publish the story as a novel, an invention. I did, and the novel served its purpose. But now, in 1934, the time has come (*the* time! a nice phrase; well then, *a* time) in which I can tell the whole truth – of those famous dinner parties in Richmond in 1891, and what really resulted from the second party.

You have met us, the guests, before. My name is George Hillyer, at that time barely known to the world as a minor writer of short stories. Doctor Browne and Ellis the Psychologist had been with us the previous Thursday, October 1. Today, October 8, we had also present the Editor, the Journalist, and the person I formerly called the Shy Man. I practised a little deception there, deliberately putting him well in the background. He was not really shy at all, simply a good listener, slow to speak unless he had something worth saying. He was young, with fair-brown hair and blue eyes; to make himself seem older, at that time he sported a trim little brown beard. He was a mathematical physicist, and he had once been a student under our friend the Time Traveller, when the latter was still a professor at London University.

The party went much as described in my novel. The Traveller was late, and we began dinner without him. We talked of what three of us had seen last week – the big Time Machine nearly finished, and the little model which disappeared. I suggested the Traveller was late now because he was travelling in time. "He left that note, so he must have anticipated—"

"Oh, stuff!" said the Editor. "If he can travel *backward in time*, why should he expect to be *late*? He need only stay on his machine a little longer, coming home – and he could be *early*."

"*Very* early!" The Journalist laughed. "Why, he could get back the previous week – and meet you fellows *last* Thursday."

"Including *himself*!" said the Editor. "Don't forget, he could meet himself too! Then there'd be two of him, one a week or so older than his brother. And, I presume, then there'd be *two* Time Machines! And if he took money with him, he could multiply that as well – a bad look-out for the Bank of England! So you see, it's all nonsense – a gaudy lie, a conjuring trick. There can't be any time travel."

"Excuse me," said the young Physicist. "Your argument holds only against travel backwards in a single time line. I see no objection to forward time travel. We do it all the time – at sixty seconds to the minute. And skipping forward in a machine is no more, logically, than hiding yourself for a while, and then coming on the scene again. It's the logical equivalent of the Rip Van Winkle coma. With clever technology, perhaps he *could go forward*."

"But what's the use of that," said the Editor, "if he couldn't come back?"

Just at that moment the door slowly opened, and the Time Traveller appeared – limping, bloodstained, ghastly. He was a man of middle age, and now he looked older, grey and worn.

He drank his wine, went out, changed, ate dinner, and told us his story. He had spent eight days in the year 802,701, and he had returned.

I need not repeat his story in detail: you have heard it before. In the far future, the human race had split into two species: above ground, the rich had turned into little mindless Eloi, living in a half-ruined fools' paradise; below ground, in caverns and tunnels, the enslaved workers had turned into foul, lemur-like Morlocks – and turned upon their former masters, turned cannibal – if that was the right word – coming out at night, especially in the dark of the moon, to eat the Eloi. He told us of his life among the Eloi: of Weena, the little Eloi girl-woman, blonde and helpless, whom he rescued from drowning when none of her companions would raise a decadent finger to save her; and how at last he had lost her, in a night of fire and torment, with Morlocks all around – lost her to death by fire – or worse. And then he added an episode still more terrifying, the episode of the sun flickering out some thirty millions of years hence.

At that point, the young Physicist objected. "Are you sure about that date, Sir? That sounds like Kelvin, and his theory of the sun's energy – or rather, lack of it. But we don't really know what makes the sun shine. I am working on the structure of the atom; at the sun's enormous temperatures, who knows what strange energies may lurk there . . . Anyway, I've read the geologists. The earth, and so the sun, must have existed for hundreds of millions of years already; and if so, why not hundreds of millions more?"

The Traveller hesitated. "I *think* it was thirty million . . . I must admit, I was rather hysterical after I left the Morlocks. All that Further Vision was like a bad dream."

"Then perhaps," said Ellis, the Psychologist, "that episode of the Eloi and Morlocks was also nothing more than a dream, though a fascinating one. The symbolism—"

"No, no! That was absolutely real. As real as this room! And – I've shown you Weena's two flowers."

The two sad little flowers lay withered upon the table. And we looked at the Traveller's scars.

"I believe you about the Morlocks," said the young Physicist suddenly. "It's exactly in line with present trends. We are really two nations, so why not later two species? And we treat our workers abominably."

"Hear, hear!" I said.

The Traveller smiled wanly. "Thank you, Welles. I know your socialist leanings – yours too, Hillyer – but thank you. As for me, I wish we could simply *abolish* the workers – be served by intelligent machines. Then certainly no Morlocks could evolve."

"But now," said Welles, the Physicist, "what do you intend to do, Sir? You've still got a working Time Machine, haven't you?"

"Go back," said the Traveller.

"Go back in time? To the past?"

"No, go back to the future. I must – I will try again to rescue Weena . . ."

"I'm afraid," said Welles, "there may be a problem about that, Sir."

"You would meet yourself," I said. "Will you wrestle with your former self over who has the honour to save Weena?"

The Traveller looked shaken. "I hadn't thought of that."

"I don't think that would happen," said Welles. "The real trouble, I think, is that you wouldn't get back to the same future."

"There is only one future!"

"No, Sir, there must be at least two. According to your hopes, one future in which Weena dies, another in which you save her. And I think something like that might happen. But not *exactly* that. You see, by coming back and telling us about the future, you have already altered the future. You have reinforced my socialist fears, and I think Hillyer's also. We will now make extra efforts – talk urgently to William Morris, to the Fabians – so the Eloi–Morlock situation may never arise, in *this* stream of time. Time is not really a single stream, a single fixed railway-track from fixed past to fixed future. There are many tracks of possibility, some close together, some far apart. And you have just proved that – by apparently *coming back* from our future."

"*Apparently* coming back. I *have* come back!"

"Not from *our* future Sir, no. From a future which *was* ours until – a moment perhaps two hours ago. When your machine stopped in the laboratory and you dismounted, while we were eating dinner – I think I know the exact moment – that was when you split time, and pushed us onto a slightly different line. Like a railwayman shifting points. We have all been running on a different line since then."

"This is preposterous!" said Doctor Browne. "We didn't feel a thing!"

"I felt dizzy at one moment," said Welles. "A slight *blurring* feeling, about 7.45. It only lasted a fraction of a second. One could easily disregard it."

It struck me then that I had felt it too – I thought at the time I might be going to faint. Nobody else would admit to it.

"Is there a piece of paper handy?" asked Welles. "I need to draw a diagram or two to explain my Theory of Time. It's my belief that backward time journeys are never straight back – always oblique. Otherwise you have circular causation."

Pencil and paper were found, and Welles drew the following sketch:

"This is the happening I deny," said Welles. "A single time-track – which I had to draw rather thick – and you, Sir, going forward to 802,701 and returning to 1891. You see that you have circular causation? For instance, we are not *all* socialists here. Your tale of purely underground workers may strike one or two of us as a *good* idea. They might push it ... Then the Morlocks in the future become the *cause* of the Morlocks in the future – practically, they are *un*caused. Or if you go less far into the future, to the advanced time, you could bring back the secret of some wonderful invention – say, anti-gravity flying machines – and publish it now. Then that invention will never have to be *invented* – the future flying machines would be their own cause. And so on ... That is why I deny any straight returns. This is how I see the true situation."

And he drew:

"You see," he said, "there is no longer any circular causation – there are only zigzags. And 802,701B awaits your next journey, Sir – that would be the dotted line. There is no fear of meeting yourself: because you have never been in 802,701B, only in 802,701A."

"It's still crazy," I said. "What if our learned friend went back a week now, as our newspaper friends suggested – to our last dinner party. Would he meet himself, and us, in that case?"

Welles smiled. "I think he could. The situation would be as follows:

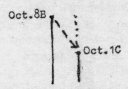

"That gets us a third time track," said Welles, "Track C. On our present track, which is Track B – also on Track A – our learned friend did not turn up last week *because we know he didn't*. Several of you lived through that party, and you know there was only one Traveller, and only one Machine. But on Track C, there is no circular causation to prevent doubling of men or machines. Maybe the conservation laws would have to be modified – one track loses matter, another gains . . . Of course, there would also be a corresponding future on Track C, a year 802,701C. I don't know what it would be like, but it might be exposed to a raid by *two* Time Machines."

"My head is splitting," said Doctor Browne. "All this airy, crazy theory!"

"It need not be only theory," said Welles. "I know it's late, but if we're not too tired to spare, say, another hour, we could experiment."

"Experiment!" said the Traveller, rousing himself. "Why not? But I'm not ready yet for another long time journey . . ."

"No, Sir, I meant short hops, fifteen minutes or so, forth and back. Could you stand that?"

"Certainly, young man!"

"Then let's go, Sir. You know, I've never even seen the Time Machine as yet . . ."

2

We all trooped into the laboratory – and there was the Machine, just as the Traveller had described, in the northwest corner: a little battered, a little stained, but wonderfully impressive. The Editor and Journalist stared and tittered, but Welles was immediately touching it here, touching it there, almost stroking it, and asking technical questions which I for one could not follow. The Traveller answered him.

"*Gravitational* energy?" said Welles at last. "My God, Sir, that – if you can touch *that* you are far beyond anything we now imagine . . . and the conversion factor?"

The Traveller gave him some numbers.

"That means, practically unlimited. You can reach the ends of Time, and only slightly reduce the earth's orbital momentum. Ah, what a glorious device!"

"For my next raid on the Future, however," said the Traveller, "I'll have to install some modifications. An extra saddle, wheels . . . But those can wait. Now, what little experiment do you want, Welles?"

"Can you go forward in time just a quarter of an hour?"

"Yes. I adjusted the fine control as I was returning. Go forward fifteen minutes, and then what?"

"Stay there, Sir. We'll just wait here, and see you reappear."

"Stand well back," said the Traveller.

He mounted his machine, pressed a lever – and vanished! A strong gust of wind blew in at the open window.

We all gaped. "God, what a trick!" said the Editor. "Better than that ghost he showed us last Christmas. I suppose its done with mirrors . . . Well now, now what do we do?"

"We could go back to the smoking room, and return," said Welles. "But I intend to stay right here, watching that empty corner."

We all agreed to stay.

"Don't move from *this* corner," said Welles. "There might be a nasty accident if he reappeared *in* one of us."

We waited. The Psychologist took up a topic he had raised the previous week. "Suppose – he went back to the Battle of Hastings – and then *saved* Harold, won the battle for the Saxons! What then?"

I laughed. "We'd be speaking a different language now, Ellis – something more like German or Dutch, with almost no French roots. And our gracious Queen would probably be called Sieglinde – or something like that!"

"Not at all," said Welles, smiling. "You're on the one-track theory again, Hillyer. No Traveller could affect the Battle of Hastings in *our* time-stream. It can't be done, because we know it *hasn't* been done. But our friend could go back to 1066 in another track – D, would it be? – and then in that stream there would be no Norman Conquest. I have a feeling that there may be very many time-streams, some very similar to our history, some very different. Perhaps these streams are diverging all the time, even without Time Machines ... I don't know. But my guess is, the ones that are very different are inaccessible to our present selves. If our friend were to go back in time and tamper with some version of history – then I'm afraid *we* would never see him again. He could return to 1891 – but it wouldn't be *our* 1891. He would exist for our counterpart selves – the ones speaking Saxon perhaps; but no longer for us."

"Perish that thought!" exclaimed Doctor Browne. "I'd hate to lose him! Even now . . ." He gazed uneasily at the empty corner.

"No, no: no danger. He has simply gone into *our* future; which any minute now will be our present."

A few seconds later, he was proved right. The Machine and the Traveller flashed into existence in the northwest corner. We felt a swirl of air.

"Still there?" said the Traveller, looking cheerfully at us. "Has anything happened? I just pressed the lever a fraction . . ."

"Fifteen minutes have passed," I said. "We had an anxious wait."

"For me," said the Traveller, "it was less than a second."

"Very good, Sir," said Welles. "Now we have proved – for those who aren't too sceptical – that forward time travel is feasible, and involves no paradoxes. But now – would you go forward again, another fifteen minutes – *and then come back*, on the machine, to a point just a few seconds ahead of now? Say, to avoid trouble, to half a minute ahead of the time you leave?"

"This will take fine tuning," said the Traveller, looking at his dials, "but – yes, I will do it. Here goes!"

Again he vanished. This time we had only a few moments to wait. Suddenly I felt dizzy, and I saw the man and the Machine flash back into their place. But now the Traveller looked troubled. He dismounted, and came over towards us.

Welles held up his hand. "Did anyone feel strange, just now?"

"Yes," said Browne, stroking his grizzled beard and looking meditative. "Now you mention it, just as our friend flashed back, I felt a little dizzy."

"So did I," said Ellis.

"And I," I said.

"The splitting of the tracks," said Welles.

"I say," the Traveller began, "what happened to you people? When I dismounted, fifteen minutes ahead, there was nobody – not in here, not in the whole house! I questioned Mrs Watchett. She said you had all gone home. Then I came back in here, got on the Machine, returned – and here you are!"

"Ah well," said Browne, smiling, "I suppose it *is* late, and we *will* depart in the next few minutes."

"No," said Welles, taking out his watch. "*I* am going to stay right here for *twenty minutes*. Why don't you all stay? That way we will prove something important."

His meaning sank in to all of us. "Prove it's all nonsense!" the Editor laughed.

"I–I didn't see you!" said the Traveller.

"No – and you didn't see yourself either, Sir, in this corner. If you'll just wait . . ."

We waited twenty minutes. And nothing whatever happened. The Traveller moved the Machine into the centre of the room. But the far corner remained empty. Everyone looked at their watches, the Traveller consulted the chronometer on his Machine. At last he looked round at us, dismayed. "It – it is five minutes past the moment I arrived and found you gone. Yet – you are *not* gone!"

"And you have not reappeared in the far corner, or anywhere else," I said. "If that had happened, five minutes ago you would have met yourself, too. Evidently, that journey has been wiped out."

"Not *wiped out*—" Welles began.

"I'll settle this!" cried the Traveller. "I'll ask Mrs Watchett!" And he rushed out of the laboratory.

"I'd like to see the housekeeper's face," said the Journalist, "when he *does* ask her. Why – there might be a story in this – in the silly column." And he ran out too.

We heard voices in the passage, and then they both re-entered – with Mrs Watchett, that motherly, elderly widow. "Oh, no Sir," she was saying, "you never did ask me any such thing. And I never told you the gentlemen had left. How could I? They've been here with you all this 'alf hour and more, lookin' at your experiments."

"All right, Mrs Watchett, you can go," said the Traveller. "I – I just had a dream, that's all. It's over now." He passed a hand wearily over his brow. He seemed quite crestfallen.

"It's high time to make our dream *departure* come true," said the Editor crisply. "Well, thank you, mine host, for showing us some diverting illusions. Maskelyne is nothing to you. I look forward to something really startling this Christmas. Perhaps you can conjure up for us the ghost of a Morlock. That'd be something – the ghost of a being who doesn't yet exist – and probably never will."

And he left, and the Journalist went with him.

"Hopeless people," said Welles savagely. "Two ancestors of the Eloi."

"But – perhaps they're right," said the Traveller. "Perhaps I did dream all this future travel. You have just shown, Welles, that one of my trips to the future was an illusion."

"*No* Sir – not at all," said Welles. "It was real, all right. But by *returning*, by slipping back those fifteen minutes and telling us about your trip, you shifted us onto another time-line. We all felt the shift as a blurring, the moment you returned. We are now on Track C – before that, we were on Track B, the one you created by your return from the Morlocks. Track B still exists – in some metaphysical dimension you have just interviewed Mrs Watchett, she has told you the house is empty, and from that track you have vanished on your Machine, I fear for ever, leaving *that* Mrs Watchett and your other servants aghast. But I don't think abandoned tracks snuff out of existence."

"What is Existence?" said Ellis. "I think Berkeley had

something. Where there are perceiving minds, there you have existence. I rather like your many-tracked world, Welles."

Welles laughed. "Consciousness is certainly a great mystery. Why do we feel confined to *this* track now? Why are we not also aware of our continuing lives in Tracks A and B? Perhaps our counterparts in Track B, who have long since gone home, are even now wondering the same thing . . . But it's no more mysterious, I think, than the odd fact that our consciousness is confined to one body. Why do I always wake up in the morning and find myself confined to the body and brain of Herbert Welles, the not-very-brilliant student of physics – and not one day find myself in the body of George Hillyer, the excellent story writer? Anyway, Sir, the world is a very strange place – and backward Time Travel makes it stranger. You came back obliquely just now, thereby creating a new track and a new future. This evening you have created two new futures, by making two backward time journeys."

"But then," said the Traveller, "Weena still exists, in what you call Future A."

"Yes, Sir."

"*But I can't get back there.*"

"Not exactly *there*. But if you go forward again to 802,701, on this Track C, you may find it not *very* different."

"Then that is just what I shall do."

He agreed with us that his next journey would be in five or six days' time – the time needed to modify the Machine, and make other preparations. And we agreed with him – Browne, Ellis, Welles and myself – that in the interval we would do nothing to disturb the far future. No political activities, no socialist meetings. Doctor Browne even promised to limit his charitable work among the poor to a minimum. And of course, we all promised to keep the projected future journey a complete secret from all outsiders. We thought alike on most matters – Browne was a Liberal, Ellis a Radical: now we had become a conspiracy.

As we were leaving the house, Welles said to us: "It's just occurred to me that *not* doing something is also a modification. To be fair to our friend – to ensure that he meets something like Eloi – I suggest we just carry on as usual, doing neither more *nor* less. I shall visit William Morris as usual – but won't say a word to him about the future triumph of capitalism."

"How do you rate our friend's chances," I said, "of finding Weena?"

"Not high. We can't suppress our own knowledge of Future A. Even those newspaper idiots . . . Trivial little actions now, smoking one cigar more or less – they must have increasing effects over 800,000 years. Unpredictable effects. I hope I'm wrong, but – I'll visit William Morris, and *try* to be unaffected by what I know."

3

In the event, only I had time to visit William Morris; Welles, unavoidably, became involved in one unusual activity; for the Traveller pressed him into service as a collaborator in modifying the Time Machine. Welles hardly resisted the Traveller's request; soon he became eager to help. For the Machine fascinated him.

By Saturday evening they had installed the four wheels which could be lowered when needed below the level of the runners. They were bicycle wheels, small size, with solid tyres. The Traveller was determined now to wheel his machine into an Eloi building, and there chain it to a pillar, safe from the prying eyes and fingers of the Morlocks.

On Monday, there was a new development. The second saddle, installed behind the Traveller's seat, was first intended for the rescued Weena. Then Welles said:

"Why don't I go too, Sir? With two of us, you'd be more than twice as secure. We could stand alternate watches, at night. And I could always cover your back."

The Traveller was half elated, half dubious. "It's very good of you. But you know the dangers?"

"Of course. But after your pioneer journey, they should be small. *Much* smaller with two of us. And a much greater chance of a successful rescue."

"Yes, yes. But it would alter things. And I want them, as far as possible, unaltered . . ."

"Sir, I would stay in the background – especially as regards Weena."

That settled it. It was agreed that they would return with Welles carrying Weena before him on a slightly lengthened saddle.

I also was given a little job. As a writer of fiction, I should have the necessary talent and the Traveller called on me to invent a story for Mrs Watchett. Silently I invoked the spirit of Dickens, to account for the sudden arrival of a young foreign female, alone, oddly clad, and unchaperoned, in the Richmond house. I think in the end my tale would have gladdened the great Charles's heart. On the Monday evening I took the housekeeper aside, in the little office-cum-sitting-room, and broke it to her.

The Traveller, I said, had an uncle – recently deceased – who had worked most of his life in Transylvania, and married there. Wife half Transylvanian, half French – also dead now. They had left an only daughter. The poor girl was utterly without resources – a wicked business partner had ruined that family, and indirectly caused the father's death . . .

When I got this far, Mrs Watchett could barely restrain her tears. "Oh, Sir, the poor little thing! How old is she?"

"We are not very sure. In her teens, I believe. She is now in France, with a relative on her mother's side – an old woman who is herself poor, and unable to travel. It is not yet at all certain, but we *think* the girl may manage to come over to England this week. She will then be utterly dependant on her cousin, your master. We hope you, Mrs Watchett, can take care of the girl – you being the only woman in this house, apart from the maid."

"Oh yes, Sir, of course, it'd be a pleasure. I had a little daughter meself once . . ."

"You must be prepared for some surprises, Mrs Watchett. Miss Driver will be *very* foreign, I'm told – not a word of English. You'll have to use sign language. And – they have rather *simple* manners in Transylvania. I don't think they use knives or forks. Oh yes – and they're vegetarians."

"Bless my soul! Sir – how will we feed her? Vegetarian . . ."

"Oh, Doctor Browne is preparing a diet sheet. Perhaps gradually we could tempt her to cheese and eggs. If you'll have the things by Wednesday . . ."

Wednesday, indeed, was fixed for the great journey. The

Traveller had cancelled all his usual Thursday parties: if we got Weena, we would have to keep her very secret for a while. Luckily, the Editor and Journalist had lost interest in us – not even a paragraph had appeared in their paper.

Ellis was unavoidably detained for most of that day, but on Wednesday morning, four of us assembled in the laboratory. It was nearly 10 a.m., a grey dismal October day, but the electric lights in that big room burned brightly. The Traveller and Welles prepared to mount the newly polished Machine in its old spot in the southeast corner; Doctor Browne and I stood well back. We two were the farewelling and, we hoped, the welcoming committee. Browne had his medical bag. "Pray it won't be needed," he muttered. I felt pangs of fear for Welles, my close friend . . .

The Traveller and Welles had large haversacks – this time they would be well equipped with revolvers, a camera, a patent lamp, extra clothing. Clothing! Welles had visited a theatrical costumier's, and now they both wore Roman tunics over trousers and boots. Welles had also shaved off his beard – and his hairless chin made him look very young, if anything less than his actual twenty-five years.

"We want to be inconspicuous this time," said the Traveller. "As much like Eloi as possible. I'm too tall, of course – but my friend might just pass as a very tall one of that people. We are going to arrive, of course, in full view of that Sphinx, and the Morlocks who live in its base may have spy-holes."

"They may also have dark goggles," said Welles.

"*My* Morlocks didn't," said the Traveller.

"Perhaps not, Sir, but perhaps *these* Morlocks will have. You know, we have been forced to do some unusual things. It can't be *exactly* the same future . . ."

"No, you proved that last Thursday night," said the Traveller, somewhat bitterly. "But we must try to repeat events as nearly as possible. We'll arrive just one day earlier, secure the Machine, check the next day that no other Traveller arrives in the middle of that thunderstorm – then wait to meet Weena at the river, so I can rescue her—"

"And then come directly back?" said Browne.

"No." The Traveller looked stubborn. "I mean to repeat things – as far as it's safe. We'll spend five more days there, so she can get to know me again – so she is willing for the ultimate rescue, from the Morlocks. She has to love and trust – so that she will not be afraid to get on our Machine."

I saw what he left half unspoken: he wanted the *same* experience as before, but with a happy ending. He would have to win, all over again, the affections of a girl in the far future – a girl who might not now even exist.

I said: "Do you all realize that today is October 14?"

"What of it?" said the Traveller.

"It's the anniversary of the Battle of Hastings. Which we talked once of changing. Well, with your return voyage today, you ought to change at least *our* future history."

"How?"

"Weena must change things a little," I said.

Later, I remembered that as the understatement of the century. Or two centuries.

4

When the Machine and its two occupants vanished, there was the usual cold blast of wind from the open window, as air rushed in to occupy the little vacuum.

"Well," said Browne, "if all goes smoothly, we shouldn't have long to wait. That's one crazy thing about this Time Travel: they can spend eight days away, but for us it should be only a few seconds. Or if they overshot . . ."

"They'd arrive in our past – on a different time track," I said. "And I think, *we* would never see them again. Because we *haven't* so seen them. Other selves of ours would meet them, greet them – but not *us*."

Browne shuddered. "I can't bear to think of that."

"Well, they agreed not to overshoot."

"Why aren't they back already?"

The question hung in the air. The laboratory remained silent and bare in the glare of the electric lights.

"Who was it," I asked, "who said, 'You can never step into the same river twice'?"

"Heraclitus."

"Heraclitus was right. But our learned friend is trying to do just that. I suppose it's what we all long to do – to re-live some moment of our lives, but live it *better*."

"Yes, indeed. You drop a precious crystal goblet, your favourite – and it shatters into a hundred pieces. Gone for ever. If only you could have ten seconds back! And once I lost a woman patient – and just afterwards thought of a different treatment, which might have saved her. Oh, to go back just one day! But one never can. Time's arrow is relentless, Hillyer. What's done is done, once and for all. And Time Travel does not alter that – as Welles proved the other night. Because of the zig-zag effect. You can never have things over again—"

As he was yet speaking, I felt a familiar qualm of dizziness, a blast of air – and there was the Time Machine, solidifying, only feet in front of me. I cried out, and reeled backward. Browne also jumped back. The Machine was moving – rolling on its wheels. As it came to a stop against the wall, I saw that there were three figures on it. The two men were in modern trousers and shirt-sleeves; Welles had the handle of a revolver drooping from his trouser pocket.

In front of Welles, almost in his lap, sat a young girl, blonde, fair-skinned, blue-eyed. She wore a short white tunic trimmed with gold, and gilded sandals. She looked terrified. She was clutching the waist of the Traveller, just ahead of her, and crying out in an unknown musical language: "Periu, Periu, puio isu olo!" In spite of her fear, the quality of her voice was strangely beautiful, and warmer than I would have expected: contralto or mezzo-soprano, clear but not shrill. As she held the Traveller by the waist, so Welles also held her firmly round her slim waist on that long saddle. I realised that he must have been holding her so through all their journey back across the years. Lucky man, I thought, to hold so sweet a little creature!

The Traveller now jumped down from his saddle, and reached up for her. "It's all right, Weena!" he laughed. "You're safe! No more Morlocks!" Then he added: "Laio, laio – pu Molokoi alo."

They were all off the Machine now, all facing us. The Traveller and the girl had their arms round each other.

"Everything is fine!" said the Traveller, laughing. "And this is certainly Weena – my Weena! I rescued her from the river, just like last time, and rescued her from the Morlocks. No second version of me appeared. I suppose Welles is right in his basic theory – just as well, or we *couldn't* have rescued her. But otherwise – it was just the same – or a little better! Weena slept on my arm, those nights in the big grey house – and by day, she crowned me with flowers . . . She's the *same* girl, I tell you – just as sweet, just as loving – but this time she's saved!"

"So much for Heraclitus," I murmured. "Doctor, you *can* have things over again."

"Well, I am glad, very glad," said Browne. "And Weena . . ."

His voice trailed away. I too, for a while, could do nothing but gaze at her. She was not quite as small as I had first thought – under five feet, certainly, but not by much. I could not tell her age at all: she might be anything between fourteen and twenty, and even of those limits I was not confident. Age seemed not to *apply* to her. Her skin was flawless, not dead white but slightly kissed by the sun; her features were symmetrical, her curly hair a rich golden colour; and her eyes were very bright, with a green sparkle within their blue. Her beauty was indeed *awesome*. Like a Greek goddess on a small scale: a nymph, immortal and ageless.

"You–you did not really tell us—" I began.

But this nymph was still frightened. She raised a shapely fair arm, and pointed at Browne. "Moloko?" she cried.

Welles laughed. "No, no." He caressed Weena's bare shoulder. "Pu Moloko, Wini – niio, pereno." He turned to Browne. "She thought you might be a Morlock, Doctor. It's your beard. I'm glad I shaved mine off. The Morlocks are – hairy."

Weena said a few more rapid musical words, looking wildly all about her. The Traveller replied quickly, reassuringly, in the same language. He stroked her hand.

"She doesn't like this place," Welles explained. "It's dark, it's enclosed. For her, it has a Morlockish feel. I don't blame her. She doesn't know about Time Travel: we told her we were taking her away to a different *place* – Beriten – Britain – where there'd be no Morlocks. It'll take her a long while before she realises the truth."

"You all seem quite *fluent*," said Browne. "I thought . . ."

The Traveller turned to us. "That was another thing that

went *better*. I at least knew some of the language from the start. We picked up much more before we even met Weena. And since . . . Now, come on – we've got to get her out of here, make her comfortable."

"After that," said Browne, "I'd like to *examine* her. Thoroughly. Superficially she looks . . . but after 800,000 years . . ."

"Not today," said the Traveller. "You'd frighten her."

"Yes, indeed," said Welles. "Where we came from, the Morlocks—"

"Enough, Welles!" said the Traveller, sharply. "Now, *out*."

So we all left the laboratory; and Weena was introduced to the household, and the household to her. The sun came out of the clouds, the house brightened, and when Weena entered the sumptuous drawing-room, she quickly lost her fear. She slipped off her sandals, and stood on the carpet in very shapely bare white feet. Mrs Watchett gasped when she saw the newcomer – "Oh, what a *pretty* young lady!" – and James the manservant goggled, and Ellen the maid, who was young, fell over in making her curtsy. Weena laughed; she had a very lovely laugh. Then she seized Ellen's hand, and kissed her on the cheek. She kissed Mrs Watchett also. Perhaps she would have kissed more of us – including James – if Mrs Watchett had not grasped her firmly by the arm.

"She's just a child, Mrs Watchett," said the Traveller.

"Oh Sir, maybe so – but she's too old to go about in them *clothes*!"

I knew what was offending the good housekeeper: Weena's tunic hem-line. It came only a little way below her knees, revealing lovely bare legs as well as feet; and in 1891, even ankles . . .

"Yes of course," said the Traveller. "You shall measure her presently, Mrs Watchett, and get proper things made. But give her a little time . . ."

Weena was now marvelling at everything she saw. She ran her hands over the furniture, and laughed when Welles demonstrated sitting on the sofa. She bounced up and down on that. Then she ran, amazed, to stare at the coal fire in the fireplace.

"Don't they have no *fires* in that Silvania?" said Mrs Watchett.

"It's a warm country," said the Traveller hastily. "They don't need them."

Now Weena wanted to know all our names. She had a great affection for the Traveller, whom she called "Periu" – a version of his first name – but she was also on very good terms with Welles, whom she called "Abio" (Herbert). "Mr Hillyer" was too much of a mouthful for her, and "George" was quite impossible, so she quickly christened me "Ilio".

"These are also meaningful words in Eloic," Welles smiled. "*Abio* means 'coloured glass' or 'jewel' and *ilio* means 'clear glass'."

"Charming," I said.

Weena also could not manage "Mrs Watchett", but took to calling her, from her first name, Meri or sometimes Meri-a.

"The *a*-ending is honorific," said Welles. "From the way Mrs Watchett is bossing her, I think she imagines *she* is the head of things here."

Weena now laughed, pointing to each of us in turn, beginning with the women. "Meri-a na Eleni . . . na Periu na Abio na Ilio . . . na Baranu na Demu. Oli perenoi, sa?"

"She asks if we are all friends," said Welles. He turned to her. "Sa, Wini – oli perenoi."

The Traveller coughed. "Really, Welles! No Socialism now, please!"

"Well, Sir, we're not enemies, are we? We're as much perenoi to each other as all the Eloi are – nearly. We don't eat, dissect or enslave each other."

"Oli laii, laii Taweloi!" exclaimed Weena.

"She says we are all good people," said Welles. "And *Taweloi* – that means, Big or Great Eloi."

The only thing Weena disliked about us was – our clothes. These she thought *ogo* – ugly. She was asking, evidently, why we wore such things – so sombre, so heavy. To that there was no answer. I noticed that though she was very lightly clad, and the day was not warm, she did not feel the cold. Mrs Watchett remarked on that.

"Oh," said Welles cheerfully, "in Transylvania, Mrs Watchett, they bring up children not to mind the cold. You'd be surprised how little the young ones wear."

The Traveller frowned. But at that moment, Weena kissed Mrs Watchett again.

"Oh, the darling little pet!" cried Mrs Watchett. "Oh, I *do* beg your pardon, Sir—"

"That's all right," said the Traveller. "See, it's exactly what I told you all before – she's just like a child."

As the servants left the room, Browne said: "A child of what age?"

"That we still don't know," said the Traveller. "Probably she won't know herself. All the Eloi who are adult look about the same age – no visible ageing. She thought the lines on my forehead were *wounds* – scars. Their youthfulness – there's probably a sinister reason for that – which we can all guess."

I shuddered, looking at lovely white-and-gold Weena. She had won all our hearts, and I was very glad that the Traveller had, after all, succeeded in saving his little girl-woman from the horrible Morlocks. Moreover, she struck me now as not altogether mindless. I had feared, from the Traveller's first tale, that we might have a sweet idiot on our hands. Not so: she was obviously full of curiosity about "Beriten" – and many of her sentences were longer than just two words.

At the cold luncheon which followed, things went on like that. According to the Traveller's custom, no servants waited at table – Browne had laid out vegetarian dishes for Weena, and we other carnivores had bread, cheese and discreetly cut up bits of ham. Weena quite liked her food. Of course, she ate at first with her hands; she laughed in astonishment when she saw us plying forks. And then she began to learn that trick too: rapidly she began impaling sections of her apple.

"It's just a game to her," said the Traveller.

"But a game she's good at," said Welles. He sat next to her, on the other side from the Traveller, and helped her to place her fingers correctly on the fork and knife. "See – we'll soon be able to pass her off as an English lady!"

Then Weena rapidly kissed him on the cheek. I laughed. "Not if she does things like that!"

"Just a child," said the Traveller. But he frowned; and Welles was flushing.

"Come now!" I said. "Your adventures in the Far Future! Surely they couldn't have been *exactly* the same as the first time?"

"Well, not *exactly*," the Traveller admitted. "The thunderstorm on our second day – corresponding to my first day, the other time – that was a very mild affair – no hail, just a little rain. And we roamed to a few different places."

"And I," said Welles, "I had to shoot a Morlock just as we were escaping. We had to wheel the machine out on to the lawn in front of the Sphinx – so as to arrive just in the laboratory – and it was broad daylight, and the Morlocks erupted out of the base of the Sphinx, wearing black goggles and shooting metal arrows at us . . . And there were – other differences."

"But not in Weena," said the Traveller. "And that's all that matters."

After that, he became rather uncommunicative; and Welles, noticing his mood, also remained silent.

When the meal was over, Browne lingered to help with arrangements; but Welles and I had our own affairs to attend to – some of them recently rather neglected. So we took our leave, Welles making it clear to Weena that he would return the next day. She gave him a fervent hug – he had difficulty getting away.

Since our lodgings were close together, in Putney, Welles and I shared a cab home. As soon as we were clip-clopping on our way, Welles leaned towards me.

"Hillyer – he is deceiving himself!"

"What do you mean?" I said

"Two things. First, she is *not* a child: I have spent enough time with her to know that. She is a bit puzzled by the way he treats her – by the things he *doesn't* do, if you take my meaning."

"I do take it, Welles. And I've known you long enough to know you would know. Well, what's the *other* thing?"

"The other thing is possibly metaphysical. Across the parallel time lines, what does it mean when we say a person is 'the same' or 'not the same'? But if you alter history – alter conditions noticeably, say, for the year 802,701 – can a person in that altered year be 'the same person'? He kept trying to convince himself, in that future world, that nothing important was different. But things *were* different. Some he might have failed to notice on his first journey, but certainly not all. Not all non-human mammals were extinct, for a start. There was a species of nocturnal deer: I saw it as I stood watch the fourth night, and the Morlocks were hunting it, with crossbows. And once in the

distance, I saw beasts like large sheep . . . There would be no
need in that world for the Morlocks to eat Eloi, and I suspect
they didn't – unless for the pleasure of revenge. The Eloi feared
them, yes. In the Grey House, they told frightening stories . . .
But the Eloi were not mindless. Each House had organization –
with a head-woman, and orchards owned by particular Houses.
And that Sphinx: even *he* agreed it was less dilapidated. And the
language: the roots were the same, but I'm sure the structure
was more complex. He is not a linguist, but I have good German
– and in the end I was becoming more fluent than he. Nouns
had plurals: singular Elo, plural Eloi. Similarly, Moloko and
Molokoi. That means, of course, 'Morlocks' – and the Eloi were
not averse to discussing them. To me, she hinted things, once
when he was not there: midnight kidnappings by Morlocks,
medical examinations in the bowels of the earth, piercings. It
sounded more like *vivisection* than cannibalism."

I shuddered. "Just as horrible – worse!"

"Yes. But it shows intelligence – in both species. Those
Morlocks were *scientists* – among other things. And in the far
distance, the London area had a *wall* round it – like the Great
Wall of China. The area inside, with the great Eloi Houses – she
called that 'Lanan' – the Land, maybe derived from 'London'.
Outside the Wall was 'pulan' – the Uncountry. I think the
Morlocks ruled there, on the surface. Once when he was tired,
she led me up a hill near the Wall. I suppose it was near Croydon,
and from the crest we saw beyond the Wall: I think, that was the
area of our Bromley. The Morlocks had great machines there,
mirrors collecting the sun's rays, I presume for power. If any
Eloi lived in the Uncountry, they were mere slaves of the
Morlocks. I think we saw a few: they were naked and brown,
herders of the big sheep-like animals. She called them 'pu-Eloi'
or 'poi-Eloi' – Unpeople, Dead People. Within the wall, the Eloi
paradise was only a reservation – or a zoo. Oh yes, and the
Morlock Uprising had happened not all that long before. I gathered from her that it was only about ten lifetimes ago: there were
traditions surviving from the time before 'the Molokoi became
great'."

"Phew," I said. "That's a lot of stuff you've gathered in a few
days from pretty little Weena."

"She is not pretty," he said, "she is beautiful. *And her name is not Weena.*"

"What!"

"No. It's *he* who keeps calling her that, and she tolerates it – it's a joke, for her, because the – *a* ending is honorific, it sounds as if he's flattering her. Her real name is Wiyeni – or Wini. Most Eloi names mean something, and *wiyeni* means something like 'female organizer', or 'junior leader of a House' – you might say, 'princess'. But she likes it when I use the short form, Wini."

"You're in love with her," I said.

"Yes," said Welles.

5

The name problem, for our nymph, was luckily soon settled, or rather evaded. The Traveller decided that to mislead the curious she ought to have a proper English name. He chose Winifred. And he told Mrs Watchett that her full name was Winifred Jane Driver – she had been christened "Winifred Jane" by her late English father, albeit in Transylvania the name had become somewhat mangled. At times he still called her "Weena", but to most other people she was "Winnie". I called her that, too; but secretly I thought of her as Wiyeni – the Princess.

She had a wild, pagan quality, which did not really disappear, not even when Mrs Watchett clothed her in Victorian garb, first in things borrowed from Ellen. Wiyeni showed her mettle over that business! The lendings dismayed her – why underclothes? And then, when the tailored things appeared, she flatly refused to wear them. "Puio, ogo!" she cried. The things were bad, ugly. And corsets – no, never; did they want to kill her? And the shoes – she would rather go barefoot, and round the house she did. (She had very beautiful feet, which certainly did not deserve to have their toes cramped, or distorted by high heels.) In the end, the matter was compromised. The hemline was taken up, daringly revealing her ankles, so that she would not trip over; and less stylish but more comfortable shoes were ordered for her. The mode of bodice and collar for ladies, that year, was a little masculine. I thought, in the end, she looked like an angelic choirboy – or like Hebe come to earth, disguised as Ganymede.

The bedroom reserved for "Winnie" was another shock for her. The bed and the other furnishings were wonderful – she had been used to sleeping on bare stone floors – but what was this? Was she to sleep *alone*? She had never done such a thing in her life! It was too frightening! That first night, she stood at the door and argued with Mrs Watchett and the Traveller. Already she had a few words of English; with those, and gestures, and some Eloic, she made her meaning plain.

No Morlocks? Maybe – hard to believe – but maybe other dangers? "You, Periu – you – why not you sleep too?" And she pointed to the bed.

Mrs Watchett nearly had a fit. "Oh, *Sir!*"

"She means no harm, Mrs Watchett," said the Traveller hastily. "She's just a child – terrified of the dark. Transylvania was a dangerous country. There were – wolves . . ."

"Maybe, Sir. But she'll have to learn. Go now, Sir – I'll soothe her."

She managed that, at last; and got the girl into a warm nightdress. Then she showed her how to lock and unlock the door. Winnie seemed delighted, and kept turning the key, one way and the other.

"Now," said the housekeeper, "goodnight, Miss Winnie. And you *lock* now – yes?"

"Sa – yes – lock-a. Goo' nigh', Meri-a." And as Mrs Watchett went out, she heard the key turn. Suspicious, she lingered a while; but the key did not turn back again. "Poor little thing," she murmured. "Master's right – an innocent baby."

What followed after that, I heard much later, from Wiyeni's own lips. Neither the Traveller nor Mrs Watchett breathed a word to anyone.

First, Wiyeni waited till Mrs Watchett's steps could no longer be heard. Then she unlocked the door, and in her nightdress slipped into the Traveller's room. He was on the point of undressing. She smiled. "Periu, dear, cannot I sleep with you here, dear friend?" But he went red in the face; he seized her arm, marched her back to her room, and made her lock herself in. Wiyeni turned from the door with a little sob.

It was dark in that bedroom: the house had electric light only in the laboratory, and they had not given her a lamp for fear of accidents. But by drawing back the curtains from her south-facing window, she let in some light from the eleven-day-old gibbous moon. The moon was high in the sky, and that surprised her: in the Eloi world it had been summer, and she knew that summer moons rode low. Still, the good light comforted her: she looked out over the strange and wonderful garden, and saw no prowling Morlocks. So she went to her lonely bed. But under the great pile of bedclothes, she felt too hot. And the nightdress, borrowed from Ellen, was coarse and scratchy. She stripped it off, and then, naked under the sheet, fell comfortably asleep.

Thursday began with a shock for Mrs Watchett.

She came about 7.30 a.m. with a tray of tea and toast to Winnie's door, and knocked. She heard a light scamper of feet, the door was unlocked, and in the half-light of the room she saw a little white form topped by golden hair. At first she took the whiteness for Winnie's nightdress. Then the rising sun emerged from a cloud, and Mrs Watchett realized that Winnie was naked.

She rushed in, almost upsetting her tray, and slammed the door shut behind her with her heel. "Oh, you *naughty* thing!" she cried.

It was a long time before Winnie could be made to understand her crime.

That same Thursday, just after breakfast, Ellis arrived. This was his second meeting with Wiyeni, and he found her fascinating. The psychology of a girl from the far future . . . Nearly as interesting, too, was the Traveller's attitude to her.

As the morning was fine, they went for a walk in the garden. Almost all the plants and trees were new to Wiyeni – she kept darting about among the yellow fallen leaves, picking up strange items. And then suddenly, as he strolled from behind a tree-trunk, she met Mrs Watchett's white cat, Tiger. Both cat and girl seemed equally startled (so Ellis told us later). She had never known a tame animal before.

"Tikuro!" she breathed – then said to the Traveller in Eloic, "Periu – this is a creature we have known, carved over the great door of one of our Houses. That House is named for the carving, House of Tikuro. I did not know they were real. Ah, Beriten is a land where old tales are true! But is it dangerous? Will it bite us?"

"Pu, pu," laughed the Traveller. "No, Weena. He is a little friend. See! – Tiger, Tiger, Tiger . . . come here, puss!"

He now made them acquainted. Soon Wiyeni was kneeling, stroking Tiger and laughing, as Tiger purred.

"Isn't she just a marvellous sweet child?" said the Traveller.

Ellis gave him a considering look. "Marvellous, yes . . ."

A similar thing happened when they came up to the hedge. Beyond, in a field, two horse were grazing.

"Osoi!" cried Wiyeni. "More carving-animals! I come from the House of the Oso. But, they are very great! Do they eat people?"

"No, Weena-child, only grass. And we ride on their backs, and they pull us in machines." He translated for Ellis. "Imagine, she thought they might eat us!"

"A reasonable guess, in the circumstances," said Ellis. "They might be omnivores – like us Great Eloi."

"She's a perfect child," said the Traveller.

"Well, she's not a perfect fool."

Immediately after that, Browne arrived, with a middle-aged nurse. And now he got his wish. In her bedroom upstairs, he and the nurse examined Wiyeni. She had lost all fear of "Baranu," and stripped naked without hesitation. Browne's examination was not intrusive; but he noted her small breasts, her little fringe of golden pubic hair, her wide hips; and he felt her bones. He decided that she was probably about eighteen years old – and should have very little trouble when she came to bear children.

Those days, those next few weeks, we were continually in and out of the Traveller's house, at many times of the day. The education of Wiyeni-Winnie was an urgent priority. Until she could pass for a nineteenth-century girl, if only a foreign one, she must remain a virtual prisoner in that house and garden, yet already she was eager to explore "Beriten". I, as a literary man, was given the primary and very agreeable task of teaching her English. Welles undertook to explore her mental skills, especially in the direction of arithmetic.

On that first Thursday forenoon, I met Welles in Putney, and we took a cab for Richmond. "Come on," I said, "now you must tell me everything. So far I've had only snippets. The Far Future! What was that like?"

His blue eyes twinkled, and he looked almost boyish. "Well, it was *fun*, you know. And some things will still be *our* future. Little bits of weather may change, but the climate is surely beyond human control, and the stars . . . It is a warm world, beyond all Ice Ages. The sea level is higher, the Thames wider. And the stars! All different! There are two Pole stars, bright blue ones which circle the actual pole like the hands of a clock . . . But *he's* told you some of that already. As for the Eloi – some of the things were really the same on his first trip, only he was too prudish to mention them. For instance, nakedness. The Eloi all bathe naked, and think nothing of it. Wini was naked, you know, when he leapt into the river and rescued her."

"Golly!"

"Yes, indeed. He was a bit embarrassed, bringing her to shore, and me there – especially as she was in no hurry to get dressed again. The Eloi are not in the least prudish. The young kids, up to about four years old, go stark naked all the time – I think it makes them very hardy against cold; and at night, when they huddle together in those Houses, most of them huddle naked. We three slept in a little side room of the Grey House, where we had the Machine chained to a pillar; and I'm sure Wini would have taken her tunic off if *he* had let her."

"What!"

"Yes. She never left us, you know, from the moment she met us, and she was very grateful for being rescued. Mind you, her cramp was only a momentary thing, and she was recovering as he got to her. And other Eloi were swimming up . . . He managed to win the credit, but only just. And she was impressed not just by the rescue, but by what he was – a benevolent giant, with wonderful powers and devices, so useful against the Morlocks. I think she expected to reward him in the obvious way, and was quite willing to do it. But he kept treating her as a child, so she – just cuddled him. I showed more willing, and that time we were alone near Bromley, coming down from the crest of the hill – she suddenly hugged me, and kissed me on the lips. She was grateful to me too, you see, and the view of the Uncountry and its Morlock machines had just frightened her. I didn't let things go any further, then, out of loyalty to *him*. But God, Hillyer, she is sweet! By the bye, I'm pretty sure she has had lovers before.

The Eloi don't seem to have marriage. Life in Lanan is so easy, apart from the Morlocks, that a woman can easily bring up her children without the help of a man. And they do it: I saw always these units of mother-and-child, with never a possessive man about. But in the house-tribes, there is plenty of help to be had when needed, and the men are gentle with children. Eloi women are not very fertile, I think, so they make sure they have plenty of lovers. I – I think this will be the greatest problem with Wini – she won't have any sense of what we call respectability."

I whistled. "A Greek goddess indeed – with the morals of one . . . But she seems so *nice*."

"She is, too. Her feelings go deeper than those of most Eloi. She may be casual about sex – but I'm sure she can also *love*. Affection . . . she has a strong *affection* for our learned friend. Let me give you one example. You know, he tried to repeat everything possible – so on our last morning there, he descended into that Morlock well, to take his flash pictures. He expected me to stay with Wini and console her. I was rather looking forward to that . . . But *she* didn't stay. She started climbing down that well after him."

"Good God! I thought they were terrified—"

"She *was* terrified. She cried out, 'They will cut him!' I'm sure she meant dissect him. The Eloi lived always with the possibility of being kidnapped one night, taken down a Morlock hole, and used in experiments. Yet she was going to risk the same fate, to save her friend. I rushed after her, stopped her, wrestled with her. It's no joke, wrestling on the rungs of an iron ladder over a bottomless pit. Luckily, in the end I convinced her that he was in no real danger. This time he had a miner's lamp . . . When he came out, we decided to evacuate at once. Just as well – the Morlocks were thoroughly alarmed, and that was when they came at us out of the Sphinx." He mused. "Wini is not in the least stupid. The Eloi as a whole, on this time track, were brighter – decadent, yes, but not idiots. But of them all, Wini struck me as exceptional. The others were placid, never thinking that their lives could ever be different. But Wini had the instincts of a fighter: she was very curious, and restless. She had left her birth-house, and now she knew many house-tribes – she'd been travelling between them – and during our days there, it was really *she* who was our leader. She realised that the Morlocks ought not to see us two. She made us avoid certain hillsides – 'The Molokoi will see'. I think she meant they had hides in there, with spyholes. Without her, I don't think we'd have lasted that many days. As it was, we stayed one day fewer than we'd planned. She slept on his arm for only four nights, not five."

"And you?"

"I watched while they slept. Then, when it was his watch, I slept close beside her. Not touching her, though I ached to, since *he* could see . . . I don't know how deeply she feels for me. She is very *fond* of me – as she is of him. I don't know if it goes beyond that. I expect she would sleep with me, given the opportunity. But I – I want more than that . . . But I do know one thing."

"What?"

"I'm very glad we did not bring back Weena – his original Weena. Wini, Wiyeni – she's an enormous improvement."

"She's also an enormous problem," I said.

"Yes, but a delightful one. She seems to have a gift for language – she began imitating English sounds even in *that* world. So, as soon as she has enough vocabulary, I think we should tell her the whole truth. And then see what she does."

"About Time Travel? Will she understand it? It was bad enough for *us*."

He laughed. "Try her, and see. She is ignorant, but not stupid. And she'll soon notice an oddity. It was midsummer in that Eloi world – now it's autumn. You can't keep the *season* a secret, not in England. And they must have had winters in the Eloi world, even if mild ones – short days and long nights. How long do you think it'll take her to notice?"

It took her, in fact, about one more day. And by Saturday morning, she was quite sure. She had seen the fallen leaves, and from her south-facing window she had watched three sunrises and three sunsets. And now, on Saturday, at a joint lesson in the breakfast room facing the garden, she tackled Welles and myself. She looked very fetching now, in her nineteenth-century garb – all but the shoes: in the house, she preferred to go barefoot. She spoke to us in a mixture of English and Eloic (for the latter, Welles translated).

"Abio, Ilio," she said, frowning with concentration, "how can it be, that it was hot time when we left my place Lanan – and now, in your great Eloi place, it is coming to the cold time? I thought it was just a few heartbeats, that wonder journey – but it must be many moons!"

"It is many moons – *months*," said Welles. "But not quite in the way you think, Wini . . ."

She could already count very well, both in Eloic and in English, and now she mastered, from twelve months, the word *year* – and a flood of illumination followed.

Yes, she could count years. "I, Wiyeni – it is twenty and one years since I come out of my mother."

Twenty-one! And Browne had thought her no more than eighteen . . .

"Yes, and my sister Isi is of thirty years, and my mother Mena is of fifty-and-three. My mother is *tamana* – great-house-mother – of the Oso House, far south near the Wall of the Uncountry. My mother, so, will die after seven years, and Isi will become Isa, and house-mother."

"Your mother will *die*?" I cried. We had shown her a dead bird in the garden. No, there was no mistake. She mimed *dying* quite well. And confirmed it by translation: in Eloic, *poi*.

"She means it," said Welles. "How do you know, Wini, that your mother will die in seven years' time?"

"Because she is fifty-and-three. People die when they are sixty years old." Suddenly she looked anxious. "O, Abio, Ilio! How old are you? Not fifty, not nearly sixty?"

I burst out laughing. "Do we look it? I am twenty-six; Abio is twenty-five."

She looked at Welles with joy. "Then you will live, Abio, my dear, near as long as me: thirty-five more years."

A little more questioning revealed the astounding truth: all Eloi, if they survived other hazards, died peaceful deaths at age sixty. Before that time, once they were full grown, they did not age visibly at all.

"*That's* why they all looked young," muttered Welles. "Not mass slaughter by Morlocks."

"It sounds like the Golden Age indeed," I said. "Like in Hesiod. 'Death came to them as sleep'."

But Welles was now greatly moved. He gripped her arm, her shoulder. "Wini – darling! You – at sixty . . ."

"Oh yes," she said brightly. "But there is nothing to fear in that, Abio, my jewel, my friend. After some years, few or many, we come out again from some other woman. So they say in the Houses."

"It is pleasant if you can believe that," he said.

"But now, Abio, Ilio, tell me how that wonderful Machine moves through months . . ."

Then we told her – that the Machine had borne her, not forward a few months, but *backward* a great many years, to a time before there were any Morlocks in Britain. After a short while, she grasped what we were saying – but could not at first believe it.

"I did not believe it at first either, Winnie," I said. "But Periu is very clever – *he* made the Machine, and he has shown us that it does truly carry people forward and backward in time."

A great light seemed to dawn in her face. "Then – then you are truly the Taweloi, those who are told of in the stories of our Houses – you who built the Houses! You are the men of our fore-mothers! O Abio, Ilio!"

And she slipped from her chair, knelt before us, and began kissing our feet. Welles hurriedly raised her. She laughed.

"Now I will find Mother Meri-a, and kiss her feet too. For she is a woman, and may be one of my foremothers, my mother's mother's foremother!"

"Wait," I said. "Do you know, Winnie, how the Morlocks started?"

"No, Ilio . . ."

We told her. Her expression became one of horror. "People made *Taweloi* into Morlocks!"

"Taweloi like James, like Ellen," I said.

"But Demu and Eleni are lovely people! Oh, that was bad, bad!"

"Is," said Welles. "It is happening now, Wini. What should we do about it?"

"Stop it – stop it from happening! Do not let anyone be pushed down out of the Sun!" said Wiyeni indignantly.

"That's exactly what we mean to do," said Welles. "Will you help us, Wini?"

"Yes, yes, yes! All I can how!"

"I think you can a lot," said Welles.

6

The secret of Winnie was confined, outside the household, to the four of us – Browne, Ellis, Welles and myself. I sent a note to the Editor saying that the Traveller's second great journey had failed – he had not found Weena. Which, in a way, was true . . .

It was agreed among us and the Traveller that we could not go public for a long time. Not even his strange photographs could be displayed as yet. Debate continued as to whether we could ever go public with the whole truth of Time Travel. The Traveller himself was in two minds about that. He liked having the monopoly of the secret and the power – not even Welles understood how the essential trick was done – but on the other hand he knew that if he published, he would become more famous than Newton or Galileo.

"Or the inventor of dynamite," said Welles at one of our conferences. "That's the true analogy. In this world of wars and rumours of wars – can the world be trusted with such a power? Can Germany – or France – or Russia? There'd be a million revisions of history, for a start. Not that we'd know about it – but still . . . If anything can happen, or has happened, nothing remains interesting, there are no serious issues. And I don't like the idea of *armies* suddenly appearing in our real future. Sir, you must not release your invention till the world has become a far more civilized place. Meanwhile, for a long time, some of us will be trying to make it so."

That argument seemed to convince even the Traveller. Browne and Ellis began some urgent social projects. Meanwhile, all of us were helping to educate Winnie. And she made very rapid progress. By early November, she was able to go out shopping with Mrs Watchett, mostly to Richmond, but occasionally to the inner areas of London. Thus she learned the hard facts of the money economy, and saw poverty, ugliness, dirt and desperation. They shocked her profoundly; and dark basements and underground railways filled her with special horror. "You – you are half Morlocks!" she once whispered. Even the Richmond house had a basement kitchen, and she often lingered there, grieving, and trying to help Ellen with her drudgery. But her relations with Welles, and partly also with me, grew ever closer as she realised how much we too hated the existing situation. Under cover of our lessons, we preached socialism to her. But she was no simple disciple: she objected to our ideas of scale.

"The whole of this land cannot be one House," she said. "It must be a friendship of many Houses – some small, some big. This House of ours, now – it is not big, but it could hold twenty people. Ellen will have children, I may have some, and we could invite a few more women, and their lovers."

"You're forgetting one thing, Winnie," I said. "This house doesn't belong to us – it belongs to Periu – as you call him."

"That is bad," she said, frowning. "Bad, bad! A House must not belong to one person – especially not to a *man*. It should belong to the people who live in it – all of them."

"Don't say anything like that to Periu," said Welles. "Not yet, anyway."

The Traveller was continuing to treat her as a child, or a very young woman. But she was fast outgrowing him. I sensed some uneasiness between him and Welles. Perturbed, I consulted Ellis.

"Rivalry?" he said. "Yes, there will be – of a kind. But don't think our learned friend will ever propose marriage to her. He is not a very sexual being. Rather like Ruskin – or Dodgson the mathematical photographer. He likes girls to be young – very young. If it comes to a contest, Welles will win."

By Christmas, Winnie's English was nearly perfect, and Welles was beginning to teach her German. That would come in handy later, he said. I was teaching her to read and write. Both came easy to her, especially as I began to teach her letters using Eloic words, one letter to one sound.

At Christmas, also, she was introduced into society, as Miss Winifred Driver, the Traveller's foreign-born cousin and ward. The Thursday dinner-parties were resumed. "Winifred" charmed everyone with her beauty, her delightful not-quite-perfect accent, and her semi-Socialist opinions. The Editor and Journalist suspected nothing, and Filby and the Mayor fell in love with her. But the Traveller became increasingly subdued.

He did not really like House Socialism. And he was beginning to admit, even to himself, that this was not the first Weena he had loved and lost.

In spring 1892 came the crisis. Winnie wanted to go out more, especially to political meetings, and unchaperoned. The Traveller forbade that.

"Then I will go away," she said calmly. "I love you, Periu, but no man tells me what I must or must not do. We did not live so in my country."

Welles came to her rescue. He got her to marry him. At first that idea also outraged her, but he explained that only the form was necessary to make her respectable. "I won't in fact own you, Wini. Of course you may love whom you like."

"I should hope so!" she said.

"But I hope," he said softly, "that I may mean a little more to you than all the rest."

She kissed him fervently. "Abio – Bertie – you know you will always be my *taleyeno* and *tapereno* – best lover, best friend."

So, after a brief civil ceremony, and now with a gold ring on her finger, she moved in with him, in his Putney lodging. There, at last, those two consummated their love.

It was in every sense a wonderful love; for both of them rich and strange. She found him gentle, but stronger and more serious than any Eloi man. She liked that. And he – he once confided: "Hillyer, she's not quite *human*. But better!"

She was faithful to him, in her own fashion. He was certainly always her best friend, as he was, in our world, her first lover.

But not by any means the last . . . I, too, have held her lovely, perfect nakedness in my arms.

Not much now remains for me to record, except the triumphs of Winnie-Wiyeni, and how they affected our world.

During the summer of 1892 she began to be famous. She remained friends with the Traveller, and often visited him at Richmond; but she also gladdened the hearts of many other people – including William Morris, whose last years she cheered considerably. He liked to call her "Jane Welles". But Jane Welles argued with him that Marxist Communism was a dreadfully bad idea. She was utterly opposed to class hatred, and she thought socialism could only work with very small-scale communes. "The workers must all be friends and lovers," she insisted.

In late 1893, in circumstances I shall describe later, she did in fact set up a small commune, and it flourished. When I married, a year later, my wife and I moved in to the same establishment, and lived there very happily. People came to call it "The Welles-Hillyer Place". Many years later, we also bought an estate in Essex, which became our main headquarters. Within our House, and the Houses other people founded in imitation, sex was a matter of free choice. Winnie sometimes persuaded men to join by making love with them; but she never went to bed with a man she really disliked. By now, she realized that men and women of our time were much more possessive and jealous than the Eloi. She shrugged her little shoulders, and made allowances and adaptations. "A House can be as small as one woman and one man," she said, "so long as it is friend to the other Houses."

In 1895, of course, I published *The Time Machine*, which made me famous – especially, I think, the illustrated edition, which used the Traveller's photographs. That book brought in plenty of money, and really launched our brand of socialism. Some people called us "the anti-Morlock movement". The Marxists hated us, but many of the Fabians came over, and Chesterton was also very friendly.

The rest is history. "Winnie Welles" became a world figure – long before her husband won his Nobel prize for atomic physics. She charmed most of the influential men in Europe and America; and also went to bed with many of them. Among her conquests, reputedly, were the German Kaiser Wilhelm II and Tsar Nicholas. The Kaiser launched a famous saying: "When is socialism not socialism? When it's in bed with Winnie Welles!"

She was also very active in the feminist movement and the Federal Peace Movement. When the Pan-European Alliance was signed in Brussels, August 4, 1914, she was present as the guest of both the Kaiser and the Tsar. That was the same year that the Liberal government in Britain gave votes to women, and Home Rule to Ireland, and passed the second round of bills establishing the welfare state. At Christmas that year, Winnie said: "Bertie, George – I think we've done it. There won't be any Morlocks in *our* future!" I am sure she will be proved right.

By then she was one of the most beloved women in the world – and not only by her lovers. Of course it helped that she remained so amazingly young and amazingly beautiful. Hollywood made her huge offers, the British government offered her a peerage in her own right – but she turned all such things down. We had enough money, partly from my writings and Welles's scientific work, to be comfortable in Richmond and Essex – and Winnie preferred before any other title to be known as the house-mother of Easton Glebe.

After X-rays came in, Doctor Browne gave her a really searching internal examination. He found that she had no appendix, and there were one or two other things which made him pronounce: "Really, she should be classified as a different species – not *Homo* (so-called) *sapiens*, but *Homo amabilis*."

We had suspected that before, especially as the years went by with no child. But in 1900 she did bear her single child – easily, with hardly any labour – a daughter whom she called Amber. Welles was certainly the father. Amber is beautiful, too, with her mother's blue-green eyes, and gold-brown hair. She is now a fine biologist, and with her special knowledge she declares that she is a sterile hybrid: she will never have children. Instead, she has adopted two, a boy Anthony and a girl Amy. Amber Welles is now thirty-four, but looks not a day over twenty.

We do not know if she will die in the same manner as her mother. Yes, that sad event happened four years ago now. There was hardly any visible change in Winnie, but one day she told us all that she was going. "Do not grieve too much, Abio," she said. "We have had a good life, thanks to you. I was a slave of the Morlocks, and you set me free to work in this world. And Amber will comfort you." Then, one fine summer's evening, she lay down in that garden in Essex, quietly closed her eyes, and did not open them again.

Her funeral was attended by an enormous number of celebrities – including the old Kaiser and the famous German painter Adolph Hitler. Hitler was a great man in the world peace movement; he was visibly in tears all through the ceremony. "She was followed to her grave," said one newspaper, "by a procession of her lovers: an exceedingly long procession."

What would the world have been like today without

Winnie-Wiyeni? Impossible to say – but surely a much worse place. Over the last forty years, through our mixture of social-ism, capitalism and distributism, the gap between rich and poor has narrowed wonderfully. And now with the World Federation strongly established, and no major war possible, I think it is safe to tell the world the truth about Time Travel. But even so, perhaps it is better that the actual invention is lost – forever, unless a genius comes on the scene again the equal of Peregrine Driver.

For that was the Traveller's name. We lost him, and his Machine, one day in October 1892. He vanished from his labo-ratory, one Thursday morning, leaving a note to say that he had gone in quest of "the real, the one and only Weena".

He also left a will which stipulated that, if he had not returned by the same date in 1893, he was to be presumed dead, and all his property was to be made over to Winifred Jane Welles. That was how, in October 1893, we acquired our first commune in Richmond.

One cannot choose but wonder: where did he go? To yet another version of the year 802,701 – to meet, perhaps, his end at the hands of some super-Morlocks? Or did he go back into the past, as a preliminary – to establish a time-line in which Welles would not be a possible rival for the affections of Weena?

Welles once suggested to me: "He may have messed us up thoroughly – so that in that world, Bertie Welles is the writer, and George Hillyer – I don't know what." I once wrote a story somewhat like that. In my tale, Professor Driver returned first to the second Thursday *morning*, October 8 about 10 a.m. There he picked up one version of himself and other Time Machine; then the two of them went back to the first Thursday dinner, October 1 – the dinner at which Welles was not present. In that time-line, the second dinner-party on October 8 never took place at all, Welles was therefore eliminated, and the raid on the far future was made by three Travellers on three Machines . . . That was fiction; but I do suspect that something *like* that may well have happened. If so, of course the Traveller disappeared completely from our own time stream.

For in our world, as everybody knows now, he has never returned.

THE WIND OVER THE WORLD

Steven Utley

One of the more popular plots associated with time travel is the possibility of returning to the age of the dinosaurs. Ray Bradbury wrote what many believe to be the definitive short story involving dinosaurs in "A Sound of Thunder" (1952), which showed how one small mistake by travellers to the past resulted in a diversity of changes in the present.

Steven Utley chose to go back even further in time, well before the age of the dinosaurs, to the Silurian Period, a geological age which lasted for over 30 million years some 400 million years ago. Life on land was comparatively minimal at that time. Utley, who sadly died while this volume was being compiled, has been writing his Silurian Tales since "There and Then" appeared in 1993 but it was not until the publication of The 400-Million-Year Itch *(2012) and* Invisible Kingdoms *(2013) that the stories were collected in book form. The following is one of the more poignant episodes.*

The attendant barely looked up from the clipboard cradled in the crook of his arm when Leveritt came in. The room was devoid of personality, but just as she entered through one door, a second man dressed in a lab coat went out through a door directly opposite, and in the instant before it swung shut, she glimpsed the room beyond – brightly lit, full of gleaming surfaces – and heard or thought that she heard a low sound like a faint pop of static or the breaking of waves against a shore. She shuddered as an electric thrill of excitement passed through her.

"Please stretch out on the gurney there." The man with the

clipboard continued writing as he spoke. "You can stow your seabag on the rack underneath."

Leveritt did as he said. She said, "I feel like I'm being prepped for surgery."

"We don't want you to black out and fall and hurt yourself." He finished writing, came around the end of the gurney to her, and turned the clipboard to show her the printed form. "This," he said, offering her his pen, "is where you log out of the present. Please sign on the line at the bottom there."

Leveritt's hand trembled as she reached for the pen. She curled her fingers into a fist and clenched it tightly for a second. She gave the attendant an apologetic smile. "I'm just a little nervous." She tried to show him that she really was just a little nervous by expanding the smile into a grin; it felt brittle and hideous on her face. "I did volunteer for this," she told him. I am more excited than scared to be doing this, she told herself.

The attendant smiled quickly, professionally. "Even volunteers have the right to be nervous. Try to relax. We've done this hundreds of times now, and there's nothing to it. Ah!"

His exclamation was by way of greeting a second attendant, so like him that Leveritt felt she would be unable to tell them apart were she to glance away for a moment, who escorted a slight figure dressed in new-looking safari clothes and carrying, instead of the high-powered rifle that would have completed his ensemble, a seabag and a laptop. He stowed the bag and climbed on to the gurney next to Leveritt's without being told, signed the log with a flourish, and lay back smiling. He turned his face toward Leveritt and said, "Looks like we're traveling companions – time-traveling companions!" He talked fast, as though afraid he would run out of breath before he finished saying what he had to say. "Allow me to introduce myself – Ed Morris."

"I'm Bonnie Leveritt."

"Pleased to meet you, Miz Leveritt – or is it Doctor?"

She wondered if he could utter sentences not punctuated with dashes. "Miz," she said, "working on Doctor. I'm on my way to join a field team from Texas A and M."

One of the attendants consulted his wristwatch and nodded to the other, and each picked up a loaded syringe. The man looming over Leveritt gave her that quick, professional smile again. "This is to keep you from going into shock."

She had no particular horror of needles but turned away, nevertheless, to watch Morris, who lay squinting against the glare of the fluorescent lights. She heard him grunt softly as the needle went into his arm.

"It'll be another few minutes," said Leveritt's attendant. He and his twin left. Leveritt and Morris waited.

After a minute or so, he asked her, "How you holding up?"

"Fine." Her voice sounded strange to her, thick, occluded, like a heavy smoker's. She cleared her throat and spoke the word again; improvement was arguable. "Actually," she confessed, "I'm nervous as hell. This is my first time. It wouldn't be so bad if I didn't have to lie here waiting."

"Supplies go through first – we're down on the priority list, below soap and toilet paper. My first time, I was nervous as hell, too. Nobody gives people in my line of work credit for much imagination. Except . . ." he made a breathless kind of chuckle ". . . when it comes to creative accounting. Yeah, I'm one of the bean-counters. But let me tell you – the night before my first time, I didn't sleep a wink. Not a wink. I kept imagining all sorts of things that might go wrong – plus, it all seemed so unreal, it was all so thrilling – and it was going to happen to me. Man! Oh, sure, the concept's more exciting than the reality. There's not much to where we're headed – a little moss and a lot of mud. Beats me why they couldn't've made a hole into some more interesting time period."

"I suppose that depends on your definition of interesting. Besides, as I understand it, they didn't make the hole, they sort of found it. We're lucky it didn't open up on somewhere we couldn't go or wouldn't want to."

"You mean, like my hometown – Dallas?"

Leveritt smiled; she was from Fort Worth. "Worse. For all but the few most recent hundred millions of years, the Earth's been pretty inhospitable – poisonous atmosphere, too much ultraviolet light, things like that."

"Spoken like a true scientist!"

"Not quite a full-blown one yet," she said, "but I guess I've got pedantry down."

"Ah. Well, anyway, as I was saying – I was nervous before my first time. Scared, in fact. You might not think it to look at me," and he paused long enough for her to realize that she was now to take a good look at him, so she did, "but I am no shrinking violet. I have a real active lifestyle – mountain climbing, sky diving. I guess I like heights."

Leveritt was willing to give Morris the benefit of the doubt, but he was a balding little fortyish man whom she could not imagine working his way up a sheer rockface. Dressed in his great-white-hunter outfit, he lay clutching the laptop to his narrow chest, drumming his middle, ring, and little fingers on the case. He looked as calm as though he were waiting for an elevator, but he also looked like what he was, an accountant.

"Still," he went on, "it's one thing to jump out of a plane at ten thousand feet – another to jump through a hole in time. Straight out of the twenty-first century – straight into the prehistoric past! So, I didn't get any sleep. The next day, when it came time for me to make the jump, I was a wreck – all because I was scared, see. But I hid the fact I was a wreck – and you know why? Because I was even more scared that if anybody found out, I wouldn't get to make the jump – getting to do it meant that much to me."

Leveritt gave him another, more heartfelt smile. "It does to me, too. But was it rough? The jump itself? I ask everyone I meet who's done it."

Morris screwed up his face and gestured dismissively. "It's no worse'n hitting a speed bump when you're driving a little too fast. Oh, sure, you hear sometimes about people who got bounced around kind of hard, but – speaking from personal experience – I honestly think I could've walked right out of the jump station afterwards with nothing more'n a headache and upset stomach. It was nothing. Now I'm less nervous about making the jump than I am about talking funding to this group of entomologists when I get there. Uh, you're not an entomologist yourself, are you?"

"Geologist."

"You ever tried to talk to an entomologist about anything but bugs?"

"Not knowingly, no."

"Then you've never had to pretend to listen to whatever gas some guy wants to vent—"

Leveritt had to laugh. "You obviously have never dated some guys!"

"Ah?" Morris frowned. "No. I sure haven't." Then he got it, or got part of it, anyway, and made another breathless chuckle. "Anyhow, I have to go talk to these entomologists, and they never can – I deal in the definite, see. All they can talk about is the great contributions they're making to science – how vital their work is. I know they're making contributions to science – that's why they're there, right? They understand all about bugs. I understand all about money – and never the twain shall meet . . ."

Leveritt found herself tuning out the sense of the words, but she could not tune out the sound of them. The drugs were taking effect; she wanted to relax and drift, but Morris's voice would not let her. She closed her eyes. Scarcely five seconds later, the attendants suddenly returned; one of them announced, "Time to go, folks," and Leveritt's gurney struck the door sharply as it lurched into motion. The air in the jump station had an unpleasant tang to it. Leveritt saw people moving briskly about, heard them muttering to one another, heard that low sound of static or surf again. A technician seated behind a console said, "One minute to next transmission."

"Doesn't matter which one of us goes through first, does it?" Morris asked his attendant, who answered with a shake of his head. The little man grinned at Leveritt. "Then I'll go first and wait for you on the other side."

"No. Please, I need to get this over with. Let me go first."

"Well, guys – you heard the lady."

Leveritt's attendant pushed her gurney quickly past Morris's, past a metal railing, on to the sending-receiving platform. He lightly touched her arm with the back of his hand. "Have a nice trip."

"Thanks."

"Deep breaths, now," he said as he stepped back off the platform.

"Standby to send," said the technician at the console. "Five seconds. Four."

Leveritt inhaled deeply.

"Three."

Morris caught her eye through the bars of the railing. She was touched by and grateful for his wink of encouragement.

"Two."

She started to exhale. Everything turned to white light.

The Navy doctor held her eye open between his thumb and forefinger and directed the beam from a penlight into it. She moved her tongue in her mouth, swallowed, and managed to say, "Where'm I?"

"Sickbay."

"I made it? To the Silurian?"

The doctor put away the penlight. "Now, what do you think?"

Leveritt moved her head experimentally and at once regretted it. When the pain had receded, she carefully took stock. She was still on the gurney. There were exposed pipes overhead and a muffled throb of machinery. The ship, she thought, I'm on the ship, in the Silurian, and after a second or two she realized that she was disappointed. She had wondered if being in Silurian time would feel somehow different. Thus far, it felt just like a hangover.

The doctor held up a knuckley finger in front of her face. "I want you to follow my finger with your eyes. Don't move your head."

It hurt her even to think about moving her head again. She watched the finger move to the left and back to the right. She said, "My head's killing me."

"You'll be fine in a little while. You're just a little shaken up. Here." He gave her two aspirin tablets and some water in a paper cup. "Stay on the gurney till those take effect. Then we'll see about getting you up on your feet."

"How soon can I get ashore?"

"We generally like to keep new arrivals under observation for at least six hours." Leveritt groaned when he said that, and he gave her a mildly reproachful look. "You can only get ashore by boat, and the next one doesn't leave until late this afternoon."

"It's just that I've been looking forward to this so long."

"Uh huh. Well, the Silurian Period's still got five or ten million years to run. You aren't going to miss out on it."

The door opened behind him, and a khaki-clad officer leaned in and asked, "Doctor White, may I talk to her now?" Visible in the passageway was an unhappy-looking man in civilian clothes.

"These gentlemen," said the doctor, "have some questions they want to ask you. Feel up to it?"

Before she could reply, the officer said, "Just a couple of routine questions."

"Sure."

The officer moved quickly toward the gurney with the civilian in tow. Doctor White said, "Miz Leveritt, this is Mister Hales—"

"How do you do?" said the officer, rather too impatiently, she thought.

"—and this is Doctor Cutsinger." The civilian slightly inclined his head in greeting and repeated her name. "The lieutenant is from our operations department. Doctor Cutsinger is one of our civilian engineers."

"Physicist," Cutsinger said, and smiled tightly.

Leveritt tried to sound good-natured. "I was hoping you were the welcoming committee. Isn't anybody going to welcome me to the Paleozoic?" Evidently, no one was. Lieutenant Hales regarded her as though her show of good-naturedness were somehow in poor taste. Cutsinger continued to look unhappy. The doctor nodded at the two men and went out, closing the door behind himself. Leveritt repressed a sigh of bafflement and said, "Well, gentlemen, ask away."

Hales said, "Miz Leveritt."

"Lieutenant?"

He was obviously uncertain as to how to proceed. The lower part of his expression suddenly twisted, rearranging itself into an approximation of a smile; at the same time, a frown intensified the upper part. Considered with his deep-set eyes and hook nose, the effect was ghastly and alarming. Finally, he said, "The, ah, experience of time-travel is never exactly the same for anyone. We like to find out, ah, make a point of finding out how it was for each person each time. Can you describe your experience in detail?"

Leveritt's eyes met Cutsinger's. He blinked and shifted his gaze to a point slightly to the right of her ear. She refocused on

Hales and said, "I'm afraid there were no details, just a blinding flash of light."

Hales seemed disappointed by her answer. "What about before the jump? Did anything in the jump station strike you as unusual?"

If you weren't so intense, Leveritt thought, that question would be funny. "It was all unusual to me, because, as you surely must know already, this was my first jump."

"Of course. We want your impressions, though. Anything you can tell us, anything at all. Before the flash of light, when they took you into the jump station – you and Ed Morris. Do you know him well?"

She saw something shift in Cutsinger's face as he glanced at the lieutenant, saw his expression of general unhappiness sharpen into one of very particular contempt. To the oblivious Hales she said, "I don't know him at all. We met a few minutes before the jump, and he talked my ear off. I think you'd do better to ask him these questions. As you surely must also know, Mister Morris'd made at least one jump before this. He can tell you if anything was unusual or not. As for me . . ." she swung her legs over the edge of the gurney and sat up ". . . if I'm going to answer any more questions, it's going to be in an upright position."

After a second's hesitation, she slid off the gurney, on to her feet. Cutsinger said, "Are you all right?"

"A little rubbery in the knees, like I just came in off the jogging trail. Otherwise . . ." She stepped away from the gurney, quickly stepped back, leaned on it for support, admitted, "Still a little wobbly." She locked eyes with the lieutenant. "What is it in particular you're driving at? I somehow can't help feeling you know something and are dying to know if I know it, too."

Hales turned the full force of his grimace on her again, and she realized with a jolt that he now intended it to be a look of reassurance. "As I said, these are just routine questions."

And possibly excepting my six-year-old nephew, you are the worst, the most unconvincing liar I've ever known. She almost said it aloud. What stopped her was the thought of all the time and effort she had put into getting this far – to a room, as she saw it, adjoining the prehistoric past – and how much farther there was to go. Fist on hip, she waited.

Hales, however, clearly was at a loss. He turned to Cutsinger, who, no less clearly, was close to losing his temper. "Anything you can think of to ask her?"

"I told you there was no point to this!"

"I wish to God," said Leveritt, "one of you would tell me what this is all about." Neither man spoke. "Fine. Have it your way. But if I don't get out of this room, I'm going to go insane. The doctor said I wouldn't be able to go ashore for hours, but if you're through, I'd at least like to take a look outside. Okay? Please?"

Cutsinger brushed past Hales. He said, "Permit me," and offered Leveritt his arm.

A romantic, she thought, taking it.

"I think," Hales said, "Miz Leveritt had better remain in sickbay."

Not looking back at him, Cutsinger said, "Take a flying leap."

"Master-at-arms!"

A bluejacket with a sidearm suddenly filled the doorway. Cutsinger sighed, shrugged, and said, "Sorry," as he directed Leveritt to a chair.

"I'm sorry, too," said Hales, "but this is a United States Navy ship, and the rules of security are in force. Miz Leveritt, I want you to understand that this interview is confidential."

"So much for the subtle approach!" Cutsinger said sourly.

Hales ignored him. "You're not to repeat any part of our conversation to anybody or make any record of it without express authorization. Any breach—"

"I'm sure she gets the idea, Lieutenant."

"Not at all," said Leveritt. "What am I not supposed to talk about?"

"We have a situation," Cutsinger said quickly, before Hales could open his mouth to answer her, "an unprecedented one, I might add, which is why Hales here's so rattled, why he's handling it in such a ham-handed manner. Ham-headed, too." The lieutenant's mouth did open now, in a threat display. Cutsinger met it with a glower and continued talking. "About all he's really going to accomplish by invoking security is to make it impossible for you to do the work you came here to do."

Leveritt gave Hales an even look. "I didn't come all this way just to fight the Navy."

"There're some thousands of people living and working here," said Hales, "and in the interest of general morale, we have got to keep rumors and misinformation from spreading and panic from breaking out."

"You're the one who's panicked! Either leave her alone or tell her. She'll hear all about it soon enough."

"Don't underestimate Navy security," Hales said stiffly.

That elicited a harsh laugh from Cutsinger. "I bet you anything it was all over the ship inside of five minutes. I bet you it's already gotten ashore, some version of it, anyhow. All you're doing is putting Miz Leveritt in a very awkward position. She'll be the only person in the whole expedition who won't have an opinion on what everybody else is talking about."

"Master-at-arms, Doctor Cutsinger is needed back at the jump station."

"Aye, aye, sir." The bluejacket stepped to Cutsinger's side.

"Tell her," Cutsinger said over his shoulder as he went out, "for God's sake, tell her."

The bluejacket closed the door behind himself, and Hales said, "Well." He looked at Leveritt; his features relaxed; he almost smiled a real smile. "Please accept my apologies on Doctor Cutsinger's behalf. As a civilian aboard a Navy ship, he naturally finds working under Navy supervision irksome at times."

"By supervision, do you mean armed guard?"

"I mean – I am not a martinet or a horse's patoot." He took a step toward the door. "Please come with me. I have enough to worry about without you going insane."

He led her down the passageway and opened a heavy steel door at the end of it. As Leveritt stepped through the doorway and on to a catwalk, a breeze touched her face and ruffled her hair. Her first, quick 180-degree survey took in the fact that the ship and some lesser vessels lay off a rocky coast. She gripped the railing with both hands and inhaled the scent of sea salt and the faintly oily smell of the ship. From a deck overhanging the catwalk came the sounds of a helicopter warming up its motor and spinning its blades. Below, waves smacked noisily against the hull. The mid-morning sun was behind the ship, in whose great angular shadow the water was blue-black, almost slate-colored. Close by, two auxiliary craft rode at anchor, and beyond them a glittering expanse of blue-green water stretched to a line of sea cliffs. Even as she stared, transfixed by the sight of that shore, another, even smaller craft – not a Navy vessel at all, but a sailboat – came into view around the headland. Against the somber cliffs, its sail looked like a blazing fire. "Oh, my." She breathed the words.

Hales had followed her on to the catwalk. He rested his elbows on the railing and did not look at her when he spoke. "Doctor Cutsinger did tell me there'd be no point in question-ing you. If there'd been any way to find out what we need to know without actually asking you . . ."

She realized after a moment that what he was saying must be important, but it took an effort of will to turn her attention from the Silurian vista, and she was scarcely able to say, "I beg your pardon?"

"He also talked me out of sending you right back to the twenty-first century. He may have talked me out of confining you to the ship until we get this, this situation straightened out."

Now Leveritt could not take her eyes off him. "I swear to you, I don't know anything and won't talk to anybody about anything; please just let me go off into the hinterlands and collect rocks like I'm supposed to."

Hales almost smiled again. "He said I'm treating everyone here like children. I'm not trying to, I'm really not. I see his point." He made a gesture that seemed meant to take in every-thing around them. "This is the greatest thing since the moon landings, and a lot less exclusive. Every single person here, Navy as well as civilian, wants to be here and volunteered to be here. Doctor Cutsinger's view is, we're all grownups and deserve to be told the truth like grownups. All the truth all the time."

Leveritt asked, "And what's your view?" and when he did not answer immediately, "Or doesn't the Navy let you have one?"

"Right the second time. All of us here, we're an extension of our nation. There're all these little communities of scientists scattered about, and there's the Navy, delivering supplies, providing transport, holding things together. The Silurian

Earth's a United States possession, Miz Leveritt, American territory, and the Navy's here to guard our national interests. It is in the national interest that the Navy decides what is classified matter. Only persons who need to know about classified matter to perform an official job for the Navy are entrusted with the information. That's rule number one, and it leaves you out. Rule number two is, persons to whom classified matter is entrusted are responsible for protecting it against unauthorized disclosure. That hems me in."

"Fine. What're you going to do with me?"

"Escort you back to sickbay. Later, I hope, see you on your way to go collect rocks."

It was late in the short Silurian day when Hales guided Leveritt through the ship to the boat bay. From a platform above that noisy grotto, she watched as the last supplies were loaded, then, with a nod to the lieutenant, descended to the boat. The coxswain helped her aboard. Hales surprised her by climbing down after her. He gave no sign that he heard her when she asked, "Are you going to keep watch on me from now on?" She found a seat amidships; he gave her a nod as he took the one next to hers but said nothing.

She was too excited, however, to resent his presence. She had had sleep, a shower, and her first food in almost twenty-four hours, and the morning's frustrations and mystifications were falling away behind her. When she ran her eye over the neatly stowed boxes and crates, the words BATHROOM TISSUE prompted something too fleeting to be called a memory. The bay's gates opened. Leveritt looked up, caught a glimpse of someone who could have been Cutsinger on the platform, and glanced at Hales to gauge his reaction. His attention, though, was directed forward rather than upward. The boat slid out, sliced across the ship's lengthening, darkening shadow, and emerged suddenly into sunlight. She gazed shoreward, at the drowned valley's rocky walls, and felt that at last she truly was entering Paleozoic time. Not even the sight of the pier, jutting out from the near shore below a cluster of Quonset huts and tents, dispelled the feeling. She spared the ship a single backward glance. Everything in its shadow, everything aboard it, contained by it – even the air circulating through it and the seawater sloshing within the confines of its boat bay – belonged to the twenty-first century. She looked shoreward again and thought of the great steel monster no more.

Several boats, including a tiny blue-hulled sailboat, were tied up at the pier. Indistinct human figures waiting there gradually resolved themselves into a small party of Navy men in tropical khakis and two civilians who stood apart both from them and from each other. Both civilians wore white suits, but one man was short, stout, and sunburnt, and the other was tall as well as thickset, tanned rather than burnt, and had a Panama hat with a purple hat band set at a rakish angle atop his squarish head. It was clear from his bearing that he considered himself to be a vision. Leveritt laughed when she saw him, waved, and called out, "Rob! Rob Brinkman!"

Brinkman waved back, and when the boat had been tied up he reached down and offered Leveritt his enormous brown hand. She was a medium-sized woman, heavier in the hips than she cared to be, but he seemed to lift her right out of the boat and on to the pier with only minimal assistance from her. His grin and voice were as big as the rest of him. "Welcome to the Silurian!"

Leveritt hugged him. She could not quite encircle his torso with her arms. "It's about time someone here said that to me. What a suit! What a hat! Is this what you wear on collecting trips now?"

"Only if pretty grad students are going along."

Behind her, somebody peevishly said, "I'm supposed to meet Ed Morris. I'm Michael Diehl, from the San Diego Natural History Museum."

As Brinkman stepped around Leveritt to ask a bluejacket to hand up her gear, she saw the other civilian peering anxiously into the boat, as though he expected to spot Ed Morris trying to hide from him among the cargo. The party of Navy men had got immediately to work unloading the boat, and their interest in Diehl did not extend beyond his keeping out of their way. Hales, however, introduced himself and said, "I regret that Mister Morris is unable to come ashore at this time."

"Eh? Why not?"

"Side-effects of the jump."

"Oh. Well, you could've radioed that piece of information and saved me an hour's wait for nothing. Could've saved yourself a boat ride, too."

Hales noticed Leveritt watching him. He favored Diehl with a mild version of his frown-above, smile-below expression. "Boat rides're what the Navy's all about."

Brinkman turned with Leveritt's seabag on his shoulder and said, "Okay," and the two of them walked away. The pier came straight off the camp's main thoroughfare, which was paved with metal matting and lined with huts. Tents had been erected along intersecting streets. There was a good deal of pedestrian traffic, both civilian and Navy. Brinkman led Leveritt past supply, generator, and administration buildings, the dispensary, the exchange, the mess – "The Navy part of camp," he told her, adding, "but we get to use the facilities, of course." Civilian personnel lived in and worked out of a group of tents he called the suburbs. "Our people're already upriver, so, tonight, you'll be the guest of a bunch of centipede enthusiasts."

"How charming."

"It'd probably be a good idea to shake out your shoes in the morning. Want some dinner?"

"I think all I want tonight," she said, "is to walk a little way past the last row of tents, where I can see pure and unadulterated Paleozoic."

"Care for a guide?"

She gave him a sidelong mock-wary lock. "Not if it's some notorious lady-killer in an ice-cream suit."

Brinkman laughed. "Just make sure you keep the camp on your left when you go out, or you'll wind up in the marsh. And don't go out too far, either. And don't stay up too late."

"Yes, Mother."

"We leave right after breakfast, and around here breakfast is at sunrise."

He showed her where she was to spend the night. None of his centipede enthusiasts was about, so Leveritt put her seabag just inside the door, bade him good night, and with no further ado set out on her walk. Not far beyond the last row of tents, the ground rose sharply; the going was not especially rough, but she did not push her luck – the sun was going down fast, and she did not fancy making her way across unfamiliar ground in the dark. Just as she reached a ledge from which she could look down into the camp, a thin bugle call announced the commencement of the evening colors ceremony. Electric lights illuminated the camp, and she had no trouble spotting the flagpole. There came a second bugle call, followed by the national anthem. The flag sank slowly out of sight behind a Quonset hut. Out on the water, the shadow of the Earth itself swallowed up the ship. Leveritt sat down on warm smooth rock, lay back to look up at the purpling, then blackening, sky, and finally felt herself part of Silurian reality, in Paleozoic time and space. Contentment filled her.

How long she remained thus, she did not know. The moon rose, the unrecognizable stars slightly shifted their positions. Eventually, she became aware that the rock had cooled without getting any softer. She got up and walked slowly toward camp.

As she came among the tents, she heard voices and music from some of them and noticed that traffic had thinned. No insects orbited the lights, unexpectedly reminding her that no birds had wheeled and screeched over the bay. She knew, of course, that the Silurian was too early for birds and insects – flying insects, at least – but until this moment she had not appreciated their absence.

Just before she reached her tent, she saw Michael Diehl approaching. His face held a sickly cast, and he appeared to have his entire attention focused on the ground before him. When she started to go inside, however, he called out, "Excuse me, these tents're reserved for the San Diego Natural History Museum."

"Rob Brinkman said there's an extra cot. He's the—"

"Brinkman. Texas A and M." Diehl was near enough now for her to catch a whiff of what he breathed out. His red complexion, she decided, was not wholly the result of too much sun.

"We're on our way upriver in the morning," she said, "so it'll only be—"

"You're the woman who came in on the boat with Lieutenant Hales. Leveritt, isn't it?"

"Yes. And your name's Diehl. Look, if there's a problem, I'm sure Doctor Brinkman can—"

"You made the jump this morning. With Ed Morris."

"Yes." She said it quickly and said no more, not wanting to be cut off again.

Diehl glanced to left and right. "I think you better come with me. I know where we can have a drink and talk in private."

"Um, thank you for the offer, but I'm very tired, and I need to—"

"You're the only one I can talk to about what's happened to Ed Morris!" There was a note of pleading in the whiskey-scented voice. "And I'm the only one you can talk to."

"What? What's happened to Ed Morris?"

Diehl looked closely at her. "You don't know? No, I can see you don't. You didn't really see it happen. I guess nobody really saw it. And Hales didn't tell you, did he? No, of course he didn't. He laid that Navy security stuff on me, too. Tried to hand me some crap, and when I raised holy hell and threatened to go straight to his commanding officer—"

"What about Ed Morris?"

"There was an accident! Come on, let's go where we can talk. We're too close to the Navy here."

She hesitated as he walked past, got as far into a protest as "I don't think I'm supposed," then followed him back the way she had just come, up the slope behind the camp, to the ledge. Diehl wiped the mouth of a small flask on his coat sleeve and offered it to her. She declined to accept. He took a drink, gasped, and replaced the screw top.

"Ed Morris," he said, "didn't come through the hole today like he was supposed to."

"What do you mean?"

"Just what I said. Hales told me – after I made him tell me – Morris made the jump one minute after you, but he never arrived here. He's gone. Lost."

"Gone, lost – where?"

Diehl shook his head. "They don't know."

"But—"

"They don't know! They honestly don't. Maybe it was some glitch in the machinery that did it, or sunspots. Maybe some quirk of the hole itself, something they don't know about. I frankly don't think they know much more about the hole now than they did in the beginning."

"But how do you *lose* somebody?"

"You gotta remember what a strange thing the hole is. When they first stumbled across it, all they knew was, here's this strange thing. This anomaly. They sent in robot probes to get specimens, photograph everything in sight. By and by, they figured out what they had was this doorway into the past. But it didn't just open up on a place on a day. It wasn't that stable. There was a sort of flutter, and it caused what they call spatial drift and temporal spread. So, two probes might go through together on our side, the twenty-first-century side, but come out miles and years apart on the Silurian side. That's why they built the jump stations. They built one of them aboard that ship and pushed the ship through the hole so they could keep things synchronized on both sides of the hole. It all worked perfectly, until today. Today, Ed Morris may've been plunked down anywhere. Far inland or far out to sea. He may've arrived a hundred years ago or a hundred years from now."

"Alive?" She was barely able to ask it.

"Not for long. Not unless he's a helluva lot smarter and luckier'n Robinson Crusoe. And if he was hurt—"

"How awful. That poor man."

"If he was really lucky, he never knew what happened. Never felt a thing. Hales says he may just've been scattered across four hundred million years."

Leveritt felt a chill of horror, though she could not have said what being scattered across four hundred million years might entail.

"He says everything's working again," Diehl went on, "they're sending and receiving again, but until they figure out what went wrong . . ." He abandoned the sentence to take another drink. "Everything we use here, food, supplies, it's all gotta come through the hole. And the hole—"

Leveritt knew what he was about to say and said it for him. "The hole's the only way home."

"You got that right! The only way!"

She looked upward. The moon was slightly higher in the sky than when she had seen it – how long before? Half an hour? Then, she had experienced happiness greater than any other she could remember. Now, she felt oppressed, weighed down.

They were silent for almost a minute. Then, as Diehl tilted his head back to drink, Leveritt said, "Well, what can we do about it?"

Diehl smacked his lips. "Indeed, what? Doesn't seem right. It isn't right. A man dies, vanishes – whatever's applicable in this case. He's got no family or friends far's I can find out, and there's nothing to bury. And nobody's supposed to talk about him, so he won't even get a memorial service. Not even if he did have family and friends."

"M-mister Diehl, I don't think we should—"

"It isn't right! Know what really sets us apart from the animals? Never mind what religion says about souls. Souls're just puffs of air. The only thing makes a man's death meaningful is remembrance. Without remembrance, he's just a wind that blew over the world and never left a trace."

"Mister Diehl! I don't think we should talk about him any more. I don't think we should meet again, either."

"Huh? Why not?"

"If Lieutenant Hales finds out we've had this conversation and that I know about Ed Morris—"

"To hell with Hales! Don't be scared of him; stand up to him like I did!"

"He may not be able to make trouble for you," Leveritt said impatiently, "but I think he can make a lot for me. It's already occurred to him to either send me back home or lock me up. Will you give me your word you won't let him find out?"

"Bastard's not gonna hear a thing from me. And if you're upriver, he can't bother you any."

"I wish I could be sure of that. I'm – listen, from the moment I learned about the hole, I wanted to join this expedition. I worked hard to get here. Now that I am here . . ."

Her voice trailed off in a sob; her throat constricted as she sensed impending, insupportable loss, and tears gathered on her eyelashes. She clenched her jaw and fists and held on, somehow, to her composure. Beside her, Diehl coughed and said in his thickened voice, "Still some left, how 'bout it?" and when she had blinked away the tears, she saw him holding the flask out to her again.

"No," she said, "thank you."

"You ever drink?"

"Hardly ever."

"Same here," and he raised the flask to his lips.

"Well," she said, and went carefully down the slope and directly to her tent. The camp had grown quiet, and most of the electric lights had been extinguished. A middle-aged woman answered her knock and let her get barely one sentence into an explanation before inviting her inside and introducing herself as Carol Hays.

"Rob Brinkman met me in the mess tent," Hays said, "and told me to expect you. Sorry nobody was here earlier, but we were probably still sluicing the mud off ourselves. We've been slogging around in the marsh all day."

Leveritt let Hays introduce her to a sleepy-looking young woman. She instantly forgot the woman's name but managed to smile and say, "Doctor Brinkman told me you're centipede enthusiasts."

Hays made a mock-horrified face and then laughed, and the young woman, affecting a tolerably good Dixie-belle drawl, said, "We have found that gentlemen do not look at us quite so askance if we refer to ourselves as entomologists."

Did either of you know Ed Morris? Leveritt wanted to ask. She was grateful that they were very tired and not such good hosts that they would stay awake on her account.

Soon, on her cot, in the dark, she lay listening to their soft, regular breathing and trying to resist falling immediately asleep. She had realized as soon as she lay her head down that she was exhausted, but she felt herself under obligation, at the end of a day she regarded as the most momentous of her life, to spend some time sifting through its events, analyzing and categorizing, summing up. She could not, however, keep everything straight on the ledger page before her mind's eye; Ed Morris kept shoving everything else aside. Then, when she thought pointedly about what must have happened to him, her imagination was drawn not to visions of accidents resulting in death, but to one of a human figure stretched like a rubber band from the top of the geologic column toward an indefinite point at the mid-Paleozoic level. The figure was alive. It writhed across almost half a billion years.

She recoiled from that image, and another promptly presented itself: Ed Morris as a straight line continually approaching a curve but never meeting it within finite distance.

But perhaps, she told herself, he met a real death instead of some exotic asymptotic fate. Perhaps he's at the bottom of the bay . . .

If I'd let him make the jump before me, it would've been me who . . .

And Morris might've been sitting out there with Diehl tonight, trying to think of something to say about a person he'd barely known for five minutes.

Or maybe not. Diehl wouldn't even have known who Morris was talking about . . .

She awoke remembering no dreams. The sky had only begun to lighten; she showered and dressed and was packed and waiting to go when Brinkman came for her. He wore old khaki now, and a hat that needed blocking. After a quick breakfast, they went directly to the pier. There was fog enough so that, viewed from the pier's end, the camp seemed obscured by curtains of gauze. Nothing could be seen of the vessels in the bay.

Leveritt and Brinkman stepped aboard the boat that was to carry them upriver. There was no ceremony, no one to see them on their way, and they were the only passengers. They sat under a white canopy and drank coffee from a thermos bottle as the lines were cast off and the boat nosed into the current. Pier and camp receded and were soon lost from sight; by the time the fog lifted, they lay behind a bend in the river. The view from the boat was of barren heights and marshy borders. Dense Lilliputian forests of primitive plants covered the low, muddy islets. At length, Brinkman put his face close to Leveritt's and said, "Hello."

She started, drew back, looked at him in astonishment.

"I said hello, Bonnie. Before that, I said I think it's going to be a beautiful day." He aimed a finger vaguely skyward. "You know, dazzling blue sky, fleecy white clouds."

"Sorry. I must've – I was in a trance."

"I'll say."

She nodded toward the marsh. "I guess I've probably seen nearly every documentary ever made about the Silurian. But I never imagined how quiet it is here. Life on Earth hasn't found its voice yet. Hasn't hit its stride." She broke into a grin. "I think I'm quoting from one of those old documentaries."

"I doubt it," said Brinkman. "I bet everybody here is secretly, mentally narrating a documentary every second of the day."

The boat bisected the silent world. Brinkman pulled his hat down over his eyes, folded his arms, and slept. After a time, Leveritt realized, and was by fast turns surprised and appalled to realize, that the vista bored her.

It can't be! she thought in panic.

It isn't, she thought a moment later. It's something else. I'm distracted.

By Ed Morris.

Leveritt sprawled on her cot, arms and legs dangling over the edge because she could not bear her own blistering touch. It was a hot evening and humid, so sticky that her face stung and her T-shirt and boxer shorts adhered to her skin, pasted to it with perspiration. Her tentmate, Gilzow, lay on the other cot, a wet handkerchief over her face. The flaps were drawn at both ends of the tent; from time to time, the air between the two women stirred discreetly, trying, it seemed to Leveritt, to attract as little attention as possible when it did so.

Finally, she delivered herself of a theatrical groan to signal that she was giving up on the notion of falling asleep. She sat up, lighted the lantern, and wiped her face and throat with a damp cloth. She said, "And I thought Texas summers were miserable."

Through her handkerchief, Gilzow said, "Look at the bright side. No mosquitoes. No fire ants, either."

"But no shade trees to sit under, and no grass to sit on. And no watermelon to eat out on the grass, out under a tree."

Gilzow lifted a corner of the handkerchief and peeked out. "You know what'd really be nice right now? Cold beer. Not that awful Navy stuff; I mean, real beer. Fine, manly beer so cold it's got ice crystals suspended in it. Or rum and Coke, in a big tall glass, with lots of ice cubes. Mm hmm. Cool us off and render us insensible at the same time." She let the corner of the handkerchief fall back into place. "I cannot believe there isn't a drop of anything to drink in this whole camp."

"Well, at least we can get Cokes and ice at the supply tent."

Gilzow sighed, barely audibly above the lantern's hiss. Then she plucked the handkerchief off her face and sat up. "I'm willing to forego insensibility," she said, "if I can only cool off. Just let me find my sandals."

Leveritt slipped outside and waited, listening. The camp was on a low bluff overlooking the river valley. Behind the bluff was a rocky flatland extending to distant hills. By day it stood revealed in all its stark desolation; nothing moved on the plain that wind or rain did not move, for only down in the valley, along the river's winding course, was there life. Between sunset and sunrise, the flatland lay vast and black, as mysterious as sea depths, while the night resounded with the cracking of cooling rocks.

Gilzow emerged. Theirs was the one undarkened tent, and the sky was overcast, but the obscured full moon cast enough light for them to see their way through the camp. No one else was about. The tents were open, however, and out of them came snatches of conversation, murmurings about heat and humidity and the day's work and the next day's prospects. When they overheard a man say, "Roger, where's that rain you predicted?" they paused, Gilzow literally in mid-step, balanced on one foot, until Roger answered, "I think the rain clouds must've gotten themselves snagged on those jumbly old hills." Leveritt walked on, Gilzow hopped and skipped to catch up, and her soft laughter hung in the unmoving air.

"Jumbly old hills!" She glanced back over her shoulder at the tent. "I don't think Roger's actually supposed to be doing what he does. I think he's a meteorologist who got lost on his way to becoming a poet."

"Listen to you!"

"It's true. He once showed me some poems he'd written, and I memorized one of them." Gilzow stopped walking, struck a pose, and recited:

> "Australopithecus' sleep
> is fitful, for it seems
> that Australopithecus
> isn't used to having dreams."

"That's not poetry," Leveritt said, "it's doggerel. And besides, I'm sure australopithecines could—"

"Oh, get a sense of humor, Bonnie."

Stung, Leveritt opened her mouth to reply, but no retort occurred to her.

"Sorry, Bonnie." Gilzow sounded sincerely contrite. "This heat and humidity—"

"It's okay," Leveritt said stiffly. "It's – I'm a born pedant."

On their way back from the supply tent, carrying a cooler between themselves and each holding an opened soft drink by its throat in her free hand, they came upon two men. Gilzow said, "Mike, Roger."

Mike Holmes and Roger Ovington turned, and the former said, "Hi, Lou. Bonnie. Hot enough for you?"

"Blah. About that rain, Roge."

"Paleozoic weather's as capricious as Cenozoic." Ovington nodded toward the hills. "But it's coming. We just saw some lightning flashes way off on the horizon."

"Bonnie 'n' I're going to have to drown our sorrows in straight Coca-Cola – unless somebody around here's got some rum or something he'd consider swapping for bizarre sexual favors."

"Sorry," said Holmes, "sorrier than I know how to tell you," and he gave a little laugh obviously intended to show that he might not be kidding. Gilzow laughed, too, to show that she definitely was. Leveritt could only marvel at her tentmate's self-possession. She herself could think of nothing to say, could think nothing, in fact, except, We're all four of us standing here in our underwear.

"Well," Gilzow said, "come sit on the cliff with us anyway. We also grabbed some crackers and a can of chicken salad."

"Then stand back, girls," Holmes said, "because we take big bites."

They sat among the rocks at the edge of the bluff and dangled their feet over an inky void – by night, the valley was abyssal. They ate and spoke of nothing in particular. All four of them started at a very loud pop of fracturing rock, and Ovington said, "It doesn't take much imagination to populate the darkness here with giant crustacean monsters clacking their claws."

Gilzow leaned close to Leveritt and said in a low voice, "I rest my case."

Holmes said to Ovington, "Sometimes you are a weird person."

Ovington laughed. "To me, prehistoric still means big ugly monsters. Hey, I'm just a weatherman, okay? I can't tell a psychophyte – what is it?"

"*Psilo*phyte," said Gilzow.

"I can't tell a psilophyte from creamed spinach. To me, a trilobite's just a waterlogged pillbug. And it doesn't matter what time period I'm in, meteorology's the same here as it is back home. Trade winds blow from the east, a high-pressure system's still – everything's different for the rest of you."

"Not for me and Bonnie," said Holmes. "Rocks is rocks."

"Still." Ovington gestured at the overcast sky. "The Milky Way's different, yet it looks the same to me here as it does back home. One of the astronomers told me once that in the time between now and the twenty-first century, our little solar system is going to travel all the way around the rim of the galaxy. A complete orbit and then some, as a matter of fact."

"You try to imagine that," Leveritt said quietly, "but you just can't."

"When I was a kid," said Gilzow, "I drove myself just about nuts trying to deal with geologic time and cosmic immensity. I started collecting models of geologic time, copying them out of science books and science-fiction novels, into a notebook. I must've ended up with a couple or three dozen. Like, if the Earth's age were compressed into twelve months, or twenty-four hours, or sixty minutes. Or how, if you put a dime on top of the world's tallest building, the height of the building would represent the entire age of the Earth, and the thickness of the dime would represent how long humans've been around."

"I like that one," Ovington said, and laughed. "I like it a lot!"

"My favorite," said Holmes, extending both arms out from his sides, "has always been the one my dad taught me when I was ten. The span of my arms, he said, was how long life had existed on Earth. And all of human history and prehistory fit on the edge of my fingernail."

"Dang," said Gilzow, "where's my notebook?"

They fell silent. Minutes passed, irregularly punctuated by the sounds of splintering rock and faint, unmistakable thunder.

"Do you suppose," Leveritt said suddenly, and tried to keep herself from asking the question that had been forming in her for weeks, since the night before the boat had brought her from the camp on the estuary, tried to make herself stop, but it had to come out now, had to, now, "do you suppose that if somebody came from the twenty-first century and died here in the Silurian, he'd cease to exist back in the future?"

The others' faces turned toward her. She could not see their expressions clearly but did not think she needed to see them to imagine their collective thought: What a truly *stupid* question!

Holmes said, "Whoa," but not sarcastically, and then, "Run that by me again."

Encouraged, she said, "I mean, would that person still be born and grow up to come back through time and die four hundred million years before he's born? Or would he be erased from existence? Would he have never been?"

"Actually," said Ovington – it was, Leveritt realized with gratitude, his kind of question – "there's a story about someone who decided to tackle that very matter. This was back in the early days of the expedition, when everybody was jittery about creating paradoxes. All this person did was bring back some lab animals and kill them."

"What happened?" Leveritt said.

"Nothing happened. You could say the experiment annihilated the animals but didn't annihilate them from having been. Or so the story goes. It may not be a true story."

"What if—" Leveritt cut herself short. What if *what*? What if somebody were to be scattered across four hundred million years, what then? "Nothing. Never mind."

Gilzow turned back to Ovington. "What you're saying, if that story's not true, is that the matter hasn't been settled."

"Well, by now, it surely has. People've been in Paleozoic time long enough."

"Long enough, anyway," said Holmes, "so nobody can tell the true stories from the weird rumors. All these myths're building up. Everybody repeats them; nobody knows if there's anything to them or not. Like the one about the government's secret plan to dump reactor waste in the Silurian."

"Actually," Ovington said, "the way I heard that story, if it is the same story, is that some generals tried to figure out a military application for a hole into the Silurian. Their plan was to sow Eurasia and Gondwanaland with nukes, so, later on, whenever the infidels and darkies got out of line—"

Holmes guffawed, and Gilzow said, "It's got to be true!"

"No," said Holmes, "it can't be, it's too stupid."

"It's so stupid it has to be true."

"Maybe it is," said Ovington, "and maybe it isn't, but this much is certain – the United States isn't sharing the hole with anybody!"

Then, Leveritt thought, there's the story about the man who jumped through – into? across? – time and never came – out? down? Anyway, he vanished as though he'd never been. No one could tell he'd ever been, because nobody was supposed to talk about him.

And there's a woman in the story who worked hard to get someplace, do something, be somebody. She found true happiness for maybe a whole hour. Afterward, she kept wondering what had happened to it, what had gone wrong. She was no quitter, never had been, but her work somehow wasn't as fulfilling as she'd expected, and everyone around her thought she was a humorless prig.

But those were just symptoms. The problem—

Thunder rolled across the flatland, louder than before. Leveritt looked and saw a lightning-shot purple sky. The air suddenly moved and grew cool, eliciting a duet of ahs from Gilzow and Holmes and a full-throated cry of "Yes!" from someone in camp. Ovington rose and shouted in that direction, "I told you it was coming!" To the others on the bluff, he said, "Gotta run. Work to do," and rushed off.

"Guess we'd better go batten down," said Holmes.

"Just toss everything into the cooler," Gilzow told him. "Bonnie 'n' I'll clean it up later."

He did as she said, and then they picked up the cooler between themselves and hurried away.

Leveritt did not follow. The problem, she sat thinking, really was that the woman thought she was in a different story, her own, instead of the one about the man who vanished. Every time she turned around, there was his ghost. She couldn't make him go away. There was no place else for him to go, no one else who would take him in. No one else knew who he was because she wasn't supposed to talk about him.

Stop haunting me, Ed Morris. Stop.

The first heavy raindrop struck Leveritt on the back of the hand. She got to her feet and found herself leaning into a stiffening wind, squinting against airborne grit, in some danger of being either blown off the bluff or else blinded and simply blundering over the edge. She saw a bobbing point of light that had to be a lantern and concentrated on walking straight at it.

The rain started coming down hard. She found her tent, but as she bent to duck under the flap, she smelled ozone and felt a tingling all over her body, a mass stirring of individual hairs. Everything around her turned white, and she jerked back. For a timeless interval, she saw or imagined that she could see every upturned, startled face and wrinkled square inch of tent fabric in camp, every convolution of the roiling clouds above, everything between herself and the faraway hills, every rock, every fat drop of water hurtling earthward. At an impossible distance from her, yet close enough for her to see his safari garb and the dark flat square object he held, was a slight man whose expression both implored and accused.

The thunderclap smashed her to the ground. She came up on hands and knees, blinded, deafened, screaming, "I *remember* you, goddammit. What do you *want?*"

Strong hands closed around her wrist and forearm and dragged her out of the rain. Someone wiped her face with a cloth. At first, she could see nothing and heard only a ringing in her ears. Gradually, she made out Gilzow's face, saw the look of concern, even alarm, in her wide blue eyes, saw her lips move and heard the sound of her voice though not the words she spoke. Leveritt shook her head. Gilzow stopped trying to talk to her and unselfconsciously helped her remove her wet underclothes. There was a second lightning strike close by the camp, and thunder as loud and sharp as a cannonade. Leveritt toweled herself dry, pulled on khaki pants and a flannel shirt, found her voice at last.

"I'm fine."

"You don't sound fine to me."

She did not sound fine to herself. "I was just dazzled by the lightning."

"You're lucky you weren't fried by it. I don't guess you'd've been yelling bloody murder if it'd hit you, but it must've hit right behind you. I'd swear I saw your silhouette right through the tent flap."

"Really, I'm fine. Really."

"Well, you lie down." Gilzow made a shivery sound. "I'm breaking out the blankets. First it's too hot for sleep, now it's too chilly."

Leveritt stretched out on her cot, and Gilzow spread a light blanket over her, tucked it around her almost tenderly, and extinguished the lantern. Leveritt lay listening to the rain's arrhythmic drumming. It shouldn't be my job, she thought, to have to remember Ed Morris. The storm passed. She slept.

The following morning was as warm and humid as though there had been no rainstorm. The normally clear and placid river had become a muddy torrent. Erosion was rapid in the Silurian; the steaming flatland, which drained through notches in the bluffs, looked the same and yet subtly changed. The camp's denizens, ten people in all, stood about in twos and threes, surveyed the valley and the plain, and talked, depending on their specialties, of turbidity or fossiliferous outcrops or possible revisions in topographical maps.

Leveritt and Holmes spent the day in a tent with the sides drawn up, consolidating survey data and incorporating it into a three-dimensional computer model of the region from the valley to the hills. Over tens of millions of years, the land had been repeatedly submerged, then raised, drained, eroded. "Up and down," Holmes said, "more times than the proverbial whore's drawers." Leveritt, her fierce concentration momentarily broken, shot him an oh-please look. They barely noticed a brief mid-morning cloudburst, barely paused for lunch, and might have skipped it but for the noise made by a couple of campmates returning muddy and ravenous from a collecting sortie into the valley. The sun was halfway down the sky when Holmes abruptly switched off his laptop, stretched, and declared that they could continue that evening, but right at that moment he needed some downtime. Leveritt glared at his retreating back until he had disappeared into the next tent; she found herself looking past the tent at the barren plain and the distant hills, and after a minute she resigned herself to thinking about Ed Morris and wondering what had become of him.

Ed Morris. Ed Morris. Maybe you arrived high and dry and unhurt out there on the plain . . .

Her catalog of the possible fates of Ed Morris had grown extensive. It occurred to her now to record them in a notebook, like Gilzow's models of geologic time. Then she remembered Lieutenant Hales's injunction against writing anything that had to do with Ed Morris. She still did not feel safe from Hales.

Ed Morris. You arrived and – what? You wasted at least a little time and energy being confused and frightened. But after a while, you gathered your wits and took stock of your predicament. And what a predicament. You've got no food, no water, no idea of where you are. You know only where you aren't. You have only the clothes on your back and the laptop in your hand.

If it's night, you learn immediately that the stars are no help at all. The constellations you know don't exist yet. You wander around in the dark, fall into a ravine, break your neck and die instantly . . .

Or break your leg and expire miserably over the course of a couple of days.

Back to the beginning. You find water, a rivulet, and follow it to a stream and follow that to the river and follow the river to the sea and find the main camp . . .

Or find nothing, if you've arrived before there is a camp.

Or you don't find water and don't fall and break any bones. You just wander around until your strength gives out.

No. You do find water, you reach the river, but you realize your strength will inevitably give out, that you're lost and doomed to die in the middle of nowhere and no two ways about it, unless you take a chance, eat some of the local flora or fauna, shellfish, millipedes, whatever you can grab, anything you can keep down. You eat it raw, because you don't have any way to make fire, but don't get sick and die. You – what do you do if you live?

You live out your life alone. Adam without Eve in paleo-Eden. Robinson Crusoe of the dawn.

Alone with your laptop.

Best-case scenario, Ed Morris. You walk into camp just around dinnertime tonight, ragged and emaciated after an epic trek, and tired of subsisting on moss and invertebrates, but alive, whole, and proud of yourself.

Not-as-good scenario, at least not as good for you, but it'd let everybody give you your due and let me be done with you. We find the cairn you built with the biggest rocks you could move. Inside the cairn, we find your laptop. The seals're intact, the circuitry isn't corroded. We can read the message you left for us . . .

Lot of work for a dying man.

Okay. First, you figure out how to survive. Then you build a cairn. You wander around building cairns all over the place, increasing the chances we'll find at least one of them.

Leveritt went quickly to her tent. She hung a canteen from her belt, put a wide-brimmed straw hat on her head, and started walking toward the hills. The wet ground crunched underfoot.

The levelness of the flatland was an illusion; the ground was all barely perceptible slopes, falling, rising, like the bosom of a calm sea. When she could no longer see the camp, she planted her fists on her hips and stood looking around at the rocky litter and thought, Now what?

Take stock, she told herself.

I've eaten, I'm not lost, my life isn't at stake here. None of which Ed Morris could say. I'm not confused and scared, either, and I haven't been injured. Besides not having eaten for ten, twelve hours before the jump, he didn't look like he had a lot of body fat to live off. On the plus side, he was a mountain climber and a skydiver, in good shape and not a physical coward.

How long would it have taken him to get over the confusion and fright? Give him the benefit of the doubt. A career in accountancy implies a well-ordered mind.

How much more time would've passed before it occurred to him to build a cairn? Then he'd have had to pick a site where a cairn would have a chance of being found, where it wouldn't get washed away, where there was an ample supply of portable rock. If he was back toward the hills, he'd have found the streambeds full of smooth stones of a particularly useful size. Out here, he'd just have had to make do with what's at hand.

How much rock could he have moved before his strength gave out?

Leveritt picked up a grapefruit-sized chunk of limestone, carried it a dozen feet, and set it down next to a slightly larger chunk. She worked her way around and outward from the two, gathering the bigger stones, carrying them back. After laboring steadily for the better part of two hours, she was soaked with perspiration, her arms, back, and legs ached, and she had erected an indefinite sort of pyramid approximately three feet high. Increasingly, she had expended time and energy locating suitable stones at ever-greater distances from the cairn and lugging them over to it. She squatted to survey her handiwork.

Ed Morris, she told herself, wouldn't have stopped working at this point, because he didn't have a camp to return to when he got tired. Still, it's a respectable start, stable, obviously the work of human hands.

She rose and walked in the direction of the camp. She paused once to look back and wonder. How long before it tumbles down?

No one in camp seemed to have noticed her absence. Typical, she thought. She discovered, however, that she could not maintain a sour mood for very long. She and Holmes worked together for an hour after dark, and then she retired to her tent and, soon, to her cot. Despite the mugginess of the evening, she had no trouble falling asleep.

For the next two days, work thoroughly involved her. On the afternoon of the third day, she returned to the cairn. She started to add to it, decided, No, moved off a hundred yards, and built a second cairn. Thereafter, she spent most of such free daylit time as she had piling up stones. She never returned to any site.

Now her absences did attract notice. Holmes trailed her past two abandoned cairns to her latest site. She answered his questions with monosyllables or shrugs or ignored the questions altogether, keeping on the move the whole while, finding, prying up, carrying, setting down stones. She refused his offer to help. Finally, he said, quite good-naturedly, "You need a hobby, Bonnie."

"This *is* my hobby, Mike." She wished aloud that he would go away, and he did.

That evening, over a dinner that tasted better than dinner usually did, Gilzow asked her what she was doing, and Leveritt replied, "Pursuing mental health." Later, she was almost unable to keep herself from laughing at one of Holmes's stupid jokes.

Two weeks and seven cairns after she had begun, as she lay on the edge of sleep, she realized with a start that she had not thought about Ed Morris all that day.

Four days later, when she had returned from building her eighth and last cairn, she asked around for a copy of *Robinson Crusoe*. Nobody had one. Gilzow offered her *Emma*, by Jane Austen. "Close enough," Leveritt said.

A month passed.

The supply boat arrived three days ahead of schedule. Everyone turned out to carry boxes; the first people to reach the boat yelled to those following, "Brinkman's here!" The big man, who had been downriver for ten weeks, stood in the bow, waving his shapeless hat. It transpired that the loud, sincere welcome was not entirely for him. He had brought a mixed case of liquor.

When the supplies had been unloaded and the camp had settled down for a round or two of good stiff drinks, Brinkman sought out Leveritt and asked her to walk with him along the bluff. They had scarcely put the camp out of earshot when he heaved a great sigh, his ebullient humor fell away from him like a cloak, and he suddenly looked tired and pale under his tan and more solemn than she could recall having seen him.

"I really came all the way up here," he said, "to tell you this personally. Two days ago, they dug something out of the marsh down by the main camp. It was one of the – part of one of the gurneys they use in the jump station."

"Ed Morris," Leveritt said bleakly. She had not said the name aloud since her conversation with Michael Diehl. Now, as though invoked by her speaking it, a humid wind swept up the valley, bearing a faint fetid breath of the estuary.

Brinkman said, "A Navy security officer named Hales told me about it."

"More surprises. I'd've thought he'd be swearing everyone to secrecy."

"It was too late for that. Everybody in camp knew it by the time he heard about it. Everybody."

"What about Ed Morris himself?"

"They're digging around. They haven't found anything else yet, and God knows if they will. The gurney's all twisted up like a pretzel, and one end's melted. God knows what that implies – besides the obvious, terrific heat. The thing was buried in a mud bank. Impacted. A botanist tripped over an exposed part."

"How long had it been there?"

Brinkman shook his head. "They're still working on that, but even the most conservative guess puts it before the manned phase of the expedition. As to how it got there – there has to be an inquest. You have to be there for it."

Leveritt groaned. "I don't have anything to tell."

"So Hales said. But people higher up're calling the shots. Everything's got to be official, and you've got to be part of it."

"I cannot get away from this thing!" Leveritt sat down on a knob of rock and angrily kicked at the ground. "Not from Hales and the Navy, and, most of all, not from Ed Morris. I thought I'd done it, finally worked it out by myself, but—"

"I'm sorry, Bonnie. You have to go back with me in the morning. I can find work for you to do until this thing's over."

"Making coffee?" She could not keep the bitterness out of her voice. "I want to be *here*, Rob."

"I've never known you not to be willing to do what you had to do so you could do what you want to do. While you're there – the San Diego bunch has talked about holding a memorial service. I kind of gather none of them knew Morris all that well, or liked him, or something. But he is the expedition's first casualty. Since you were almost the last person to see him, perhaps you could—"

Leveritt shook her head emphatically. "No."

"Bonnie, the man is dead."

"I couldn't eulogize him if my life depended on it. What I know about him wouldn't fill half a dozen sentences. He talked too fast and dressed like Jungle Jim. He said he liked mountain climbing and sky diving. And I'm very sorry about what happened to him, but it wasn't my fault."

"Who said it was your fault?" Brinkman knelt beside her and picked at his cuticle. "There has to be one meaningful thing you could say about him."

Leveritt sighed. She looked down at the supply boat and imagined herself on it again, sitting, as before, under the white canopy with Brinkman, drinking coffee from a thermos bottle, and glimpsing the pier and the cluster of tents and Quonset huts through the fog. She saw it all as though it were a movie being shown in reverse. She would have to go back and back and back, until she reached a point before Ed Morris had taken over her life, and start anew. This time, she told herself, I will make things happen the way they're supposed to happen. I will be the hero of my own story.

She said, "When he found out how nervous I was, he gave me a pep talk. And just before I went through the hole, he gave me a wink of encouragement."

"Well, then, if nothing else, you owe him for that wink." Brinkman could not have spoken more softly and been heard.

Leveritt closed her eyes and thought of the scene in the jump station, the purposeful technicians, Ed Morris's face framed by the bars of the railing. She looked helplessly at Brinkman, who said, "What?"

The humid wind moved up the valley again, and again she smelled the estuary's attenuated fetor of death and of life coming out of death. She exhaled harshly and said, "Nothing." She had meant to say that she could not recall the color of Ed Morris's eyes. "Never mind. I'll think of something." The wind passed across the rocky plain, toward the ancient crumbled hills and beyond.

SCREAM QUIETLY

Sheila Crosby

Time travel does not have to involve huge time spans as the following story, set during the Victorian period, demonstrates. It also introduces us to the crucial question that if time travel is possible and is eventually perfected then surely we would have been visited at some time by people from the future.

Sheila Crosby is a British astronomer long resident in the Canary Islands. She has to date written only a handful of short stories, mostly for small press magazines.

Oaklands,
Cathedral Rise,
Lincolnshire, England
7th July, 1849

My Dearest Joanne,

Sweet sister, my husband grows more violent. Little Julian greatly admired the wooden horse you sent for his first birthday, and he gave me a wonderful present, by taking his first steps! Naturally I was delighted, but then he tripped, fell, and wept a little. I thought them very few tears for the lump on his head, but in an instant George charged upstairs to us. He knocked Julian out of my arms entirely, roaring that a man had a right to peace in his own home. And does Julian have no right to peace in his house? I will not say "home"; this has never been a home to either of us. Of course, Julian screamed (which at the time I believed to be largely from terror) and George picked him up by one arm and flung him into a wardrobe, locking the door and pocketing the key. Julian was abruptly silent, which terrified me.

Naturally I protested.

George pushed his face within an inch of mine and screamed, "I will not have my son mollycoddled like a baby!"

I replied, "But he is twelve months old. It is natural that he should cry when he falls."

"Then he must learn, I tell you!" shouted George with his face growing ever redder. I thought he would have apoplexy.

"George, release him! Give me the key."

He made to go, and I stood in front of him. "The key, George. I beg you." Perhaps you will think it rash, and indeed I was terrified, but I was desperate to rescue my child.

He pushed me violently, and I fell over the alphabet blocks. I managed not to scream, so the neighbours will have no cause for gossip this time.

"You brought it on yourself," said George, and quit the house.

He was drunk, of course, and it was not yet ten in the morning. At least on this occasion the bruises do not show, being entirely on my back.

Lucy helped me to my feet, with many a "Poor Madam!" and "Lord have mercy!" and we surveyed the wardrobe. To my inexpressible relief, poor Julian started to whimper within.

At length I said, "The hinges are inside. I believe we must send for a locksmith, Lucy. Julian may need the apothecary for his hurts."

Lucy bit her lip & shuffled her feet. "Please, Ma'am. I think I might open it," and she did so, using my fine crochet hook. You may imagine my severe disquiet over a maid who can pick locks, but at the same time, I am very grateful to her.

Julian was severely concussed & his collar bone was broken. The apothecary bound his arm while the collar bone heals. He suspects that the skull may have a small fracture, and recommends that he stay abed for at least a week. You know my son. Do you believe I can keep him confined for a week?

George will doubtless be most repentant when he comes home. He blames the drink, but will not stop drinking. Oh, it is a bitter thing to be owned as a slave is owned!

I have walked around the room to calm myself a little. It is true that my lot is far better than a slave. Whatever else I may have to bear, I am well fed & clothed, and nobody requires sixteen hours of hard labour from me each day, merely a vast amount of fawning & cringing. I still wish most fervently that George had no part in such a cruel and illegal trade, but George sees no difference between carrying slaves to America in his ships and carrying bolts of cloth home. I confess, I should be delighted were the West Africa Squadron to capture one of his clippers and free the slaves, though George should be ruined, and I with him.

Well, I have a little lighter news also. Do you remember Mary Dunn at school? She is Mary Bassom now, having married a farmer, and lives in Yorkshire. You probably remember her as I do, a good-hearted girl, but solemn & unimaginative. We have corresponded since we left Miss Bainbridge's Academy, although I do not open my heart to her as I do to you. In her last letter, she assures me that she has recently had visits from faeries! Can you credit it? I confess, I know not what to think, unless she has left her wits. Her letter seemed rational and collected enough. At any event, she says her fey guests do not speak English, but German, and are clearly anxious to communicate something. Since I was so very clever at foreign languages, she says, would I do her the kindness of visiting? Though I cannot conceive that faeries (if faeries they be!) would speak German, I should cheerfully live in Newgate jail to escape George for a while. (My Dear, that is not a hint. I am perfectly aware that your employers consider it unthinkable for a governess to have visitors, and my thoughts are with you, always. Alas, I should find your company very much more congenial than Mary's. Doubtless I shall hear a good more than I care for about what the baker's wife's second cousin said to the haberdashery assistant's sister on Thursday. Or was it Wednesday?)

I shall use all my charm to persuade George to permit this visit, as soon as possible, even though Julian is scarcely fit to travel. At some wayside inn he would be safe from violence, if not from bedbugs.

Your loving sister,
Sophie

The Nag's Head Inn,
Nether Grassmeade,
Lincolnshire, England
8th July, evening

My Dearest Joanne,

My circumstances are greatly altered and Julian & I left for Windscour Farm this morning. I have explained to everyone that George is travelling on business and I do not expect his return in the near future. Would that I could write more! But all explanations must wait.

As we entered the coach, a gentlewoman of middle years approached and called me by name. I thought her familiar, but could not place her at all. At all events, she looked deep into my eyes and said, "All will turn out for the best, my dear. But you will need all your courage."

Would that I could believe her! And yet I cannot forget her either.

Your loving sister,
Sophie

Windscour Farm,
Otley,
W. Yorkshire, England
14th July, 1849

My Dear Joanne,

The journey was less dreadful than I expected. We brought our own sheets, and travelled but twenty miles each day. I had expected Julian to be a sore trial, confined for so many hours each day to the jolting coach, but he was enchanted with the changing view, and when he tired of that, Lucy & I sang to him and he would sleep. At each inn they immediately ascribed his hurts to an upset of the coach, and couldn't do enough for him. Poor Frank came in for a good deal of scolding from innkeepers' wives for his supposed reckless driving. He nobly forbore from telling otherwise.

On arrival, we bathed, of course, and after some bread & milk, I left Julian sleeping under Lucy's watchful eye, while I went to take tea with Mary. She was most concerned about Julian, and recommended that I find a new coachman. In justice to Frank, I had to tell her that Julian came by his wounds before our journey began. Then she was horrified that I subjected the child to a journey in such a condition, whereupon the whole story of my marriage came out. Mary & Mr Bassom were loud in their sympathy, and warm in their offer of a refuge here as long as possible. In short, until George positively insists on my return. Mr Bassom opined that the law is unjust to women, that it is unreasonable that George may do anything to Julian & I short of murder. "A woman is not a pair of boots, and should not be treated thus!" he said.

Naturally, I was most moved by their kindness, and I repent my last letter's attempt at wit at Mary's expense.

Once I had recovered some calm, we talked of the faeries. Mary tells me her visitors are shy, and invariably appear a little before dawn by the druid stone. I distrusted their choice of place but Mary assured me that they are nothing demoniac in appearance or action. She says I am not to picture tiny ladies with butterfly wings, nor little men with beards & green clothes, but strange creatures almost our own height. Accordingly, I shall retire to bed early, and meet them in the morning, to find out what manner of folk they may be.

Your loving sister,
Sophie

Windscour Farm,
Otley,
15th July, 1849

My Dear Joanne,

We arose early, and we walked up to the druid stone in the pearly light before dawn. The wind was sharp, and I was glad of my shawl, but the heather was abloom, smelling of mead, and curlews were calling. Their song always raises a longing in me to fly away. Alas, I have sufficient reason to flee: would that I had a nest to fly to! But you will be agog to hear about the faeries.

Their mode of transportation was most curious. At first I mistook it for one of those curious lens-shaped clouds which form downwind of certain hills, and I only realized my mistake as it flew closer and landed. As God is my witness, Joanne, it flew. It was perhaps a score of feet across, completely smooth, and, most startling of all, completely silent. I was somewhat nervous, as you may well imagine, but I reminded myself that I had faced George in many a rage, and I could face this, and besides, Mary had met her visitors on a dozen occasions, and suffered no hurt.

There came a faint hum, no louder than a spinning wheel, and a door appeared in the side of the faery coach, almost as though an invisible hand drew a pencil line. The door opened, and a ramp extended, and two faeries strolled out.

I had imagined many strange things as I tossed in my bed the previous night, yet these faeries were stranger. Do you remember our stillborn brother, William, who arrived four months too early? A foolish question. I am sure you cannot forget; no more can I. These faeries reminded me forcibly of the poor mite, although while William was no bigger than my hand, these were perhaps four feet tall, and very much alive. I mean they had the same pale skin, and overlarge head, and feeble-looking limbs, and delicate features. Oh but their eyes were different! I have never seen such beautiful eyes, preternaturally large, silver and multifaceted like a fly's. They wore curious clothes, all of a piece, and yet divided at the legs; I believe they would allow great comfort & freedom of movement.

They approached us, and bowed, hands folded, as Chinamen do. The taller said, "Ik wood stonden in yore grace."

I blinked & curtsied to cover my confusion.

Mary said, "Do you understand them? Is it not German?"

I replied, "I think it may be Dutch, for it is not German, though it sounds somewhat alike. I shall try to speak with them in German." Whereupon I directed myself to the visitors saying, "Wilkommen meinen herren. Sprechen Sie Deutsch?"

The faeries looked at each other, and the smaller one said, "We knowen not thys spekyng."

I turned to Mary. "Of all things most strange! I do believe they are talking Middle English!" In truth they were. As you know, I am a poor scholar, but we contrived a halting conversation. I said, "Ik clepe Sophie," and they told me they were Zondliss (the larger) and Mica.

They said they were not faeries, but men, "even as yourselne," from the far distant future, and they were journeying in time! They were most astonished to hear this was the year of our Lord 1849, for they had believed themselves in 1343 and were in great fear of being burned as witches. It took no little time to enlighten them, and I suspect there may have been some confusion with the Mohammedan system of counting years. They claim to come from over a million years in the future. I could scarcely credit it, but as Mary observed, "Consider how slowly the careful breeding of cattle does change their form. If these are indeed men, it would take many, many centuries for them to change so."

"True," I said. "And it seems unlikely that men will fly within a thousand years, much less travel in time."

We were interrupted by the larger traveller bowing again. "Please your Ladyshyp, wir be enfamyned." Seeing my lack of comprehension he continued, "Wir be soure dystressed & deyen for lak of vitaille."

"Oh Mary," I cried, "they are starving!"

Mary hastened home and returned with bread & cheese & milk, but they will need far greater provision for a journey, especially should they lose their way again.

In short we are to meet them again on the morrow, bearing food for them. They must indeed have been sore afraid not to ask for succour here, there, & yonder. Oh Joanne, shall I ask them for passage? My case is desperate, and we could not be followed, but how should I live in the future? And how should Julian? Besides, they are lost by five hundred years and their navigation is clearly not to be trusted.

Your loving sister,
Sophie

Windscour Farm,
Otley,
16th July, 1849, pre-dawn

My Dear Joanne,

I have lain awake most of the night, but I am finally decided. My situation is more desperate than even you know. I am no longer fleeing George, but rather justice, or at least the law of England.

Dearest Joanne, prepare yourself for a shock. George has been dead for nine days.

The day he fractured Julian's skull he returned home after my letter was posted, & announced he must travel for business, ordering Lucy to pack all Julian's clothes & his own, but none of mine. He drank a vast deal of port over dinner, slurring his words before we had finished the fish course, and I was alarmed for the consequences for myself. In spite of this, when we retired for the night, I sought an explanation. George said he was "blue-devilled with my fawning on the child," and the only way I would give him my "proper attention" was by sending our child away. He had found someone who would foster him cheaply enough, & would leave Julian there on the first stage of his journey.

You may imagine my emotions. My heart's Darling hidden away as though he were born out of wedlock! Do you know how many children so fostered do not survive to their fifth birthday? So many foster parents take the money and spend it on gin rather than food for their charges. I begged. I wept. Nothing availed. He knocked me to the floor.

And then I screamed as George forcibly asserted his marital rights over my body. I was still weeping when he fell into a drunken slumber. I still do not clearly recall what followed. I lost my wits entirely, or perhaps I finally found them. At all events, I untied George's cravat and retied it in a noose which I then tightened around his neck, with fatal result. He never even awoke.

I remember only too clearly my struggle to get his mortal remains into his travelling trunk. In the morning I feigned normality, telling the servants that George had departed already, and ordered his trunk sent on. I invented the address, and hoped it would be quite some time before anyone opened it. I packed whatever jewellery and money I could find in haste, and we came here, a normal-seeming journey. My first plan was to flee from here to Bavaria, where I might hope to earn my bread by teaching English. Alas, we should be conspicuous, and I fear the law must eventually discover us. For myself, I no longer care, but I took comfort that Julian might be somewhat older by the time I was hanged.

My plan has changed. I have spent hours contriving an account of my troubles (but not my crime!) in Middle English, and I shall beg the time travellers to take me to the end of the millennium. The world should not have become unrecognizable in that time – men should scarcely be flying – but I shall escape.

You would, I am sure, urge caution, and you would be right. What do I know of these strange folk beyond their own account? They are clearly not to be trusted to find the year 2000 or any other. It grieves me to leave you alone. And yet what else am I to do? I pray that the strange woman in Lincoln was right, and that all will indeed turn out for the best. Certainly, I shall need courage, as she said.

I shall leave this letter in my room. If you receive it, you will know that I could not return to destroy it, and therefore I have gone to the future. Please burn this missive.

Good-bye forever, my heart.

Your loving sister,

Sophie

4 Rue des anemones,
Nantes, France
18th July, 1849

My Dear Joanne,

How shall I begin to explain? I fear my last letter will have distressed you greatly. Although you will receive my letters only two days apart, a score of years has passed for me. But I am well, and I am now forty-eight years old. If you believe I should pay for my crime, I will understand, but I misdoubt that you will find any to believe your tale.

You will have gathered from receiving it that the time travellers did indeed agree to convey us, but not to the destination I anticipated, nor in the manner.

Naturally my Middle English greatly improved with constant use. I shall tell you the whole as I finally understood it, and leave out the many misunderstandings & misconceptions under which I long laboured.

Mica and Zondliss are historians, attempting to research witchcraft. They had a companion, Bordan, who sadly succumbed to the Black Death. I think Bordan must have been the practical member of the crew. Zondliss is pleasant natured & hopelessly incompetent. Mica is sweetness itself and utterly impractical – which accounts for their unplanned detour to 1849. Do you remember Mr Cartlight, who knew everything about Babylon but could never open his own boiled egg without assistance, nor find his handkerchief, nor his spectacles? Mica is cut from the same cloth. They have a wondrous device aboard their time carriage which produces food from wood shavings. This had a cord ending in a curious six-pronged contrivance. Beside it on the wall was a curious six-hollowed depression. I fitted the prongs into the hollows and the contraption immediately began producing roast beef with potatoes & carrots. Since nobody dared to adjust it, we continued with roast beef until Julian indulged his curiosity while none of us observed him, whereupon every meal became poached salmon with spinach. You may not credit it, but one can tire of such luxury, especially for breakfast.

Zondliss endeavoured to bring us to the year he & Mica left, with remarkable incompetence. I was sent to inquire into the date on a number of occasions. You may imagine the reaction I obtained by approaching utter strangers in what they considered Carnival dress, and inquiring, please what year was this? Consequently I once spent a whole shilling on a newspaper to discover the year was 1970. I still preserve the newspaper and it delights me. Flying machines & horseless carriages & men walking on the moon! Truly Joanne, the moon! And yet perhaps more wonderful to me was the situation of women: divorcing husbands, debating in Parliament and campaigning for equal pay with men. I seriously considered staying, but I could scarcely repay Mica & Zondliss with abandonment.

At length we arrived in the far future where everyone looked like Mica & Zondliss. I was confounded to discover that we were still one thousand years from Mica's time, but then she obtained a competent coachman, and thus we reached her home year.

I declare my entire sojourn was one long perplexity & bewilderment. I was sorely puzzled to distinguish one future-dweller from another, and they arrived with a "pop" from thin air and departed the same way. It gave me palpitations every time, although Julian chuckled with glee. We visited cities floating in the air, and an utterly vast hollow sphere around a sun. I cannot begin to make you understand the strangeness of it all, for I could not begin to understand it myself.

It was obvious that we could not live in such a time. Even had I learned to fit in, where would Julian find a wife? And yet, if we were returned to 1849 I should be hanged, and then what would become of Julian? Finally the notion occurred to me to return to before George's murder, when there should be no hue & cry. Accordingly I told them I came from 1829, and to 1829 they returned me. I pawned my jewels, and obtained a position as governess to a French family who originally came to Otley to escape Bonaparte. You do not need me to tell you of the trials of a governess's life, being only too familiar with them yourself. The family regarded me as a servant, and the servants regarded me as a spy for the family.

And then the master's younger brother visited. Truly Joanne, I did not set out to ensnare him. Having married once under the influence of Mammon, I should scarcely rush to repeat the experiment! I merely thought (and still think) François to be the most kind & charming & agreeable man I had ever met. It seemed extraordinary to me that he was unwed, notwithstanding his shyness. When at last I confided to him some of the truth of my first marriage, he declared that God gave men muscles to protect their families, and not to bully them. On another occasion he opined that a woman's talents were no less than a man's, merely distinct. Men have muscles while women have clever, sensitive fingers; men are able to concentrate on one thing with great energy, while a woman can attend to many things at once. Thus man & woman were complete when together. That is how he makes me feel, Joanne, complete.

And so I became Madame Verne, at the cost of no small scandal, and we are still happy and complete together. We had another four children and all are well. At François's suggestion, we changed Julian's name to the French equivalent, Jules, to save him from cruel comments when he should begin his schooling.

I wrote my younger self a letter, warning against marriage to George, but I forbore to post it. If I never married George, what should become of Jules? Would he cease to exist? I could not bear to venture such a circumstance. I shudder to think what paradoxes I may have caused by my untruths already. Yet I have just returned from Lincoln where I talked to my younger self as I entered the coach. I remembered how the words gave a glimmer of hope in my darkest days, and I could not forbear.

Jules, of course, has no memory of his natural father, nor of our extraordinary adventures. How could he, at those tender years? And yet he writes the most extraordinary novels of the future.

Your loving sister,
Sophie

DARWIN'S SUITCASE

Elisabeth Malartre

Some hope that even if time travel is not possible, there may be a way of capturing residual images of the past in some kind of time viewer. Witnessing the past and the future as distinct from actually being there was how Charles Dickens ingeniously handled the revelations to Ebenezer Scrooge by the ghosts in A Christmas Carol *(1843). A rather more scientific (albeit unrealistic) basis was proposed by the French astronomer Camille Flammarion in* Lumen *(1872) where he suggested that if you travel faster than light you would be able to witness past events by "historic light", though of course everything would be seen backwards. However, if a time viewer ever with unlimited scope is invented then all privacy would be lost, an idea that was emphatically demonstrated in such stories as "The Dead Past" (1956) by Isaac Asimov, "I See You" (1976) by Damon Knight and the novel,* The Light of Other Days *(2000) by Arthur C. Clarke and Stephen Baxter.*

The following story is a double whammy since it uses a time viewer to witness an encounter between a time traveller and an historic personality. Elisabeth Malartre is the wife of author Gregory Benford and has co-authored with him a number of short stories plus the non-fiction Beyond Human: Living with Robots and Cyborgs *(2007).*

"Our English sphinx moths have proboscides as long as their bodies, but in Madagascar, there must be moths with proboscides capable of extension to a length of between 10 and 11 inches."

> *On the Various Contrivances by which British and*
> *Foreign Orchids are Fertilised by Insects, and*
> *on the Good Effects of Intercrossing*, Charles Darwin, 1862

Sister Solange checked herself just before she nodded off. She stared bleary-eyed at the balky Temporal ViewScreen.

It was before matins, and she was never bright in the early morning. And if someone should find her here . . . the sister who ran the library would never allow this observation during regular research hours. It wasn't on the Approved List.

Not many of the sisters were even allowed to touch the machine. Solange was still new to the convent, so it was a great privilege for her to TimeView.

Forty minutes before matins.

She reached out again to the control panel. Maybe this time she'd get it set correctly. She was not very gifted with these new electronics, and far too impatient at their eccentricities. She stared at the crumpled sheet: "Charles Darwin during the writing of *The Origin of Species*, 1858."

She ran her finger back and forth over the keyboard in frustration. Still nothing on the screen, but it triggered a recorded warning: "*Caution. The Temporal Viewer is a delicate instrument. Please use it carefully.*"

She looked at the ancient clock on the wall. Thirty-eight minutes left.

She rapped her knuckles on the screen. The time-code indicator light flickered and a chime sounded. A toneless voice announced, "The new setting is 1866. Please confirm by pressing the return key."

Sister Solange groaned. "Oh, no, what have I done?"

She reached for the Year Control knob and turned it back. The time-code indicator flickered again. She briefly saw 1859, then it returned to 1866. In frustration she yanked the knob smartly to the left. It came off in her hand.

She stared in horror at the knob. Too late she remembered what Sister Marthe the Librarian had said. There were nodes in the time stream that seemed to attract the Temporal Viewer. Maybe 1866 was one of them.

Sister Solange sighed. Her impatience had gotten her into trouble once again. Penance, surely, maybe even . . . she stopped as the screen cleared suddenly, showing a figure dressed in dark clothes.

"Oh, it's working. Thank you, Lord. I am so unworthy of your beneficence." She resolved to do penance anyway.

She squinted at the screen. A middle-aged man was walking with a stick in the countryside. She looked at the paper again. *Darwin walked and thought things through in an open field called the Sandwalk near his home in England, Down House.*

He looked ordinary enough for such an evil man.

She wondered what he was thinking. Was he plotting his terrible attack on the Church?

She adjusted the fine focus gingerly. It seemed like magic – but Holy magic, she corrected herself, to see something that had happened over two hundred years ago.

She bent closer to the screen, wishing for the morning coffee of her pre-convent days.

With a crackling sound, the screen erupted in diagonal stripes.

"Oh, no, please not now." As suddenly as it started, the lines stopped. Sister Solange stared anxiously at the screen.

There were two people in the field – one walking, the second one standing a little way off.

"Funny, I didn't see him there before." She shrugged. "But this is so much better. I'll be able to hear them talking. I'll actually hear Darwin's voice! Oh, thank you Lord!" Despite the Church's interdiction on viewing Darwin, this had to be Divine intervention, she thought. But no recording – this one was strictly off the record.

She hunched over the screen, absentmindedly tucking a stray red curl under the edge of her severe black wimple.

Thwack!
Clink.

Norman Albright hesitated, heart hammering. Through the early morning Kentish fog, he recognized the man wielding the walking stick and approaching at a steady pace.

He cleared his throat and stepped forward. "Ahem, Mr Darwin, sir . . ."

He hoped he wasn't too startling a figure. His clothes had been carefully researched. The unfamiliar wool overcoat was heavy on his shoulders; in the damp air it exuded a musky smell. The stiff shirt collar was uncomfortable, and through the thick cotton of the shirt he felt the box in his breast pocket.

The middle-aged man in front of him looked as Albright had anticipated: balding on top, heavy eyebrows, and a short beard streaked with grey. The few surviving photos had been morphed to this age to aid recognition. Overall, an unassuming man for so pivotal a figure. But the gaze from his pale eyes blazed forth with an intensity at odds with the rest of the body. This was indeed The Darwin.

"You have the advantage, sir."

Albright proffered his hand awkwardly. "Norman Albright. An honor to meet you, sir. I've traveled far for this." His words sounded stilted, archaic; his tongue was thick with nervousness. But Research assured him this was about right for 1866. He'd gone through a lot of coaching to get the language right.

Darwin's hand shot out, and his grasp was firm. "Pleased, I'm sure. How may I be of assistance?"

"I . . . I have urgent need to ask you questions . . . about your work. Perhaps I could walk with you for a while."

"That would be agreeable. It does a man good to compose his thoughts with a walk before breakfast."

Albright fell into step beside Darwin. It was hard to concentrate. He was actually here, on the famous Sandwalk, with the Founder, where, tradition held, Darwin had done much of the thinking on his famous Theory of Natural Selection. The Temporal Voyager worked! He looked around. The land itself was unexceptional – a narrow strip of about one and a half acres, bordered by a gravel walk. On one side large broad-leafed trees shaded the gravel. But what trees! They appeared to be poplars, but much larger, and with many more leaves than the ones at home. On the other side of a low hedge was an adjoining grassy field. He stared at it. The grass was so green and lush! And the smells – so sweet. This was how country air used to smell, he understood. Unfamiliar notes hung in the air. Birdsong!

Darwin walked steadily as Albright got his bearings and took in the scene around him. As he walked he punctuated his steps with blows from the walking stick.

There was a period of silence as they fell into rhythm.

Then Darwin turned to him. "Do tell me how you came to be here so early. Are you stopping nearby?"

"No, I started out this morning from . . . London."

"Indeed. I myself prefer not to travel, but when I must do so, I find it preferable also in the early morning. I trust the journey was not too tiring?"

"No, not at all. It was most pleasant, and of course, I was looking forward to this meeting, so my thoughts were well occupied."

"Very kind of you. How did you find me here? Did you first call at Down House?"

"No, sir," said the younger man. "Your work is well known among my colleagues, and your regular habits have been chronicled. I knew you would be here at this time of day."

Darwin seemed taken aback. He looked at Albright's collar. "Your colleagues, you say." He pursed his lips and frowned. "But you are a man of the cloth?"

"Well naturally. Who is not these days?" A slight hesitation. "The Order of Scientism." To Darwin's puzzled look he added, "Protestant, of course."

"Scientism. Pardon my confusion, I am not aware . . ."

"Nor could you be. The Order was founded after you – your time."

Thwack! As they rounded the last corner, the battered iron tip of the briar wood cane flipped the top flint off the pile. The rough-hewn grey stone landed solidly on the stony ground. *Clink.*

"After my time? What do you mean?"

Albright sighed. Time was short. He'd better start his pitch. "The Order of Scientism was formed in 1943. I appear in the guise of a Victorian clergyman, but I am from the future. From 2156, to be exact."

*   *   *

Sister Solange started. Had she heard correctly? This man Albright claimed to be from ... eighteen years in the future! What was he doing there? Indulging himself, as she was, or trying to change something? She felt suddenly uneasy. Perhaps he was the reason the Temporal Viewer had picked this time.

Darwin stopped and looked at him sternly. "This conversation has taken a most remarkable turn."

"I assure you, I am most earnest."

"Yet you claim to be—"

"From the future, yes, sir."

"Whose future?"

"Well, everyone's, I guess." He smiled briefly. To Darwin's puzzled look he added, "It's the future you helped to bring about. And that's why I'm here."

"Indeed." Darwin frowned. "This is a prank, is it not?"

"No, sir, not at all. I'm really from the future, and I'm prepared to prove it." He reached into his inside pocket and withdrew a small, carefully wrapped parcel which he handed to Darwin. "Please, sir, unwrap it."

Albright watched anxiously as Darwin took the proffered parcel, fumbled with the paper and opened the small cardboard box. With a soft cry he gently lifted out its contents.

With relief, Albright continued. "In 1862 you published a book on orchid fertilization, including a description of *Angraecum sesquipedale*, a Madagascar orchid species with an eleven and a half inch nectary. You predicted that there must be a sphinx moth with a proboscis long enough to reach the nectar.

"In 1903, just before the Church clamped down all the way on biological inquiries, a collector named Morgan found the moth in Madagascar. He named it *Xanthopan morgani praedicta* to honor your prediction." He looked at the small brown object in Darwin's palm. "We thought you might like to see it."

"Most remarkable. I am most gratified to see this." Darwin looked it over carefully before replacing it in the box. "I should like to study this more fully. The proboscis is curled, but it does appear to be fully long enough to extract nectar from the comet orchid." He looked at Albright. "Was this what you wanted to discuss?"

"No, sir, this was for your pleasure only."

Darwin straightened up with a jerk. "Of course, this lovely specimen does not, in itself, prove that you are what you say. The moth does not evince a date of discovery."

"I am aware of that. On the other hand, you have not heard of the discovery, so I could be telling the truth." Albright smiled. "But in either case it indicates sincerity on my part."

"That is indeed a reasonable argument. Do you have any other . . . proofs?"

Albright's smile faded. "We thought long and hard about that. There are few objects which cannot be falsified – books and newspapers with later dates could have been printed at any time, for example. Same with coins. Also, there are certain limitations on objects that may be carried back into the past. We are only beginning to learn about them by experimentation, but it appears as though future technology cannot go backwards in time. In other words, it cannot exist before it was invented."

He looked up with a pleading expression. "That also seems reasonable, does it not? We hoped that the moth would make the journey, because others of its kind exist in 1866. And, I, of course, for the same reason." He smiled nervously. "Humans are an old technology. So I bring only my argument, which I beg to be allowed to present."

Darwin drew out a watch on a chain and squinted at it before tucking it back into his vest pocket. "Very well, I'm willing to continue our discussion, although I withhold judgment on your fantastic claim." They resumed walking. "So, what part of my work *did* you wish to discuss?"

"A work that you are contemplating, but have not yet written. A work that is unnecessary to the acceptance of your theory, but which will cause a great deal of harm to the future of science. A great deal of harm. I am here to beg you not to pursue this work. And I have but little time to do it."

"Really? You know of a work I have not yet written? I am confounded."

"Our records are not complete, for reasons which I shall attempt to make clear, but they lead us to believe that about now you are working on a book entitled, *An Answer to the Religious Opposition to the Origin of Species and the Descent of Man.*"

"Your knowledge is not quite precise. I have made a few notes about the subject, solely to keep track of arguments in opposition. I believe I have said so in a letter or two."

"Yes, sir, I know, but trust me, that book *will* be published, in 1884."

Darwin looked unhappily at Albright. "So far in the future, then, the attacks will continue?"

"I'm afraid so."

Thwack!

Clink. Another circuit of the Sandwalk completed, another flint knocked off the pile.

"I admit to initially being puzzled, then irked, by the blind rejection of my Theory by a rigid biblical interpretation by . . . by certain minds. And then Captain FitzRoy's suicide has preyed heavily on my mind these last months." He looked up. "You know of Captain FitzRoy?"

FitzRoy! If only Darwin knew how much he despised that name! He had been brought up under the gaze of that ubiquitous face! He had grown to hate the mutton chop sideburns, the disdainful expression, the deep-set eyes with their arrogant stare. *Darwin spent five pleasant years with the man, but I have been forced to live by FitzRoy's tyrannical pronouncements all of my life!* He stifled the passionate tirade that threatened to burst from his lips. Instead he nodded mutely.

Darwin seemed not to notice his companion's anguish. He continued, "Despite our initial camaraderie on the *Beagle*, we argued much during the voyage. I disappointed him severely by not finding substantiation for the Book of Genesis in my observations of the natural world. As I found more variation among the species, so he became more and more rigid and resisted all interpretations that conflicted in any way with the most literal reading of the Bible." He shook his head. "We last met as friends in 1857, when he came to stay at Down House for two nights, but the visit was not a success. We parted coolly, and never met again."

1857. A visit with FitzRoy. Albright made a mental note. As a leading Darwin scholar, even he hadn't been aware that the two had continued on social terms after the voyage. A familiar ache gripped him. *So much has been lost.*

Seemingly gripped by memories, Darwin continued his monologue, an intense expression on his face. "After the publication of the *Origin*, he became a violent objector to my work. I, on the other hand, could not see why Natural Selection threatened his religion. Finally, he became convinced that he had nurtured a blasphemer on board the *Beagle*, and he turned it over and over in his mind until I fear it unhinged him. In despair at what he viewed as the triumph of my satanic views, he took his life most cruelly April last."

"It was a tragedy," Albright said with vehemence. "His suicide created one of the most powerful martyrs in history."

Darwin turned to him with a perplexed look, but continued, "I feel compelled to set down the arguments pro and con my theory, in the hope that others of his religious rigidity might be dissuaded from this unfortunate act. The Church must not be used as an impediment to thinking!"

"And yet such an intended act of mercy will have such terrible consequences," murmured Albright.

"Indeed? My book?"

"Absolutely. That book started a chain of events that became a crusade against science throughout Europe and the Americas that continues even today, some three hundred years later."

"Three hundred years—"

Albright waved away his objections, plunged on. "Imagine, sir, that it is 1884, and your book – the book you are going to write – has just been published. As they did for the *Origin*, your old supporters, Huxley and Hooker, defended you most ably. And by then there were others convinced by your arguments and evidence."

"Most gratifying."

"Yes, but more importantly, the Church hierarchy took the criticism very badly. The bishops accused you of setting man's ingenuity against God's word. Worse, the public supported them, especially in the face of the very unpopular Neanderthal fossils from Germany. People did not want to believe they were descended from apes and barbarous tribes of men."

"Indeed, it is perhaps an unpopular idea, but inescapable. Man is not exempted from the rest of the animal kingdom in this regard."

"I agree, but it fueled the flames of the rebellion. Many men like FitzRoy joined together in a campaign to expunge what they termed the 'heresy of evolution'. They called themselves the Fitzrovians, and demanded a literal interpretation of the events set forth in Genesis."

"And who spoke against them?"

"Nobody, there's the tragedy. Men of science thought it would pass, and that they could safely ignore what they saw to be religious zealots. But those ideas started to snowball, and what ensued was a great resurgence of fundamentalist religion, and a suppression of science. Schools were forbidden to teach about evolution and natural selection; then it spread to the other sciences. For over two centuries, men of science have had to labor secretly, in great peril."

"I cannot believe that account, Mr Albright. Rational thought and scientific endeavor are seen as honorable professions in Europe and have for some three hundred years. Tycho Brahe and Johannes Kepler were great astronomers in the sixteenth century, well respected and rewarded by the Danish crown."

Thwack!

Clink.

Albright was sure those two sounds would be indelibly burned into his memory no matter what happened. That, and the sounds of the birds.

"Yes, but Kepler's mother was tried as a witch in Germany, Giordano Bruno was burned at the stake in Rome for insisting that the Earth circles the sun, and well into the seventeenth century, Galileo was forced to recant that same doctrine."

Darwin looked at him sharply. "You know your history well, for a man from so far in the future."

"We have learned the whole history of suppression these long years. Oh, we are desperate to be free! Believe this if nothing else." In anguish Albright tore open his shirt to reveal an elaborate, garishly colored tattoo of a cross.

"I am an acolyte of the Holy Order of Scientism, for over two centuries the only way for a few to keep alive the flame of learning untainted by religious dogma. We seek to know the world the way it *is*, not the way it is ordained to be by the Hierarchy of Fitzrovians. Only now are we beginning to move out from the shadow of the Church. But we have lost so much time, and it may be too late."

Darwin was visibly taken aback, and stammered, "Is that . . . adornment real?"

"The tattoo? Yes, and another like it on my back. I'll take them with me to the grave."

"But . . . why? Of what use is such . . . adornment?"

"Fealty, for some. For others such as myself, disguise. Although it is true that the hold of the Church is gradually loosening, we have lost over two centuries of scientific understanding. Two centuries! Our climate is changing and we don't know why, the world's population is soaring, the forests were cut or burned, the deserts advance, the air is brown, the waters are poisoned and the people sicken."

"Surely, the leaders—"

"Either the Hierarchy doesn't care or they are unable to manage the crisis. Whichever it is, there is little expectation that we can cure the world with our present state of knowledge anyway. It was a desperate hope, but perhaps by changing the past we can recapture that lost time."

"You speak of lost time, yet you claim to be from the future, therefore you have the ability to travel through time. Surely that is remarkably advanced science."

"The time travel device was an accidental discovery. We don't know how it works, but it does, at least for short trips. If I am able to change our past, by dissuading you from publishing that book, we don't know what will happen. We hope it will change the future for the better. But maybe it cannot be changed. Our philosophers have debated long and deeply about this: maybe I exist only because the events in my past unfurled as they have. Perhaps in another—" He stopped short as a wave of dizziness hit him.

Wha—? Oh no, not yet. He peeled back his sleeve to look at his watch. *It's not time yet!*

Darwin was looking at him sharply. "Are you ill, sir?"

"No, just . . . dizzy. Perhaps the temporal travel device has affected me."

"Young man, your tale is most persuasive, although I can scarcely believe one book of mine could be so pivotal in history."

Albright recovered himself. "All our historical research indicates just that, sir. What we know of causality tells us that the form the future takes has a sensitive dependence on initial conditions. Even a seemingly minor event can have great consequences. And, for a man of your renown, that new book was not a minor event."

Darwin stared at him intently. "Just how did you plan to dissuade me?"

"By doing what I just did, telling you what is going to happen if you *do* publish it."

"What if I refuse, or am not convinced? I admit that it irks me greatly that certain bishops are so opposed to my ideas." He looked at Albright sharply. "Are you prepared to accept failure?"

Albright hesitated, suddenly aware of the heavy lump in his overcoat pocket. "Mr Darwin, sir, I . . . we wish you no harm, but we are determined not to fail our world."

"I see. You will stop me by force if necessary." Darwin looked at him as if appraising what means Albright would use.

Albright nodded slightly. *I'm losing him*, he thought unhappily. "If I can persuade you that there is independent proof of your theory, would you be satisfied?"

Darwin drew himself up. "Proof? Young man, I have labored for decades on my theory of Natural Selection. I truly believe that I have amassed an overwhelming body of evidence—"

"Someone has found the *mechanism* for inheritance."

Darwin stopped short. "The mechanism? What do you mean?"

"Well, not the actual . . . ah . . ." He fought back another wave of dizziness. "Well, you understand, not the actual, uh, bodies in the cell, but the *mathematics* of inheritance."

Darwin stared uncomprehendingly.

Albright rushed on. "There's a book, just published, by Gregor Mendel, about experiments he did with garden pea plants. He has established that there is a unit of heredity, some . . . factor passed from parent to offspring, in a regular and repeatable way. Some of these factors are transmitted visibly, and are called dominant. Others become, ah, latent in the process and are called recessive. With the correct crosses, Mendel could make them reappear in later generations, so he knew they were still there, albeit hidden."

A look of awe slowly washed over the older man's face and his mouth worked as he silently wrestled with the implications.

"So you see," continued Albright, "if an organism exhibits an unfavorable factor and dies because of it, and this happens to all the other individuals with the same factor, it will be eliminated from the population." Bright sparks flashed across his eyes. He reached into his coat and clutched the weapon. "It's the mechanism for nashural s'lection!"

"The mechanism for natural selection. Yes. It could very well be. I will need to see that book! Tell me again who is the author?"

"M ... M ... Mendel," he slurred. "G ... G ... Gregor Mendel, a m ... m ... monk, an Augush ... tini ... tian."

"What did you say? I couldn't understand. Speak up, please!"

Albright stared fuzzily. The scene around him was becoming grainy. *Still time*. In desperation he yanked his arm out of his pocket, aimed the antique pistol at Darwin. *God help me*. He squeezed the trigger as greyness descended.

The crackling noise awakened her. Solange started up, feeling woozy and a bit unclear. She absentmindedly put her hand up to her hair to tuck a stray red curl into ... nothing.

"Rats, must've dozed off."

The screen in front of her was full of diagonal lines.

"That does it. I can't do any assignment if the freaking Viewer conks out on me."

Electronics never worked for her. This morning already her chronometer had failed to network with her wakeup implant. She'd almost missed her session with the TVS. She'd rushed to the library in the nick of time, shouldered her way past the waiting students and jammed her ID thumbprint down just as the robo-librarian was about to give her slot away. As it was she'd lost fifteen minutes.

Someone pounded on the door. "Two minutes!"

She checked the big chronometer.

"Hell, my session's over! What'd I see anyway?"

The vidrecorder was still running. She shut it off and removed the spool.

The door opened suddenly. The librarian rolled in. "Time's up," it rumbled. "Please relinquish the Temporal ViewScreen."

"Okay, okay, keep your treads on," she muttered. "I'm leaving."

Her eye fell on the assignment sheet. "Observation of Charles Darwin during writing of *The Origin of Species*, 1858."

It was clearly marked "Easy". Hell, she hadn't even been able to tune the freaking gizmo to that date. It'd stuck on 1866. Well, she'd done something different. But what? She felt for the spool in her pocket.

Whatever I see, I'll just be creative with my interpretation, she thought. After all, what difference could it make what some old guy was thinking three hundred years ago?

She hurried out into the bright new morning in search of coffee.

TRY AND CHANGE THE PAST

Fritz Leiber

The following is the oldest story in the book, first published in 1958, but it is such a classic, yet surprisingly little known, that I could not leave it out. The story was the first of what would become Leiber's Change War series, which included his novel The Big Time *(1961) and stories collected as* The Change War *(1978). The series explores a war raging across the space-time continuum between two factions each seeking to protect their version of reality. There are only hints of that in this story, which is arguably the definitive story on whether it is possible to change the past or whether causality and fate are so powerful that the past is somehow protected. It's a theme we'll return to a few more times in this volume.*

Fritz Leiber (1910–92) was one of the giants of the science-fiction and fantasy fields from the 1940s up until his death. He may be best remembered now for his long-running heroic fantasy series featuring the Grey Mouser and Fafhrd, but Leiber was as equally adept at science fiction and his novels include The Green Millennium *(1953),* The Wanderer *(1964) and* A Specter is Haunting Texas *(1969).*

No, I wouldn't advise anyone to try to change the past, at least not his *personal* past, although changing the *general* past is my business, my fighting business. You see, I'm a Snake in the Change War. Don't back off – human beings, even Resurrected ones engaged in time-fighting, aren't built for outward wriggling and their poison is mostly psychological. "Snake" is slang for the soldiers on our side, like Hun or Reb or Ghibbelin. In the Change War we're trying to alter the past – and it's tricky, brutal work, believe me – at points all over the cosmos, anywhere and anywhen, so that history will be warped to make our side defeat the Spiders. But that's a much bigger story, the biggest in fact, and I'll leave it occupying several planets of microfilm and two asteroids of coded molecules in the files of the High Command.

Change one event in the past and you get a brand new future? Erase the conquests of Alexander by nudging a Neolithic pebble? Extirpate America by pulling up a shoot of Sumerian grain? Brother, that isn't the way it works at all! The space-time continuum's built of stubborn stuff and change is anything but a chain-reaction. Change the past and you start a wave of changes moving futurewards, but it damps out mighty fast. Haven't you ever heard of temporal reluctance, or of the Law of the Conservation of Reality?

Here's a little story that will illustrate my point: This guy was fresh recruited, the Resurrection sweat still wet in his armpits, when he got the idea he'd use the time-traveling power to go back and make a couple of little changes in his past so that his life would take a happier course and maybe, he thought, he wouldn't have to die and get mixed up with Snakes and Spiders at all. It was as if a new-enlisted feuding hillbilly soldier should light out with the high-power rifle they issued him to go back to his mountains and pick off his pet enemies.

Normally it couldn't ever have happened. Normally, to avoid just this sort of thing, he'd have been shipped straight off to some place a few thousand or million years distant from his point of enlistment and maybe a few light-years, too. But there was a local crisis in the Change War and a lot of routine operations got held up and one new recruit was simply forgotten.

Normally, too, he'd never have been left alone a moment in the Dispatching Room, never even have glimpsed the place except to be rushed through it on arrival and reshipment. But, as I say, there happened to be a crisis, the Snakes were short-handed, and several soldiers were careless. Afterwards two N.C.s were busted because of what happened and a First Looey not only lost his commission but was transferred outside the galaxy and the era. But during the crisis this recruit I'm telling you about had opportunity and more to fool around with forbidden things and try out one of his schemes.

He also had all the details on the last part of his life back in the real world, on his death and its consequences, to mull over and be tempted to change. This wasn't anybody's carelessness. The Snakes give every candidate that information as part of the recruiting pitch. They spot a death coming and the Resurrection Men go back and recruit the person from a point a few minutes or at most a few hours earlier. They explain in uncomfortable detail what's going to happen and wouldn't he rather take the oath and put on scales? I never heard of anybody turning down that offer. Then they lift him from his lifeline in the form of a Doubleganger and from then on, brother, he's a Snake.

So this guy had a clearer picture of his death than of the day he bought his first car, and a masterpiece of morbid irony it was. He was living in a classy penthouse that had belonged to a crazy uncle of his – it even had a midget astronomical observatory, unused for years – but he was stony broke, up to the top hair in debt, and due to be dispossessed next day. He'd never had a real job, always lived off his rich relatives and his wife's, but now he was getting a little too mature for his stern dedication to a life of sponging to be cute. His charming personality, which had been his only asset, was deader from overuse and abuse than he himself would be in a few hours. His crazy uncle would not have anything to do with him any more. His wife was responsible for a lot of the wear and tear on his social-butterfly wings; she had hated him for years, had screamed at him morning to night the way you can only get away with in a penthouse, and was going batty herself. He'd been playing around with another woman, who'd just given him the gate, though he knew his wife would never believe that and would only add a scornful note to her screaming if she did.

It was a lousy evening, smack in the middle of an August heat wave. The Giants were playing a night game with Brooklyn. Two long-run musicals had closed. Wheat had hit a new high. There was a brush fire in California and a war scare in Iran. And tonight a meteor shower was due, according to an astronomical bulletin that had arrived in the morning mail addressed to his uncle – he generally dumped such stuff in the fireplace unopened, but today he had looked at it because he had nothing else to do, either more useful or more interesting.

The phone rang. It was a lawyer. His crazy uncle was dead and in the will there wasn't a word about an Asteroid Search Foundation. Every penny of the fortune went to the no-good nephew.

This same character finally hung up the phone, fighting a tendency for his heart to spring giddily out of his chest and through the ceiling. Just then his wife came screeching out of the bedroom. She'd received a cute, commiserating, tell-all note from the other woman; she had a gun and announced that she was going to finish him off.

The sweltering atmosphere provided a good background for sardonic catastrophe. The French doors to the roof were open behind him but the air that drifted through was muggy as death. Unnoticed, a couple of meteors streaked faintly across the night sky.

Figuring it would sure dissuade her, he told her about the inheritance. She screamed that he'd just use the money to buy more other women – not an unreasonable prediction – and pulled the trigger.

The danger was minimal. She was at the other end of a big living room, and her hand wasn't just shaking; she was waving the nickel-plated revolver as if it were a fan.

The bullet took him right between the eyes. He flopped down, deader than his hopes were before he got the phone call. He saw it happen because as a clincher the Resurrection Men brought him forward as a Doubleganger to witness it invisibly – also standard Snake procedure and not productive of time-complications, incidentally, since Doublegangers don't imprint on reality unless they want to.

They stuck around a bit. His wife looked at the body for a couple of seconds, went to her bedroom, blonded her graying hair by dousing it with two bottles of undiluted peroxide, put on a tarnished gold-lamé evening gown and a bucket of make-up, went back to the living room, sat down at the piano, played "Country Gardens" and then shot herself, too.

So that was the little skit, the little double blackout, he had to mull over outside the empty and unguarded Dispatching Room, quite forgotten by its twice-depleted skeleton crew while every available Snake in the sector was helping deal with the local crisis, which centered around the planet Alpha Centauri Four, two million years minus.

Naturally it didn't take him long to figure out that if he went back and gimmicked things so that the first blackout didn't occur, but the second still did, he would be sitting pretty back in the real world and able to devote his inheritance to fulfilling his wife's prediction and other pastimes. He didn't know much about Doublegangers yet and had it figured out that if he didn't die in the real world he'd have no trouble resuming his existence there – maybe it'd even happen automatically.

So this Snake – name kind of fits him, doesn't it? – crossed his fingers and slipped into the Dispatching Room. Dispatching is so simple a child could learn it in five minutes from studying the board. He went back to a point a couple of hours before the tragedy, carefully avoiding the spot where the Resurrection Men had lifted him from his lifeline. He found the revolver in a dresser drawer, unloaded it, checked to make sure there weren't any more cartridges lying around, and then went ahead a couple of hours, arriving just in time to see himself get the slug between the eyes same as before.

As soon as he got over his disappointment, he'd learned something about Doublegangers he should have known all along, if his mind had been clicking. The bullets he'd lifted were Doublegangers, too; they had disappeared from the real world only at the point in space-time where he'd lifted them, and they had continued to exist, as real as ever, in the earlier and later sections of their lifelines – with the result that the gun was loaded again by the time his wife had grabbed it up.

So this time he set the board so he'd arrive just a few minutes before the tragedy. He lifted the gun, bullets and all, and waited around to make sure it stayed lifted. He figured – rightly – that if he left this space-time sector the gun would reappear in the dresser drawer, and he didn't want his wife getting hold of any gun, even one with a broken lifeline. Afterwards – after his own death was averted, that is – he figured he'd put the gun back in his wife's hand.

Two things reassured him a lot, although he'd been expecting the one and hoping for the other: his wife didn't notice his presence as a Doubleganger and when she went to grab the gun she acted as if it weren't gone and held her right hand just as if there were a gun in it. If he'd studied philosophy, he'd have realized that he was witnessing a proof of Leibniz's theory of Pre-established Harmony: that neither atoms nor human beings really affect each other; they just look as if they do.

But anyway he had no time for theories. Still holding the gun, he drifted out into the living room to get a box seat right next to Himself for the big act. Himself didn't notice him any more than his wife had.

His wife came out and spoke her piece same as ever. Himself cringed as if she still had the gun and started to babble about the inheritance; his wife sneered and made as if she were shooting Himself.

Sure enough, there was no shot this time, *and* no mysteriously appearing bullet hole – which was something he'd been afraid of. Himself just stood there dully while his wife made as if she were looking down at a dead body and went back to her bedroom.

He was pretty pleased: this time he actually *had* changed the past. Then Himself slowly glanced around at him, still with that dull look, and slowly came toward him. He was more pleased than ever because he figured now they'd melt together into one man and one lifeline again, and he'd be able to hurry out somewhere and establish an alibi, just to be on the safe side, while his wife suicided.

But it didn't happen quite that way. Himself's look changed from dull to desperate, he came up close ... and suddenly grabbed the gun and quick as a wink put a thumb to the trigger and shot himself between the eyes. And flopped, same as ever.

Right there he was starting to learn a little – and it was an unpleasant and shivery sort of learning – about the Law of the Conservation of Reality. The four-dimensional space-time universe doesn't *like* to be changed, any more than it likes to lose or gain energy or matter. If it *has* to be changed, it'll adjust itself just enough to accept that change and no more. The Conservation of Reality is a sort of Law of Least Action, too. It doesn't matter how improbable the events involved in the adjustment are, just so long as they're possible at all and can be used to patch the established pattern. His death, at this point, was part of the established pattern. If he lived on instead of dying, billions of other compensatory changes would have to be made, covering many years, perhaps centuries, before the old pattern could be re-established, the snarled lifelines woven back into it – and the universe finally go on the same as if his wife had shot him on schedule.

This way the pattern was hardly affected at all. There were powder burns on his forehead that weren't there before, but there weren't any witnesses to the shooting in the first place, so the presence or absence of powder burns didn't matter. The gun was lying on the floor instead of being in his wife's hands, but he had the feeling that when the time came for her to die, she'd wake enough from the Pre-established Harmony trance to find it, just as Himself did.

So he'd learned a little about the Conservation of Reality. He also had learned a little about his own character, especially from Himself's last look and act. He'd got a hint that he had been trying to destroy himself for years by the way he'd lived, so that inherited fortune or accidental success couldn't save him, and if his wife hadn't shot him he'd have done it himself in any case. He'd got a hint that Himself hadn't merely been acting as an agent for a self-correcting universe when he grabbed the gun; he'd been acting on his own account, too – the universe, you know, operates by getting people to cooperate.

But, although these ideas occurred to him, he didn't dwell on them, for he figured he'd had a partial success the second time, and the third time if he kept the gun away from Himself; if he dominated Himself, as it were, the melting-together would take place and everything else would go forward as planned.

He had the dim realization that the universe, like a huge sleepy animal, knew what he was trying to do and was trying to thwart him. This feeling of opposition made him determined to outmaneuver the universe – not the first guy to yield to such a temptation, of course.

And up to a point his tactics worked. The third time he gimmicked the past, everything started to happen just as it did the second time. Himself dragged miserably over to him, looking for the gun, but he had it tucked away and was prepared to hold on to it. Encouragingly, Himself didn't grapple. The look of desperation changed to one of utter hopelessness, and Himself turned away from him and very slowly walked to the French doors and stood looking out into the sweating night. He figured Himself was just getting used to the idea of not dying. There wasn't a breath of air. A couple of meteors streaked across the sky. Then, mixed with the up-seeping night sounds of the city, there was a low whirring whistle.

Himself shook a bit, as if he'd had a sudden chill. Then Himself turned around and slumped to the floor in one movement. Between his eyes was a black hole.

Then and there this Snake I'm telling you about decided never again to try and change the past, as least not his personal past. He'd had it, and he'd also acquired a healthy respect for a High Command able to change the past, albeit with difficulty. He scooted back to the Dispatching Room, where a sleepy and surprised Snake gave him a terrific chewing-out and confined him to quarters. The chewing-out didn't bother him too much – he'd acquired a certain fatalism about things. A person's got to learn to accept reality as it is, you know – just as you'd best not be surprised at the way I disappear in a moment or two – I'm a Snake too, remember.

If a statistician is looking for an example of a highly improbable event, he can hardly pick a more vivid one than the chance of a man being hit by a meteorite. And, if he adds the condition that the meteorite hit him between the eyes so as to counterfeit the wound made by a 32-caliber bullet, the improbability becomes astronomical cubed. So how's a person going to outmaneuver a universe that finds it easier to drill a man through the head that way rather than postpone the date of his death?

NEEDLE IN A TIMESTACK

Robert Silverberg

With Fritz Leiber's story having introduced us to the idea of trying to change the past, we enter into a sequence of stories that explores that whole concept, not in a big way, such as murdering Adolf Hitler before the outbreak of the Second World War, or trying to stop the crucifixion of Christ, but in much smaller, more personal ways.

Robert Silverberg's writing career now spans more than sixty years during which time he has written hundreds of short stories, novels and reference works – a small library in its own right. A not inconsiderable number of these involve time travel, most notably his novels Hawksbill Station *(1968),* Up the Line *(1969) and* Project Pendulum *(1987), all three of which are available in an omnibus edition,* Times Three *(2011). The following story first appeared in 1983 but confusingly borrowed its title from an earlier collection of Silverberg's stories,* Needle in a Timestack *(1966), which contained no story under that name. But why let a good title go to waste, Silverberg thought, and so at last a story by that name appeared in* Playboy *in 1983 and was collected in* The Conglomeroid Cocktail Party *(1984). Confused? Not as much as the lead character in this story.*

Between one moment and the next the taste of cotton came into his mouth, and Mikkelsen knew that Tommy Hambleton had been tinkering with his past again. The cotton-in-the-mouth sensation was the standard tip-off for Mikkelsen. For other people it might be a ringing in the ears, a tremor of the little finger, a tightness in the shoulders. Whatever the symptom, it always meant the same thing: your time-track has been meddled with; your life has been retroactively transformed. It happened all the time. One of the little annoyances of modern life, everyone always said. Generally, the changes didn't amount to much.

But Tommy Hambleton was out to destroy Mikkelsen's marriage, or, more accurately, he was determined to unhappen it altogether, and that went beyond Mikkelsen's limits of tolerance. In something close to panic he phoned home to find out if he still had Janine.

Her lovely features blossomed on the screen – glossy dark hair, elegant cheekbones, cool sardonic eyes. She looked tense and strained, and Mikkelsen knew she had felt the backlash of this latest attempt too.

"Nick?" she said. "Is it a phasing?"

"I think so. Tommy's taken another whack at us, and Christ only knows how much chaos he's caused this time."

"Let's run through everything."

"All right," Mikkelsen said. "What's your name?"

"Janine."

"And mine?"

"Nick. Nicholas Perry Mikkelsen. You see? Nothing important has changed."

"Are you married?"

"Yes, of course, darling. To you."

"Keep going. What's our address?"

"11 Lantana Crescent."

"Do we have children?"

"Dana and Elise. Dana's five, Elise is three. Our cat's name is Minibelle, and—"

"Okay," Mikkelsen said, relieved. "That much checks out. But I tasted the cotton, Janine. Where has he done it to us this time? What's been changed?"

"It can't be anything major, love. We'll find it if we keep checking. Just stay calm."

"Calm. Yes." He closed his eyes. He took a deep breath. The little annoyances of modern life, he thought. In the old days, when time was just a linear flow from *then* to *now*, did anyone get bored with all that stability? For better or for worse it was different now. You go to bed a Dartmouth man and wake up Columbia, never the wiser. You board a plane that blows up over Cyprus, but then your insurance agent goes back and gets you to miss the flight. In the new fluid way of life there was always a second chance, a third, a fourth, now that the past was open to anyone with the price of a ticket. But what good is any of that, Mikkelsen wondered, if Tommy Hambleton can use it to disappear me and marry Janine again himself?

They punched for readouts and checked all their vital data against what they remembered. When your past is altered through time-phasing, all records of your life are automatically altered too, of course, but there's a period of two or three hours when memories of your previous existence still linger in your brain, like the phantom twitches of an amputated limb. They checked the date of Mikkelsen's birth, parents' names, his nine genetic coordinates, his educational record. Everything seemed right. But when they got to their wedding date the readout said 8 Feb 2017, and Mikkelsen heard warning chimes in his mind. "I remember a summer wedding," he said. "Outdoors in Dan Levy's garden, the hills all dry and brown, the 24th of August."

"So do I, Nick. The hills wouldn't have been brown in February. But I can see it – that hot dusty day—"

"Then five months of our marriage are gone, Janine. He couldn't unmarry us altogether, but he managed to hold us up from summer to winter." Rage made his head spin, and he had to ask his desk for a quick buzz of tranks. Etiquette called for one to be cool about a phasing. But he couldn't be cool when the phasing was a deliberate and malevolent blow at the center of his life. He wanted to shout, to break things, to kick Tommy Hambleton's ass. He wanted his marriage left alone. He said, "You know what I'm going to do one of these days? I'm going to go back about fifty years and eradicate Tommy completely. Just arrange things so his parents never get to meet, and—"

"No, Nick. You mustn't."

"I know. But I'd love to." He knew he couldn't, and not just because it would be murder. It was essential that Tommy Hambleton be born and grow up and meet Janine and marry her, so that when the marriage came apart she would meet and marry Mikkelsen. If he changed Hambleton's past, he would change hers too, and if he changed hers, he would change his own, and anything might happen. Anything. But all the same he was furious. "Five months of our past, Janine—"

"We don't need them, love. Keeping the present and the future safe is the main priority. By tomorrow we'll always think we were married in February of 2017, and it won't matter. Promise me you won't try to phase him."

"I hate the idea that he can simply—"

"So do I. But I want you to promise you'll leave things as they are."

"Well—"

"Promise."

"All right," he said. "I promise."

Little phasings happened all the time. Someone in Illinois makes a trip to eleventh-century Arizona and sets up tiny ripple currents in time that have a tangential and peripheral effect on a lot of lives, and someone in California finds himself driving a silver BMW instead of a gray Toyota. No one minded trifling changes like that. But this was the third time in the last twelve months, so far as Mikkelsen was able to tell, that Tommy Hambleton had committed a deliberate phasing intended to break the chain of events that had brought about Mikkelsen's marriage to Janine.

The first phasing happened on a splendid spring day – coming home from work, sudden taste of cotton in mouth, sense of mysterious disorientation. Mikkelsen walked down the steps looking for his old ginger tomcat, Gus, who always ran out to greet him as though he thought he was a dog. No Gus. Instead a calico female, very pregnant, sitting placidly in the front hall.

"Where's Gus?" Mikkelsen asked Janine.

"Gus? Gus who?"

"Our cat."

"You mean Max?"

"Gus," he said. "Sort of orange, crooked tail—"

"That's right. But Max is his name. I'm sure it's Max. He must be around somewhere. Look, here's Minibelle." Janine knelt and stroked the fat calico. "Minibelle, where's Max?"

"Gus," Mikkelsen said. "Not Max. And who's this Minibelle?"

"She's our cat, Nick," Janine said, sounding surprised. They stared at each other.

"Something's happened, Nick."

"I think we've been time-phased," he said.

Sensation as of dropping through trapdoor – shock, confusion, terror. Followed by hasty and scary inventory of basic life-data to see what had changed. Everything appeared in order except for the switch of cats. He didn't remember having a female calico. Neither did Janine, although she had accepted the presence of the cat without surprise. As for Gus – Max – he was getting foggier about his name, and Janine couldn't even remember what he looked like. But she did recall that he had been a wedding gift from some close friend, and Mikkelsen remembered that the friend was Gus Stark, for whom they had named him, and Janine was then able to dredge up the dimming fact that Gus was a close friend of Mikkelsen's and also of Hambleton and Janine in the days when they were married, and that Gus had introduced Janine to Mikkelsen ten years ago when they were all on holiday in Hawaii.

Mikkelsen accessed the household callmaster and found no Gus Stark listed. So the phasing had erased him from their roster of friends. The general phone directory turned up a Gus Stark in Costa Mesa. Mikkelsen called him and got a freckle-faced man with fading red hair, who looked more or less familiar. But he didn't know Mikkelsen at all, and only after some puzzling around in his memory did he decide that they had been distantly acquainted way back when, but had had some kind of trifling quarrel and had lost touch with each other years ago.

"That's not how I think I remember it," Mikkelsen said. "I remember us as friends for years, really close. You and Donna and Janine and I were out to dinner only last week, is what I remember, over in Newport Beach."

"Donna?"

"Your wife."

"My wife's name is Karen. Jesus, this has been one hell of a phasing, hasn't it?" He didn't sound upset.

"I'll say. Blew away your marriage, our friendship, and who knows what-all else."

"Well, these things happen. Listen, if I can help you any way, fella, just call. But right now Karen and I were on our way out, and—"

"Yeah. Sure. Sorry to have bothered you," Mikkelsen told him.

He blanked the screen.

Donna. Karen. Gus. Max. He looked at Janine.

"Tommy did it," she said.

She had it all figured out. Tommy, she said, had never forgiven Mikkelsen for marrying her. He wanted her back. He still sent her birthday cards, coy little gifts, postcards from exotic ports.

"You never mentioned them," Mikkelsen said.

She shrugged. "I thought you'd only get annoyed. You've always disliked Tommy."

"No," Mikkelsen said, "I think he's interesting in his oddball way, flamboyant, unusual. What I dislike is his unwillingness to accept the notion that you stopped being his wife a dozen years ago."

"You'd dislike him more if you knew how hard he's been trying to get me back."

"Oh?"

"When we broke up," she said, "he phased me four times. This was before I met you. He kept jaunting back to our final quarrel, trying to patch it up so that the separation wouldn't have happened. I began feeling the phasings and I knew what must be going on, and I told him to quit it or I'd report him and get his jaunt-license revoked. That scared him, I guess, because he's been pretty well behaved ever since, except for all the little hints and innuendoes and invitations to leave you and marry him again."

"Christ," Mikkelsen said. "How long were you and he married? Six months?"

"Seven. But he's an obsessive personality. He never lets go."

"And now he's started phasing again?"

"That's my guess. He's probably decided that you're the obstacle, that I really do still love you, that I want to spend the rest of my life with you. So he needs to make us unmeet. He's taken his first shot by somehow engineering a breach between you and your friend Gus a dozen years back, a breach so severe that you never really became friends and Gus never fixed you up with me. Only it didn't work out the way Tommy hoped. We went to that party at Dave Cushman's place and I got pushed into the pool on top of you and you introduced yourself and one thing led to another and here we still are."

"Not all of us are," Mikkelsen said. "My friend Gus is married to somebody else now."

"That didn't seem to trouble him much."

"Maybe not. But he isn't my friend any more, either, and that troubles *me*. My whole past is at Tommy Hambleton's mercy, Janine! And Gus the cat is gone too. Gus was a damned good cat. I miss him."

"Five minutes ago you weren't sure whether his name was Gus or Max. Two hours from now you won't know you ever had any such cat, and it won't matter at all."

"But suppose the same thing had happened to you and me as happened to Gus and Donna?"

"It didn't, though."

"It might the next time," Mikkelsen said.

But it didn't. The next time, which was about six months later, they came out of it still married to each other. What they lost was their collection of twentieth-century artifacts – the black-and-white television set and the funny old dial telephone and the transistor radio and the little computer with the typewriter keyboard. All those treasures vanished between one instant and the next, leaving Mikkelsen with the telltale cottony taste in his mouth, Janine with a short-lived tic below her left eye, and both of them with the nagging awareness that a phasing had occurred.

At once they did what they could to see where the alteration had been made. For the moment they both remembered the artifacts they once had owned, and how eagerly they had collected them in '21 and '22, when the craze for such things was just beginning. But there were no sales receipts in their files and already their memories of what they had bought were becoming blurry and contradictory. There was a grouping of glittery sonic sculptures to the corner, now, where the artifacts had been. What change had been effected in the pattern of their past to put those things in the place of the others?

They never really were sure – there was no certain way of knowing – but Mikkelsen had a theory. The big expense he remembered for 2021 was the time jaunt that he and Janine had taken to Aztec Mexico, just before she got pregnant with Dana. Things had been a little wobbly between the Mikkelsens back then, and the time jaunt was supposed to be a second honeymoon. But their guide on the jaunt had been a hot little item named Elena Schmidt, who had made a very determined play for Mikkelsen and who had had him considering, for at least half an hour of lively fantasy, leaving Janine for her.

"Suppose," he said, "that on our original time-track we never went back to the Aztecs at all, but put the money into the artifact collection. But then Tommy went back and maneuvered things to get us interested in time jaunting, and at the same time persuaded that Schmidt cookie to show an interest in me. We couldn't afford both the antiques and the trip; we opted for the trip, Elena did her little number on me, it didn't cause the split that Tommy was hoping for, and now we have some gaudy memories of Moctezuma's empire and no collection of early electronic devices. What do you think?"

"Makes sense," Janine said.

"Will you report him, or should I?"

"But we have no proof, Nick!"

He frowned. Proving a charge of time-crime, he knew, was almost impossible, and risky besides. The very act of investigating the alleged crime could cause an even worse phase-shift and scramble their pasts beyond repair. To enter the past is like poking a baseball bat into a spiderweb: it can't be done subtly or delicately.

"Do we just sit and wait for Tommy to figure out a way to get rid of me that really works?" Mikkelsen asked.

"We can't just confront him with suspicions, Nick."

"You did it once."

"Long ago. The risks are greater now. We have more past to lose. What if he's not responsible? What if he gets scared of being blamed for something that's just coincidence, and *really* sets out to phase us? He's so damned volatile, so unstable – if he feels threatened, he's likely to do anything. He could wreck our lives entirely."

"If *he* feels threatened? What about—"

"Please, Nick. I've got a hunch Tommy won't try it again. He's had two shots and they've both failed. He'll quit it now. I'm sure he will."

Grudgingly Mikkelsen yielded, and after a time he stopped worrying about a third phasing. Over the next few weeks, other effects of the second phasing kept turning up, the way losses gradually make themselves known after a burglary. The same thing had happened after the first one. A serious attempt at altering the past could never have just one consequence; there was always a host of trivial – or not so trivial – secondary shifts, a ramifying web of transformations reaching out into any number of other lives. New chains of associations were formed in the Mikkelsens' lives as a result of the erasure of their plan to collect electronic artifacts and the substitution of a trip to pre-Columbian Mexico. People they had met on that trip now were good friends, with whom they exchanged gifts, spent other holidays, shared the burdens and joys of parenthood. A certain hollowness at first marked all those newly ingrafted old friend-ships, making them seem curiously insubstantial and marked by odd inconsistencies. But after a time everything felt real again, everything appeared to fit.

Then the third phasing happened, the one that pushed the beginning of their marriage from August to the following February, and did six or seven other troublesome little things, as they shortly discovered, to the contours of their existence.

"I'm going to talk to him," Mikkelsen said.

"Nick, don't do anything foolish."

"I don't intend to. But he's got to be made to see that this can't go on."

"Remember that he can be dangerous if he's forced into a corner," Janine said. "Don't threaten him. Don't push him."

"I'll tickle him," Mikkelsen said.

He met Hambleton for drinks at the Top of the Marina, Hambleton's favorite pub, swiveling at the end of a jointed stalk a thousand feet long rising from the harbor at Balboa Lagoon. Hambleton was there when Mikkelsen came in – a small sleek man, six inches shorter than Mikkelsen, with a slick confident manner. He was the richest man Mikkelsen knew, gliding through life on one of the big microprocessor fortunes of two generations back, and that in itself made him faintly menacing, as though he might try simply to buy back, one of these days, the wife he had loved and lost a dozen years ago when all of them had been so very young.

Hambleton's overriding passion, Mikkelsen knew, was time-travel. He was an inveterate jaunter – a compulsive jaunter, in fact, with that faintly hyperthyroid goggle-eyed look that frequent travelers get. He was always either just back from a jaunt or getting his affairs in order for his next one. It was as though the only use he had for the humdrum real-time event horizon was to serve as his springboard into the past. That was odd. What was odder still was where he jaunted. Mikkelsen could understand people who went zooming off to watch the battle of Waterloo, or shot a bundle on a first-hand view of the sack of Rome. If he had anything like Hambleton's money, that was what he would do. But according to Janine, Hambleton was forever going back seven weeks in time, or maybe to last Christmas, or occasionally to his eleventh birthday party. Time-travel as tourism held no interest for him. Let others roam the ferny glades of the Mesozoic: he spent fortunes doubling back along his own time-track, and never went anywhen other. The purpose of Tommy Hambleton's time-travel, it seemed, was to edit his past to make his life more perfect. He went back to eliminate every little contretemps and faux pas, to recover fumbles, to take advantage of the new opportunities that hindsight provides – to retouch, to correct, to emend. To Mikkelsen that was crazy, but also somehow charming. Hambleton was nothing if not charming. And Mikkelsen admired anyone who could invent his own new species of obsessive behavior, instead of going in for the standard hand-washing routines, or stamp-collecting or sitting with your back to the wall in restaurants.

The moment Mikkelsen arrived, Hambleton punched the autobar for cocktails and said, "Splendid to see you, Mikkelsen. How's the elegant Janine?"

"Elegant."

"What a lucky man you are. The one great mistake of my life was letting that woman slip through my grasp."

"For which I remain forever grateful, Tommy. I've been working hard lately to hang on to her, too."

Hambleton's eyes widened. "Yes? Are you two having problems?"

"Not with each other. Time-track troubles. You know, we were caught in a couple of phasings last year. Pretty serious ones. Now there's been another one. We lost five months of our marriage."

"Ah, the little annoyances of—"

"—modern life," Mikkelsen said. "Yes. A very familiar phrase. But these are what I'd call frightening annoyances. I don't need to tell you, of all people, what a splendid woman Janine is, how terrifying it is to me to think of losing her in some random twitch of the time-track."

"Of course. I quite understand."

"I wish I understood these phasings. They're driving us crazy. And that's what I wanted to talk to you about."

He studied Hambleton closely, searching for some trace of guilt or at least uneasiness. But Hambleton remained serene.

"How can I be of help?"

Mikkelsen said, "I thought that perhaps you, with all your vast experience in the theory and practice of time-jaunting, could give me some clue to what's causing them, so that I can head the next one off."

Hambleton shrugged elaborately. "My dear Nick, it could be anything! There's no reliable way of tracing phasing effects back to their cause. All our lives are interconnected in ways we never suspect. You say this last phasing delayed your marriage by a few months? Well, then, suppose that as a result of the phasing you decided to take a last bachelor fling and went off for a weekend in Banff, say, and met some lovely person with whom you spent three absolutely casual and nonsignificant but delightful days, thereby preventing her from meeting someone else that weekend with whom in the original time-track she had fallen in love and married. You then went home and married Janine, a little later than originally scheduled, and lived happily ever after; but the Banff woman's life was totally switched around, all as a consequence of the phasing that delayed your wedding. Do you see? There's never any telling how a shift in one chain of events can cause interlocking upheavals in the lives of utter strangers."

"So I realize. But why should we be hit with three phasings in a year, each one jeopardizing the whole structure of our marriage?"

"I'm sure I don't know," said Hambleton. "I suppose it's just bad luck, and bad luck always changes, don't you think? Probably you've been at the edge of some nexus of negative phases that has just about run its course." He smiled dazzlingly. "Let's hope so, anyway. Would you care for another filtered rum?"

He was smooth, Mikkelsen thought. And impervious. There was no way to slip past his defenses, and even a direct attack – an outright accusation that he was the one causing the phasings – would most likely bring into play a whole new line of defense. Mikkelsen did not intend to risk that. A man who used time jaunting so ruthlessly to tidy up his past was too slippery to confront. Pressed, Hambleton would simply deny everything and hasten backward to clear away any traces of his crime that might remain. In any case, making an accusation of time-crime stick was exceedingly difficult, because the crime by definition had to have taken place on a track that no longer existed. Mikkelsen chose to retreat. He accepted another drink from Hambleton; they talked in a desultory way for a while about phasing theory, the weather, the stock market, the excellences of the woman they both had married, and the good old days of 2014 or so when they all used to hang out down in dear old La Jolla, living golden lives of wondrous irresponsibility. Then he extricated himself from the conversation and headed for home in a dark and brooding mood. He had no doubt that Hambleton would strike again, perhaps quite soon. How could he be held at bay? Some sort of preemptive strike, Mikkelsen wondered? Some bold leap into the past that would neutralize the menace of Tommy Hambleton forever? Chancy, Mikkelsen thought. You could lose as much as you gained, sometimes, in that sort of maneuver. But perhaps it was the only hope.

He spent the next few days trying to work out a strategy. Something that would get rid of Hambleton without disrupting the frail chain of circumstance that bound his own life to that of

Janine – was it possible? Mikkelsen sketched out ideas, rejected them, tried again. He began to think he saw a way.

Then came a new phasing on a warm and brilliantly sunny morning that struck him like a thunderbolt and left him dazed and numbed. When he finally shook away the grogginess, he found himself in a bachelor flat ninety stories above Mission Bay, a thick taste of cotton in his mouth, and bewildering memories already growing thin of a lovely wife and two kids and a cat and a sweet home in mellow old Corona del Mar.

Janine? Dana? Elise? Minibelle?

Gone. All gone. He knew that he had been living in this condo since '22, after the breakup with Yvonne, and that Melanie was supposed to be dropping in about six. That much was reality. And yet another reality still lingered in his mind, fading vanishing.

So it had happened. Hambleton had really done it, this time.

There was no time for panic or even for pain. He spent the first half hour desperately scribbling down notes, every detail of his lost life that he still remembered, phone numbers, addresses, names, descriptions. He set down whatever he could recall of his life with Janine and of the series of phasings that had led up to this one. Just as he was running dry the telephone rang. Janine, he prayed.

But it was Gus Stark. "Listen," he began, "Donna and I got to cancel for tonight, on account of she's got a bad headache, but I hope you and Melanie aren't too disappointed, and . . ." He paused. "Hey, guy, are you okay?"

"There's been a bad phasing," Mikkelsen said.

"Uh-oh."

"I've got to find Janine."

"Janine?"

"Janine – Carter," Mikkelsen said. "Slender, high cheekbones, dark hair – you know."

"Janine," said Stark. "Do I know a Janine? Hey, you and Melanie on the outs? I thought—"

"This had nothing to do with Melanie," said Mikkelsen.

"Janine Carter." Gus grinned. "You mean Tommy Hambleton's girl? The little rich guy who was part of the La Jolla crowd ten-twelve years back when—"

"That's the one. Where do you think I'd find her now?"

"Married Hambleton, I think. Moved to the Riviera, unless I'm mistaken. Look, about tonight, Nick—"

"Screw tonight," Mikkelsen said. "Get off the phone. I'll talk to you later."

He broke the circuit and put the phone into search mode, all directories worldwide, Thomas and Janine Hambleton. While he waited, the shock and anguish of loss began at last to get to him, and he started to sweat. His hands shook; his heart raced in double time. I won't find her, he thought. He's got her hidden behind seven layers of privacy networks and it's crazy to think the phone number is listed, for Christ's sake, and—

The telephone. He hit the button. Janine calling, this time.

She looked stunned and disoriented, as though she were working hard to keep her eyes in focus. "Nick?" she said faintly. "Oh, God, Nick, it's you, isn't it?"

"Where are you?"

"A villa outside Nice. In Cap d'Antibes, actually. Oh, Nick – the kids – they're gone, aren't they? Dana. Elise. They never were born, isn't that so?"

"I'm afraid it is. He really nailed us, this time."

"I can still remember just as though they were real – as though we spent ten years together – oh, Nick—"

"Tell me how to find you. I'll be on the next plane out of San Diego."

She was silent a moment.

"No. No, Nick. What's the use? We aren't the same people we were when we were married. An hour or two more and we'll forget we ever were together."

"Janine—"

"We've got no past left, Nick. And no future."

"Let me come to you!"

"I'm Tommy's wife. My past's with him. Oh, Nick, I'm so sorry, so awfully sorry – I can still remember, a little, how it was with us, the fun, the running along the beach, the kids, the little fat calico cat – but it's all gone, isn't it? I've got my life here, you've got yours. I just wanted to tell you—"

"We can try to put it back together. You don't love Tommy. You and I belong with each other. We—"

"He's a lot different, Nick. He's not the man you remember from the La Jolla days. Kinder, more considerate, more of a human being, you know? It's been ten years, after all."

Mikkelsen closed his eyes and gripped the edge of the couch to keep from falling. "It's been two hours," he said. "Tommy phased us. He just tore up our life, and we can't ever have that part of it back, but still we can salvage something, Janine, we can rebuild, if you'll just get the hell out of that villa and—"

"I'm sorry, Nick." Her voice was tender, throaty, distant, almost unfamiliar. "Oh, God, Nick, it's such a mess. I loved you so. I'm sorry, Nick. I'm so sorry."

The screen went blank.

Mikkelsen had not time-jaunted in years, not since the Aztec trip, and he was amazed at what it cost now. But he was carrying the usual credit cards and evidently his credit lines were okay, because they approved his application in five minutes. He told them where he wanted to go and how he wanted to look, and for another few hundred the makeup man worked him over, taking that dusting of early gray out of his hair and smoothing the lines from his face and spraying him with the good old Southern California tan that you tend to lose when you're in your late thirties and spending more time in your office than on the beach. He looked at least eight years younger, close enough to pass. As long as he took care to keep from running into his own younger self while he was back there, there should be no problems.

He stepped into the cubicle and sweet-scented fog enshrouded him and when he stepped out again it was a mild December day in the year 2012, with a faint hint of rain in the northern sky. Only fourteen years back, and yet the world looked prehistoric to him, the clothing and the haircuts and the cars all wrong, the buildings heavy and clumsy, the advertisements floating overhead offering archaic and absurd products in blaring gaudy colors. Odd that the world of 2012 had not looked so crude to him the first time he had lived through it; but then the present never looks crude, he thought, except through the eyes of the future. He enjoyed the strangeness of it: it told him that he had really gone backward in time. It was like walking into an old movie. He felt very calm. All the pain was behind him now; he remembered nothing of the life that he had lost, only that it was important for him to take certain countermeasures against the man who had stolen something precious from him. He rented a car and drove quickly up to La Jolla. As he expected, everybody was at the beach club except for young Nick Mikkelsen, who was back in Palm Beach with his parents. Mikkelsen had put this jaunt together quickly but not without careful planning.

They were all amazed to see him – Gus, Dan, Leo, Christie, Sal, the whole crowd. How young they looked! Kids, just kids, barely into their twenties; all that hair, all that baby fat. He had never before realized how young you were when you were *young*. "Hey," Gus said, "I thought you were in Florida!" Someone handed him a popper. Someone slipped a capsule to his ear and raucous overload music began to pound against his cheekbone. He made the rounds, grinning hugging, explaining that Palm Beach had been a bore, that he had come back early to be with the gang. "Where's Yvonne?" he asked.

"She'll be here in a little while," Christie said.

Tommy Hambleton walked in five minutes after Mikkelsen. For one jarring instant Mikkelsen thought that the man he saw was the Hambleton of his own time, thirty-five years old, but no: there were little signs, and certain lack of tension in this man's face, a certain callowness about the lips, that marked him as younger. The truth, Mikkelsen realized, is that Hambleton had *never* looked really young, that he was ageless, timeless, sleek and plump and unchanging. It would have been very satisfying to Mikkelsen to plunge a knife into that impeccably shaven throat, but murder was not his style, nor was it an ideal solution to his problem. Instead, he called Hambleton aside, bought him a drink and said quietly, "I just thought you'd like to know that Yvonne and I are breaking up."

"Really, Nick? Oh, that's so sad! I thought you two were the most solid couple here!"

"We were. We were. But it's all over, man. I'll be with someone else New Year's Eve. Don't know who, but it won't be Yvonne."

Hambleton looked solemn. "That's so sad, Nick."

"No. Not for me and not for you." Mikkelsen smiled and

nudged Hambleton amiably. "Look, Tommy, it's no secret to me that you've had your eye on Yvonne for months. She knows it too. I just wanted to let you know that I'm stepping out of the picture, I'm very gracefully withdrawing, no hard feelings at all. And if she asks my advice, I'll tell her that you're absolutely the best man she could find. I mean it, Tommy."

"That's very decent of you, old fellow. That's extraordinary!"

"I want her to be happy," Mikkelsen said.

Yvonne showed up just as night was falling. Mikkelsen had not seen her for years, and he was startled at how uninteresting she seemed, how bland, how unformed, almost adolescent. Of course, she was very pretty, close-cropped blonde hair, merry greenish-blue eyes, pert little nose, but she seemed girlish and alien to him, and he wondered how he could ever have become so involved with her. But of course all that was before Janine. Mikkelsen's unscheduled return from Palm Beach surprised her, but not very much, and when he took her down to the beach to tell her that he had come to realize that she was really in love with Hambleton and he was not going to make a fuss about it, she blinked and said sweetly, "In love with Tommy? Well, I suppose I *could* be – though I never actually saw it like that. But I could give it a try, couldn't I? That is, if you truly are tired of me, Nick." She didn't seem offended. She didn't seem heart-broken. She didn't seem to care much at all.

He left the club soon afterward and got an express-fax message off to his younger self in Palm Beach: *Yvonne has fallen for Tommy Hambleton. However upset you are, for God's sake get over it fast, and if you happen to meet a young woman named Janine Carter, give her a close look. You won't regret it, believe me. I'm in a position to know.*

He signed it *A Friend*, but added a little squiggle in the corner that had always been his own special signature-glyph. He didn't dare go further than that. He hoped young Nick would be smart enough to figure out the score.

Not a bad hour's work, he decided. He drove back to the jaunt-shop in downtown San Diego and hopped back to his proper point in time.

*　　*　　*

There was the taste of cotton in his mouth when he emerged. So it feels that way even when you phase *yourself*, he thought. He wondered what changes he had brought about by his jaunt. As he remembered it, he had made the hop in order to phase himself back into a marriage with a woman named Janine, who apparently he had loved quite considerably until she had been snatched away from him in a phasing. Evidently the unphasing had not happened, because he knew he was still unmarried, with three or four regular companions – Cindy, Melanie, Elena and someone else – and none of them was named Janine. Paula, yes, that was the other one. Yet he was carrying a note, already starting to fade, that said: *You won't remember any of this, but you were married in 2016 or 17 to the former Janine Carter, Tommy Hambleton's ex-wife, and however much you may like your present life, you were a lot better off when you were with her.* Maybe so, Mikkelsen thought. God knows he was getting weary of the bachelor life, and now that Gus and Donna were making it legal, he was the only singleton left in the whole crowd. That was a little awkward. But he hadn't ever met anyone he genuinely wanted to spend the rest of his life with, or even as much as a year with. So he had been married, had he, before the phasing? Janine? How strange, how unlike him.

He was home before dark. Showered, shaved, dressed, headed over to the Top of the Marina. Tommy Hambleton and Yvonne were in town, and he had agreed to meet them for drinks. Hadn't seen them for years, not since Tommy had taken over his brother's villa on the Riviera. Good old Tommy, Mikkelsen thought. Great to see him again. And Yvonne. He recalled her clearly, little snub-nosed blonde, good game of tennis, trim compact body. He'd been pretty hot for her himself, eleven or twelve years ago, back before Adrienne, before Charlene, before Georgiana, before Nedra, before Cindy, Melanie, Elena, Paula. Good to see them both again. He stepped into the skylift and went shooting blithely up the long swivel-stalk to the gilded little cupola high above the lagoon. Hambleton and Yvonne were already there.

Tommy hadn't changed much – same old smooth slickly dressed little guy – but Mikkelsen was astonished at how time and money had altered Yvonne. She was poised, chic, sinuous, all that baby-fat burned away, and when she spoke there was the smallest hint of a French accent in her voice. Mikkelsen embraced them both and let himself be swept off to the bar.

"So glad I was able to find you," Hambleton said. "It's been years! Years, Nick!"

"Practically forever."

"Still going great with the women, are you?"

"More or less," Mikkelsen said. "And you? Still running back in time to wipe your nose three days ago, Tommy?"

Hambleton chuckled. "Oh, I don't do much of that any more. Yvonne and I went to the Fall of Troy last winter, but the short-hop stuff doesn't interest me these days. I . . . oh. How amazing?"

"What is it?" Mikkelsen asked, seeing Hambleton's gaze go past him into the darker corners of the room.

"An old friend," Hambleton said. "I'm sure it's she! Someone I once knew – briefly, glancingly . . ." He looked toward Yvonne and said, "I met her a few months after you and I began seeing each other, love. Of course, there was nothing to it, but there could have been – there could have been . . ." A distant wistful look swiftly crossed Hambleton's features and was gone. His smile returned. He said, "You should meet her, Nick. If it's really she, I know she'll be just your type. How amazing! After all these years! Come with me, man!"

He seized Mikkelsen by the wrist and drew him, astounded, across the room.

"Janine?" Hambleton cried. "Janine Carter?"

She was a dark-haired woman, elegant, perhaps a year or two younger than Mikkelsen, with cool perceptive eyes. She looked up, surprised. "Tommy? Is that you?"

"Of course, of course. That's my wife, Yvonne, over there. And this – this is one of my oldest and dearest friends, Nick Mikkelsen. Nick . . . Janine . . ."

She stared up at him. "This sounds absurd," she said, "but don't I know you from somewhere?"

Mikkelsen felt a warm flood of mysterious energy surging through him as their eyes met. "It's a long story," he said. "Let's have a drink and I'll tell you all about it."

DEAR TOMORROW

Simon Clark

If time travel ever is perfected in the future, might not people of the future be able to rectify problems of today and, if so, would they respond to a direct appeal? That was the idea that prompted Simon Clark to write the following very subtle story which makes its first appearance in this anthology.

Although Clark has been writing science fiction since 1985 he is probably best known for his horror novels, which include Nailed by the Heart *(1995),* Vampyrrhic *(1998) and its sequels, and* Ghost Monster *(2009). Amongst his other work is the DrWho novella* The Dalek Factor *(2004) and the sequel to John Wyndham's classic,* The Day of the Triffids – The Night of the Triffids *(2001).*

Ten

His name was – is – or will be John Salvin. The worst time of his life began when he waved goodbye to his wife and daughter. On that July evening, Kerry and ten-year-old Laurel climbed into a light aircraft that would take them on a sight-seeing flight over a Norwegian fjord.

The plane lifted off from the airfield before soaring out over the calm body of water that perfectly reflected the mountains. The last John saw of the plane – the last anyone saw of the plane – was as it climbed into a deep blue sky. The aircraft resembled a tiny, silver star as it gradually grew smaller, and smaller, and then vanished.

Nine

From the *TV Times: Impossible, Isn't It?* The reality show that turns unreality on its head. This week the presenters go time-travelling.

Eight

London: Friday afternoon. Mr and Mrs Banerjee called in at a pizza takeaway to ask directions to a hotel. Mrs Kamana Banerjee had secretly planned a thirtieth birthday treat at the theatre for her husband. They were followed into the takeaway by a youth, who'd fled from a rival gang. One of the youth's pursuers fired six rounds from a pistol. None of the bullets struck their intended target. Murad Banerjee, however, was, by sheer chance, hit in the throat. When the wounded man turned to his wife, his expression, she remembers, was apologetic, as if this incident was his mistake.

The instant Murad fell Kamana was beside him, cradling his head in her lap. Meanwhile, the hunted youth made good his escape over the pizza-seller's counter and out the back.

Kamana Banerjee constantly replayed the lethal thirty seconds over and over in her head. The image of that unwarranted and unneeded expression of apology on her husband's face haunted her ever since he'd died on the takeaway floor three years ago. Every time she recalled the circumstances of the killing she'd ask herself: *Why did we choose that particular place to ask directions? Why didn't we ask in the supermarket next door? Why didn't we just walk further along the street?* And she'd always offer up this heartfelt prayer to her pantheon of many gods: "Please turn back the clock. Please let me be back there in London with my husband, just before we go into the takeaway. Give me the chance to do things differently this time."

Seven

Every so often, the tiny face of a child will peer out from a mass of starving people in Africa and touch humanity's conscience. Might our "Dear Tomorrow" messages touch a nerve a thousand years from now? Just as the first, viable time machine shivers into life? So, why not join us, and be part of the greatest experiment in the history of humankind.

Press release for *Impossible, Isn't It?*

Six

John Salvin hadn't yet acquired the knack of living alone, even though five years had passed since his wife, Kerry, and daughter, Laurel, had vanished. This evening, he heard the drone of a light aircraft flying over the house. Instantly, he found himself transported back to the Norwegian airfield. In his imagination, he stood there again near the control tower, watching the single-engine plane dwindle into the distance, eventually turning into a silver speck that resembled a lone star drifting above the fjord.

John sighed. For as long as he heard the plane, which appeared to be doggedly circling above him, he would continue to inhabit that moment when the ill-fated machine carried his wife and daughter off the radar screens and out of his life forever. Quickly he set the tablet computer down on the sofa beside him, grabbed the TV remote then punched up the volume. Television didn't interest him these days; however, laughter from an excited audience was enough to drown the memory-provoking sound of the aircraft above his house.

John never even glanced at the TV screen. Instead, he returned to the small screen that he balanced on his lap. Working in admin for a publisher of school textbooks kept him busy by day. Evenings were dangerous places, though. All too quickly he could find himself picturing what had become of Kerry and Laurel, so he'd managed to interest the company's editors in his idea for a history book with an unusual twist.

Now here he was, gratefully busy with *Voices from the Past – Letters from Long Ago*. For six months he'd been carefully reading, winnowing, and listing items for an anthology of letters, missives and epistles written centuries ago. He preferred letters sent by ordinary people to family and friends, rather than those stilted communiqués emperors despatched to their civil servants. He scrolled down to find a choice example of a more homely missive – this particular one sent from a Byzantine mother to her son during the reign of Empress Theodora, circa AD 1056, in what is present-day Turkey: *My son, to meet with your wishes I shall describe our house in Tarsus, which you have yet to see. From the street, we enter through a blue door into a cool hallway that has a floor of marble. To continue along a passageway brings you to the kitchen. This a pleasant place, and smells deliciously of fresh bread that Zoe bakes. The old chap that served us in Nicaea still tends the garden. We watch him munching grapes from the vine. Later he shouts loudly, shakes his arms, and performs such a drama to suggest that birds have stolen our grapes. This old greybeard is strange in his ways now.*

John Salvin had been reading this vintage correspondence for several minutes before he realized that someone on television was talking about letters being like little time machines: that they often contain vivid glimpses of the past. John pretty much shared the same thought as he'd worked on his anthology of ancient writings, so the programme tweaked his interest; he looked up as the show's presenter, a woman with a winning smile and clear, intelligent eyes, spoke to camera.

"Time travel machines don't exist yet," she said. "But what if they become a reality in the future? With that thought in mind, this show will conduct the most exciting and the most important experiment in the history of the human race."

"Hyperbole," John murmured, before adding a more resonant sounding, "Bollocks."

The presenter continued, "Our experiment is beautiful in its simplicity. We ask viewers to record a short video that contains their message to the future. Here's your opportunity to tell your descendants why you are speaking to them. When you've done that, I want you to upload the video to the *Impossible, Isn't It?* website. We'll be there at the rendezvous point on the big day, and our cameras will record what happens next. Now, over to Greg at the video wall."

Bright and bouncy, Greg at the video wall described how TV programmes had acquired an immortality all of their own. With the aid of computer animations, he demonstrated how the viewers' messages "will, indeed, be little time machines in their own right. Yes, okay, they will travel slowly into the future – just as slowly as you, me, Uncle Tom Cobley and all; nevertheless, your video messages will eventually be viewed sometime hence

– perhaps a thousand years from now, when time travel is as straightforward as it is for us to nip down to the supermarket. So consider your letter to your descendants as being like a message in a bottle tossed into the sea of time."

The female presenter returned to sum up the experiment. "Next week's *Impossible, Isn't It?* will feature a selection of your Dear Tomorrow messages. Archived recordings of the show will undoubtedly be watched centuries from now. What's more, it's my personal belief that time machines will be invented one day; that's why I'm inviting time-travelling viewers from the distant future to visit us at our rendezvous point on Mount Snowdon in North Wales, on the tenth of July – that's just twelve days away. We intend to broadcast a special live edition of the programme from the very top of the mountain. With us will be the vigil team, consisting of members of the public who have uploaded what we deem to be the most compelling and moving videogrammes. So will our unique invitation be a success? Will I be greeting people from those far off tomorrows? Find out for yourselves by joining us live on Mount Snowdon for the greatest experiment of all time."

"Bollocks. Temporal, fourth dimensional bollocks," John muttered as he selected a letter from his tablet that was written eighteen hundred years ago – one sent by a soldier stationed on Hadrian's Wall to his girlfriend in Rome; the disgruntled spear-carrier complained bitterly about his cold feet and asked her to send thicker socks.

John Salvin tried to dismiss the TV show's frivolous time travel experiment from his mind. He didn't succeed. Instead, he began to wonder, *What if . . .*

Five

Five years ago, John used his phone to video Kerry and Laurel when they walked toward the four-seater aircraft. Even though he'd watched the clip hundreds of times before, he replayed those haunting images yet again on his phone as he sat at the kitchen table to eat dinner. The recording lasted just nineteen seconds. Eventually, he'd come to refer to this poignant little film as the "Parting Shot". Whenever he watched the video, which forever preserved his final view of Kerry and Laurel, he would study their every gesture, every movement, every smile. Therefore, the screen completely held his attention when he touched "play". With each repeat viewing, he'd suck in a pained lungful of air as if he watched it for the very first time . . . because there walked Kerry and Laurel again: two living human beings; mother and daughter looking so much alike with the same blonde hair and excited smiles. As the pair followed the pilot to the aircraft, he could tell they were eager to see Sognefjord from the air. Behind them, lay a wilderness landscape, mountains soared into a clear blue sky.

At the plane, both turned and waved; Kerry had the new pink camera in her hand, and she called out happily: "We'll be back by one. See you then."

A second later, both had climbed into the plane; that's when the Parting Shot faded to black, and John's heart, as always, gave a sickening plunge, because he remembered how he'd caught his last glimpse of his wife and daughter on that fateful day, and he knew only too well that he'd be with them no more.

Four

The woman spoke softly: "Dear Tomorrow. My name is Kamana Banerjee. Three years ago, my husband died when he was shot by a stranger. Murad Banerjee was a good man who loved me so much. This will appear selfish of me, because nobody deserves to die, and all of us wish to save the lives of people we love, but I am sending this message to you in the future to let you know that I intend to join the vigil on Mount Snowdon. I am begging that you not only appear to us on the mountain, but you will take me back to that day in London when my husband was killed. I wish with all my heart to arrive just five minutes before he was murdered. Please give me a chance to save Murad."

John Salvin had watched the video at least a dozen times on the *Impossible, Isn't It?* website. Later, he'd paced the lawn and swore at himself for even entertaining the notion of doing something similar. After that, he'd held a photograph of his wife and daughter in his hands and wept.

Okay, he'd make himself look ridiculous. Work colleagues would be embarrassed for him. Strangers might ridicule him in the street. Of course, none of those scenarios might actually happen. His videogramme might not even be chosen for the programme's website, and highly unlikely to be aired on tomorrow's episode. Nevertheless, he recorded his message anyway.

"Dear Tomorrow," he began. "I want to hitch a lift in your time machine, too. My wife, Kerry, and my daughter, Laurel, disappeared five years ago. The plane they were travelling in vanished during a sightseeing trip in Norway."

Yes, okay, so he'd become the proverbial drowning man clutching at straws on the water. Yet this question had started to obsess him: *What if the time travel experiment is a success?* John knew that he'd eagerly grab at the rarest of chances to save the two people he loved most in the world.

The show's producers disabled the comments facility on their website when individuals began to post malicious or downright bizarre responses to the videos:

Murad Banerjee was blasted by assassins from the future cos he's a fuckin' terrorist. Him and his bitch were going to nuke London.

And: *Salvin's wife isn't dead. She shacked up with the pilot man, right?*

And this one: *They were all transfigured by higher beings: *STENDEC**

Val Garner, presenter of *Impossible, Isn't It?*, had read these comments, and others, including one that accused John Salvin of murdering his family, and then lying about the missing aeroplane. Val promptly emailed the director: *Thank God, we're going to broadcast from the top of Snowdon, otherwise we'd have all kinds of idiots turning up to spoil things☹ BTW I'm still SERIOUSLY worried about interference from the public – can we close footpaths to the summit?*

Be sure to tank-up-your-tum at Pete's Eats in Llanberis. It's going to be a LONG day!!!

Three

Brothers can reach the essential point of a conversation with a speed that might appear brutal to others. When Robert Salvin visited his brother he immediately asked this question: "Why are you torturing yourself?"

"I'm not."

"You are, John. Just because the plane was never found doesn't mean that Kerry and Laurel, or even the pilot, are still alive."

"I never said they were."

As Robert followed John into the lounge he sighed. "But, deep down, you believe that somehow they survived."

"The programme's just about to start."

"You have to accept that Kerry and Laurel are dead."

"Don't nag, Robert."

"You're a young man for God's sake. Find another wife. Father another child."

John said nothing. On television, the opening credits rolled for *Impossible, Isn't It?* As applause from the studio audience faded Val Garner smiled into the camera. "Good evening. Tonight we'll present our selection of messages that will be preserved for viewers in the distant future. So, if you're watching this programme a hundred years from now, or a thousand years from now, I'd like to give you a very warm welcome. And if you have that time machine please, *please* visit us in person on Saturday, the tenth of July – we will be eagerly awaiting your appearance."

Robert harrumphed. "We're always seeing objects as they were in the past. We never see the moon as it is now—"

"I'd like to hear the television."

"It takes one and a quarter seconds for moonlight to reach the earth. Most stars are thousands of light-years away, so we're seeing them as they were thousands of years ago."

"Robert, you asked to watch this programme with me. Now you're talking over it."

"I don't want you to entertain unrealistic hopes for the experiment. It's just a novelty cooked up for television. So . . . any chance of a beer?"

"Be my guest."

Robert paused in the doorway. "You're my brother. I'd hate for you to be disappointed when this experiment on Mount Snowdon is a flop, as it inevitably will be."

"Shush. They're starting to show the videogrammes."

Robert grunted his distaste as he headed for the kitchen. Meanwhile, John kept his focus on the TV. First of all, some comical videos were broadcast; these were the ice-breakers to settle the viewer in for more thoughtful recordings. Soon Robert was back with a glass of beer.

John pointed at the screen. "I've seen this one before. That woman's husband was murdered. He only went into a fast-food shop to ask for directions."

On screen, a dark-haired woman looked deep into the lens. "Dear Tomorrow. My name is Kamana Banerjee. Three years ago, my husband died when he was shot by a stranger. Murad Banerjee was a good man who loved me so much."

Robert's grim expression stated clearly enough that he didn't approve of the programme. Nevertheless, he remained silent, although the next face that flashed up onscreen startled him so much that beer slopped from the glass on to his lap.

A familiar voice came from the TV. "Dear Tomorrow. I want to hitch a lift in your time machine, too. My wife, Kerry, and my daughter, Laurel, disappeared five years ago . . ."

"My God," Robert gasped in amazement. "They picked you. They actually picked you!"

Two

John heard the voice of old on the phone – a voice that managed to interweave sighs of disappointment as his brother, Robert, criticized what he identified as yet another of John's fatally flawed plans. "So you're going to prance up to the top of Mount Snowdon? You're actually going to stand in front of TV cameras so everyone in the country can see you make a damn fool of yourself?"

"Robert—"

"You do realize that crap will be broadcast live? This ridiculous time travel experiment's going to be an embarrassing fiasco."

"Robert, what's the harm in trying?"

"The harm? You'll be harmed, John. Do you know why? Everyone in the country will be laughing, as you stand there on the bloody mountain, hoping that A) a time machine is going to land from the future; B) that you'll hitch a ride back five years ago; and C) that somehow you're going to stop Kerry and Laurel from boarding a plane which is going to vanish into the sea. God above, John, get real. Quit this fantasy; you're becoming pathetic."

"Ever since we were boys you hated me having something you didn't."

"Rubbish."

"You always took my toys off me. I'm not letting you take this away."

After hanging up on his brother, John watched the video clip that he'd drily named the Parting Shot, which captured those final images of Kerry and ten-year-old Laurel as they walked toward the waiting aircraft. When the ritual was over John took a walk through the village of Llanberis that nestled between a lake and the foot of Mount Snowdon. A cloudless July evening rendered the summit clearly visible.

Immediately after his videogramme had been screened on *Impossible, Isn't It?* he'd been telephoned by a production assistant, who'd invited him to take part in the live broadcast. Apparently, John's video was one of thousands uploaded; however, he and just another eleven people had been selected to take part in the televised vigil, which would take place tomorrow evening. The man had explained to John how the minutes would be dramatically counted down to zero hour at nine p.m. That was the moment when everyone hoped the time machine would appear. "Of course, this is a tongue-in-cheek experiment," the man had confessed. "If time machines are invented in the future, why haven't we seen them already? After all, the *Titanic*'s passengers could have been warned, couldn't they? Someone could have shot Hitler." When John suddenly went quiet, as he wondered if the entire programme was a practical joke on the viewing public, the man interpreted the silence as another concern. "Don't worry about the cost. Everyone taking part in the show will be booked into a hotel in Llanberis. We're covering travel expenses, too. Now, any questions?"

John Salvin rested both hands on top of the stone wall as he watched the stream flow by. With it being such a warm evening, people were sipping drinks on the hotel lawn. He, however, preferred the solitude of the lane that ran beside the stream. Besides, here he enjoyed a little time travel moment all of his own, because scratched there on the wall were the names of visitors to Llanberis from the past. The oldest was a Billy Smith, RN, who'd carved 1913 after his name. Billy must be long in his grave; yet his personal message to the future had survived, stating clearly that he'd stood here next to the stream in the year before the start of World War I.

"You look as if you're asking yourself if you're doing the right thing."

At the sound of the voice he turned to see a woman with long, black hair.

"Mrs Banerjee?"

"We recognize each other from our videogrammes, don't we, Mr Salvin?"

"Seeing as we're both part of what's supposed to be the greatest experiment of all time then you best call me John."

"I'm Kamana."

Smiling, they shook hands. After that, they stood in the evening sunshine, chatting about what the production team had planned.

"Have they told you much about the vigil?" Kamana asked.

"Not much, other than we head up the mountain tomorrow, and that twelve of us were chosen because of our messages."

She flicked back her long hair. "Then we wait for zero hour."

"While being shown live on primetime television. Nervous?"

"You mean, am I afraid of being made a fool of?" She shook her head. "If there is a billion-to-one chance I can somehow save my husband retrospectively, as it were, then I will do whatever it takes."

"It's strange. My head says nobody will miraculously appear from the future. But my heart's whispering: *Maybe, just maybe.*"

"Look, more members of our team." Kamana nodded in the direction of the High Street where a woman pushed a fragile-looking teenager in a wheelchair. "The girl is Wendy Matlock. Her grandmother asked for drugs to be sent back from the future to cure a terminal illness."

"I have a terrible feeling about tomorrow night when we hit zero hour."

"You mean if the experiment should fail?"

"I'm terrified it will be a success. Imagine if people arrive from a thousand years in the future? Nothing in this world will ever be the same again." John lightly ran his fingers over names etched into the wall by individuals who were probably dead by now. John's fingertips tingled – he could almost sense the hopes and fears enshrined in the hearts of those who'd stood here before him, and chosen to mark their presence here.

"*John ... John Salvin!*"

John turned to see a middle-aged man running down the lane. His face streamed with sweat and he was clearly anxious.

The man stopped ten paces short of them. "John Salvin?" he panted.

"Yes."

"Thank God I've found you! I've arrived a day early."

"*What?*" An emotional electricity snapped along John's spine.

"I'm here a day early." The man sucked in a lungful of air. "I'm from the future."

Kamana's dark eyes were wide with shock.

The stranger beckoned. "John, hurry. I've brought your daughter with me."

"My daughter?" John felt as if the ground had opened beneath him.

"Yes, Laurel's with me. Your daughter, Laurel! The one who disappeared! For God's sake, hurry! I can only keep her here for a few more minutes." He ran back up the hill, shouting for John to follow.

John raced after him, his heart pounding wildly. He'd run about a hundred paces or so when the man opened the back doors of a van, parked beside the lane.

"Hurry!" shouted the stranger. "She's in here! I can't hold it back for much longer!".

Laurel's in there ... I'm going to see Laurel. She'll be fifteen now. Will she still recognize me? These thoughts sped through John's head as he peered into the van's gloomy interior. *God, I don't want to frighten her ... she's come so far ...*

There, in the back of the vehicle, on a grubby mattress sat a teenage girl, hair tightly scraped back into a pony tail, while her eyes resembled large balls of glass in her gaunt face. She stared back at John without speaking.

"Laurel?" This seemed like a dream to John. "Laurel, are you all right?"

"Get in the van," the stranger ordered. "Get in. Hurry!"

Just then, a figure hurtled into this bizarre scene, and gripped John's arm.

Kamana roared at the stranger. "Go away! If you don't, I'll call the police!"

The man sprinted to the driver's seat. Seconds later, the van screeched away.

John shook his head in confusion. "That didn't look like Laurel . . ." He shrugged, utterly baffled.

"John." Kamana took his hand. "Forget about those two. They'll have been trying to get money out of you."

"He used my daughter's name. He knew her."

"No, he didn't, John. He watched your video on television, just as millions of others have done. He's a bad man; he was trying to exploit you."

John allowed himself to be led back to the main street. Only then did he realize that Kamana still held his hand.

"Sorry." He began to feel his old self again. "For a minute back there, I was in a state of shock."

"Don't worry." She smiled. "We're getting a lot of attention. Look at all those people."

John had assumed that Llanberis was always this busy on a Friday evening. However, he realized that the people in the cars, which trundled bumper-to-bumper along the street, from the direction of the mountain railway station all the way to Pete's Eats, were watching not only John and Kamana with fascination, but the girl in the wheelchair and other individuals whose videogrammes had being broadcast on *Impossible, Isn't It?* Many began to wave from the cars.

"My God," breathed John. "We're famous, aren't we?" He waved back. "We're actually famous."

Kamana waved, too. "And depending on what happens twenty-four hours from now, we might become the most famous people on the planet."

One

The next morning John Salvin found Kamana sitting alone in the hotel dining room. The place buzzed with film crew, production staff, invited journalists and those members of the public who had been chosen to take part in the show, and who hoped that futurity would hear their prayer . . . or, rather, their messages from the here and now.

John smiled. "Good morning, Kamana. Mind if I join you for breakfast?"

"Good morning, John. I was hoping you would."

A waiter appeared for their order. Kamana chose fruit, cereals and tea; John ordered a full cooked breakfast and coffee. Prospects for the day ahead excited him, and that excitement had ignited a ferocious appetite.

When the plate arrived heaped with sausages, fried eggs, tomatoes and succulent mushrooms he said, "Weren't you tempted by all this?" He attacked the steaming food.

"Holy Cow."

"Pardon?"

"The sausages are beef."

"I'm sorry, I don't . . . oh." The proverbial penny dropped.

"That's right. I'm Hindu . . . a case of Hindus vis-à-vis cows."

"So you don't eat cow – sorry, I mean beef." He pushed the sausages to one side.

"Thank you for being so considerate, but go ahead, enjoy your breakfast."

He realized she was touched by his gesture of not eating beef sausage in front of her; that, in turn, touched something deep inside of him. He realized he liked Kamana. What's more, he hadn't thanked her properly for saving him from the conman, or drug addict, or whatever the stranger was yesterday.

"Kamana," he began, "we're here until Monday, so I wondered if you'd have lunch with me tomorrow?" Her expression revealed that she was examining his invitation from different angles. Subtext as well as overt meaning. "We could drive down to Caernarfon."

The moment she opened her mouth to reply was the moment a scream killed all the conversations in the room stone dead.

People in the act of eating suddenly froze. A woman brandished a long-bladed knife as she advanced through the tables toward one occupied by the show's director. John recognized the lady with the knife. Yesterday, she'd pushed her sick granddaughter through Llanberis in a wheelchair.

"The experiment's been hijacked!" the woman shrieked. "They're working for the government! Even if people do arrive from the future we won't be allowed to see them. Wendy needs medicine to keep her alive. She won't get it! We've all been tricked into helping with this experiment, and we're going to get nothing for ourselves!"

She lunged at the director; the knife flashed in the air. Plates and cutlery seemed to explode from tables nearby as the production team leapt up to tackle the woman. Within seconds she was bundled sobbing out of the room. Fortunately, nobody seemed to have been hurt during the attack, and soon spilt teas and coffees were being mopped up by the hotel staff.

The show's presenter, Val Garner, appeared. "I'm terribly sorry about that. Wendy Matlock was taken poorly last night, so she can't participate in our vigil. Don't worry, I'm sure everything will be all right and Wendy will be feeling better soon." She smiled warmly, confident that the force of her personality had restored calm. "So, ladies and gentlemen, here we are at last: D-Day as it were. I'm sure you're all looking forward to this evening as much as I am." She checked her watch. "The countdown has begun. We're just thirteen hours from Zero Hour."

Twelve people were due to take part in the vigil. Now the number had been reduced to eleven. Later that morning, John Salvin strolled across the hotel lawn in the company of the decidedly attractive Kamana Banerjee. Both gazed up at the summit of Mount Snowdon as clouds parted to reveal that enormous body of rock – one that resembled the humped back of a colossal beast rising up above the Welsh landscape.

"Eleven hours until Zero Hour," murmured John.

Just for a second, Kamana reached out to take his hand before releasing it again. A little fix of reassurance? A physical signal that this lovely woman was at ease with him? He wondered if reading body language was a precise science. Meanwhile, the now famous time-travel experiment had well and truly caught the public's imagination. Cars streamed into the village to choke its High Street and side roads. He decided that whatever the result of the experiment tonight, the next few hours were about to become extremely interesting.

A prediction that was reinforced by Kamana suddenly turning to him and saying, "Thank you for the invitation to lunch in Caernarfon tomorrow, John. Yes, I'd love to come."

Despite preparations for the live broadcast, John Salvin still adhered to his routine of watching the Parting Shot film – something he invariably did at least twice a day. So, in the seclusion of his hotel room, John took the phone from his pocket, brought up that precious video, and touched "play". As always, he'd flinch as if stung by the sight of Kerry and Laurel, walking toward the single-engine plane where they'd wave their farewell. Kerry, forever enshrined in the phone's memory card (and a host of backup devices) would sing out: "We'll be back by one. See you then." After they boarded the plane John felt the same painful tug of grief as the nineteen-second film came to an end.

He sat down on the bed to watch the clip again, and hoped with every atom of his heart that the experiment would be a success.

Ten hours to Zero Hour.

After the drama of the woman apparently trying to murder the show's director, those members of staff assigned to take care of the "civilian" component of the show acted pretty much like sheepdogs. John found himself, along with Kamana and the rest of the vigil party, being herded to the hotel lounge for a briefing. There were plans indicating where they'd wait on Mount Snowdon, where the cameras would be positioned, and the location of the summit café and toilets. And after that, instead of being left to roam the village (and perhaps develop cold feet over taking part in tonight's live broadcast), everyone was ushered into the cinema at Snowdon's railway station – there they watched a film about the history of the rack-and-pinion railway, and its sturdy little engines that hauled carriages full of visitors three-and-a-half thousand feet to the barren summit.

Even though their movements were slickly managed, John had ample opportunity to witness the growing number of men and women gathering in the streets, as if this was the approach of Judgement Day. When the vigil party sat outdoors for lunch at the station café John watched the influx of spectators with astonishment.

Kamana whispered to him in awe, "These crowds remind me of a scene from that film *Quatermass and the Pit* – just before all hell breaks loose."

Meanwhile, steam engines regularly pulled out of the station; they made a ferocious panting sound as they began their ascent of the mountainside. Carriages were crammed with film crew, cameras, and equipment – the TV entertainment army was heading to the frontline, ready to fight the ratings war.

Kamana shivered, and her bare arms went to gooseflesh. "It'll soon be our turn for the train."

John checked the station clock. "Eight hours to Zero Hour."

At six o' clock the vigil party gathered at the muster point. By this time, crowds filled the area outside the little platform where the locomotive waited, hissing steam. When a production assistant called out the names of those taking part in the broadcast, John and Kamana, and the others, had to find a way through dense clumps of men and women – these were members of the public that had decided to get as close to the time-travel experiment as possible. After nearly being abducted yesterday John remained alert to any sudden outburst of strange behaviour, or even attack. However, most people nodded and smiled as he and his group passed by. Of course, the show's participants were being recognized from their videogrammes that been broadcast on Thursday's edition of *Impossible, Isn't It?* Strangers even reached out to shake hands with John and the rest of the vigil team during their short walk to the waiting train. There were comments of "Good luck", "I hope it all goes well", and a tongue-in-cheek, "Say hello to them from me, won't you?"

Just then, an old man gently took Kamana's arm so he could have a word. "What I don't understand," he began, "is how did they send your telly messages into the future?"

Kamana answered good naturedly, "There's no special fast way of transmitting them forwards through time. They're like time capsules. They'll reach the future just like anything else."

"So the video messages aren't there yet?" he asked with a puzzled frown.

An eager young man answered on Kamana's behalf, "The recordings will be found eventually. Our descendants will see the videogrammes, and know the experiment's date and location. The idea is that scientists hundreds of years from now might have discovered the secret of time, and they'll travel back here to meet these people. Isn't that right, Mrs Banerjee?"

Before she could respond, the minder ushered the party through the platform gate and into a snug little railway carriage.

"Next stop, the summit!" declared their minder before slamming the door shut.

Kamana sat down next to John, shot him a telling look and shivered. "Three hours to go until Zero Hour, and I am starting to feel terrified."

Zero

The rack-and-pinion railway journey to the summit of Mount Snowdon takes around sixty minutes. Their speed up the gradient never exceeded five miles per hour, and the clatter of steel cogs engaging with teeth in the track meant that John Salvin could hear very little in the way of the other passengers' conversations. Most, however, would be discussing the televised vigil that grew ever closer. Kamana sat beside him on the bench seat, one hip touching his, which was as much to do with the limitations of space as any hint of growing intimacy between them. Nevertheless, John enjoyed the closeness. They were forming a bond. *Due to us having a shared agenda in this experiment,* he asked himself, *or is this the start of something bigger?* Once again, he wondered if he could accurately read her body language. Were there tell-signs that she liked him, too?

A man in a straw hat debated the experiment with a woman in a red dress. On this occasion his voice succeeded in reaching John over the train's vigorous clanking. "They say the purpose of time is to stop everything happening at once."

"What if people come from the future?" the woman asked. "Isn't there a danger that they'll bring a dangerous virus with them? What if we're all infected?"

Another chipped in, a guy with a sun-reddened bald head: "Listen. The past ceases to exist the second it becomes the past – so will we see folk in golden suits from AD 3000? No, we're going to see bugger-all. This experiment will be a total failure."

Smiling happily, the man in the straw hat gazed at the mountains. "I'm glad I brought the camera; it'd be a complete waste of a journey if I hadn't brought the camera."

John spoke to Kamana, "If nothing happens up there at Zero Hour, no visitors materialize from tomorrow, what will you do?"

"Continue my life as a widow. What else can I do?"

John experienced intense disappointment that she was prepared to surrender to a life of widowhood. He glanced sideways at the woman, her black hair rippling beautifully in the warm breeze flowing through the open window. Her dark eyes gazed in the direction of a shining lake, and at that moment he knew that Kamana Banerjee didn't see the lake . . . no, in her mind's eye, she saw herself being catapulted back three years to the London street where her husband was just about to step through a door and be killed by a bullet meant for someone else. No doubt Kamana visualized herself pulling Mr Banerjee away to safety before the fatal shot was fired. Kamana still loved her husband. John winced at the futility of his powerful desire for this woman, because he knew she wouldn't be interested in him – not while Murad Banerjee still remained alive in her mind.

He gazed at those vistas of rocky slopes, immense mountains and serene valleys in the evening sunlight. They were breathtaking. Yet he soon found himself thinking about his own wife who'd gone missing five years ago. True, his legal status was very much *Single*; however, he experienced a sudden agonising spasm of guilt, because he'd been planning to try and . . . what's the right word? *Seduce* Kamana? No, "seduce" had connotations of exploitation. Instead, John had entertained warm, romantic hopes of developing a relationship with her. He realized his feelings toward Kamana had usurped thoughts about the arrival of visitors from the future this evening. This fantasy about somehow begging a lift back five years to stop his wife and daughter boarding the plane in Norway seemed not only absurd, but childishly unrealistic. What's more, had he been so arrogant to believe that some powerful individual from the future would slam the flow of time into reverse gear so he could reclaim two lives? He loved Kerry and Laurel. Yet the simple truth is they were dead. Now here he was, sitting beside this lovely woman. Here were two living human beings who had the marvellous opportunity to build a new future for themselves. But no . . . Kamana was shackled to her dead husband. While he, John Salvin, had become the gutless puppet of his dead wife and his dead daughter. A sudden rage blazed inside him. How he craved to yell, or kick out at something – *anything!* Conflicting emotions smashed against one another – guilt, jealousy, anger. As he sat there, he clenched his fists, and furiously willed his imagination to carry him back into the past.

It is five years ago. Kerry and Laurel are following the pilot to where a light aircraft is waiting. My wife carries the new pink camera. Within moments, the plane will soar away in the direction of the fjord. Soon the machine and its passengers will vanish from the radar, never be seen again. Today I have been given this miraculous opportunity to save them. All I need do is stop Kerry and Laurel boarding the aircraft. I can pretend I feel ill and must return to the hotel straightaway. The sightseeing flight will be cancelled. My wife and daughter will still be alive.

I call out, "Kerry, wait!"

Instead of climbing aboard, she turns to face me. "John? What's wrong?"

"Just be sure to take some good photographs up there, won't you?"

Laughing, she brandishes the camera. "Don't worry. We'll get plenty."

With that, Kerry follows Laurel on to the plane. Within seconds it takes off, just as it always does in my memory, and quickly dwindles into a silver star in the sky. "Yes, I had the chance to save you both, but I didn't. Because, if you were still alive, I would never have met Kamana."

"John? Are you all right?" Kamana's large eyes were full of concern. "You don't look at all well."

"Kamana, I have an important confession. The man who shot your husband was me. Three years ago, I murdered him, knowing that his death would bring us together. I want you."

John thought: *Now what? How will she react to a statement like that? That I gunned down Murad? Go on, take a guess. Shocked and silent? Hurt and tearful? Anger and throwing punches?*

She touched his hand. "John, what's the matter?"

He blinked. No, he hadn't actually voiced that admission about slaying her husband. Those words had all been inside his head. He smiled. "Maybe it's the altitude. I feel dizzy."

"Breathe deeply, try and relax."

Okay, some brutal instinct had urged John to make a confession about killing her husband. Not that he'd actually murdered the man, of course. What he wanted, with a violent passion, was to slaughter the memory ghost that kept its deathly grip on this woman. If she did not fully accept Murad's death, and the *permanence* of his death, she'd never be able to fully reclaim her own life.

"I was thinking about my wife and daughter." John decided not to reveal what he'd really been thinking; instead, he diluted those raw scenarios with a lighter comparison. "We might never travel back in time, but in a way Kerry and Laurel are constantly moving forward into the present to be with me. What's more, I can't help but picture what my wife's response would be if she materialized tonight and I admitted to her that I needed to find someone new to have in my life."

"You hold imaginary conversations with your wife?" She gave a solemn nod. "Inside my head, I talk for hours with Murad."

"Maybe we should tell these memory ghosts of ours to leave us alone?"

Her expression snapped to one of shock, but not in response to what he'd just said. Instead, she exclaimed, "John, your nose is bleeding."

"The altitude," he said, though he knew it was nothing to do with that. He visualized his blood vessels bursting one after another due to the sheer emotional pressure building inside him. In truth, he wanted to free them both from their past tragedies – only he didn't know how. The intensity of that frustration was the real cause of the nasal haemorrhage.

"Here, these are clean tissues."

The rest of the journey became dominated by attempts to stop the cascade of blood. Others in the carriage offered handkerchiefs and good advice. "Hold your head back," suggested the man in the straw hat. "Pinch the bridge of your nose," advised the woman in the red dress.

At last, the clanking of the train abruptly stopped. In the silence that followed an excited voice shouted, "*We're here!*"

Immediately after that, John noticed the haunting drone of an aeroplane circling high overhead. Zero Hour was almost upon them.

Kamana helped John from the carriage as production staff rushed forward, eager as sheepdogs, to round up the vigil party. Swiftly, they herded everyone from the station to the mountain-top café, which stood just feet away. John's nose still bled so copiously he wondered if a major artery had exploded inside his head. Rather than dousing the café floor with his lifeblood he decided to remain outside.

The show's director hurtled forward. "My God! What happened to you?"

John could only manage grunts through the fistful of tissue he pressed against his face so Kamana answered for him, "A nose bleed."

"Thank goodness! I thought he'd been shot. We'll have to find him a clean shirt."

"Mr Salvin needs medical treatment." Kamana sounded annoyed with the man. "He can't take part in the show like this."

"We're one down already with the girl in hospital. He must take part."

"Then get him some first aid."

"Okay, just trundle him over there to those seats. Our first-aider will be along as soon as. We're having our usual frantic five minutes. Happens before every show." He waved at a techni-cian. "Tom! Make sure the monitors are properly shaded. I can't see a blessed thing in this sunlight." The director whirled away to impose order on chaos.

Kamana spoke softly, "Don't worry, John. I'll find someone to take a look at you."

John left bloody splotches on the ground as he headed toward a line of plastic chairs. Here, the summit of Mount Snowdon buzzed with activity. Technicians fiddled with cameras that had been set on tripods. Cables snaked to a large tent that served as the control centre. A satellite dish, which would beam live transmissions to the outside world, had been erected beside the café. The much-publicized *Greatest Experiment of All Time* would begin shortly, with the presenter interviewing the vigil party live on TV, perhaps trying to elicit heart-breaking stories and tears. Those "Dear Tomorrow" videogrammes would be replayed again, and the viewing public would be reminded about the nature of the experiment: that it's hoped the video messages will be unearthed centuries from now when the first viable time machines are ready to set sail for the distant past. The presenter would repeat the invitation to time travellers "to please visit us here on Mount Snowdon at 9 p.m., on the tenth of July" with the year flashing brightly onscreen.

To John Salvin it seemed as if he watched technical preparations for the show from faraway; the sound of voices grew fainter. Meanwhile, a frighteningly large pool of blood continued to grow on the ground between his feet.

Kamana strove to remain calm, yet there was a distinct note of tension in her voice. "Sit here, John. I'll bring help."

The evening sun dazzled him. Above the mountain, a light aircraft circled with determined persistence, the sound of its engine somehow becoming more penetrating and unsettling. Blood loss made his mind so light it seemed to detach himself from the Earth to float up there, high above the landscape where the aeroplane flew. In fact, when he opened his eyes he found himself occupying the seat beside the pilot; in the two seats behind him were Kerry and Laurel. They *ooohed* at the gorgeous scenery spread out below them. Kerry used the pink camera that she was so proud of to take photographs for her husband to see later. John had imagined hundreds of times before that this is how they'd be on that fatal flight out over the Norwegian fjord. Yet he'd always stopped himself from visualizing what happened to the plane, causing it to disappear. Today, however, he made the decision to keep the images rolling. On board, the engine grew louder, a sustained note of such power that the sound alone appeared to hold the plane high above the water. But just a moment later the engine died – this was followed by an alarming silence.

"Don't worry," said the pilot. "This isn't a problem. I can restart her."

Kerry and Laurel's expressions were forensic studies in absolute horror. Their eyes had grown shockingly large in their faces.

"Not long now." The pilot flicked switches in front of him, his movements becoming progressively faster. "The engine will soon be running again."

However, that powerful sustained note of the aircraft's one and only engine didn't return. Apart from air rushing over the wings there was no other sound. Kerry put her arm around Laurel and held the ten-year-old girl tightly.

Then Kerry spoke gently, yet firmly, "Laurel, listen to me. I love you. Your daddy loves you. Now close your eyes. I want you to picture your daddy's face."

A calm ocean greeted the plane. The machine vanished beneath its surface the instant it struck. And John Salvin rode all the way down into that turquoise, undersea world with his family. Five years later they were still there – the pilot, Kerry and Laurel – one thousand feet deep on the ocean bed. Not lost as such. Because how can three dead people know what it feels like to be lost? Only those who are still alive and are still grieving are lost when such a tragedy occurs.

A colossal explosion of sound snatched John Salvin back to the here and now. Men and women ran for the shelter of the café. Lightning blazed from a black cloud that bruised the once flawless, blue sky. More thunder bellowed across the face of the mountain. A distinct odour of rain filled the air, prompting technicians to rush and cover the cameras before the deluge came.

John's head felt as if his skull had emptied of blood – after all, so much had poured out of him in the last few minutes. Even so, he managed to voice what was on his mind: "I was on the plane with them . . . five years ago . . .'

"What plane? Sorry, John, I can't make out what you're saying."

He smiled up at Kamana. "Oh? I didn't know you'd come back."

Thunder boomed across the Welsh landscape. Savage gusts of wind tore apart the tent that housed the broadcast equipment. Debris whipped through the air as people covered their eyes and fled for cover. The director stood on a rock and waved everyone toward the café.

The man yelled in frustration, "It's over! We can't do the broadcast in this! The show's cancelled! Everyone get inside! For pity's sake, don't get yourselves struck by lightning!"

As Kamana helped John to his feet, her dark eyes brimmed with concern. "I think the bleeding's stopped. But I want someone to take a look at you."

Even though lightheaded, John managed a smile. "You know something? I'm relieved that the show's been cancelled."

"And so has their very expensive time travel experiment." She shrugged and smiled. "Though it would have been a complete failure, wouldn't it?"

"I suppose it would."

"What have you got there in your hand?"

"Just a camera. Someone must have left it back there on a chair. I think it belongs to the man in the straw hat."

"The man in the straw hat?"

"He was in the same carriage as us. Looked pleased with himself. Always smiling."

Kamana gave a puzzled shake of her head. "No, I didn't notice a man wearing a straw hat."

John paused at the café doorway. "You go ahead; I'll give the camera to the director. He can find whoever it belongs to."

"Are you sure you're all right?"

"I'll be fine."

Had she noticed something significant in his face? Because she tilted her head as she glanced at him before going inside.

Blustery winds tugged John's hair as he walked along the path. It's funny how imagination can be so vivid, he thought. When he'd pictured himself in the plane he'd watched his wife take hold of that powder-pink camera of hers. Then she'd leaned forward from the back seat, handed him the camera, locked her eyes on to his, and said, "John, you decide whether you keep this. But if you'll take my advice: get rid of it." Then she'd leaned forwards even further so she could kiss him on the cheek.

John gazed at the camera in his hand – the one he'd found just a moment ago on the chair. He thought about all the photographs Kerry had taken to preserve those happy moments of their Norwegian holiday. If, by some extraordinary chance, he could recover those photographs – for example, if the lost camera could be miraculously returned to his possession – what would he do? Yes, they'd be precious mementos. But wasn't there a danger that those snapshots would become nails that even more securely fixed him to the dead, if not forgotten, past? Ultimately, the decision wasn't a difficult one to make. Without a shred of hesitation, he thrust the camera that he'd found, with its distinctive powder-pink livery, deep into a litter bin. Logic dictated that the camera wasn't the one that belonged to Kerry, but this had become one of those extraordinary occasions when the rules of logic could be so easily broken. He didn't want to take the chance of allowing the past to haunt him anymore than it did already.

As John walked through the storm to the café, he passed the man from the train – the winds blew harder and the stranger needed to hold his straw hat tight to his head.

The man's expression was one of childish delight as he chuckled and spoke in an odd accent that John couldn't quite place. "Well – so ends our famous experiment. *Phew!* Isn't it about time that we all went home now?" Without waiting for a reply, the stranger hurried away through a sudden onslaught of rain; though why he headed out across the barren mountainside John couldn't say.

John Salvin pulled out his phone – the one that contained the Parting Shot. With the storm breaking overhead this might not, he acknowledged, be the ideal place to watch the footage again ... although in the past, he'd felt compelled to view the film at odder times than this, and in stranger places. So he touched "play" and focused his attention on the screen, which quickly became speckled with raindrops. The video clip revealed Kerry and Laurel once more, following the pilot to the aircraft. Raindrops beading on the screen acted as tiny magnifying lenses, enlarging random parts of the image. Kerry's face seemed to loom into striking close-up as she called out her usual farewell. Or what should have been her usual farewell.

Only the words "*We'll be back at one. See you then*" failed to emerge from Kerry's mouth in the way he remembered so well. Instead, with a different expression on her face, this one utterly serious, she said: "You must not grieve forever, John. Don't let the rest of your life slip away through your fingers and be wasted. Move on. Move on."

Rain falling on the phone's screen distorted the image, blood loss fuddled his thoughts to the point where the boundary between the real and the unreal had all but melted away. Surely, this must be the case, because just for a moment he thought he glimpsed, there onscreen, that same man again – the one in the straw hat – only on this occasion he stood next to the plane that would take Kerry and Laurel away. The stranger appeared to gaze out of the film into John's eyes. He didn't move or say anything; in fact, he resembled a mourner standing beside a grave.

The haemorrhage, the distorting effect of raindrops on the video footage – surely they were creating this particular miracle, weren't they? Perhaps no one from tomorrow would ever reach back and touch the actual fabric of this, our present world. However, he wondered, at some point in the future, will there be a remarkable invention that can reach back into the past to touch our minds, hearts and memories? What would our descendants' motivation be to do this? For their amusement? Or a charitable desire to administer emotional first aid? If he allowed his imagination to wander further he might suppose that the savage thunderstorm had been triggered by the backwash from such a time-ship. Then, of course, imagination can conjure all sorts of magnificent possibilities, as well as disturbing outcomes. He could even picture himself deleting the Parting Shot film, but no . . . there would be no need for that, because from now on he suspected he wouldn't feel compelled to watch it at least twice a day. Okay, yes, he would replay the Parting Shot every now again, and shed a tear or two. But he would no longer be enslaved by those nineteen seconds of heartache.

John Salvin put the phone back into his pocket and went in search of Kamana. Water running over the boulders transformed them into shining, silvery forms that seemed to be in the process of evolving into living creatures. Their brightness was dazzling. Meanwhile, the easing rain became a strangely soothing, melodious sound, and at that moment he realized he could no longer hear the haunting note of the aeroplane circling overhead. After glancing upwards into an empty sky he looked down to find Kamana standing there in front of him.

She had an extraordinary revelation of her own. "Until a moment ago, I couldn't remember that as my husband lay dying in my arms he spoke to me. Isn't that a remarkable thing to forget? Especially, when I recall every other detail so precisely? But just now I remembered his exact words." Her calm eyes met his. "Murad said: '*Kamana, I'm so sorry to leave you like this. Promise me that you'll be happy again one day.*'" A sad smile touched her lips. "Then I asked myself, did I imagine those words of his?"

"Ever since we started this trip up the mountain I've been imagining all kinds of things," he confessed. 'I even pictured myself starting a new life after losing Kerry and Laurel."

"You know something, John? What you said on the train is perfectly true. Yes, we must tell those memory ghosts of ours to leave us alone. We should not let the rest of our lives slip away through our fingers. I now realize it's time I moved on."

He paused. Hadn't he imagined Kerry using pretty much the same words? In any event, Kaman's statement, as well as its significance, acquired a special glow in John's mind as he thought about all that had happened today.

From up here, high on Mount Snowdon, it's said that you can see many kingdoms, including the Kingdom of Heaven. What he could see clearly was the sun breaking through the cloud to shine on the hills, and into hidden valleys, and a moment later the sunlight illuminated Kamana's face. What he could not see, of course, was any guarantee, or omen, or even a hint that he and this woman, for whom he had developed such a depth of feeling, would have any kind of future together. Such matters lie concealed, as they always have done, in the lap of the gods.

And yet, as they made their way toward the waiting train, that would take them on to the next chapter of their lives, he found, to his surprise, that he was smiling. After all, who knows what tomorrow might bring?

TIME GYPSY

Ellen Klages

Ellen Klages has been writing reference books for children since 1991 but in 1998 branched out into fiction, mostly science fiction and fantasy but including a novel set at the time of the construction of the first atom bomb, The Green Glass Sea *(2006). Many of her stories have been nominated for awards, including the following, and a selection of them can be found in* Portable Childhoods *(2007), which was itself shortlisted for the World Fantasy Award. Once again we are exploring the manipulation of the past, for good or for ill.*

1

Friday, February 10, 1995. 5:00 p.m.

As soon as I walk in the door, my officemate Ted starts in on me. Again. "What do you know about radiation equilibrium," he asks. "Nothing. Why?" "That figures." He holds up a faded green volume. "I just found this insanely great article by Chandrasekhar in the '45 *Astrophysical Journal*. And get this – when I go to check it out, the librarian tells me I'm the first person to take it off the shelf since 1955. Can you believe that? Nobody reads anymore." He opens the book again. "Oh, by the way, Chambers was here looking for you."

I drop my armload of books on my desk with a thud. D. Raymond Chambers is the chairman of the Physics department, and a Nobel Prize winner, which even at Berkeley is a very, very big deal. Rumor has it he's working on some top secret government project that's a shoe-in for a second trip to Sweden. "Yeah, he wants to see you in his office, pronto. He said something about Sara Baxter Clarke. She's that crackpot from the 50s, right? The one who died mysteriously."

I wince. "That's her. I did my dissertation on her and her work." I wish I'd brought another sweater. This one has holes in both elbows. I'd planned a day in the library, not a visit with the head of the department.

Ted looks at me with his mouth open. "Not many chick scientists to choose from, huh? And you got a post-doc here doing that? Crazy world." He puts his book down and stretches. "Gotta run. I'm a week behind in my lab work. Real science, you know."

I don't even react. It's only a month into the term, and he's been on my case about one thing or another – being a woman, being a dyke, being close to thirty – from day one. He's a jerk, but I've got other things to worry about. Like D. Chambers, and whether I'm about to lose my job because he found out I'm an expert on a crackpot. Sara Baxter Clarke has been my hero since I was a kid. My pop was an army technician. He worked on radar systems, and we traveled a lot – six months in Reykjavik, then the next six in Fort Lee, New Jersey. Mom always told us we were gypsies, and tried to make it seem like an adventure. But when I was eight, Mom and my brother Jeff were killed in a bus accident on Guam. After that it didn't seem like an adventure any more.

Pop was a lot better with radar than he was with little girls. He couldn't quite figure me out. I think I had too many variables for him. When I was ten, he bought me dresses and dolls, and couldn't understand why I wanted a stack of old physics magazines the base library was throwing out. I liked science. It was about the only thing that stayed the same wherever we moved. I told Pop I wanted to be a scientist when I grew up, but he said scientists were men, and I'd just get married.

I believed him, until I discovered Sara Baxter Clarke in one of those old magazines. She was British, went to MIT, had her doctorate in theoretical physics at twenty-two. At Berkeley, she published three brilliant articles in very, very obscure journals. In 1956, she was scheduled to deliver a controversial fourth paper at an international physics conference at Stanford. She was the only woman on the program, and she was just twenty-eight.

No one knows what was in her last paper. The night before she was supposed to speak, her car went out of control and plunged over a cliff at Devil's Slide – a remote stretch of coast south of San Francisco. Her body was washed out to sea. The accident rated two inches on the inside of the paper the next day – right under a headline about some vice raid – but made a small uproar in the physics world. None of her papers or notes were ever found; her lab had been ransacked. The mystery was never solved.

I was fascinated by the mystery of her the way other kids were intrigued by Amelia Earhart. Except nobody'd ever heard of my hero. In my imagination, Sara Baxter Clarke and I were very much alike. I spent a lot of days pretending I was a scientist just like her, and even more lonely nights talking to her until I fell asleep.

So after a Master's in Physics, I got a PhD in the History of Science – studying her. Maybe if my obsession had been a little more practical, I wouldn't be sitting on a couch outside Dr Chambers's office, picking imaginary lint off my sweater, trying to pretend I'm not panicking. I taught science in a junior high for a year. If I lose this fellowship, I suppose I could do that again. It's a depressing thought.

The great man's secretary finally buzzes me into his office. Dr Chambers is a balding, pouchy man in an immaculate, perfect suit. His office smells like lemon furniture polish and pipe tobacco. It's wood-paneled, plushly carpeted, with about an acre of mahogany desk. A copy of my dissertation sits on one corner.

"Dr McCullough." He waves me to a chair. "You seem to be quite an expert on Sara Baxter Clarke."

"She was a brilliant woman," I say nervously, and hope that's the right direction for the conversation.

"Indeed. What do you make of her last paper, the one she never presented?" He picks up my work and turns to a page marked with a pale green Post-it. "'An Argument for a Practical Tempokinetics?'" He lights his pipe and looks at me through the smoke.

"I'd certainly love to read it," I say, taking a gamble. I'd give anything for a copy of that paper. I wait for the inevitable lecture about wasting my academic career studying a long-dead crackpot.

"You would? Do you actually believe Clarke had discovered a method for time travel?" he asks. "Time travel, Dr McCullough?"

I take a bigger gamble. "Yes, I do."

Then Dr Chambers surprises me. "So do I. I'm certain of it. I was working with her assistant, Jim Kennedy. He retired a few months after the accident. It's taken me forty years to rediscover what was tragically lost back then."

I stare at him in disbelief. "You've perfected time travel?"

He shakes his head. "Not perfected. But I assure you, tempokinetics is a reality."

Suddenly my knees won't quite hold me. I sit down in the padded leather chair next to his desk and stare at him. "You've actually done it?"

He nods. "There's been a great deal of research on tempokinetics in the last forty years. Very hush-hush, of course. A lot of government money. But recently, several key discoveries in high-intensity gravitational field theory have made it possible for us to finally construct a working tempokinetic chamber."

I'm having a hard time taking this all in. "Why did you want to see *me*?" I ask.

He leans against the corner of his desk. "We need someone to talk to Dr Clarke."

"You mean she's alive?" My heart skips several beats.

He shakes his head. "No."

"Then—?"

"Dr McCullough, I approved your application to this university because you know more about Sara Clarke and her work than anyone else we've found. I'm offering you a once in a lifetime opportunity." He clears his throat. "I'm offering to send you back in time to attend the 1956 International Conference for Experimental Physics. I need a copy of Clarke's last paper."

I just stare at him. This feels likes some sort of test, but I have no idea what the right response is. "Why?" I ask finally.

"Because our apparatus works, but it's not practical," Dr Chambers says, tamping his pipe. "The energy requirements for the gravitational field are enormous. The only material that's even remotely feasible is an isotope they've developed up at the Lawrence lab, and there's only enough of it for one round trip. I believe Clarke's missing paper contains the solution to our energy problem."

After all these years, it's confusing to hear someone taking Dr Clarke's work seriously. I'm so used to being on the defensive about her, I don't know how to react. I slip automatically into scientist mode – detached and rational. "Assuming your tempokinetic chamber is operational, how do you propose that I locate Dr Clarke?"

He picks up a piece of stiff ivory paper and hands it to me. "This is my invitation to the opening reception of the confer-ence Friday night, at the St Francis Hotel. Unfortunately I couldn't attend. I was back east that week. Family matters."

I look at the engraved paper in my hand. Somewhere in my files is a Xerox copy of one of these invitations. It's odd to hold a real one. "This will get me into the party. Then you'd like me to introduce myself to Sara Baxter Clarke, and ask her for a copy of her unpublished paper?"

"In a nutshell. I can give you some cash to help, er, convince her if necessary. Frankly, I don't care how you do it. I *want* that paper, Dr McCullough."

He looks a little agitated now, and there's a shrill undertone to his voice. I suspect Dr Chambers is planning to take credit for what's in the paper, maybe even hoping for that second Nobel. I think for a minute. Dr Clarke's will left everything to Jim Kennedy, her assistant and fiancé. Even if Chambers gets the credit, maybe there's a way to reward the people who actually did the work. I make up a large, random number.

"I think $30,000 should do it." I clutch the arm of the chair and rub my thumb nervously over the smooth polished wood.

Dr Chambers starts to protest, then just waves his hand. "Fine. Fine. Whatever it takes. Funding for this project is not an issue. As I said, we only have enough of the isotope to power one trip into the past and back – yours. If you recover the paper successfully, we'll be able to develop the technology for many, many more excursions. If not . . ." he lets his sentence trail off.

"Other people *have* tried this?" I ask, warily. It occurs to me I may be the guinea pig, usually an expendable item.

He pauses for a long moment. "No. You'll be the first. Your records indicate you have no family, is that correct?"

I nod. My father died two years ago, and the longest relationship I've ever had only lasted six months. But Chambers doesn't strike me as a liberal. Even if I was still living with Nancy, I doubt if he would count her as family. "It's a big risk. What if I decline?"

"Your post-doc application will be reviewed," he shrugs. "I'm sure you'll be happy at some other university."

So it's all or nothing. I try to weigh all the variables, make a reasoned decision. But I can't. I don't feel like a scientist right now. I feel like a ten-year-old kid, being offered the only thing I've ever wanted – the chance to meet Sara Baxter Clarke.

"I'll do it," I say.

"Excellent." Chambers switches gears, assuming a brisk, businesslike manner. "You'll leave a week from today at precisely 6:32 a.m. You cannot take anything – underwear, clothes, shoes, watch – that was manufactured after 1956. My secretary has a list of antique clothing stores in the area, and some fashion magazines of the times." He looks at my jeans with distaste. "Please choose something appropriate for the reception. Can you do anything with your hair?"

My hair is short. Nothing radical, not in Berkeley in the 90s. It's more like early Beatles – what they called a pixie cut when I was a little girl – except I was always too tall and gawky to be a pixie. I run my fingers self-consciously through it and shake my head.

Chambers sighs and continues. "Very well. Now, since we have to allow for the return of Clarke's manuscript, you must take something of equivalent mass – and also of that era. I'll give you the draft copy of my own dissertation. You will also be supplied with a driver's license and university faculty card from the period, along with packets of vintage currency. You'll return with the manuscript at exactly 11:37 Monday morning. There will be no second chance. Do you understand?"

I nod, a little annoyed at his patronizing tone of voice. "If I miss the deadline, I'll be stuck in the past forever. Dr Clarke is the only other person who could possibly send me home, and she won't be around on Monday morning. Unless . . .?" I let the question hang in the air.

"Absolutely not. There is one immutable law of tempokinetics, Dr McCullough. You cannot change the past. I trust you'll remember that?" he says, standing.

Our meeting is over. I leave his office with the biggest news of my life. I wish I had someone to call and share it with. I'd settle for someone to help me shop for clothes.

Friday, February 17, 1995. 6:20 a.m.

The supply closet on the ground floor of LeConte Hall is narrow and dimly lit, filled with boxes of rubber gloves, lab coats, shop towels. Unlike many places on campus, the Physics building hasn't been remodeled in the last forty years. This has always been a closet, and it isn't likely to be occupied at 6:30 on any Friday morning.

I sit on the concrete floor, my back against a wall, dressed in an appropriate period costume. I think I should feel nervous, but I feel oddly detached. I sip from a cup of lukewarm 7-eleven coffee and observe. I don't have any role in this part of the experiment – I'm just the guinea pig. Dr Chambers's assistants step carefully over my outstretched legs and make the final adjustments to the battery of apparatus that surrounds me.

At exactly 6:28 by my antique Timex, Dr Chambers himself appears in the doorway. He shows me a thick packet of worn bills and the bulky, rubber-banded typescript of his dissertation, then slips both of them into a battered leather briefcase. He places the case on my lap and extends his hand. But when I reach up to shake it, he frowns and takes the 7-eleven cup.

"Good luck, Dr McCullough," he says formally. Nothing more. What more would he say to a guinea pig? He looks at his watch, then hands the cup to a young man in a black T-shirt, who types in one last line of code, turns off the light, and closes the door.

I sit in the dark and begin to get the willies. No one has ever done this. I don't know if the cool linoleum under my legs is the last thing I will ever feel. Sweat drips down between my breasts as the apparatus begins to hum. There is a moment of intense – sensation. It's not sound, or vibration, or anything I can quantify. It's as if all the fingernails in the world are suddenly raked down all the blackboards, and in the same moment oxygen is transmuted to lead. I am pressed to the floor by a monstrous force, but every hair on my body is erect. Just when I feel I can't stand it any more, the humming stops.

My pulse is racing, and I feel dizzy, a little nauseous. I sit for a minute, half-expecting Dr Chambers to come in and tell me the experiment has failed, but no one comes. I try to stand – my right leg has fallen asleep – and grope for the light switch near the door.

In the light from the single bulb, I see that the apparatus is gone, but the gray metal shelves are stacked with the same boxes of gloves and shop towels. My leg all pins and needles; I lean against a brown cardboard box stenciled Bayside Laundry Service, San Francisco 3, California.

It takes me a minute before I realize what's odd. Either those are very old towels, or I'm somewhere pre-ZIP code.

I let myself out of the closet, and walk awkwardly down the empty hallway, my spectator pumps echoing on the linoleum. I search for further confirmation. The first room I peer into is a lab – high stools in front of black slab tables with Bunsen burners, gray boxes full of dials and switches. A slide rule at every station.

I've made it.

Friday, February 17, 1956. 7:00 a.m.

The campus is deserted on this drizzly February dawn, as is Telegraph Avenue. The streetlights are still on – white lights, not yellow sodium – and through the mist I can see faint lines of red and green neon on stores down the avenue. I feel like Marco Polo as I navigate through a world that is both alien and familiar. The buildings are the same, but the storefronts and signs look like stage sets or photos from old *Life* magazines.

It takes me more than an hour to walk downtown. I am disoriented by each shop window, each passing car. I feel as if I'm a little drunk, walking too attentively through the landscape, and not connected to it. Maybe it's the colors. Everything looks too real. I grew up with grainy black-and-white TV reruns and 50s technicolor films that have faded over time, and it's disconcerting that this world is not overlaid with that pink-orange tinge.

The warm aromas of coffee and bacon lure me into a hole-in-the-wall café. I order the special – eggs, bacon, hash browns and toast. The toast comes dripping with butter and the jelly is in a glass jar, not a little plastic tub. When the bill comes it is 55¢. I leave a generous dime tip then catch the yellow F bus and ride down Shattuck Avenue, staring at the round-fendered black Chevys and occasional pink Studebakers that fill the streets.

The bus is full of morning commuters – men in dark jackets and hats, women in dresses and hats. In my tailored suit I fit right in. I'm surprised that no one looks 50s – retro 50s – the 50s that filtered down to the 90s. No poodle skirts, no DA haircuts. All the men remind me of my pop. A man in a gray felt hat has the *Chronicle*, and I read over his shoulder. Eisenhower is considering a second term. The San Francisco police chief promises a crack-down on vice. *Peanuts* tops the comics page and there's a Rock Hudson movie playing at the Castro Theatre. Nothing new there.

As we cross the Bay Bridge I'm amazed at how small San Francisco looks – the skyline is carved stone, not glass and steel towers. A green Muni streetcar takes me down the middle of Market Street to Powell. I check into the St Francis, the city's finest hotel. My room costs less than I've paid for a night in a Motel 6.

All my worldly goods fit on the desktop – Chambers's manu-script; a brown leather wallet with a driver's license, a Berkeley faculty card, and twenty-three dollars in small bills; the invita-tion to the reception tonight; and 30,000 dollars in banded stacks of 50-dollar bills. I pull three bills off the top of one stack and put the rest in the drawer, under the cream-colored hotel stationery. I have to get out of this suit and these shoes.

Woolworth's has a toothbrush and other plastic toiletries, and a tin "Tom Corbett, Space Cadet" alarm clock. I find a pair of pleated pants, an Oxford cloth shirt, and wool sweater at the City of Paris. Macy's Men's Shop yields a pair of "dungarees" and two T-shirts I can sleep in – 69 cents each. A snippy clerk gives me the eye in the Boys department, so I invent a nephew, little Billy, and buy him black basketball sneakers that are just my size.

After a shower and a change of clothes, I try to collect my thoughts, but I'm too keyed up to sit still. In a few hours I'll actually be in the same room as Sara Baxter Clarke. I can't distinguish between fear and excitement, and spend the afternoon wandering aimlessly around the city, gawking like a tourist.

Friday, February 17, 1956. 7:00 p.m.

Back in my spectator pumps and my tailored navy suit, I present myself at the doorway of the reception ballroom and surrender my invitation. The tuxedoed young man looks over my shoulder, as if he's expecting someone behind me. After a moment he clears his throat.

"And you're Mrs—?" he asks, looking down at his typewritten list.

"Dr McCullough," I say coolly, and give him an even stare. "Mr Chambers is out of town. He asked me to take his place."

After a moment's hesitation he nods, and writes my name on a white card, pinning it to my lapel like a corsage.

Ballroom A is a sea of gray suits, crew cuts, bow-ties and heavy black-rimmed glasses. Almost everyone is male, as I expected, and almost everyone is smoking, which surprises me. Over in one corner is a knot of women in bright cocktail dresses, each with a lacquered football helmet of hair. Barbie's cultural foremothers.

I accept a canapé from a passing waiter and ease my way to the corner. Which one is Dr Clarke? I stand a few feet back, scanning nametags. Mrs Niels Bohr. Mrs Richard Feynman. Mrs Ernest Lawrence. I am impressed by the company I'm in, and dismayed that none of the women has a name of her own. I smile an empty cocktail party smile as I move away from the wives and scan the room. Gray suits with a sprinkling of blue, but all male. Did I arrive too early?

I am looking for a safe corner, one with a large, sheltering potted palm, when I hear a blustery male voice say, "So, Dr Clarke. Trying the H. G. Wells route, are you? Waste of the taxpayer's money, all that science fiction stuff, don't you think?"

A woman's voice answers. "Not at all. Perhaps I can change your mind at Monday's session." I can't see her yet, but her voice is smooth and rich, with a bit of a lilt or a brogue – one of those vocal clues that says, "I'm not an American." I stand rooted to the carpet, so awestruck I'm unable to move.

"Jimmy, will you see if there's more champagne about?" I hear her ask. I see a motion in the sea of gray and astonish myself by flagging a waiter and taking two slender flutes from his tray. I step forward in the direction of her voice. "Here you go," I say, trying to keep my hand from shaking. "I've got an extra."

"How very resourceful of you," she laughs. I am surprised that she is a few inches shorter than me. I'd forgotten she'd be about my age. She takes the glass and offers me her other hand. "Sara Clarke," she says.

"Carol McCullough." I touch her palm. The room seems suddenly bright and the voices around me fade into a murmur. I think for a moment that I'm dematerializing back to 1995, but nothing so dramatic happens. I'm just so stunned that I forget to breathe while I look at her.

Since I was ten years old, no matter where we lived, I have had a picture of Sara Baxter Clarke over my desk. I cut it out of that old physics magazine. It is grainy, black and white, the only photo of her I've ever found. In it, she's who I always wanted to be – competent, serious, every inch a scientist. She wears a white lab coat and a pair of rimless glasses, her hair pulled back from her face. A bald man in an identical lab coat is showing her a piece of equipment. Neither of them is smiling.

I know every inch of that picture by heart. But I didn't know that her hair was a coppery red, or that her eyes were such a deep, clear green. And until this moment, it had never occurred to me that she could laugh.

The slender blond man standing next to her interrupts my reverie. "I'm Jim Kennedy, Sara's assistant."

Jim Kennedy. Her fiancé. I feel like the characters in my favorite novel are all coming to life, one by one.

"You're not a wife, are you?" he asks.

I shake my head. "Post doc. I've only been at Cal a month."

He smiles. "We're neighbors, then. What's your field?"

I take a deep breath. "Tempokinetics. I'm a great admirer of Dr Clarke's work." The blustery man scowls at me and leaves in search of other prey.

"Really?" Dr Clarke turns, raising one eyebrow in surprise. "Well then we should have a chat. Are you—?" She stops in mid-sentence and swears almost inaudibly. "Damn. It's Dr Wilkins and I must be pleasant. He's quite a muckety-muck at the NSF, and I need the funding." She takes a long swallow of champagne, draining the crystal flute. "Jimmy, why don't you get Dr McCullough another drink and see if you can persuade her to join us for supper."

I start to make a polite protest, but Jimmy takes my elbow and steers me through the crowd to an unoccupied sofa. Half an hour later we are deep in a discussion of quantum field theory when Dr Clarke appears and says, "Let's make a discreet exit, shall we? I'm famished."

Like conspirators, we slip out a side door and down a flight of service stairs. The Powell Street cable car takes us over Nob Hill into North Beach, the Italian section of town. We walk up Columbus to one of my favorite restaurants – the New Pisa – where I discover that nothing much has changed in forty years except the prices.

The waiter brings a carafe of red wine and a trio of squat drinking glasses and we eat family style – bowls of pasta with red sauce and steaming loaves of crusty garlic bread. I am speechless as Sara Baxter Clarke talks about her work, blithely answering questions I have wanted to ask my whole life. She is brilliant, fascinating. And beautiful. My food disappears without me noticing a single mouthful.

Over coffee and spumoni she insists, for the third time, that I call her Sara, and asks me about my own studies. I have to catch myself a few times, biting back citations from Stephen Hawking and other works that won't be published for decades. It is such an engrossing, exhilarating conversation, I can't bring myself to shift it to Chambers's agenda. We leave when we notice the restaurant has no other customers.

"How about a nightcap?" she suggests when we reach the sidewalk.

"Not for me," Jimmy begs off. "I've got an 8:30 symposium tomorrow morning. But why don't you two go on ahead. The Paper Doll is just around the corner."

Sara gives him an odd, cold look and shakes her head. "Not funny, James," she says and glances over at me. I shrug noncommittally. It's seems they have a private joke I'm not in on.

"Just a thought," he says, then kisses her on the cheek and leaves. Sara and I walk down to Vesuvio's, one of the bars where Kerouac, Ferlinghetti, and Ginsberg spawned the Beat Generation. Make that *will* spawn. I think we're a few months too early.

Sara orders another carafe of raw red wine. I feel shy around her, intimidated, I guess. I've dreamed of meeting her for so long, and I want her to like me. As we begin to talk, we discover how similar, and lonely, our childhoods were. We were raised as only children. We both begged for chemistry sets we never got. We were expected to know how to iron, not know about ions. Midway through her second glass of wine, Sara sighs.

"Oh, bugger it all. Nothing's really changed, you know. It's still just snickers and snubs. I'm tired of fighting for a seat in the old boys' club. Monday's paper represents five years of hard work, and there aren't a handful of people at this entire conference who've had the decency to treat me as anything but a joke." She squeezes her napkin into a tighter and tighter wad, and a tear trickles down her cheek. "How do you stand it, Carol?"

How can I tell her? I've stood it because of you. You're my hero. I've always asked myself what Sara Baxter Clarke would do, and steeled myself to push through. But now she's not a hero. She's real, this woman across the table from me. This Sara's not the invincible, ever-practical scientist I always thought she was. She's as young and as vulnerable as I am.

I want to ease her pain the way that she, as my imaginary mentor, has always eased mine. I reach over and put my hand over hers; she stiffens, but she doesn't pull away. Her hand is soft under mine, and I think of touching her hair, gently brushing the red tendrils off the back of her neck, kissing the salty tears on her cheek.

Maybe I've always had a crush on Sara Baxter Clarke. But I can't be falling in love with her. She's straight. She's forty years older than I am. And in the back of my mind, the chilling voice of reality reminds me that she'll also be dead in two days. I can't reconcile that with the vibrant woman sitting in this smoky North Beach bar. I don't want to. I drink two more glasses of wine and hope that will silence the voice long enough for me to enjoy these few moments.

We are still talking, our fingertips brushing on the scarred wooden tabletop, when the bartender announces last call. "Oh, bloody hell," she says. "I've been having such a lovely time I've gone and missed the last ferry. I hope I have enough for the cab fare. My Chevy's over in the car park at Berkeley."

"That's ridiculous," I hear myself say. "I've got a room at the hotel. Come back with me and catch the ferry in the morning." It's the wine talking. I don't know what I'll do if she says yes. I want her to say yes so much.

"No, I couldn't impose. I'll simply—" she protests, and then stops. "Oh, yes, then. Thank you. It's very generous."

So here we are. At 2:00 a.m. the hotel lobby is plush and utterly empty. We ride up in the elevator in a sleepy silence that becomes awkward as soon as we are alone in the room. I nervously gather my new clothes off the only bed and gesture to her to sit down. I pull a T-shirt out of its crinkly cellophane wrapper. "Here," I hand it to her. "It's not elegant, but it'll have to do as a nightgown."

She looks at the T-shirt in her lap, and at the dungarees and black sneakers in my arms, an odd expression on her face. Then she sighs, a deep, achy sounding sigh. It's the oddest reaction to a T-shirt I've ever heard.

"The Paper Doll would have been all right, wouldn't it?" she asks softly.

Puzzled, I stop crinkling the other cellophane wrapper and lean against the dresser. "I guess so. I've never been there." She looks worried, so I keep talking. "But there are a lot of places I haven't been. I'm new in town. Just got here. Don't know anybody yet, haven't really gotten around. What kind of place is it?"

She freezes for a moment, then says, almost in a whisper, "It's a bar for women."

"Oh," I nod. "Well, that's okay." Why would Jimmy suggest a gay bar? It's an odd thing to tell your fiancée. Did he guess about me somehow? Or maybe he just thought we'd be safer there late at night, since—

My musings – and any other rational thoughts – come to a dead stop when Sara Baxter Clarke stands up, cups my face in both her hands and kisses me gently on the lips. She pulls away, just a few inches, and looks at me.

I can't believe this is happening. "Aren't you . . . isn't Jimmy . . .?"

"He's my dearest chum, and my partner in the lab. But romantically? No. Protective camouflage. For both of us," she answers, stroking my face.

I don't know what to do. Every dream I've ever had is coming true tonight. But how can I kiss her? How can I begin something I know is doomed? She must see the indecision in my face, because she looks scared, and starts to take a step backwards. And I can't let her go. Not yet. I put my hand on the back of her neck and pull her into a second, longer kiss.

We move to the bed after a few minutes. I feel shy, not wanting to make a wrong move. But she kisses my face, my neck, and pulls me down on to her. We begin slowly, cautiously undressing each other. I fumble at the unfamiliar garter belts and stockings, and she smiles, undoing the rubber clasps for me. Her slender body is pale and freckled, her breasts small with dusty pink nipples.

Her fingers gently stroke my arms, my thighs. When I hesitantly put my mouth on her breast, she moans, deep in her throat, and laces her fingers through my hair. After a minute her hands ease my head down her body. The hair between her legs is ginger, the ends dark and wet. I taste the salty musk of her when I part her lips with my tongue. She moans again, almost a growl. When she comes it is a single, fierce explosion.

We finally fall into an exhausted sleep, spooned around each other, both T-shirts still crumpled on the floor.

Saturday, February 18, 1956. 7:00 a.m.

Light comes through a crack in the curtains. I'm alone in a strange bed. I'm sure last night was a dream, but then I hear the shower come on in the bathroom. Sara emerges a few minutes later, toweling her hair. She smiles and leans over me – warm and wet and smelling of soap.

"I have to go," she whispers, and kisses me.

I want to ask if I'll see her again, want to pull her down next to me and hold her for hours. But I just stroke her hair and say nothing.

She sits on the edge of the bed. "I've got an eleven o'clock lab, and there's another dreadful cocktail thing at Stanford this evening. I'd give it a miss, but Shockley's going to be there, and he's front runner for the next Nobel, so I have to make an appearance. Meet me after?"

"Yes," I say, breathing again. "Where?"

"Why don't you take the train down. I'll pick you up at the Palo Alto station at half-past seven and we can drive to the coast for dinner. Wear those nice black trousers. If it's not too dreary, we'll walk on the beach."

She picks up her wrinkled suit from the floor where it landed last night, and gets dressed. "Half past seven, then?" she says, and kisses my cheek. The door clicks shut and she's gone.

I lie tangled in the sheets, and curl up into the pillow like a contented cat. I am almost asleep again when an image intrudes – a crumpled Chevy on the rocks below Devil's Slide. It's like a fragment of a nightmare, not quite real in the morning light. But which dream is real now?

Until last night, part of what had made Sara Baxter Clarke so compelling was her enigmatic death. Like Amelia Earhart or James Dean, she had been a brilliant star that ended so abruptly she became legendary. Larger than life. But I can still feel where her lips brushed my cheek. Now she's very much life-size, and despite Chambers's warnings, I will do anything to keep her that way.

Saturday, February 18, 1956. 7:20 p.m.

The platform at the Palo Alto train station is cold and windy. I'm glad I've got a sweater, but it makes my suit jacket uncomfortably tight across my shoulders. I've finished the newspaper and am reading the train schedule when Sara comes up behind me.

"Hullo there," she says. She's wearing a nubby beige dress under a dark wool coat and looks quite elegant.

"Hi." I reach to give her a hug, but she steps back.

"Have you gone mad?" she says, scowling. She crosses her arms over her chest. "What on earth were you thinking?"

"Sorry." I'm not sure what I've done. "It's nice to see you," I say hesitantly.

"Yes, well, me too. But you can't just . . . oh, you know," she says, waving her hand.

I don't, so I shrug. She gives me an annoyed look, then turns and opens the car door. I stand on the pavement for a minute, bewildered, then get in.

Her Chevy feels huge compared to the Toyota I drive at home, and there are no seat belts. We drive in uncomfortable silence all through Palo Alto and on to the winding, two-lane road that leads to the coast. Our second date isn't going well.

After about ten minutes, I can't stand it any more. "I'm sorry about the hug. I guess it's still a big deal here, huh?"

She turns her head slightly, still keeping her eyes on the road. "Here?" she asks. "What utopia are you from, then?"

I spent the day wandering the city in a kind of haze, alternately giddy in love and worrying about this moment. How can I tell her where – when – I'm from? And how much should I tell her about why? I count to three, and then count again before I answer. "From the future."

"Very funny," she says. I can hear in her voice that she's hurt. She stares straight ahead again.

"Sara, I'm serious. Your work on time travel isn't just theory. I'm a post-doc at Cal. In 1995. The head of the physics department, Dr Chambers, sent me back here to talk to you. He says he worked with you and Jimmy, back before he won the Nobel Prize."

She doesn't say anything for a minute, then pulls over on to a wide place at the side of the road. She switches off the engine and turns towards me.

"Ray Chambers? The Nobel Prize? Jimmy says he can barely do his own lab work." She shakes her head, then lights a cigarette, flicking the match out the window into the darkness. "Ray set you up for this, didn't he? To get back at Jimmy for last term's grade? Well it's a terrible joke," she says turning away, "and you are one of the cruelest people I have ever met."

"Sara, it's not a joke. Please believe me." I reach across the seat to take her hand, but she jerks it away.

I take a deep breath, trying desperately to think of something that will convince her. "Look, I know it sounds crazy, but hear me out. In September, *Modern Physics* is going to publish an article about you and your work. When I was ten years old – in 1975 – I read it sitting on the back porch of my father's quarters at Fort Ord. That article inspired me to go into science. I read about you, and I knew when I grew up I wanted to travel through time."

She stubs out her cigarette. "Go on."

So I tell her all about my academic career, and my "assignment" from Chambers. She listens without interrupting me. I can't see her expression in the darkened car.

After I finish, she says nothing, then sighs. "This is rather a lot to digest, you know. But I can't very well believe in my work without giving your story some credence, can I?" She lights another cigarette, then asks the question I've been dreading. "So if you've come all this way to offer me an enormous sum for my paper, does that mean something happened to it – or to me?" I still can't see her face, but her voice is shaking.

I can't do it. I can't tell her. I grope for a convincing lie. "There was a fire. A lot of papers were lost. Yours is the one they want."

"I'm not a faculty member at *your* Cal, am I?"

"No."

She takes a long drag on her cigarette, then asks, so softly I can barely hear her, "Am I . . . ?" She lets her question trail off and is silent for a minute, then sighs again. "No, I won't ask. I think I prefer to bumble about like other mortals. You're a dangerous woman, Carol McCullough. I'm afraid you can tell me too many things I have no right to know." She reaches for the ignition key, then stops. "There is one thing I must know, though. Was last night as carefully planned as everything else?"

"Jesus, no." I reach over and touch her hand. She lets me hold it this time. "No, I had no idea. Other than finding you at the reception, last night had nothing to do with science."

To my great relief, she chuckles. "Well, perhaps chemistry, don't you think?" She glances in the rearview mirror then pulls me across the wide front seat and into her arms. We hold each other in the darkness for a long time, and kiss for even longer. Her lips taste faintly of gin.

We have a leisurely dinner at a restaurant overlooking the beach in Half Moon Bay. Fresh fish and a dry white wine. I have the urge to tell her about the picture, about how important she's been to me. But as I start to speak, I realize she's more important to me now, so I just tell her that. We finish the meal gazing at each other as if we were ordinary lovers.

Outside the restaurant, the sky is cloudy and cold, the breeze tangy with salt and kelp. Sara pulls off her high heels and we walk down a sandy path, holding hands in the darkness. Within minutes we are both freezing. I pull her to me and lean down to kiss her on the deserted beach. "You know what I'd like," I say, over the roar of the surf.

"What?" she murmurs into my neck.

"I'd like to take you dancing."

She shakes her head. "We can't. Not here. Not now. It's against the law, you know. Or perhaps you don't. But it is, I'm afraid. And the police have been on a rampage in the city lately. One bar lost its license just because two men were holding hands. They arrested both as sexual vagrants and for being – oh, what was the phrase – lewd and dissolute persons."

"Sexual vagrants? That's outrageous!"

"Exactly what the newspapers said. An outrage to public decency. Jimmy knew one of the poor chaps. He was in Engineering at Stanford, but after his name and address were published in the paper, he lost his job. Does that still go on where you're from?"

"I don't think so. Maybe in some places. I don't really know. I'm afraid I don't pay any attention to politics. I've never needed to."

Sara sighs. "What a wonderful luxury that must be, not having to be so careful all the time."

"I guess so." I feel a little guilty that it's not something I worry about. But I was four years old when Stonewall happened. By the time I came out, in college, being gay was more of a lifestyle than a perversion. At least in San Francisco.

"It's sure a lot more public," I say after a minute. "Last year there were a quarter of a million people at the Gay Pride parade. Dancing down Market Street and carrying signs about how great it is to be queer."

"You're pulling my leg now. Aren't you?" When I shake my head she smiles. "Well, I'm glad. I'm glad that this witch hunt ends. And in a few months, when I get my equipment up and running, perhaps I shall travel to dance at your parade. But for tonight, why don't we just go to my house? At least I've got a new hi-fi."

So we head back up the coast. One advantage to these old cars, the front seat is as big as a couch; we drive up Highway 1 sitting next to each other, my arm resting on her thigh. The ocean is a flat, black void on our left, until the road begins to climb and the water disappears behind jagged cliffs. On the driver's side the road drops off steeply as we approach Devil's Slide.

I feel like I'm coming to the scary part of a movie I've seen before. I'm afraid I know what happens next. My right hand grips the upholstery and I brace myself for the oncoming car or the loose patch of gravel or whatever it is that will send us skidding off the road and on to the rocks.

But nothing happens. Sara hums as she drives, and I realize that although this is the spot I dread, it means nothing to her. At least not tonight.

As the road levels out again, it is desolate, with few signs of civilization. Just beyond a sign that says "Sharp Park" is a trailer camp with a string of bare light bulbs outlining its perimeter. Across the road is a seedy looking roadhouse with a neon sign that blinks "Hazel's." The parking lot is jammed with cars. Saturday night in the middle of nowhere.

We drive another hundred yards when Sara suddenly snaps her fingers and does a U-turn.

Please don't go back to the cliffs, I beg silently. "What's up?" I ask out loud.

"Hazel's. Jimmy was telling me about it last week. It's become a rather gay club, and since it's over the county line, out here in the boondocks, he says anything goes. Including dancing. Besides, I thought I spotted his car."

"Are you sure?"

"No, but there aren't that many '39 Packards still on the road. If it isn't, we'll just continue on." She pulls into the parking lot and finds a space at the back, between the trash cans and the ocean.

Hazel's is a noisy, smoky place – a small, single room with a bar along one side – jammed wall-to-wall with people. Hundreds of them: mostly men, but more than a few women. When I look closer, I realize that some of the "men" are actually women with slicked-back hair, ties, and sportcoats.

We manage to get two beers, and find Jimmy on the edge of the dance floor – a minuscule square of linoleum, not more than 10 x 10, where dozens of people are dancing to Bill Haley & the Comets blasting from the jukebox. Jimmy's in a tweed jacket and chinos, his arm around the waist of a young Latino man in a tight white T-shirt and even tighter blue jeans. We elbow our way through to them and Sara gives Jimmy a kiss on the cheek. "Hullo, love," she says.

He's obviously surprised – shocked – to see Sara, but when he sees me behind her, he grins. "I told you so."

"James, you don't know the half of it," Sara says, smiling, and puts her arm around me.

We dance for a few songs in the hot, crowded bar. I take off my jacket, then my sweater, draping them over the railing next to the bottles of beer. After the next song I roll up the sleeves of my button-down shirt. When Jimmy offers to buy another round of beers, I look at my watch and shake my head. It's midnight, and as much as I wanted to dance with Sara, I want to sleep with her even more.

"One last dance, then let's go, okay?" I ask, shouting to be heard over the noise of the crowd and the jukebox. "I'm bushed."

She nods. Johnny Mathis starts to sing, and we slow dance, our arms around each other. My eyes are closed and Sara's head is resting on my shoulder when the first of the cops bursts through the front door.

Sunday, February 19, 1956. 12:05 a.m.

A small army of uniformed men storms into the bar. Everywhere around us people are screaming in panic, and I'm buffeted by the bodies running in all directions. People near the back race for the rear door. A red-faced, heavy-set man in khaki, a gold star on his chest, climbs on to the bar. "This is a raid," he shouts. He has brought reporters with him, and flashbulbs suddenly illuminate the stunned, terrified faces of people who had been sipping their drinks moments before.

Khaki-shirted deputies, nightsticks in hand, block the front door. There are so many uniforms. At least forty men – highway patrol, sheriff's department, and even some army MPs – begin to form a gauntlet leading to the back door, now the only exit.

Jimmy grabs my shoulders. "Dance with Antonio," he says urgently. "I've just met him, but it's our best chance of getting out of here. I'll take Sara."

I nod and the Latino man's muscular arms are around my waist. He smiles shyly just as someone pulls the plug on the jukebox and Johnny Mathis stops in mid-croon. The room is quiet for a moment, then the cops begin barking orders. We stand against the railing, Jimmy's arm curled protectively around Sara's shoulders, Antonio's around mine. Other people have done the same thing, but there are not enough women, and men who had been dancing now stand apart from each other, looking scared.

The uniforms are lining people up, herding them like sheep toward the back. We join the line and inch forward. The glare of headlights through the half-open back door cuts through the smoky room like the beam from a movie projector. There is an icy draft and I reach back for my sweater, but the railing is too far away, and the crush of people too solid to move any direction but forward. Jimmy sees me shivering and drapes his sportcoat over my shoulders.

We are in line for more than an hour, as the cops at the back door check everyone's ID. Sara leans against Jimmy's chest, squeezing my hand tightly once or twice, when no one's looking. I am scared, shaking, but the uniforms seem to be letting most people go. Every few seconds, a car starts up in the parking lot, and I can hear the crunch of tires on gravel as someone leaves Hazel's for the freedom of the highway.

As we get closer to the door, I can see a line of black vans parked just outside, ringing the exit. They are paneled with wooden benches, filled with the men who are not going home, most of them sitting with their shoulders sagging. One van holds a few women with crew cuts or slicked-back hair, who glare defiantly into the night.

We are ten people back from the door when Jimmy slips a key into my hand and whispers into my ear. "We'll have to take separate cars. Drive Sara's back to the city and we'll meet at the lobby bar in your hotel."

"The bar will be closed," I whisper back. "Take my key and meet me in the room. I'll get another at the desk." He nods as I hand it to him.

The cop at the door looks at Sara's elegant dress and coat, barely glances at her outstretched ID, and waves her and Jimmy outside without a word. She pauses at the door and looks back at me, but an MP shakes his head and points to the parking lot. "Now or never, lady," he says, and Sara and Jimmy disappear into the night.

I'm alone. Antonio is a total stranger, but his strong arm is my only support until a man in a suit pulls him away. "Nice try, sweetie," the man says to him. "But I've seen you in here before, dancing with your pansy friends." He turns to the khaki-shirted deputy and says, "He's one of the perverts. Book him." The cop pulls Antonio's arm up between his shoulder blades, then cuffs his hands behind his back. "Time for a little ride, pretty boy," he grins, and drags Antonio out into one of the black vans.

Without thinking, I take a step towards his retreating back. "Not so fast," says another cop, with acne scars across both cheeks. He looks at Jimmy's jacket, and down at my pants and my black basketball shoes with a sneer. Then he puts his hands on my breasts, groping me. "Loose ones. Not all tied down like those other he-shes. I like that." He leers and pinches one of my nipples.

I yell for help, and try to pull away, but he laughs and shoves me up against the stack of beer cases that line the back hallway. He pokes his nightstick between my legs. "So you want to be a man, huh, butchie? Well just what do you think you've got in there?" He jerks his nightstick up into my crotch so hard tears come to my eyes.

I stare at him, in pain, in disbelief. I am too stunned to move or to say anything. He cuffs my hands and pushes me out the back door and into the van with the other glaring women.

Sunday, February 19, 1956. 10:00 a.m.

I plead guilty to being a sex offender, and pay the $50 fine. Being arrested can't ruin *my* life. I don't even exist here.

Sara and Jimmy are waiting on a wooden bench outside the holding cell of the San Mateo County jail. "Are you all right, love?" she asks.

I shrug. "I'm exhausted. I didn't sleep. There were ten of us in one cell. The woman next to me – a stone butch? – really tough, Frankie – she had a pompadour – two cops took her down the hall – when she came back the whole side of her face was swollen, and after that she didn't say anything to anyone, but I'm okay, I just—" I start to shake. Sara takes one arm and Jimmy takes the other, and they walk me gently out to the parking lot.

The three of us sit in the front seat of Jimmy's car, and as soon as we are out of sight of the jail, Sara puts her arms around me and holds me, brushing the hair off my forehead. When Jimmy takes the turnoff to the San Mateo bridge, she says, "We checked you out of the hotel this morning. Precious little to check, actually, except for the briefcase. Anyway, I thought you'd be more comfortable at my house. We need to get you some breakfast and a bed." She kisses me on the cheek. "I've told Jimmy everything, by the way."

I nod sleepily, and the next thing I know we're standing on the front steps of a brown shingled cottage and Jimmy's pulling away. I don't think I'm hungry, but Sara makes scrambled eggs and bacon and toast, and I eat every scrap of it. She runs a hot bath, grimacing at the purpling, thumb-shaped bruises on my upper arms, and gently washes my hair and my back. When she tucks me into bed, pulling a blue quilt around me, and curls up beside me, I start to cry. I feel so battered and so fragile, and I can't remember the last time someone took care of me this way.

Sunday, February 19, 1956. 5:00 p.m.

I wake up to the sound of rain and the enticing smell of pot roast baking in the oven. Sara has laid out my jeans and a brown sweater at the end of the bed. I put them on, then pad barefoot into the kitchen. There are cardboard boxes piled in one corner, and Jimmy and Sara are sitting at the yellow formica table with cups of tea, talking intently.

"Oh good, you're awake." She stands and gives me a hug. "There's tea in the pot. If you think you're up to it, Jimmy and I need to tell you a few things."

"I'm a little sore, but I'll be okay. I'm not crazy about the 50s, though." I pour from the heavy ceramic pot. The tea is some sort of Chinese blend, fragrant and smoky. "What's up?"

"First a question. If my paper isn't entirely – complete – could there possibly be any repercussions for you?"

I think for a minute. "I don't think so. If anyone knew exactly what was in it, they wouldn't have sent me."

"Splendid. In that case, I've come to a decision." She pats the battered brown briefcase. "In exchange for the extraordinary wad of cash in here, we shall send back a perfectly reasonable sounding paper. What only the three of us will know is that I have left a few things out. This, for example." She picks up a pen, scribbles a complex series of numbers and symbols on a piece of paper, and hands it to me.

I study it for a minute. It's very high-level stuff, but I know enough physics to get the gist of it. "If this really works, it's the answer to the energy problem. It's exactly the piece Chambers needs."

"Very, very good," she says smiling. "It's also the part I will never give him."

I raise one eyebrow.

"I read the first few chapters of his dissertation this afternoon while you were sleeping," she says, tapping the manuscript with her pen. "It's a bit uneven, although parts of it are quite good. Unfortunately, the good parts were written by a graduate student named Gilbert Young."

I raise the other eyebrow. "But that paper's what Chambers wins the Nobel for."

"Son of a bitch." Jimmy slaps his hand down onto the table. "Gil was working for me while he finished the last of his dissertation. He was a bright guy, original research, solid future – but he started having these headaches. The tumor was inoperable, and he died six months ago. Ray said he'd clean out Gil's office for me. I just figured he was trying to get back on my good side."

"We can't change what Ray does with Gil's work. But I won't give him *my* work to steal in the future." Sara shoves Chambers's manuscript to the other side of the table. "Or now. I've decided not to present my paper in the morning."

I feel very lightheaded. I *know* she doesn't give her paper, but . . . "Why not?" I ask.

"While I was reading the manuscript this afternoon, I heard that fat sheriff interviewed on the radio. They arrested ninety people at Hazel's last night, Carol, people like us. People who only wanted to dance with each other. But he kept bragging about how they cleaned out a nest of perverts. And I realized – in a blinding moment of clarity – that the university is a branch of the state, and the sheriff is enforcing the state's laws. I'm working for people who believe it's morally right to abuse you – or me – or Jimmy. And I can't do that any more."

"Here, here!" Jimmy says, smiling. "The only problem is, as I explained to her this morning, the administration is likely to take a very dim view of being embarrassed in front of every major physicist in the country. Not to mention they feel Sara's research is university property." He looks at me and takes a sip of tea. "So we decided it might be best if Sara disappeared for a while."

I stare at both of them, my mouth open. I have that same odd feeling of déjà vu that I did in the car last night.

"I've cleaned everything that's hers out our office and the lab," Jimmy says. "It's all in the trunk of my car."

"And those," Sara says, gesturing to the boxes in the corner, "are what I value from my desk and my library here. Other than my Nana's teapot and some clothes, it's all I'll really need for a while. Jimmy's family has a vacation home out in West Marin, so I won't have to worry about rent – or privacy."

I'm still staring. "What about your career?"

Sara puts down her teacup with a bang and begins pacing the floor. "Oh, bugger my career. I'm not giving up my *work*, just the university – and its hypocrisy. If one of my colleagues had a little fling, nothing much would come of it. But as a woman, I'm supposed to be some sort of paragon of unsullied Victorian virtue. Just by being *in* that bar last night, I put my 'career' in jeopardy. They'd crucify me if they knew who – or what – I am. I don't want to live that way any more."

She brings the teapot to the table and sits down, pouring us each another cup. "End of tirade. But that's why I had to ask about your money. It's enough to live on for a good long while, and to buy all the equipment I need. In a few months, with a decent lab, I should be this close," she says, holding her thumb and forefinger together, "to time travel in practice as well as in theory. And that discovery will be mine – ours. Not the university's. Not the government's."

Jimmy nods. "I'll stay down here and finish this term. That way I can keep tabs on things and order equipment without arousing suspicion."

"Won't they come looking for you?" I ask Sara. I feel very surreal. Part of me has always wanted to know *why* this all happened, and part of me feels like I'm just prompting the part I know comes next.

"Not if they think there's no reason to look," Jimmy says. "We'll take my car back to Hazel's and pick up hers. Devil's Slide is only a few miles up the road. It's—"

"It's a rainy night," I finish. "Treacherous stretch of highway. Accidents happen there all the time. They'll find Sara's car in the morning, but no body. Washed out to sea. Everyone will think it's tragic that she died so young," I say softly. My throat is tight and I'm fighting back tears. "At least I always have."

They both stare at me. Sara gets up and stands behind me, wrapping her arms around my shoulders. "So that *is* how it happens?" she asks, hugging me tight. "All along you've assumed I'd be dead in the morning?"

I nod. I don't trust my voice enough to say anything.

To my great surprise, she laughs. "Well, I'm not going to be. One of the first lessons you should have learned as a scientist is never assume," she says, kissing the top of my head. "But what a terrible secret for you to have been carting about. Thank you for not telling me. It would have ruined a perfectly lovely weekend. Now let's all have some supper. We've a lot to do tonight."

Monday, February 20, 1956. 12:05 a.m.

"What on earth are you doing?" Sara asks, coming into the kitchen and talking around the toothbrush in her mouth. "It's our last night – at least for a while. I was rather hoping you'd be waiting in bed when I came out of the bathroom."

"I will. Two more minutes." I'm sitting at the kitchen table, rolling a blank sheet of paper into her typewriter. I haven't let myself think about going back in the morning, about leaving Sara, and I'm delaying our inevitable conversation about it for as long as I can. "While we were driving back from wrecking your car, I had an idea about how to nail Chambers."

She takes the toothbrush out of her mouth. "It's a lovely thought, but you know you can't change anything that happens."

"I can't change the past," I agree. "But I *can* set a bomb with a very long fuse. Like forty years."

"What? You look like the cat that's eaten the canary." She sits down next to me.

"I've retyped the title page to Chambers's dissertation – with your name on it. First thing in the morning, I'm going to rent a large safe deposit box at the Wells Fargo Bank downtown, and pay the rent in advance. Sometime in 1995, there'll be a miraculous discovery of a complete Sara Baxter Clarke manuscript. The bomb is that, after her tragic death, the esteemed Dr Chambers appears to have published it under his own name – and won the Nobel Prize for it."

"No, you can't. It's not my work either, it's Gil's and—" she stops in mid-sentence, staring at me. "And he really *is* dead. I don't suppose I dare give a fig about academic credit anymore, should I?"

"I hope not. Besides, Chambers can't prove it's *not* yours. What's he going to say – Carol McCullough went back to the past and set me up? He'll look like a total idiot. Without your formula, all he's got is a time ·machine that won't work. Remember, you never present your paper. Where I come from it may be okay to be queer, but time travel is still just science fiction."

She laughs. "Well, given a choice, I suppose that's preferable, isn't it?"

I nod and pull the sheet of paper out of the typewriter.

"You're quite a resourceful girl, aren't you?" Sara says, smiling. "I could use an assistant like you." Then her smile fades and she puts her hand over mine. "I don't suppose you'd consider staying on for a few months and helping me set up the lab? I know we've only known each other for two days. But this . . . I . . . us . . . Oh, dammit, what I'm trying to say is I'm going to miss you."

I squeeze her hand in return, and we sit silent for a few minutes. I don't know what to say. Or to do. I don't want to go back to my own time. There's nothing for me in that life. A dissertation that I now know isn't true. An office with a black and white photo of the only person I've ever really loved – who's sitting next to me, holding my hand. I could sit like this forever. But could I stand to live the rest of my life in the closet, hiding who I am and who I love? I'm used to the 90s – I've never done research without a computer, or cooked much without a microwave. I'm afraid if I don't go back tomorrow, I'll be trapped in this reactionary past forever.

"Sara," I ask finally. "Are you sure your experiments will work?"

She looks at me, her eyes warm and gentle. "If you're asking if I can promise you an escape back to your own time someday, the answer is no. I can't promise you anything, love. But if you're asking if I believe in my work, then yes. I do. Are you thinking of staying, then?"

I nod. "I want to. I just don't know if I can."

"Because of last night?" she asks softly.

"That's part of it. I was raised in a world that's so different. I don't feel right here. I don't belong."

She kisses my cheek. "I know. But gypsies never belong to the places they travel. They only belong to other gypsies."

My eyes are misty as she takes my hand and leads me to the bedroom.

Monday, February 20, 1956. 11:30 a.m.

I put the battered leather briefcase on the floor of the supply closet in LeConte Hall and close the door behind me. At 11:37

exactly, I hear the humming start, and when it stops, my shoulders sag with relief. What's done is done, and all the dies are cast. In Palo Alto an audience of restless physicists is waiting to hear a paper that will never be read. And in Berkeley, far in the future, an equally restless physicist is waiting for a messenger to finally deliver that paper.

But the messenger isn't coming back. And that may be the least of Chambers's worries.

This morning I taped the key to the safe deposit box – and a little note about the dissertation inside – into the 1945 bound volume of *The Astrophysical Journal*. My officemate Ted was outraged that no one had checked it out of the Physics library since 1955. I'm hoping he'll be even more outraged when he discovers the secret that's hidden inside it.

I walk out of LeConte and across campus to the coffee shop where Sara is waiting for me. I don't like the political climate here, but at least I know that it will change, slowly but surely. Besides, we don't have to stay in the 50s all the time – in a few months, Sara and I plan to do a lot of traveling. Maybe one day some graduate student will want to study the mysterious disappearance of Dr Carol McCullough. Stranger things have happened.

My only regret is not being able to see Chambers's face when he opens that briefcase and there's no manuscript. Sara and I decided that even sending back an incomplete version of her paper was dangerous. It would give Chambers enough proof that his tempokinetic experiment worked for him to get more funding and try again. So the only thing in the case is an anonymous, undated postcard of the St Francis Hotel that says:

"Having a wonderful time. Thanks for the ride."

THE CATCH

Kage Baker

Science-fiction writers soon realized that in order to prevent, or at least minimize, the creation of paradoxes by manipulating the past there needed to be some kind of time police, someway of monitoring the entirety of time to retain equilibrium. Isaac Asimov created the existence of Eternity, an organization that monitored time in The End of Eternity *(1955), and there have been many similar stories and books since then including* Guardians of Time *(1960) by Poul Anderson,* Times Without Number *(1962) by John Brunner and* Lord Kalvan of Otherwhen *(1965) by H. Beam Piper. The most famous Time Lord of all is, of course, Dr Who.*

With In the Garden of Iden *(1997), Kage Baker (1952– 2010) introduced what became a long-running series about the Company, or more accurately the Zeus Corporation, run by the mysterious Dr Zeus. The Company does not so much patrol the past as seek to preserve its treasures, both living and manufactured. The enterprise is extremely expensive, because the agents of the Company are not normal humans but ones who have been genetically engineered to withstand the rigours of time travel. Consequently the Company seeks to preserve its agents at all costs, and that's the subject of "The Catch", one of the more complex and convoluted of the Company stories.*

The barn stands high in the middle of back-country nowhere, shimmering in summer heat. It's an old barn, empty a long time, and its broad planks are silvered. Nothing much around it but yellow hills and red rock.

Long ago, somebody painted it with a mural. Still visible along its broad wall are the blobs representing massed crowds, the green diamond of a baseball park, and the primitive-heroic figure of an outfielder leaping, glove raised high. His cartoon eyes are wide and happy. The ball, radiating black lines of force, is sailing into his glove. Above him is painted the legend:

WHAT A CATCH!

And, in smaller letters below it:

1951, The Golden Year!

The old highway snakes just below the barn, where once the mural must have edified a long cavalcade of DeSotos, Packards and Oldsmobiles. But the old road is white and empty now, with thistles pushing through its cracks. The new highway runs straight across the plain below.

Down on the new highway, eighteen-wheeler rigs hurtle through, roaring like locomotives, and they are the only things to disturb the vast silence. The circling hawk makes no sound. The cottonwood trees by the edge of the dry stream are silent too, not a rustle or a creak along the whole row; but they do cast a thin gray shade, and the men waiting in the Volkswagen Bug are grateful for that.

They might be two cops on stakeout. They aren't. Not exactly.

"Are you going to tell me why we're sitting here, now?" asks the younger man, finishing his candy bar.

His name is Clete. The older man's name is Porfirio.

The older man shifts in his seat and looks askance at his partner. He doesn't approve of getting stoned on the job. But he shrugs, checks his weapon, settles into the most comfortable position he can find.

He points through the dusty windshield at the barn. "See up there? June 30, 1958, family of five killed. '46 Plymouth Club Coupe. Driver lost control of the car and went off the edge of the road. Car rolled seventy meters down that hill and hit the rocks, right there. Gas tank blew. Mr and Mrs William T. Ross of Visalia, California identified from dental records. Kids didn't have any dental records. No relatives to identify bodies.

"Articles in the local and Visalia papers, grave with the whole family's names and dates on one marker in a cemetery in Visalia.

Some blackening on the rocks up there. That's all there is to show it ever happened."

"Okay," say the younger man, nodding thoughtfully. "No witnesses, right?"

"That's right."

"The accident happened on a lonely road, and state troopers or whoever found the wreck after the fact?"

"Yeah."

"And the bodies were so badly burned they all went in one grave?" Clete looks pleased with himself. "So . . . forensic medicine being what it was in 1958, maybe there weren't five bodies in the car after all? Maybe one of the kids was thrown clear on the way down the hill? And if there was *somebody* in the future going through historical records, looking for incidents where children vanished without a trace, this might draw their attention, right?"

"It might," agrees Porfirio.

"So the Company sent an operative to see if any survivors could be salvaged," says Clete. "Okay, that's standard Company procedure. The Company took one of the kids alive, and he became an operative. So why are we here?"

Porfirio sighs, watching the barn.

"Because the kid didn't become an operative," he says. "He became a problem."

1958. Bobby Ross, all-American boy, was ten years old, and he loved baseball and cowboy movies and riding his bicycle. All-American boys get bored on long trips. Bobby got bored. He was leaning out the window of his parents' car when he saw the baseball mural on the side of the barn.

"Hey, look!" he yelled, and leaned *way* out the window to see better. He slipped.

"Jesus Christ!" screamed his mom, and lunging into the back she tried to grab the seat of his pants. She collided with his dad's arm. His dad cursed; the car swerved. Bobby felt himself gripped, briefly, and then all his mom had was one of his sneakers, and then the sneaker came off his foot. Bobby flew from the car just as it went over the edge of the road.

He remembered afterward standing there, clutching his broken arm, staring down the hill at the fire, and the pavement was hot as fire too on his sneakerless foot. His mind seemed to be stuck in a little circular track. He was really hurt bad, so what he had to do now was run to his mom and dad, who would yell at him and drive him to Dr Werts, and he'd have to sit in the cool green waiting room that smelled scarily of rubbing alcohol and look at dumb *Humpty Dumpty Magazine* until the doctor made everything all right again.

But that wasn't going to happen now, because . . .

But he was really hurt bad, so he needed to run to his mom and dad—

But he couldn't do that ever again, because—

But he was really hurt bad—

His mind just went round and round like that, until the spacemen came for him.

They wore silver suits, and they said, "Greetings, Earth Boy; we have come to rescue you and take you to Mars," but they looked just like ordinary people and in fact gave Bobby the impression they were embarrassed. Their space ship was real enough, though. They carried Bobby into it on a stretcher and took off, and a space doctor fixed his broken arm, and he was given space soda pop to drink, and he never even noticed that the silver ship had risen clear of the hillside, one step ahead of the state troopers, until he looked out and saw the curve of the Earth. He'd been lifted from history, as neatly as a fly ball smacking into an outfielder's mitt.

The spacemen didn't take Bobby Ross to Mars, though. It turned out to be some place in Australia. But it might just as well have been Mars. Because, instead of starting fifth grade, and then going onto high school, and getting interested in girls, and winning a baseball scholarship, and being drafted, and blown to pieces in Viet Nam – Bobby Ross became an immortal.

"Well, that happened to all of us," says Clete, shifting restively. "One way or another. Except I've never heard of the Company recruiting a kid as old as ten."

"That's right." Keeping his eyes on the barn, Porfirio reaches into the back seat and gropes in a cooler half-full of rapidly melting ice. He finds and draws out a bottle of soda. "So what does that tell you?"

Clete considers the problem. "Well, everybody knows you can't work the immortality process on somebody that old. You hear rumors, you know, like when the Company was starting out, that there were problems with some of the first test cases—" He stops himself and turns to stare at Porfirio. Porfirio meets his gaze but says nothing, twisting the top off his soda bottle.

"*This* guy was one of the test cases!" Clete exclaims. "And the Company didn't have the immortality process completely figured out yet, so they made a mistake."

Several mistakes had been made with Bobby Ross.

The first, of course, was that he was indeed too old to be made immortal. If two-year-old Patty or even five-year-old Jimmy had survived the crash, the process might have been worked successfully on them. Seat belts not having been invented in 1946, however, the Company had only Bobby with whom to work.

The second mistake had been in sending "spacemen" to collect Bobby. Bobby, as it happened, didn't like science fiction. He liked cowboys and baseball, but rocket ships left him cold. Movie posters and magazine covers featuring bug-eyed monsters scared him. If the operatives who had rescued him had come galloping over the hill on horseback, and had called him Pardner instead of Earth Boy, he'd undoubtedly have been as enchanted as they meant him to be and bought into the rest of the experience with a receptive mind. As it was, by the time he was offloaded into a laboratory in a hot red rocky landscape, he was far enough out of shock to have begun to be angry, and his anger focused on the bogusness of the spacemen.

The third mistake had been in the Company's choice of a mentor for Bobby.

Because the Company hadn't been in business very long – at least, as far as its stockholders knew – a lot of important things about the education of young immortals had yet to be discovered, such as: no mortal can train an immortal. Only another immortal understands the discipline needed, the pitfalls to be avoided when getting a child accustomed to the idea of eternal life.

But when Bobby was being made immortal, there weren't any other immortals yet – not successful ones, anyway – so the Company might be excused that error, at least. And if Professor Bill Riverdale was the last person who should have been in charge of Bobby, worse errors are made all the time. Especially by persons responsible for the welfare of young children.

After all, Professor Riverdale was a good, kind man. It was true that he was romantically obsessed with the idyll of all-American freckle-faced boyhood to an unhealthy degree, but he was so far in denial about it that he would never have done anything in the least improper.

All he wanted to do, when he sat down at Bobby's bedside, was help Bobby get over the tragedy. So he started with pleasant conversation. He told Bobby all about the wonderful scientists in the far future, who had discovered the secret of time travel, and how they were now working to find a way to make people live forever.

And Bobby, lucky boy, had been selected to help them. Instead of going to an orphanage, Bobby would be transformed into, well, nearly into a superhero! It was almost as though Bobby would never have to grow up. It was every boy's dream! He'd have super-strength and super-intelligence and never have to wash behind his ears, if he didn't feel like it! And, because he'd live forever, one day he really would get to go to the planet Mars.

If the immortality experiment worked. But Professor Riverdale – or Professor Bill, as he encouraged Bobby to call him – was sure the experiment would work this time, because such a lot had been learned from the last time it had been attempted.

Professor Bill moved quickly onto speak with enthusiasm of how wonderful the future was, and how happy Bobby would be when he got there. Why, it was a wonderful place, according to what he'd heard! People lived on the moon and on Mars too, and the problems of poverty and disease and war had been licked, by gosh, and there were *no Communists!* And boys could ride their bicycles down the tree-lined streets of that perfect world, and float down summer rivers on rafts, and camp out in the woods, and dream of going to the stars . . .

Observing, however, that Bobby lay there silent and withdrawn, Professor Bill cut his rhapsody short. He concluded that Bobby needed psychiatric therapy to get over the guilt he felt at having caused the deaths of his parents and siblings.

And this was a profound mistake, because Bobby Ross – being a normal ten-year-old all-American boy – had no more conscience than Pinocchio before the Cricket showed up, and it had never occurred to him that he had been responsible for the accident. Once Professor Bill pointed it out, however, he burst into furious tears.

So poor old Professor Bill had a lot to do to help Bobby through his pain, both the grief of his loss and the physical pain of his transformation into an immortal, of which there turned out to be a lot more than anybody had thought there would be, regardless of how much had been learned from the last attempt.

He studied Bobby's case, paying particular attention to the details of his recruitment. He looked carefully at the footage taken by the operatives who had collected Bobby, and the mural on the barn caught his attention. Tears came to his eyes when he realized that the sight of the ballplayer must have been Bobby's last happy memory, the final golden moment of his innocence.

"What'd he do?" asks Clete, taking his turn at rummaging in the ice chest. "Wait, I'll bet I know. He used the image of the mural in the kid's therapy, right? Something to focus on when the pain got too bad? Pretending he was going to a happy place in his head, as an escape valve."

"Yeah. That was what he did."

"There's only root beer left. You want one?"

"No, thanks."

"Well, so why was this such a bad idea? I remember having to do mental exercises like that, myself, at the Base school. You probably did, too."

"It was a bad idea because the Professor didn't know what the hell he was doing," says Porfirio. The distant barn is wavering in the heat, but he never takes his eyes off it.

Bobby's other doctors didn't know what the hell they were doing either. They'd figured out how to augment Bobby's intelligence pretty well, and they already knew how to give him unbreakable bones. They did a great job of convincing his body it would never die, and taught it how to ward off viruses and bacteria.

But they didn't know yet that even a healthy ten-year-old's DNA has already begun to deteriorate, that it's already too subject to replication errors for the immortality process to be successful. And Bobby Ross, being an all-American kid, had got all those freckles from playing unshielded in ultraviolet light. He'd gulped down soda pop full of chemicals and inhaled smoke from his dad's Lucky Strikes and hunted for tadpoles in the creek that flowed past the paper mill.

And then the doctors introduced millions of nanobots into Bobby's system, and the nanobots' job was to keep him perfect. But the doctors didn't know yet that the nanobots had to be programmed with an example to copy. So the nanobots latched onto the first DNA helix they encountered, and made it their pattern for everything Bobby ought to be. Unfortunately, it was a damaged DNA helix, but the nanobots didn't know that.

Bobby Ross grew up at the secret laboratory, and as he grew it became painfully obvious that there were still a few bugs to be worked out of the immortality process. There were lumps, there were bumps, there were skin cancers and deformities. His production of pineal tribrantine three was sporadic. Sometimes, after months of misery, his body's chemistry would right itself. The joint pain would ease, the glands would work properly again.

Or not.

Professor Bill was so, so sorry, because he adored Bobby. He'd sit with Bobby when the pain was bad, and talk soothingly to send Bobby back to that dear good year, 1951 – and what a golden age 1951 seemed by this time, because it was now 1964, and Bobby had become Robert, and the world seemed to be lurching into madness. Professor Bill himself wished he could escape back into 1951. But he sent Robert there often, into that beautiful summer afternoon when Hank Bauer had leaped so high from the green diamond – and the ball had *smacked* into his leather glove – and the crowds went wild!

Though only in Robert's head, of course, because all this was being done with hypnosis.

Nobody ever formally announced that Robert Ross had failed the immortality process, because it was by no means certain he wasn't immortal. But it had become plain he would never be the flawless super-agent the Company had been solving for, so less and less of the laboratory budget was allotted to Robert's upkeep.

What did the Company do with unsuccessful experiments? Who knows what might have happened to Robert, if Professor Bill hadn't taken the lad under his wing?

He brought Robert to live with him in his own quarters on the Base, and continued his education himself. This proved that Professor Bill really was a good man and had no ulterior interest in Robert whatsoever; for Bobby, the slender kid with skin like a sun-speckled apricot, was long gone. Robert by this time was a wizened, stooping, scarred thing with hair in unlikely places.

Professor Bill tried to make it up to Robert by giving him a rich interior life. He went rafting with Robert on the great river of numbers, under the cold and sparkling stars of theory. He tossed him physics problems compact and weighty as a baseball, and beamed with pride when Robert smacked them out of the park of human understanding. It made him feel young again, himself.

He taught the boy all he knew, and when he found that Robert shone at Temporal Physics with unsuspected brilliance, he told his superiors. This pleased the Company managers. It meant that Robert could be made to earn back the money he had cost the Company, after all. So he became an employee, and was even paid a modest stipend to exercise his genius by fiddling around with temporal equations on the Company's behalf.

"And the only problem was, he was a psycho?" guesses Clete. "He went berserk, blew away poor old Professor Riverdale and ran off into the sunset?"

"He was emotionally unstable," Porfirio admits. "Nobody was surprised by that, after what he'd been through. But he didn't kill Professor Riverdale. He did run away, though. Walked, actually. He walked through a solid wall, in front of the Professor and about fifteen other people in the audience. He'd been giving them a lecture in advanced temporal paradox theory. Just smiled at them suddenly, put down his chalk, and stepped right through the blackboard. He wasn't on the other side, when they ran into the next room to see."

"Damn," says Clete, impressed. "*We* can't do that."

"We sure can't," says Porfirio. He stiffens, suddenly, seeing something move on the wall of the barn. It's only the shadow of the circling hawk, though, and he relaxes.

Clete's eyes have widened, and he looks worried.

"You just threw me a grenade," he says. *Catching a grenade* is security slang for being made privy to secrets so classified one's own safety is compromised.

"You needed to know," says Porfirio.

The search for Robert Ross had gone on for years, in the laborious switchback system of time within which the Company operated. The mortals running the 1964 operation had hunted him with predictable lack of success. After the ripples from that particular causal wave had subsided, the mortal masters up in the twenty-fourth century set their immortal agents on the problem.

The ones who were security technicals, that is. The rank-and-file Preservers and Facilitators weren't supposed to know that there had ever been mistakes like Robert Ross. This made searching for him that much harder, but secrecy has its price.

It was assumed that Robert, being a genius in Temporal Physics, had somehow managed to escape into Time. Limitless as Time was, Robert might still be found within it. The operatives in charge of the case reasoned that a needle dropped into a haystack must gravitate toward any magnets concealed in the straw. Were there any magnets that might attract Robert Ross?

"Baseball!" croaked Professor Riverdale, when Security Executive Tvashtar had gone to the nursing home to interview him. "Bobby just loved baseball. You mark my words, he'll be at some baseball game somewhere. If he's in remission, he'll even be on some little town team."

With trembling hands he drew a baseball from the pocket of his dressing gown and held it up, cupping it in both hands as though he presented Tvashtar with a crystal wherein the future was revealed.

"He and I used to play catch with this. You might say it's the egg out of which all our hopes and dreams hatch. Peanuts and Crackerjack! The crack of the bat! The boys of summer. Bobby was the boy of summer. Sweet Bobby ... He'd have given anything to have played the game ... It's a symbol, young man, of everything that's fine and good and American."

Tvashtar nodded courteously, wondering why mortals in this era assumed the Company was run by Americans, and why they took it for granted that a stick-and-ball game had deep mystical significance. But he thanked Professor Riverdale, and left the 1970s gratefully. Then he organized a sweep through Time, centering on baseball.

"And it didn't pan out," says Clete. "Obviously."

"It didn't pan out," Porfirio agrees. "The biggest search operation the Company ever staged, up to that point. You know how much work was involved?"

It had been a lot of work. The operatives had to check out every obscure minor-league player who ever lived, to say nothing of investigating every batboy and ballpark janitor and even bums who slept under the bleachers, from 1845 to 1965. Nor was it safe to assume Robert might not be lurking beyond the fruited plains and amber waves of grain; there were Mexican, Cuban and Japanese leagues to be investigated. Porfirio, based at that time in California, had spent the Great Depression sweeping up peanut shells from Stockton to San Diego, but neither he nor anyone else ever caught a glimpse of Robert Ross.

It was reluctantly concluded that Professor Riverdale hadn't had a clue about what was going on in Robert's head. But, since Robert had never shown up again anywhere, the investigation was quietly dropped.

Robert Ross might never have existed, or indeed died with his mortal family. The only traces left of him were in the refinements made to the immortality process after his disappearance, and in the new rules made concerning recruitment of young operatives.

The Company never acknowledged that it had made any defectives.

*   *   *

"Just like that, they dropped the investigation?" Clete demands. "When this guy knew how to go places without getting into a time transcendence chamber? Apparently?"

"What do you think?" says Porfirio.

Clete mutters something mildly profane and reaches down into the paper bag between his feet. He pulls out a can of potato chips and pops the lid. He eats fifteen chips in rapid succession, gulps root beer, and then says:

"Well, obviously they *didn't* drop the investigation, because here we are. Or something happened to make them open it again. They got a new lead?"

Porfirio nods.

1951. Porfirio was on standby in Los Angeles. Saturday morning in a quiet neighborhood, each little house on its square of lawn, rows of them along tree-lined streets. In most houses, kids were sprawled on the floor reading comic books or listening to Uncle Whoa-Bill on the radio, as long low morning sunlight slanted in through screen doors. In one or two houses, though, kids sat staring at a cabinet in which was displayed a small glowing image brought by orthicon tube; for the Future, or a piece of it anyway, had arrived.

Porfirio was in the breakfast room, with a cup of coffee and the sports sections from the *Times*, the *Herald Express*, the *Examiner* and the *Citizen News*, and he was scanning for a certain profile, a certain configuration of features. He was doing this purely out of habit, because he'd been off the case for years; but, being immortal, he had a lot of time on his hands. Besides, he had all the instincts of a good cop.

But he had other instincts, too, even more deeply ingrained than hunting, and so he noticed the clamor from the living room, though it wasn't very loud. He looked up, scowling, as three-year-old Isabel rushed into the room in her nightgown.

"What is it, mi hija?"

She pointed into the living room. "Maria's bad! The scary man is on the TV," she said tearfully. He opened his arms and she ran to him.

"Maria, are you scaring your sister?" he called.

"She's just being a dope," an impatient little voice responded.

He carried Isabel into the living room, and she gave a scream and turned her face over his shoulder so she wouldn't see the television screen. Six-year-old Maria, on the other hand, stared at it as though hypnotized. Before her on the coffee table, two little bowls of Cheerios sat untasted, rapidly going soggy in their milk.

Porfirio frowned down at his great-great-great-great-(and several more greats) grand-niece. "Don't call your sister a dope. What's going on? It sounded like a rat fight in here."

"She's scared of the Amazing No Man, so she wanted me to turn him off, but he's *not* scary," said Maria. "And I want to see him."

"You were supposed to be watching *Cartoon Circus*," said Porfirio, glancing at the screen.

"Uh-huh, but Mr Ringmaster has people on sometimes too," Maria replied. "See?

Porfirio looked again. Then he sat down beside Maria on the couch and stared very hard at the screen. On his arm, Isabel kicked and made tiny complaining noises over his shoulder until he absently fished a stick of gum from his shirt pocket and offered it to her.

"Who is this guy?" he asked Maria.

"The Amazing No Man," she explained. "Isn't he *strange*?"

"Yeah," he said, watching. "Eat your cereal, honey."

And he sat there beside her as she ate, though when she dripped milk from her spoon all over her nightgown because she wasn't paying attention as she ate, he didn't notice, because he wasn't paying attention either. It was hard to look away from the TV.

A wizened little person wandered to and fro before the camera, singing nonsense in an eerily high-pitched voice. Every so often he would stop, as though he had just remembered something, and grope inside his baggy clothing. He would then produce something improbable from an inner pocket: a string of sausages. A bunch of bananas. A bottle of milk. An immense cello and bow. A kite, complete with string and tail.

He greeted each item with widely pantomimed surprise, and a cry of "*Woooowwwwww!*" He pretended he was offering the sausages to an invisible dog, and made them disappear from his hand as though it were really eating them. He played a few notes on the cello. He made the kite hover in midair beside him, and did a little soft-shoe dance, and the kite bobbed along with him as though it were alive. His wordless music never stopped, never developed into a melody, just modulated to the occasional *Wowww* as he pretended to make another discovery.

More and more stuff came out of the depths of his coat, to join a growing heap on the floor: sixteen bunches of bananas. A dressmaker's dummy. A live sheep on a leash. An old-fashioned Victrola, complete with horn. A stuffed penguin. A bouquet of flowers. A suit of armor. At last, the pile was taller than the man himself. He turned, looked full into the camera with a weird smile, and winked.

Behind Porfirio's eyes, a red light flashed. A readout overlaid his vision momentarily, giving measurements, points of similarity and statistical percentages of matchup. Then it receded, but Porfirio had already figured out the truth.

The man proceeded to stuff each item back into his coat, one after another.

"See? Where does he make them all go?" asked Maria, in a shaky voice. "They can't all fit in there!"

"It's just stage magicians' tricks, mi hija," said Porfirio. He observed that her knuckles were white, her eyes wide. "I think this is maybe too scary for you. Let's turn it off, okay?"

"I'm not scared! He's just . . . funny," she said.

"Well, your little sister is scared," Porfirio told her, and rose and changed the channel, just as Hector wandered from the bedroom in his pajamas, blinking like an owl.

"Popi, Uncle Frio won't let me watch Amazing No Man!" Maria complained.

"What, the scary clown?" Hector rolled his eyes. "Honey, you know that guy gives you nightmares."

"I have to go out," said Porfirio, handing Isabel over to her father.

"You were living with mortals? Who were these people?" asks Clete.

"I had a brother, when I was mortal," says Porfirio. "I check up on his descendants now and then. Which has nothing to do with this case, okay? But that's where I was when I spotted Robert Ross. All the time we'd been looking for a baseball player, he'd been working as the Amazing Gnomon."

"And a gnomon is the piece on a sundial that throws the shadow," says Clete promptly. He grins. "Sundials. Time. Temporal physics. They just can't resist leaving clues, can they?"

Porfirio shakes his head. Clete finishes the potato chips, tilting the can to get the last bits.

"So when the guy was programmed with a Happy Place, it wasn't baseball he fixated on," he speculates. "It was 1951. 'The Golden Year'. He had a compulsion to be there in 1951, maybe?"

Porfirio says nothing.

"So, how did it go down?" says Clete, looking expectant.

It hadn't gone down, at least not then.

Porfirio had called for backup, because it would have been fatally stupid to have done otherwise, and by the time he presented his LAPD badge at the studio door, the Amazing Gnomon had long since finished his part of the broadcast and gone home.

The station manager at KTLA couldn't tell him much. The Amazing Gnomon had his checks sent to a post office box. He didn't have an agent. Nobody knew where he lived. He just showed up on time every third Saturday and hit his mark, and he worked on a closed set, but that wasn't unusual with stage magicians.

"Besides," said the mortal with a shudder, "he never launders that costume. He gets under those lights and believe me, brother, we're glad to clear the set. The cameraman has to put Vapo-rub up his nose before he can stand to be near the guy. Hell of an act, though, isn't it?"

The scent trail had been encouraging, even if it had only led to a locker in a downtown bus station. The locker, when opened, proved to contain the Amazing Gnomon's stage costume: a threadbare old overcoat, a pair of checked trousers, and clown shoes. They were painfully foul, but contained no hidden pockets or double linings where anything might be concealed, nor any clue to their owner's whereabouts.

By this time, however, the Company had marshaled all available security techs on the West Coast, so it wasn't long before they tracked down Robert Ross.

Then all they had to do was figure out what the hell to do next.

Clete's worried look has returned.

"Holy shit, I never thought about that. How do you arrest one of *us*?" he asks.

Porfirio snarls in disgust. His anger is not with Clete, but with the executive who saddled him with Clete.

"Are you ready to catch another grenade, kid?" he inquires, and without waiting for Clete's answer he extends his arm forward, stiffly, with the palm up. He has to lean back in his seat to avoid hitting the Volkswagen's windshield. He drops his hand sharply backward, like Spiderman shooting web fluid, and Clete just glimpses the bright point of a weapon emerging from Porfirio's sleeve. Pop, like a cobra's fang, it hits the windshield and retracts again, out of sight. It leaves a bead of something pale pink on the glass.

"Too cool," says Clete, though he is uneasily aware that he has no weapon like that. He clears his throat, wondering how he can ask what the pink stuff is without sounding frightened. He has always been told operatives are immune to any poison.

"It's not poison," says Porfirio, reading his mind. "It's derived from Theobromos. If I stick you in the leg with this, you'll sleep like a baby for twelve hours. That's all."

"Oh. Okay," says Clete, and it very much isn't okay, because a part of the foundation of his world has just crumbled.

"You can put it in another operative's drink, or you can inject it with an arm-mounted rig like this one," Porfirio explains patiently. "You can't shoot it in a dart, because any one of us could grab the dart out of the air, right? You have to close with whoever it is you're supposed to take down, go hand to hand.

"But first, you have to get the other guy in a trap."

Robert Ross had been in a trap. He seemed to have chosen it.

He turned out to be living in Hollywood, in an old residency hotel below Franklin. The building was squarely massive, stone, and sat like a megalith under the hill. Robert had a basement apartment with one tiny window on street level, at the back. He might have seen daylight for an hour at high summer down in there, but he'd have to stand on a stool to do it. And wash the window first.

· The sub-executive in charge of the operation had looked at the reconnaissance reports and shaken his head. If an operative wanted a safe place to hide, he'd choose a flimsy frame building, preferably surrounding himself with mortals. There were a hundred cheap boarding houses in Los Angeles that would have protected Robert Ross. The last place any sane immortal would try to conceal himself would be a basement dug into granite with exactly one door, where he might be penned in by other immortals and unable to break out through a wall.

The sub-executive decided that Robert *wanted* to be brought in.

It seemed to make a certain sense. Living in a place like that, advertising his presence on television; Robert must be secretly longing for some kindly mentor to find him and tell him it was time to come home. Alternatively, he might be daring the Company problem solvers to catch him. Either way, he wasn't playing with a full deck.

So the sub-executive made the decision to send in a psychologist. A *mortal* psychologist. Not a security tech with experience in apprehending immortal fugitives, though several ringed the building and one – Porfirio, in fact – was stationed outside the single tiny window that opened below the sidewalk on Franklin Avenue.

Porfirio had leaned against the wall, pretending to smoke and watch the traffic zooming by. He could hear Robert Ross breathing in the room below. He could hear his heartbeat. He heard the polite double knock on the door, and the slight intake of breath; he heard the gentle voice saying, "Bobby, may I come in?"

"It's not locked," was the reply, and Porfirio started. The voice belonged to a ten-year-old boy.

He heard the click and creak as the door opened, and the sound of two heartbeats within the room, and the psychologist saying: "We had quite a time finding you, Bobby. May I sit down?"

"Sure," said the child's voice.

"Thank you, Bobby," said the other, and Porfirio heard the scrape of a chair. "Oh, dear, are you all right? You're bleeding through your bandage."

"I'm all right. That's just where I had the tumor removed. It grows back a lot. I go up to the twenty-first century for laser surgery. Little clinics in out-of-the-way places, you know? I go there all the time, but you never notice."

"You've been very clever at hiding from us, Bobby. We'd never have found you if you hadn't been on television. We've been searching for you for years."

"In your space ships?" said the child's voice, with adult contempt.

"In our time machines," said the psychologist. "Professor Riverdale was sure you'd run away to become a baseball player."

"I can't ever be a baseball player," replied Robert Ross coldly. "I can't run fast enough. One of my legs grew shorter than the other. Professor Bill never noticed that, though, did he?"

"I'm so sorry, Bobby."

"Good old Professor Bill, huh? I tried being a cowboy, and a soldier, and a fireman, and a bunch of other stuff. Now I'm a clown. But I can't ever be a baseball player. No home runs for Bobby."

Out of the corner of his eye, Porfirio saw someone laboring up the hill toward him from Highland Avenue. He turned his head and saw the cop.

The too-patient adult voice continued:

"Bobby, there are a lot of other things you can be in the Future."

"I hate the Future."

Porfirio watched the cop's progress as the psychologist hesitated, then pushed on:

"Do you like being a clown, Bobby?"

"I guess so," said Robert. "At least people *see* me when they look at me now. The man outside the window saw me, too."

There was a pause. The cop was red-faced from the heat and his climb, but he was grinning at Porfirio.

"Well, Bobby, that's one of our security men, out there to keep you safe."

"I know perfectly well why he's there," Robert said. "He doesn't scare me. I want him to hear what I have to say, so he can tell Professor Bill and the rest of them."

"What do you want to tell us, Bobby?" said the psychologist, a little shakily.

There was a creak, as though someone had leaned forward in a chair.

"You know why you haven't caught me? Because I figured out how to go to 1951 all by myself. And I've been living in it, over and over and over. The Company doesn't think that's possible, because of the variable permeability of temporal fabric, but it is. The trick is to go to a different *place* every *time*. There's just one catch."

The cop paused to wipe sweat off his brow, but he kept his eyes on Porfirio.

"What's the catch, Bobby?"

"Do you know what happens when you send something back to the same year often enough?" Robert sounded amused. "Like, about a hundred million times?"

"No, Bobby, I don't know."

"I know. I experimented. I tried it the first time with a wheel off a toy car. I sent it to 1912, over and over, until . . . do you know where Tunguska is?"

"What are you trying to tell me, Bobby?" The psychologist was losing his professional voice.

"Then," said Robert, "I increased the mass of the object. I sent a baseball back. Way back. Do you know what really killed off the dinosaurs?"

"Hey there, zoot suit," said the cop, when he was close enough. "You wouldn't be loitering, would you?"

". . . You can wear a hole in the fabric of space and time," Robert was saying. "And it just might destroy everything in the whole world. You included. And if you were pretty sick of being alive, but you couldn't die, that might seem like a great idea. Don't you think?"

There was the sound of a chair being pushed back.

Porfirio grimaced and reached into his jacket for his badge, but the cop pinned Porfirio's hand to his chest with the tip of his nightstick.

"Bobby, we can help you!" cried the psychologist.

"I'm not little Bobby anymore, you asshole," said the child's voice, rising. "I'm a million, million years old."

Porfirio looked the cop in the eye.

"Vice squad," he said. The cop sagged. Porfirio produced his badge.

"But I got a tip from one of the residents here—" said the cop.

"*Woooowwwww*," said the weird little singsong voice, and there was a brief scream.

"What happened?" demands Clete. He has gone very pale.

"We never found out," says Porfirio. "By the time I got the patrolman to leave and ran around to the front of the building, the other techs had already gone in and secured the room. The only problem was, there was nothing to secure. The room was empty. No sign of Ross, or the mortal either. No furniture, even, except a couple of wooden chairs. He hadn't been living there. He'd just used the place to lure us in."

"Did anybody ever find the mortal?"

"Yeah, as a matter of fact," Porfirio replies. "Fifty years later. In London."

"He'd gone forward in time?" Clete exclaims. "But that's supposed to be impossible. Isn't it?"

Porfirio sighs.

"So they say, kid. Anyway, he hadn't gone forward in time. Remember, about ten years ago, when archaeologists were excavating that medieval hospital over there? They found hundreds of skeletons in its cemetery. Layers and layers of the dead. And – though this didn't make it into the news, not even into the *Fortean Times* – one of the skeletons was wearing a Timex."

Clete giggles shrilly.

"Was it still ticking?" he asks. "What the hell are you telling me? There's this crazy immortal guy on the loose, and he's able to time-travel just using his brain, and he wants to destroy the whole world and he's figured out how, *and we're just sitting here?*"

"You have a better idea?" says Porfirio. "Please tell me if you do, okay?"

Clete controls himself with effort.

"All right, what did the Company do?" he asks. "There's a plan, isn't there, for taking him out? There must be, or we wouldn't be here now."

Porfirio nods.

"But what are we doing here *now*?" says Clete. "Shouldn't we be in 1951, where he's hiding? Wait, no, we probably shouldn't, because that'd place even more strain on the fabric of time and space. Or whatever."

"It would," Porfirio agrees.

"So ... here we are at the place where Bobby Ross was recruited. The Company must expect he's going to come back here. Because this is where he caused the accident. Because the criminal always returns to the scene of the crime, right?" Clete babbles.

"Maybe," says Porfirio. "The Company already knows he leaves 1951 sometimes, for medical treatment."

"And sooner or later he'll be driven to come *here*," says Clete, and now he too is staring fixedly at the barn. "And – and today is June 30, 2008. The car crash happened fifty years ago today. That's why we're here."

"He might come," says Porfirio. "So we just wait—" He stiffens, stares hard, and Clete stares hard too and sees the little limping figure walking up the old road, just visible through the high weeds.

"Goddamn," says Clete, and is out of the car in a blur, ejecting candy bar wrappers and potato chip cans as he goes, and Porfirio curses and tells him to wait, but it's too late; Clete has crossed the highway in a bound and is running across the valley, as fast as only an immortal can go. Porfirio races after him, up that bare yellow hill with its red rocks that still bear faint carbon traces of horror, and he clears the edge of the road in time to hear Clete bellow:

"Security! Freeze!"

"Don't—" says Porfirio, just as Clete launches himself forward to tackle Robert Ross.

Robert is smiling, lifting his arms as though in a gesture of surrender. Despite the heat, he is wearing a long overcoat. Its lining is torn, just under his arm, and where the sweat-stained rayon satin hangs down Porfirio glimpses fathomless black night, white stars.

"*Lalala la la*. Woooowww," says Robert Ross, just as Clete hits him. Clete shrieks and then is gone, sucked into the void of stars.

Porfirio stands very still. Robert winks at him.

"What a catch!" he says, in ten-year-old Bobby's voice.

It's hot up there, on the old white road, under the blue summer sky. Porfirio feels sweat prickling between his shoulderblades.

"Hey, Mr Policeman," says Robert, "I remember you. Did you tell the Company what you heard? Have they been thinking about what I'm going to do? Have they been scared, all these years?"

"Sure they have, Mr Ross," says Porfirio, flexing his hands.

Robert frowns. "Come on, *Mr Ross* was my father. I'm Bobby."

"Oh, I get it. That would be the Mr Ross who died right down there?" Porfirio points. "In the crash? Because his kid was so stupid he didn't know better than to lean out the window of a moving car?"

An expression of amazement crosses the wrinkled, dirty little face, to be replaced with white-hot rage.

"Faggot! Don't you call me stupid!" screams Robert. "I'm brilliant! I can make the whole world come to an end if I want to!"

"You made it come to an end for your family, anyway," says Porfirio.

"No, I didn't," says Robert, clenching his fists. "Professor Bill explained about that. It just happened. Accidents happen all the time. I was innocent."

"Yeah, but Professor Bill lied to you, didn't he?" says Porfirio. "Like, about how wonderful it would be to live forever?"

His voice is calm, almost bored. Robert says nothing. He looks at Porfirio with tears in his eyes, but there is hate there too.

"Hey, Bobby," says Porfirio, moving a step closer. "Did it ever once occur to you to come back here and prevent the accident? I mean, it's impossible, sure, but didn't you even think of giving it a try? Messing with causality? It might have been easy, for a super-powered genius kid like you. But you didn't, did you? I can see it in your eyes."

Robert glances uncertainly down the hill, where in some dimension a 1946 Plymouth is still blackening, windows shattering, popping, and the dry summer grass is vanishing around it as the fire spreads outward like a black pool.

"What do you think, Bobby? Maybe pushed the grandfather paradox, huh? Gone back to see if you couldn't bend the rules, burn down this barn before the mural was painted? Or even broken Hank Bauer's arm, so the Yankees didn't win the World Series in 1951? I can think of a couple of dozen different things I'd have tried, Bobby, if I'd had superpowers like you.

"But you never even tried. Why was that, Bobby?"

"*La la la*," murmurs Robert, opening his arms again and stepping toward Porfirio. Porfirio doesn't move. He looks Robert in the face and says:

"You're stupid. Unfinished. You never grew up, Bobby."

"Professor Bill said never growing up was a good thing," says Robert.

"Professor Bill said that because he never grew up either," says Porfirio. "You weren't real to him, Bobby. He never saw *you* when he looked at you."

"No, he never did," says Robert, in a thick voice because he is crying. "He just saw what he wanted me to be. Freckle-faced kid!" He points bitterly at the brown discoloration that covers half his cheek. "Look at me now!"

"Yeah, and you'll never be a baseball player. And you're still so mad about that, all you can think of to do is to pay the Company back," says Porfirio, taking a step toward him.

"That's right!" sobs Robert.

"With the whole eternal world to explore, and a million other ways to be happy – still, all you want is to pay them back," says Porfirio, watching him carefully.

"Yeah!" cries Robert, panting. He wipes his nose on his dirty sleeve. He looks up again, sharply. "I mean . . . I mean . . ."

"See? Stupid. And you're not a good boy, Bobby," says Porfirio gently. "You're a goddamn monster. You're trying to blow up a whole world full of innocent people. You know what should happen, now? Your dad ought to come walking up that hill, madder than hell, and punish you."

Robert looks down the hillside.

"But he can't, ever again," he says. He sounds tired.

Porfirio has already moved, and before the last weary syllable is out of his mouth Robert feels the scorpion-sting in his arm.

He whirls around, but Porfirio has already retreated, withdrawn up the hillside. He stands before the mural, and the painted outfielder smiles over his shoulder. Robert clutches his arm, beginning to cry afresh.

"No fair," he protests. But he knows it's more than fair. It is even a relief.

He falls to his knees, whimpering at the heat of the old road's surface. He crawls to the side and collapses, in the yellow summer grass.

"Will I have to go to the Future now?" Robert asks piteously.

"No, son. No Future," Porfirio replies.

Robert nods and closes his eyes. He could sink through the rotating earth if he tried, escape once again into 1951; instead he floats away from time itself, into the back of his father's hand.

Porfirio walks down the hill toward him. As he does so, an all-terrain vehicle comes barreling up the old road, mowing down thistles in its path.

It shudders to a halt and Clete leaps out, leaving the door open in his headlong rush up the hill. He is not wearing the same suit he wore when last seen by Porfirio.

"You stinking son of a bitch *defective*," he roars, and aims a kick at Robert's head. Porfirio grabs his arm.

"Take it easy," he says.

"He sent me back six hundred thousand years! Do you know how long I had to wait before the Company even opened a damn transport depot?" says Clete, and looking at his smooth ageless face Porfirio can see that ages have passed over it. Clete now has permanently furious eyes. Their glare bores into Porfirio like acid. *No convenience stores in 598,000 BC, huh?* Porfirio thinks to himself.

"You knew he was going to do this to me, didn't you?" demands Clete.

"No," says Porfirio. "All I was told was, there'd be complications to the arrest. And you should have known better than to rush the guy."

"You got that right," says Clete, shrugging off his hand. "So why don't you do the honors?"

He goes stalking back to his transport, and hauls a body bag from the back seat. Porfirio sighs. He reaches into his coat and withdraws what looks like a screwdriver handle. When he thumbs a button on its side, however, a half-circle of blue light forms at one end. He tests it with a random slice through a thistle, which falls over at once. He leans down and scans Robert Ross carefully, because he wants to be certain he is unconscious.

"I'm sorry," he murmurs.

Working with the swiftness of long practice, he does his job. Clete returns, body bag under his arm, watching with grim satisfaction. Hank Bauer is still smiling down from the mural.

When the disassembly is finished, Porfirio loads the body bag into the car and climbs in beside it. Clete gets behind the wheel and backs carefully down the road. Bobby Ross may not be able to die, but he is finally on his way to eternal rest.

The Volkswagen sits there rusting for a month before it is stolen.

The blood remains on the old road for four months, before autumn rains wash it away, but they do wash it away. By the next summer the yellow grass is high, and the road as white as innocence once more.

REAL TIME

Lawrence Watt Evans

Patrolling the past will not be without its hazards and the following story is all the more powerful and memorable because of its brevity.

Lawrence Watt Evans established his reputation as a writer of high fantasy with The Lure of the Basilisk *(1980), the first of his Lords of Dus series, but he has since written many science-fiction stories and novels, starting with* The Chromosomal Code *(1984).*

Someone was tampering with time again; I could feel it, in my head and in my gut, that sick, queasy sensation of unreality.

I put my head down and gulped air, waiting for the discomfort to pass, but it only got worse.

This was a bad one. Someone was tampering with something serious. This wasn't just someone reading tomorrow's papers and playing the stock market; this was *serious*. Someone was trying to change history.

I couldn't allow that. Not only might his tampering interfere with my own past, change my whole life, possibly even wipe me out of existence, but I'd be shirking my job. I couldn't do that.

Not that anyone would know. They must think I'm dead. I haven't been contacted in years now, not since I was stranded in this century. They must think I was lost when my machine and my partner vanished in the flux.

But I'm not dead, and I had a job to do. With help from head-quarters or without, with a partner or without, even with my machine or without, I had a job to do, a reality to preserve, a whole world to safeguard. I knew my duty. I *know* my duty. The past can't take tampering.

They might send someone else, but they might not. The tampering might have already changed things too much. They might not spot it in time. Or they might simply not have the manpower. Time travel lets you use your manpower efficiently, with 100 per cent efficiency, putting it anywhere you need it instantly, but that's not enough when you have all of the past to guard, everything from the dawn of time to the present – not *this* present, the *real* present – you'd need a million men to guard it all, and they've always had trouble recruiting. The temptations are too great. The dangers are too great. Look at me, stuck here in the past, for the dangers – and as for the temptations, look at what I have to do. People trying to *change* everything, trying to benefit themselves at the cost of reality itself – they need men they can *trust*, men like me, and there can never be enough of us.

I sat up straight again and I looked at the mirror behind the bar and I knew what I had to do. I had to stop the tampering. Just as I had stopped it before, three – no, four – four times now.

They might send someone else, but they might not, and I couldn't take that chance.

I had to find the tamperer myself, and deal with him. If I couldn't find him directly, if he wasn't in this time period but later, then I might need to tamper with time myself, to change *his* past without hurting *mine*.

That's tricky, but I've done it.

I slid off the stool and stood up, gulped the rest of my drink, and laid a bill on the bar – five dollars in the currency of the day. I shrugged, straightening my coat, and I stepped out into the cool of a summer night.

Insects sang somewhere, strange insects extinct before I was born, and the streetlights pooled pale grey across the black sidewalks. I turned my head slowly, feeling the flux, feeling the shape of the time-stream, of my reality.

Downtown was firm, solid, still rooted in the past and the present and secure in the future. Facing in the opposite direction I felt my gut twist. I crossed the empty street to my car.

I drove out the avenues, ignoring the highways. I can't feel as well on the highways; they're too far out of the city's life-flow.

I went north, then east, and the nausea gripped me tighter with every block. It became a gnawing pain in my belly as the world shimmered and shifted around me, an unstable reality. I stopped the car by the side of the street and forced the pain down, forced my perception of the world to steady itself.

When I was ready to go on I leaned over and checked in the glove compartment. No gloves – the name was already an anachronism even in this time period. But my gun was there. Not my service weapon; that's an anachronism, too advanced. I don't dare use it. The knowledge of its existence could be dangerous. No, I had bought a gun here, in this era.

I pulled it out and put it in my coat pocket. The weight of it, that hard, metal tugging at my side, felt oddly comforting.

I had a knife, too. I was dealing with primitives, with savages, not with civilized people. These final decades of the twentieth century, with their brushfire wars and nuclear arms races, were a jungle, even in the great cities of North America. I had a knife, a good one, with a six-inch blade I had sharpened myself.

Armed, I drove on, and two blocks later I had to leave the avenue, turn onto the quiet side-streets, tree-lined and peaceful.

Somewhere, in that peace, someone was working to destroy my home, my life, my *self*.

I turned again, and felt the queasiness and pain leap within me, and I knew I was very close.

I stopped the car and got out, the gun in my pocket and my hand on the gun, my other hand holding the knife.

One house had a light in the window; the homes on either side were dark. I scanned, and I knew that that light was it, the center of the unreality – maybe not the tamperer himself, but something, a focus for the disturbance of the flow of history.

Perhaps it was an ancestor of the tamperer; I had encountered that before.

I walked up the front path and rang the bell.

I braced myself, the knife in one hand, the gun in the other.

The porch light came on, and the door started to open. I threw myself against it.

It burst in, and I went through it, and I was standing in a hallway. A man in his forties was staring at me, holding his wrist where the door had slammed into it as it pulled out of his grip. There had been no chain-bolt; my violence had, perhaps, been more than was necessary.

I couldn't take risks, though. I pointed the gun at his face and squeezed the trigger.

The thing made a report like the end of the world, and the man fell, blood and tissue sprayed across the wall behind him.

A woman screamed from a nearby doorway, and I pointed the gun at her, unsure.

The pain was still there. It came from the woman. I pulled the trigger again.

She fell, blood red on her blouse, and I looked down at her as the pain faded, as stability returned.

I was *real* again.

If the man were her husband, perhaps she was destined to remarry, or to be unfaithful – *she* would have been the tamperer's ancestor, but *he* might not have been. The twisting of time had stopped only when the woman fell.

I regretted shooting him, then, but I had had no choice. Any delay might have been fatal. The life of an individual is precious, but not as precious as history itself.

A twinge ran through my stomach; perhaps only an aftereffect, but I had to be certain. I knelt, and went quickly to work with my knife.

When I was done, there could be no doubt that the two were dead, and that neither could ever have children.

Finished, I turned and fled, before the fumbling police of this era could interfere.

I knew the papers would report it the next day as the work of a lunatic, of a deranged thief who panicked before he could take anything, or of someone killing for perverted pleasure. I didn't worry about that.

I had saved history again.

I wish there were another way, though.

Sometimes I have nightmares about what I do; sometimes I dream that I've made a mistake, killed the wrong person, that I stranded myself here. What if it wasn't a mechanical failure that sent the machine into flux. What if I changed my own past and did that to myself?

I have those nightmares sometimes.

Worse, though, the very worst nightmares, are the ones where I dream that I never changed the past at all, that I never lived in any time but this one, that I grew up here, alone, through an unhappy childhood and a miserable adolescence and a sorry adulthood – that I never travelled in time, that it's all in my mind, that I killed those people for nothing.

That's the worst of all, and I wake up from that one sweating, ready to scream.

Thank God it's not true.

THE CHRONOLOGY PROTECTION CASE

Paul Levinson

We close this short sequence with a story that takes the basic concept of Fritz Leiber's "Try and Change the Past" and develops it to the ultimate, exploring how time and the universe protects itself.

Paul Levinson is Professor of Communication and Media Studies at Fordham University in New York City and has written extensively on the subject in Mind at Large *(1988),* The Soft Edge *(1997),* New New Media *(2009) and many similar books. He also finds the time to broadcast regularly on radio and TV, write songs and the occasional science-fiction story. The following introduced his forensic scientist and investigator Phil D'Amato, who finds himself up against the mysteries of the universe and the perils of alternate sciences. He features in two more short stories and the novels* The Silk Code *(1999),* The Consciousness Plague *(2002) and* The Pixel Eye *(2003). Amongst his other novels is the time-travel adventure* The Plot to Save Socrates *(2006).*

Carl put the call through just as I was packing up for the day. "She says she's some kind of physicist," he said, and although I rarely took calls from the public, I jumped on this one.

"Dr D'Amato?" she asked.

"Yes?"

"I saw you on television last week – on that cable talk show. You said you had a passion for physics." Her voice had a breathy elegance.

"True," I said. Forensic science was my profession, but cutting-edge physics was my love. Too bad there wasn't a way to nab rapist murderers with spectral traces. "And you're a physicist?" I asked.

"Oh yes, sorry," she said. "I should introduce myself. I'm Lauren Goldring. Do you know my work?"

"Ahm . . ." The name did sound familiar. I ran through the rolodex in my head, though these days my computer was becoming more reliable than my brain. "Yes!" I snapped my fingers. "You had an article in *Scientific American* last month about some Hubble data."

"That's right," she said, and I could hear her relax just a bit. "Look, I'm calling you about my husband – he's disappeared. I haven't heard from him in two days."

"Oh," I said. "Well that's really not my department. I can connect you to—"

"No, please," she said. "It's not what you think. I'm sure his disappearance has something to do with his work. He's a physicist too."

I was in my car forty minutes later on my way to her house, when I should have been home with pizza and the cat. No contest: a physicist in distress always wins.

Her Bronxville address wasn't too far from mine in Yonkers.

"Dr D'Amato?" she opened the door.

I nodded. "Phil."

"Thank you so much for coming," she said, and ushered me in. Her eyes looked red, like she suffered from allergies or had been crying. But few people have allergies in March.

The house had a quiet appealing beauty. As did she.

"I know the usual expectations in these things," she said. "He has another woman; we've been fighting. And I'm sure that most women whose vanished husbands *have* been having affairs are quick to profess their certainty that that's not what's going on in *their* cases."

I smiled. "OK, I'm willing to start with the assumption that your case is different. Tell me how."

"Would you like a drink, some wine?" she walked over to a cabinet, must've been turn of the century.

"Just ginger ale, if you have it," I said, leaning back in the plush Morris chair she'd shown me into.

She returned with the ginger ale, and some sort of sparkling water for herself. "Well, as I told you on the phone, Ian and I are physicists—"

"Is his last name Goldring, like yours?"

Lauren nodded. "And, well, I'm sure this has something to do with his project."

"You two don't do the same work?" I asked.

"No," she said. "My area's the cosmos at large – big bang theory, blackholes in space, the big picture. Ian's was, is, on the other end of the spectrum. Literally. His area's quantum mechanics." She started to sob.

"It's OK," I said. I got up and put my hand on her shoulder. Quantum mechanics could be frustrating, I knew, but not *that* bad.

"No," she said. "It isn't OK. Why am I using the past tense for Ian?"

"You think some harm's come to him?"

"I don't know," her lips quivered. She did know, or thought she knew.

"And you feel this has something to do with his work with tiny particles? Was he exposed to dangerous radiation?"

"No," she said. "That's not it. He was working on something called quantum signalling. He always told me everything about his work – and I told him everything about mine – we had that kind of relationship. And then a few months ago, he suddenly got silent. At first I thought maybe he *was* having an affair . . ."

And the thought popped into my head: if I had a woman with your class, an affair with someone else would be the last thing on my mind.

"But then I realized it was deeper than that. It was something, something that frightened him, in his work. Something that I think he wanted to shield me from."

"I'm pretty much of an amiable amateur when it comes to quantum mechanics," I said, "but I know something about it. Suppose you tell me all you know about Ian's work, and why it could be dangerous."

*   *   *

What I in fact fully grasped about quantum mechanics I could write on a postcard to my sister in Boston and it would likely fit. It had to do with light and particles so small that they were often indistinguishable in their behavior, and prone to paradox at every turn. A particularly vexing aspect that even Einstein and his colleagues tried to tackle in the 1930s involved two particles that at first collided and then travelled at sublight speeds in opposite directions: would observation of one have an instantaneous effect on the other? Did the two particles, having once collided, now exist ever after in some sort of mysterious relationship or field, a bond between them so potent that just to measure one was to influence the other, regardless of how far away? Einstein wondered about this in a thought experiment. Did interaction of subatomic particles tie their futures together forever, even if one stayed on Earth and the other wound up beyond Pluto? Real experiments in the 1960s and after suggested that's just what was happening, at least in local areas, and this supported Heisenberg's and Bohr's classic "Copenhagen" interpretation that quantum mechanics was some kind of mind-over-matter deal – that just looking at a quantum or tiny particle, maybe even thinking about it, could affect not only it but related particles. Einstein would've preferred to find another cause – non-mental – for such phenomena. But that could lead to an interpretation of quantum mechanics as faster-than-light action – the particle on Earth somehow sent an instant signal to the particle in space – which of course ran counter to Einstein's relativity theories.

Well, I guess that would fill more than your average postcard. The truth is blood and semen and DNA evidence were a lot easier to make sense of than quantum mechanics, which was one reason that kind of esoteric science was just a hobby with me. Of course, one way that QM had it over forensics is that it rarely had to do with dead bodies. But Lauren Goldring was wanting to tell me that maybe it did in at least one case, her husband's.

"Ian was part of a small group of physicists working to demonstrate that QM was evidence of faster-than-light travel, time travel, maybe both," she said.

"Not a product of the mind?" I asked.

"No," she said, "not as in the traditional interpretation."

"But doesn't faster-than-light travel contradict Einstein?" I asked.

"Not necessarily," Lauren said. "It seems to contradict the simplest interpretations, but there may be some loopholes."

"Go on," I said.

"Well, there's a lot of disagreement even among the small group of people Ian was working with. Some think the data supports both faster-than-light *and* time travel. Others are sure that time travel is impossible even though—"

"You're not saying that you think some crazy envious scientist killed him?" I asked.

"No," Lauren said. "It's much deeper than that."

A favorite phrase of hers. "I don't understand," I said.

"Well, Stephen Hawking, for one, says that although the equations suggest that time travel might be possible on the quantum level, the universe wouldn't let this happen ..." She paused and looked at me. "You've heard about Hawking's work in this area?"

"I know about Hawking in general," I said. "I'm not that much of an amateur. But not about his work in time travel."

"You're very unusual for a forensic scientist," she said, with an admiring edge I very much liked. "Anyway, Hawking thinks that whatever quantum mechanics may permit, the universe just won't allow time travel – because the level of paradox time travel would create would just unravel the whole universe."

"You mean like if I could get a message back to JFK that he would be killed, and he believed me and acted upon that information and didn't go to Dallas and wasn't killed, this would create a world in which I would grow up with no knowledge that JFK had ever been killed, which would mean I would have no motive to send the message that saved JFK, but if I didn't send that message then JFK would be killed—"

"That's it," Lauren said. "Except on the quantum level you might achieve that paradox by sending back information just a few seconds in time – say, in the form of a command that would shut down the generating circuit and prevent the information from being sent in the first place—"

"I see," I said.

"And, well, because things like that, if they could happen, if they happened all the time, would lead to a constantly remade, inside-out, self-effacing universe, Hawking promulgated his 'Chronology Protection Conjecture' – the universe protects the existing timeline, whatever the theoretical possibilities of time travel."

"How does your husband fit into this?" I asked.

"He was working on a device, an experiment, to disprove Hawking's conjecture," she said. "He was trying to create a local wormhole with temporal effects."

"And you think he somehow disappeared into this?" Jeez, this was beginning to sound like a bad episode of *Star Trek*. But she seemed rational, everything she'd outlined made sense, and something in her manner continued to compel my attention.

"I don't know," she looked like she was close to tears again.

"All right," I said. "Here's what I think we should do. I'm going to call in Ian's disappearance to a friend in the department. He's a precinct captain, and he'll take this seriously. He'll contact all the airports, get Ian's picture out to cops on the beat—"

"But I don't think—"

"I know," I said. "You've got a gut feeling that something more profound is going on. And maybe you're right. But we've got to cover all the bases."

"OK," she said quietly, and I noticed that her lips were quivering again.

"Will you be OK tonight? I'll be back to you tomorrow morning." I took her hand.

"I guess so," she said huskily, and squeezed my hand.

I didn't feel like letting go, but I did.

The news the next morning was terrible. I don't care what the shrinks say: flat-out confirmed death is always worse than ambiguous, unresolved disappearance. I couldn't bring myself to just call her on the phone. I drove to her home, hoping she was in.

She opened the door. I tried to keep a calm face, but I'm not that good an actor.

She understood immediately. "Oh no!" she cried out. She staggered and collapsed in my arms. "Please no."

"I'm sorry," I said, and touched her hair. I felt like kissing her forehead, but didn't. I hardly knew her, yet I felt very close to her, a part of her world. "They found him a few hours ago near Columbia University. Looks like another stupid, senseless, goddamned random drive-by shooting. That's the kind of world we live in." I didn't know whether this would in any way lessen her pain. At least his death had nothing to do with his work.

"No, not random," she said, sobbing. "Not random."

"OK," I said, "you need to rest. I'm going to call someone over here to give you a sedative. I'll stay with you till then."

The medic was over in fifteen minutes. He gave her a shot, and she was asleep a few minutes later. "Not random. Not random," she mumbled.

I called the captain, and asked if he could send a uniform over to stay with Lauren for the afternoon. He wasn't happy – his people were overworked, like everyone – but he owed me. Many's the time I'd saved his butt with some piece of evidence I'd uncovered in the back of an orifice.

I dropped by the autopsy. Nothing unusual there. Three bullets from a cheap punk's gun, one shattered the heart, did all the damage, Ian Goldring's dead. No sign of radiation damage, no strange chemistry in the body. No possible connection that I could see to anything Lauren had told me. Still, the coroner was a friend, I explained to him that the victim was the husband of a friend, and asked if he could run any and every conceivable test at his disposal to determine if there was anything different about this corpse. He said sure. I knew he wouldn't find anything though.

I went back to my office. I thought of calling Lauren and telling her about the autopsy, but she'd be better off if I let her rest. I was tired of looking at dead bodies. I turned on my computer and looked at its screen instead. I was on a few physics lists on the Internet. I logged on and did some reading about Hawking and his chronology protection conjecture.

"Lady physicist on the phone for you again," Carl called out. It was late afternoon already. I logged off and rubbed my eyes.

"Hi," Lauren said.

"You OK?" I asked.

"Yeah," she said. "I just got off the phone with one of the other researchers in Ian's group, and I think I've got part of this figured out." She sounded less tentative than yesterday – like she was indeed more on top of what was actually going on, or thought she was – but more worried.

I started to tell her, gently as I could, about the autopsy.

"Doesn't matter," she interrupted me. "I mean, I don't think the *way* that Ian was killed has any relevance to this. It's the fact that he *was* killed that counts – the reason he was killed."

The reason – everyone wants reasons in this irrational society. Science in the laboratory deals with reason. In the outside world, you're lucky if you can find a reason. "I know it's painful," I said. "But Ian's death had no reason – his killer was likely just a high-flying kid with a gun. Happens all the time. Ian was just in the wrong place. A random victim in the murder lottery."

"No, not random," Lauren said.

She'd said the same thing this morning. I could hear her starting to sob again.

"Look, Phil," she continued. "I really think I'm close to understanding this. I'm going to make a few more calls. I, uh, we hardly know each other, but I feel good talking this out with you. Our conversation last night helped me a lot. Can I call you back in an hour? Or maybe – I don't know, if you're not busy tonight – could you come over again?"

She didn't have to ask twice. "I'll see you at seven. I'll also bring some food in case you're hungry – you have to eat."

I knew even before I drove up that something was wrong. I guess my eyes after all these years of looking around crime scenes are especially sensitive to the weak flicker of police lights on the evening sky at a distance. The flicker still turns my stomach.

"What's going on here?" I got out of my car, Chinese food in hand, and asked the uniform.

"Who the hell are you?" he replied.

I fumbled for my ID.

"He's OK," Janny Murphy, the uniform who'd come to stay with Lauren in the afternoon, walked over. "He's forensics."

The food dropped from my hand when I saw the expression on her face. Brown moo-shoo pork juice dribbled down the driveway.

"It's crazy," Janny said. "Doc says it's less than one in ten thousand. Some rare allergy to the shot the medic gave her. It wasn't his fault. It somehow brings out an asthma attack hours later. Fifty per cent fatality."

"And Lauren – Dr Goldring – was in the unlucky part of the curve."

Janny nodded.

"I don't believe this," I said, shaking my head.

"I know," Janny said. "Helluva coincidence. Physicist and his wife, also a physicist, both dying like that."

"Maybe it's not a coincidence," I said.

"What do you mean?" Janny said.

"I don't know what I mean," I said. "Is Lauren – is the body – still here? I'd like to have a look at her."

"Help yourself," Janny gestured inside the house.

I can't say Lauren looked at peace in death. I could almost still see her lips quivering, straining to tell me something, though they were as sealed as the deadest night now. I had an urge again to kiss her face. I'd known her all of two days, wanted as many times to kiss her.

I was aware of Janny standing beside me.

"I'm going home now," I said.

"Sure," Janny said. "The captain says he'd like to talk to you tomorrow morning. Just to wrap this whole mess up. Bad karma."

Yeah, karma, like in Fritz Capra's *Tao of Physics*. Like in two entities crossing each other's paths and then ever more touching each other's destinies. Like me and this soul with the soft, still lips. Except I had no power to influence Lauren, to make things better for her any more. And the truth is, I hadn't done much for her when she was alive.

I was awake all night. I logged onto a few more fringy physics lists with my computer and did more reading. Finally it was light outside. I thought about calling Stephen Hawking. He was where? California? Cambridge, England? I wasn't sure. I knew he'd be able to talk to me if I could reach him – I'd seen a video of him talking through a special device – but he'd probably think I was crazy when I told him what I had to say. So I called Jack Donovan instead. He was another friend who owed me. I had lots of friends like that in the city. Jack was a science reporter for

Newsday, and I'd come through for him with off-the-record background on murder investigations in my bailiwick lots of times. I hoped he'd come through for me now. I was starting to get worried. He had lots of connections in the field – he could talk to scientists who'd shy away from me, my being in the Department and all.

It was seven in the morning. I expected to get his answering machine, but I got him. I told him my story.

"OK," he said. "Why don't you go see the captain at the precinct, and then come over to see me? I'll do some checking around in the meantime."

I did what Jack said. I kept strictly to the facts with the captain – no suppositions, no chronological or any other protection schemes – and he took it all in with his customary frown.

"Damn shame," he muttered. "Nice lady like that. They oughta take that sedative off the market. Damn drug companies are too greedy."

"Right," I said.

"You look exhausted," he said. "You oughta take the rest of the day off."

"More or less what I had in mind," I said, and left for Jack's.

I thought *my* office was high-tech, but Jack's Hempstead newsroom looked like something well into the next century. Computer screens everywhere you looked, sounds of modems chirping on and off like the patter of tiny raindrops.

Jack looked concerned. "You're not going to like this," he said.

"What else is new," I said. "Try me."

"Well, you were right about my having better entrée to these physicists than you. I did a lot of checking," Jack said. "There were six people working actively in conjunction with Ian on this project. A few more, of course, if you take into account the usual complement of graduate student assistants. But outside of that, the project was sealed up pretty tightly – not by the government or any agency, but by the researchers themselves. Sometimes they do that when the research gets really fringy – like they don't want anyone to know what they're really doing until they're sure they have a reliable effect. You wouldn't believe some of the wild

things people have been getting into in the past few years –
especially the physicists – now that they have the Internet to
yammer at each other."

"I'm tired, Jack. Please get to the point."

"Well, four of the seven – that includes Ian Goldring – are
now dead. One had a heart attack – the day after his doctor told
him his cholesterol was in the bottom 10 per cent. I guess that's
not so strange. Another fell off his roof – he was cleaning out his
gutters – and severed his carotid artery on a sharp piece of flag-
stone that was sticking up on his walk. He bled to death before
anyone found him. Another was struck by a car – DOA. And
then there's Ian. I could write a story on this even without your
conjecture—"

"Please don't," I said.

"It's a weird situation all right. Four out of seven dying like
that – and also Goldring's wife."

"How are the spouses of the other fatalities?" I asked.

"All OK," Jack said. "But none are physicists. None knew
anything at all about their husbands' work – all of the dead were
men. Lauren Goldring is the only one who had any idea what
her husband was up to."

"She wasn't sure," I said. "But I think she figured it out just
before she died."

"Maybe they all picked up some virus at a conference they
attended – something which threw off their sense of balance,
caused their heart rate to speed up," Sam Abrahmson, Jack's
editor, strolled by and jumped in. Clearly he'd been listening on
the periphery of our conversation. "That could explain the two
accidents and the heart attack," he added. "Maybe even the
sedative death."

"But not the drive-by shooting of Goldring," I said.

"No," Abrahmson admitted. "But it could be an interesting
story anyway. Think about it," he said to Jack and strolled away.

I looked at Jack. "Please, I'm begging you. If I'm right—"

"It's likely something completely different," Jack said. "Some
completely different hidden variable."

Hidden variables. I'd been reading about them all night.
"What about the other three? Have you been able to get in touch
with them?" I asked.

"Nope," Jack said. "Hays and Strauss refused to talk to me about it. Both had their secretaries tell me they were aware of some of the deaths, had decided not to do any more work on the local wormhole project, had no plans to publish what they'd already done, didn't want to talk to me about it or hear from me again. Each claimed to be involved now in something completely different."

"Does that sound to you like the usual behavior of research scientists?" I asked.

"No," Jack said. "The ones I know eat up publicity, and they'd hang on to a project like this for decades, like a dog worrying a bone."

I nodded. "And the third physicist?"

"Fenwick? She's in a small plane somewhere in the outback of Australia. I couldn't reach her at all."

"Call me immediately if you hear the plane crashes," I said. I really meant "when" not "if", but I didn't want Jack to think I was even more far gone than I was. "Please try to hold off on any story for now," I said and made to leave.

"I'll do what I can," Jack said. "Try to get some rest. I think there's something going on here all right, but not what you think."

The drive back to Westchester was harrowing. Two cars nearly sideswiped me, and one big-ass truck stopped so suddenly in front of me that I had all I could do to swerve out of crashing into it and becoming an instant Long Island Expressway pancake.

Let's say the QM time-travel people were right. Particles are able to influence each other travelling away from each other at huge distances, because they're actually travelling back in time to an earlier position when they were in immediate physical contact. So time travel on the quantum mechanical level is possible – technically.

But let's say Hawking was also right. The universe can't allow time travel – for to do so would unravel its very being. So it protects itself from dissemination of information backwards in time.

That wouldn't be so crazy. People are saying the universe can be considered one huge organism – a Gaia writ large. Makes sense then, that this organism, like all other organisms, would have tendencies to act on behalf of its own survival – would act to prevent its dissolution via time travel.

But how would such protection express itself? A physicist figures out a way of creating a local wormhole that can send some information back in time – back to his earlier self and equipment – in some non-blatantly paradoxical way. It doesn't shut off the circuit that sent it. So this information is in fact sent and in fact received – by the scientist. But the universe can't allow that information transfer to stand. So what happens?

Hawking says the universe's first line of defense is to create energy disturbances severe enough at the mouths of the wormhole to destroy it and its time-channelling ability. OK. But let's say the physicist is smart or lucky enough to create a wormhole that can withstand these self-disruptive forces. What does the universe do then?

Maybe it makes the scientist forget this information. Maybe causes a minor stroke in the scientist's brain. Maybe causes the equipment to irreparably break down. Maybe the lucky physicist is really unlucky. Maybe this already happened lots of times.

But what happens when a group of scientists around the world who achieve this time travel transfer reach a critical mass – a mass that will soon publish its findings, and make them known, irrevocably, to the world?

Jeez! – I jammed the heel of my hand into my car horn and swerved. The damn Volkswagen driver must be drunk out of his mind . . .

So what happens when this group of scientists gets information from its own future? Has proof of time travel, information that can't be? The universe regulates itself, polices its timeline, in a more drastic way. All existence is equilibrium – a stronger threat to existence evokes a stronger reaction. A freak fatal accident. A sudden massive heart attack. Another no-motive, drive-by shooting that the universe already dishes out to all too many people in this hapless world of ours. Except in this case, the universe's motive is quite clear and strong: it must protect its chronology, conserve its current existence.

Maybe this already happened too. How many physicists on the cutting edges of this science died too young in recent years? Jeez, here was a story for Jack all right.

But why Lauren? Why did she have to die?

Maybe because the universe's protection level went beyond just those who received illicit future information. Maybe it extended to those who understood just what it was doing, just—

Whamp! Something big had smashed into the rear of my car, and I was skidding way out of control towards the edge of the Throggs Neck Bridge, towards where some workers had removed the barriers to fix some corrosion or something. I was strangely calm, above it all. I told myself to go easy on the brakes, but my leg clamped down anyway and my speed increased. I wrenched my wheel around, but all that did was spin me into a backward skid off the bridge. My car sailed way the hell out over the black-and-blue Long Island Sound.

The way down took a long time. They'd say I was overwrought, over tired, that I lost control. But I knew the truth, knew exactly why this was happening. I knew too much, just like Lauren.

Or maybe there was a way out, a weird little corner of my brain piped up.

Maybe I didn't know the truth. Maybe I was wrong. Maybe if I could convince myself of that, the universe wouldn't have to protect itself from me. Maybe it would give me a second chance.

My car hit the water.

I was still alive.

I was a pretty fair swimmer.

If only I could force myself never to think of certain things, maybe I had a shot.

Maybe the deaths of the physicists were coincidental after all . . .

I lost consciousness thinking no, I couldn't just forget what I already knew so well . . . How could I will myself not to think of that very thing I was trying to will myself not to think about . . . that blared in my mind now like a broken car horn . . . But if I died, what I knew wouldn't matter anyway . . .

I awoke fighting sheets . . . of water. No, these were too white. Maybe hospital sheets. Yeah, white hospital sheets. They smelled like that too.

I opened my eyes. Hospital rooms were hell – I knew better than most the truth of that – but this was just a hospital room.

I was sure of that. I was alive.

And I remembered everything. With a spasm that both energized and frightened me, I realized that I recalled everything I'd been thinking about the universe and its protective clutch . . .

But I was still alive.

So maybe my reasoning was not completely right . . .

"Dr D'Amato," a female voice, soft but very much in command, said to me. "Good to see you awake."

"Good to *be* awake, Nurse, ah, Johnson," I squinted at her name tag, then her face. "Uhm, what's my situation? How long have I been here?"

She looked at the chart next to my bed. "Just a day and a half," she said. "They fished you out of the Sound. You were suffering from shock. Here," she gave me a cup of water. "Now that you're awake, you can take these orally." She gave me three pills, and turned off the intravenous that I'd just realized was attached to me. She disconnected the tubing from my vein.

I held the pills in my hand. I thought about the universe again. I envisioned it, rightly or wrongly, as a personal antagonist now. Let's say I was right about the reach of its chronology protection after all. Let's say it had spared me in the water, because I was on the verge of willing myself to forget. Let's say it had allowed me to get medicine and nutrition intravenously, while I was unconscious, because while I was unconscious I posed no threat. But let's say now that I was awake, and remembered, it would—

"Dr D'Amato. Are you falling back asleep on me?" She smiled. "Come on now, be a good boy and take your pills."

They burned in my palm. Maybe they were poison. Maybe something I had a lethal allergy to. Like Lauren. "No," I said. "I'm OK, now, really. I don't need them." I put the pills on the table, and swung my legs out of bed.

"I don't believe this," Johnson said. "It's true – you doctors make the worst God-awful patients. You just stay put now – hear me?" She gave me a look of exasperation and stalked out the door, likely to get the resident on duty, or, who knew, security.

I looked around for my clothes. They were on a chair, a dried out crumpled mess. They stank of oil and saltwater. At least my wallet was still inside my jacket pocket, money damp but intact. Good to see there was still some honesty left in this town.

I dressed quickly and opened the door. The corridor was clear. Goddamn it, I could leave if I wanted to. I was a patient not a prisoner.

At least insofar as the hospital was concerned. As for the larger realm of being, I couldn't say any more.

I took a cab straight home. The most important new piece of evidence – to this whole case, as well as to me personally – was that I was alive. This meant that my assessment of the universe's vindictiveness was missing something. Or maybe the universe was just a less effective assassin of forensic scientists than quantum physicists and their knowing wives.

I called Jack to see if there was anything new.

"Oh, just a second please," the *Newsday* receptionist said. I didn't like the tone of her voice.

"Hello, can I help you?" This was a man's voice, but not Jack's. He sounded familiar but I couldn't place him.

"Yes, I'm Dr Phil D'Amato of NYPD Forensics calling Jack Donovan."

Silence. Then, "Hello, Phil. I'm Sam Abrahmson. You still in the hospital?"

Right. Abrahmson. That was the voice. "No. I'm out. Where's Jack?"

Abrahmson cleared his throat. "He was killed with Dave Strauss this morning. He'd talked Strauss into going public with this – Strauss supported your story. He'd picked Strauss up at his summer cottage in Ellenville – Strauss had been hiding out there – and was driving him back to the city. They got blown off a small bridge. Freak accident."

"No freakin' accident," I said. "You know that as well as I do." Another particle who'd danced this sick quantum twist with me. Another particle dead. But this one was completely my fault – I'd brought Jack into this.

"I don't know what I know," Abrahmson said. "Except that at this point the story's on hold. Until we find out more."

I was glad to hear he sounded scared. "That's a good idea," I said. "I'll be back to you."

"Take care of yourself," Abrahmson said. "God knows what that subatomic radiation can do to the body and mind. Or maybe it's all just coincidence. God only knows. Take care of yourself."

"Right." Subatomic radiation. Abrahmson's latest culprit. First it was a virus; now it was radiation. I'd said the same stupid thing to Lauren, hadn't I? People like to latch on to something they know when faced with something they don't know – especially something that kills some physicists here, a reporter there, who knew who else. But radiation had nothing to do with this. Stopping it would take a lot more than lead shields.

I tracked down Richard Hays. I was beginning to get a further inkling of what might be going on, and I needed to talk it out with one of the principals. One of the last remaining principals. It could save both our lives.

I used my NYPD clout to intimidate enough secretaries and assistants to get directly through to him.

"Look, I don't care if you're the bleeding head of the FBI," he said. He was British. "I'm going to talk to you about this just once, now, and then never again."

"Thank you, Doctor. So please tell me what you think is happening here. Then I'll tell you what I know, or think I know."

"What's happening is this," Hays said. "I was working on a project with my colleagues. That's true. But I came to realize the project was a dead-end – that the phenomena we were investigating weren't real. So I ceased my involvement in that research. I have no intention of ever picking up that research again – of ever publishing about it, or even talking about it, except to indicate that it was a waste of time. I'd strongly advise you to do the same."

I had no idea how he talked ordinarily, but his words on the phone sounded like each had been chosen with the utmost care. "Why do I feel like you're reading from a script, Dr Hays?"

"I assure you everything I'm saying is real. As you no doubt already have evidence of yourself," Hays said.

"Now you look," I raised my voice. "You can't just sweep this under the rug. If the universe *is* at work here in some way, you think you can just avoid it by pretending you don't know about it? The universe would know about your pretense too – it's after all still part of the universe. And word of this will get out anyway – someone will sooner or later publish something. If you want to live, you've got to face this, find out what's really happening here, and—"

"I believe you are seriously mistaken, my friend. And that, I'm afraid, concludes our interview, now and forever." He hung up.

I held on to the disconnected phone, which beeped like a seal, for a long time. I realized that the left side of my body hurt, from my chest up through my shoulder and down my arm. The pain had come on, I thought, at the end of my futile lecture to Hays. Right when I'd talked about publishing. Maybe publishing was the key – maybe talk about dissemination of this information, as opposed to just thinking about it, is what triggered the universe's backlash. But I was also sure I was right in what I'd said to Hays about the need to confront this, about not running away . . .

I put the phone back in its receiver and lay down. I was bone tired. Maybe I was getting a heart attack, maybe I wasn't. Maybe I was still in shock from my dip in the Sound. I couldn't fight this all on my own much longer.

The phone rang. I fumbled with the receiver. How long had I been sleeping? "Hello?"

"Dr D'Amato?" a female voice, maybe Lauren's, maybe Nurse Johnson's. No, someone else.

"Yes?"

"I'm Jennifer Fenwick."

Fenwick, Fenwick – yes, Jennifer Fenwick, the last quantum physicist on this project. I'd wheedled her number from Abrahmson's secretary and left a message for her in Australia – the girl at the hotel wasn't sure if she'd already left. "Dr Fenwick, I'm glad you called. I, uhm, had some ideas I wanted to talk to you about – regarding the quantum signalling project." I wasn't sure how much she knew, and didn't want to scare her off.

She laughed, oddly. "Well, I'm wide open for ideas. I'll take help wherever I can get it. I'm the only damn person left alive from our research group."

"Only person?" So she knew – apparently more than I.

I looked at the clock. It was tomorrow morning already – I'd slept right through the afternoon and night. Good thing I'd called my office and gotten the week off, the absurd part of me that kept track of such trivia noted.

"Richard Hays committed suicide last night," Fenwick's voice cracked. "He left a note saying he couldn't pull it off any longer – couldn't surmount the paradox of deliberately not thinking of something – couldn't overcome his lifelong urge as a scientist to tell the world what he'd discovered. He'd prepared a paper for publication – begged his wife to have it published posthumously if he didn't make it. I spoke to her this morning. I told her to destroy it. And the note too. Fortunately for her, she had no idea what the paper was about. She's a simple woman – Richard didn't marry her for her brains."

"I see," I said slowly. "Where are you now?"

"I'm in New York," she said. "I wanted to come home – I didn't want to die in Australia."

"Look, you're still alive," I said. "That means you've still got a chance. How about meeting me for lunch" – I looked at the clock again – "in about an hour? The Trattoria Il Bambino on 12th Street in the Village is good. As far as I know, no one there has died from the food as yet." How I could bring myself to make a crack like that at a time like this, I didn't know.

"OK," Fenwick said.

She was waiting for me when I arrived. On the way down, I'd fantasized that she'd look just like Lauren. But in fact she looked a little older and wiser. And even more frightened.

"All right," I said after we'd ordered and gotten rid of the waiter. "Here's what I have in mind. You tell me as a physicist where this might not add up. First, everyone who's attempted to publish something about your work has died."

Jennifer nodded. "I spoke to Lauren Goldring the afternoon she died. She told me she was going to the press."

I sighed. "I didn't know that – but it supports my point. In fact, the two times I even toyed with going public about this, I had fleeting interviews with death. The first time in the water, the second with some sort of pre-heart attack, I'm sure."

Jennifer nodded again. "Same for me. Wheeler wrote about cosmic censorship. Maybe he was on to the same thing as Hawking."

"All right, so what does that tell us?" I said. "Even thinking about publishing this is dangerous. But apparently it's not a capital offense – knowing about this is in itself not fatal. We're still alive. It's as if the universe allows private, crackpot knowledge in this area – cause no one takes crackpots seriously, even scientific ones. It's the danger of public dissemination that draws the response – the threat of an objectively accepted scientific theory. Our private knowledge isn't the real problem here. Communication is. The definite intention to publish. That's what kills you. Yeah, cosmic censorship is a good way of putting it."

"OK," Jennifer said.

"OK," I said. "But it's also clear that we can't just ignore this – can't expect to suppress it in our minds. Not having any particular plan to publish won't be enough to save us – not in the long run. Sooner or later after a dark silent night we'd get the urge to shout it out. It's human nature. It's inside of us. Hays's suicide proves it – his note spells it out. You can't just not think of something. You can't just will an idea into oblivion. It's self-defeating. It makes you want to get up on the rooftop and scream it to the world even more – like a repressed love."

"Agreed," Jennifer said. "So what do we do, then?"

"Well, we can't go public with this story, and we can't will ourselves to forget it. But maybe there's a third way. Here's what I was thinking. I can tell you – in strict confidence – that we sometimes do this in forensics." I lowered my voice. "Let's say we have someone who was killed in a certain way, but we don't want the murderer to know that we know how the murder took place. We just deliberately at first publicly interpret the evidence in a different way – after all, there's usually more than one trauma that can result in a given fatal injury to a body – more than one plausible explanation of how someone was killed. Slipped and hit your head on a rock, or someone hit you in the head with a rock – sometimes there's not much difference between the results of the two."

"The universe is murderous, all right, I can see that, but I don't see how what you're saying would work in our situation," Jennifer said.

"Well, you tell me," I said. "Your group thinks it built a worm-hole that allows signalling through time. But couldn't you find another phenomenon to attribute those effects to? After all, we only have time travel on the brain because of H. G. Wells and his literary offspring. Let's say Wells had never written *The Time Machine*. Let's say science fiction had taken a different turn. Then your group would likely have come up with another explanation for your findings. And you can do this now anyway!" I took a sip of wine and realized I felt pretty good. "You can publish an article on your work, and attribute your findings to something other than time travel. Indicate they're some sort of other physical effect. Come up with the equivalent of a false phlogiston theory, an attractive bogus conception for this tiny sliver of subatomic phenomena, to account for the time-travel effects. The truth is, few if any serious scientists actually believe that time travel is possible anyway, right? Most think it's just science fiction, nothing else. Who would have reason to suspect a time-travel effect here unless you specifically called attention to it?"

Jennifer considered. "The graduate research assistants worked only on the data acquisition level. Only the project principals, the seven of us," she caught her breath, winced – "only the seven of us knew this was about time travel. No one else. Ours were supposedly the best minds in this area. Lot of good it did us."

"I know," I tried to be as reassuring as I could. "But then without that time-travel label, all you've got is another of a hundred little experiments in this area per year – jeez, I checked the litera-ture, there are a lot more than that – and your study would likely get lost in the wash. That should shut the universe up. That should keep it safe from time travel – send the scientific commu-nity off on the wrong track, in a different direction – maybe not send them off in any direction all. Could you do that?"

Jennifer sipped her wine slowly. Her glass was shaking. Her lips clung to the rim. She was no doubt thinking that her life depended on what she decided to do now. She was probably right. Mine too.

"Exotic matter is what makes the effect possible," she said at last. "Exotic matter keeps the wormhole open long enough. No one knows much about how it works – in fact, as far as I know, our group created this kind of exotic matter, in which weak forces are suspended, for the first time in our project. I guess I could make a case that a peculiar property of this exotic matter is that it creates effects that mimic time travel in artificial wormholes – I could make a persuasive argument that we didn't really see time travel through that wormhole at all; what we have instead is a reversal of processes to earlier stages when they come in contact with our exotic matter; no signalling from the future. You know – we thought the glass was half full, but it was really half empty."

"No," I said. "That's still not going far enough. You've got to be more daring in your deception – come up with something that doesn't invoke time travel at all, even in the negative. Publishing a paper with results that are explicitly said not to demonstrate time travel is akin to someone the police never heard of coming into the station and saying he didn't do it – that only arouses our suspicion. I'm sorry to be so blunt, Jennifer. But you've got to do more. Can't you come up with some effects of exotic matter that have nothing to do with time travel at all?"

She drained her wine glass and put it down, neither half full nor half empty. Completely empty. "This goes against everything in my life and training as a scientist," she said. "I'm supposed to pursue the truth, wherever it takes me."

"Right," I said. "And how much truth will you be able to pursue when you're like Hays and Strauss and the others?"

"Einstein said the universe wasn't malicious," she said. "This is unbelievable."

"Maybe Einstein was saying the glass was half empty when he knew it was half full. Maybe he knew just what he was doing – knew which side his bread was buttered on – maybe he wanted to live past middle age."

"God Almighty!" She slammed her hand on the table. Glasses rattled. "Couldn't I just swear before you and the universe never to publish anything about this? Wouldn't that be enough?"

"Maybe, maybe not," I said. "From the universe's point of view, your publishing a paper that explicitly attributes the effects to something other than time travel seems much safer – to you as well as the universe. Let's say you change your mind, years from now, and try to publish a paper that says you succeeded with time travel after all. You'd already be on record in the literature as attributing those effects to something else – you'd be much less likely to be believed then. Safer for the universe. Safer for you. A paper with a false lead is not only our best bet now, it's an insurance policy for our future."

Jennifer nodded, very slowly. "I guess I could come up with something – some phenomenon unrelated to time travel – unsuggestive of it. The connection of quantum effects to human thought has always had great appeal, and even though I personally never saw much more than wishful thinking in that direction."

"That's better," I said quietly.

"But how can we be sure no one else will want to look into these effects?" Jennifer asked.

I shrugged. "Guarantees of anything are beyond us in this situation. The best we can hope for are probabilities – that's how the QM realm operates anyway, isn't it? – likelihoods of our success, statistics in favor of our survival. As for your effects, well, effects don't have much impact outside of a supportive context of theory. Psalm 51 says, 'Cleanse me with hyssop and I shall be clean' – the penicillin mold was first identified on a piece of decayed hyssop by a Swedish chemist – but none of this led to antibiotics until spores from a mold landed in Fleming's Petri dish, and he place them in the right scientific perspective. Scientists thought they had evidence of spontaneous generation of maggots in old meat, until they learned how maggots make love. Astronomers saw lots of evidence for aluminiferous ether, until Michelson-Morley decisively proved that wrong. You're working on the cutting edge of physics with your wormholes. No one knows what to expect – you said it yourself – yours were the best minds in this area. *You* can create the context. No one's left to contradict you. Let's face it, if you word your paper properly, it will likely go unnoticed. But if not, it will point people in the wrong direction – and once pointed that way, away from time travel, the world could take years, decades, longer, to look at time travel as a real scientific possibility again. The history of science is filled with wrong glittering paths, tenaciously taken and defended. That's the path of life for us. I'm not happy about it, but there it is."

Our food arrived. Jennifer looked away from me, and down at her veal. I hadn't completely won her over yet. But she'd stopped objecting. I understood how she felt. To theoretical scientists, pursuit of truth was sometimes more important than life itself. Maybe that's why I went into flesh-and-blood forensics. I pushed on.

"The truth is, we've all been getting along quite well without time travel anyway – it could wreak far more havoc in everyone's lives than nuclear weapons ever did. The universe may not be wrong here."

She looked up at me.

"It's all up to you now," I said. "I'm not a physicist. I can't pull this off. I can take care of the general media, but not the scientific journals." I thought about Abrahmson at *Newsday*. He hadn't a clue which way was up in this thing. He'd just as soon believe this nightmare was all coincidence – the ever popular placeholder for things people didn't want to understand. I could easily pitch it to him in that way.

She gave me a weak smile. "OK, I'll try it. I'll write the article with the mental spin on the exotic effects. *Physics Review D* was given some general info that we were doing something on exotic matter, and is waiting for our report. It'll have maximum impact on other physicists there. The human mind in control of matter will be catnip for a lot them anyway."

"Good," I smiled back. I knew she meant it. I knew because I suddenly felt very hungry, and dug into my own veal with a zest I hadn't felt for anything in a while. It tasted great. Two particles of humanity had connected again. Maybe this time the relationship would go somewhere.

It occurred to me, as I took Jennifer's hand and squeezed it with relief, that maybe this was just what the universe had wanted all along.

As they say in the Department, an ongoing string of deaths is a poor way to keep a secret.

WOMEN ON THE BRINK
OF A CATACLYSM

Molly Brown

One of the hardest types of time-travel story to write is that involving a time loop, a kind of endless knot or Shrivatsa which has no beginning or end but, like the serpent Ouroboros, seems to be chasing or even consuming its own tail. The classic examples are "By His Bootstraps" (1941) and "All You Zombies ..." (1959) by Robert A. Heinlein, both of which are too easily available to reprint here. Instead I wanted to use this lesser known but equally complex, and much more amusing, example.

Molly Brown is an American writer and occasional stand-up comedienne, long resident in Britain. Her novels have included the historical mystery Invitation to a Funeral *(1995) and a children's science-fiction thriller,* Virus *(1994), and you will find other time-travel stories in her collection* Bad Timing *(2001).*

I felt like I was going through a meat grinder. Then there was a blinding flash of light – bright orange – and I felt like I was going through a meat grinder backwards. And there I was, back in one piece. Slightly dizzy, a little stiff around the joints. Swearing I'd never do that again.

The digital display inside the capsule read: 29 April 1995, 6:03 p.m., E.S.T. If that was true, then I was furious. Toni promised she would only set the timer forward by two minutes, and I'd gone forward by a year! A whole year, wasted. Didn't she realize I had work to do? And then I thought: oh my God, the exhibition! I was supposed to have an exhibition in July, 1994 – if I've really gone forward a year, I missed my one-woman show at Gallery Alfredo!

I opened the capsule door, bent on murder. And then I froze. This wasn't my studio.

I live and work on the top floor of an old warehouse in lower Manhattan, and I do sculpture. Abstract sculpture. I take scrapped auto parts and turn them into something beautiful. I twist industrial rubbish into exquisite shapes. I can mount a bicycle wheel onto a wooden platform and make it speak volumes about the meaning of life. I once placed a headless Barbie doll inside a fish tank and sold it for five thousand dollars, and that was before I was famous – I hear the same piece recently fetched more than forty.

I'd been working on a new piece called "Women on the Brink of a Cataclysm": an arrangement of six black and white television sets, each showing a video loop of a woman scrubbing a floor, when Toni Fisher rang the doorbell. I've known Toni off and on since we were kids. We grew up in the same town and went to the same high school before going our separate ways after graduation, in 1966. I went to art school in California; she got a scholarship to study physics at Cambridge in England. It would be twenty years before we met again, at the launch party for *Gutsy Ladies: Women making their mark in the 80s*, the latest book by Arabella Winstein.

It was one of those dreadful media circuses; I remember a PR woman in a geometric haircut dragging me around the room for a round of introductions: "Hey there, gutsy lady, come and meet some other gutsy ladies." I was there in my capacity as "Gutsy Lady of the Art World" and Toni had been profiled in a chapter entitled: "Gutsy Lady on the Cutting Edge of Science".

I saw her leaning against a wall in the corner: a tall, stick-thin character with spikey blonde hair, gulping champagne. I could see she was a kindred spirit – we were the only ones not wearing neat little suits with boxy jackets – but I had no idea who she was; in high school she'd been a chubby brunette with glasses. She saw me looking at her, and waved me over.

We leaned against the wall together, jangling the chains on our identical black leather jackets. "I'm working on a calculation," she said, "that will show density of shoulder pad to be in directly inverse proportion to level of intelligence. I'm drunk by the way."

"I'm Joanna Krenski."

"I know who you are. I've still got the charcoal portrait you did of me for your senior year art project. The damn thing must be worth a fortune now; I keep meaning to get it valued."

That was the start of our friendship, the second time around.

Eight years later, I was sitting inside this metal egg, surrounded by my work and my tools and the huge amount of dust they always seem to generate, and Toni was shouting, okay, push the button. Then I opened the capsule door and Toni was gone and all my work was gone and even the dust was gone.

I was in a huge, open-plan loft with floor to ceiling windows – that much was like my studio – but everything had been polished and swept and there were flowers everywhere. Flowers in vases, flowers in pots, flowers in a window-box. And then there were paintings of flowers. Dozens of delicate little water-colours depicting roses and lilies and lilacs completely covered one wall, each framed behind a pane of sparkling glass. Unframed oils on canvas stood leaning against every wall, apparently divided into categories: fluffy kittens, cute children, puppies with big sad eyes. I could have puked.

A woman was standing with her back to me, painting some-thing on a medium-sized canvas mounted on a wooden easel. It looked like it was going to be another puppy. The woman had tightly permed hair cut just above the collar – mouse brown gone mostly grey – and she was wearing a white smock over a knee-length dress. I also noticed she was wearing high heels. To paint.

Oh God, I thought, just like my mother. I remembered her putting on a hat and a little string of pearls to attend her first evening art class; she was like something out of a '50s TV sitcom. And how proud she was of her little pictures of birds. My mother used to paint birds: little red robins and yellow canaries, with musical notes coming out of their beaks. She hung them all over the living room walls. It was embarrassing.

I was going to have to handle this very carefully. The woman was obviously some old dear of my mother's generation and I was a disembodied head sticking out of a metallic egg. I didn't want to give the poor woman a heart attack. I cleared my throat. "Excuse me," I said. "Please don't be frightened. I'm not a burglar or anything." Even as I said it, I realized how stupid it must have sounded: a burglar in a metal egg.

The woman swung around, and I gasped.

"You again," she said, quite calmly. "I never expected you to turn up here."

I felt my mouth open and close half a dozen times, but no words came out. I just sat there, inside the capsule, gaping like a mackerel. The woman had my face. She'd let her hair go grey – something I've refused to do – and she was wearing a string of pearls just like my mother's and a dress I wouldn't be caught dead in, but based on her face – and even her voice – she could have been my sister. My twin.

There was an odd smell in the air; I'd noticed it the moment I opened the capsule door and now I realized what it was. It was bread, baking. Something very strange was going on here.

"I don't know how you did it," she went on. "Toni said we were both stuck where we were. She was very apologetic about it, of course." She put her palette and brush down on a table beside the easel, then crossed her arms and looked at me. She seemed angry. "Well, you can forget it."

I finally managed to get my vocal cords working. "Huh? Forget what?"

"Even if you've found a way, I'm not going back," she said. "No way am I going back. Ever. This is my life now, my world, and I like it. Though . . ." she paused a moment, and her face – my face – crumpled into a mass of lines. Oh God, I thought, I don't look as old as her, do I? She blinked hard, several times, as if she was trying not to cry. "How's Katie? Is she all right?"

I shook my head; the only Katie I knew was a drama critic, and I didn't think that was who she meant.

"The boys I don't worry about so much; they're grown up now. I know they'll be okay. But Katie . . . she's just a kid, isn't she?"

"Katie who? And who are you? I mean you look so much like . . . like my mother. Are we related or something?"

Her eyes opened wide. "You mean you don't know? But . . . but you've been there. Isn't that where you came from just now?"

"Been where?"

"But you must have! Or how could I be here?"

This woman was talking nonsense; I figured she must be crazy, maybe even dangerous. Maybe she was one of those fanatical fans who get plastic surgery to look like their idols. Okay, maybe a forty-five year-old sculptor doesn't have that kind of fan. Even a forty-five year-old sculptor who appeared in two Warhol films and has had her picture on the cover of everything from *Newsweek* to *Rolling Stone* (twice), probably doesn't have that kind of fan. I still figured the only thing for me to do was to get the hell away from her in a hurry.

I leaned forward, trying to pull myself out of the capsule, but she grabbed me by the shoulders, shoved me back down inside it, and held me there. I struggled and swore, but I couldn't get up. I don't think she was any stronger than me, but she had the major advantage of not being curled into an almost foetal position inside a metal egg.

Her face hovered inches above mine, mouth twisted with rage, eyes narrow and shining with something that might have been hate or might even have been fear; I couldn't tell. It was like looking into one of those distorted fairground mirrors.

"But you have been there," she insisted. "You arrived there a year ago today. That's when the switch took place."

"What switch?"

"This switch," she said, slamming the capsule door down over my head.

It was worse the second time. My head was pounding; my whole body ached. It took a few seconds for my eyes to come back into focus – then I saw the digital display. I was back where I started; 29 April, 1994, 6:01 p.m., E.S.T. I sighed with relief. I was home and I still had three months to get ready for my show at Gallery Alfredo; I hadn't missed it after all.

I shoved the door open, expecting to see my studio, and Toni waiting by the capsule. I had a few choice words in store for Toni! But she wasn't there. And my studio wasn't there.

I couldn't tell where I was at first; it was dark. But as my eyes began to adjust, I saw that I was in a windowless room lined with crowded shelves.

"Hello!" I shouted. "Is anybody there?"

No answer.

"Shit." I took a deep breath, gathered all my strength, and slowly began to extricate myself from Toni's infernal machine. I never felt so stiff and sore; I could hardly move. My jeans felt tighter than usual, as if my body was swollen. And my poor legs! I had to massage them to get the blood moving again, and then there was an unbearable sensation of pins and needles. I finally managed to stand up.

The shelves around me were stacked with jars of homemade preserves and chocolate chip cookies. There were bags of flour, a tinned baked ham, fresh coffee beans, baskets of fruit and vegetables, various pots and pans. It looked like some kind of a pantry.

I reached for the door, praying it wasn't locked. It wasn't, and I stepped into a kitchen that would have been the height of technology in 1956. The brand names were all ones I remembered from my childhood, the appliances were all big and white and clunky, except for the toaster, which was small and round and covered in shiny chrome, and the coffee percolator, which was switched on and bubbling away.

There was nothing in that room that would have been out of place when I was five years old. No microwave oven, no food processor, no espresso machine. There was a meat grinder and a coffee grinder, each with a handle you needed to crank. You needed a match to light the stove. You had to defrost the fridge.

And it was all brand new.

"Hello! Anybody home?" I wandered through the dining room – a printed sign on the wall above the sideboard read, "Give us this day our daily bread" – and into a living room with a picture window and clear plastic covers over all the furniture. An embroidered sampler above the fireplace proclaimed, "Bless this house and everyone in it." I shook my head.

I looked out the window and saw women in cotton dresses hanging laundry, men in white shirts mowing lawns, kids on one-speed bikes with little tinkling bells and metal baskets. There was at least one big, gas-guzzling automobile in every driveway.

It was 1950s suburbia, even worse than I remembered it. I had walked straight into an episode of *Leave It to Beaver*. I shook my head in disbelief; Toni's time machine had actually worked.

I heard a crash, coming from the kitchen. I ran back, pausing in the kitchen doorway. The back door was open. I looked around the room. There was no one there. Nothing seemed to be missing. I took a couple of cautious steps onto the linoleum floor. Then a couple more. Everything seemed okay; the door probably wasn't properly closed in the first place, and a gust of wind had blown it open. It wouldn't be that unusual back in the '50s; we never used to lock the doors when I was a kid. I crossed the room and pulled the door shut. I realized I'd been holding my breath, and let it out.

There was a sudden high-pitched sound, and I nearly jumped a mile. I swung around, clutching my chest and cursing myself for being such an idiot. It was only the telephone. The phone was mounted on the kitchen wall behind me, big and white, with an old-fashioned dial. I walked towards it, then decided to let the answering machine pick it up. I listened to it ringing and ringing, until it finally struck me they didn't have answering machines in the 1950s. I lifted the receiver. "Hello?"

"Joanna, what kept you so long? I was just about to hang up."

I knew that voice! "Toni? Oh thank God. How did you find me? How did you know what number to call?"

There was a long pause. "Joanna, are you all right?"

"I'm stuck inside a forty-year-old copy of *Better Homes and Gardens*, and you're asking me if I'm all right?"

"Joanna, you sound a little strange. Is Bob there?"

"Bob? Who the hell is Bob?"

"You're having one of your little turns again, aren't you? Now do me favour. I want you to sit down, or, better yet, why don't you lie down? Take some good deep breaths, and try to relax." I could not believe the way she was talking to me, in this slow, soothing murmur, like I was some kind of nutcase. She might as well have been saying, "Now put that gun down, Joanna."

"You said you were going to send me two minutes forward, not forty years back! I don't want to lie down and relax. I want to get out of here! And what do you mean, 'turns'? I do not have 'turns'!"

"I'll be there as soon as I can, okay? Just try and stay calm; I'm on my way." There was a click.

"Wait a minute, Toni! Toni?" There was no one there; she'd hung up. I leaned against the wall, rubbing my throbbing temples. Nothing made sense. If I was really in the 1950s, and I'd left Toni back in the '90s, then how could she phone me?

I heard a door open and slam shut, then a man's voice: "Honey, I'm home!"

I didn't know what to do. One half of me said I should walk right up to the man, introduce myself and calmly explain what I was doing in his house. The other half said I should hide. I heard footsteps, moving towards me. Heavy footsteps.

I decided to hide.

I tiptoed backwards into the pantry, pulling the door closed behind me, trying hard not to breathe. I turned around and saw a second metal egg. I raised a hand to my mouth and bit it to keep myself from screaming. Where had that other egg come from? I bent down to examine it. Like mine, the digital display must have been broken; it still said 1994. But this egg was nearly twice as big, and looked a lot more comfortable. It even had a padded lining.

So that was how Toni found me; she'd followed me back into time. She'd had a second egg the whole time, and she'd obviously saved the better one for herself, the selfish bitch. But if she was here, in the same house, then why did she have to phone me?

And where was she now?

I heard the man's voice again: "Joanna, sweetheart! Jo-aaann-a!" Who was this guy and how did he know my name? "Joanna!"

The voice was louder, he was getting closer. I heard footsteps moving across the kitchen floor. They stopped in front of the pantry door. I watched the doorknob turn. I tensed, unsure what to do.

"Who's there?" I said.

The voice sounded relieved. "Oh there you are! Didn't you hear me?" The door opened and I saw a middle-aged man with his mouth hanging open. "Oh my God, Joanna! What have you done?"

"Huh?"

"Your hair! What have you done to your hair? It's ... it's purple!"

I couldn't believe it; this guy catches an intruder cowering in a closet, and his only reaction is to comment on her hair colour? And my hair isn't purple, by the way. The tint I use is called Flickering Flame, and the packet describes it as a deep burgundy red. The guy was so busy gawking at my hair, he didn't even notice the pair of metal ovals sitting in the middle of his pantry floor. I stepped out into the kitchen, pulling the pantry door closed behind me.

"You ... you look positively indecent," the man went on, following me across the kitchen. "Look at you! Hair sticking up all over the place, like you haven't combed it in a week!" I positioned myself with my back to what I assumed was the cutlery drawer; I wanted to be within reach of something I could use as a weapon, just in case. "You look like some kind of a ... a ... a hussy! No wife of mine is going around looking like a hussy."

Wife? I thought, this man thinks I'm his wife?

"And where did you get those awful clothes? You look like some kind of a greasy mechanic!"

I was ready to punch the guy. First my hair, and now my clothes. There was nothing wrong with my clothes. I was wearing black designer jeans – strategically ripped at the knees – that cost me nearly five hundred dollars, and an understated, plain black T-shirt that was a bargain at $57.99.

Hussy? I thought. Greasy mechanic? What kind of bigoted moron uses words like that, and more important, what kind of moron mistakes a complete stranger for his wife? The man looked normal enough – almost too normal. Forty-something, thinning hair, brown tinged with grey, bit of a paunch, dressed like he just came home from an office.

"What if the neighbours saw you looking like that? And what about Katie?"

Katie. That rang a bell. "Ah," I said, remembering what the woman who looked like my mother had told me, "Katie's just a kid, isn't she?"

The man sighed and shook his head. "You're having hot flushes again, aren't you?" He touched my forehead as if he was checking for a fever. I slid my hand into the drawer behind me, grabbed hold of something I hoped was a knife, and waited to see what he would do next. But all he did was bend slightly forward, and stare open-mouthed at my feet. "You're wearing tennis shoes."

"Tennis shoes? I'll have you know these are Nikes!"

"Nikes?" he repeated, obviously confused. "But I thought you must be wearing heels . . ." His eyes moved upwards along my body, finally stopping at my eyes. "Joanna, I don't understand what's going on." Neither do I, I felt like saying, but I didn't get the chance because he carried straight on without a pause. "How could you possibly be taller?"

"Taller than who?"

"Than you were when I left you this morning. And you're thinner, too."

"Ha! Don't I wish." I took my hand out of the drawer. The guy didn't seem violent, just confused. And standing as close to him as I was, something about the guy was awfully familiar. I thought, I know him. If I could just see past the bald patch and the beer gut, and concentrate on the voice and the eyes, I knew it would come back to me. Then it hit me.

"Bobby!" I said, "Bobby Callahan! You took me to my senior prom."

His eyes went very wide. "Yes, dear," he said cautiously, "why are you bringing that up now?"

"I didn't recognize you at first; it's been a long time. It's gotta be twenty-five years. No, closer to thirty. God, Bobby, I can't believe it! So what are you doing with yourself these days?" I reached out to shake his hand.

Bobby went ever so pale. "Joanna, darling. I think you should lie down."

A few minutes later, I was leaning against a stack of frilly pillows, embroidered with sayings like "I Love Mom" and "Home Is Where The Heart Is", on one of a pair of narrow twin beds, separated by a twee little night table with two separate lamps and two individual wind-up alarm clocks, listening to Bobby clatter around in the kitchen below. He obviously wasn't used to cooking. My sudden appearance in the pantry apparently hadn't surprised him at all, but the fact that I hadn't made dinner seemed a shock beyond belief.

There was a loud crash, an "Ouch!" and a "Dammit!", then footsteps moving back up the stairs. Bobby poked his head into the bedroom and said he was driving down to the Chinese. The last thing he told me was that I should try and get some sleep.

I jumped up the minute I heard the downstairs door close; I had no intention of hanging around until he came back. Then the wardrobe doors flew wide open, and a hand shoved me back onto the mattress.

For the second time in less than ten minutes, I found myself staring open-mouthed at someone with my face. This one was even dressed the same as me: the same jeans, same T-shirt, same Nike sneakers. She had the same blunt haircut, the same shade of Flickering Flame. "Snap!" she said.

I raised my head and took a long, careful look at her. I noticed two slight differences between us: she had a blue canvas shoulder-bag draped across her arm, and a bad case of sunburn. The sunburn looked painful; the skin on her nose was peeling.

"Who are you?" I said. "Is this your house?"

"Let me address your second question first. If this was my house, do you really think I would be hiding in the wardrobe? And as to your first: who do you think I am? I know it's a little difficult, so I'll give you a clue. Who do I look like?"

"Like me?"

"Bingo!" she said, "You got it in one." She flopped down on the other bed, stretching her arms high over her head. "God, my back is killing me!"

I swung my legs around and sat up, facing the other bed.

"Let me get this straight," I said. "You're saying that you're me?"

She rolled onto her side, propping her head up with one arm. "That's one way of putting it. Though as far as I'm concerned, it's you that's me, not me that's you. A subtle distinction, I admit, but a significant one. To me, at least." There was something slightly different about her voice, too. It was a little deeper than mine, and a little harsher, as if she wanted to scream but was struggling to control herself. I guess the fact I didn't understand a word she was saying showed on my face, because she gave me a look of pure disgust. "Don't tell me you don't get it! Look, I'm an alternate you from a parallel universe, capiche?"

I couldn't believe what I had just heard. "A parallel universe?" I said. "Then how the hell did you get here?"

She got up and started looking through the various jars and bottles on the dresser. She opened one of the jars and spread some cream on her face. "How do you think I got here? The same way as you: inside that damn machine of Toni's. She made one in my universe as well, you know. A slightly better one, if you don't mind me saying so; I've seen yours down in the pantry, and it does look a bit poor."

I got up and stood by the window, watching wives in cotton dresses calling children and husbands in for dinner, and I knew this wasn't my universe, either. "So this is what the universe would have been like if I'd married Bobby Callahan."

"Oh get real!" the other Joanna said, disgusted. "Cultural and scientific stagnation is the basis of this type of universe, not who married Bobby Callahan."

"I don't understand how I got here. Toni's machine was supposed to send me forward in time, not sideways through space."

"That wasn't the machine's fault; it was that woman!"

"Woman? What woman?"

Her hands tightened into fists and her eyes became narrow slits. "The bitch that set the timer on Toni's machine to go backwards. Don't you see? As long you only move forward, you remain in the same universe. But if you try to go backwards, even by a fraction of a second, you end up in a parallel world. They tell me this is to stop you murdering your grandmother so you were never born. Anyway, she set the timer backwards on purpose to get me out of the way, so she could take over my life in my universe."

"How do you know this?"

"Because she told me! I met her. I talked to her; she's living in my studio, and I tell you she's ruined it. Cleared out all my stuff, and covered every available space with pictures of flowers and kittens. Disgusting!"

I sank down onto the nearest bed. "What did she look like?"

"Like me with grey hair and a perm, dressed in my mother's clothes. She's an alternate me from one of these oppressive suburban worlds and now she's living it up in mine, spending my money, using my name and reputation to exhibit her nauseating little pictures at all the best galleries."

Suddenly it all made sense. The woman in my studio, talking about a switch. "I've met her, too. She slammed the capsule door down on my head and the next thing I knew I was here."

"Isn't that always the way?" said the other Joanna, nodding in sympathy.

"But I still don't understand. I mean, how did she get there in the first place?"

"I have a theory about that," said the other Joanna. "I think one of us – meaning one in a world where Toni has invented a time machine – pushed the wrong button and went back by accident, maybe by only a couple of seconds. She ended up in a world like this one, and came face to face with her parallel self, a housewife who always dreamed of being an artist but never did anything about it. The Joanna like us explained who she was and how she got there. The parallel Joanna saw her chance at wealth and fame and stole the machine, leaving the other one stranded. Maybe this happened more than once, and one of these parallel Joannas ended up in your world and one in mine."

"Well, Toni will know what to do when she gets here."

"Toni? Here?"

"Yeah, she phoned just a little while ago. She said she was on her way over."

"Oh, you mean the Toni that lives here. You can forget about any help from that direction. Not the right sort of Toni."

"The right sort?"

"I've met most of the Tonis you get in this sort of world. Sometimes she's a widow with a grown-up son – usually in the army – sometimes she's a librarian, and if you're really lucky, she might be a high school science teacher."

"You've been in other worlds like this one?"

"Sure. I've been in loads of 'em. I always arrive on the same date: 29 April, 1994, and the same time: just after 6 p.m. Because that's when the first switch took place – in one of this infinite number of universes. And eventually, I'm going to be there when that first switch is about to happen, and I'm going to stop it before it does, and then none of this will ever have happened."

"How will you stop it happening?"

She smiled, patting the canvas bag that still hung from her shoulder. "I have my methods."

So she was going to make everything all right again. I should have been thrilled, but I couldn't help feeling resentful; I didn't like being made to feel stupid. Maybe I hadn't grasped all the nuances of quantum theory, and instantly figured out what was going on and how to fix it, but I was still a famous artist, and very rich. Didn't that count for anything anymore?

"I'm having an affair with a twenty-two year-old male model," I said, leaning back on the bed. "We might even do a TV commercial together; they want him to play a gorgeous young man at an exhibition opening, and me to play myself. Then he picks up a bottle of . . ."

"Shut up!" she said.

"Ooh, hit a sore point, have I? In my world, I'm often seen with much younger men."

"Will you be quiet? There's somebody coming." She moved to one side of the window, flattening herself against the wall.

"Who is it?" I whispered, sitting up.

She raised a finger to her mouth to signal silence. I got up and headed for the window.

"Get back!" she hissed, then mouthed the words, "It's her."

I flattened myself against the wall on the other side of the window from her, and peered cautiously around the frame. A woman was walking towards the house, struggling with several large shopping bags. She had my face. I looked across to the other Joanna, and saw her reach inside her canvas bag and take out a gun. She reached in again, and took out a silencer.

"What are you doing?" I whispered.

She ignored me, raising the gun and taking aim at a defence-less woman. I couldn't stand by and let this happen; I picked up one of those twee little table lamps, and broke it over her head. The gun went off, missing the woman, but sending a bullet tearing through one of her shopping bags, spilling groceries all over the pavement. The Joanna that married her high school sweetheart stopped in her tracks, staring at the shredded bag. "Move!" I shouted. "She'll kill you!"

Unfortunately, the lamp didn't knock my other self out; it just made her mad. She swung around, blood streaming from several cuts on her scalp, and pointed the gun right at me. "You stupid bitch! I fucking had her!"

"You were going to kill her!"

"I'll kill every one of them, until I get the right one. And no one's going to stop me."

I swung my right leg back and around, kicking the gun from her hand just as it went off a second time, sending chunks of plaster flying from the wall beside her. I'd taken a course in jiu-jitsu about fifteen years earlier, and this was the first time I'd ever used it. Of course she'd taken it, too, and two seconds later I was being thrown head first over her shoulder. I landed on the bedroom floor with a thud, and looked up to see my other self with a gun once more pointed at my head. She was smiling. "It isn't murder, you know. It's more like suicide by proxy."

I closed my eyes, and waited to die. There was a sound like an explosion, and I thought, is that it? Am I dead? Then I thought, that can't be it; I've got a lap full of glass.

I opened my eyes again, and saw a grey-haired woman with my face, holding what was left of the second table lamp. Bobby was right; she was about an inch or two shorter than me, and maybe five pounds heavier. She reached down and picked the gun up from the floor beside the other, unconscious, Joanna, and pointed it at me. "I think you owe me an explanation, don't you?"

I told her everything. She didn't believe me of course, until I showed her the two metal eggs in her pantry. "I'm a bit of an artist myself," she said. "One of my paintings was in an exhibition at the town hall. Maybe you'd like to have a look at some of my paintings later; they're up in the attic."

Then there was the problem of what to do with the other Joanna. When we went back up to the bedroom, she was starting to wake up. "Wha'?" she said, "What happened? Where am I?" Joanna Callahan and I stood on either side of the bed where we'd left her firmly tied down with a length of laundry-line. She looked from one side of the bed to the other. "Who are you guys supposed to be, the Bobsey Twins?"

"Maybe I shouldn't have hit her so hard," said Joanna Callahan.

"I'd be dead if you hadn't," I reminded her.

"And so would I, if what you say is true," she sighed.

"What's going on?" said Joanna on the bed. "Who are you bozos?"

"Don't you know me?" I asked her.

"I never saw you in my life!"

"Do you know who you are?" Joanna Callahan asked her.

"Of course I do! I'm . . ." She frowned in concentration. "Oh shit."

"You stay with her," Joanna Callahan told me. "I'll just run and get my first aid kit from the kitchen."

Before I could think to ask her what she had in a first aid kit for amnesia, she was gone.

"Why don't I remember who I am?" asked Joanna on the bed.

"You've had a nasty crack on the head," I told her. "You fell down the stairs."

"Why am I all tied up?"

"To keep you from falling down again. Stay there, I'll be right back." I ran downstairs to the kitchen. The pantry door was open, and there was only one metal egg: the one I came in. Joanna Callahan had stolen the nicer one, with the padded lining.

"Bitch!" I shouted, kicking the refrigerator. "Fucking bitch!"

Then Joanna upstairs started screaming for help. She was making a hell of a racket; someone would call the police if she kept that up. I ran back up the stairs and found the bed tipped over onto its side, and Joanna wriggling around on the floor, trying to break loose. "Help!" she kept screaming, "Somebody help me!"

The front doorbell rang, and Joanna started screaming even louder. I stuffed a pillowcase down her mouth; that shut her up. The doorbell kept ringing and I heard a woman's voice call my name. "Joanna! Open up! Are you okay?" Toni. I grabbed a scarf out of the wardrobe to hide my Flickering Flame hair, then I ran to the window. "Toni!" I called down, faking a yawn. "Sorry, I must have been asleep."

A large, dark-haired woman wearing a brown cardigan sweater over a white blouse and brown skirt looked up from the street. She was wearing a pair of horn-rimmed glasses so thick they reminded me of Mister Magoo. She had "small town librarian" written all over her. Definitely not the right sort of Toni.

"Joanna, are you all right? I thought I heard you screaming for help!" Joanna with the pillowcase in her mouth was trying to stand up with a bed tied to her back.

"I was having the worst nightmare! Hold on, I'll be right down." I ran down the stairs to the kitchen, then remembered something and ran back up again. The other Joanna was squirming around more than ever, making a lot of "Hmph!" and "MMMMMM!" sort of noises. I had to admire her determination. "Don't worry, Joanna. Someone will untie you in a minute, I promise. But it won't be me." I put the gun back inside her blue canvas bag, and slung it over my shoulder.

I was halfway down the stairs when I heard Toni say, "Bob! Thank God you're home! There's something wrong with Joanna!" I reached the bottom just as his key turned in the lock. By the time they reached the bedroom, I was already in the pantry, squeezing myself back inside my uncomfortable, unpadded, metal egg. There was a lot of screaming and shouting going on upstairs.

I heard Toni say she was calling the police, and then I heard heavy footsteps on the stairs. I pulled the capsule door down over my head, and stared at a row of unlabelled buttons. I didn't have the slightest idea which one to press, so I pressed them all. I heard Toni's voice outside the capsule, saying, "What the . . ." and then I was ripped into a million pieces.

I pushed the door open and found myself staring up at a cactus. I was dizzy and more than a little nauseous; I waited for the cactus to stop spinning before I tried to sit up. The moment I raised my head, the cactus started whirling again, faster than ever. I'd been broken down and reassembled for the third time in less than half an hour, and I didn't think my body could take a fourth; at least not yet. I pulled myself out of the capsule, fell to my knees, and vomited onto scorching hot dust. I crawled on all fours towards a clump of stunted bushes a few yards away, and rested in the tiny patch of shade they provided.

I don't know how long I was there; I think I must have fallen asleep. All I know is when I opened my eyes again, a man was standing over me, his face a mixture of surprise and concern. "You all right?" he said. He had white hair down to his shoulders, a full white beard, a round face with chubby red cheeks, sparkling brown eyes, and an enormous belly. Santa Claus in blue jeans.

"No, I'm not all right. I feel like hell and I don't have the slightest idea where I am."

The man knelt down beside me. "My house is just the other side of that hill. Don't try to move; I'll carry you."

"No, it's okay. I can walk."

"Now you just lean on me," he said, helping me to my feet. "And don't you worry 'bout a thing; my old lady'll get you fixed up in no time. She'll be interested to see you. Real interested, I'll tell you that for nothing."

"What do you mean, interested?"

"You'll see. Believe you me, you'll see."

A pair of large dogs – one black, one brown – lunged forward to greet us as we approached a large adobe house painted in a myriad of colours. Each of the outside walls was like a mural, one side adorned with children running through a field, another with a cityscape of high-rise buildings lit by a reddish-gold setting sun, another a series of geometric shapes in primary colours. Behind the house was another building, a bright red barn almost as big as the house.

"Down Horace! Get down, Charlemagne! Down boys," the man said as the dogs leapt around us, barking excitedly. "This here lady doesn't feel too well." Then he raised his voice to a shout: "Jo-aaannn-a!"

A woman appeared in the doorway. Wearing an ankle-length denim dress and a string of beads. Centre-parted, waist-length hair. Brown, streaked with grey. "Who you got there, Mark?"

"This lady's sick. Help me get her inside the house."

She ran forward, and slid an arm around my back. I closed my eyes; I didn't want to look at her face.

"Oh my God, Mark," she said.

"Yeah, I know. Ain't it the strangest thing?"

I woke up with a dreadful case of sunburn; my face and arms were bright red. I raised my head and saw the woman who had introduced herself as Joanna Hansen standing in the bedroom doorway, holding a mug of coffee. Her salt-and-pepper hair was tied back in a long ponytail, and she was wearing sandals and a cotton kimono. I looked around for my clothes, and didn't see them.

"I put them in the wash," she told me. "Borrow anything you want from that closet."

I pulled on a pair of jeans and a denim shirt, and went down to the kitchen. Mark was making hotcakes in honour of my visit. He was under the impression I was a long lost cousin of Joanna's – at least that's what I'd told him the night before.

I'd known Mark Hansen back in 1967, when we were both art students in San Francisco. It was the Summer of Love, and he had long black hair and drove a VW van. So there actually was a universe where I'd said yes when he asked me to go and live with him in the desert. In his day, he was every bit as gorgeous as any twenty-two year-old male model. I wondered if there was a universe where he hadn't ended up looking like Father Christmas.

"I can't get over it," he said to Joanna. "All these years you had a cousin that's your spitting image and you never even knew she existed!"

"Yeah," said Joanna, eyeing me suspiciously, "I can't get over it, either."

I had told them both the most ridiculous pack of lies the night before, how I'd been on my way to visit Joanna and my rented car had broken down in the middle of the desert, and Mark, at least, seemed to believe it. I knew Joanna was waiting for the chance to get me alone; that's what I would have done.

Her chance came that afternoon, when Mark drove into town to get the shopping. We were sitting on the front step, sipping iced tea with slices of lemon, when she finally said it: "Isn't it time you told me the truth?"

"I don't know what you mean."

"I don't have a cousin named Annabel." (Annabel was the first name that popped into my head the night before; I don't know why.) "Not even a long-lost one, like you claim to be. So who are you, and what were you doing out in the middle of nowhere, covered in plaster dust and broken glass? And how come you look so much like me? I'm warning you, I want the truth."

"You'll never believe it."

"Try me."

"Okay." I put down my glass of iced tea, and looked her right in the eye. "Do you ever wonder what your life would have been like if you'd made some different decisions along the way?"

"I haven't done acid since 1975," she said when I was finished. "Don't you think it's time for you to give it up, too?"

"I told you you'd never believe me. Maybe if we could contact Toni; she might be working on something similar in this world. Maybe she even got it right in this one."

Joanna Hansen shook her head. "Toni's dead. She died a long time ago," she said. "O.D.'d."

"What? She can't be dead!"

"Why not? If I'm supposed to believe you, then where you come from, my two kids were never even born!" Mark had shown me pictures of them the night before: two extremely dishy young men, one twenty-five years old, the other only twenty-one. Then I remembered whose children they were.

"Oh yeah," I said, "Joanna Callahan apparently had some kids as well."

"And she just up and left them."

"More than once," I said. "I mean, more than one version of her left more than one version of them."

"How do you know I won't steal your machine, so I can be rich and famous in New York?"

"You don't know where I left it."

"You think I couldn't find it if I wanted to?" She laughed. "You ought to see your face; you've gone bright green. Well, you sit out here and worry yourself sick about whether I think being you is such an attractive prospect or not. Meanwhile, I've got work to do. Help yourself to anything you want from the fridge."

And then she left me, sitting alone on the step.

I was still there when Mark came back, two hours later. The dogs leapt out of the truck and ran towards me, barking and wagging their tails. A second later, I was on my back, having my face licked. "I've never known those dogs to take to someone as quick as they've taken to you," Mark said. "It's like they've known you all their lives."

"I noticed," I said, pushing them away.

"Where's Joanna?"

"She said she had some work to do."

"Then she'll be in her studio. Haven't you been in there yet?"

I shook my head.

"I thought she'd have given you the grand tour by now," he said. "Never mind. Help me get the groceries in, and I'll take you around."

A short while later, he led me around the back of the house to the large building I'd assumed was a barn. "Please don't think she's being rude, abandoning you like that. It's just that she's got this big show coming up in a couple of months, and she reckons she's nowhere near ready."

"Show? What kind of show?"

"Joanna's an artist; didn't she tell you?"

Of course, I thought, Mark and I had met in art school. So what was this Joanna's art like? More puppies and flowers? No, I thought, this one's an old hippie; I'll bet she weaves native-style blankets and sells them at craft fairs. Then Mark opened the door and my mouth dropped open.

This Joanna, like me, was a sculptor, and like me, she worked mostly in metal, and – this is a hard admission for me to make – she was every bit as good as me. Maybe even – this is an even harder admission – a little better.

I touched the twisted trunk of a metal tree with shiny flat leaves. Tiny men hung like fruit from its branches, each with a noose around his neck, each with a completely different and individual expression of pain or horror on his face. I wished I'd done it. Though in a way, I had.

"That one's already sold," Mark told me. "Some museum in Europe's offered her a couple million for it, and she's told 'em they can have it after the show."

At the sound of the words: "couple million", my heart almost did a flip-flop. It was all I could do not to clutch at my chest. I took a few deep breaths, counting to ten on each inhalation.

"So where is this show of hers?" I asked him, trying to sound nonchalant.

"The Museum of Contemporary Art," he told me, adding, "That's in New York." As if I didn't know. And I'd been so worried this Joanna might want to trade places with me. "Didn't you see that TV show they did about her?" he asked me. "It was on prime time, coast to coast."

"I'm afraid I missed it."

We found her at the far end of the building, working on a rather familiar arrangement of six black and white television sets called "Women on the Brink of a Cataclysm". She couldn't figure out why I thought that was funny.

Then she switched it on, and I saw that unlike mine, each of her screens showed a different woman doing a different repetitious task: one scrubbing a floor, one doing dishes, one hanging laundry, one ironing shirts, one chopping vegetables, and one slashing her wrists, over and over again, in an endless loop.

I wished I'd done mine like that – though of course I would, now. There was nothing in Joanna Hansen's work I wouldn't be proud to call my own. If I couldn't get back to my own world – and I was beginning to doubt I ever would – then this one would suit me just fine. But making the switch might be difficult with Mark around; it would have to be done gradually.

I offered to help Joanna in her studio, and learned exactly where she kept everything. I got her to tell me her complete history under the pretext of trying to figure out just where our paths had diverged. I got Mark to tell me everything I'd need to know about him under the pretext of finding him a fascinating conversationalist, which he never was, even when we were students. I went through every photo album and every scrap book, memorizing the details. I sat through slides and home movies. And I nagged Joanna about her hair, told her it made her look much older than she was, and reminded her of all the photographers that would be at her opening party in New York. "Just trim the ends a little," I told her. "Just cover the grey." I finally convinced her to let me cut it – a much quicker process than waiting for mine to grow – but I couldn't get her to colour it; I had to let myself go grey.

Within three weeks of my arrival, Joanna Hansen and I were indistinguishable.

One morning when Mark had driven into town, I told Joanna it was time for me to leave. I put on the clothes I had arrived in, slung the blue canvas bag with the gun in it over my shoulder, and thanked her for everything. Then, as though it were an afterthought, I asked her if she'd like to see the time machine.

I led her out into the desert, to the spot where Toni's metal egg sat hidden behind a cactus plant. "That's it," I said.

"It doesn't look very comfortable."

"Why don't you try it for yourself?" I said. "Get inside, see how it feels."

"No thanks."

I pointed the gun at her. "Get inside."

"You can't shoot me," she said.

"I can and I will if you don't do what I tell you."

"No, you can't. That gun isn't loaded; I took the bullets out ages ago."

I pointed the gun straight at her and pulled the trigger.

Nothing happened. "You bitch! You've been through my things!"

"Damn right. I did that the first night you turned up. You think I'm stupid or something? Now," she reached into one of the pockets in her denim skirt, "this gun is loaded." She was holding a little semi-automatic pistol. "As you were saying, Joanna, it's time you went back to your own world."

"Wait a minute," I said. "That was only a joke with the gun; I was never going to shoot you. What I was going to suggest is that we work together, sort of interchangeably. You could get twice as much done, and nobody would ever know."

"Good-bye, Joanna."

I got inside the machine, and the next thing I knew it was the 29th of April, 1994, a little after 6 p.m., and I was back in Joanna Callahan's pantry, with swollen joints and a raging headache. As I struggled to pull myself up, I noticed another metal egg. This one not only had a padded interior, but a row of little flashing lights along the outside.

Someone was coming. I ran through the kitchen and out the back door. I crouched down outside the open kitchen window and listened to the phone ringing, then my voice: "Toni! Thank God! How did you find me? How did you know what number to call?"

I was about to go back inside and talk to this woman, when I heard a car pull into the front drive. I crept along the wall towards the front of the house and saw Bob Callahan put his key in the front door. "Honey! I'm home!"

He'd head straight back to the kitchen and find the other me cowering in the pantry, where I'd left my only method of escape. I had to get back inside the house; I reached the door just before it swung completely closed, and crept into the hallway. I heard voices coming from the kitchen, then I heard Bobby say, "I think you'd better lie down."

I ran upstairs to the bedroom. It was different than I remembered. There was only one bed, a double. I looked out the window and saw a long-haired guy in black leather tinkering with his motorcycle, watched by a bunch of kids in baggy clothes and baseball caps worn backwards. I breathed a sigh of relief. This was more like the 1994 I knew. But it still wasn't the right one; Bobby Callahan was leading one of the alternate me's up the stairs.

"If this was my house, do you really think I'd be hiding in the wardrobe?" I said a short while later. "And as to your second question: who do I look like?"

"Like me, I guess. But older."

"Older?" I rushed over to the mirror. She was right. That grey hair put ten years on me, and my time in the desert hadn't done my complexion any good; I noticed several new lines around my eyes and mouth. I opened a jar of Joanna Callahan's moisturizer and spread it on my face.

"You look a lot like that woman who was in my studio," said the other Joanna – she was reaching for something inside a canvas bag just like mine, only hers was green. "Or at least I think it was my studio."

The downstairs door opened and slammed shut. Bobby couldn't be back already. I whispered to the other Joanna to stay where she was and keep quiet, then I tiptoed into the hall. A teenage girl with blonde hair, black roots, and thick black eyeliner, stomped up the stairs in a pair of platform boots. She had four or five earrings on each ear, and one through her right nostril.

"Fuck off, Mom. Don't hassle me," she said, opening one of the other doors and slamming it behind her. So this was Katie. A moment later, the walls were vibrating with music by some band I'd never heard of.

I went downstairs and had another look at the house. There was a stack of videos next to the television, a microwave oven and food processor in the kitchen. All those "Bless This House" embroideries were gone, replaced by paintings of a grey-haired woman in varying states of depression. They weren't bad. I flipped one over and read the neatly printed words: Number Three in a Series of Women on the Brink of a Cataclysm.

Well, Joanna, I thought, meaning both of them – the one I'd left upstairs, and the one who'd be home any minute now – you're on your own. I opened the pantry door and sank down inside a padded machine with a row of lovely flashing lights. The machine was a joy. I didn't feel a thing. No stiffness, no swelling, no dizziness. I opened the door and found myself back in the desert. April 29, 1994, just after 6 p.m. New York time – the middle of a scorching afternoon out west. I had been given a second chance. And this time I would do it right. I wouldn't let Mark see me; I'd get Joanna on her own and do the switch immediately. Then I'd have my exhibition, collect my millions, and give poor Mark an amicable divorce settlement – in this world, I could afford to be generous.

I climbed the little hill that hid the house from view and saw a shack. A dilapidated little house, like something out of Ma and Pa Kettle. I'm in the wrong place, I thought; I made a wrong turn somewhere out in the desert. Then two large dogs ran towards me, leaping and barking. One was black and one was brown. A man chased after them, shouting, "Charlemagne! Horace! Get back here!"

He looked at me and stopped dead in his tracks. "Joanna! Come outside!"

She appeared in the doorway, dressed in jeans and a transparent gauze top. "Wow!" she said.

They offered me a glass of home brew and a joint. Joanna told me she made native-style blankets and sold them at craft fairs.

I left after dinner.

I pushed the capsule door open, and breathed a huge sigh of relief. I was back in New York, surrounded by noise and dirt and traffic. I was home, though for some reason I wasn't in my studio. I had landed in an alley, surrounded by overflowing metal garbage cans and stacks of cardboard boxes.

I heard a rustling sound coming from one of the cardboard boxes – the closest one. Rats, I thought, cringing. I hate rats.

I leaned forward to pull myself up, and came face to face with a pair of bloodshot eyes, staring through a little hole in the nearest box. My own eyes watered at the pungent, combined aromas of alcohol and stale perspiration.

"So you've come for me, at last."

Oh no, I thought. There was something horribly familiar about that voice. "Maybe," I said. "That depends on who you think I am."

"You're the angel of death, aren't you?"

"Your name isn't Joanna, by any chance?"

"You are the angel of death!" The box lid flew open and a woman rose before me. Toothless. Matted grey hair crawling with insects. Dressed in layer upon layer of dirty, ragged clothing: a winter coat over a man's shirt over a sweater over a dress over a pair of trousers. Eyes shining with madness, hands clutching a pair of heavily laden shopping bags. "I'm ready. Take me to a better world than this one."

I slammed down the lid and pressed every button. I knew I must have arrived someplace else, but I couldn't bring myself to look. I just sat there, curled up inside my padded metal egg, and shook.

How could I have ended up like that? Me, Joanna Krenski. Talented, attractive, intelligent. Whatever could have happened to bring me down to that level? Homeless. Penniless. Living in a box. And then I realized why I couldn't stop shaking. I, Joanna Krenski – the Joanna Krenski – was in exactly the same position. Homeless and penniless, living inside a box – it's just that mine was made of metal instead of cardboard. Joanna the bag lady had lost her mind; how long would it be before I lost mine? If I dared to think about it, I knew I was already on the way.

All my life I'd thought of myself as an essentially good person, but all I'd been was comfortable. The moment I realized I'd lost my place in my world, meaning my material security (not the so-called friends I'd chosen on the basis of what they could do for me, not the young lover I only regarded as a trophy), I'd been ready to lie, steal, and even kill. I had almost murdered the only alternate Joanna to treat me with any kindness. Now I thanked God the gun hadn't been loaded. I felt disgusted and ashamed. I hated myself. Over and over again.

I didn't care where I had landed this time – the desert, the suburbs, my studio, a sewer – it didn't matter. I would stay curled inside my egg; I was never coming out again. And I wouldn't have come out, if someone else hadn't pulled the capsule door open.

"Please," a familiar woman's voice said in a whisper. "You've got to help me."

I lay back inside the egg, looking up at one of the Joanna Callahans. She was trying to squeeze into the machine with me.

"Why should I help you with anything?" I said, wedging my legs across the opening. "Everything that's happened is your fault. If you didn't like your own world, you should have done something to change it from within, not try to steal someone else's."

"I know that now. I know," she whispered, leaning down over me, "and I'm sorry. Really I am. But you've got to move over. There's room in here for both of us. Please. She's killed the others; I saw her do it!"

So I had come full circle. One of me was killing off all the Joanna Callahans so the whole thing would never have happened. It didn't seem like such a bad idea to me now, and I said so. "No, you don't understand! She's the one that started it! She's—" she looked up at something I couldn't see, a look of pure terror on her face. "Press the button," she said, slamming the lid down.

"Save yourself!" Then I heard the most horrible scream: an animal sound that would haunt me forever, through every time and every universe.

I pushed the door open and raised my head in time to see a woman in a silver catsuit drag Joanna Callahan across the floor and through a giant hoop, by means of a grappling hook stuck into her back. As Joanna passed, howling, through the hoop, there was a blinding flash of light. She covered her eyes, shrieking and floundering helplessly. There was a final tug on the hook, and then she stopped screaming.

Joanna Callahan lay dead in a pool of blood at the feet of a woman with long black hair tied into a knot at the top of her head, a taut, muscular body, an unlined face with implanted cheekbones out to there, and the cruellest eyes I have ever seen. Me with plastic surgery, a personal trainer, and an advanced state of psychosis. She smiled at me and licked her lips; I slammed the capsule door shut and carefully pressed what I hoped were the right buttons.

I didn't want to switch universes this time, I wanted to stay in this one. Whatever this me was doing, she had to be stopped.

I opened the capsule just a crack; it was dark. I opened it a little further, and listened.

Silence.

The digital display inside the capsule read: April 29, 1994, 11:59 p.m., E.S.T. I had gone forward almost six hours. I stepped out of the capsule and examined my surroundings. I was in a large, square room with a bare concrete floor, furnished with a combination of electronic equipment and implements of torture.

The giant hoop leaned against one wall. It was about six and a half feet high, and three inches deep, lined with hundreds of tiny light bulbs. I still had no idea what it was. I walked to the window and looked down at the twinkling lights of Manhattan. At least I assumed it was Manhattan; I didn't recognize any of the buildings. All I knew was I was very high up – at least ninety floors. I opened the only door in the room and peered down a long, dark hallway lined with doors. No lights on anywhere. It was a Friday night; she'd probably gone out.

I shoved the egg behind something that looked like an Iron Maiden with electrical cabling, and stepped out into the hall. Two Doberman Pinschers raced at me from the shadows, barking and growling. Stay calm, I told myself; dogs can smell fear. And then I remembered: smell. Joanna Hansen's dogs had taken to me because I smelled exactly like her. "Down boys," I said firmly, holding out my hand for them to sniff. They slunk away as if they were terrified.

I stood where I was, listening and waiting. Then I switched on the lights; if those dogs hadn't roused anyone, there was no one around to rouse.

I opened one door after another, peering into a seemingly endless succession of huge, opulently furnished rooms. This Joanna was seriously rich. Then I came to a door that had no visible lock or handle; on the wall beside it was a small glass plate showing the outline of a hand. I pressed my hand flat against it, a little sign flashed "palmprint cleared for access", the door slid silently open, and I stepped into an armoury. There were guns of every description, hundreds of them, lined up on racks inside huge glass cases. There was every type of sword, machete, axe, knife, and razor, also behind glass. There were stacks of drawers marked "ammo". And, mounted on the wall: the grappling hook, Joanna Callahan's blood still visible on two of its iron claws.

To get into the weapons cases required a voiceprint identification. That was easy, all I had to do was say "open". I don't know anything about guns, so I just took one that felt fairly light and easy to handle, a smallish rifle. I loaded both the rifle and the handgun I'd stolen from that other Joanna back in the suburbs, and filled my canvas bag with extra ammunition.

I pushed the last door open, at the end of the hall, and felt around in the dark for the light switch. There was a slight humming sound, followed by a "whoosh", before the room came into view.

The walls, floor, and ceiling were velvet black; the only light came from inside the glass display cases scattered around the room. Each contained a moving, three-dimensional figure. They were better than any holograms I had ever seen. There was no angle at which they appeared to lose their definition; they were every bit as convincing from the back as they were from the front. And as I said before, they moved.

I stopped in front of one and watched a man pounding against the glass, his face contorted into a howl of hysteria. I could almost hear his screams, almost believe he was alive. I waved my hand in front of his face; he kept on pounding, his hands raw and bloody, his eyes glazed with desperation, staring at something I couldn't see. An engraved plate at the base of the display read: Trapped. J. Krenski, 1987.

I paused beside another case. Its occupant lunged towards me, holding a knife, and I leapt back, raising my rifle. I shook my head, cursing myself for being so jumpy, but the damn thing was incredibly realistic. The slobbering face pressed against the glass seemed to be leering directly at me. I looked at the title plate: Slasher.

In one display, a child was shooting up. In another, a hideous couple performed continuous sex, in another, an animal gnawed at its own foot, caught in a metal clamp above the title plate: Trapped 2.

There were rows and rows of cases, each more grotesque than the last. Finally I came to the arrangement of six glass cases, titled: Women on the Brink of a Cataclysm: 6 Variations on the Theme of Suicide by Proxy. Joanna Callahan was there, sliding across the floor with a grappling hook in her back. A version of Joanna Hansen was there, twitching at the end of a noose. A platinum blonde Joanna in a waitress uniform clutched at a knife in her chest. A brown-haired Joanna in a business suit appeared to be suffocating. One like me was in the process of being shot repeatedly, and one with black hair and fake cheek-bones stood motionless, pointing a sub-machine gun directly at my chest.

"Drop the rifle, Joanna," she said.

I dropped it.

"And the bag."

The bag hit the floor. "I don't get it," I said. "What's the point of all this?"

"The point?" She raised both eyebrows. "The point, my dear, is art! I brought you here to be part of my exhibition."

"But how?"

"That was amazingly easy. When Toni first came up with the idea for her time machine, she decided it was extremely likely that at least one or two parallel versions of herself might be working along the same lines, and that at least a few parallel versions of myself might have one or two fundamental character flaws. So we sent out one empty machine, pre-set to go backwards, and it took exactly ten seconds to round up half-a-dozen of you, who'd been bouncing back and forth between your various universes, doing everything from ripping each other off to committing mass murder. And the minute you were all in one room, how you went for each other's throats! It was all Toni and I could do to keep you apart." She threw her head back and laughed. "I'd say every single one of you deserved her place here."

"You don't want me for that piece, though, do you?" I said. "I mean, you've already got one like me; I'd throw the visual balance off."

She shrugged. "You'll look different by the time I'm finished with you. Toni!"

Toni entered the room, pushing the giant hoop on a set of wheels. She had an American flag tattooed across her shaven head.

"What is that thing?" I asked.

"It's a three-dimensional camera," Joanna explained. "It photographs you from all directions at once."

The blinding light I'd seen was the flash going off. "So everything in here is just a photographic image, kind of like a 3-D movie."

"More or less, though we enhance it on a computer."

"So why did you have to kill them? Couldn't you just simulate the whole thing on a computer?"

She snorted in disgust. "That would be cheating."

I leaned against the 95th floor lobby wall, watching Toni set up. There was nothing else I could do with Joanna pointing a machine-gun at me. As she'd already pointed out, there was no point in screaming because there was no one around to hear; this was an office building and no one else lived here but her, because she owned the entire block.

"Okay," Toni said. "It's all ready."

She had the elevator doors propped open. The 3-D hoop camera was wedged on its side inside the shaft, three floors down. The elevator car was stopped one floor above us.

"This is going to be such a brilliant image," Joanna said, motioning me towards the elevator shaft.

"How can you do this to me? I'm you, you stupid bitch! How can you do this to yourself?"

"No, dear," she said, shaking her head. "Only I am me. You are merely a variation on a theme. Now are you going to jump, or am I going to push you?"

I clung to the wall either side of the shaft with all my strength. "You're gonna have to push me."

I heard a horrible cackling laugh. That was Toni. Then I heard at least a dozen gunshots in rapid succession. I turned around and saw a bag lady holding an automatic assault rifle.

It turned out one of the other Joannas had landed in an alley and left her machine unattended for less than a minute. Joanna the bag lady turned out to be just as much a thief as the rest of us – thank God – and much better at staying out of sight, having had a lot more practice. She'd spent most of the last six hours under a stack of towels inside a cupboard, which she told me was a lot more space than she was used to.

We found her machine and the ones the others had arrived in, in a workroom behind the exhibition. They were each quite different – some weren't even egg-shaped at all. We used one of the larger ones to dispose of Joanna and Toni; we sent their bodies three hundred years into the future.

"So what will you do now?" I asked my bag lady self.

"Treat myself to a bath and a change of clothing," she said. "Then a long sleep, in a real bed, and breakfast in the kitchen in the morning. Maybe I'll just stay here permanently and stage an exhibition of my own. I'm a bit of an artist myself, you know. I mean, I am Joanna Krenski, and I seem to be extremely rich."

She smiled and nudged me towards one of the eggs, at gunpoint.

*   *   *

I found myself back in the Callahan's pantry, pushing the door of my little padded capsule open just as Joanna Callahan herself was settling down into another egg directly beside me. "Don't do it," I told her. "On behalf of all your possible selves, I beg you not to do this." She ignored me.

I got up and walked through the house. The kitchen was shiny and white, the dining room decorated with watercolour paintings of daisies and the living room walls covered in pastel sketches of guinea pigs and bunny rabbits.

I went upstairs and found one of me sitting on the edge of a narrow twin bed. Bobby was right – her hair was purple. And so was her canvas bag. "She's done it again," I said, "She's stolen your egg. Why are we all so horrible to each other? To ourselves? I don't understand it."

"What did you say?"

"I said she's stolen your egg. Though I can't say I'm surprised. I'm not surprised by anything any of us do any more."

She got up and ran downstairs. "Wait!" I said, running after her. By the time I reached the kitchen she was gone. I stared at the empty pantry floor for a minute or two and then I sighed. "Well that's it, then," I said. I went upstairs and put on a cotton dress, a little big around the waist and hips. "Toni!" I said when she arrived, "I'm sorry if I sounded a little strange on the phone . . ."

I don't check the pantry for eggs any more; if anyone was coming, they'd have been here by now. Bob's finally getting used to the idea that if he wants a shirt ironed or the house vacuumed, he'll just have to do it himself. And the same goes for sex. I don't feel sorry for him any more; his wife walked out on him more than six months ago, leaving him with a stranger from another universe, and he still hasn't noticed.

The Katie in this world is just too sweet for words: little brown pigtails, knee socks, freckles, and pleated skirts. I preferred the other one. Bob Junior just turned twenty-eight. He and his wife live a couple of blocks away, and he has a little construction business. He helped me convert the garage into a studio, then he gave me a complete set of tools – including a welding torch – as a "studio warming" present.

My other son, Harold, lives in New York, but comes to visit most weekends. He wants to be my manager; he says he loves what I'm doing, especially the metal tree with the little men hanging from it like fruit. He says he doesn't know where I get my ideas.

I have an appointment with one of the major gallery owners tomorrow. I'm taking my latest piece to show him: a headless Barbie doll stuck inside a fish tank.

Well, it worked the last time.

LEGIONS IN TIME

Michael Swanwick

The title of the following story is an affectionate tribute to the classic novel, The Legion of Time, *by Jack Williamson, first serialized in 1938. The novel revealed the conflict between two variant futures each seeking to protect their own timeline, both of which stem from a key moment when a young boy, John Barr, picked up either a magnet or a stone. From this came the phrase, "Jonbar Point", meaning a critical moment which can generate a variant future. Michael Swanwick takes the concept much further in this story, melding it with the mood and scale of the time-war stories by A. E. van Vogt, notably "Recruiting Station" (1942) and "The Changeling" (1944) later collected as* Masters of Time *(1950). The result is a genuine tour de force that looks back to the Golden Age of magazine science fiction.*

Michael Swanwick is a multi-award-winning American writer whose books have included Vacuum Flowers *(1987),* Stations of the Tide *(1991) and, of special interest to this volume in its portrayal of an alternate United States,* In the Drift *(1985).*

Eleanor Voigt had the oddest job of anyone she knew. She worked eight hours a day in an office where no business was done. Her job was to sit at a desk and stare at the closet door. There was a button on the desk which she was to push if anybody came out that door. There was a big clock on the wall and precisely at noon, once a day, she went over to the door and unlocked it with a key she had been given. Inside was an empty closet. There were no trap doors or secret panels in it – she had looked. It was just an empty closet.

If she noticed anything unusual, she was supposed to go back to her desk and press the button.

"Unusual in what way?" she'd asked when she'd been hired. "I don't understand. What am I looking for?"

"You'll know it when you see it," Mr Tarblecko had said in that odd accent of his. Mr Tarblecko was her employer, and some kind of foreigner. He was the creepiest thing imaginable. He had pasty white skin and no hair at all on his head, so that when he took his hat off he looked like some species of mushroom. His ears were small and almost pointed. Ellie thought he might have some kind of disease. But he paid two dollars an hour, which was good money nowadays for a woman of her age.

At the end of her shift, she was relieved by an unkempt young man who had once blurted out to her that he was a poet. When she came in, in the morning, a heavy Negress would stand up wordlessly, take her coat and hat from the rack, and with enormous dignity leave.

So all day Ellie sat behind the desk with nothing to do. She wasn't allowed to read a book, for fear she might get so involved in it that she would stop watching the door. Crosswords were allowed, because they weren't as engrossing. She got a lot of knitting done, and was considering taking up tatting.

Over time the door began to loom large in her imagination. She pictured herself unlocking it at some forbidden not-noon time and seeing – what? Her imagination failed her. No matter how vividly she visualized it, the door would open onto something mundane. Brooms and mops. Sports equipment. Galoshes and old clothes. What else would there be in a closet? What else could there be?

Sometimes, caught up in her imaginings, she would find herself on her feet. Sometimes, she walked to the door. Once she actually put her hand on the knob before drawing away. But always the thought of losing her job stopped her.

It was maddening.

Twice, Mr Tarblecko had come to the office while she was on duty. Each time he was wearing that same black suit with that same narrow black tie. "You have a watch?" he'd asked.

"Yes, sir." The first time, she'd held forth her wrist to show it to him. The disdainful way he ignored the gesture ensured she did not repeat it on his second visit.

"Go away. Come back in forty minutes."

So she had gone out to a little tearoom nearby. She had a bag lunch back in her desk, with a baloney-and-mayonnaise sandwich and an apple, but she'd been so flustered she'd forgotten it, and then feared to go back after it. She treated herself to a dainty "lady lunch" that she was in no mood to appreciate, left a dime tip for the waitress, and was back in front of the office door exactly thirty-eight minutes after she'd left.

At forty minutes, exactly, she reached for the door.

As if he'd been waiting for her to do so, Mr Tarblecko breezed through the door, putting on his hat. He didn't acknowledge her promptness *or* her presence. He just strode briskly past, as though she didn't exist.

Stunned, she went inside, closed the door, and returned to her desk.

She realized then that Mr Tarblecko was genuinely, fabulously rich. He had the arrogance of those who are so wealthy that they inevitably get their way in all small matters because there's always somebody there to *arrange* things that way. His type was never grateful for anything and never bothered to be polite, because it never even occurred to them that things could be otherwise.

The more she thought about it, the madder she got. She was no Bolshevik, but it seemed to her that people had certain rights, and that one of these was the right to a little common courtesy. It diminished one to be treated like a stick of furniture. It was degrading. She was damned if she was going to take it.

Six months went by.

The door opened and Mr Tarblecko strode in, as if he'd left only minutes ago. "You have a watch?"

Ellie slid open a drawer and dropped her knitting into it. She opened another and took out her bag lunch. "Yes."

"Go away. Come back in forty minutes."

So she went outside. It was May, and Central Park was only a short walk away, so she ate there, by the little pond where children floated their toy sailboats. But all the while she fumed. She was a good employee – she really was! She was conscientious, punctual, and she never called in sick. Mr Tarblecko ought to appreciate that. He had no business treating her the way he did.

Almost, she wanted to overstay lunch, but her conscience wouldn't allow that. When she got back to the office, precisely thirty-nine and a half minutes after she'd left, she planted herself squarely in front of the door so that when Mr Tarblecko left he would have no choice but to confront her. It might well lose her her job, but . . . well, if it did, it did. That's how strongly she felt about it.

Thirty seconds later, the door opened and Mr Tarblecko strode briskly out. Without breaking his stride or, indeed, showing the least sign of emotion, he picked her up by her two arms, swivelled effortlessly, and deposited her to the side.

Then he was gone. Ellie heard his footsteps dwindling down the hall.

The nerve! The sheer, raw *gall* of the man!

Ellie went back in the office, but she couldn't make herself sit down at the desk. She was far too upset. Instead, she walked back and forth the length of the room, arguing with herself, saying aloud those things she should have said and would have said if only Mr Tarblecko had stood still for them. To be picked up and set aside like that . . . Well, it was really quite upsetting. It was intolerable.

What was particularly distressing was that there wasn't even any way to make her displeasure known.

At last, though, she calmed down enough to think clearly, and realized that she was wrong. There *was* something – something more symbolic than substantive, admittedly – that she could do.

She could open that door.

Ellie did not act on impulse. She was a methodical woman. So she thought the matter through before she did anything. Mr Tarblecko very rarely showed up at the office – only twice in all the time she'd been here, and she'd been here over a year. Moreover, the odds of him returning to the office a third time only minutes after leaving it were negligible. He had left nothing behind – she could see that at a glance; the office was almost Spartan in its emptiness. Nor was there any work here for him to return to.

Just to be safe, though, she locked the office door. Then she got her chair out from behind the desk and chocked it up under the doorknob so that even if somebody had a key, he couldn't get in. She put her ear to the door and listened for noises in the hall.

Nothing.

It was strange how, now that she had decided to do the deed, time seemed to slow and the office to expand. It took forever to cross the vast expanses of empty space between her and the closet door. Her hand reaching for its knob pushed through air as thick as molasses. Her fingers closed about it, one by one, and in the time it took for them to do so there was room enough for a hundred second thoughts. Faintly, she heard the sound of . . . machinery? A low humming noise.

She placed the key in the lock, and opened the door.

There stood Mr Tarblecko.

Ellie shrieked, and staggered backward. One of her heels hit the floor wrong, and her ankle twisted, and she almost fell. Her heart was hammering so furiously her chest hurt.

Mr Tarblecko glared at her from within the closet. His face was as white as a sheet of paper. "One rule," he said coldly, tonelessly. "You had only one rule, and you broke it." He stepped out. "You are a very bad slave."

"I . . . I . . . I . . ." Ellie found herself gasping from the shock. "I'm not a slave at all!"

"There is where you are wrong, Eleanor Voigt. There is where you are very wrong indeed," said Mr Tarblecko. "Open the window."

Ellie went to the window and pulled up the blinds. There was a little cactus in a pot on the windowsill. She moved it to her desk. Then she opened the window. It stuck a little, so she had to put all her strength into it. The lower sash went up slowly at first and then, with a rush, slammed to the top. A light, fresh breeze touched her.

"Climb onto the windowsill."

"I most certainly will—" *not*, she was going to say. But to her complete astonishment, she found herself climbing up onto the sill. She could not help herself. It was as if her will were not her own.

"Sit down with your feet outside the window."

It was like a hideous nightmare, the kind that you know can't be real and struggle to awaken from, but cannot. Her body did exactly as it was told to do. She had absolutely no control over it.

"Do not jump until I tell you to do so."

"Are you going to tell me to jump?" she asked quaveringly. "Oh, *please*, Mr Tarblecko . . ."

"Now look down."

The office was on the ninth floor. Ellie was a lifelong New Yorker, so that had never seemed to her a particularly great height before. Now it did. The people on the sidewalk were as small as ants. The buses and automobiles on the street were the size of matchboxes. The sounds of horns and engines drifted up to her, and birdsong as well, the lazy background noises of a spring day in the city. The ground was so terribly far away! And there was nothing between her and it but air! Nothing holding her back from death but her fingers desperately clutching the window frame!

Ellie could feel all the world's gravity willing her toward the distant concrete. She was dizzy with vertigo and a sick, stomach-tugging urge to simply let go and, briefly, fly. She squeezed her eyes shut tight, and felt hot tears streaming down her face.

She could tell from Mr Tarblecko's voice that he was standing right behind her. "If I told you to jump, Eleanor Voigt, would you do so?"

"Yes," she squeaked.

"What kind of person jumps to her death simply because she's been told to do so?"

"A . . . a slave!"

"Then what are you?"

"A slave! A slave! I'm a slave!" She was weeping openly now, as much from humiliation as from fear. "I don't want to die! I'll be your slave, anything, whatever you say!"

"If you're a slave, then what kind of slave should you be?"

"A . . . a . . . *good* slave."

"Come back inside."

Gratefully, she twisted around, and climbed back into the office. Her knees buckled when she tried to stand, and she had to grab at the windowsill to keep from falling. Mr Tarblecko stared at her, sternly and steadily.

"You have been given your only warning," he said. "If you disobey again – or if you ever try to quit – I will order you out the window."

He walked into the closet and closed the door behind him.

There were two hours left on her shift – time enough, barely, to compose herself. When the disheveled young poet showed up, she dropped her key in her purse and walked past him without so much as a glance. Then she went straight to the nearest hotel bar and ordered a gin and tonic.

She had a lot of thinking to do.

Eleanor Voigt was not without resources. She had been an executive secretary before meeting her late husband, and everyone knew that a good executive secretary effectively runs her boss's business for him. Before the Crash, she had run a household with three servants. She had entertained. Some of her parties had required weeks of planning and preparation. If it weren't for the Depression, she was sure she'd be in a much better-paid position than the one she held.

She was *not* going to be a slave.

But before she could find a way out of her predicament, she had to understand it. First, the closet. Mr Tarblecko had left the office and then, minutes later, popped up inside it. A hidden passage of some kind? No – that was simultaneously too complicated and not complicated enough. She had heard machinery, just before she opened the door. So . . . some kind of transportation device, then. Something that a day ago she would have sworn couldn't exist. A teleporter, perhaps, or a time machine.

The more she thought of it, the better she liked the thought of the time machine. It was not just that teleporters were the stuff of Sunday funnies and Buck Rogers serials, while *The Time Machine* was a distinguished philosophical work by Mr H. G. Wells. Though she had to admit that figured in there. But a teleportation device required a twin somewhere, and Mr Tarblecko hadn't had the time even to leave the building.

A time machine, however, would explain so much! Her employer's long absences. The necessity that the device be watched when not in use, lest it be employed by Someone Else. Mr Tarblecko's abrupt appearance today, and his possession of a coercive power that no human being on Earth had.

The fact that she could no longer think of Mr Tarblecko as human.

She had barely touched her drink, but now she found herself too impatient to finish it. She slapped a dollar bill down on the bar and, without waiting for her change, left.

During the time it took to walk the block and a half to the office building and ride the elevator up to the ninth floor, Ellie made her plans. She strode briskly down the hallway and opened the door without knocking. The unkempt young man looked up, startled, from a scribbled sheet of paper.

"You have a watch?"

"Y-yes, but . . . Mr Tarblecko . . ."

"Get out. Come back in forty minutes."

With grim satisfaction, she watched the young man cram his key into one pocket and the sheet of paper into another and leave. *Good slave*, she thought to herself. Perhaps he'd already been through the little charade Mr Tarblecko had just played on her. Doubtless every employee underwent ritual enslavement as a way of keeping them in line. The problem with having slaves, however, was that they couldn't be expected to display any initiative . . . Not on the master's behalf, anyway.

Ellie opened her purse and got out the key. She walked to the closet.

For an instant she hesitated. Was she really sure enough to risk her life? But the logic was unassailable. She had been given no second chance. If Mr Tarblecko *knew* she was about to open the door a second time, he would simply have ordered her out the window on her first offense. The fact that he hadn't, meant that he didn't know.

She took a deep breath and opened the door.

There was a world inside.

For what seemed like forever, Ellie stood staring at the bleak metropolis so completely unlike New York City. Its buildings were taller than any she had ever seen – miles high! – and interlaced with skywalks, like those in *Metropolis*. But the buildings in the movie had been breathtaking, and these were the opposite of beautiful. They were ugly as sin: windowless, grey, stained, and discolored. There were monotonous lines of harsh lights along every street, and under their glare trudged men and women as uniform and lifeless as robots. Outside the office, it was a beautiful bright day. But on the other side of the closet, the world was dark as night.

And it was snowing.

Gingerly, she stepped into the closet. The instant her foot touched the floor, it seemed to expand to all sides. She stood at the center of a great wheel of doors, with all but two of them – to her office and to the winter world – shut. There were hooks beside each door, and hanging from them were costumes of a hundred different cultures. She thought she recognized togas, Victorian opera dress, kimonos . . . But most of the clothing was unfamiliar.

Beside the door into winter, there was a long cape. Ellie wrapped it around herself, and discovered a knob on the inside. She twisted it to the right, and suddenly the coat was hot as hot. Quickly, she twisted the knob to the left, and it grew cold. She fiddled with the thing until the cape felt just right. Then she straightened her shoulders, took a deep breath, and stepped out into the forbidding city.

There was a slight electric sizzle, and she was standing in the street.

Ellie spun around to see what was behind her: a rectangle of some glassy black material. She rapped it with her knuckles. It was solid. But when she brought her key near its surface, it shimmered and opened into that strange space between worlds again.

So she had a way back home.

To either side of her rectangle were identical glassy rectangles faceted slightly away from it. They were the exterior of an enormous kiosk, or perhaps a very low building, at the center of a large, featureless square. She walked all the way around it, rapping each rectangle with her key. Only the one would open for her.

The first thing to do was to find out where – or, rather, *when* – she was. Ellie stepped in front of one of the hunched, slow-walking men. "Excuse me, sir, could you answer a few questions for me?"

The man raised a face that was utterly bleak and without hope. A ring of grey metal glinted from his neck. "Hawrzat dagtiknut?" he asked.

Ellie stepped back in horror and, like a wind-up toy temporarily halted by a hand or a foot, the man resumed his plodding gait.

She cursed herself. Of *course* language would have changed in the however-many-centuries future she found herself in. Well . . . that was going to make gathering information more difficult. But she was used to difficult tasks. The evening of John's suicide, she had been the one to clean the walls and the floor. After that, she'd known that she was capable of doing anything she set her mind to.

Above all, it was important that she not get lost. She scanned the square with the doorways in time at its center – mentally, she dubbed it Times Square – and chose at random one of the broad avenues converging on it. That, she decided would be Broadway.

Ellie started down Broadway, watching everybody and everything. Some of the drone-folk were dragging sledges with complex machinery on them. Others were hunched under soft, translucent bags filled with murky fluid and vague biomorphic shapes. The air smelled bad, but in ways she was not familiar with.

She had gotten perhaps three blocks when the sirens went off – great piercing blasts of noise that assailed the ears and echoed from the building walls. All the streetlights flashed off and on and off again in a one-two rhythm. From unseen loudspeakers, an authoritative voice blared, "*Akgang! Akgang! Kronzvarbrakar! Zawzawkstrag! Akgang! Akgang . . .*"

Without hurry, the people in the street began turning away, touching their hands to dull grey plates beside nondescript doors and disappearing into the buildings.

"Oh, cripes!" Ellie muttered. She'd best—

There was a disturbance behind her. Ellie turned and saw the strangest thing yet.

It was a girl of eighteen or nineteen, wearing summer clothes – a man's trousers, a short-sleeved flower-print blouse – and she was running down the street in a panic. She grabbed at the uncaring drones, begging for help. "Please!" she cried. "Can't you help me? Somebody! Please . . . you have to help me!" Puffs of steam came from her mouth with each breath. Once or twice she made a sudden dart for one of the doorways and slapped her hand on the greasy plates. But the doors would not open for her.

Now the girl had reached Ellie. In a voice that expected nothing, she said, "Please?"

"I'll help you, dear," Ellie said.

The girl shrieked, then convulsively hugged her. "Oh, thank you, thank you, thank you," she babbled.

"Follow close behind me." Ellie strode up behind one of the lifeless un-men and, just after he had slapped his hand on the plate, but before he could enter, grabbed his rough tunic and gave it a yank. He turned.

"Vamoose!" she said in her sternest voice, and jerked a thumb over her shoulder.

The un-man turned away. He might not understand the word, but the tone and the gesture sufficed.

Ellie stepped inside, pulling the girl after her. The door closed behind them.

"Wow," said the girl wonderingly. "How did you do that?"

"This is a slave culture. For a slave to survive, he's got to obey anyone who acts like a master. It's that simple. Now, what's your name and how did you get here?" As she spoke, Ellie took in her surroundings. The room they were in was dim, grimy – and vast. So far as she could see, there were no interior walls, only the occasional pillar and here and there a set of functional metal stairs without railings.

"Nadine Shepard. I . . . I . . . There was a door! And I walked through it and I found myself *here*! I . . ."

The child was close to hysteria. "I know, dear. Tell me, when are you from?"

"Chicago. On the North Side, near—"

"Not where, dear, when? What year is it?"

"Uh . . . 2004. Isn't it?"

"Not here. Not now." The grey people were everywhere, moving sluggishly, yet always keeping within sets of yellow lines painted on the concrete floor. Their smell was pervasive, and far from pleasant. Still . . .

Ellie stepped directly into the path of one of the sad creatures, a woman. When she stopped, Ellie took the tunic from her shoulders and then stepped back. Without so much as an expression of annoyance, the woman resumed her plodding walk.

"Here you are." She handed the tunic to young Nadine. "Put this on, dear, you must be freezing. Your skin is positively blue." And, indeed, it was not much warmer inside than it had been outdoors. "I'm Eleanor Voigt. Mrs Eleanor Voigt."

Shivering, Nadine donned the rough garment. But instead of thanking Ellie, she said, "You look familiar."

Ellie returned her gaze. She was a pretty enough creature though, strangely, she wore no makeup at all. Her features were regular, intelligent – "You look familiar too. I can't quite put my finger on it, but . . ."

"Okay," Nadine said, "now tell me. Please. Where and when am I, and what's going on?"

"I honestly don't know," Ellie said. Dimly, through the walls, she could hear the sirens and the loudspeaker-voice. If only it weren't so murky in here! She couldn't get any clear idea of the building's layout or function.

"But you *must* know! You're so . . . so capable, so in control. You . . ."

"I'm a castaway like you, dear. Just figuring things out as I go along." She continued to peer. "But I can tell you this much: We are far, far in the future. The poor degraded beings you saw on the street are the slaves of a superior race – let's call them the Aftermen. The Aftermen are very cruel, and they can travel through time as easily as you or I can travel from city to city via inter-urban rail. And that's all I know. So far."

Nadine was peering out a little slot in the door that Ellie hadn't noticed. Now she said, "What's this?"

Ellie took her place at the slot, and saw a great bulbous street-filling machine pull to a halt a block from the building. Insectoid creatures that might be robots or might be men in body armor poured out of it, and swarmed down the street, examining every door. The sirens and the loudspeakers cut off. The streetlights returned to normal. "It's time we left," Ellie said.

An enormous artificial voice shook the building. *Akbang! Akbang! Zawzawksbild! Alzowt! Zawzawksbild! Akbang!*

"Quickly!"

She seized Nadine's hand, and they were running.

Without emotion, the grey folk turned from their prior courses and unhurriedly made for the exits.

Ellie and Nadine tried to stay off the walkways entirely. But the air began to tingle, more on the side away from the walkways than the side toward, and then to burn and then to sting. They were quickly forced between the yellow lines. At first they were able to push their way past the drones, and then to shoulder their way through their numbers. But more and more came dead-stepping their way down the metal stairways. More and more descended from the upper levels via lifts that abruptly descended from the ceiling to disgorge them by the hundreds. More and more flowed outward from the building's dim interior.

Passage against the current of flesh became first difficult, and then impossible. They were swept backwards, helpless as corks in a rain-swollen river. Outward they were forced and through the exit into the street.

The "police" were waiting there.

At the sight of Ellie and Nadine – they could not have been difficult to discern among the uniform drabness of the others – two of the armored figures stepped forward with long poles and brought them down on the women.

Ellie raised her arm to block the pole, and it landed solidly on her wrist.

Horrid, searing pain shot through her, greater than anything she had ever experienced before. For a giddy instant, Ellie felt a strange elevated sense of being, and she thought, *If I can put up with this, I can endure anything.* Then the world went away.

Ellie came to in a jail cell.

At least that's what she thought it was. The room was small, square, and doorless. A featureless ceiling gave off a drab, even light. A bench ran around the perimeter, and there was a hole in the middle of the room whose stench advertised its purpose.

She sat up.

On the bench across from her, Nadine was weeping silently into her hands.

So her brave little adventure had ended. She had rebelled against Mr Tarblecko's tyranny and come to the same end that awaited most rebels. It was her own foolish fault. She had acted without sufficient forethought, without adequate planning, without scouting out the opposition and gathering information first. She had gone up against a Power that could range effortlessly across time and space, armed only with a pocket handkerchief and a spare set of glasses, and inevitably that Power had swatted her down with a contemptuous minimum of their awesome force.

They hadn't even bothered to take away her purse.

Ellie dug through it, found a cellophane-wrapped hard candy, and popped it into her mouth. She sucked on it joylessly. All hope whatsoever was gone from her.

Still, even when one has no hope, one's obligations remain. "Are you all right, Nadine?" she forced herself to ask. "Is there anything I can do to help?"

Nadine lifted her tear-stained face. "I just went through a door," she said. "That's all. I didn't do anything bad or wrong or . . . or anything. And now I'm here!" Fury blazed up in her. "Damn you, damn you, damn you!"

"Me?" Ellie said, astonished.

"You! You shouldn't have let them get us. You should've taken us to some hiding place, and then gotten us back home. But you didn't. You're a stupid, useless old woman!"

It was all Ellie could do to keep from smacking the young lady. But Nadine was practically a child, she told herself, and it didn't seem like they raised girls to have much gumption in the year 2004. They were probably weak and spoiled people, up there in the twenty-first century, who had robots to do all their work for them, and nothing to do but sit around and listen to the radio all day. So she held not only her hand, but her tongue. "Don't worry, dear," she said soothingly. "We'll get out of this. Somehow."

Nadine stared at her bleakly, disbelievingly. "*How*?" she demanded.

But to this Ellie had no answer.

*   *   *

Time passed. Hours, by Ellie's estimation, and perhaps many hours. And with its passage, she found herself, more out of boredom than from the belief that it would be of any use whatsoever, looking at the situation analytically again.

How had the Aftermen tracked her down?

Some sort of device on the time-door might perhaps warn them that an unauthorized person had passed through. But the "police" had located her so swiftly and surely! They had clearly known exactly where she was. Their machine had come straight toward the building they'd entered. The floods of non-men had flushed her right out into their arms.

So it was something about her, or _on_ her, that had brought the Aftermen so quickly.

Ellie looked at her purse with new suspicion. She dumped its contents on the ledge beside her, and pawed through them, looking for the guilty culprit. A few hard candies, a lace hankie, half a pack of cigarettes, fountain pen, glasses case, bottle of aspirin, house key ... and the key to the time closet. The only thing in all she owned that had come to her direct from Mr Tarblecko. She snatched it up.

It looked ordinary enough. Ellie rubbed it, sniffed it, touched it gently to her tongue.

It tasted sour.

Sour, the way a small battery tasted if you touched your tongue to it. There was a faint trickle of electricity coming from the thing. It was clearly no ordinary key.

She pushed her glasses up on her forehead, held the thing to her eye, and squinted. It looked exactly like a common everyday key. Almost. It had no manufacturer's name on it, and that was unexpected, given that the key looked new and unworn. The top part of it was covered with irregular geometric decorations.

Or _were_ they decorations?

She looked up to see Nadine studying her steadily, unblinkingly, like a cat. "Nadine, honey, your eyes are younger than mine – would you take a look at this? Are those tiny ... _switches_ on this thing?"

"What?" Nadine accepted the key from her, examined it, poked at it with one nail.

Flash.

When Ellie stopped blinking and could see again, one wall of their cell had disappeared.

Nadine stepped to the very edge of the cell, peering outward. A cold wind whipped bitter flakes of snow about her. "Look!" she cried. Then, when Ellie stood beside her to see what she saw, Nadine wrapped her arms about the older woman and stepped out into the abyss.

Ellie screamed.

The two women piloted the police vehicle up Broadway, toward Times Square. Though a multiplicity of instruments surrounded the windshield, the controls were simplicity itself: a single stick which when pushed forward accelerated the vehicle and when pushed to either side turned it. Apparently the police did not need to be particularly smart. Neither the steering mechanism nor the doors had any locks on them, so far as Ellie could tell. Apparently the drone-men had so little initiative that locks weren't required. Which would help explain how she and Nadine had escaped so easily.

"How did you know this vehicle was beneath us?" Ellie asked. "How did you know we'd be able to drive it? I almost had a heart attack when you pushed me out on top of it."

"Way gnarly, wasn't it? Straight out of a Hong Kong video." Nadine grinned. "Just call me Michelle Yeoh."

"If you say so." She was beginning to rethink her hasty judgment of the lass. Apparently the people of 2004 weren't quite the shrinking violets she'd made them out to be.

With a flicker and a hum, a square sheet of glass below the windshield came to life. Little white dots of light danced, jittered, and coalesced to form a face.

It was Mr Tarblecko.

"*Time criminals of the Dawn Era,*" his voice thundered from a hidden speaker. "*Listen and obey.*"

Ellie shrieked, and threw her purse over the visi-plate. "Don't listen to him!" she ordered Nadine. "See if you can find a way of turning this thing off!"

"*Bring the stolen vehicle to a complete halt immediately!*"

To her horror, if not her surprise, Ellie found herself pulling the steering-bar back, slowing the police car to a stop. But then

Nadine, in blind obedience to Mr Tarblecko's compulsive voice, grabbed for the bar as well. Simultaneously, she stumbled and, with a little *eep* noise, lurched against the bar, pushing it sideways.

The vehicle slewed to one side, smashed into a building wall, and toppled over.

Then Nadine had the roof-hatch open and was pulling her through it. "C'mon!" she shouted. "I can see the black doorway-thingie – the, you know, place!"

Following, Ellie had to wonder about the educational standards of the year 2004. The young lady didn't seem to have a very firm grasp on the English language.

Then they had reached Times Square and the circle of doorways at its center. The streetlights were flashing and loudspeakers were shouting, "*Akbang! Akbang!*" and police vehicles were converging upon them from every direction, but there was still time. Ellie tapped the nearest doorway with her key. Nothing. The next. Nothing. Then she was running around the building, scraping the key against each doorway, and . . . there it was!

She seized Nadine's hand, and they plunged through.

The space inside expanded in a great wheel to all sides. Ellie spun about. There were doors everywhere – and all of them closed. She had not the faintest idea which one led back to her own New York City.

Wait, though! There were costumes appropriate to each time hanging by their doors. If she just went down them until she found a business suit . . .

Nadine gripped her arm. "Oh, my God!"

Ellie turned, looked, saw. A doorway – the one they had come through, obviously – had opened behind them. In it stood Mr Tarblecko. Or, to be more precise, *three* Mr Tarbleckos. They were all as identical as peas in a pod. She had no way of knowing which one, if any, was hers.

"Through here! Quick!" Nadine shrieked. She'd snatched open the nearest door.

Together, they fled through it.

"Oolohstullalu ashulalumoota!" a woman sang out. She wore a jumpsuit and carried a clipboard, which she thrust into Ellie's face. "Oolalulaswula ulalulin."

"I . . . I don't understand what you're saying," Ellie faltered. They stood on the green lawn of a gentle slope that led down to the ocean. Down by the beach, enormous construction machines, operated by both men and women (women! of all the astonishing sights she had seen, this was strangest), were rearing an enormous, enigmatic structure, reminiscent to Ellie's eye of Sunday school illustrations of the Tower of Babel. Gentle tropical breezes stirred her hair.

"Dawn Era, Amerlingo," the clipboard said. "Exact period uncertain. Answer these questions. Gas – for lights or for cars?"

"For cars, mostly. Although there are still a few—"

"Apples – for eating or computing?"

"Eating," Ellie said, while simultaneously Nadine said, "Both."

"Scopes – for dreaming or for resurrecting?"

Neither woman said anything.

The clipboard chirped in a satisfied way. "Early Atomic Age, pre- and post-Hiroshima, one each. You will experience a moment's discomfort. Do not be alarmed. It is for your own good."

"Please." Ellie turned from the woman to the clipboard and back, uncertain which to address. "What's going on? Where are we? We have so many—"

"There's no time for questions," the woman said impatiently. Her accent was unlike anything Ellie had ever heard before. "You must undergo indoctrination, loyalty imprinting, and chronomilitary training immediately. We need all the time-warriors we can get. This base is going to be destroyed in the morning."

"What? I . . ."

"Hand me your key."

Without thinking, Ellie gave the thing to the woman. Then a black nausea overcame her. She swayed, fell, and was unconscious before she hit the ground.

"Would you like some heroin?"

The man sitting opposite her had a face that was covered with blackwork tattoo eels. He grinned, showing teeth that had all been filed to a point.

"I beg your pardon?" Ellie was not at all certain where she was, or how she had gotten here. Nor did she comprehend how she could have understood this alarming fellow's words, for he most certainly had *not* been speaking English.

"Heroin." He thrust the open metal box of white powder at her. "Do you want a snort?"

"No, thank you." Ellie spoke carefully, trying not to give offense. "I find that it gives me spots."

With a disgusted noise, the man turned away.

Then the young woman sitting beside her said in a puzzled way, "Don't I know you?"

She turned. It was Nadine. "Well, my dear, I should certainly hope you haven't forgotten me so soon."

"Mrs Voigt?" Nadine said wonderingly. "But you're ... you're ... young!"

Involuntarily, Ellie's hands went up to her face. The skin was taut and smooth. The incipient softening of her chin was gone. Her hair, when she brushed her hands through it, was sleek and full.

She found herself desperately wishing she had a mirror.

"They must have done something. While I was asleep." She lightly touched her temples, the skin around her eyes. "I'm not wearing any glasses! I can see perfectly!" She looked around her. The room she was in was even more spartan than the jail cell had been. There were two metal benches facing each other, and on them sat as motley a collection of men and women as she had ever seen. There was a woman who must have weighed three hundred pounds – and every ounce of it muscle. Beside her sat an albino lad so slight and elfin he hardly seemed there at all. Until, that is, one looked at his clever face and burning eyes. *Then* one knew him to be easily the most dangerous person in the room. As for the others, well, none of them had horns or tails, but that was about it.

The elf leaned forward. "Dawn Era, aren't you?" he said. "If you survive this, you'll have to tell me how you got here."

"I—"

"They want you to think you're as good as dead already. Don't believe them! I wouldn't have signed up in the first place, if I hadn't come back afterwards and told myself I'd come through it all intact." He winked and settled back. "The situation is hopeless, of course. But I wouldn't take it seriously."

Ellie blinked. Was everybody mad here?

In that same instant, a visi-plate very much like the one in the police car lowered from the ceiling, and a woman appeared on it. "Hero mercenaries," she said, "I salute you! As you already know, we are at the very front lines of the War. The Aftermen Empire has been slowly, inexorably moving backwards into their past, our present, a year at time. So far, the Optimized Rationality of True Men has lost 5314 years to their onslaught." Her eyes blazed. "That advance ends here! That advance ends now! We have lost so far because, living down-time from the Aftermen, we cannot obtain a technological superiority to them. Every weapon we invent passes effortlessly into their hands.

"So we are going to fight and defeat them, not with technology but with the one quality that, not being human, they lack – human character! Our researches into the far past have shown that superior technology can be defeated by raw courage and sheer numbers. One man with a sunstroker can be overwhelmed by savages equipped with nothing more than neutron bombs – *if* there are enough of them, and they don't mind dying! An army with energy guns can be destroyed by rocks and sticks and determination.

"In a minute, your transporter and a million more like it will arrive at staging areas afloat in null-time. You will don respirators and disembark. There you will find the time-torpedoes. Each one requires two operators – a pilot and a button-pusher. The pilot will bring you in as close as possible to the Aftermen time-dreadnoughts. The button-pusher will then set off the chronomordant explosives."

This is madness, Ellie thought. *I'll do no such thing.* Simultaneous with the thought came the realization that she had the complex skills needed to serve as either pilot or button-pusher. They must have been given to her at the same time she had been made young again and her eyesight improved.

"Not one in a thousand of you will live to make it anywhere near the time-dreadnoughts. But those few who do will justify the sacrifices of the rest. For with your deaths, you will be preserving humanity from enslavement and destruction!

Martyrs, I salute you." She clenched her fist. "We are nothing! The Rationality is all!"

Then everyone was on his or her feet, all facing the visi-screen, all raising clenched fists in response to the salute, and all chanting as one, "*We are nothing! The Rationality is all!*"

To her horror and disbelief, Ellie discovered herself chanting the oath of self-abnegation in unison with the others, and, worse, meaning every word of it.

The woman who had taken the key away from her had said something about "loyalty imprinting". Now Ellie understood what that term entailed.

In the grey not-space of null-time, Ellie kicked her way into the time-torpedo. It was to her newly sophisticated eyes, rather a primitive thing: Fifteen grams of nano-mechanism welded to a collapsteel hull equipped with a noninertial propulsion unit and packed with five tons of something her mental translator rendered as "annihilatium". This last, she knew to the core of her being, was ferociously destructive stuff.

Nadine wriggled in after her. "Let me pilot," she said. "I've been playing video games since Mario was the villain in Donkey Kong."

"Nadine, dear, there's something I've been meaning to ask you." Ellie settled into the button-pusher slot. There were twenty-three steps to setting off the annihilatium, each one finicky, and if were even one step taken out of order, nothing would happen. She had absolutely no doubt she could do it correctly, swiftly, efficiently.

"Yes?"

"Does all that futuristic jargon of yours actually *mean* anything?"

Nadine's laughter was cut off by a *squawk* from the visi-plate. The woman who had lectured them earlier appeared, looking stern. "Launch in twenty-three seconds," she said. "For the Rationality!"

"For the Rationality!" Ellie responded fervently and in unison with Nadine. Inside, however, she was thinking, *How did I get into this?* and then, ruefully, *Well, there's no fool like an old fool.*

"Eleven seconds . . . seven seconds . . . three seconds . . . one second."

Nadine launched.

Without time and space, there can be neither sequence nor pattern. The battle between the Aftermen dreadnoughts and the time-torpedoes of the Rationality, for all its shifts and feints and evasions, could be reduced to a single blip of instantaneous action and then rendered into a single binary datum: win/ lose.

The Rationality lost.

The time-dreadnoughts of the Aftermen crept another year into the past.

But somewhere in the very heart of that not-terribly-important battle, two torpedoes, one of which was piloted by Nadine, converged upon the hot-spot of guiding consciousness that empowered and drove the flagship of the Aftermen time-armada. Two button-pushers set off their explosives. Two shock-waves bowed outward, met, meshed, and merged with the expanding shockwave of the countermeasure launched by the dreadnought's tutelary awareness.

Something terribly complicated happened.

Then Ellie found herself sitting at a table in the bar of the Algonquin Hotel, back in New York City. Nadine was sitting opposite her. To either side of them were the clever albino and the man with the tattooed face and the filed teeth.

The albino smiled widely. "Ah, the primitives! Of all who could have survived – myself excepted, of course – you are the most welcome."

His tattooed companion frowned. "Please show some more tact, Sev. However they may appear to us, these folk are not primitives to *themselves*."

"You are right as always, Dun Jal. Permit me to introduce myself. I am Seventh-Clone of House Orpen, Lord Extratemporal of the Centuries 3197 through 3992 Inclusive, Backup Heir Potential to the Indeterminate Throne. Sev, for short."

"Dun Jal. Mercenary. From the early days of the Rationality. Before it grew decadent."

"Eleanor Voigt, Nadine Shepard. I'm from 1936, and she's from 2004. Where – if that's the right word – are we?"

"Neither where nor when, delightful aboriginal. We have obviously been thrown into hypertime, that no-longer-theoretical state informing and supporting the more mundane seven dimensions of time with which you are doubtless familiar. Had we minds capable of perceiving it directly without going mad, who knows what we should see? As it is," he waved a hand, "all this is to me as my One-Father's clonatorium, in which so many of I spent our minority."

"I see a workshop," Dun Jal said.

"I see—" Nadine began.

Dun Jal turned pale. "A Tarbleck-null!" He bolted to his feet, hand instinctively going for a sidearm which, in their current state, did not exist.

"Mr Tarblecko!" Ellie gasped. It was the first time she had thought of him since her imprinted technical training in the time-fortress of the Rationality, and speaking his name brought up floods of related information: That there were seven classes of Aftermen, or Tarblecks as they called themselves. That the least of them, the Tarbleck-sixes, were brutal and domineering overlords. That the greatest of them, the Tarbleck-nulls, commanded the obedience of millions. That the maximum power a Tarbleck-null could call upon at an instant's notice was four quads per second per second. That the physical expression of that power was so great that, had she known, Ellie would never have gone through that closet door in the first place.

Sev gestured toward an empty chair. "Yes, I thought it was about time for you to show up."

The sinister grey Afterman drew up the chair and sat down to their table. "The small one knows why I am here," he said. "The others do not. It is degrading to explain myself to such as you, so he shall have to."

"I am so privileged as to have studied the more obscure workings of time, yes." The little man put his fingertips together and smiled a fey, foxy smile over their tips. "So I know that physical force is useless here. Only argument can prevail. Thus . . . trial by persuasion it is. I shall go first."

He stood up. "My argument is simple: As I told our dear, savage friends here earlier, an heir-potential to the Indeterminate Throne is too valuable to risk on uncertain adventures. Before I was allowed to enlist as a mercenary, my elder self had to return from the experience to testify I would survive it unscathed. I did. Therefore, I will."

He sat.

There was a moment's silence. "That's all you have to say?" Dun Jal asked.

"It is enough."

"Well." Dun Jal cleared his throat and stood. "Then it is my turn. The Empire of the Aftermen is inherently unstable at all points. Perhaps it was a natural phenomenon – *once*. Perhaps the Aftermen arose from the workings of ordinary evolutionary processes, and could at one time claim that therefore they had a natural place in this continuum. That changed when they began to expand their Empire into their own past. In order to enable their back-conquests, they had to send agents to all prior periods in time to influence and corrupt, to change the flow of history into something terrible and terrifying, from which they might arise. And so they did.

"Massacres, death-camps, genocide, World Wars . . ." (There were other terms that did not translate, concepts more horrible than Ellie had words for.) "You don't really think those were the work of *human beings*, do you? We're much too sensible a race for that sort of thing – when we're left to our own devices. No, all the worst of our miseries are instigated by the Aftermen. We are far from perfect, and the best example of this is the cruel handling of the War in the final years of the Optimized Rationality of True Men, where our leaders have become almost as terrible as the Aftermen themselves – because it is from their very ranks that the Aftermen shall arise. But what *might* we have been?

"Without the interference of the Aftermen might we not have become something truly admirable? Might we not have become not the Last Men, but the First truly worthy of the name?" He sat down.

Lightly, sardonically, Sev applauded. "Next?"

The Tarbleck-null placed both hands heavily on the table and, leaning forward, pushed himself up. "Does the tiger explain himself to the sheep?" he asked. "Does he *need* to explain? The sheep understand well enough that Death has come to walk among them, to eat those it will and spare the rest only because he is not yet hungry. So too do men understand that they have met their master. I do not enslave men because it is right or proper but because I *can*. The proof of which is that I *have*!

"Strength needs no justification. It exists or it does not. I exist. Who here can say that I am not your superior? Who here can deny that Death has come to walk among you? Natural selection chose the fittest among men to become a new race. Evolution has set my foot upon your necks, and I will not take it off."

To universal silence, he sat down. The very slightest of glances he threw Ellie's way, as if to challenge her to refute him. Nor could she! Her thoughts were all confusion, her tongue all in a knot. She knew he was wrong – she was sure of it! – and yet she could not put her arguments together. She simply couldn't think clearly and quickly enough.

Nadine laughed lightly.

"Poor superman!" she said. "Evolution isn't linear, like that chart that has a fish crawling out of the water at one end and a man in a business suit at the other. All species are constantly trying to evolve in all directions at once – a little taller, a little shorter, a little faster, a little slower. When that distinction proves advantageous, it tends to be passed along. The Aftermen aren't any smarter than Men are – less so, in some ways. Less flexible, less innovative . . . Look what a stagnant world they've created! What they *are* is more forceful."

"Forceful?" Ellie said, startled. "Is that all?"

"That's enough. Think of all the trouble caused by men like Hitler, Mussolini, Caligula, Pol Pot, Archers-Wang 43 . . . All they had was the force of their personality, the ability to get others to do what they wanted. Well, the Aftermen are the descendants of exactly such people, only with the force of will squared and cubed. That afternoon when the Tarbleck-null ordered you to sit in the window? It was the easiest thing in the world to one of them. As easy as breathing.

"That's why the Rationality can't win. Oh, they *could* win, if they were willing to root out that streak of persuasive coercion within themselves. But they're fighting a war, and in times of war one uses whatever weapons one has. The ability to tell millions of soldiers to sacrifice themselves for the common good is simply too useful to be thrown away. But all the time they're fighting the external enemy, the Aftermen are evolving within their own numbers."

"You admit it," the Tarbleck said.

"Oh, be still! You're a foolish little creature, and you have no idea what you're up against. Have you ever asked the Aftermen from the leading edge of your Empire why you're expanding backwards into the past rather than forward into the future? Obviously because there are bigger and more dangerous things up ahead of you than you dare face. You're afraid to go there – afraid that you might find *me*!" Nadine took something out of her pocket. "Now go away, all of you."

Flash.

Nothing changed. Everything changed.

Ellie was still sitting in the Algonquin with Nadine. But Sev, Dun Jal, and the Tarbleck-null were all gone. More significantly, the bar felt *real* in a way it hadn't an instant before. She was back home, in her own now and her own when.

Ellie dug into her purse and came up with a crumpled pack of Lucky Strike Greens, teased one out, and lit it. She took a deep drag on the cigarette and then exhaled. "All right," she said, "who are you?"

The girl's eyes sparkled with amusement. "Why, Ellie, dear, don't you know? I'm *you*!"

So it was that Eleanor Voigt was recruited into the most exclusive organization in all Time – an organization that was comprised in hundreds of thousands of instances entirely and solely of herself. Over the course of millions of years she grew and evolved, of course, so that her ultimate terrifying and glorious self was not even remotely human. But everything starts somewhere, and Ellie of necessity had to start small.

The Aftermen were one of the simpler enemies of the humane future she felt that Humanity deserved. Nevertheless they had to be – gently and nonviolently, which made the task more difficult – opposed.

After fourteen months of training and the restoration of all her shed age, Ellie was returned to New York City on the morning she had first answered the odd help wanted ad in the *Times*.

Her original self had been detoured away from the situation, to be recruited if necessary at a later time.

"Unusual in what way?" she asked. "I don't understand. What am I looking for?"

"You'll know it when you see it," the Tarbleck-null said.

He handed her the key.

She accepted it. There were tools hidden within her body whose powers dwarfed those of this primitive chronotransfer device. But the encoded information the key contained would lay open the workings of the Aftermen Empire to her. Working right under their noses, she would be able to undo their schemes, diminish their power, and, ultimately, prevent them from ever coming into existence in the first place.

Ellie had only the vaguest idea how she was supposed to accomplish all this. But she was confident she could figure it out, given time. And she had the time.

All the time in the world.

COMING BACK

Damien Broderick

The next few stories take us down other convolutions of time, starting with a different type of time loop where you are trapped in a constant repetitive cycle of time. This idea was popularized in the film Groundhog Day *(1993), but has been around much longer than that, notably in Kurt Vonnegut's* Slaughterhouse Five *(1969) and Ken Grimwood's* Replay *(1987).*

Damien Broderick is an Australian writer and commentator upon the fields of science fiction and speculative science, such as in The Spike *(1997), which considers how we mere mortals are coping with rapidly advancing technologies. Broderick was one of the first writers to explore the concept of virtual reality in* The Judas Mandala, *written in 1975 but not published until 1982. The latter volume, together with* The Dreaming Dragons *(1980), subtitled "A Time Opera", displays a complex weave of alternate timelines and paradoxes.*

Yes, by now he admits that Jennifer is not deliberately driving him crazy. Quit laying it on her, Rostow chides himself. His Bastilled lunacy is self-evidently self-inflicted. There can be no doubt, as Tania had always insisted, that his is a personality gruesomely at risk, pumping through spasms of mania and depression, elation and reproach. As he glances up, the bulwarks of censure shear free of their hinges. The three coil techs, finishing up, share his appreciation with ogles and grins.

Descending the worn rubber treads of the catwalk, its non-magnetic structure faintly creaking and spronging in ludicrous counterpoint, Jennifer's legs are golden with undepilated summer hairs. Certainly he will lose his reason. It is her innocent, unconscious hauteur that propels Rostow's intolerable aspirations.

Who would believe that less than three weeks ago, governed by hard liquor and soft drugs, his hands had crept like pussycats over those shins, pounced past her knees to her thighs and beyond, while all the while dexterous Auberon Mountbatten Singh, D.Sc., coolly worked at the far end of her torso with mysterious expertise, soothing her brow, the edges of her jaw, the latent weakness at her throat, the revealed swell of her breasts? Even at this moment Rostow can scarcely credit his role in that maniacal and tasteless contest. Was it a contest? As she steps from the catwalk to her computer terminal, Rostow groans at an ambiguity only he perceives.

If even once she took stock; fixed him with, say, a single killing glance of rebuke and rejection . . . that would put an end to it. He might flail himself definitively and be done. Instead, she moves with languid competence in his marginal survival spaces like a neutrino beam wafting through a mountain of solid lead.

"Hi," she offers, settling herself in a molded seat. Her gaze penetrates him for an instant, moving after a beat to her keyboard. "Stan's on his way with the entire entourage. I spied."

"Jambo," says Rostow. It's all there, bolted into his larynx. Dutifully he runs the coded sequence of knobs and toggles which shunts the system from Latent to Standby. He nods to the departing technicians. There is a Parkinsonian tremor in his stupid fingers. "Pouring spirits down their throats, I guess. Softening them up."

Neat square indicators simmer vividly as the control instrumentation, swift bleats from his console to hers and back, patch into readiness. "This little number should sober them," she observes. "'Jambo'?"

"Swahili for 'Hello, sailor.'" A thread of mush in his voice and his brain tells his ear that the inflection was wrong. I blew it. Every time I blow it. With a mental fist he clouts his forehead. There is no time for limping second guesses. Stan Donaldson's abrasive voice precedes the man by half a second as the door swings wide for the expensive feet of the Board of Directors.

"We acquired it from Princeton, Senator," the department head is saying. "ERDA paid out a quarter of a billion dollars for a Tokamak Fusion Test reactor that was obsoleted overnight when Sandia secured sustained fusion by inertial confinement."

It seems to Rostow, squinting from the side of his eye and jittery with alarm, that this approach is a mistake. The senator is notorious for his loathing of costly obsolescence. Uh-huh. Buonacelli halts in midstride, pokes a finger into Donaldson's chubby chest. "Another sonofabitch Ivy League boondoggle. By the Lord, that's the kind of crap I won't abide."

Donaldson stands his ground. His own rasp is melodic after the senator's gravel hurtling from a tip-truck.

"Their blunder was our good fortune, sir," he says. "They were going to haul off the toroidal coils for recycling, but I managed to have them diverted to this laboratory. Everything is surplus or off-the-shelf. It made for a considerable saving."

Somewhat mollified, Buonacelli pushes forward to loom over Jennifer Barton's supervisor terminal, his minnows in attendance. "I'm still god-damned if I know what your magnets are for. Come straight out with it, man. The trustees won't be slow to scrap any project that smacks of self-indulgent tinkering." The set of his agribiz frame shows approval of Jennifer at least. "Convince us, and fast. This is the third department we've been dragged through today, and my feet are killing me."

"Miss Barton, could you fetch the senator a chair?"

Incredulous on her behalf, Rostow burns. Buonacelli holds the woman's biceps as she rises. "That's fine, honey, I'll stand." An arm goes around her shoulders in a friendly squeeze nobody in his right mind could construe as avuncular. Eddie Rostow damages his tooth enamel. "Don't bother buttering me up, Dr Donaldson. Let's get straight to the meat. What does this pile of junk do? Why do you deserve more megabucks?"

Rostow's chagrin buckles to delight as Stan's moist, unhealthy jowls darken. No doubt this will be the third or fourth time Donaldson has tried to explain the advanced-wave mirror to the accountants. Probably, Eddie decides, Buonacelli is just baiting him. The old bastard might know zilch about high-energy physics, but he's nobody's fool.

There again, it would serve Donaldson right if they haven't followed a word he's been saying. The man revels in pretentious jargon. Rostow hears a scurry of furry feet in the cardboard box near his own, cranes his neck, breaks up in silent mirth. The white bunny rabbit in the box is making its own critical observations. Cottontail high, it's dropping a stream of dry pellets into the shredded lettuce that litters the box.

Florid, Stan has decided to simplify his spiel. He's saying: "A totally new branch of technology, gentlemen. Perhaps my previous remarks were overly technical."

"New like Princeton?"

"New like Sandia," the professor says, grasping thankfully at the straight line. "Yet thoroughly rooted in classical theory. What we have here, gentlemen, is the answer to a puzzle provoked by James Clerk Maxwell more than a century ago. Maxwell," he glosses, "was the genius who first showed that electricity and magnetism were one and the same. His equations are the basis of all electronic technology."

"For history we fund historians," one of the committee says coldly, currying favor, and recoils slightly when Buonacelli growls.

Irritated and emboldened, the great physicist states loftily: "Physics is precisely the accumulated history of great physicists. My point, Senator, is that Maxwell's equations for electromagnetic wave motion have two sets of solutions. One set describes what we term *retarded* waves, where fluctuations are broadcast outward due to the acceleration of a charged particle. Radio waves from a transmitter are retarded waves, akin to the ripples from a stone dropped in a pond."

Rostow monitors surges of power in the system, holding it in equilibrium. He seeks Jennifer Barton's eye, hoping for a shared long-suffering grimace, but her attention is directed to the listening senator.

Donaldson is creeping into pomposity again. "The other solutions, equally valid in theoretical terms, we call *advanced* waves. Until now they have never been detected, let alone utilized."

"Radio waves get drawn back into a transmitter?" Buonacelli poses acutely, puzzled.

"Exactly." Donaldson rewards him with a satisfied pout. "Advanced waves converge to a point. Another way of looking at it is to say that they travel backwards in time. They put time into reverse. Normally, for complex reasons, the two sets of waves interfere, yielding no more than the retarded component. What I've done here with this equipment—"

Unnoticed, Eddie Rostow sits bolt upright and his face distorts in a throttled shriek. What *you've* done, you thieving sonofabitch?

But Buonacelli's scandalized roar has filled the lab. Suddenly it is obvious that indeed he had not grasped the earlier explanations. "Who in hell do you think you are, Professor – H. G. Wells? Don't you ever learn? How dare you stand there and shamelessly tell us you've been spending the university's endowment on a *time* machine? Credit me with the sense I was born with."

As Rostow spins in his chair, the dignitaries are stomping toward the door. Before Donaldson finds words, Jennifer Barton has magically slipped into Buonacelli's path. "Surely you're not leaving yet, Senator. Won't you at least wait for the demonstrations we've prepared for you?" She blinks as if something is in her eye.

"Harrumph!" Buonacelli lifts her hands in his beefy paws. "I don't know how they've taken you in, my dear. Never trust a scientist. If they're not lunatics, they're swindlers. Either way, it's a waste of good tax revenue."

"Why, Senator! I'm a scientist myself."

He releases one hand, strokes his jaw. "My apologies, dear lady. To tell the truth, my eldest son is a chemist at Dow." Gallantly he bows, retaining one of her hands. "Very well, gentlemen. To please this charming lady, let's take a look at the professor's so-called demonstration."

Wincing, Rostow spins quickly back to his station. He knows he'll be the butt of Stan's fuming humiliation the moment the directors are on their way. Why do I put up with it?

Tersely, the professor tells Buonacelli, "You may examine this equipment thoroughly." He leads them to the mirror chamber buried between gigantic doughnut-shaped magnets, slides open the weighty hatch. With heavy sarcasm he says, "Assure yourselves it's quite empty. There are no hidden trapdoors or disappearing rabbits." Rostow swallows a snigger, his eye on the white bunny munching in its box between his feet. Poor little beast, he thinks an instant later. I hate that part of it. But it's going to rock Buonacelli on his heels and open his wallet.

"Advanced waves are generated in every molecular interaction. Within these confines they are reflected almost totally. The crystalline surface of the chamber constitutes an *array* of laser-like amplifiers which augment the advanced-wave component." My idea, Eddie Rostow wants to shout. Without that, you'd have a big magnetic field going absolutely nowhere. But whose name will go on the paper? He says nothing. Donaldson puts his head inside the chamber. Dully, as he twists back and forth, his muffled voice states: "As you see, it's perfectly safe at the moment." An almost irresistible impulse floods Rostow. Regretfully, he pulls his finger back from the power switches.

"Okay," growls Buonacelli, "it's empty. So?"

Jennifer Barton leaves her terminal and returns with a flask of boiling water in one hand and a tray of ice cubes in the other.

"This will be simple but graphic, Senator," she says. It is Stan's notion of theatrics to have her fetch the props. "As you can see, this water is very hot. Would you care to dip in your pinky to test it, sir?"

"Thank you, honey, but I guess I recognize hot water when I see it."

A crony adds, unnecessarily, "You've been in plenty of it in your time." Everyone laughs ingratiatingly. Jenny drops two large ice cubes into the flask, places it inside the chamber. She goes at once to her terminal, and her features blank out in the inert Zen concentration of perfect egoless programming. The assembled company stare foolishly at the sight of two ice cubes slowly dissolving. Donaldson dogs the hatch. An enhanced but rudimentary image of the interior comes to life on an adjacent TV screen. It shows two ice cubes slowly dissolving.

"Ideally," the professor says, fists clenched at his sides, "the chamber would be absolutely shielded. We've sacrificed some signal purity so you can see what's going on inside. The process will still work reasonably well. Is the system on-line, Eddie?"

"Yeah." Rostow's own palms are wet. The whole performance is premature. Five successful tests and two fails. Donaldson's a yo-yo, bobbing from an obsession for publicity at any cost through close-mouthed paranoia and back. It'd almost be nice if the damned thing blew out. Bite your tongue. It's my baby. Go, go.

"Well, don't just sit there."

"Right, Stan," says Rostow through his teeth, and smashes the toggle closed.

There is no new sound, no deep shuddering hum or rising whine. Current in the magnetic coils goes to fifty thousand amps, and there is a faint creaking as monstrously thick non-magnetic structural members crave one another's company in the embrace of the stupendous field. Sometimes, with the lights dimmed, Rostow has seen phantom bars of pale light crossing his line of sight. Field strengths of this magnitude can screw with the visual cortex. Or maybe the magnets bend cosmic radiation through the soft tissues of his eyeballs and brain, nibbling tiny explosions of pseudolight in his synapses. It isn't happening now. Everyone stares at the TV monitor, waiting for something apocalyptic. Caught by the mood, Rostow abandons his console and steals across to join them.

"I'm still waiting," Buonacelli barks.

"Watch the ice cubes, Senator," Jennifer tells him.

"Dear God." It is one of the accountants who first grasps what is happening. "The bastards are getting bigger!"

"Just so," Donaldson says, loosening his fists. "The basic conservation law: heat can't pass from a cold object to a hot one. But time inside the mirror is now running backwards, gentlemen, for all practical purposes. Advanced Maxwell radiation, amplified by the lasing action, is converging on the flask. The Second Law of Thermodynamics is repealed."

Rostow's body thumps to his pulse. Steam is rising once more from the flask. A pair of unblemished cubes jounce at the surface of the boiling water.

"Fantastic," Buonacelli groans. "I take it all back. Dr Donaldson, this is the wonder of the age."

"You have yet to witness the more dramatic part of our demonstration." Turning abruptly, the professor stumbles into

Rostow. "Wouldn't it be better if you were at your console, Eddie? Please power the system down immediately and put it on Standby. Where's that animal?"

Rostow chews at part of his face. "I'll get him for you." He slouches in his seat, runs the current down, feels in the box with his left hand for the bunny. Helplessly he glances at Jennifer Barton. She is watching him. Fingers tight around the bunny's ears, he hoists it from the box and feels acid in his stomach as he identifies the flash of emotion in her face.

Taking the bunny, Donaldson suggests: "Remove the flask and then stand by for my mark." Rostow seethes, but welcomes the distraction. Behind him the bunny squeals. Nothing wrong with its memory at any rate. There's a meaty thunk. When he turns back with the remelted cubes, Rostow finds the professor marching toward him with the bunny's bloody, guillotined corpse in a sterile glass dish. One of the accountants, no great white hunter, is averting squeamish eyes. Buonacelli's are narrowed in wild surmise.

Resurrection is at once prosaic, electrifying, impossible to comprehend. On the monitor, the bunny's grainy sopping fur lightens as untold trillions of randomly bustling molecules reverse their paths. As the flow staunches, its poor partitioned head rolls upward from the glass bowl and fits itself seamlessly to its unmarked neck. Prestidigitation. The bunny blinks spasmodically, slow lids snapping upward, wiggles his ass, and disgorges a strip of unchewed lettuce. The lab thunders crazily with applause.

"By the Lord, you're a genius!" Color has drained from Buonacelli's seamed features; it surges back, as he beats Donaldson's shoulders. "Reviving the dead . . ." He pauses and adds slowly, with avaricious appetite: "A man could live forever."

"I doubt it," Rostow tell him. "We can put people back together, and heal wounds. But unfortunately it won't help those who die of natural causes."

"Rejuvenate them!"

"It'll rub out your memory."

"Not your financial holdings, by God." The senator flexes his fingers, thickened by incipient arthritis. "Plenty of memories I could happily live without. You could brief yourself – leave notes, tapes . . ."

"Sorry. Reversed time passes at the conventional rate. Do you want to spend forty years in solitary confinement? Besides, even the immensely rich couldn't run this machine nonstop for that long."

Donaldson is nodding his agreement, until it occurs to him that he's no longer the center of attention. "I did ask you to stay at your console, Eddie. Miss Barton, thank you, that will be all today." With smiles all around, he ushers the committeemen away from the mirror into a cozy space of his own contriving. Eddie Rostow watches them troop toward the door. They remain in shock, their several minds no doubt working like maniacs as each tries to figure himself in and the rest out. "Truly astounding," one says as the door closes.

Rostow covers his face. In the huge empty lab he hears Jennifer Barton rise from her seat. He opens his fingers for a peek. She is regarding him across her deactivated terminal; he cannot read her expression with certainty. Once more he covers his eyes and listens to the tap of her shoes, the click of her exit. Wistfully he sniffs the air for a trace of her scent, more natural pheromone than applied cosmetic. On the monitor screen, the bunny is scratching at the walls of the mirror chamber. Poor little beast. Dazed by anger, lust, remorse and sympathy, Rostow strides to the chamber and plucks the bunny to freedom and mortality.

A dizzying aura of bloody light spangled with pinpoints of imploding radiance momentarily blinds him. "Cretin," he mouths, dropping the rabbit and slamming the hatch. He runs toward the console, clutching his eyes, and barks his shin on the back of his chair.

Nothing explodes. When his vision clears he scans the bank of square lights on the system he had left running at full power without computer supervision. Christ Almighty, we need a fail-safe on that. Who'd expect anyone to be so dumb? Shuddering, he runs through the step-down with scrupulous attention to detail, double-checking every item.

As he finishes, he notes the bunny lumping near his numb toes, trying to get back into its box. The stupid bastard is hungry again. He heaves it in.

The afternoon is only half done. This is insane. Did Roentgen finish off his full day's work after the first exhibition of X-rays?

Surely Watson and Crick didn't quietly mop up the lab after they'd confirmed the DNA helix. I'll take myself off and tie one on, he decides. I'll get drunk as a skunk. He'd done just that after the first successful trial of the advanced-wave mirror: alone, bound to secrecy by his nervous department head, he'd sat in a downtown bar and poured bourbon into his belly until the trembling urge to howl with joy dopplered into a morose blur. And paid for it next day. Oh, no, not that again. I'll march down to Jennifer's room and lay it all out for her. Invite her to a movie, a plate of *Fricassée de Poulet* at Chez Marius and a bottle or two of Riesling. We'll get smashed together, bemoan Donaldson's bastardy; hell we'll leave Donaldson out of it; we'll go to her apartment and screw our tiny pink asses off.

His hand had been all the way up her skirt, and the next day she'd acted as if nothing had ever passed between them. Did goddamned Auberon Mountbatten Singh have his evil Anglo-Indian way with her that night, rotating through ingenious positions? It doesn't bear thinking about.

For a moment, to his horror, Rostow finds himself regretting his divorce. Worse, he finds his baffled free-floating lust drifting in the direction of the image of his ex-wife. Swiftly, before he damages his brain beyond repair, he puts a stop to that.

With effort he levers up from the dead console and mooches to the foot of the catwalk, leaning on its handrail. I have to stop brooding about Jennifer. I could have killed myself shoving my hand into the powered mirror, through the temporal interface. I do not interest her strangely. Undoubtedly only fantastic self-restraint prevented her from smashing my impertinent jaw with her knee. My God, how can I look her in the eye?

This kind of maundering unreels through Rostow's head until he is so bored with it that he turns back to check the data for tomorrow's log of tests. Glancing at the wall clock, he sees that he's wasted half an hour in useless self-laceration. Maybe, after all, he should simply run out the door, burst into her office, and screw her until the sweat pops from her admiring brow. Oh my God. He drags a heavy battered mathematical cookbook from the bench where the bunny rabbit was murdered and resigns himself to the honorable discharge of his employment. A dizzying aura of bloody light spangled with pinpoints of imploding radiance momentarily blinds him. "Cretin," he mouths, dropping the rabbit and slamming the hatch. He runs toward the console, clutching his eyes, and barks his shins on the back of his chair.

Nothing explodes. A startled, unconvinced element in his mind asks itself: Hasn't this all happened before?

He notes the bunny lumping near his numb toes trying to get back into its box. The stupid bastard is – Oh Jesus. A small disjointed part of him watches the wind-up golem, as detached as the bunny's head after its sacrifice. This isn't déjà vu. It's too sustained. I'll take myself off and tie one on, he decides. I'll get drunk as a skunk. Oh my God, I'm tracking through the same temporal sequence twice. But that's truly insane, delusional. Time isn't repeating itself. I'm using the advanced-wave mirror system as a metaphor, at some profoundly cracked-up level of my unconscious. Didn't my dear sweet brilliant wife complain that I'm a cyclothymic personality, a marginal manic-depressive, obsessively driven to repeat my laments? I've careened into a rut. A conditioned habit of thought. Jennifer Barton is driving me nuts. I can't even see her in the same room without brooding on the same stupefying regrets and fantasies. I'll march down to Jennifer's room and lay it all out for her. Invite her to a movie, a plate of *Fricassée de*—

All his sensations are scrambled. The terror in his head clangs against the lugubrious mood of his hormones. I looked at the clock, he tells himself desperately, clutching for a falsifiable test. Sound scientific method. What did it say? 4:37. Last time round. He grips that single datum, while his mutinous corpse leans on the railing of the catwalk, one foot propped on a rubber tread. Glancing at the wall clock, he sees that he's wasted half an hour—

Oh God Almighty. 4:37. Exultation bursts in his mind, leaving his flesh to plod like lead. Hold it, that doesn't mean you haven't flipped your cranium. Everyone has a built-in clock. Three Major Biorhythms Ordain Your Fate, that sort of thing. He wants to giggle, but his chest and jaw don't respond to the wish. His frail flesh has resigned itself to the honorable discharge of his employment. A dizzying aura of bloody light spangled with pinpoints of imploding radiance momentarily blinds him.

No! the small anarchic part screams silently. I can't stand it. It's happening again. I'm stuck in a loop of time. Wait, I can prove it. I dropped the rabbit. Any moment now I'll glance down and see it . . .

. . . trying to get back into its box. The stupid bastard is hungry again. He heaves it in—

Rostow tells himself: this is the third time round. Or is it? Were he in control of his programmed muscles, he would shudder. Maybe I've been caught in this loop for all eternity, or at any rate long enough for random quantum variations in one part of my brain to set up an isolated observing subprogram. Jesus, how much pseudo-duration would that take? Ludwig Bolzmann's *Stosszahlansatz* postulate: ordered particles spontaneously decay into chaos, but given enough interactions they can swirl together again into a new order, or even the old order. Suppose I'm at the bottom of a local fluctuation from unordered equilibrium. What's the Poincaré recurrence time for a human being and his lab? Say 10 to the 10th power raised to the 30th power. That's *absolutely* grotesque. The entire universe would have evaporated into dead cold soot. So I'm re-cycling. I stuck my mitt in the hatch and screwed up the mirror. I'm looping through the same thirty minutes forever, knowing exactly what's due next and unable to do anything about it. Maybe I'm not crazy – but I will be soon.

I'm a prisoner, Rostow realizes, in my own past.

For a moment, to his horror, he finds himself regretting his divorce. Worse, he finds—

Hold it, the isolated segment thinks. If I'm patched into the lasing system, the additional mass of my body is pushing the mirror into a singularity on an asymptotic curve, tending to the limit at thirty-odd minutes duration. But Hawking has shown that quantum effects re-enter powerfully under such conditions. After all, Rostow debates with himself, they must, or I'd be unaware of what's happening. The human brain has crucial quantum-scale interactions. Hadn't Popper and Eccles been arguing that case for years? So maybe I can break free of my prior actions. What's to stop me *deciding* to cross the room and pick up the flask from the bench where I put it?

Jenny, you bitch, he thinks, why are you doing this to me? Bitterly, he wanders to the bench and lifts the lukewarm flask of melted ice-cubes to his lips. It tastes terrible. He puts it down with revulsion, then picks it up once more and stares in amazement. I'm not thirsty. Something *made* me do that—

—the flask slips out of his fingers and shatters. The twin sectors of consciousness fuse.

Eddie Rostow goes stealthily to his console chair and lowers himself with infinite delicacy.

Aloud, he mutters: "I'm not out of it yet. Or am I? Is one change in the cause-and-effect sequence sufficient to take me off the loop?" Mellowing afternoon light slants across his fists from the barred skylight, a sympathetic doubling to the shadow from harsh white fluoros, and his voice echoes wanly. Rostow flushes. If Donaldson comes through that door to hear him mumbling to himself—

But that isn't on the agenda, is it? If anyone in the entire world has a certified lease on his own immediate future, it's Edward Theodore Rostow, doctoral candidate and imbecile. The sparkling impossible conjecture has come belatedly on tiptoes to smash him behind the ear. With a glad cry he leaps to his feet. "I can do anything! *Anything* I wish!"

I'm not trapped. I thought I was a prisoner, but I'm the first man in history to be genuinely liberated. Set free from consequences. *Do it.* If you don't like the results, scrub it on the next cycle and *try again.*

Rostow grabs up paper and calculator, scrawls figures. Start by establishing the exact parameters. See if the loop is decaying or elongating. It's aggravating, but he rounds out the cycle with his eyes clamped to the clock. The bloody aura flashes a half-minute after the digital clock jumps to 4:37. With iron control he keeps hold of the rabbit and wrenches his head around as vision clears. Three minutes after four. His endocrine fluids are telling him to panic, sluggishly stuck in the original sequence. Rostow's excited mind shouts them down. Denying the inertia of previous events, he takes the wriggling bunny to his console and places it carefully in its cardboard home. A thirty-four minute loop, forsooth.

Considerable effort is required initially. Rostow's First Theorem, he thinks, grinning. Any action will continue to be repeated indefinitely unless a volitional force is applied to counter that action. Fortunately, the energy necessary to alter intention and will is in the microvolt range. Yes. The brain *is* a quantum machine for making choices, once you understand that choice is possible.

He halts with his hand on the door latch. Think this through. Stan Donaldson, esteemed head of department and professor, is the last sonofabitch who deserves to know. Will I fall off the loop if I wander away from the mirror? Leaving the loop is suddenly a most undesirable prospect. Yet some obscure prompting dispels these trepidations. Rostow opens the door and enters the long colorless corridor.

Led by bombastic Donaldson, the Board of Directors is taking the stairs to the free hooch. Jennifer Barton's thick mane swirls as she shakes her head, freeing her arm from the senator's grip. On the bottom step she pivots and turns right, toward her small office in the Software Center. Not celebrating? Eddie shuts the lab door and pursues her down the corridor.

I can't tell her about it. She'd be obliged to call for the men in white. Up ahead, she slips into her office without looking in his direction. Arousal stirs in him, fecklessly.

Not truly believing it, he reminds himself: Anything is possible. There are no payoffs. The world's a stage, tra-la. "I'll just lay it on the line," he mutters seriously. A passing student blinks at him. With an inane giggle, Rostow nods. Loudly, in a crisp tone, he tells the student: "I'll ask her what the hell it is between us."

"Oh," says the student, and walks on, swiveling his brows.

High out of his gourd on freedom unchecked by restraint, Rostow zooms toward joy with the woman of his dreams. In a magical slalom on the vinyl tiles, he bursts through Jennifer Barton's door and thrusts his hands on the desk's edge. Her lab coat lies on a filing cabinet; she stands at her window, brushing her hair. "Tell me, for Christ's sake," Eddie barks before his vocabulary can freeze up, "what the hell it is between us."

His secret sweetheart narrows her eyes. With deflated, acute perception, Rostow surmises that perhaps he is not *her* secret sweetheart. "I hate it with the rabbit," she tells him, putting the brush in a drawer. "But it was a sensational *coup de théâtre*. Coming up for a drink?"

"Didn't you notice? I wasn't invited."

"Surely it was understood." She is being patient with him. Rostow closes the door at his back and sits on the desk. Stress is winding him tight. Has the stoned euphoria gone already?

"Jennifer," he says.

She waits. Then she rolls the caster-footed chair forward, sits before her impressive stacks of hard copy, and waits some more.

"Look. Jennifer, something went wrong with my upbringing. The only time I'm fluent is when I'm smashed, and then I turn into the maddened wolfman. So I don't go out very often. For example. Six months ago, after a horrible divorce, I ventured to a party without a keeper. Nobody tied me up or shoved a gag in my face. I failed conspicuously to recognize an old acquaintance, and then hectored him about the polarity of his sexual cravings. In the crudest possible terms. With no provocation, I noisily engaged a stern feminist on the matter of her tits, which I found noteworthy. I ended by shouting in a proprietorial manner from one end of the host's house to the other, at three in the morning, inviting young bearded people and their companions to drink up and depart swiftly, in what seemed to me a hearty and engaging fashion. When I got home I fell down in my own puke."

After a further silence, Jennifer lights a cigarette. "How horrible."

"Doubtless I'm a horrible person in every respect."

"That's not what I meant."

Rostow starts to yell, then lowers his voice in confusion. "I stumble over you sprawled on a fat bean-bag in the middle of a room of colleagues and strangers having your tits massaged by a swarthy blackamoor—"

She's on her feet. "Okay, sport. Enough. Out." Eddie is taken aback at the power of her extended arm as she hoists him off the desk. He thumps down heavily, barring the door with one leg.

"No, goddamn it. So I sit down beside you and toy with your wonderfully hairy leg. You smile and extend your limbs. I can't believe it. Up goes my little hand, hoppity-scamp—"

"Shut up, you creep."

For this, Rostow is utterly unprepared. He gapes.

Jennifer refuses to lower her eyes. Blotches of color stand out on her cheekbones. "You're right, Rostow, you are a horrible person. Incredibly enough, I once found you rather piquant. Your crass behavior the other night might have been forgivable as whimsy." In authentic rage she clamps her teeth together and wrenches the door open. "Stay or go as you please." Then the room is vacant, and Rostow slumps on the desk with his guts spilling out of his wounds and his brain whirling into sawdust and aloes.

The bloody aura is a jolt from one awful dream to another. With iron control he keeps hold of the rabbit and wrenches his head around as vision clears. Three minutes after four. Yet the appalling encounter echoes like a double image, a triple image in fact. His chemistry overloads and he vomits uncontrollably. Finally sourness sweeps away hallucination; he totters to the console and runs the mirror system down to Latent.

Aghast, he tells himself: "Scrub it out. Make it didn't happen." Regressing to childhood. His mouth tastes repulsive; he wipes his lips on the back of his hand. I can't take much more of this, he thinks. The human frame wasn't meant to handle the strain of dual sets of information. It'd take a Zen roshi to cope with this weirdness. The bitch, the lousy bitch.

But it isn't Jennifer Barton's doing. Rostow is doomed by his oafishness. I've got to keep away from her. I'd shred myself into a million messy bits. It is clear, though, that he cannot cower forever in the lab with only a canonized rabbit for company. Enough, he tells himself. Out. The clock shows a quarter after four. Cyclic time is slipping away. Down the corridor, unharassed, Jennifer Barton is presumably finalizing her coiffure.

Rostow slams the door, running for the stairs. As he expects, Buonacelli and his claque are milling in the Senior Faculty Bar. Donaldson dispenses whiskies in their midst, jovial, exonerated, cautioning them all to reticence under the rubric of security.

"A wonderful experience, Dr, uh, Rostow?" says one of the directors, a pleasant administrator. Eddie turns convulsively. "I'm Harrison Macintyre, Ford Foundation." The man holds out his hand. "No problems with funding," he smiles, "after today."

"Oh. Thank you. Not 'doctor', I'm afraid. I've never had time to write anything up." Stan seems to be explaining how the advanced-wave project sprang fully armed from his professorial brow. Adrenalin begins a fresh surge.

Macintyre puts liquor into his hand and says, "I've been wondering about that. Publication, I mean. Surely today wasn't your first trial with the equipment."

"No. No, Harrison. Call me Eddie. We knew it was going to work. It's been operational for some weeks." Across the russet carpet, Buonacelli is laughing boomingly. "The Nobel Prize for Physics, Stan," says the senator. "The Nobel Prize for Medicine," adds a beaming director. "Hot damn," cries another "they'll make it a hat trick and give you the Nobel Prize for Literature when your paper comes out."

Rostow scowls hideously. "Normally we would indeed have published by now, Harrison," he says loudly. "But after the tachyon fiasco, Professor Donaldson developed some misgivings about shooting his mouth off prematurely, you see." Faces turn. "You must remember. Every man and his dog was hunting faster-than-light particles. The great physicist spied his chance at glory." The Ford Foundation man, scandalized, tries to hush him. Eddie drains his glass, gestures for another. "But the professor blew it. His tachyons were actually pickup calls from the Green Cab Company. They snuck in through his Faraday cage. Someone didn't check that out until after the press conference did we, Stan?"

Donaldson is peering at the half-full glass in Rostow's grasp; slowly, he allows his gaze to rise until he studies a point somewhere near Eddie's left ear. "Mr Rostow," he says from the depths of his soul, "hired hands are rarely invited into this room. Those who gain that privilege generally comport themselves with civility and a due measure of deference. Those who have just been fired without a reference do not linger here under any circumstances. Get out of my sight."

Jennifer Barton arrives at that moment, smiling, hair lustrous. At the door she hesitates, scanning shocked faces. Their eyes meet. Her presence – oblivious of edited outrage, witness to new humiliation – sends Rostow into a frenzy. He throws down his glass and catches Donaldson by his lapels.

"I wish you wouldn't shout, Frog-face," he says, every sinew on fire. "You astounding hypocrite," he says, jouncing the man back on his heels. "What's a Nobel Prize or two between hired hands?" he says, thumping Donaldson heavily in the breast. Two or three of the directors have come to their senses by now and grapple with Rostow, dragging him away from his gasping and empurpled victim. "It happens all the time, doesn't it?" Eddie squirms, kicking at targets of opportunity. "We poor bastards break our asses so some ludicrous discredited figure-head can whiz off to Stockholm to meet the king."

Even in his own ears, Rostow's outburst sounds thin, thin. Where righteousness should ring, only a stale peevishness lingers. Tears of anger and mortification star the pendant cut-glass lamps. He breaks free and pushes through business suits. Jennifer stares at him, off balance. "You don't want to stay with these vultures," he cries, seizing her arm. It seems that she stud-ies his scarlet face for minutes of silence. With a minimal move-ment she dislodges his hand.

"Eddie," she says regretfully, "when are you going to grow up?"

Bitch. Bitch, bitch.

And the bloody aura. He is holding the rabbit, wrenching his head around to check the clock. This time the shock of recur-rence is curiously attenuated, as if lunatic hostility sits better than misery with a physiology keyed to fright. Rostow's heart rattles, catches its beat; the pulse thunders in his neck and wrists. The rabbit struggles free. He moves with Tarquin's ravishing stride to the console, at a pitch of emotion. Icily he shuts down the mirror system. There are cracks in the concrete where the supports for the magnetic coils are embedded. A faint regular buzzing comes from the fluoros. His skin is crawling, as if each hair on his body is a nipple, erect and preternaturally sensitive. Gagging, he closes the door and paces remorselessly down the corridor.

Jennifer Barton stands on the bottom step of the carved stairs, deflecting Senator Buonacelli's horseplay. Rostow storms past them. "Hey, boy, that was a great show," cries the senator. "Why don't you and this little lady come up and join us in a drink?" Rostow hardly hears the man. His feet are at the ends of his legs. Jennifer's door is not locked. He leaves it wide for her. Staring out into the afternoon light. Three tall blacks fake and run, dribbling a ball.

"Well, Jambo!" As Eddie faces her, Jennifer is closing the door, meeting him with an infectious smile. "It's taken you long enough to find my office, sailor."

"What?" he says, uncomprehending. He pushes her roughly back against the crowded desk and takes her thigh with cruel pressure. Speechless and instantly afraid, she repudiates his hand. He thrusts it higher and tugs at her underwear.

"Let's pick up where we left off," he informs her. An absolute chill pervades his flesh. Nothing had prepared him to expect this of himself. Everything he calls himself is outraged, shrunken in loathing at his own actions.

"Stop it," she says distantly. "You fucking asshole." Tactically her posture is not favorable; when she drives up her right knee, its bruising force is deflected from his leg. I can have whatever I want. The whole universe is a scourge slashing at my vulnerable back. Very well, let those be the rules. He imagines he is laughing. I have nothing to offer but fear itself. As she begins to scream and batter his neck, his cheek, his temple, he clouts her savagely into semi consciousness. Oh Jesus, you can't be blamed for what happens during a nightmare. In the absence of causality, Fyodor, all things are permitted. She is bent backward, moving feebly. One of his hands clamps her mouth, hard against her teeth, the other unzips. I'm the Primary Process Man, oh, wow. But he is so cold. There is no blood under his skin. Rostow batters at her thighs with his limp flesh. He slides to his knees. The edge of the desk furrows his nose.

"You," Jenny grunts. She is blank with detestation. Tenderly, she touches her skull. "You."

Eddie Rostow lurches upright. Swaying, exposed, he falls into the corridor. The same young student, returning, regards him with astonishment and abhorrence. The boy reaches out a hand, changes his mind and pelts away in search of aid. It is all a grainy picture show, a world-sized monitor screen. They'll fire him for this. Oh, shit, Jenny, you don't understand; I *love* you.

In fugue, Rostow pitches down the corridor.

The cleaver is lying where Donaldson left it on the bench, a ripple of bunny blood standing back from its surgical edge. Rostow's self-contempt has no bounds. As he lifts the blade, there is one final lucid thought. I'm an animal, he tells himself. We can't be trusted. The cleaver's handle slips in his sweating fingers. He tightens his grip and with a kind of concentration brings the thing in a whirling silvery arc into the tilted column of his neck. Shearing through the heavy sterno-mastoid muscle, in one blow it slashes the carotid artery, the internal jugular and the vagus nerve, before it's stopped by the banded cartilage of the trachea. He scarcely feels his flesh open: all pain is in the intolerable impact. A brilliant crimson jet spears and spatters, but Rostow fails to see it: he collapses in shock, and the fluid pulses out of his torpid body until he is dead.

His corpse lies cooling until half a minute after 4:37.

A dizzying aura of bloody light spangled with pinpoints of imploding radiance momentarily blinds him.

Rostow screams.

There is nothing banal in this plunge upward into instantaneous rebirth. It is overwhelming. It is transcendental. It is a jackhammer on Rostow's soul.

Like a thousand micrograms of White Lightning, life detonates every cell of his brain and body. He has been to hell, and died afterwards. Let me stay dead. Let me be dead.

Catharsis purges him of every thought. Eddie cradles the white rabbit in his arms and sobs his heart out.

At length he is sufficiently composed to reflect: I never cried when Tania left. Everything wise within me insisted that I should cry, but I turned my back. He realizes that he hasn't wept freely since he was a child. Dear Jesus, does it take this abomination to lance my constricted soul?

And his spirits do indeed soar. Without denying the reality of what he has done, his pettiness and spite and ignominy, he encompasses a mood of redemptive benediction. It brings a wide, silly grin to his mouth.

"Bunny rabbit," he declares, lofting the animal high over his head, laughing as its big grubby hind feet thump the air, "ain't nobody been where we wuz, baby. Let me tell you, buster, I like this side a lot better."

Eddie feeds the rabbit a strip of lettuce and steps through the tedious details of shutdown. He meditates on his humbling and his bestiality, flinching at memory.

The frailty at his core yearns to interpret it all as a stress nightmare, an hallucination. Denial would be not merely futile and cowardly; it would betray what has been offered him. Rather piquant, eh? Holy shit. Still, it is a point of access. Eddie Rostow confesses to his worst self that he needs all the help he can get.

The next cycle brings swifter recovery. Rostow splashes tepid water from the flask into his face, dabbing at his reddened eyelids. Soon he must spend some time figuring how to replicate the loop condition after he gets off this one. Fertile conjectures multiply; he suppresses them for the moment. Nerving himself, he walks edgily to the Software Center, nodding companionably to the passing student. The directors have ascended to their solace. His knock is tentative.

Jennifer's smile startles him with its warmth. She lowers her hairbrush. "Well, hello, sailor."

Eddie stands in the doorway, drinking her unbruised face. Despite himself he flushes.

"Don't just loiter there with intent, man. You're the unsung hero of the moment. It was sensational." She frowns. "I hated it with the rabbit, though."

"Jennifer," he says in a rush, "I'm sorry about the party. You know."

"That. Yeah. You were rather blunt."

"You inspire the village idiot in me."

"Sailor, that's the sweetest thing anyone ever. Coming up to poach on the Professorial Entertainment Allowance Fund?"

Eddie melts disgustingly within, wallowing in amnesty. "I happen to know a place."

"You've got a fifth of Jack Daniels squirreled in your locker."

"I've always admired your mind. Passionately."

"That wasn't the part you molested in public."

"I am," he tells her, "truly sorry." Her hair flows in his fingers and he puts his face against hers for a moment. Jenny touches his hand.

"While we dally," she tells him, "Stan is up there screwing you,"

"No argument. He's like that. All scientists are lunatics and swindlers. I intend to fight. More to the point, are you screwing Dr Singh? Oh Christ, don't answer that."

"I will not. It's none of your business. For God's sake, don't get snotty. Here, let me help you off with your—"

"Shouldn't we shut the door?"

"Kick it, you're closer. Why did it take you so long to get here?"

"Don't ask."

"Hmm. You know, I thought you were going to throw a tantrum in the lab."

Eddie tries to keep his tone light. "Upon my soul, Miss Barton, that'd be no way for a besotted genius to contest his rights." Shortly he asks: "Won't the printouts get runkled?"

"There's more in the computer, you fool."

On the next loop, abandoning his dazed inertia for an instant, Eddie glances at Jennifer's wrist watch and ensures that the flash comes as the flash comes as the flash comes . . .

THE VERY SLOW TIME MACHINE

Ian Watson

Back in 1935 Murray Leinster was the first to suggest, in "The Morrison Monument", that if time travel was possible then the time machine itself, and therefore the traveller, would be visible through the entirety of its journey from point A in time to point B. The idea hasn't been much considered since, but the ever reliable Ian Watson resurrected it with considerable ingenuity to create what I believe is the definitive treatment of the idea.

Ian Watson is one of those renegade writers of science fiction who constantly pushes the boundaries, seeking to create original and thought-provoking work. His one time-travel novel is Oracle *(1997) but a selection of his short stories involving time in all its manifestations can be found in the collections* The Very Slow Time Machine *(1979) and* Slow Birds *(1985).*

(1990)

The Very Slow Time Machine – for convenience: the VSTM* – made its first appearance at exactly midday 1 December 1985 in an unoccupied space at the National Physical Laboratory. It signalled its arrival with a loud bang and a squall of expelled air. Dr Kelvin, who happened to be looking in its direction, reported that the VSTM did not exactly *spring* into existence instantly, but rather expanded very rapidly from a point source, presumably explaining the absence of a more devastating explosion as the VSTM jostled with the air already present in the room.

---

* *The term VSTM is introduced retrospectively in view of our subsequent understanding of the problem (2019).*

Later, Kelvin declared that what he had actually seen was the *implosion* of the VSTM. Doors were sucked shut by the rush of air, instead of bursting open, after all. However it was a most confused moment – and the confusion persisted, since the occupant of the VSTM (who alone could shed light on its nature) was not only time-reversed with regard to us, but also quite crazy.

One infuriating thing is that the occupant visibly grows saner and more presentable (in his reversed way) the more that time passes. We feel that all the hard work and thought devoted to the enigma of the VSTM is so much energy poured down the entropy sink – because the answer is going to come from him, from inside, not from us; so that we may as well just have bided our time until his condition improved (or, from his point of view, began to degenerate). And in the meantime his arrival distorted and perverted essential research at our laboratory from its course without providing any tangible return for it.

The VSTM was the size of a small caravan; but it had the shape of a huge lead sulphide, or galena, crystal – which is, in crystallographer's jargon, an octahedron-with-cube formation consisting of eight large hexagonal faces with six smaller square faces filling in the gaps. It perched precariously – but immovably – on the base square, the four lower hexagons bellying up and out towards its waist where four more squares (oblique, vertically) connected with the mirror-image upper hemisphere, rising to a square north pole. Indeed it looked like a kind of world globe, lopped and sheered into flat planes, and has remained very much a separate, private world to this day, along with its passenger.

All faces were blank metal except for one equatorial square facing southwards into the main body of the laboratory. This was a window – of glass as thick as that of a deep-ocean diving bell – which could apparently be opened from inside, and only from inside.

The passenger within looked as ragged and tattered as a tramp; as crazy, dirty, woe-begone and tangle-haired as any lunatic in an ancient Bedlam cell. He was apparently very old; or at any rate long solitary confinement in that cell made him seem so. He was pallid, crookbacked, skinny and rotten-toothed. He raved and mumbled soundlessly at our spotlights. Or maybe he only mouthed his ravings and mumbles, since we could hear nothing whatever through the thick glass. When we obtained the services of a lipreader two days later the mad old man seemed to be mouthing mere garbage, a mishmash of sounds. Or was he? Obviously no one could be expected to lip-read backwards; already, from his actions and gestures, Dr Yang had suggested that the man was time-reversed. So we video-taped the passenger's mouthings and played the tapes backwards for our lipreader. Well, it was still garbage. Backwards, or forwards, the unfortunate passenger had visibly cracked up. Indeed, one proof of his insanity was that he should be trying to talk to us at all at this late stage of his journey rather than communicate by holding up written messages – as he has now begun to do. (But more of these messages later; they only begin – or, from his point of view, *cease* as he descends further into madness – in the summer of 1989.)

Abandoning hope of enlightenment from him, we set out on the track of scientific explanations. (Fruitlessly. Ruining our other, more important work. Overturning our laboratory projects – and the whole of physics in the process.)

To indicate the way in which we wasted our time, I might record that the first "clue" came from the shape of the VSTM, which, as I said, was that of a lead sulphide or galena crystal. Yang emphasized that galena is used as a semiconductor in crystal rectifiers: devices for transforming alternating current into direct current. They set up a much higher resistance to an electric current flowing in one direction than another. Was there an analogy with the current of time? Could the geometry of the VSTM – or the geometry of energies circulating in its metal walls, presumably interlaid with printed circuits – effectively impede the forward flow of time, and reverse it? We had no way to break into the VSTM. Attempts to cut into it proved quite ineffective and were soon discontinued, while X-raying it was foiled, conceivably by lead alloyed in the walls. Sonic scanning provided rough pictures of internal shapes, but nothing as intricate as circuitry; so we had to rely on what we could see of the outward shape, or through the window – and on pure theory.

Yang also stressed that galena rectifiers operate in the same manner as diode valves. Besides transforming the flow of an electric current they can also *demodulate*. They separate information out from a modulated carrier wave – as in a radio or TV set. Were we witnessing, in the VSTM, a machine for separating out "information" – in the form of the physical vehicle itself, with its passenger – from a carrier wave stretching back through time? Was the VSTM a solid, tangible analogy of a three-dimensional TV picture, played backwards?

We made many models of VSTMs based on these ideas and tried to send them off into the past, or the future – or anywhere for that matter! They all stayed monotonously present in the laboratory, stubbornly locked to our space and time.

Kelvin, recalling his impression that the VSTM had seemed to expand outward from a point, remarked that this was how three-dimensional beings such as ourselves might well perceive a four-dimensional object first impinging on us. Thus a 4-D sphere would appear as a point and swell into a full sphere then contract again to a point. But a 4-D octahedron-and-cube? According to our maths this shape couldn't have a regular analogue in 4-D space; only a simple octahedron could. Besides, what would be the use of a 4-D time machine which shrank to a point at precisely the moment when the passenger needed to mount it? No, the VSTM wasn't a genuine four-dimensional body; though we wasted many weeks running computer programs to describe it as one, and arguing that its passenger was a normal 3-D space man imprisoned within a 4-D space structure – the discrepancy of one dimension between him and his vehicle effectively isolating him from the rest of the universe so that he could travel hindwards.

That he was indeed travelling hindwards was by now absolutely clear from his feeding habits (i.e. he regurgitated) though his extreme furtiveness about bodily functions coupled with his filthy condition meant that it took several months before we were positive, on these grounds.

All this, in turn, raised another unanswerable question: if the VSTM was indeed travelling backwards through time, precisely where did it *disappear* to, in that instant of its arrival on 1 December 1985? The passenger was hardly on an archaeological jaunt, or he would have tried to climb out.

At long last, on midsummer day 1989, our passenger held up a notice printed on a big plastic eraser slate.

CRAWLING DOWNHILL, SLIDING UPHILL!

He held this up for ten minutes, against the window. The printing was spidery and ragged; so was he.

This could well have been his last lucid moment before the final descent into madness, in despair at the pointlessness of trying to communicate with us. Thereafter it would be *downhill all the way*, we interpreted. Seeing us with all our still eager, still baffled faces, he could only gibber incoherently thenceforth like an enraged monkey at our sheer stupidity.

He didn't communicate for another three months.

When he held up his next (i.e. penultimate) sign, he looked slightly sprucer, a little less crazy (though only comparatively so, having regard to his final mumbling squalor).

THE LONELINESS! BUT LEAVE ME ALONE!
IGNORE ME UNTIL 1995!

We held up signs (to which we soon realized, his sign was a response):

ARE YOU TRAVELLING BACK THROUGH TIME? HOW? WHY?

We would have also dearly loved to ask: where do you disappear to on December 1 1985? But we judged it unwise to ask this most pertinent of all questions in case his disappearance was some sort of disaster, so that we would in effect be foredooming him, accelerating his mental breakdown. Dr Franklin insisted that this was nonsense; he broke down *anyway*. Still, if we *had* held up that sign, what remorse we would have felt: because we *might* have caused his breakdown and ruined some magnificent undertaking . . . We were certain that it had to be a magnificent undertaking to involve such personal sacrifice, such abnegation, such a cutting-off of oneself from the rest of the human race. This is about all we were certain of.

(1995)

No progress with our enigma. All our research is dedicated to solving it, but we keep this out of sight of him. While rotas of postgraduate students observe him round the clock, our best brains get on with the real thinking elsewhere in the building. He sits inside his vehicle, less dirty and dishevelled now, but monumentally taciturn: a trappist monk under a vow of silence. He spends most of his time re-reading the same dog-eared books, which have fallen to pieces back in our past: Defoe's *Journal of the Plague Year* and *Robinson Crusoe* and Jules Verne's *Journey to the Centre of the Earth*; and listening to what is presumably taped music – which he shreds from the cassettes back in 1989, flinging streamers around his tiny living quarters in a brief mad fiesta (which of course we see as a sudden frenzy of disentangling and repackaging, with maniacal speed and neatness, of tapes which have lain around, trodden underfoot, for years).

Superficially we have ignored him (and he, us) until 1995: assuming that his last sign had some significance. Having got nowhere ourselves, we expect something from him now.

Since he is cleaner, tidier and saner now, in this year 1995 (not to mention ten years younger) we have a better idea of how old he actually is; thus some clue as to when he might have started his journey.

He must be in his late forties or early fifties – though he aged dreadfully in the last ten years, looking more like seventy or eighty when he reached 1985. Assuming that the future does not hold in store any longevity drugs (in which case he might be a century old, or more!) he should have entered the VSTM sometime between 2010 and 2025. The later date, putting him in his very early twenties if not teens, does rather suggest a "suicide volunteer" who is merely a passenger in the vehicle. The earlier date suggests a more mature researcher who played a major role in the development of the VSTM and was only prepared to test it on his own person. Certainly, now that his madness has abated into a tight, meditative fixity of posture, accompanied by normal activities such as reading, we incline to think him a man of moral stature rather than a time-kamikaze; so we put the date of commencement of the journey around

2010 to 2015 (only fifteen to twenty years ahead) when he will be in his thirties.

Besides theoretical physics, basic space science has by now been hugely sidetracked by his presence.

The lead hope of getting man to the stars was the development of some deep-sleep or refrigeration system. Plainly this does not exist by 2015 or so – or our passenger would be using it. Only a lunatic would voluntarily sit in a tiny compartment for decades on ends, ageing and rotting, if he could sleep the time away just as well, and awake as young as the day he set off. On the other hand, his life-support systems seem so impeccable that he can exist for decades within the narrow confines of that vehicle using recycled air, water and solid matter to 100 per cent efficiency. This represents no inconsiderable outlay in research and development – which must have been borrowed from another field, obviously the space sciences. Therefore the astronauts of 2015 or thereabouts require very long-term life support systems capable of sustaining them for years and decades, up and awake. What kind of space travel must they be engaged in, to need these? Well, they can only be going to the stars – the slow way; though not a *very* slow way. Not hundreds of years; but decades. Highly dedicated men must be spending many years cooped up alone in tiny spacecraft to reach Alpha Centaurus, Tau Ceti, Epsilon Eridani or wherever. If their surroundings are so tiny, then any extra payload costs prohibitively. Now who would contemplate such a journey merely out of curiosity? No one. The notion is ridiculous – *unless* these heroes are carrying something to their destinations which will then link it inexorably and instantaneously with Earth. A tachyon descrambler is the only obvious explanation. They are carrying with them the other end of a tachyon-transmission system for beaming material objects, and even living human beings, out to the stars!

So, while one half of physics nowadays grapples with the problems of reverse-time, the other half, funded by most of the money from the space vote, pre-empting the whole previously extant space programme, is trying to work out ways to harness and modulate tachyons.

These faster-than-light particles certainly *seem* to exist; we're fairly certain of that now. The main problem is that the technology for harnessing them is needed *beforehand*, to prove that they do exist and so to work out exactly *how* to harness them.

All these reorientations of science – because of *him* sitting in his enigmatic vehicle in deliberate alienation from us, reading *Robinson Crusoe*, a strained expression on his face as he slowly approaches his own personal crack-up.

(1996)

If you were locked up in a VSTM for X years, would you want a calendar on permanent display – or not? Would it be consoling or taunting? Obviously his instruments are calibrated – unless it was completely fortuitous that his journey ended on 1 December 1985 at precisely midday! But can he see the calibrations? Or would he prefer to be overtaken suddenly by the end of his journey, rather than have the slow grind of years unwind itself? You see, we are trying to explain why he did not communicate with us in 1995.

Convicts in solitary confinement keep their sanity by scratching five-barred gates of days on the walls with their fingernails; the sense of time passing keeps their spirits up. But on the other hand, tests of time perception carried out on potholers who volunteered to stay below ground for several months on end show that the internal clock lags grossly – by as much as two weeks in a three month period. Our VSTM passenger might gain a reprieve of a year – or five years! – on his total subjective journey time, by ignoring the passing of time. The potholers had no clue to night and day; but then, neither does he! Ever since his arrival, lights have been burning constantly in the laboratory; he has been under constant observation . . .

He isn't a convict, or he would surely protest, beg to be let out, throw himself on our mercy, give us some clue to the nature of his predicament. Is he the carrier of some fatal disease – a disease so incredibly infectious that it must affect the whole human race unless he were isolated? Which can only be isolated by a time capsule? Which even isolation on the Moon or Mars would not keep from spreading to the human race? He hardly appears to be . . .

Suppose that he had to be isolated for some very good reason, and suppose that he concurs in his own isolation (which he visibly does, sitting there reading Defoe for the *n*th time), what demands .this unique dissection of one man from the whole continuum of human life and from his own time and space? Medicine, psychiatry, sociology, all the human sciences are being drawn into the problem in the wake of physics and space science. Sitting there doing nothing, he has become a kind of funnel for all the physical and social sciences: a human black hole into which vast energy pours, for a very slight increase in our radius of understanding. That single individual has accumulated as much disruptive potential as a single atom accelerated to the speed of light – which requires all the available energy in the universe to sustain it in its impermissible state.

Meanwhile the orbiting tachyon laboratories report that they are just on the point of uniting quantum mechanics, gravitational theory and relativity; whereupon they will at last "jump" the first high-speed particle packages over the C-barrier into a faster-than-light mode, and back again into our space. But they reported *that* last year – only to have their particle packages "jump back" as antimatter, annihilating five billion dollars' worth of equipment and taking thirty lives. They hadn't jumped into a tachyon mode at all, but had "möbiused" themselves through wormholes in the space-time fabric.

Nevertheless, prisoner of conscience (his own conscience, surely!) or whatever he is, our VSTM passenger seems nobler year by year. As we move away from his terminal madness, increasingly what strikes us is his dedication, his self-sacrifice (for a cause still beyond our comprehension), his Wittgensteinian spirituality. "Take him for all in all, he is a Man. We shall not look upon his like . . ." Again? We shall look upon his like. Upon the man himself, gaining stature every year! That's the wonderful thing. It's as though Christ, fully exonerated as the Son of God, is uncrucified and his whole life re-enacted before our eyes in full and certain knowledge of his true role. (Except . . . that this man's role is silence.)

(1997)

Undoubtedly he is a holy man who will suffer mental crucifixion for the sake of some great human project. Now he re-reads Defoe's *Plague Year*, that classic of collective incarceration and the resistance of the human spirit and human organizing ability. Surely the "plague" hint in the title is irrelevant. It's the sheer force of spirit which beat the Great Plague of London – that is the real keynote of the book.

Our passenger is the object of popular cults by now – a focus for finer feelings. In this way his mere presence has drawn the world's peoples closer together, cultivating respect and dignity, pulling us back from the brink of war, liberating tens of thousands from their concentration camps. These cults extend from purely fashionable manifestations – shirts printed with his face, now neatly shaven in a Vandyke style; rings and worry-beads made from galena crystals – through the architectural (octahedron-and-cube meditation modules) to life-styles themselves: a Zen-like "sitting quietly, doing nothing".

He's Rodin's *Thinker*, the *Belvedere Apollo*, and Michelangelo's *David* rolled into one for our world as the millennium draws to its close. Never have so many copies of Defoe's two books and the Jules Verne been in print before. People memorize them as meditation exercises and recite them as the supremely lucid, rational Western mantras.

The National Physical Laboratory has become a place of pilgrimage, our lawns and grounds a vast camping site – Woodstock and Avalon, Rome and Arlington all in one. About the sheer tattered degradation of his final days less is said; though that has its cultists too, its late twentieth-century anchorites, its Saint Anthonies pole-squatting or cave-immuring themselves in the midst of the urban desert, bringing austere spirituality back to a world which appeared to have lost its soul – though this latter is a fringe phenomenon; the general keynote is nobility, restraint, quiet consideration for others.

And now he holds up a notice.

I IMPLY NOTHING. PAY NO ATTENTION TO MY PRESENCE.
KINDLY GET ON DOING YOUR OWN THINGS. I CANNOT EXPLAIN
TILL 2000.

He holds it up for a whole day, looking not exactly angry, but
slightly pained. The whole world, hearing of it, sighs with joy at
his modesty, his self-containment, his reticence, his humility.
This must be the promised 1995 message, two years late (or two
years early; obviously he still has a long way to come). Now he
is Oracle; he is the Millennium. This place is Delphi.

The orbiting laboratories run into more difficulties with their
tachyon research; but still funds pour into them, private dona-
tions too on an unprecedented scale. The world strips itself of
excess wealth to strip matter and propel it over the interface
between sub-light and trans-light.

The development of closed-cycle living pods for the carriers
of those tachyon receivers to the stars is coming along well; a fact
which naturally raises the paradoxical question of whether his
presence has in fact stimulated the development of the technology by which he himself survives. We at the National Physical
Laboratory and at all other such laboratories around the world
are convinced that we shall soon make a breakthrough in our
understanding of time-reversal – which, intuitively, should
connect with that other universal interface in the realm of matter,
between our world and the tachyon world – and we feel too,
paradoxically, that our current research must surely lead to the
development of the VSTM which will then become so oppor-
tunely necessary to us, for reasons yet unknown. No one feels
they are wasting their time. He is the Future. His presence here
vindicates our every effort – even the blindest of blind alleys.

What kind of Messiah must he be, by the time he enters the
VSTM? How much charisma, respect, adoration and wonder
must he have accrued by his starting point? Why, the whole
world will send him off! He will be the focus of so much collective hope and worship that we even start to investigate *Psi*
phenomena seriously: the concept of group mental thrust as a
hypothesis for his mode of travel – as though he is vectored not
through time or 4-D space at all but down the waveguide of
human will-power and desire.

(2001)

The millennium comes and goes without any revelation. Of course that is predictable; he is lagging by a year or eighteen months. (Obviously he can't see the calibrations on his instruments; it was his choice – that was his way to keep sane on the long haul.)

But finally, now in the autumn of 2001, he holds up a sign, with a certain quiet jubilation:

WILL I LEAVE 1985 SOUND IN WIND & LIMB?

Quiet jubilation, because we have already (from his point of view) held up the sign in answer:

YES! YES!

We're all rooting for him passionately. It isn't really a lie that we tell him. He did leave relatively sound in wind and limb. It was just his mind that was in tatters . . . Maybe that is inessential, irrelevant, or he wouldn't have phrased his question to refer merely to his physical body.

He must be approaching his take-off point. He's having a mild fit of tenth-year blues, first decade anxiety, self-doubt, which we clear up for him . . .

Why doesn't he know what shape he arrived in? Surely that must be a matter of record before he sets off . . . *No!* Time can not be invariable, determined. Not even the Past. Time is probabilistic. He has refrained from comment for all these years so as not to unpluck the strands of time past and reweave them in another, undesirable way. A tower of strength he has been. *Ein' feste Burg ist unser Zeitgänger!* Well, back to the drawing board, and to probabilistic equations for (a) tachyon-scatter out normal space (b) time-reversal.

A few weeks later he holds up another sign, which must be his promised Delphic revelation:

I AM THE MATRIX OF MAN.

Of course! Of course! He has made himself that over the years. What else?

A matrix is a mould for shaping a cast. And indeed, out of him have been moulded increasingly since the late 1990s, such has been his influence.

Was he sent hindwards to save the world from self-slaughter by presenting such a perfect paradigm – which only frayed and tattered in the eighties when it did not matter any more; when he had already succeeded?

But a matrix is also an array of components for translating from one code into another. So Yang's demodulation of information hypothesis is revived, coupled now with the idea that the VSTM is perhaps a matrix for transmitting the "information" contained in a man across space and time (and the man-transmitter experiments in orbit redouble their efforts); with the corollary (though this could hardly be voiced to the enraptured world at large) that perhaps the passenger was *not there* at all in any real sense; and he had never been; that we merely were witnessing an experiment in the possibility of transmitting a man across the galaxy, performed on a future Earth by future science to test out the degradation factor: the decay of information – mapped from space on to time so that it could be observed by us, their predecessors! Thus the onset of madness (i.e. information decay) in our passenger, timed in years from his starting point, might set a physical limit in *light-years* to the distance to which a man could be beamed (tachyonically?). And this was at once a terrible kick in the teeth to space science – and a great boost. A kick in the teeth, as this suggested that physical travel through interstellar space must be impossible, perhaps because of Man's frailty in face of cosmic ray bombardment; and thus the whole development of intensive closed-cycle life-pods for single astronaut couriers must be deemed irrelevant. Yet a great boost too, since the possibility of a receiverless transmitter loomed. The now elderly Yang suggested that 1 December 1985 was actually a moment of lift-off to the stars. Where our passenger went then, in all his madness, was to a point in space thirty or forty light-years distant. The VSTM was thus the testing to destruction of a future man-beaming system and practical future models would only deal in distances (in times) of the order of seven or eight years. (Hence no other VSTMs had imploded into existence, hitherto.)

(2010)

I am tired with a lifetime's fruitless work; however, the human race at large is at once calmly loving and frenetic with hope. For we must be nearing our goal. Our passenger is in his thirties now (whether a live individual, or only an epiphenomenon of a system for transmitting the information present in a human being: literally a "ghost in the machine"). This sets a limit. It sets a limit. He couldn't have set off with such strength of mind much earlier than his twenties or (I sincerely hope not) his late teens. Although the teens *are* a prime time for taking vows of chastity, for entering monasteries, for pledging one's life to a cause . . .

(2015)

Boosted out of my weariness by the general euphoria, I have successfully put off my retirement for another four years. Our passenger is now in his middle twenties and a curious inversion in his "worship" is taking place, representing (I think) a subconscious groundswell of anxiety as well as joy. Joy, obviously, that the moment is coming when he makes his choice and steps into the VSTM, as Christ gave up carpentry and stepped out from Nazareth. Anxiety, though, at the possibility that he may pass beyond this critical point, towards infancy; ridiculous as this seems! He knows how to read books; he couldn't have taught himself to read. Nor could he have taught himself how to speak *in vitro* – and he has certainly delivered lucid, if mysterious, messages to us from time to time. The hit song of the whole world, nevertheless, this year is William Blake's "The Mental Traveller" set to sitar and gongs and glockenspiel . . .

> *For as he eats and drinks he grows*
> *Younger and younger every day;*
> *And on the desert wild they both*
> *Wander in terror and dismay . . .*

The unvoiced fear represented by this song's sweeping of the world being that he may yet evade us; that he may slide down towards infancy, and at the moment of his birth (whatever life-support mechanisms extrude to keep him alive till then!) the VSTM will implode back whence it came: sick joke of some alien superconsciousness, intervening in human affairs with a scientific "miracle" to make all human striving meaningless and pointless. Not many people feel this way openly. It isn't a popular view. A man could be torn limb from limb for espousing it in public. The human mind will never accept it; and purges this fear in a long song of joy which at once mocks and copies and adores the mystery of the VSTM.

Men put this supreme *man* into the machine. Even so, Madonna and Child does haunt the world's mind . . . and a soft femininity prevails – men's skirts are the new soft gracious mode of dress in the West. Yet he is now so noble, so handsome in his youth, so glowing and strong; such a Zarathustra, locked up in there.

(2018)

He can only be twenty-one or twenty-two. The world adores him, mothers him, across the unbridgeable gulf of reversed time. No progress in the Solar System, let alone on the interstellar front. Why should we travel out and away, even as far as Mars, let alone Pluto, when a revelation is at hand; when all the secrets will be unlocked here on Earth? No progress on the tachyon or negative-time fronts, either. Nor any further messages from him. But he *is* his own message. His presence alone is sufficient to express Mankind: hopes, courage, holiness, determination.

(2019)

I am called back from retirement, for he is holding up signs again: the athlete holding up the Olympic Flame.

He holds them up for half an hour at a stretch – as though we are not all eyes agog, filming every moment in case we miss something, anything.

When I arrive, the signs that he has already held up have announced:

(*Sign One*) THIS IS A VERY SLOW TIME MACHINE. (And I amend accordingly, crossing out all the other titles we had bestowed on it successively, over the years. For a few seconds I wonder whether he was really naming the machine – defining it – or complaining about it! As though he'd been fooled into being its passenger on the assumption that a time machine should proceed to its destination *instanter* instead of at a snail's pace. But no. He was naming it.) TO TRAVEL INTO THE FUTURE, YOU MUST FIRST TRAVEL INTO THE PAST, ACCUMULATING HINDWARD POTENTIAL. (THIS IS CRAWLING DOWNHILL.)

(*Sign Two*) AS SOON AS YOU ACCUMULATE ONE LARGE QUANTUM OF TIME, YOU LEAP FORWARD BY THE SAME TIMESPAN AHEAD OF YOUR STARTING POINT. (THIS IS SLIDING UPHILL.)

(*Sign Three*) YOUR JOURNEY INTO THE FUTURE TAKES THE SAME TIME AS IT WOULD TAKE TO LIVE THROUGH THE YEARS IN REAL-TIME; YET YOU ALSO OMIT THE INTERVENING YEARS, ARRIVING AHEAD INSTANTLY. (PRINCIPLE OF CONSERVATION OF TIME.)

(*Sign Four*) SO, TO LEAP THE GAP, YOU MUST CRAWL THE OTHER WAY.

(*Sign Five*) TIME DIVIDES INTO ELEMENTARY QUANTA. NO MEASURING ROD CAN BE SMALLER THAN THE INDIVISIBLE ELEMENTARY ELECTRON; THIS IS ONE "ELEMENTARY LENGTH" (EL). THE TIME TAKEN FOR LIGHT TO TRAVEL ONE EL IS "ELEMENTARY TIME" (ET): I.E. 10^{-23} SECONDS, THIS IS ONE ELEMENTARY QUANTUM OF TIME. TIME CONSTANTLY LEAPS AHEAD BY THESE TINY QUANTA FOR EVERY PARTICLE; BUT, NOT BEING SYNCHRONIZED, THESE FORM A CONTINUOUS TIME-OCEAN RATHER THAN SUCCESSIVE DISCRETE "MOMENTS", OR WE WOULD HAVE NO CONNECTED UNIVERSE.

(*Sign Six*) TIME REVERSAL OCCURS NORMALLY IN STRONG NUCLEAR INTERACTIONS I.E. IN EVENTS OF ORDER 10^{-23} SECS. THIS REPRESENTS THE "FROZEN GHOST" OF THE FIRST MOMENT OF UNIVERSE WHEN AN "ARROW OF TIME" WAS FIRST STOCHASTICALLY DETERMINED.

(*Sign Seven*) (And this is when I arrived, to be shown Polaroid photographs of the first seven signs. Remarkably, he is holding up each sign in a linear sequence from *our* point of view; a considerable feat of forethought and memory, though no less than we expect of him.) NOW, ET IS INVARIABLE & FROZEN IN; YET UNIVERSE AGES. STRETCHING OF SPACE-TIME BY EXPANSION PROPAGATES "WAVES" IN THE SEA OF TIME, CARRYING TIME-ENERGY WITH PERIOD (X) PROPORTIONAL TO THE RATE OF EXPANSION, AND TO RATIO OF TIME ELAPSED TO TOTAL TIME AVAILABLE FOR THIS COSMOS FROM INITIAL CONSTANTS. EQUATIONS FOR X YIELD A PERIOD OF THIRTY-FIVE YEARS CURRENTLY AS ONE MOMENT OF MACRO-TIME WITHIN WHICH MACRO-SCOPIC TIME REVERSAL BECOMES POSSIBLE.

(*Sign Eight*) CONSTRUCT AN "ELECTRON SHELL" BY SYNCHRO-NIZING ELECTRON REVERSAL. THE LOCAL SYSTEM WILL THEN FORM A TIME-REVERSED MINI-COSMOS & PROCEED HIND-WARDS TILL X ELAPSES WHEN TIME CONSERVATION OF THE TOTAL UNIVERSE WILL PULL THE MINI-COSMOS (OF THE VSTM) FORWARD INTO MESH WITH UNIVERSE AGAIN I.E. BY THIRTY-FIVE PLUS THIRTY-FIVE YEARS.

"But how?" we all cried. "How do you synchronize such an infinity of electrons? We haven't the slightest idea!"

Now at least we knew when he had set off: from thirty-five years after 1985. From *next year*. We are supposed to know all this by next year! Why has he waited so long to give us the proper clues?

And he is heading for the year 2055. What is there in the year 2055 that matters so much?

(*Sign Nine*) I DO NOT GIVE THIS INFORMATION TO YOU BECAUSE IT WILL LEAD TO YOUR INVENTING THE VSTM. THE

SITUATION IS QUITE OTHERWISE. TIME IS PROBABILISTIC, AS SOME OF YOU MAY SUSPECT. I REALIZE THAT I WILL PROBABLY PERVERT THE COURSE OF HISTORY & SCIENCE BY MY ARRIVAL IN YOUR PAST (MY MOMENT OF DEPARTURE FOR THE FUTURE); IT IS IMPORTANT THAT YOU DO NOT KNOW YOUR PREDICAMENT TOO EARLY, OR YOUR FRANTIC EFFORTS TO AVOID IT WOULD GENERATE A TIME LINE WHICH WOULD UNPREPARE YOU FOR MY SETTING OFF. AND IT IS IMPORTANT THAT IT DOES ENDURE, FOR I AM THE MATRIX OF MAN. I AM LEGION. I SHALL CONTAIN MULTITUDES.

MY RETICENCE IS SOLELY TO KEEP THE WORLD ON TOLERABLY STABLE TRACKS SO THAT I CAN TRAVEL BACK ALONG THEM. I TELL YOU THIS OUT OF COMPASSION, AND TO PREPARE YOUR MINDS FOR THE ARRIVAL OF GOD ON EARTH.

"He's insane. He's been insane from the start."

"He's been isolated in there for some very good reason. Contagious insanity, yes."

"Suppose that a madman could project his madness—"

"He already has done that, for decades!"

"—no, I mean really project it, into the consciousness of the whole world; a madman with a mind so strong that he acted as a template, yes a matrix for everyone else, and made them all his dummies, his copies; and only a few people stayed immune who could build this VSTM to isolate him—"

"But there isn't time to research it now!"

"What good would it do shucking off the problem for another thirty-five years? He would only reappear—"

"Without his strength. Shorn. Senile. Broken. Starved of his connections with the human race. Dried up. A mental leech. Oh, he tried to conserve his strength. Sitting quietly. Reading, waiting. But he broke! Thank God for that. It was vital to the future that he went insane."

"Ridiculous! To enter the machine next year he must already be alive! He must already be out there in the world projecting this supposed madness of his. But he isn't. We're all separate sane individuals, all free to think what we want—"

"*Are we?* The whole world has been increasingly obsessed with him these last twenty years. Fashions, religions, life-styles:

the whole world has been skewed by him ever since he was born!
He must have been born about twenty years ago. Around 1995.
Until then there was a lot of research into him. The tachyon
hunt. All that. But he only began to *obsess* the world as a spiritual
figure after that. From around 1995 or 6. When he was born as
a baby. Only, we didn't focus our minds on his own infantile
urges – because we had him here as an adult to obsess ourselves
with—"

"Why should he have been born with infantile urges? If he's
so unusual, why shouldn't he have been born already leeching
on the world's mind; already knowing, already experiencing
everything around him?"

"Yes, but the real charisma started then! All the emotional
intoxication with him!"

"All the mothering. All the fear and adoration of his infancy.
All the Bethlehem hysteria. Picking up as he grew and gained
projective strength. We've been just as obsessed with Bethlehem
as with Nazareth, haven't we? The two have gone hand in hand."

(*Sign Ten*) I AM GOD. AND I MUST SET YOU FREE. I MUST CUT
MYSELF OFF FROM MY PEOPLE; CAST MYSELF INTO THIS HELL
OF ISOLATION.

I CAME TOO SOON; YOU WERE NOT READY FOR ME.

We begin to feel very cold; yet we cannot feel cold. Something
prevents us – a kind of malign contagious tranquillity.

It is all so *right*. It slots into our heads so exactly, like the missing jigsaw piece for which the hole lies cut and waiting, that we
know what he said is true; that he is growing up out there in our
obsessed, blessèd world, only waiting to come to us.

(*Sign Eleven*) (Even though the order of the signs was time-
reversed from his point of view, there was the sense of a real
dialogue now between him and us, as though we were both
synchronized. Yet this wasn't because the past was inflexi-
ble, and he was simply acting out a role he knew "from
history". He was really as distant from us as ever. It was the
looming presence of *himself* in the real world which cast its
shadow on us, moulded our thoughts and fitted our

questions to his responses; and we all realized this now, as though scales fell from our eyes. We weren't guessing or fishing in the dark any longer; we were being dictated to by an overwhelming presence of which we were all conscious – and which wasn't locked up in the VSTM. The VSTM was Nazareth, the setting-off point; yet the whole world was also Bethlehem, womb of the embryonic God, his babyhood, childhood and youth combined into one synchronous sequence by his all-knowingness, with the accent on his wonderful birth that filtered through into human consciousness ever more saturatingly.)

MY OTHER SELF HAS ACCESS TO ALL THE SCIENTIFIC SPECULATIONS WHICH I HAVE GENERATED; AND ALREADY I HAVE THE SOLUTION OF THE TIME EQUATIONS. I SHALL ARRIVE SOON & YOU SHALL BUILD MY VSTM & I SHALL ENTER IT; YOU SHALL BUILD IT INSIDE AN EXACT REPLICA OF THIS LABORATORY, SOUTHWEST SIDE. THERE IS SPACE THERE. (Indeed it had been planned to extend the National Physical Laboratory that way, but the plans had never been taken up, because of the skewing of all our research which the VSTM had brought about.) WHEN I REACH MY TIME OF SETTING OUT, WHEN TIME REVERSES, THE PROBABILITY OF THIS LABORATORY WILL VANISH, & THE OTHER WILL ALWAYS HAVE BEEN THE TRUE LABORATORY THAT I AM IN, INSIDE THIS VSTM. THE WASTE LAND WHERE YOU BUILD, WILL NOW BE HERE. YOU CAN WITNESS THE INVERSION; IT WILL BE MY FIRST PROBABILISTIC MIRACLE. THERE ARE HYPERDIMENSIONAL REASONS FOR THE PROBABILISTIC INVERSION, AT THE INSTANT OF TIME REVERSAL. BE WARNED NOT TO BE INSIDE THIS LABORATORY WHEN I SET OUT, WHEN I CHANGE TRACKS, FOR THIS SEGMENT OF REALITY HERE WILL ALSO CHANGE TRACKS, BECOMING IMPROBABLE, SQUEEZED OUT.

(*Sign Twelve*) I WAS BORN TO INCORPORATE YOU IN MY BOSOM; TO UNITE YOU IN A WORLD MIND, IN THE PHASE SPACE OF GOD. THOUGH YOUR INDIVIDUAL SOULS PERSIST, WITHIN THE FUSION. BUT YOU ARE NOT READY. YOU MUST BECOME READY IN THIRTY-FIVE YEARS TIME BY FOLLOWING THE MENTAL EXERCISES WHICH I SHALL DELIVER TO YOU, MY

MEDITATIONS. IF I REMAINED WITH YOU NOW, AS I GAIN
STRENGTH, YOU WOULD LOSE YOUR SOULS. THEY WOULD BE
SUCKED INTO ME, INCOHERENTLY. BUT IF YOU GAIN STRENGTH,
I CAN INCORPORATE YOU COHERENTLY WITHOUT LOSING YOU.
I LOVE YOU ALL, YOU ARE PRECIOUS TO ME, SO I EXILE MYSELF.

THEN I WILL COME AGAIN IN 2055. I SHALL RISE FROM
TIME, FROM THE USELESS HARROWING OF A LIMBO WHICH
HOLDS NO SOULS PRISONER, FOR YOU ARE ALL HERE, ON
EARTH.

That was the last sign. He sits reading again and listening to
taped music. He is radiant; glorious. We yearn to fall upon him
and be within him.

We hate and fear him too; but the Love washes over the Hate,
losing it a mile deep.

He is gathering strength outside somewhere: in Wichita or
Washington or Woodstock. He will come in a few weeks to reveal
himself to us. We all know it now.

And then? Could we kill him? Our minds would halt our
hands. As it is, we know that the sense of loss, the sheer bereave-
ment of his departure hindwards into time will all but tear our
souls apart.

And yet . . . I will come again in 2055, he has promised. And
incorporate us, unite us, as separate thinking souls – if we follow
all his meditations; or else he will suck us into him as dummies,
as robots if we do not prepare ourselves. What then, when God
rises from the grave of time, *insane*?

Surely he knows that he will end his journey in madness!
That he will incorporate us all, as conscious living beings, into
the matrix of his own insanity?

It is a fact of history that he arrived in 1985 ragged, jibbering
and lunatic – tortured beyond endurance by being deprived of
us.

Yet he demanded, jubilantly, in 1997, confirmation of his safe
arrival; jubilantly, and we lied to him and said YES! YES! And he
must have believed us. (Was he already going mad from
deprivation?)

If a laboratory building can rotate into the probability of that
same building adjacent to itself: if time is probabilistic (which

we can never prove or disprove concretely with any measuring rod, for we can never see *what has not been*, all the alternative possibilities, though they might have been) we have to wish what we know to be the truth, not to have been the truth. We can only have faith that there will be another probabilistic miracle, beyond the promised inversion of laboratories that he speaks of, and that he will indeed arrive back in 1985 calm, well-kept, radiantly sane, his mind composed. And what is this but an entrée into madness for rational beings such as us? We must perpetrate an act of madness; we must believe the world to be other than what it was – so that we can receive among us a Sane, Blessèd, Loving God in 2055. A fine preparation for the coming of a mad God! For if we drive ourselves mad, believing passionately what was not true, will we not infect him with our madness, so that he is/has to be/will be/and always was mad too?

Credo quia impossible; we have to believe because it is impossible. The alternative is hideous.

Soon He will be coming. Soon. A few days, a few dozen hours. We all feel it. We are overwhelmed with bliss.

Then we must put Him in a chamber, and lose Him, and drive Him mad with loss, in the sure and certain hope of a sane and loving resurrection thirty years hence – so that He does not harrow Hell, and carry it back to Earth with Him.

AFTER-IMAGES

Malcolm Edwards

Probably the master of the time-dislocation story was J. G. Ballard. His view, evident in much of his short fiction, was that time was degrading and this resulted in an increasingly distorted view of the world. You will find this disturbing imagery repeated in stories ranging from "The Voices of Time" (1960) and "The Terminal Beach" (1964) through to "News from the Sun" (1981) and "Memories of the Space Age" (1982). All of these stories are now readily available in Ballard's The Complete Short Stories *(2001) and for this anthology I wanted a story that captured the essential mood and imagery of Ballard's work but was little known and not easily available. The answer came with "After-Images", the only short story by publisher, editor and critic Malcolm Edwards, who actually worked with Ballard on the publication of his best-known book,* Empire of the Sun *(1984). Edwards is the Deputy Chief Executive and Group Publisher of the Orion Publishing Group and, amongst his many responsibilities, he is the editor of the Science Fiction Masterworks series.*

After the events of the previous day Norton slept only fitfully, his dreams filled with grotesque images of Richard Carver, and he was grateful when his bedside clock showed him that it was nominally morning again. He always experienced difficulty sleeping in anything less than total darkness, so the unvarying sunlight, cutting through chinks in the curtains and striking across the floor, marking it with lines that might have been drawn by an incandescent knife, added to his restlessness. He had tried to draw the curtains as closely as possible, but they were cheap and of skimpy manufacture – a legacy from the previous owner of the flat, who for obvious reasons could not be bothered to take them with her when she moved – and even when, after much manoeuvring, they could be persuaded to meet along much of their length, narrow gaps would always appear at the top, near the pleating.

Norton felt gripped by a lassitude born of futility, but as on the eight other mornings of this unexpected coda to his existence, fought off the feeling and slid wearily out of bed. After dressing quickly and without much thought, he pulled back the curtains to admit the brightness of the early-afternoon summer sun.

The sun was exactly where it had been for the last eight days, poised a few degrees above the peaked roof of the terraced house across the road. It had been a stormy day, and a few minutes before everything had stopped a heavy shower had been sweeping across London; but the squall had passed and the sun had appeared – momentarily, one would have supposed – through a break in the cloud. The visible sky was still largely occupied by lowering, soot-coloured clouds, which enfolded the light and gave it the peculiar penetrating luminosity which presages a storm; but the sun sat in its patch of blue sky like an unblinking eye in the face of the heavens, and Norton and the others spent their last days and nights in a malign parody of the mythical, eternally sunlit English summer.

Outside the heat was stale and oppressive and seemed to settle heavily in his temples. Drifts of rubbish, untended now for several weeks, gave off a ripe odour of decay and attracted buzzing platoons of flies. Marlborough Street, where Norton lived, was one of a patchwork of late-Victorian and Edwardian terraces filling an unfashionable lacuna in the map of north London. At one end of the road was a slightly wider avenue which called itself a High Road on account of a bus route and a scattering of down-at-heel shops. Norton walked towards it, past houses which gave evidence of their owners' hasty departure, doors and windows left open. The house across the road, which for three days had been the scene of an increasingly wild party held by most of the few teenagers remaining in the area, was now silent again. They had probably collapsed from exhaustion, or drugs, or both, Norton thought.

At the corner Norton paused. To the north – his left – the street curved away sharply, lined on both sides by shabby three-storey houses with mock-Georgian facades. To the south it was straight, but about a hundred yards away was blocked off by the great baleful flickering wall of the interface, rising into the sky and curving back on itself like a surreal bubble. As always he was drawn to look at it, though his eyes resisted as if under autonomous control and tried to focus themselves elsewhere.

It was impossible to say precisely what it looked like, for its surface seemed to be an *absence* of colour. When he closed his eyes it left swimming variegated after-images: protoplasmic shapes which crossed and intermingled and blended. When Norton forced himself to stare at it, his optic nerves attempted to deny its presence, warping together the flanking images of shopfronts so that the road seemed to narrow to a point.

Norton suffered occasional migraine headaches and often experienced an analogous phenomenon as the prelude to an attack: he would find that parts of his field of vision had been excised, but that the edges of the blanks were somehow pulled together, so it was difficult to be sure something *was* missing. Just as then it was necessary sometimes to turn sideways and look obliquely to see an object sitting directly in front of him, so now, as he turned away, he could see the interface as a curving wall the colour of a bruise from which pinpricks of intense light occasionally escaped as if through faults in its fabric. Then, too, he could glimpse more clearly the three human images printed, as though by some sophisticated holographic process, upon the interface. In the centre of the road were the backs of Carver and himself as they disappeared beyond the interface, the images already starting to become fuzzy as the wavefront slowly advanced; to one side, slightly sharper, was the record of his lone re-emergence, his expression clearly pale and strained despite the heavy polarized goggles which covered half his face.

Norton had been sitting the previous morning at a table outside the Cafe Hellenika, slowly drinking a tiny cup of Greek coffee.

He had little enthusiasm for the sweet, muddy drink, but was unwilling as yet to move on to beer or wine.

The café's Greek Cypriot proprietor had reacted to the changed conditions in a manner which under other circumstances would have seemed quite enterprising. He had shifted all his tables and chairs out on to the pavement, leaving the cooler interior free for the perennial pool players and creating outside a passable imitation of a street café remembered from happier days in Athens or Nicosia. Many of the remaining local residents were of Greek origin, and the men gathered here, playing cards and chess, drinking cheap Demestica, and talking in sharp bursts which sounded dramatic however banal and ordinary the conversation. There was a timelessness to the scene which Norton found oddly apposite.

He was staring into his coffee, thinking studiously about nothing, when a shadow fell across him and he simultaneously heard the chair next to his being scraped across the pavement. He looked up to see Carver easing himself into the seat. He was dressed bizarrely in a thickly padded white suit which looked as though it should belong to an astronaut or a polar explorer. He was carrying a pair of thick goggles which he placed on the formica surface of the table. He signalled the café owner to bring him a coffee.

Norton didn't want company, but he was intrigued despite himself. "What on Earth is that outfit?" he asked.

"Explorer's gear . . . bloody hot, too," said Carver, dragging the sleeve cumbersomely across his perspiring forehead.

"What's to explore, for God's sake?"

"The . . . whatever you call it. The bubble. The interface. I've been into it."

Norton felt irritated. Carver seemed incapable of taking their situation seriously. He had attached himself to Norton four days ago as he sat getting drunk and had sought him out every day since, full of jokes of dubious merit and colourful stories of his life in some unspecified, but probably menial, branch of the diplomatic service. He was the sort of person Norton hated finding himself next to in a bar. Now he was obviously fantasizing.

"Don't be ridiculous. You'd be dead."

"Do I look dead?" Carver gestured at himself. His face, tanned and plump with eyes of a disconcertingly pure aquamarine, looked as healthy as ever.

"It's impossible," Norton repeated.

"Don't you want to know what I found?"

Losing patience, Norton shouted: "I *know* what you'd have found. You'd have found a fucking nuclear explosion. Don't tell me you went for a stroll through *that*!"

The café owner came up and slapped a cup on to the table in front of Carver, slopping the coffee into the saucer. Carver took a long slow sip of the dark liquid, looking at Norton expressionlessly over the rim of the cup as he did so. Norton subsided, feeling foolish.

"But I did, Norton," Carver finally said calmly. "I did."

Norton remained silent, stubbornly refusing to play his part in the choreography of the conversation, knowing that Carver would carry on without further prompting.

"I didn't just walk in," Carver said, after a few seconds. "I'm not suicidal. I tried probing first, with a stick. I waggled it about a bit, pulled it out. It wasn't damaged. That set me thinking. So I tried with a pet mouse of mine. No damage – except that its eyes were burned out, poor little sod. So I thought, all right, it's very bright, but nothing more. What does that suggest?"

Norton shrugged.

"It suggested to me that the whole process is slowed down in there, that there's a whole series of wavefronts – the light flash, the fireball, the blastwave – all expanding slowly, but all separate."

"It seems incredible."

"Well, the whole situation isn't precisely normal, you know—"

They were interrupted by a commotion at another table. There seemed to be some disagreement between two men over a hand of cards. One of them, a heavy-set middle-aged man wearing a greying string vest through which his bodily hair sprouted abundantly, was standing and waving a handful of cards. The other, an older man, remained seated, banging his fist repeatedly on the table. Their voices rose in a fast, threatening gabble. Then the man in the vest threw the cards across the table with a furious jerk of his arm and stamped into the café.

The other continued to talk loudly and aggrievedly to the onlookers, his words augmented by a complex mime of gesture.

Norton was glad of the distraction. He couldn't understand what Carver was getting at, and wasn't sure he wanted to. "It's amazing the way they carry on," he said. "It's as though nothing had happened, as though everything *was* normal."

"Very sensible of them. At least they're consistent."

"Are you serious?"

"Of course I am. The whole thing has been inevitable for years. We all knew that, but we tried to pretend otherwise even while we carried on preparing for it. We said that it wouldn't happen, because so far it hadn't happened – some logic! We buried our heads like ostriches and pretended as hard as we could. Now it's here – it's just down the road and we can see it coming and we know there's no escape. But we knew that all along. If you tie yourself to a railway line you don't have to wait until you can see the train coming before you start to think you're in danger. So why not just carry on as usual?"

"I didn't know you felt like that."

"Of course you didn't. As far as you're concerned I'm just the old fool in the saloon bar. End of story."

Carver had a point, Norton supposed. If anyone had asked him whether there was going to be a nuclear war in his lifetime he would probably have said yes. If anyone had asked what he was doing about it he would have shrugged and said, well, what could you do? He had friends active in the various protest movements, but couldn't help viewing their efforts as futile. Some of them would virtually admit as much sometimes, if pressed. The difference was that they couldn't bear to sit still while some hope – however remote – remained, whereas he couldn't be bothered with gestures which seemed extremely unlikely to produce results. He would rather watch TV or spend the evening in the pub.

The other difficulty was that he couldn't really picture it in his mind's eye, couldn't visualize London consumed by blast and fire, couldn't imagine the millions of deaths, the survivors of the blast explosion dying in fallout shelters, the ensuing chaos and anarchy. And because he found it unimaginable, on some level he told himself it could never happen, not here, not to him.

Being apathetic about politics – especially Middle-Eastern politics – he hadn't even been properly aware of the crisis developing until it reached flashpoint, with Russian and American troops clashing outside Riyadh. Then there had been government announcements, states of emergency, panic. Despite advice to stay at home the great mass of the population had headed out of the cities; unconfirmed rumours filtered back of clashes with troops on roads commandeered for military use. A few had stayed behind: some dutifully obeying government instructions, some doubtless oblivious to the whole thing, some, like Norton, unable to imagine an aftermath they would want to live in.

And then the sirens had sounded and he had sat waiting for the end; and they had stopped, and there was a silence which went on and on and on until Norton, like others, had gone into the streets and found himself in the middle of a situation far stranger than anything he could have imagined. The small urban island in which they stood – an irregular triangle no more than half a mile on a side – was bracketed by three virtually simultaneous groundburst explosions which had caused . . . what? A local fracture in space-time? That was as good an explanation as any. Whatever the cause, the effect was to slow down subjective time in the locality by a factor of millions, reducing the spread of the detonations to a matter of a few yards every day, hemming them into their strange and fragile-seeming shells.

At first people hoped that the miracle – for so it seemed – allowed some possibility of rescue, but they soon learned better. Between two of the wavefronts was a narrow corridor which coincided with a side road and led apparently to safety. One family, who had miscalculated their evacuation plans, piled into a car and drove off down the corridor, but halfway their car seemed suddenly to halt, as if frozen. Norton still looked at it occasionally. Through the rear window could be seen two young children, faces caught in smiles, hands arrested in mid-wave. It was clear that the phenomenon was only local, and crossing some invisible threshold they had emerged into the real-time world. At least, he thought, they would never have time to realise that their escape attempt had failed; it was left to those still trapped to experience anguish on their behalf.

Norton wondered what one of the many spy satellites which he supposed crossed overhead would make of the scene, if any of their equipment was sensitive enough to register anything. Perhaps some future historian, analysing the destruction of London, would slow down the film and wonder at an apparent burst of high-speed motion in the area on which the explosions converged. The historian would probably rub his or her eyes in puzzlement and dismiss it as an optical trick, like the after-images which played behind one's eyelids after staring into a bright light.

"So will you come?" Carver was saying.

Norton dragged his attention back to the conversation, aware that Carver had been talking and that he had not been taking in what he was saying.

"Come? Where?"

"Through the interface. I want somebody else to see this. It's amazing, Norton. The experience of a lifetime. The *last* experience of a lifetime. Why miss it?"

Norton's first instinct was to protest that he wasn't interested, that there seemed little point in seeking out new experiences when extinction was, at best, days away, but then he realized that in fact some purposeful action – even a pretence at purposeful action *would* be welcome. Terminal patients given the bad news by their doctors didn't just lie down and wait to die, if they had any spirit; they got up and got on with their lives for as long as they could. In the last analysis that was all anyone could do, and here everybody – the Greek card players, the partygoers, Carver – seemed to be doing it except him.

"Sure," he said. "But what about protective clothing? You've got all that . . ." He gestured at Carver's bulky and absurd-looking outfit.

"It's unnecessary. In fact it's hotter out here than it is there. I don't know what I was thinking about – if I had run into the heat a thousand of these would have been no protection. All you need is goggles, and I've got a spare pair at home."

Carver got up, tossed a £5 note on the table and walked away, gesturing Norton to follow. He lived just off the High

Road, in a large, double-fronted redbrick Victorian house, most of whose neighbours had been turned into bedsits. His house was still intact, though the front garden was a tangle of hollyhocks choking amid brambles, and the wood in the window sashes was visibly rotten. Little attention was evidently paid to its upkeep.

Inside was a dim hallway floored with cracked brown linoleum and cluttered with coatstands and hatracks. There was a heavy odour of dust, old leather and indefinable decay.

Carver went through into one of the rear rooms. Norton followed, then paused in the open doorway. It was a large room, with French windows opening on to the garden. It was impossible to tell what the decorations might have once been like, because the whole room was choked with a profusion of different objects. All the walls were lined from floor to ceiling with books, old and expensive bindings jammed alongside garish paperbacks seemingly at random. More books were heaped on the floor, in chairs and on tables. The rest of the room was a wild assortment of clocks, globes, stuffed animals, model ships and engines, old scientific and medical equipment, porcelain, musical instruments and countless other items. Carver made his way – almost wading through the detritus – to a desk, where some of the clutter had been pushed aside and a second pair of goggles lay amid knives, glues and offcuts of polarized plastic.

"Don't mind the mess," he said jovially, seeing Norton still hovering uncertainly by the door. "The whole house is like this, I'm afraid. Never could stop accumulating stuff. Never could throw anything out. My wife used to say I'd been a jackdaw in my previous lives. That's why I didn't leave, you know. I couldn't start off again somewhere else without all this. Sometimes I think there's more of me here—" his gesture took in the room, and the other rooms beyond it – "than *here*." He tapped the side of his skull.

Norton suddenly warmed to the man, seeing him properly for the first time as another human being, not just an irritating presence. Carver seemed to sense this and turned to fiddle with the goggles for long seconds while embarrassment dispersed from the atmosphere. "I made these up myself," he said. "Ordinary dark glasses are no good. You need extra thicknesses, lots of them. Trouble is, if you put the things on anywhere else you can't see a damn thing."

Carver insisted on showing Norton the place where he had gone exploring earlier, though he was equally adamant that this time they would cross over somewhere else. He had stripped off the cumbersome protective suit and now cut an unlikely figure as a pioneer in a Hawaiian-style shirt and corduroy slacks. He had uprooted two stout wooden poles, giving one to Norton and keeping the other himself. They walked away from the High Road, took the second turning on the left, and came face to face with another wall of shimmering, eye-wrenching colourlessness. On its surface, as if holographic images had been pasted to it, were images of Carver's back as he crossed the interface and his front view as he returned.

"You see," Carver said, "light can't escape, so the image is trapped there like a fly in amber until the thing moves forward far enough for it to break up. It's already starting to happen."

Looking closely Norton could see that indeed the images were taking on a slightly unfocused aspect, as though viewed through a wavering heat haze.

They walked back to the High Road, passed the café – where a group of men were standing round a table watching five more play out an obviously tense card game; side bets were apparently being exchanged – and approached the interface which blocked the street.

"Right," Carver said. "Keep close by me. If in doubt wave the stick in front of you. If not in doubt *still* wave the stick in front of you." He laughed, and Norton smiled in return. They pulled on their goggles and then, like blind men, tapping their way with their sticks, they walked through the interface, leaving their departing images stuck to its surface so that to anyone casually watching from the café it would have looked as if they had both suddenly and improbably halted in mid-stride.

Norton found himself enveloped in a soundless blizzard of brilliant light. Even through the thick laminations of polarized plastic the luminosity was almost painful; it was like looking too near to the sun, except that there was nowhere to turn away. The light seemed to bounce and swirl around him, to cascade on his head and fountain up from the ground. There was a singing in his ears, and he felt as though he was walking into a wind, a zephyr of pure incandescence, its photon pressure sufficient to resist his progress.

He felt exhilarated, almost ecstatic, as if he was coming face to face with God. The light was cleansing, purifying. He found that he was moving with an involuntary swimming motion of his arms, propelling himself into the cool heart of this artificial sun with a clumsy breaststroke.

"Norton! Be careful!" Carver's voice came as if from under water, far away; it splashed faintly against his ears but was washed away in the radiant tide.

Carver was at his side, tugging at his shirt. He turned and looked at the other man. Carver seemed to glow, to fluoresce. The intense effulgence overpowered ordinary colour, making him a surreal sculpture in degrees of brilliant white. His skin seemed luminous and translucent, and when Norton lifted his own hand he found it was the same; he fancied he could see dim outlines of bone through the flesh. When Carver moved he cut swathes through the light; a sudden motion of his stick sent splintered refractions in all directions.

"Carver—" Norton said, and his words seemed to be snatched away as if he was talking into a silent hurricane. "This is extraordinary . . . incredible . . ." The sentence trailed away; he had no words to describe the experience.

Carver laughed. "Who'd have thought that this lay in the heart of a nuclear explosion, eh? I don't know, though – those slow-motion films always *were* beautiful if you could forget what they were."

"How far can we go?" Norton shouted, turning away and moving towards the heart of the radiance, using his cane like a mine-detector.

"Only a few yards. You'll see."

Norton moved on a dozen paces, then the tip of his stick abruptly exploded into brilliant fire, like a sparkler on Guy Fawkes' Night. He withdrew it, stamped on the burning end. Several inches had vanished from its tip in an instant.

"It's here," he called in warning. "Just ahead."

Peering forwards he fancied he could see the further interface, the fireball advancing at its own slow, inexorable pace
behind the light flash. Even through the radiance he thought he
could detect flickering patterns of orange flame dancing across
its surface. Norton was suddenly reminded of what lay beyond
there ... but for now it was enough to be drifting, clad in a
nimbus of cool white fire.

Carver, a pale haloed ghost of a figure, was at his side. He
swished his stick playfully through the fireball's surface, coming
away each time with a couple of inches less on the tip. He was
like a lion-tamer, holding inconceivable energy at bay with just
the stick and the force of his personality.

"Don't get too close," Norton warned, as the other man
edged forward. Carver took no notice, so Norton tapped him on
the shoulder with his own stick. Carver began to turn, but as he
did so his foot caught on the kerbstone. He teetered, began to
fall backwards, mouth widening in surprise: fell faster than
Norton could lunge forwards, into the fireball.

Everything seemed to be happening in slow motion, as though
Carver had fallen into still another time anomaly. He appeared
to hang suspended as his hair burst into flame and his skin
began to char. Puffs of steam rose from his body. His shirt was
consumed so quickly that it simply seemed to vanish. His lips
drew back as if he was about to say something, but they were
only shrivelling with the heat. Behind them the gums burned
away, exposing bone that blackened swiftly, though the teeth
remained anomalously white until the enamel cracked and
burst. The goggles melted, exposing steaming sockets in a face
that was turning into a skull even as he fell. His body cooked,
as if Norton was watching an accelerated film of meat being
roasted. The skin crisped, then peeled away; the flesh followed,
crumbling and flaking away from bones that snapped and
popped from their sockets and themselves began to burn. By
the time Carver hit the ground all that was left of him was a
charred heap of smouldering detritus which blew away in
clouds of ash even as it settled. It had taken only seconds; the
only sound which reached Norton was a soft, almost plaintive
sigh.

Norton watched, transfixed with horror. Then as nausea rose in him he stumbled away, dropping his stick. He burst out of the interface into total darkness – then ripped off the goggles and squatted by the pavement, retching until all he could wring from his stomach was a thin trickle of sour yellow bile.

Now, as Norton looked sidelong at the images recording the beginning and end of yesterday's tragic adventure, he saw that the interface was undergoing a change. Patterns played more vigorously across its surface; fans of light sprayed outwards briefly; it seemed to vibrate, as if to a deep bass tone. *It's breaking down*, he thought. *It won't be long now.*

To his surprise his major feeling was not fear but relief. He understood now why condemned prisoners sometimes sacked their lawyers and actively sought their execution rather than trying to delay it.

He felt he would prefer to be at home when it happened, so he turned back into Marlborough Street. As he passed number 6 a voice called out his name. It was Mr McDonald, a friendly and gregarious pensioner who lived there with his equally good-natured wife. Norton had always got on well with them on a pleasant superficial level. Lacking transport, the McDonalds had been unable to evacuate even if they had wanted to.

Mr McDonald was busily giving the sitting room windows a second coat of whitewash. "Just putting the final touches," he said cheerily. The McDonalds had spent the last eight days as they had spent the week before, turning part of their house into a fallout shelter, following an official instruction leaflet. To them the last week seemed to be a God-given opportunity to finish the job properly. Their house did not have a cellar, so they had fitted out the large cupboard under the stairs, protecting it with countless black dustbin bags filled with earth. Inside were carefully arranged supplies of food, water and medicine; bedding and primitive cooking equipment; and even a portable chemical toilet. Before retirement made such recreations impossible to afford the McDonalds had been keen campers, and regarded their expertise and lovingly stored equipment as particular good fortune. A few days ago Mr McDonald had insisted on showing off their impressively well-organised shelter to Norton; had even offered to squeeze up and make room for three if he hadn't the materials to build his own defences. What was more, although the offer was made only out of politeness, Norton was sure the McDonalds would have gone through with it if he had pressed them. But he had declined politely, assuring them of the adequacy of his own preparations.

Now, with the image of Carver vivid in his mind, he felt like shouting at Mr McDonald, shocking him into a realisation of how futile his efforts were in the face of the kind of forces held delicately in check all around him. But it would only hurt and confuse the old man, who was simply following the instructions which he had been told would keep him safe.

Norton waved goodbye to Mr McDonald and started to walk away. But even as his foot lifted, the air seemed to shudder and split around him, and before his senses were able properly to register the phenomenon the world was filled with an instantaneous, consuming brilliance, a white fire that was neither cool nor pure.

"IN THE BEGINNING, NOTHING LASTS . . ."

Mike Strahan

I have already made reference to Camille Flammarion's Lumen *(1872) which suggested (wrongly) that if you could travel faster than light you would, via historic light, see events in the past, though those events would be in reverse. The idea that various catastrophes on Earth might disrupt time and start it running backwards was explored by Albert Robida in* L'horloge des siècles *(1902), only recently translated as* The Clock of the Centuries *(2008). Other writers have related it to individuals who find their lives running backwards as in* The Tower of Oblivion *(1921) by Oliver Onions, "The Curious Case of Benjamin Button" (1922) by F. Scott Fitzgerald or, more recently,* Time's Arrow *(1991) by Martin Amis. There are many more examples, but I have not encountered one so powerful or as potent as the following. The author tells me that it was his desire to correct his mistakes that inspired this story.*

April 7, 1936

Beulah Irene wept as the workers pulled up shovels of rust red dirt from her son's grave. She covered her dark face with her hands, not wanting the men to see her. Thick bandages wrapped her arms from fingers to elbows; the skin underneath burned and itched.

The four gravediggers gave her odd glances between pulls. They were all grim men, with dirty faces and hands. Patches of sweat and red mud stained their denim trousers and cotton shirts.

Irene removed her hands from her face and focused her eyes on the men, wanting to watch until they finished. It was important to her, even though her son would not die until yesterday.

His headstone was a pitiful thing, a small square of concrete embedded in the grass and lined with dead leaves. A tall, worn, bent-back tree cast little shade. Her husband's old grave was a few feet away, empty for decades.

She closed her eyes again, and remembered her son. He had always been a pleasant child, and clever.

His first word had been coffee.

He took his first step when he was eleven months old.

His secret tickle spot was on the back of his thigh.

He was three years old when he died.

The memories had stuffed Irene's brain since her resurrection. On the surface, they were pleasant thoughts, but time played funny tricks on her these days. Old memories would crop up, pop in her head like long forgotten debts. They treated her all the same, no matter where she was, what she was doing; she would often turn to tears.

"We're done for the day, ma'am." One of the men interrupted her thoughts. Despite the dust covering his face, his eyes and smile were bright. Behind him, his friends were collecting their shovels and brooms, their jackets and lunch refuse.

"Thank you." Her mouth was dry. She turned around to look toward the eastern horizon and was surprised to see the sun a hand or so from setting. The morning was clear and hot, with a strong breeze tugging at the dry Oklahoma yellow grass. *Where has the time gone?* She wondered.

"You okay, ma'am?" He asked.

Irene shook her head and shrugged, "Just nervous." Her bandages itched; they were dirty again. Red dirt rimmed the frayed edges of the white gauze covering her arms. It looked like dried blood.

"Reckon so. It's hard sometimes." The laborer turned and raised a hand in goodbye to his departing friends. A spare denim coat and a dusty lunch pail remained. "Don't know if you recall, but I was one of the fellas that worked on your husband." His mouth creased, as though he wanted to say more.

Irene looked closely at him and shook her head, "I'm sorry, I don't remember you." Irene had a hard time remembering. Like most people, the future was a harsh muddle; she remembered senses better than events. Colors, smells, textures. Sounds. It surprised her when someone remembered something so far ahead.

"No offense taken, ma'am." He held up his hands. "I was blessed with a good memory, must've been forty years."

"It's been that long?" She asked.

"Sure has. Easier then. Job like this would've taken an hour, back when we had machines." He scratched at his ear again and looked over Irene's shoulder to the East. His eyes fell on her and for a moment, he held her gaze. "Should head home, ma'am. I'll see you."

He stepped toward the edge of the open grave and crouched down to pick up his jacket and pail. Without giving Irene another glance, he walked away with his coat flung over his shoulder.

"Thank you! For today!" Irene remembered.

He turned, walked backwards, smiled. "It's never easy, ma'am."

Irene nodded and looked down at the open grave. She was alone with her son.

Sparing a shudder, she walked home. The road into town was straight, wide enough for two autos to squeeze past each other. Most of the houses and farms she passed were empty, the families having left for the West, to work healthier land. There had been no rain in months.

The sun was almost beyond the horizon when she reached town. The buildings lining the street sagged against each other, their wooden siding faded the color of driftwood. The town's main street was a packed dirt road of choked, blood red dust.

A group of children rushed by her on the sidewalk, chasing a mongrel with an aluminum can tied to its neck. Irene gave them a sad smile as they passed.

The young were always so full of life, the first time because they thought they were immortal, the second time because they knew exactly when their end would come. Irene found it hard to watch children. They reminded her of her son.

There were other people on the street, walking dogs or riding horses, and a few older automobiles. Most of the machines from the future were artifacts now, their metal skeletons wired together in museums, the leather and rubber and plastic all rotted away.

Others had tried to rebuild things, piece back together what little the future had left them. The results were nothing but showpieces, sad monuments to a time they would never see again.

Her house was two blocks off the center of town, on the wrong side of the railroad tracks. It was a Sears's kit home, an ugly square of faded white stucco walls and sticky brown shingles. It had three rooms: a den, a kitchen, a bedroom.

She pushed open their crooked screen door. Her husband was in the den, sitting in an old easy chair, a hulk of a radio mirroring him across the room. He sighed when she entered and set yesterday's paper across his lap.

Irene ignored him. She could sense her anger from earlier in the afternoon, but the memory of their argument had faded.

He folded his arms hard across his chest and said nothing, but kept his eyes on her, his mouth set in a scowl.

Irene stepped over to the sink, and unwound her dirty bandages. She bit her lip as the heavy gauze separated from her arms and fingers, leaving behind ugly purple flesh. The doctor had been surprised that she could do anything with her hands. Her body was remembering the accident that had killed her son and scarred her for life.

The doctor had said that the resurrected body was like a book; whether you read it backward or forward, the words were always the same. If you broke a bone, or suffered a cut in your first life, your body would suffer the hurt again in the second.

Our son will suffer his hurts again, too, she reminded herself for the thousandth time.

Irene dipped her arms into a stainless steel bowl of water. The muscles in her back relaxed as the cool water took some of the edge off her pain. She pulled her bandages off the wood counter and ran them under. She had to grit her teeth as she rubbed out the dirt between her thumb and forefinger. The pain was getting worse.

Nothing lasts forever. Things will get better, easier. The thought was a salve, calming.

She tried to reapply the bandages herself, but only grew frustrated as the gauze clung awkwardly to her tender flesh.

"Can you help me?" She finally asked, her back to her husband. Her voice was raw, cracked.

Her husband pushed himself up from his chair. He was a big man; strong, with wide set shoulders and large hands. He was getting younger, and had just gotten his full head of black hair back. He had another twenty-five years until his birthday, until he returned to his mother, giving himself up to her pregnant embrace. Irene doubted that was what he wanted, but it would be his mother's decision.

Resurrection always led back to the beginning: death, life, birth. She had already decided that when her son's birth came, she would take him back into her, because she couldn't bear the thought of burying him again.

She hissed as her husband took her right arm into his rough hands and coiled the first bandage around her forearm and between her fingers. The cool, clean cloth comforted her skin.

He dipped the second bandage into the metal basin. It was one of their few prized possessions, an artifact from the future. Metal and stone and wood from older trees were the only things that could survive their own creation; everything else rotted away at the anniversary of its making.

Irene looked up at him, then away. "He's our son," she said, recalling their argument. She closed her eyes. *How could I forget?*

"I know." His voice was quiet and firm.

"Our baby," she added.

"I know."

"Then show it!" Irene turned her head up again, the muscles in her arms tensed. She wanted to lash out. "Why don't you want this?"

"It's a hard world," he sighed. His eyes shifted right, then closed, "The pain isn't worth it. Not for us to lose him again in three years."

"That's not an excuse! I've been waiting seventy years for this." Irene's words choked in her throat. "I need him. I need to see him again, even if it's only three years."

Her husband shook his head and crossed his arms, "He never had a first chance at life. With only three years, he won't have a second."

"No. No. No!" Irene wanted to hit something, to strike out at his indifference. "You don't want him back because you resent me, you resent what God has given us. You wish you had never been resurrected!"

"I do not . . ."

"You do," Irene continued, the heat building in her throat. "You've been miserable ever since you came back. You've been mad at me ever since I let them pull you from the ground!"

"No, I—"

"You—" Irene interrupted.

"Let me finish." Her husband jutted a finger in her face. He towered over her, his cheeks flushed red. "I don't think any such thing. I love you. I love our son." His breath was heavy; his words were even.

"Say his name," she ordered.

"What?"

"Say his name. It's been forty years and you have called him your kid, your boy, your son." Irene held up a fist and jutted out her fingers, counting the strikes. "You have never called him by his name. His Christian name that we gave him the day he was born. You have never said that name in this house. You've been back for forty years and you have never said his name. Not once."

"Stop it," her husband turned away from her and clenched his fists. "I don't need this."

"What's his name?!" Irene cried.

"I don't need this." He stalked away. He grabbed his coat off a peg next to the stove and slammed the screen behind him, rattling the door's wooden frame.

Run away! Irene thought. *That's all you do is run!*

Irene stumbled toward the table and pulled out a chair. She collapsed on it and laid her head on their red and white checkered tablecloth. Great racking sobs constricted her lungs as she wept. *He resents me,* she thought.

Do you blame him? she chided.

Her husband had suffered through black depression since he had returned to the living. The doctor thought there was a problem when his body was regenerating, as if the brain had not wired itself back together properly.

But that wasn't the answer. Her husband had not been happy before his death, living a life of failure and depression until he passed away in 1978. When he was reborn, it came as a shock, like a sick joke that he would have to relive his miserable life again as punishment. If anyone had wanted to remain in the ground, absent from the second chance God had given them, it was her husband, even if that meant waking up from death buried, suffocating, and dying again.

It was a predicament Irene had no problem remembering. She bore witness to his bitterness every day.

He thought it was a better alternative for him, thought it was best for their son. *He can say what he wants, about pain, about how hard the world is, but in the end, he's afraid. He's afraid of being hurt again.*

Aren't you afraid? she argued.

Irene didn't let her husband stay in the ground; when his time came she had the diggers uncover his grave. She needed him, to share the burden she carried, to help her life feel normal again.

And he has resented it ever since.

What her husband wanted for their son was horrible. She couldn't stand to imagine it: her son, waking up from his resurrection in his coffin, buried alive. He would survive for hours, in the dark, in the heat, alone, before he would succumb to death again.

Irene wept at the thought, and imagined what it would be like to have six feet of dirt separating her from her resurrected son, to hear his muffled cries, to claw at the red ground until her fingers were nothing but wells of blood.

She had failed him once, and couldn't fail him again.

The kitchen was dark when her husband returned, scraping the metal screen against the wood door. Outside, the crickets sang in the green of late morning.

Irene had fallen asleep at the table, her head cradled in her arms, her chin resting on the tablecloth. She woke up when her husband entered.

"Back already?" She yawned, stretching her sore arms across the table, their fight almost forgotten. She shook herself and grimaced. She hated that, when the passage of time made her forget.

"Bar was closed. Dick had an accident or something." He hung his coat up on its peg and tossed his billfold onto the counter.

"Is he alright?" Her husband had found a bottle somewhere. The stench of scotch clung to him, and permeated the tight kitchen air.

"I don't know." He coughed; "they were closed." He crossed to the other side of the table and collapsed into the chair opposite her. When he was sitting at their table he always looked like a giant, with his shoulders towering above the surface and his knees packed in tight underneath. He placed his head in his hands.

"I'm sorry," she said, without meaning it.

"He's been gone a long time," he said.

"I need this, Del, more than anything. I miss him."

Her husband rubbed at his eyes with the palms of his hands. "I'm sorry." He grimaced.

They looked at each other, silent.

"Please?" Irene asked. "Please?"

The quiet stretched, and Irene knew not to interrupt again. She kept her eyes on the tablecloth, focusing on a yellow stain near the table's edge. Her husband couldn't stop her, but she wanted him there, needed him. Their son was coming home.

April 6, 1936

The wind was blowing again like the day before, pushing Irene's skirt hard against her knees, shaking the tall tree that stood sentinel over her son's grave. The high grass of the plain was flat from the wind. In the distance, a farmer trawled his field for seeds to use the next fall, to resurrect the wheat.

The morning was hot for late spring. The cemetery wasn't far from town, but the heat and the dirt road made the journey difficult. Thick beads of sweat coated Irene's neck and daubed at the armpits of her dress. She waved her thin hands at her face absently, using the motion to settle the nervousness boiling in her belly. Her arms had been stiff and sore all afternoon, and the motion loosened them. The burning sensation had worsened through the night, waking her up several times from her shallow sleep.

Her husband was next to her, dressed for the occasion. He had slicked his hair back with leftover cooking fat, and he was wearing his only suit, the one he wore on their wedding day. The hem was ragged, and two of the buttons on his three-button coat bent at odd angles. He muttered and took a draw from his flask. They had stopped at Dick's that afternoon to fill it up. She could smell the heavy scotch on his breath. His walk was stuttering and uneven, so bad that Irene had to push the buggy they had brought for their son half of the way.

They both stepped near the edge of the grave. Her son's coffin was at the bottom, and while the laborers had cleaned and polished the surface of the lid, a light dusting of red dirt had settled on it overnight. The casket itself was a plain wood, stained a dark brown. To Irene, it looked too small.

"When are they coming?" Her husband asked, uncomfortable.

"Soon. Any minute," she replied, adjusting her hat. Her dress was a simple black. She could not remember, but imagined she wore it during her son's funeral. The thought lashed at Irene, but she pushed it down. *It'll be over soon. My baby is coming home.*

She kept her eyes on the casket, until the Reverend and the laborers arrived, and relaxed a little. *Patience,* she reminded herself.

The Reverend was the youngest of them. He was a little boy, with rosy cheeks and sandy hair, his priest's collar loose on his thin neck. Irene didn't know how much longer he had, but guessed it was less than a decade. He was one of the few children that had not retired, and Irene admired him for it.

"Irene, Delbert." The Reverend spoke with a child's falsetto and offered up a hand to her husband. "We've been waiting for this one." Behind him, the workers filed past. The men were familiar, and Irene imagined that they had been the ones who helped uncover her son tomorrow.

Irene didn't answer the Reverend, but instead turned her attention back to the coffin. Two of the workers jumped down into the hole. They worked a little space for themselves, bent down and lifted the coffin up with ease.

The casket crested the grave's edge, where the remaining two laborers picked it up and moved it to the side, setting it down next to the large pile of dirt they had dug. Irene had tensed when they brought the coffin up, worrying that the men might jostle her son. Most times, people left the casket in the ground to prevent such problems, but her son's casket was so small that lifting it out would make his recovery easier.

"How much time do we have?" The Reverend asked.

"A few minutes." Irene replied.

"Best hurry, then." The Reverend smiled. Irene's stomach gurgled. A few more minutes and her son's wait would be over. Her wait would be over. The pain in her arms intensified. She could feel it in the tips of her fingers.

The Reverend opened his bible. Behind him, the laborers removed their denim caps and stuffed them into empty pockets. Irene moved closer to her husband and clutched his arm. Her knees felt weak and her nose was growing numb.

"You okay?" her husband asked. "You're breathing hard."

"I'm fine." She tightened her grip. The skin of her arms felt as though it were on fire. *Was this what my son felt?* She hissed at the pain in her arms and closed her eyes. She had forgotten how much it hurt. It would be worse for her son, she realized. The scalding water had covered his entire body.

The Reverend began his prayer, and Irene could not focus on his words. Her breath came in short, rapid spurts. She would catch snippets, "Blessed us with his soul ... new life ... in resurrection ... happy moments to cherish ... serve out your plan ... repentance for sins ..." The words held little meaning for her. She tried focusing her mind, but her eyes kept wandering to the casket.

The Reverend clasped his Bible shut when he finished. "The Lord gives his blessing." He smiled at Irene.

Irene nodded and turned her attention to the setting sun on the Eastern horizon. Soon her son would be back. The workers moved to the large pile of dirt, and began to shovel it back into the empty grave. The Reverend stepped up to the coffin and flashed the sign of the cross in blessing, then moved away to make room for Irene and her husband.

She blinked and her vision blurred with tears. Everything was quiet, save her husband's steady breathing and the scrape of shovels against the ground. Her husband placed an arm over her shoulder and gripped her tight.

THUMP.

The sound came from the coffin, shaking loose some of the dirt.

THUMP.

THUMP.

THUMP.

Irene shuttered each time, her heart skipping a beat.

"Momma!" A muffled voice coughed through the thick wood. It was hoarse, edged with pain. "Momma! I hurt!"

Irene screamed and fell before her husband could catch her. Her knees sank into the dry grass as she wailed, placing her head in both bandaged hands as fire burned up her arms. She had forgotten how bad the pain was, the burning so hot that it washed her vision white. She knew it would hurt, but thought her joy would push it down, make it smaller.

But the pain cut both ways, she realized, as her son's scream echoed hers. *What kind of mother am I?*

"MOMMA!" Her little boy wailed again.

"Irene." Her husband was crouched next to her, his voice was thick. He stuck an arm underneath her to help her to her feet.

She looked at him, and saw the worry in the lines of his face. *He remembers. Is three years worth it?*

Irene shook the thought from her head; she had made her decision. Her son needed her now, more than ever. She let her husband guide her to the edge of his coffin as she gasped between sobs. The casket rocked back and forth on the ground, sending particles of red dirt shimmering through the air. The wind picked them up and pushed them out of sight.

"MOMMA!"

She fell to her knees again, this time at the center of the casket. Her husband knelt beside her to work at the coffin's latch. With heavy, fumbling hands he sprung the lock and lifted the lid.

Her son's face was still bright with the undertaker's makeup. He was in a simple black suit, with bare feet. His hands were bright red. He writhed on the ivory lining, his torso twisting back and forth like a rag wrung of all its water.

"MOMMA!" His voice hit her unblocked and she nearly fell on her hands.

"He will heal." The Reverend spoke up behind them. "The pain will go." His voice was calm, soothing, confident.

Irene shut her eyes, wishing the pain would come to a quick end. She leaned into the casket, moving her hands slowly. She reached for her son's hand and gripped onto it. She gasped when she felt her son grip back, feeling the bones protruding from his sharp knuckles and the tension wrought by his thin fingers. The skin of his hands was raw and angry, and he gripped hers with a force that made her cry out through the pain.

"Momma!" The boy cried again, weaker. His eyes were clenched shut. His head and his feet were the only parts that the water had not touched.

"Shhh, baby. Momma's right here." His writhing slowed, his limbs slackened and his breathing evened. Irene reached out and straightened his hair, pushing a few stray hairs on his forehead up and over his ear with a bandaged finger.

"Your father's here too," her husband croaked, fumbling the words. He leaned next to her, his knuckles bright white against the coffin's dark wood.

Her son's eyes flashed open, searching wild. His body writhed again, until his eyes found his father.

"*Why?*" her son screamed. His eyes were wide and accusing. His body lost its tension as he passed out from the pain.

Irene dropped his hand.

Her husband fell away from the casket, knocking up a cloud of blood red dust.

"What does he mean?" Irene whispered. Her husband choked out a groan. She stood up from the casket, raised her voice. "What does he mean?!"

Looming over her husband, her mind tugged at the memory, reliving it in agonizing detail.

It had been just like every Monday: She filled the laundry tub, heated it to scalding. It was early, the sun well above the horizon.

Her husband was in bed, out of work, sleeping off the Okie scotch Dick made in his giant backyard kiln.

Her son had been in the other room, playing with a new wooden train that his father had bought for him on a recent job scouting trip to Kingfisher. She could still hear the sound, the *CLICK-CLACK* of wood striking wood.

CLICK-CLACK went the train. Irene could see him now, pushing it across the worn linoleum of their kitchen floor.

He played there all the time.

He knew to stay away from that awful heat.

CLICK-CLACK.

Irene closed her eyes, remembered the sounds. She had moved to the den; there had been a knock at the door.

CLICK-CLACK.

CLICK-CLACK.

THUMP. THUMP. THUMP.

CLICK-CLACK.

Then the hiss of water, like bacon thrown on a griddle, followed by her son's scream. So close together that they played out simultaneously in her head.

She ran to the kitchen, her husband in the opposite doorway, three steps from their bed. She dove after her son, burning her arms as she pulled him from the water. Her husband was behind her, sober, frozen in indecision, fear. She did not remember hearing him get up.

"Did you . . . do this?" She cried at the completion of the memory.

Her husband's eyes shut tight, he let loose a sob.

Irene screamed. "You whoreson!" She ran behind the casket and tore a shovel from a laborer's hands, the pain in her arms forgotten.

She turned on her husband, the shovel held high. He had not moved. Tears ran tracks through the dirt on his face. "I'm sorry," he said. "I didn't mean to."

Irene charged him. She swung for his head, but was stopped short as a pair of hard arms wrapped round her waist. She was lifted in the air, carried off beyond the grave, beyond the sight of her husband. She screamed and kicked, dropping the shovel so she could press down on her captor's forearms.

"Stop." The man behind her gasped. She tossed her head to see him. It was one of the diggers, caked in red dirt. He grimaced, flashing bright teeth. "Please. Stop."

". . . kill . . . him," Irene screamed through labored breath.

"No." The Reverend followed them, staying beyond Irene's kicking legs. His black slacks were stained dirt red and a few wisps of hair were out of place. "No."

"I will!"

"I know." He held up a hand, and the laborer loosened his grip and set her feet on the ground. His arms still locked around her waist. "What good will come of it?"

"He killed my son!" Irene drove against the worker's arms. He stumbled, but did not break.

"Your son is alive." The Reverend pointed at the casket. "In time, he will forget. You will forget."

"No! I will never forget." Irene scratched at the worker's arms. He released her and Irene fell forward, to her knees. Pain shot through her arms as she landed on her wounded hands.

The Reverend forced a smile and placed his hands on her shoulders. A dimple formed against his young cheek. "That is the promise of resurrection. That is the gift the Lord has given us, why he resurrected us, to wipe the slate clean. All of our sins will be forgiven. Forgotten. As our lives roll back, all the things we have done, will be undone. In a few hours, a day, you will forget. It will be as if it never happened."

Irene did not want to forget.

"I am sorry." The Reverend's high voice broke for a moment, and he wiped away tears of his own. "In resurrection all things, all of life's mysteries, become clear. I will speak to your husband. I think it is best for you to spend this first day away from your son. By yesterday, he will be fine, and this horrible memory will be gone."

Irene screamed and lunged to her feet, only to fall flat in the dust as the laborer forced her back down by her shoulders. The remaining three diggers gathered around the casket.

The Reverend took Irene by her tender hands, and guided her to her feet. Standing, Irene was a head taller than he.

Her son was still in his casket, his eyes closed. He tossed his head and murmured something against the soft lining of his coffin. Her husband was still on his knees, his head held tight in his thick hands.

He looked up. "Please," he begged. "Please?"

Irene shook her head, bit her lip. The pain cut through her consciousness.

The Reverend broke the intervening silence. "In our lives we all do things that we regret. Monstrous things. It pays nothing to dwell on them. I want you, Irene, and you, Delbert, to spend the night here, contemplating this."

"What about my son?"

"I will take him. In a few hours, his wounds will heal. He will remember nothing of this tragedy. Neither will you."

"I need him," Irene shook her head. "I don't want to forget!"

"Irene. Please." The Reverend spread his arms. "This is for the best."

The Reverend turned to the four laborers and pointed to Irene's husband. "Bind his hands and feet. He will spend the night here, by his son's grave." He looked sideways at Irene. "Lock her in the caretaker's home."

Irene watched as the men lifted her wounded son out of his coffin and into his buggy. He did not stir. Moments later the Reverend pushed her son away, across the uneven field, toward the setting sun.

"Will you come with me, ma'am?" The worker that held her back asked. "Please?"

She nodded her head, and watched as her husband's feet and hands were bound with hemp.

She closed her eyes and allowed herself to be led away by the digger's hard, calloused hand. *I will not forget*, she swore to herself. *I will not forget.* She repeated the mantra over and over. *Your husband did this . . . he took your son away from you.*

Irene waited until dark before breaking out. The caretaker's house was little more than a shanty, four walls cobbled together by spare pieces of wood, stone and metal. The walls had many soft spots. Irene spent a few minutes working on one, pushing on loose stones, pulling rotted wood, until she formed a space wide enough to squeeze her thin body out of the house, dragging her torso and legs against the ground. The laborers had left long before. The night was silent, dry, without wind.

Remember! Irene closed her eyes, and forced herself to recall the details of the day.

The moon cast long shadows against the graves of the cemetery. Irene used the light of the moon and stars to guide her way to her son's gravesite. Her arms were fully recovered, the skin soft, supple, new, flawless, perfect.

She felt out of breath, robbed of her joy. She should be celebrating the resurrection of her son, at home, with her husband.

Today, everything was meant to be fixed. Instead, it was shattered.

Her son's grave was filled, with a small indentation and her son's headstone the only proof it ever existed. Irene saw no sign of her husband.

Where did he go?

She began to panic. *What if he escaped? What if he tries to hurt my son again?*

He was bound, she reminded herself. *Four strong men. You saw it yourself.*

She crouched at the grave, and let her hands linger over the memory of her son still etched in the stone. If she had a hammer, she would destroy it, break it down to dust. She worked the stone with her hands, pressing it until it fell over in a muffled thump.

Irene stood and ran her eyes around the small graveyard, looking for her husband. She did not know what she would do once she found him. Her mind refused to answer any time she asked. *What will you do?* she chided herself. *Scream at him? Hit him? Kill him?*

"Delbert!" She called into the darkness. "Where are you, you whoreson?!"

Above her, the old sentinel tree groaned in answer. Irene looked up.

Remember!

Her husband's body swung from the tree, his legs twisting one way in the wind, then another. He had fashioned a rude noose from the scraps of hemp the diggers had used to bind him. His fingers were raw and bloody. The purple sheen of his face was hard to pick out against the backdrop of the night sky.

Irene fell to her knees and broke her eyes away from her dead husband, letting her vision fall to the tree's trunk. Her husband had cut into the wood, worked at the dry, dead bark with his bare hands.

The words he left behind were simple, covered in blood:

LOOK AFTER HIM.

Her husband had not forgotten.

"I'm sorry," Irene whispered.

February 13, 1933

Irene had dreaded this day. Unlike the future, the past was inevitable.

She panted through exertion, her body covered in a clammy sheen of sweat. There was little heat in the hospital, and she only had a thin cotton gown to separate her skin from the cold. Goosebumps pebbled her exposed arms and thighs, and her spread legs were high above her body, mounted in stirrups.

"We're almost there, Irene." The doctor smiled from between her legs. He was an older man, with well-styled whiskers and a bald head.

"You're doing great," a nurse echoed, dressed in a white apron and cap. She was standing next to her, holding her hand as she took in large gasps of air.

She gritted her teeth and balled her fists as the doctor pushed her son deeper. She recalled the pain of childbirth, and knew that it was nothing compared to this. She could feel her son struggling as he went higher into her uterus, with his sharp feet and hard elbows.

Irene had dreaded this day, but not for the pain.

She cried out in grief. These three years had been wonderful, an era of brightness where her life held few flaws.

Yet the anniversary of her son's birth always hung over Irene, like dark storm clouds on the horizon, a constant reminder that his end was coming. Now her son was on the final path of his life. He would live another nine months, until he became a part of her.

Irene could feel him struggling, his limbs searching for room in her cramped stomach. She cried out as her son flipped, planting a hard heel up against her diaphragm.

"And we're done. You did a great job, kid," the doctor said. He turned and scrubbed his hands in a metal basin, a wan smile on his lips.

Irene ran a hand across her bulging belly and rested her sweat-soaked hair on the over-starched hospital pillow. Her smile was sad. There was little joy in it.

Irene still remembered.

She would never forget.

TRAVELLER'S REST

David I. Masson

David I. Masson (1915–2007), who was a Scottish librarian and curator, only published one volume of stories, The Caltraps of Time *(1968), but its contents include some of the most compelling and unusual stories dealing with time and time travel that you will find anywhere. One of the strangest and densest is the following, which many regard as the definitive story dealing with the dislocation and compression of time, making it run at different speeds in different locales.*

It was an apocalyptic sector. Out of the red-black curtain of the forward sight-barrier, which at this distance from the Frontier shut down a mere twenty metres north, came every sort of meteoric horror: fission and fusion explosions, chemical detonations, a super-hail of projectiles of all sizes and basic velocities, sprays of nerve-paralysants and thalamic dopes. The impact devices burst on the barren rock of the slopes or the concrete of the forward stations, some of which were disintegrated or eviscerated every other minute. The surviving installations kept up an equally intense and nearly vertical fire of rockets and shells. Here and there a protectivized figure could be seen "sprinting" up, down or along the slopes on its mechanical "walker" like a frantic ant from an anthill attacked by flamethrowers. Some of the visible oncoming trajectories could be seen snaking overhead into the indigo gloom of the rear sight-curtain, perhaps fifty metres south, which met the steep-falling rock surface forty-odd metres below the observer's eye. The whole scene was as if bathed in a gigantic, straight, rainbow. East and west, as far as the eye could see, perhaps some forty miles in this clear mountain air despite the debris of explosion (but cut off to west by a spur from the range) the visibility-corridor witnessed a continual onslaught and counter-onslaught of devices. The visible pandemonium was shut in by the sight-barriers' titanic canyon-walls of black, reaching the slim pale strip of horizon-spanning light at some immense height. The audibility-corridor was vastly wider than that of sight; the many-pitched din, even through left ear in helm, was considerable.

"Computer-sent, must be," said H's transceiver into his right ear. No sigil preceded this statement, but H knew the tones of B, his next-up, who in any case could be seen a metre away saying it, in the large concrete bubble whence they watched, using a plaspex window and an infrared northviewer with a range of some hundreds of metres forward. His next-up had been in the bunker for three minutes, apparently overchecking, probably for an appreciation to two-up who might be in station VV now.

"Else how can they get minute-ly impacts here, you mean?" said H.

"Well, of course it could be longrange low-frequency – we don't really know how Time works over There."

"But if the conceleration runs asymptotically to the Frontier, as it should if Their Time works in mirror-image, would anything ever have got over?"

"Doesn't have to, far's I can see – maybe it steepens a lot, then just falls back at the same angle the other Side," said B's voice; "anyway, I didn't come to talk science: I've news for you, if we hold out the next few seconds here: you're Relieved."

H felt a black inner sight-barrier beginning to engulf him, and a roaring in his ears swallowed up the noise of the bombardment. He bent double as his knees began to buckle, and regained full consciousness. He could see his replacement now, an uncertain-looking figure in protsuit (like everybody else up here) at the far side of the bunker.

"XN 3, what orders then?" he said crisply, his pulse accelerating.

"XN 2: pick em-kit now, repeat now, rocket 3333 to VV, present tag" – holding out a luminous orange label printed with a few coarse black characters – "and proceed as ordered thence."

H stuck up his right thumb from his fist held sideways at elbow length, in salute. It was no situation for facial gestures or unnecessary speech. "XN 3, yes, em-kit, 3333 rocket, tag" (he had taken it in his left glove) "and VV orders; parting!"

He missed B's nod as he skimmed on soles to the exit, grabbed a small bundle hanging (one of fifteen) from the fourth hook along, slid down the greasy slide underground ten metres to a fuel-cell-lit cavern, pressed a luminous button in the wall, watched a lit symbol passing a series of marks, jumped into the low "car" as it ground round the corner, and curled up foetus-wise. His weight having set off the cardoor mechanism, the car shut, slipped down and (its clamps setting on H's body) roared off down the chute.

Twenty-five seconds after his "parting" word H uncurled at the forward receiver cell of station VV nearly half a mile downs-lope. He crawled out as the rocket ground off again, walked ten steps onward in this larger version of his northward habitat, saluted thumb-up and presented his tag to two-up (recognized from helm-tint and helm-sign), saying simultaneously, "XN 3 rep, Relieved."

"XN 1 to XN 3: take this" (holding out a similar orange tag plucked from his pocket) "and take mag-lev train down, in – seventy seconds. By the way, ever seen a prehis?"

"No, sir."

"Spot through here, then; look like pteros but more primitive."

The infrared telescopic viewer looking north-west passed through the forward sight-barrier which due north was about forty metres away here; well upslope yet still well clear of the dark infrared-radiation barrier could be seen, soundlessly screaming and yammering, two scaly animals about the size of large dogs, but with two legs and heavy wings, flopping around a hump or boulder on the rock. They might have been hit on their way along, and could hardly have had any business on that barren spot, H thought.

"Thanks; odd," he said. Eleven seconds of the seventy had gone. He pulled out a squirter-cup from the wall and took a drink from the machine, through his helm. Seventeen seconds gone, fifty-three to go.

"XN 1 to XN 3: how are things up there?"

Naturally a report was called for: XN 2 might never return, and communication up-time and down-time was nearly impossible at these latitudes over more than a few metres.

"XN 3. Things have been hotting up all day; I'm afraid a burst through may be attempted in the next hour or so – only my guess, of course. But I've never seen anything like it all this time up here. I suppose you'll have noticed it in VV too?"

"XN 1, thanks for report," was all the answer he got. But he could hear for himself that the blitz was much more intense than any he had known at this level either.

Only twenty-seven seconds remained. He saluted and strode off across the bunker with his em-kit and the new tag. He showed the tag to the guard, who stamped it and pointed wordlessly down a corridor. H ran down this, arriving many metres down the far end at a little gallery. An underslung railguided vehicle with slide-doors opening into cubicles glided quietly alongside. A gallery-guard waved as H and two others waiting opened doors whose indicators were unlit, the doors slid to, and H found himself gently clamped in on a back-tilted seat as the mag-lev train accelerated downhill. After ten seconds it stopped at the next checkhalt; a panel in the cubicle ceiling lit up to state "DIVERSION, LEFT", presumably because the direct route had been destroyed. The train now appeared to accelerate but more gently, swung away to left (as H could feel), and stopped at two more checkhalts before swinging back to right and finally decelerating, coming to rest and opening some 480 seconds after its start, by Had's personal chronograph, instead of the 200 he had expected.

At this point daylight could again be seen. From the top bunker where XN 2 had discharged him, Had had now gone some ten miles south and nearly 3,000 metres down, not counting detours. The forward sight-barrier here was hidden by a shoulder of mountain covered in giant lichen, but the southern barrier was evident as a violet-black fog-wall a quarter of a mile off. Lichens and some sort of grass-like vegetation covered much of the neighbouring landscape, a series of hollows and ravines. Noise of war was still audible, mingled with that of a storm, but nearby crashes were not frequent and comparatively little damage could be seen. The sky overhead was turbulent.

Some very odd-looking animals, perhaps between a lizard and a stoat in general appearance, were swarming up and down a tree-fern nearby. Six men in all got out of the mag-lev train, besides Had. Two and three marched off in two groups down a track eastward. One (not one of those who had got in at VV) stayed with Had.

"I'm going down to the Great Valley; haven't seen it for twenty days; everything'll be changed. Are you sent far?" said the other man's voice in Had's right ear through the transceiver.

"I – I – I'm Relieved," tried Had uncertainly.

"Well I'm ... disintegrated!" was all the other man could manage. Then, after a minute, "Where will you go?"

"Set up a business way south, I think. Heat is what suits me, heat and vegetation. I have a few techniques I could put to good use in management of one sort or another. I'm sorry – I never meant to plume it over you with this – but you did ask me."

"That's all right. You certainly must have Luck, though. I never met a man who was Relieved. Make good use of it, won't you? It helps to make the Game worthwhile, up here – I mean, to have met a man who is joining all those others we're supposed to be protecting – it makes them real to us in a way."

"Very fine of you to take it that way," said Had.

"No – I mean it. Otherwise we'd wonder if there was any people to hold the Front for."

"Well, if there weren't, how'd the techniques have developed for holding on up here?" put in Had.

"Some of the Teccols I remember in the Great Valley might have developed enough techniques for that."

"Yes, but think of all the pure science you need to work up the techniques from; I doubt if that could have been studied inside the Valley Teccols."

"Possibly not – that's a bit beyond me," said the other's voice a trifle huffily, and they stood on in silence till the next cable-car came up and round at the foot of the station. Had let the man get in it – he felt he owed him that – and a minute later (five seconds only, up in his first bunker, he suddenly thought ironically and parenthetically) the next car appeared. He swung himself in just as a very queer-looking purple bird with a long bare neck alighted on the stoat-lizards' tree-fern. The cable-car sped down above the ravines and hollows, the violet southern curtain backing still more swiftly away from it. As the time-gradient became less steep his brain began to function better and a sense of well-being and meaningfulness grew in him. The car's speed slackened.

Had was glad he still wore his protsuit when a couple of chemical explosions burst close to the cable line, presumably by chance, only fifty metres below him. He was even more glad of it when flying material from a third broke the cable itself well downslope and the emergency cable stopped him at the next pylon. He slid down the pylon's lift and spoke with his transceiver close to the telephone at the foot. He was told to make west two miles to the next cable-car line. His interlocutor, he supposed, must be speaking from an exchange more or less on the same latitude as that of his pylon, since communication even here was still almost impossible north-south except at ranges of some metres. Even so, there was a squeaky sound about the other voice and its speech came out clipped and rapid. He supposed his own voice would sound gruff and drawled to the other.

Using his "walker", he picked his way across ravines and gullies, steering by compass and watching the sight-barriers and the Doppler tint-equator ahead for yawing. "All very well for that man to talk about Teccols," he thought, "but he must realize that no civilization could have evolved from anywhere as far north as the Great Valley: it's far too young to have even evolved Men by itself – at least at this end; I'm not sure how far south the eastern end goes."

The journey was not without its hazards: there were several nearby explosions, and what looked like a suspicious artificial miasma, easily overlooked, lay in two hollows which he decided to go round. Moreover, an enraged giant bear-sloth came at him in a mauve shrub-thicket and had to be eliminated with his quickgun. But to one who had just come down from that mountain-hell all this seemed like a pleasant stroll.

Finally he came upon the line of pylons and pressed the telephone button at the foot of the nearest, after checking that its latitude-number was nearly right. The same voice, a little less outlandish and rapid, told him a car would arrive in three-quarters of a minute and would be arranged to stop at his pylon; if it did not, he was to press the emergency button nearby. Despite his "walker", nearly an hour had gone by since he set out by it. Perhaps ninety minutes had passed since he first left the top bunker – well over a minute and a half of their time there.

The car came and stopped, he scrambled up and in, and this time the journey passed without incident, except for occasional sudden squalls, and the passage of flocks of nervous crows, until the car arrived at its terminus, a squat tower on the heathy slopes. The car below was coming up, and a man in it called through his transceiver as they crept past each other, "First of a bunch!" Sure enough the terminus interior was filled with some twenty men all equipped – almost enough to have warranted sending them up by polyheli, thought Hadol, rather than wait for cars at long intervals. They looked excited and not at all cast down, but Hadol refrained from giving away his future. He passed on to the ratchet-car way and found himself one of a group of men more curious about the landscape than about their fellows. A deep reddish curtain of indeterminate thickness absorbed the shoulders of the heights about a quarter-mile northward, and the bluish fog terminated the view over the valley at nearly half a mile southward, but between the two the latitudinal zone was tolerably clear and devoid of obvious signs of war. Forests of pine and lower down of oak and ash covered the slopes, until finally these disappeared in the steepening edge of the Great Valley, whose meadows could however be glimpsed past the bluff. Swirling cloud-shadows played over the ground, skirts and tassels of rain and hail swept across it, and there was the occasional flash and rumble of a storm. Deer could be seen briefly here and there, and dense clouds of gnats danced above the trees.

A journey of some fifty minutes took them down, past two empty stations, through two looped tunnels and among waterfalls and under cliffs where squirrels leapt across from dangling root to root, through a steadily warmer and warmer air to the pastures and cornfields of the Great Valley, where a narrow village of concrete huts and wooden cabins, Emmel, nestled on a knoll above the winding river, and a great road ran straight to the east, parallel to a railway. The river was not, indeed, large here – a shallow, stony but attractive stream, and the Great Valley (all of whose breadth could now be seen) was at this western point no more than a third of a mile across. The south-ward slopes terminating the North-Western Plateau, now them-selves visible, were rich in shrubland.

The utter contrast with what was going on above and, in top bunker time, perhaps four minutes ago, made Hadolar nearly drunk with enjoyment. However, he presented his luminous tag and had it (and his permanent checktab) checked for radiation, countersigned and stamped by the guard commander at the military terminal. The detachable piece at the end of the tag was given back to him to be slipped into the identity disc which was, as always, let into a slot in one of his ribs; the other portion was filed away. He got out of his protsuit and "walker", gave up his gun, ammunition and em-kit, was given two wallets of 1,000 credit tokens each and a temporary civsuit. An orderly achieved the identity-disc operation. The whole ceremony from his arrival took 250 seconds flat – two seconds up in the top bunker. He walked out like an heir to the earth.

The air was full of scents of hay, berries, flowers, manure. He took intoxicated gulps of it. At the freshouse he ordered, paid for, and drank four decis of light ale, then ordered a sandwich and an apple, paid and ate. The next train east, he was told, would be in a quarter of an hour. He had been in the place perhaps half an hour. No time to spend watching the stream, but he walked to the railhead, asked for a ticket to Veruam by the Sea some 400 miles east and, as the detailed station map showed him, about thirty miles south, paid, and selected a compartment when the train arrived from its shed.

A farm girl and a sleepy-looking male civilian, probably an army contractor, got in one after the other close behind Hadolar, and the compartment contained just these three when the train left. He looked at the farm girl with interest – she was blonde and placid – as the first female he had seen for a hundred days. Fashions had not changed radically in thirty-odd years, he saw, at least among Emmel farm-girls. After a while he averted his gaze and considered the landscape. The valley was edged by bluffs of yellowish stone now to north and now to south. Even here their difference in hue was perceptible – the valley had broadened slightly; or perhaps he was being fanciful and the difference was due solely to normal light-effects. The river meandered gracefully from side to side and from cliff to cliff, with occasional islands, small and crowned with hazel. Here and there a fisher could be seen by the bank, or wading in the stream. Farm houses passed at intervals. North above the valley rose the great slopes, apparently devoid of signs of human life except for funicular stations and the occasional heliport, until they vanished into the vast crimson-bronze curtain of nothingness which grew insensibly out of a half cloud-covered green sky near the zenith. Swirls of whirlwind among the clouds told of the effects of the time-gradient on weather, and odd lightning-streaks, unnoticed further north amid the war, appeared to pirouette among them. To the south the plateau was still hidden by the height of the bluffs, but the beginnings of the dark blue haze grew out of the sky above the valley skyline. The train stopped at a station and the girl, Hadolar saw with a pang, got out. Two soldiers got in in light dress and swapped minor reminiscences: they were on short-term leave to the next stop, a small town, Granev, and eyed Hadolar's temporary suit but said nothing.

Granev was mostly built of steel and glass: not an exciting place. It made a one-block twenty-storey five-mile strip on either side of the road, with over-pass-canopy. (How lucky, thought Hadolar, that speech and travel could go so far down this Great Valley without interlatitude problems: virtually the whole 450 miles.) Industry and some of the Teccols now appeared. The valley had broadened until, from the line, its southern cliffs began to drown in the blue haze half a mile off. Soon the northern slopes loomed a smoky ruddy brown before they, too, were swallowed up. The river, swollen by tributaries, was a few hundred metres across now and deep whenever the line crossed it. So far they had only gone fifty-odd miles. The air was warmer again and the vegetation more lush. Almost all the passengers were civilians now, and some noted Hadolar's temporary suit ironically. He would buy himself a wardrobe at Veruam at the first opportunity, he decided. But at the moment he wished to put as many miles as possible between himself and that bunker in the shortest personal time.

Some hours later the train arrived at Veruam by the North-Eastern Sea. Thirty miles long, forty storeys high, and 500 metres broad north-south, it was an imposing city. Nothing but plain was to be seen in the outskirts, for the reddish fog still obliterated everything about four miles to the north, and the bluish one smothered the view southward some seven. A well-fed Hadolaris visited one of the city's Rehabilitation Advisors, for civilian techniques and material resources had advanced enormously since his last acquaintance with them, and idioms and speech-sounds had changed bewilderingly, while the whole code of social behaviour was terrifyingly different. Armed with some manuals, a pocket recorder, and some standard speechform and folkway tapes, he rapidly purchased thin clothing, stormwear, writing implements, further recording tools, lugbags and other personal gear. After a night at a good guestery, Hadolaris sought interviews with the employing offices of seven subtropical development agencies, was tested and, armed with seven letters of introduction, boarded the night liner mag-lev train for the south past the shore of the North-Eastern Sea and to Oluluetang some 360 miles south. One of the tailors who had fitted him up had revealed that on quiet nights very low-pitched rumblings were to be heard from, presumably, the mountains northward. Hadolaris wanted to get as far from that North as he conveniently could.

He awoke among palms and savannah-reeds. There was no sign of either sight-barrier down here. The city was dispersed into compact blocks of multistorey buildings, blocks separated by belts of rich woodland and drive-like roadways and monorails. Unlike the towns of the Great Valley, it was not arranged on an east–west strip, though its north–south axis was still relatively short. Hadolarisóndamo found himself a small guestery, studied a plan of the city and its factory areas, bought a guide to the district and settled down to several days of exploration and inquiry before visiting the seven agencies themselves. His evenings were spent in adult classes, his nights absorbing the speech-form recordings unconsciously in sleep. In the end after nineteen days (about four hours at Veruam's latitude, four minutes at that of Emmel, less than two seconds at the higher bunker, he reflected) he obtained employment as a minor sales manager of vegetable products in one of the organizations.

Communication north and south, he found, was possible verbally for quite a number of miles, provided one knew the rules. In consequence the zoning here was far from severe and travel and social facilities covered a very wide area. One rarely saw the military here. Hadolarisóndamo bought an automob and, as he rose in the organization's hierarchy, a second one for pleasure. He found himself well liked and soon had a circle of friends and a number of hobbies. After a number of love-affairs he married a girl whose father was higher up in the organization, and, some five years after his arrival in the city, became the father of a boy.

"Arisón!" called his wife from the boat. Their son, aged five, was puttering at the warm surface of the lake with his fists over the gunwale. Hadolarisóndamo was painting on the little island, quick lines and sweeps across the easelled canvas, a pattern of light and shade bursting out of the swamp trees over a little bay. "Arisón! I can't get this thing to start. Could you swim over and try?"

"Five minutes more, Mihányo. Must get this down."

Sighing, Karamihányolàsve continued, but without much hope, to fish from the bows with her horizontal yo-yo gadget. Too quiet round here for a bite. A parakeet flashed in the branches to right. Derestó, the boy, stopped hitting the water, and pulled over the tube-window, let it into the lake and got Mihányo to slide on its lightswitch. Then he peered this way and that under the surface, giving little exclamations as tiny fish of various shapes and hues shot across. Presently Arisón called over, folded up his easel, pulled off his trousers, propped paints and canvas on top of everything, and swam over. There were no crocs in this lake, hippo were far off, filariasis and bilharzia had been eliminated here. Twenty minutes' rather tense tinkering got things going, and the silent fuel-cell driven screw was ready to pilot them over to the painting island and thence across the lake to where a little stream's current pushed out into the expanse. They caught four. Presently back under the westering sun to the jetty, tie-up and home in the automob.

By the time Derestó was eight and ready to be formally named Lafonderestónami, he had a sister of three and a baby brother of one. He was a keen swimmer and boatman, and was developing into a minor organizer, both at home and in school. Arisón was now third in the firm, but kept his balance. Holidays were spent either in the deep tropics (where one could gain on the time-exchange) or among the promontories on the southern shores of the North-Eastern Sea (where one had to lose), or, increasingly, in the agricultural stream-scored western uplands, where a wide vista of the world could in many areas be seen and the cloudscapes had full play. Even there the sight-barriers were a mere fogginess near the north and south horizons, backed by a darkness in the sky.

Now and then, during a bad night, Arisón thought about the "past". He generally concluded that, even if a breakthrough had been imminent in, say, half an hour from his departure, this could hardly affect the lives of himself and his wife, or even of their children, down here in the south, in view of the time-contraction southwards. Also, he reflected, since nothing ever struck further south than a point north of Emmel's latitude, the ballistic attacks must be mounted close to the Frontier; or if they were not, then the Enemy must lack all knowledge of either southern time-gradients or southern geography, so that the launching of missiles from well north of the Frontier to pass well south of it would not be worthwhile. And even the fastest heli which could be piloted against time conceleration would, he supposed, never get through.

Always adaptable, Arisón had never suffered long from the disabilities incident on having returned after a time at the Front. Mag-lev train travel and other communications had tended to unify the speech and the ethos, though naturally the upper reaches of the Great Valley and the military zone in the mountains of the North were linguistically and sociologically somewhat isolated. In the western uplands, too, pockets of older linguistic forms and old-fashioned attitudes still remained, as the family found on its holidays. By and large, however, the whole land spoke the tongue of the "contemporary" subtropical lowlands, inevitably modified of course by the onomatosyntomy or "shortmouth" of latitude. A "contemporary" ethical and social code had also spread. The southern present may be said to have colonized the northern past, even geological past, somewhat as the birds and other travelling animals had done, but with the greater resources of human wits, flexibility, traditions and techniques.

Ordinary people bothered little about the war. Time concel-eration was on their side. Their spare mental energies were spent in a vast selection of plays and ploys, making, representing, creating, relishing, criticizing, theorizing, discussing, arranging, organizing, cooperating, but not so often out of their own zone. Arisón found himself the member of a dozen interweaving circles, and Mihányo was even more involved. Not that they were never alone: the easy tempo of work and life with double "week" of five days' work, two days free, seven days' work and six days free, the whole staggered across the population and in the organizations, left much leisure time which could be spent on their own selves. Arisón took up texture-sculpting, then returned after two years to painting, but with magneto-brush instead of spraypen; purified by his texture-sculpting period, he achieved a powerful area control and won something of a name for himself. Mihányo, on the other hand, became a musician. Derestó, it was evident, was going to be a handler of men and societies, besides having, at thirteen, entered the athletic age. His sister of eight was a great talker and arguer. The boy of six was, they hoped, going to be a writer, at least in his spare time: he had a keen eye for things, and a keen interest in telling about them. Arisón was content to remain, when he had reached it, second in the firm: a chiefship would have told on him too much. He occasionally lent his voice to the administration of local affairs, but took no major part.

Mihányo and Arisón were watching a firework festival on the North-Eastern Sea from their launch, off one of the southern promontories. Up here, a fine velvety backdrop for the display was made by the inky black of the northern sight-barrier, which cut off the stars in a gigantic arc. Fortunately the weather was fine. The silhouettes of the firework boats could just be discerned. In a world which knew no moon the pleasures of a "white night" were often only to be got by such displays. The girl and Derestó were swimming round and round the launch. Even the small boy had been brought out, and was rather blearily staring north-ward. Eventually the triple green star went up and the exhibition was over; at the firework boats a midnight had been reached. Derestó and Venoyyè were called in, located by a flare, and ultimately prevailed on to climb in, shivering slightly, and dry off in the hot-air blaster, dancing about like two imps. Arisón turned the launch for the shore and Silarrè was found to be asleep. So was Venoyyè when they touched the jetty. Their parents had each to carry one in and up to the beachouse.

Next morning they packed and set out in the automob for home. Their twenty days' holiday had cost 160 days of Oluluetang time. Heavy rain was falling when they reached the city. Mihányo, when the children were settled in, had a long talk on the opsiphone with her friend across the breadth of Oluluetang: she (the friend) had been with her husband badger-watching in the western uplands. Finally Arisón chipped in and, after general conversation, exchanged some views with the husband on developments in local politics.

"Pity one grows old so fast down here," lamented Mihányo that evening; "if only life could go on for ever!"

"Forever is a big word. Besides, being down here makes no difference to the feeling – you don't feel it any slower up on the Sea, do you, now?"

"I suppose not. But if only . . ."

To switch her mood, Arisón began to talk about Derestó and his future. Soon they were planning their children's lives for them in the way parents cannot resist doing. With his salary and investments in the firm they would set up the boy for a great administrator, and still have enough to give the others every opportunity.

Next morning it was still in something of a glow that Arisón bade farewell to his wife and went off to take up his work in the offices. He had an extremely busy day and was coming out of the gates in the waning light to his automob in its stall, when he found standing round it three of the military. He looked inquiringly at them as he approached with his personal pulse-key in hand.

"You are VSQ 389 MLD 194 RV 27 XN 3, known as Hadolarisóndamo, resident at" (naming the address) "and subpresident today in this firm." The cold tones of the leader were a statement, not a question.

"Yes," whispered Arisón as soon as he could speak.

"I have a warrant for your immediate re-employment with our Forces in the place at which you first received your order for Release. You must come with us forthwith." The leader produced a luminous orange tag with black markings.

"But my wife and family!"

"They are being informed. We have no time."

"My firm?"

"Your chief is being informed. Come now."

"I – I – I must set my affairs in order."

"Impossible. No time. Urgent situation. Your family and firm must do all that between them. Our orders override everything."

"Wh – wh – what is your authority? Can I see it please?"

"This tag should suffice. It corresponds to the tagend which I hope you still have in your identity disc – we will check all that en route. Come on now."

"But I must see your authority. How do I know, for instance, that you are not trying to rob me, or something?"

"If you know the code you'll realize that these symbols can only fit one situation. But I'll stretch a point: you may look at this warrant, but don't touch it."

The other two closed in. Arisón saw that they had their quick-guns trained on him. The leader pulled out a broad screed. Arisón, as well as the dancing characters would let him, resolved them in the light of the leader's torch into an order to collect him, Arisón, by today at such and such a time, local Time, if possible immediately on his leaving his place of work (speci-fied); and below, that one man be detailed to call Mihányo by opsiphone simultaneously, and another to call the president of the organization. The Remployee and escort to join the military mag-lev train to Veruam (which was leaving within about fifteen minutes). The Remployee to be taken as expeditiously as possi-ble to the bunker (VV) and thence to the higher bunker (from which he had come some twenty years before, but only about ten minutes in the Time of that bunker, it flashed through Arisón's brain – apart from six or seven minutes corresponding to his journey south).

"How do they know if I'm fit enough for this job after all these years?"

"They've kept checks on you, no doubt."

Arisón thought of tripping one and slugging two and doing a bolt, but the quickguns of the two were certainly trained upon him. Besides, what would that gain him? A few hours' start, with unnecessary pain, disgrace and ruin on Mihányo, his children and himself, for he was sure to be caught.

"The automob," he said ridiculously.

"A small matter. Your firm will deal with that."

"How can I settle my children's future?"

"Come on, no use arguing. You are coming now, alive or dead, fit or unfit."

Speechless, Arisón let himself be marched off to a light military vehicle.

In five minutes he was in the mag-lev train, an armoured affair with strong windows. In ten more minutes, with the train moving off, he was stripped of his civilian clothes and possessions (to be returned later to his wife, he learnt), had his identity disc extracted and checked and its Relief tagend removed, and a medical checkup was begun on him. Apparently this was satisfactory to the military authorities. He was given military clothing.

He spent a sleepless night in the train trying to work out what he had done with this, what would be made of that, who Mihányo could call upon in need, who would be likely to help her, how she would manage with the children, what (as nearly as he could work it out) they would get from a pension which he was led to understand would be forthcoming from his firm, how far they could carry on with their expected future.

A grey pre-dawn saw the train's arrival at Veruam. Foodless (he had been unable to eat any of the rations) and without sleep, he gazed vacantly at the marshalling-yards. The body of men travelling on the train (apparently only a few were Remployees) were got into closed trucks and the long convoy set out for Emmel.

At this moment Hadolaris's brain began to re-register the conceleration situation. About half a minute must have passed since his departure from Oluluetang, he supposed, in the Time of his top bunker. The journey to Emmel might take up another two minutes. The route from Emmel to that bunker might take a further two and a half minutes there, as far as one could work

out the calculus. Add the twenty-years' (and southward journey's) sixteen to seventeen minutes, and he would find himself
in that bunker not more than some twenty-two minutes after he
had left it. (Mihan, Deres and the other two would all be nearly
ten years older and the children would have begun to forget
him.) The blitz was unprecedentedly intense when he had left,
and he could recall (indeed it had figured in several nightmares
since) his prophecy to XN 1 that a breakthrough might be
expected within the hour. If he survived the blitz, he was unlikely
to survive a breakthrough; and a breakthrough of what? No one
had ever seen the Enemy, this Enemy that for Time immemorial
had been striving to get across the Frontier. If it got right over,
the twilight of the race was at hand. No horror, it was believed
at the Front, could equal the horror of that moment. After a
hundred miles or so he slept, from pure exhaustion, sitting up in
a cramped position, wedged against the next man. Stops and
starts and swerves woke him at intervals. The convoy was driving at maximum speeds.

At Emmel he stumbled out to find a storm lashing down. The
river was in spate. The column was marched to the depot.
Hadolar was separated out and taken in to the terminal building
where he was given inoculations, issued with "walker", quickgun, em-kit, protsuit and other impedimenta, and in a quarter of
an hour (perhaps seven or eight seconds up at the top bunker)
found himself entering a polyheli with thirty other men. This
had barely topped the first rise and into sunlight when explosions and flarings were visible on all sides. The machine forged
on, the sight-curtains gradually closing up behind and retreating grudgingly before it. The old Northern vertigo and somnam-
bulism re-engulfed Had. To think of Kar and their offspring
now was to tap the agony of a ghost who shared his brain and
body. After twenty-five minutes they landed close to the foot of
a mag-lev train line. The top-bunker lapse of "twenty-two
minutes" was going, Had saw, to be something less. He was the
third to be bundled into the mag-lev train compartments, and
190 seconds saw him emerging at the top and heading for
bunker VV. XN 1 greeted his salute merely with a curt command
to proceed by rocket to the top bunker. A few moments more
and he was facing XN 2.

"Ah, here you are. Your Relief was killed so we sent back for you. You'd only left a few seconds." A ragged hole in the bunker wall testified to the incident. The relief's cadaver, stripped, was being carted off to the disposal machine.

"XN 2. Things are livelier than ever. They certainly are hot stuff. Every new offensive from here is pitched back at us in the same style within minutes, I notice. That new cannon had only just started up when back came the same shells – I never knew They had them. Tit for tat."

Into H's brain, seemingly clarified by hunger and exhaustion and much emotion, flashed an unspeakable suspicion, one that he could never prove or disprove, having too little knowledge and experience, too little overall view. No one had ever seen the Enemy. No one knew how or when the War had begun. Information and communication were paralysingly difficult up here. No one knew what really happened to Time as one came close to the Frontier, or beyond it. Could it be that the concel-eration there became infinite and that there was nothing beyond the Frontier? Could all the supposed missiles of the Enemy be their own, somehow returning? Perhaps the war had started with a peasant explorer lightheartedly flinging a stone north-wards, which returned and struck him. Perhaps there was, then, no Enemy.

"XN 3. Couldn't that gun's own shells be reflected back from the Frontier, then?"

"XN 2. Impossible. Now you are to try to reach that forward missile post by the surface – our tunnel is destroyed – at 15° 40' East – you can just see the hump near the edge of the I/R viewer's limit – with this message; and tell him verbally to treble output."

The ragged hole was too small. H left by the forward port. He ran, on his "walker", into a ribbon of landscape which became a thicket of fire, a porcupine of fire, a Nessus-shirt to the Earth, as in a dream. Into an unbelievable supercrescendo of sound, light, heat, pressure and impacts he ran, on and on up the now almost invisible slope . . .

TWEMBER

Steve Rasnic Tem

Continuing the theme of the previous story we have another example of the disruption of time, this time trying to depict some kind of force that has corrupted time like the weather and caused disturbances across the Earth.

Steve Rasnic Tem has been writing novels and short stories since 1979, mostly in the fields of supernatural and horror fiction but sometimes straying into science fiction. Some of his stories can be found in the collections The Far Side of the Lake *(2001) and* In Concert *(2010), the latter in collaboration with his wife, Melanie.*

Will observed through the kitchen window of his parent's farmhouse as the towering escarpment, its many strata glittering relative to their contents, moved inescapably through the fields several hundred yards away. He held his breath as it passed over and through fences, barns, tractors, and an abandoned house long shed of paint. Its trespass was apparently without effect, although some of the objects in its wake had appeared to tremble ever so slightly, shining as if washed in a recent, cleansing rain.

"It might be beautiful," his mother said beside him, her palsy magnified by the exertion of standing, "if it weren't so frightening."

"You're pushing yourself." He helped her into one of the old ladder-back kitchen chairs. "You're going to make yourself sick."

"A body needs to see what she's up against." She closed her eyes.

He got back to the window in time to see a single tree in the escarpment's wake sway, shake, and fall over. Between the long spells of disabling interference he had heard television commentators relate how, other than the symptomatic "cosmetic" impact on climate, sometimes nearby objects *were* affected, possibly even destroyed, when touched by the escarpments, or the walls, or the roaming cliffs – whatever you cared to call the phenomena. These effects were still poorly understood, and "under investigation" and there had been "no official conclusions". Will wondered if there ever would be, but no one would ever again be able to convince him that the consequences of these massive, beautiful, and strange escarpments as they journeyed across the world were merely cosmetic.

His mother insisted that the television be kept on, even late at night, and even though it was no better than a white noise machine most of the time. "We can't afford to miss anything important," she'd said. "It's like when there's a tornado coming – you keep your TV on."

"These aren't like tornadoes, Mom. They can't predict them."

"Well, maybe they'll at least figure out what they are, why they're here."

"They've talked about a hundred theories, two hundred. Time disruption, alien invasion, dimensional shifts at the earth's core. Why are tsunamis here? Does it matter? You still can't stop them." At least the constant static on the TV had helped him sleep better.

"They're getting closer." Tracy had come up behind him. There was a time when she would have put her arms around him at this point, but that affectionate gesture didn't appear to be in his wife's repertoire anymore.

"Maybe. But it's not like they have intelligence," he said, not really wanting to continue their old argument, but unable to simply let it go.

"See how it changes course, just slightly?" she said. "And there's enough tilt from vertical, I'm *sure* that can't just be an optical illusion. It leans toward occupied areas. I've been watching this one off and on all day, whenever it's visible, almost from the time it came out of the ground."

"They don't really come out of the ground." He tried to sound neutral, patient, but he doubted he was succeeding. "They've said it just looks that way. They're forming from the ground up, that's all."

"We don't know that much about them. No one does," she snapped.

"It's not like it's some predator surfacing, like a shark or a snake, prowling for victims." He was unable to soften the tone of his voice.

"You don't know that for sure."

Will watched as the escarpment either flowed out of visual range or dematerialized; it was hard to tell. "No. I guess I don't."

"Some of the people around here are saying that those things sense where there are people living, that they're drawn there, like sharks to bait. They say they learn."

"I don't know." He didn't want to talk about it anymore. "I hope not." Of course she was entitled to her opinion, and it wasn't that he knew any more than she did. But they used to know how to disagree.

He could hear his father stirring in the bedroom. The old man shuffled out, his eyes wet, unfocused. The way he moved past, Will wasn't sure if he even knew they were there. His father gazed out the window, and not for the first time Will wondered what exactly he was seeing. In the hazy distance another escarpment seemed to be making its appearance, but it might simply be the dust blown up from the ground, meeting the low-lying, streaked clouds. Then his father said "chugchugchugchugchug", and made a whooh whoohing sound, like a train. Then he made his way on out to the porch.

In his bedroom, Jeff began to whimper. Tracy went in to check on him. Will knew he should join her there – he'd barely looked at his son in days, except to say goodnight after the boy was already asleep – but considering how awkward it would be with the three of them he instead grabbed the keys to his dad's pickup and went out looking for the place where the escarpment had passed through and touched that tree.

Will had grown up here in eastern Colorado, gone to school, helped his parents out on the farm. It really hadn't changed that much over the decades, until recently, with that confusion of seasons that frequently followed the passage of escarpments through a region. The actual temperatures might vary only a few degrees from the norm, but the accompanying visual clues were often deceptive and disorienting. Stretches of this past summer had felt almost wintery, what with reduced sunlight, a deadening of plant color, and even the ghostly manifestation of a kind of faux snow which disintegrated into a shower of minute light-reflecting particles when touched.

Those suffering from seasonal affective disorder had had no summer reprieve this year. He'd heard stories that a few of the more sensitive victims had taken to their beds for most of the entire year. Colorado had a reputation for unpredictable weather, but these outbreaks, these "invasions" as some people called them, had taken this tendency toward meteorological unreliability to a new extreme.

Now it was, or at least should have been, September, with autumn on the way but still a few pretty hot days, but there were – or at least there appeared to be – almost no leaves on the trees, and no indications that there ever had been, and a gray-white sky had developed over the past few weeks, an immense amorphous shroud hanging just above the tops of the trees, as if the entire world had gone into storage. Dead of winter, or so he would have thought, if he'd actually lost track of the weeks, which he dare not do. He studied the calendar at least once a day and tried to make what he saw outside conform with memories of seasons past, as if he might will a return to normalcy.

Thankfully there had been few signs as yet of that fake snow. The official word was that the snow-like manifestation was harmless for incidental contact, and safe for children. Will wasn't yet convinced – the very existence of it gave him the creeps, thinking that some sort of metaphysical infection might have infiltrated the very atomic structure of the world, and haunted it.

"Twember," was what his mother called this new mixing of the seasons. "It's all betwixt and between. Pretty soon we're going to have just this one season. It won't matter when you plant, or what; it's all going to look like it died."

He thought he was probably in the correct vicinity now. Parts of the ground had this vaguely rubbed, not quite polished appearance, as if the path had been heated and ever-so-slightly glazed by the friction of the escarpment's passing. The air was charged – it seemed to push back, making his skin tingle and his hair stir. A small tree slightly to one side of the path had been bent the opposite way, several of its branches fresh and shiny as spring, as if they had been gently renewed, lovingly washed, but the rest with that flat, dead look he'd come to hate.

Spotting a patch of glitter on the ground, Will pulled off onto the shoulder and got out of the truck. As he walked closer he could see how here and there sprays of the shiny stuff must have spewed out of the passing escarpment, suggesting contents escaping under pressure, like plumes of steam. He dropped to one knee and examined the spot: a mix of old coins, buttons, bits of glass, small metal figures, toys, vacation mementos, souvenirs, suggesting the random debris left in the bottom of the miscellanea drawer after the good stuff has been packed away for some major household move – the stuff you threw in the trash or left behind for the next tenants.

The strong scent of persimmons permeated the air. The funny thing was, he had no idea how he knew this. Will didn't think he'd ever seen one, much less smelled it. Was it a flower, or a fruit?

For a few minutes he thought there were no other signs of the escarpment's passing, but then he began to notice things. A reflection a few yards away turned out to be an antique oil lamp. He supposed it was remotely possible such a thing could have been lost or discarded and still remain relatively intact, but this lamp was pristine, with at least an inch of oil still in its reservoir. And a few feet beyond were a pair of women's shoes, covered in white satin, delicate and expensive-looking, set upright on the pale dust as if the owner had stepped out of them but moments before, racing for the party she could not afford to miss.

The old house had been abandoned sometime in the seventies, the structure variously adapted since then to store equipment, hay, even as a makeshift shelter for a small herd of goats. From the outside it looked very much the same, and Will might have passed it by, but then he saw the ornate bedpost through one of the broken windows, and the look of fresh blue paint over part of one exterior wall, and knew that something had occurred here out of the ordinary.

The house hadn't had a door in a decade or more, and still did not, but the framing around the door opening appeared almost new, and was of metal – which it had never been – attached to a ragged border of brick which had incongruously blended in to the edges of the original wood-framed wall. Two enormous, shiny brass hinges stood out from this frame like the flags of some new, insurgent government. The effect was as if a door were about to materialize, or else had almost completed its disappearance.

Once he was past the door frame, the small abandoned house appeared as he might normally expect. Islands of dirt, drifted in through the opening or blown through the missing windows, looked to have eaten through the floorboards, some sprouting prairie grass and gray aster. There were also the scat of some wild animal or other, probably fox or coyote, small pieces of old hay from back when the building had been used for feed storage, and a variety of vulgar graffiti on the ruined walls, none of it appearing to be of recent vintage.

A short hallway led from this front room into the back of the house, and as he passed through Will began to notice a more remarkable sort of misalignment, a clear discrepancy between what was and what should have been.

A broken piece of shelf hung on the wall approximately midway through the brief hallway. It had a couple of small objects on it. On closer inspection he saw that it wasn't broken at all – the edges of the wood actually appeared finely frayed, the threads of what was alternating with the threads of what was not. Along the frayed edge lay approximately one-third of an old daguerreotype – although not at all old, it seemed. Shiny-new, glass sealed around the intact edges with rolled copper, laid inside a wood and leather case. A large portion of the entire package bitten off, missing, not torn exactly, or broken, for the missing bite of it too was delicately, wispily frayed, glass fibers floating into empty air as if pulled away. The image under the glass was of a newly married couple in Victorian-style clothing, their expressions like those under duress: the bride straining out a thin smile, the groom stiffly erect, as if his neck were braced.

A piece of pale gauze covered the opening at the end of the short hall. Now lifting on a cool breeze, the gauze slapped the walls on both sides, the ceiling. Will stepped forward and gently pulled it aside, feeling like an intruder.

A four-poster bed sat diagonally in the ruined room, the incongruous scent of the perfumed linen still strong despite faint traces of an abandoned staleness and animal decay. The bed looked recently slept in, the covers just pulled back, the missing woman – he figured it was probably a woman – having stepped out for a moment. Peering closer, he found a long, copper-colored hair on the pillow. He picked it up gently, holding it like something precious against the fading afternoon light drifting lazily in through the broken window. He wanted to take it with him, but he didn't know exactly why, or how he could, or if he should. So he laid it carefully back down on the pillow, in its approximate original location.

Half a mirror torn lengthwise was propped against a wide gap in the outer wall. Beyond was simply more of the eastern Colorado plains, scrub grass and scattered stone, but somewhat smoother than normal, shinier, and Will surmised that the escarpment had exited the farm house at this point.

He found himself creeping up to the mirror, nervous to look inside. Will never looked at mirrors much, even under normal conditions. He wasn't that old – in his fifties still and, as far as he knew, the same person inside, thinking the same thoughts he'd had at seventeen, eighteen, twenty. But what he saw in the mirror had stopped matching the self-image in his brain some time long ago.

He stopped a couple of feet away, focusing on the ragged edge where the escarpment had cut through and obliterated the present, or the past. More of that floating raggedness, suggesting a kind of yearning for completion, for what was missing. His reluctance to find his reflection made him reel a bit. What if he looked down and it was himself as a teenager looking up, with obvious signs of disappointment on his face?

But it was himself, although perhaps a bit older, paler, as if the color were being leached out and eventually he would disappear. The problem with avoiding your image in the mirror was that when you finally did see it, it was a bit of a shock, really, because of how much you had changed. Who was this old man with his thoughts?

He left the abandoned house and strolled slowly toward the pickup, watching the ground, looking for additional leavings but finding nothing. The empty ground looked like it always did out here, as it probably did in any open, unsettled place, as if it were ageless, unfixed, and yet fundamentally unchangeable. Whatever might be done to it, it would always return to this.

He wanted to describe to Tracy what he'd seen here, but what, exactly, had he seen? Time had passed this way, and left some things behind, then gone on its way. And the world was fundamentally unchanged. His mother might understand better, but Tracy was the one he wanted to tell, even though she might not hear him.

He felt the pressure change inside his ears, and he turned part of the way around, looking, but not seeing. Suddenly the world roared up behind him, passed him, and he shook.

He bent slightly backwards, looking up, terrified he might lose his balance, and having no idea of what the possible consequences might be. The moving escarpment towered high above him, shaking in and out of focus as it passed, and shaking him, seemingly shaking the ground, but clearly this wasn't a physical shaking, clearly this was no earthquake, but a violent vibration of the senses, and the consciousness behind them. Closing his eyes minimized the sensation, but he didn't want to miss anything, so other than a few involuntary blinks he kept them open. He turned his body around as best he could, as quickly, to get a better view.

He could make out the top of the escarpment, at least he could see that it did have a top, an edge indicating that it had stopped its vertical climb, but he could tell little more than that. As his eyes traveled further down he was able to focus on more detail, and taking a few steps back gave him a better perspective.

There were numerous more or less clearly defined strata, each in movement seemingly independent of the others, sometimes in an opposite flow from those adjacent, and sometimes the same but at a different speed. Like a multilayered roulette wheel, he thought, which seemed appropriate.

Trapped in most of these layers were visible figures – some of them blurred, but some of them so clear and vivid that when they were looking in his direction, as if from a wide window in the side of a building, he attempted to gain their attention by waving. None responded in any definitive way, although here and there the possibility that they might have seen him certainly seemed to be there.

The vast majority of these figures appeared to be ordinary people engaged in ordinary activities – fixing or eating dinner, housecleaning, working in offices, factories, on farms – but occasionally he'd see something indicating that an unusual event was occurring or had recently occurred. A man lying on his back, people gathered around, some attending to the fallen figure but most bearing witness. A couple being chased by a crowd. A woman in obvious anguish, screaming in a foreign language. A blurred figure in freefall from a tall building.

The settings for these dramas, suspenseful or otherwise, were most often sketchily drawn: some vague furniture, the outlines of a building, or not indicated at all. The figures sometimes acted their parts on a backdrop of floating abstractions. In a few cases, however, it was like looking out his front door – at random locations a tree branch or a roof eave actually penetrated the outer plane of the escarpment and hung there like a three-dimensional projection in the contemporary air.

It was like a gigantic three-dimensional time-line/cruise ship passing through the eastern Colorado plains, each level representing a different era. It was like a giant fault in time, shifting the temporal balance of the world in an attempt to rectify past mistakes. But there was no compelling reason to believe any of these theories. It was an enormous, fracturing mystery traveling through the world.

And just as suddenly as it had appeared, becoming so dramatically *there* it sucked up all the available reality of its environment, it was gone, reduced to a series of windy, dust-filled eddies that dissipated within a few seconds. Will shakily examined himself with eyes and hands. Would he lose his mind the way his Jeff had?

*   *   *

If they'd pulled their son out of school when these storms first began he'd be okay right now. That's what they'd been called at first, "storms", because of their sudden evolution, and the occasional accompanying wind, and the original belief that they were an atmospheric phenomenon of some sort, an optical illusion much like sunlight making a rainbow when it passed through moisture-laden cloud, although they couldn't imagine why it was so detailed, or the mechanism of its projection. Tracy had wanted to pull Jeff out until the world better understood what all this was about, and a few other parents, a very few, had already done so. But Will couldn't see the reasoning. If there was a danger how would Jeff be any safer at home? These insubstantial moving walls came out of nowhere, impossible to predict, and as far as anyone knew they weren't harmful. There had been that case of the farmer in Texas, but he'd been old, and practically senile anyway, and it must have been a terrible shock when it passed through his barn.

Tracy inevitably blamed Will, because in Jeff's case it certainly hadn't been harmless, and then Will had compounded things by being late that day. Will was often late. He had always worked at being some sort of success, even though the right combination of jobs and investments had always eluded him. He'd been selling spas and real estate, filling in the gaps with various accounting and IT consulting. Too many clients, too many little puzzle pieces of time, everything overlapping slightly so that at times his life was multidimensional, unfocused, and he was always late to wherever he was scheduled to be.

He'd pulled up to the school twenty minutes late that day to pick up Jeff. Normally it wouldn't have mattered that much – Jeff liked hanging out in the school library using their computers. And if that's where he'd been he would have probably been okay. But that particular afternoon Jeff had decided to hang out on the playground, shooting hoops until his dad came to pick him up. And that's where he'd been when the towering wall came through. One of the teachers who'd witnessed the event said later that the wall appeared so suddenly no one had time to move, and it ran over Jeff much like a runaway truck, looking scarily solid, seemingly obliterating everything in its path as it thundered across the concrete and asphalt.

Will had arrived just in time to see that rapidly moving wall vanishing into a dusty brown mist, bending gel-like, quickly losing resolution as it leaned precariously like some old building coming down in an earthquake, but silently – the roar and the shaking were entirely visual, the trauma entirely mental. He had raced into the last of its shimmering eddies and scooped his drooling boy off the ground.

Will drove the pickup back toward his parents' farm more slowly, and with more care than he had when he left. The ambient light of the day had dimmed only slightly, but the canopy of sky appeared even lower than before, only a hundred yards up or so. The landscape looked flattened, stretched out under the pressure of the low-hanging clouds. He could hear rumbles in the distance, and could see the brief glimmer of escarpments appearing, disappearing, surfacing, diving back into the world. Time escaping, time buried and sealed.

Another pickup approached on the narrow gravel road, identical, or almost identical to his. He held his breath, wondering how he would handle it if he encountered a younger or an older version of himself driving the same pickup on the road. Surely that would still be impossible, even during Twember? And if it did occur, might that not shatter the world?

The pickup slowed as it came up alongside him. He stared at the driver. Because it was Lana Sumpter, much as she'd been when she was seventeen years old – her face so new, fresh, and shiny with a soft-lipped smile cradling her words. "Will? Will Cotton? Is that you?"

Both trucks stopped; his head still shook. "I, I'm not sure," he replied. "Probably not the same one. Lana, are any of us the same one?" He was babbling, just like he used to with her. He'd loved her so much his bones used to ache, making his skin seem ill-fitting. He'd never loved anyone that much before, or since.

Lana gazed at him, cheeks slightly flushed. The dark blue of the truck appeared to fade, to lighten, to whiten. Will blinked, then could see the individual bits of faux snow accumulating, layering the truck with a sugary coating, and the white air looking crisp, brittle, about to break. She laughed, but it wasn't really a laugh. It was like words escaping under stress. "I, I guess not,

Will. Not these days. Seems like only yesterday I felt too young. Now I feel too old."

Lana's face still flushed, her eyes looking uncomfortable, her smile struggling to remain. And her lips not moving. She wasn't the one speaking.

Will shifted his head a bit to the side and peered past the lovely young girl to the older woman sitting in the shadows on the passenger side. The woman leaned forward, and although the face was somewhat puffy, and makeup had cracked in not the most flattering ways, there was a ghost of a resemblance, and as if a mask of reluctance had been peeled away, Will recognized her with a jolting, almost sickening sensation.

He felt ashamed of himself. He'd never been one to care much about people's appearances, so why did it bother him that he might have passed Lana – at one time the love of his life – on the street and not even recognize her. It was as if he'd been in love with a different person.

"This is my daughter Julie. Julie this is Will, an old friend. We knew each other when we were kids."

"Hi, Julie," he said, and had to take a breath. "You look like your mother."

"*Everybody* says that." The girl didn't sound as friendly, or as sweet, as Will had first thought.

"Are you out from Denver for awhile?" Lana asked.

"Me and the family. I don't know for how long. I don't know when we should go back, or if."

She nodded, frowned. "A lot of the old crowd came back here. Jimmie, Carol, Suze. I don't know if they wanted to be home at a time like this, if it even still feels like home, or if they thought it'd be better here. It's *not* really, I don't think. But it's more open out here. Maybe they figure these things will be easier to dodge out in the open." She shook her head.

"I know. But they come up so quickly. Maybe they're not dangerous, but maybe they are."

"I was sorry to hear about your dad," she said. "He didn't run into one of these things, did he?"

"No, he started getting confused, I don't know, at least a year before the first one appeared. I don't see how there could be a connection." She didn't say anything about Jeff, so Will figured she didn't know. Will wasn't about to bring him up. "The doctor prescribed a couple of drugs – they don't seem to help much, but I still make sure he takes them. And for now at least, the pharmacy here still gets them. And the grocery store still gets his favorite chocolate candies. If he didn't get those, well, he'd aggravate us all, I reckon." Will forced a chuckle, and was embarrassed by the fakeness of it.

"Do you think we'll have shortages? My sister does. She says we'll probably see the last supply deliveries any day now. She says, why would people continue to do their jobs with all this going on?"

So here they were talking about illnesses and medicines and disasters freely roaming the world threatening everything. Just like old people. Why hadn't they worried about those things when they were younger? Maybe when you were young you really didn't understand what time it was, or how late it could all get to be. "What else are they going to do?" he asked. "It's like the president said – no one knows how long this will last, what it means, or what the final outcome will be, so people need to go on with their lives." It sounded stupid saying it, but he imagined it was still true.

"But that broadcast was three weeks ago. How's your television reception? We have a dish, and we're getting nothing."

"Nothing much at our place either. What does Ray say about all this?" He hoped he had the name right – he hadn't been there when she'd married, only heard about it.

The girl, Julie, looked flushed, and turned her head away. Lana's face fell back into the shadows, and her voice came out shakily. "My Ray died about three months back. COPD. He said it got a lot worse with this new weather, or whatever you want to call it. I don't know, Will – it was already pretty bad."

And again Will felt shame, because along with his sadness for her came this vaguely formed notion that there might be a new opportunity for him in this. What was wrong with him? He wasn't going to leave his wife and son, so why think about it? He apologized, but of course did not fully explain why, and continued home toward Tracy, his family, and his present.

*   *   *

His eighth grade teacher Mrs Anderson used to emphasize in her social studies class that even kids from a small town school could become anything they wanted to be if only they applied themselves. "Dream big!" she'd say. "Your dreams are the only thing that will limit you." In order to back up her thesis, throughout the school year she would sprinkle in inspirational stories about people from small towns who had "made a difference", who had made it "big".

Halfway in to high school Will, and many of his friends, had concluded that this was all just so much propaganda, the purpose of which was – well – he wasn't sure, maybe to make Mrs Anderson feel better about teaching in such a small town. But they heard similar messages from other teachers, parents, pretty much anyone who came to speak to their class. Like relatively recent graduates on their way to the army or the peace corps.

Big dreams were great, but they almost always seemed to shrink when you talked to guidance counselors, recruiters, or anyone else charged with evaluating your prospects realistically. There were some important, socially-conscious things you could do with your life, certainly, but not *here*, and not for much monetary compensation. And these other careers, the ones Mrs Anderson talked about – the thinkers and writers and scientists and actors – well, all you had to be was somebody else, somebody else entirely, and from some other place.

On the trip back to his parents' farm it was relatively easy for Will to imagine himself, and this land, as something else entirely. The road, the fields, were bleached, as white as he could imagine, and as far as he could see. The whiteness intensified at times to such transparency Will imagined he could almost see to where life both entered the plants and exited them, where time ate through the world and transformed it all into something else. He might have been traveling across Russia before the revolution in his wagon, his buggy, or in middle Europe as it began its entry into the ice age, in nineteenth century Oklahoma in the dead of winter, the children starving, the wife suffering in their bed, a new baby on the way. And Will couldn't do much more than observe, and try to live, and keep his four wheels on the road, steady toward home.

The farmhouse looked as it had during that long-remembered blizzard the winter he was nine years old, when so many of the cows had died, and a stiffened pheasant stared at him from the front yard, its shining eyes frozen into jewels. A series of flashes drew his own eyes to that distant horizon line in the direction of Denver, and he considered it might be lightning, even though he knew better. Great blocks shifted there, weaving in and out of each other's way as if they had some sort of rudimentary intelligence. They appeared closer by the second, as if that city's buildings themselves were slowly advancing toward him across the eastern plains.

He pulled into the yard at the side of the house and jumped down onto the snow-laden ground, which cracked like layers of candy, allowing a white powdery residue to explode into the air with each of his steps. Of course this wasn't snow – it was nothing like snow. It was like the moments had been snatched from the air and allowed to die, left to litter the ground. He tried to step carefully, but still they fractured with very little force.

Inside the house there was the strong smell of cooking apples. A tree had been propped up in one corner. There were a few decorations on it, and his mother was sitting on the couch singing to herself and stringing popcorn into a garland.

Tracy pushed Jeff into the room and set the wheelchair brake. Their son's moaning stopped and he gazed at the tree. Will looked around for his father, found him in the corner by the front window, staring outside, motionless. Tracy came up to Will and stood there. She didn't smile, but for the first time in a long time she didn't look furious. "What's all this?" he asked.

"Christmas," she replied. "At least according to your mother."

"But it's not Christmas," he said, although truthfully he wasn't completely sure anymore.

"Maybe, maybe not. Is there going to be another Christmas this year, Will? I certainly don't know. Do you?"

He shrugged. "I guess it won't hurt anything. It sure seems to have helped Jeff."

"'Hold on to the moment.' You used to say that a lot, remember? Why did you stop saying it – was it because of me?"

He shrugged again. "You know I used to like it when you hummed in the bathroom? But the last few years it really annoyed me. That was something I shouldn't have held on to. I mean really, why would that bother me so much?"

"You used to turn the dumbest things into a celebration. Remember when it was Thomas Edison's birthday, and you turned on all the lights in the house?"

"That was before Jeff's – accident. He'd had a really bad day. I ordered pizza and made a pretty bad birthday cake. It cheered him up."

"You wore a lamp on your head, plugged in and turned on. I thought you were going to electrocute yourself! I got so mad."

"You didn't want to be married to a child. I burned my ear pretty badly taking that contraption off."

"Your mother thought this would be a perfect thing, give us all a little something to look forward to. Is that where you got the idea to create all those special holidays? From her?"

"It was my dad," Will replied. "One day he bought my mother an alligator handbag. From that year on we celebrated 'Alligator Handbag Day'. There were special sandwiches. We wore tails made out of newspaper and did a little dance. Actually, my mother didn't always fully appreciate Alligator Handbag Day."

"I can believe that."

There were several moments of awkward silence, then Will said, "This doesn't mean you still love me, does it? I mean, this celebration, this stolen moment, doesn't change anything fundamentally, does it?"

"I don't think I blame you for Jeff anymore. I really don't."

"Things change, moments get away from you, the past pays a visit, and although there's no blame, still nothing is forgiven. It's hard to live here. It always has been," he said.

"Will—"she started to say, but his father drowned her out.

"Whooh whooh!" his father yelled by the window. "Whooh whooh!" The house shook with thunder.

A great striated wall moved past the glass. Will wondered if his healthy son was trapped inside there somewhere, if inside that wall he might find his wife's love again, or some other Will, some other life. He tried to say something to Tracy, but he couldn't even hear himself, so loud everything had suddenly become. He could feel time circling outside the house, circling again, raising its voice and ready to run them down.

THE PUSHER

John Varley

If we ever achieve interstellar flight with velocities approaching the speed of light then we may at last achieve time travel, at least for the individuals on that voyage, though still only one way. It will be a significant factor to consider once that is achieved, because those volunteering for interstellar travel will never see their contemporaries again. Not unless they make special arrangements.

John Varley has been one of the giants of the past forty years of science fiction, exploding on the scene in 1974 with a rush of brilliant short stories followed by such groundbreaking novels as The Ophiuchi Hotline *(1977),* Titan *(1979) and its sequels, and, most relevant to this volume,* Millennium *(1989), a time-travel novel based on his earlier story "Air Raid" (1977) and expanded to tie in to the film* Millennium *for which Varley wrote the screenplay. A more recent time-travel novel, but one far less complex, is* Mammoth *(2005).*

Things change. Ian Haise expected that. Yet there are certain constants, dictated by function and use. Ian looked for those and he seldom went wrong.

The playground was not much like the ones he had known as a child. But playgrounds are built to entertain children. They will always have something to swing on, something to slide down, something to climb. This one had all those things, and more. Part of it was thickly wooded. There was a swimming hole. The stationary apparatus was combined with dazzling light sculptures that darted in and out of reality. There were animals, too: pygmy rhinoceros and elegant gazelles no taller than your knee. They seemed unnaturally gentle and unafraid.

But most of all, the playground had children.

Ian liked children.

He sat on a wooden park bench at the edge of the trees, in the shadows, and watched them. They came in all colors and all sizes, in both sexes. There were black ones like animated licorice jellybeans and white ones like bunny rabbits, and brown ones with curly hair and more brown ones with slanted eyes and straight black hair and some who had been white but were now toasted browner than some of the brown ones.

Ian concentrated on the girls. He had tried with boys before, long ago, but it had not worked out.

He watched one black child for a time, trying to estimate her age. He thought it was around eight or nine. Too young. Another one was more like thirteen, judging from her shirt. A possibility, but he'd prefer something younger. Somebody less sophisticated, less suspicious.

Finally he found a girl he liked. She was brown, but with startling blonde hair. Ten? Possibly eleven. Young enough, at any rate.

He concentrated on her and did the strange thing he did when he had selected the right one. He didn't know what it was, but it usually worked. Mostly it was just a matter of looking at her, keeping his eyes fixed on her no matter where she went or what she did, not allowing himself to be distracted by anything. And sure enough, in a few minutes she looked up, looked around, and her eyes locked with his. She held his gaze for a moment, then went back to her play.

He relaxed. Possibly what he did was nothing at all. He had noticed, with adult women, that if one really caught his eye so he found himself staring at her she would usually look up from what she was doing and catch him. It never seemed to fail. Talking to other men, he had found it to be a common experience. It was almost as if they could feel his gaze. Women had told him it was nonsense, or if not, it was just reaction to things seen peripherally by people trained to alertness for sexual signals. Merely an unconscious observation penetrating to the awareness; nothing mysterious, like ESP.

Perhaps. Still, Ian was very good at this sort of eye contact. Several times he had noticed the girls rubbing the backs of their necks while he observed them, or hunching their shoulders. Maybe they'd developed some kind of ESP and just didn't recognize it as such.

Now he merely watched her. He was smiling, so that every time she looked up to see him – which she did with increasing frequency – she saw a friendly, slightly graying man with a broken nose and powerful shoulders. His hands were strong, too. He kept them clasped in his lap.

Presently she began to wander in his direction.

No one watching her would have thought she was coming toward him. She probably didn't know it herself. On her way, she found reasons to stop and tumble, jump on the soft rubber mats, or chase a flock of noisy geese. But she was coming toward him, and she would end up on the park bench beside him.

He glanced around quickly. As before, there were few adults in this playground. It had surprised him when he arrived. Apparently the new conditioning techniques had reduced the numbers of the violent and twisted to the point that parents felt it safe to allow their children to run without supervision. The adults present were involved with each other. No one had given him a second glance when he arrived.

That was fine with Ian. It made what he planned to do much easier. He had his excuses ready, of course, but it could be embarrassing to be confronted with the questions representatives of the law ask single, middle-aged men who hang around playgrounds.

For a moment he considered, with real concern, how the parents of these children could feel so confident, even with mental conditioning. After all, no one was conditioned until he had first done something. New maniacs were presumably being produced every day. Typically, they looked just like everyone else until they proved their difference by some demented act.

Somebody ought to give those parents a stern lecture, he thought.

* * *

"Who are you?"

Ian frowned. Not eleven, surely, not seen up this close. Maybe not even ten. She might be as young as eight.

Would eight be all right? He tasted the idea with his usual caution, looked around again for curious eyes. He saw none.

"My name is Ian. What's yours?"

"*No.* Not your *name.* Who are *you*?"

"You mean what do I do?"

"Yes."

"I'm a pusher."

She thought that over, then smiled. She had her permanent teeth, crowded into a small jaw.

"You give away pills?"

He laughed. "Very good," he said. "You must do a lot of reading." She said nothing, but her manner indicated she was pleased.

"No," he said. "That's an old kind of pusher. I'm the other kind. But you knew that, didn't you?" When he smiled she broke into giggles. She was doing the pointless things with her hands that little girls do. He thought she had a pretty good idea of how cute she was, but no inkling of her forbidden eroticism. She was a ripe seed with sexuality ready to burst to the surface. Her body was a bony sketch, a framework on which to build a woman.

"How old are you?" he asked.

"That's a secret. What happened to your nose?"

"I broke it a long time ago. I'll bet you're twelve."

She giggled, then nodded. Eleven, then. And just barely.

"Do you want some candy?" He reached into his pocket and pulled out the pink and white striped paper bag.

She shook her head solemnly. "My mother says not to take candy from strangers."

"But we're not strangers. I'm Ian, the pusher."

She thought that over. While she hesitated he reached into the bag and picked out a chocolate thing so thick and gooey it was almost obscene. He bit into it, forcing himself to chew. He hated sweets.

"Okay," she said, and reached toward the bag. He pulled it away. She looked at him in innocent surprise.

"I just thought of something," he said. "I don't know your name. So I guess we *are* strangers."

She caught on to the game when she saw the twinkle in his eye. He'd practiced that. It was a good twinkle.

"My name is Radiant. Radiant Shiningstar Smith."

"A very fancy name," he said, thinking how names had changed. "For a very pretty girl." He paused, and cocked his head. "No, I don't think so. You're Radiant . . . Starr. With two *r's* . . . *Captain* Radiant Starr, of the Star Patrol."

She was dubious for a moment. He wondered if he'd judged her wrong. Perhaps she was really Mizz Radiant Faintingheart Belle, or Mrs Radiant Motherhood. But her fingernails were a bit dirty for that.

She pointed a finger at him and made a Donald Duck sound as her thumbs worked back and forth. He put his hand to his heart and fell over sideways, and she dissolved in laughter. She was careful, however, to keep her weapon firmly trained on him.

"And you'd better give me that candy or I'll shoot you again."

The playground was darker now, and not so crowded. She sat beside him on the bench, swinging her legs. Her bare feet did not quite touch the dirt.

She was going to be quite beautiful. He could see it clearly in her face. As for the body . . . who could tell?

Not that he really gave a damn.

She was dressed in a little of this and a little of that, worn here and there without much regard for his concepts of modesty. Many of the children wore nothing. It had been something of a shock when he arrived. Now he was almost used to it, but he still thought it incautious on the part of her parents. Did they really think the world was that safe, to let an eleven-year-old girl go practically naked in a public place?

He sat there listening to her prattle about her friends – the ones she hated and the one or two she simply adored – with only part of his attention.

He inserted ums and uh-huhs in the right places.

She was cute, there was no denying it. She seemed as sweet as a child that age ever gets, which can be very sweet and as poisonous as a rattlesnake, almost at the same moment. She had the capacity to be warm, but it was on the surface. Underneath, she cared mostly about herself. Her loyalty would be a transitory thing, bestowed easily, just as easily forgotten.

And why not? She was young. It was perfectly healthy for her to be that way.

But did he dare try to touch her?

It was crazy. It was as insane as they all told him it was. It worked so seldom. Why would it work with her? He felt a weight of defeat.

"Are you okay?"

"Huh? Me? Oh, sure, I'm all right. Isn't your mother going to be worried about you?"

"I don't have to be in for hours and hours yet." For a moment she looked so grown up he almost believed the lie.

"Well, I'm getting tired of sitting here. And the candy's all gone." He looked at her face. Most of the chocolate had ended up in a big circle around her mouth, except where she had wiped it daintily on her shoulder or forearm. "What's back there?"

She turned.

"That? That's the swimming hole."

"Why don't we go over there? I'll tell you a story."

The promise of a story was not enough to keep her out of the water. He didn't know if that was good or bad. He knew she was smart, a reader, and she had an imagination. But she was also active. That pull was too strong for him. He sat far from the water, under some bushes, and watched her swim with the three other children still in the park this late in the evening.

Maybe she would come back to him, and maybe she wouldn't. It wouldn't change his life either way, but it might change hers.

She emerged dripping and infinitely cleaner from the murky water. She dressed again in her random scraps, for whatever good it did her, and came to him, shivering.

"I'm cold," she said.

"Here." He took off his jacket. She looked at his hands as he wrapped it around her, and she reached out and touched the hardness of his shoulder.

"You sure must be strong," she commented.

"Pretty strong. I work hard, being a pusher."

"Just what *is* a pusher?" she said and stifled a yawn.

"Come sit on my lap, and I'll tell you."

He did tell her, and it was a very good story that no adventurous child could resist. He had practiced that story, refined it, told it many times into a recorder until he had the rhythms and cadences just right, until he found just the right words – not too difficult words, but words with some fire and juice in them.

And once more he grew encouraged. She had been tired when he started, but he gradually caught her attention. It was possible no one had ever told her a story in quite that way. She was used to sitting before the screen and having a story shoved into her eyes and ears. It was something new to be able to interrupt with questions and get answers. Even reading was not like that. It was the oral tradition of storytelling, and it could still mesmerize the *n*th generation of the electronic age.

"That sounds great," she said, when she was sure he was through.

"You liked it?"

"I really truly did. I think I want to be a pusher when I grow up. That was a really neat story."

"Well, that's not actually the story I was going to tell you. That's just what it's like to be a pusher."

"You mean you have another story?"

"Sure." He looked at his watch. "But I'm afraid it's getting late. It's almost dark, and everybody's gone home. You'd probably better go, too."

She was in agony, torn between what she was supposed to do and what she wanted. It really should be no contest, if she was who he thought she was.

"Well . . . but – but I'll come back here tomorrow and you—"

He was shaking his head.

"My ship leaves in the morning," he said. "There's no time."

"Then tell me now! I can stay out. Tell me now. Please please please?"

He coyly resisted, harrumphed, protested, but in the end allowed himself to be seduced. He felt very good. He had her like a five-pound trout on a twenty-pound line. It wasn't sporting. But, then, he wasn't playing a game.

⋆　　⋆　　⋆

So at last he got to his specialty.

He sometimes wished he could claim the story for his own, but the fact was he could not make up stories. He no longer tried to. Instead, he cribbed from every fairy tale and fantasy story he could find. If he had a genius, it was in adapting some of the elements to fit the world she knew – while keeping it strange enough to enthrall her – and in ad-libbing the end to personalize it.

It was a wonderful tale he told. It had enchanted castles sitting on mountains of glass, moist caverns beneath the sea, fleets of starships and shining riders astride horses that flew the galaxy. There were evil alien creatures, and others with much good in them. There were drugged potions. Scaled beasts roared out of hyperspace to devour planets.

Amid all the turmoil strode the Prince and Princess. They got into frightful jams and helped each other out of them.

The story was never quite the same. He watched her eyes. When they wandered, he threw away whole chunks of story. When they widened, he knew what parts to plug in later. He tailored it to her reactions.

The child was sleepy. Sooner or later she would surrender. He needed her in a trance state, neither awake nor asleep. That is when the story would end.

". . . and though the healers labored long and hard, they could not save the Princess. She died that night, far from her Prince."

Her mouth was a little round *o*. Stories were not supposed to end that way.

"Is that *all*? She died, and she never saw the Prince again?"

"Well, not quite all. But the rest of it probably isn't true, and I shouldn't tell it to you." Ian felt pleasantly tired. His throat was a little raw, making him hoarse. Radiant was a warm weight on his lap.

"You *have* to tell me, you know," she said, reasonably. He supposed she was right. He took a deep breath.

"All right. At the funeral, all the greatest people from that part of the galaxy were in attendance. Among them was the greatest Sorcerer who ever lived. His name . . . but I really shouldn't tell you his name. I'm sure he'd be very cross if I did.

"This Sorcerer passed by the Princess's bier . . . that's a—"

"I know, I *know*, Ian. Go on!"

"Suddenly he frowned and leaned over her pale form. 'What is this?' he thundered. 'Why was I not told?' Everyone was very concerned. This Sorcerer was a dangerous man. One time when someone insulted him he made a spell that turned everyone's heads backwards so they had to walk around with rear-view mirrors. No one knew what he would do if he got really angry.

"'This Princess is wearing the Starstone,' he said, and drew himself up and frowned all around as if he were surrounded by idiots. I'm sure he thought he was, and maybe he was right. Because he went on to tell them just what the Starstone was, and what it did, something no one there had ever heard before. And this is the part I'm not sure of. Because, though everyone knew the Sorcerer was a wise and powerful man, he was also known as a great liar.

"He said that the Starstone was capable of capturing the essence of a person at the moment of her death. All her wisdom, all her power, all her knowledge and beauty and strength would flow into the stone and be held there, timelessly."

"In suspended animation," Radiant breathed.

"Precisely. When they heard this, the people were amazed. They buffeted the Sorcerer with questions, to which he gave few answers, and those only grudgingly. Finally he left in a huff. When he was gone everyone talked long into the night about the things he had said. Some felt the Sorcerer had held out hope that the Princess might yet live on. That if her body were frozen, the Prince, upon his return, might somehow infuse her essence back within her. Others thought the Sorcerer had said that was impossible, that the Princess was doomed to a half-life, locked in the stone.

"But the opinion that prevailed was this:

"The Princess would probably never come fully back to life. But her essence might flow from the Starstone and into another, if the right person could be found. All agreed this person must be a young maiden. She must be beautiful, very smart, swift of foot, loving, kind . . . oh, my, the list was very long. Everyone doubted such a person could be found. Many did not even want to try.

"But at last it was decided the Starstone should be given to a faithful friend of the Prince. He would search the galaxy for this maiden. If she existed, he would find her.

"So he departed with the blessings of many worlds behind him, vowing to find the maiden and give her the Starstone."

He stopped again, cleared his throat, and let the silence grow.

"Is that all?" she said, at last, in a whisper.

"Not quite all," he admitted. "I'm afraid I tricked you."

"Tricked me?"

He opened the front of his coat, which was still draped around her shoulders. He reached in past her bony chest and down into an inner pocket of the coat. He came up with the crystal. It was oval, with one side flat. It pulsed ruby light as it sat in the palm of his hand.

"It shines," she said, looking at it wide-eyed and open-mouthed.

"Yes, it does. And that means you're the one."

"Me?"

"Yes. Take it." He handed it to her, and as he did so, he nicked it with his thumbnail. Red light spilled into her hands, flowed between her fingers, seemed to soak into her skin. When it was over, the crystal still pulsed, but dimmed. Her hands were trembling.

"It felt very, very hot," she said.

"That was the essence of the Princess."

"And the Prince? Is he still looking for her?"

"No one knows. I think he's still out there, and some day he will come back for her."

"And what then?"

He looked away from her. "I can't say. I think, even though you are lovely, and even though you have the Starstone, that he will just pine away. He loved her very much."

"I'd take care of him," she promised.

"Maybe that would help. But I have a problem now. I don't have the heart to tell the Prince that she is dead. Yet I feel that the Starstone will draw him to it one day. If he comes and finds you, I fear for him. I think perhaps I should take the stone to a far part of the galaxy, some place he could never find it. Then at least he would never know. It might be better that way."

"But I'd help him," she said, earnestly. "I promise. I'd wait for him, and when he came, I'd take her place. You'll see."

He studied her. Perhaps she would. He looked into her eyes for a long time, and at last let her see his satisfaction.

"Very well. You can keep it then."

"I'll wait for him," she said. "You'll see."

She was very tired, almost asleep.

"You should go home now," he suggested.

"Maybe I could just lie down for a moment," she said.

"All right." He lifted her gently and placed her prone on the ground. He stood looking at her, then knelt beside her and began to gently stroke her forehead. She opened her eyes with no alarm, then closed them again. He continued to stroke her.

Twenty minutes later he left the playground, alone.

He was always depressed afterwards. It was worse than usual this time. She had been much nicer than he had imagined at first. Who could have guessed such a romantic heart beat beneath all that dirt?

He found a phone booth several blocks away. Punching her name into information yielded a fifteen-digit number, which he called. He held his hand over the camera eye.

A woman's face appeared on his screen.

"Your daughter is in the playground, at the south end by the pool, under the bushes," he said. He gave the address of the playground.

"We were so worried! What : . . . is she . . . who is—"

He hung up and hurried away.

Most of the other pushers thought he was sick. Not that it mattered. Pushers were a tolerant group when it came to other pushers, and especially when it came to anything a pusher might care to do to a puller. He wished he had never told anyone how he spent his leave time, but he had, and now he had to live with it.

So, while they didn't care if he amused himself by pulling the legs and arms off infant puller pups, they were all just back from ground leave and couldn't pass up an opportunity to get on each other's nerves. They ragged him mercilessly.

"How were the swing-sets this trip, Ian?"

"Did you bring me those dirty knickers I asked for?"

"Was it good for you, honey? Did she pant and slobber?"

"My ten-year-old baby, she's a pullin' me back home . . ."

Ian bore it stoically. It was in extremely bad taste, and he was the brunt of it, but it really didn't matter. It would end as soon as they lifted again. They would never understand what he sought, but he felt he understood them. They hated coming to Earth. There was nothing for them there, and perhaps they wished there was.

And he was a pusher himself. He didn't care for pullers. He agreed with the sentiment expressed by Marian, shortly after lift-off. Marian had just finished her first ground leave after her first voyage. So naturally she was the drunkest of them all.

"Gravity sucks," she said, and threw up.

It was three months to Amity, and three months back. He hadn't the foggiest idea of how far it was in miles; after the tenth or eleventh zero his mind clicked off.

Amity. Shit City. He didn't even get off the ship. Why bother? The planet was peopled with things that looked a little like ten-ton caterpillars and a little like sentient green turds. Toilets were a revolutionary idea to the Amiti; so were ice cream bars, sherbets, sugar donuts, and peppermint. Plumbing had never caught on, but sweets had, and fancy desserts from every nation on Earth. In addition, there was a pouch of reassuring mail for the forlorn human embassy. The cargo for the return trip was some grayish sludge that Ian supposed someone on Earth found tremendously valuable, and a packet of desperate mail for the folks back home. Ian didn't need to read the letters to know what was in them. They could all be summed up as "Get me *out* of here!"

He sat at the viewport and watched an Amiti family lumbering and farting its way down the spaceport road. They paused every so often to do something that looked like an alien clusterfuck. The road was brown. The land around it was brown, and in the distance were brown, unremarkable hills. There was a brown haze in the air, and the sun was yellow-brown.

He thought of castles perched on mountains of glass, of Princes and Princesses, of shining white horses galloping among the stars.

He spent the return trip just as he had on the way out: sweating down in the gargantuan pipes of the stardrive. Just beyond the metal walls unimaginable energies pulsed. And on the walls themselves, tiny plasmoids grew into bigger plasmoids. The process was too slow to see, but if left unchecked the encrustations would soon impair the engines. His job was to scrape them off.

Not everyone was cut out to be an astrogator.

And what of it? It was honest work. He had made his choices long ago. You spent your life either pulling gees or pushing *c*. And when you got tired, you grabbed some *z*'s. If there was a pushers' code, that was it.

The plasmoids were red and crystalline, teardrop-shaped. When he broke them free of the walls, they had one flat side. They were full of a liquid light that felt as hot as the center of the sun.

It was always hard to get off the ship. A lot of pushers never did. One day, he wouldn't either.

He stood for a few moments looking at it all. It was necessary to soak it in passively at first, get used to the changes. Big changes didn't bother him. Buildings were just the world's furniture, and he didn't care how it was arranged. Small changes worried the shit out of him. Ears, for instance. Very few of the people he saw had earlobes. Each time he returned he felt a little more like an ape who has fallen from his tree. One day he'd return to find everybody had three eyes or six fingers, or that little girls no longer cared to hear stories of adventure.

He stood there, dithering, getting used to the way people were painting their faces, listening to what sounded like Spanish being spoken all around him. Occasional English or Arabic words seasoned it. He grabbed a crewmate's arm and asked him where they were. The man didn't know. So he asked the captain, and she said it was Argentina, or it had been when they left.

*   *   *

The phone booths were smaller. He wondered why.

There were four names in his book. He sat there facing the phone, wondering which name to call first. His eyes were drawn to Radiant Shiningstar Smith, so he punched that name into the phone. He got a number and an address in Novosibirsk.

Checking the timetable he had picked – putting off making the call – he found the antipodean shuttle left on the hour. Then he wiped his hands on his pants and took a deep breath and looked up to see her standing outside the phone booth. They regarded each other silently for a moment. She saw a man much shorter than she remembered, but powerfully built, with big hands and shoulders and a pitted face that would have been forbidding but for the gentle eyes. He saw a tall woman around forty years old who was fully as beautiful as he had expected she would be. The hand of age had just begun to touch her. He thought she was fighting that waistline and fretting about those wrinkles, but none of that mattered to him. Only one thing mattered, and he would know it soon enough.

"You *are* Ian Haise, aren't you?" she said, at last.

"It was sheer luck I remembered you again," she was saying. He noted the choice of words. She could have said coincidence.

"It was two years ago. We were moving again and I was sorting through some things and I came across that plasmoid. I hadn't thought about you in . . . oh, it must have been fifteen years."

He said something noncommittal. They were in a restaurant, away from most of the other patrons, at a booth near a glass wall beyond which spaceships were being trundled to and from the blast pits.

"I hope I didn't get you into trouble," he said.

She shrugged it away.

"You did, some, but that was so long ago. I certainly wouldn't bear a grudge that long. And the fact is, I thought it was all worth it at the time."

She went on to tell him of the uproar he had caused in her family, of the visits by the police, the interrogation, puzzlement, and final helplessness. No one knew quite what to make of her story. They had identified him quickly enough, only to find he had left Earth, not to return for a long, long time.

"I didn't break any laws," he pointed out.

"That's what no one could understand. I told them you had talked to me and told me a long story, and then I went to sleep. None of them seemed interested in what the story was about. So I didn't tell them. And I didn't tell them about the . . . the Starstone." She smiled. "Actually, I was relieved they hadn't asked. I was determined not to tell them, but I was a little afraid of holding it all back. I thought they were agents of the . . . who were the villains in your story? I've forgotten."

"It's not important."

"I guess not. But something is."

"Yes."

"Maybe you should tell me what it is. Maybe you can answer the question that's been in the back of my mind for twenty-five years, ever since I found out that thing you gave me was just the scrapings from a starship engine."

"Was it?" he said, looking into her eyes. "Don't get me wrong. I'm not saying it *was* more than that. I'm asking *you* if it wasn't more."

"Yes, I guess it was more," she said, at last.

"I'm glad."

"I believed in that story passionately for . . . oh, years and years. Then I stopped believing it."

"All at once?"

"No. Gradually. It didn't hurt much. Part of growing up, I guess."

"And you remembered me."

"Well, that took some work. I went to a hypnotist when I was twenty-five and recovered your name and the name of your ship. Did you know—"

"Yes. I mentioned them on purpose."

She nodded, and they fell silent again. When she looked at him now, he saw more sympathy, less defensiveness. But there was still a question.

"Why?" she said.

He nodded, then looked away from her, out to the starships. He wished he was on one of them, pushing *c*. It wasn't working. He knew it wasn't. He was a weird problem to her, something to get straightened out, a loose end in her life that would irritate until it was made to fit in, then be forgotten.

To hell with it.

"Hoping to get laid," he said. When he looked up she was slowly shaking her head back and forth.

"Don't trifle with me, Haise. You're not as stupid as you look. You knew I'd be married, leading my own life. You knew I wouldn't drop it all because of some half-remembered fairy tale thirty years ago. *Why?*"

And how could he explain the strangeness of it all to her?

"What do you do?" He recalled something, and rephrased it. "Who *are* you?"

She looked startled. "I'm a mysteliologist."

He spread his hands. "I don't even know what that is."

"Come to think of it, there was no such thing when you left."

"That's it, in a way," he said. He felt helpless again. "Obviously, I had no way of knowing what you'd do, what you'd become, what would happen to you that you had no control over. All I was gambling on was that you'd remember me. Because that way . . ." He saw the planet Earth looming once more out the viewport. So many, many years and only six months later. A planet full of strangers. It didn't matter that Amity was full of strangers. But Earth was home, if that word still had any meaning for him.

"I wanted somebody my own age I could talk to," he said. "That's all. All I want is a friend."

He could see her trying to understand what it was like. She wouldn't, but maybe she'd come close enough to think she did.

"Maybe you've found one," she said, and smiled. "At least I'm willing to get to know you, considering the effort you've put into this."

"It wasn't much effort. It seems so long-term to you, but it wasn't to me. I held you on my lap six months ago."

"How long is your leave?" she asked.

"Two months."

"Would you like to come stay with us for a while? We have room in our house."

"Will your husband mind?"

"Neither my husband nor my wife. That's them sitting over there, pretending to ignore us." Ian looked, caught the eye of a woman in her late twenties. She was sitting across from a man Ian's age, who now turned and looked at Ian with some suspicion but no active animosity. The woman smiled; the man reserved judgment.

Radiant had a wife. Well, times change.

"Those two in the red skirts are police," Radiant was saying. "So is that man over by the wall, and the one at the end of the bar."

"I spotted two of them," Ian said. When she looked surprised, he said, "Cops always have a look about them. That's one of the things that don't change."

"You go back quite a ways, don't you? I'll bet you have some good stories."

Ian thought about it, and nodded. "Some, I suppose."

"I should tell the police they can go home. I hope you don't mind that we brought them in."

"Of course not."

"I'll do that, and then we can go. Oh, and I guess I should call the children and tell them we'll be home soon." She laughed, reached across the table and touched his hand. "See what can happen in six months? I have three children, and Gillian has two."

He looked up, interested.

"Are any of them girls?"

PALELY LOITERING

Christopher Priest

We close with two more stories that look at the manipulation of time. I have saved them to the end because of their unusual scenarios which I will let the authors unfold.

Christopher Priest is one of Britain's most respected writers of science fiction and the fantastic. His 1995 novel, The Prestige, *about the rivalry between two stage magicians, was filmed by Christopher Nolan in 2006 and has since been adapted for the stage. His other work, some of which incorporates elements of time and a psychic distortion of reality, includes* The Inverted World *(1974),* The Space Machine *(1976),* A Dream of Wessex *(1977) and* The Separation *(2002).*

i

During the summers of my childhood, the best treat of all was our annual picnic in Flux Channel Park, which lay some fifty miles from home. Because my father was set in his ways, and for him no picnic would be worthy of its name without a joint of freshly roasted cold ham, the first clue we children had was always, therefore, when Cook began her preparations. I made a point every day of slipping down unnoticed to the cellar to count the hams that hung from steel hooks in the ceiling, and as soon as I found one was missing I would hurry to my sisters and share the news. The next day, the house would fill with the rich aroma of ham roasting in cloves, and we three children would enter an elaborate charade: inside we would be brimming over with excitement at the thought of the adventure, but at the same time restraining ourselves to act normally, because Father's announcement of his plans at breakfast on the chosen day was an important part of the fun.

We grew up in awe and dread of our father, for he was a distant and strict man. Throughout the winter months, when his work made its greatest demands, we hardly saw him, and all we knew of him were the instructions passed on to us by Mother or the governor. In the summer months he chose to maintain the distance, joining us only for meals, and spending the evenings alone in his study. However, once a year my father would mellow, and for this alone the excursions to the Park would have been cause for joy. He knew the excitement the trip held for us and he played up to it, revealing the instinct of showman and actor.

Sometimes he would start by pretending to scold or punish us for some imaginary misdemeanour, or would ask Mother a misleading question, such as whether it was that day the servants were taking a holiday, or he would affect absent-mindedness; through all this we would hug our knees under the table, knowing what was to come. Then at last he would utter the magic words "Flux Channel Park", and, abandoning our charade with glee, we children would squeal with delight and run to Mother, the servants would bustle in and clear away the breakfast, there would be a clatter of dishes and the creak of the wicker hamper from the kitchen . . . and at long last the crunching of hooves and steel-rimmed wheels would sound on the gravel drive outside, as the taxi-carriage arrived to take us to the station.

ii

I believe that my parents went to the Park from the year they were married, but my own first clear memory of a picnic is when I was seven years old. We went as a family every year until I was fifteen. For nine summers that I can remember, then, the picnic was the happiest day of the year, fusing in memory into one composite day, each picnic much like all the others, so carefully did Father orchestrate the treat for us. And yet one day stands out from all the others because of a moment of disobedience and mischief, and after that those summery days in Flux Channel Park were never quite the same again.

It happened when I was ten years old. The day had started like any other picnic day, and by the time the taxi arrived the servants had gone on ahead to reserve a train compartment for us. As we clambered into the carriage, Cook ran out of the house to wave us away, and she gave each of us children a freshly peeled carrot to gnaw on. I took mine whole into my mouth, distending my cheeks, and sucking and nibbling at it slowly, mashing it gradually into a juicy pulp. As we rattled down to the station I saw Father glancing at me once or twice, as if to tell me not to make so much noise with my mouth . . . but it was a holiday from everything, and he said nothing.

My mother, sitting opposite us in the carriage, issued her usual instructions to my sisters. "Salleen," (my elder sister), "you're to keep an eye on Mykle. You know how he runs around." (I, sucking my carrot, made a face at Salleen, bulging a cheek with the carrot and squinting my eyes.) "And you, Therese, you must stay by me. None of you is to go too close to the Channel." Her instructions came too soon – the train-ride was of second-order interest, but it came between us and the Park.

I enjoyed the train, smelling the sooty smoke and watching the steam curl past the compartment window like an attendant white wraith, but my sisters, especially Salleen, were unaccustomed to the motion and felt sick. While Mother fussed over the girls and summoned the servants from their compartment further down the train, Father and I sat gravely beside each other. When Salleen had been taken away down the train and Therese had quietened I started to fidget in my seat, craning my neck to peer forward, seeking that first magical glimpse of the silvery ribbon of the Channel.

"Father, which bridge shall we cross this time?" And, "Can we cross *two* bridges today, like last year?"

Always the same answer. "We shall decide when we arrive. Keep still, Mykle."

And so we arrived, tugging at our parents' hands to hurry them, waiting anxiously by the gate as the entrance fees were paid. The first dashing run down the sloping green sward of the Park grounds, dodging the trees and jumping high to see along the Channel, shouting disappointment because there were too many people there already, or not enough. Father beamed at us and lit his pipe, flicking back the flaps of his frock-coat and thrusting his thumbs into his waistcoat, then strolled beside Mother as she held his arm. My sisters and I walked or ran, depending on our constitutional state, heading towards the Channel, but slowing when awed by its closeness, not daring to approach. Looking back, we saw Father and Mother waving to us from the shade of the trees, needlessly warning us of the dangers.

As always, we hurried to the tollbooths for the time bridges that crossed the Channel, for it was these bridges that were the whole reason for the day's trip. A line of people were waiting at each booth, moving forward slowly to pay the entrance fee: families like ourselves with children dancing, young couples holding hands, single men and women glancing speculatively at each other. We counted the people in each queue, eagerly checked the results with each other, then ran back to our parents.

"Father, there are only twenty-six people at the Tomorrow Bridge!"

"There's *no one* at the Yesterday Bridge!" Salleen, exaggerating as usual.

"Can we cross into Tomorrow, Mother?"

"We did that last year." Salleen, still disgruntled from the train, kicked out feebly at me. "Mykle *always* wants to go to Tomorrow!"

"No I don't. The queue is longer for Yesterday!"

Mother, soothingly, "We'll decide after lunch. The queues will be shorter then."

Father, watching the servants laying our cloth beneath a dark old cedar tree, said, "Let us walk for a while, my dear. The children can come too. We will have luncheon in an hour or so."

Our second exploration of the Park was more orderly, conducted, as it was, under Father's eye. We walked again to the nearest part of the Channel – it seemed less risky now, with parents there – and followed one of the paths that ran parallel to the bank. We stared at the people on the other side.

"Father, are they in Yesterday or Tomorrow?"

"I can't say, Mykle. It could be either."

"They're nearer to the Yesterday Bridge, stupid!" Salleen, pushing me from behind.

"That doesn't mean anything, stupid!" Jabbing back at her with an elbow.

The sun reflecting from the silvery surface of the flux fluid (we sometimes called it water, to my father's despair) made it glitter and sparkle like rippling quicksilver. Mother would not look at it, saying the reflections hurt her eyes, but there was always something dreadful about its presence so that no one could look too long. In the still patches, where the mystifying currents below briefly let the surface settle, we sometimes saw upside-down reflections of the people on the other side.

Later: we edged around the tolls, where the lines of people were longer than before, and walked further along the bank towards the east.

Then later: we returned to the shade and the trees, and sat in a demure group while lunch was served. My father carved ham with the precision of the expert chef: one cut down at an angle towards the bone, another horizontally across to the bone, and the wedge of meat so produced taken away on a plate by one of the servants. Then the slow, meticulous carving beneath the notch. One slice after another, each one slightly wider and rounder than the one before.

As soon as lunch was finished we made our way to the toll-booths and queued with the other people. There were always fewer people waiting at this time of the afternoon, a fact that surprised us but which our parents took for granted. This day we had chosen the Tomorrow Bridge. Whatever the preferences we children expressed Father always had the last word. It did not, however, prevent Salleen from sulking, nor me from letting her see the joys of victory.

This particular day was the first time I had been to the Park with any understanding of the Flux Channel and its real purpose. Earlier in the summer, the governor had instructed us in the rudiments of spatio-temporal physics . . . although that was not the name he gave to it. My sisters had been bored with the subject (it was boys' stuff, they declared), but to learn how and why the Channel had been built was fascinating to me.

I had grown up with a general understanding that we lived in a world where our ancestors had built many marvellous things that we no longer used or had need for. This awareness, gleaned from the few other children I knew, was of astonishing and miraculous achievements, and was, as might be expected, wildly inaccurate. I knew as a fact, for instance, that the Flux Channel had been built in a matter of days, that jet-propelled aircraft could circumnavigate the world in a matter of minutes, and that houses and automobiles and railway trains could be built in a matter of seconds. Of course the truth was quite different, and our education in the scientific age and its history was constantly interesting to me.

In the case of the Flux Channel, I knew by my tenth birthday that it had taken more than two decades to build, that its construction had cost many human lives, and that it had taxed the resources and intelligence of many different countries.

Furthermore, the principle on which it worked was well understood today, even though we had no use for it as it was intended.

We lived in the age of starflight, but by the time I was born mankind had long lost the desire to travel in space.

The governor had shown us a slowed-down film of the launching of the craft that had flown to the stars: the surface of the Flux Channel undulating as the starship was propelled through its deeps like a huge whale trying to navigate a canal. Then the hump of its hull bursting through the surface in a shimmering spray of exploding foam, and the gushing wake sluicing over the banks of the Channel and vanishing instantaneously. Then the actual launch, with the starship soaring into the sky, leaving a trail of brilliant droplets in the air behind it.

All this had taken place in under one-tenth of a second. Anyone within twenty-five miles of the launch would have been killed by the shockwave, and it is said that the thunder of the starship's passage could be heard in every country of the Neuropean Union. Only the automatic high-speed cameras were there to witness the launching. The men and women who crewed the ship – their metabolic functions frozen for most of the flight – would not have felt the strain of such a tremendous acceleration even if they had been conscious. The flux field distorted time and space, changed the nature of matter. The ship was launched at such a high relative velocity that by the time the technicians returned to the Flux Channel it would have been outside the Solar System. By the time I was born, seventy years after this, the starship would have been ... who knows where?

Behind it, churning and eddying with temporal mystery, the Flux Channel lay across more than a hundred miles of the land, a scintillating, dazzling ribbon of light, like a slit in the world that looked towards another dimension.

There were no more starships after the first and that one had never returned. When the disturbance of the launching had calmed to a degree where the flux field was no longer a threat to human life, the stations that tapped the electricity had been built along part of its banks. A few years later, when the flux field had stabilized completely, an area of the countryside was landscaped to create the Park and the time bridges were built.

One of these traversed the Channel at an angle of exactly ninety degrees, and to walk across it was no different from crossing any bridge across any ordinary river.

One bridge was built slightly obtuse of the right-angle, and to cross it was to climb the temporal gradient of the flux field; when one emerged on the other side of the Channel, twenty-four hours had elapsed.

The third bridge was built slightly acute of the right-angle, and to cross to the other side was to walk twenty-four hours into the past. Yesterday, Today and Tomorrow existed on the far side of the Flux Channel, and one could walk at will among them.

iii

While waiting in line at the tollbooth, we had another argument about Father's decision to cross into Tomorrow. The Park management had posted a board above the paydesk, describing the weather conditions on the other side. There was wind, low cloud, sudden showers. My mother said that she did not wish to get wet. Salleen, watching me, quietly repeated that we had been to Tomorrow last year. I stayed quiet, looking across the Channel to the other side.

(Over there the weather seemed to be as it was here: a high, bright sky, hot sunshine. But what I could see was Today: yesterday's Tomorrow, tomorrow's Yesterday, today's Today.)

Behind us the queue was thinning as other, less hardy, people drifted away to the other bridges. I was content, because the only one that did not interest me was the Today Bridge, but to rub in my accidental victory I whispered to Salleen that the weather was good on the Yesterday side. She, in no mood for subtle perversity, kicked out at my shins and we squabbled stupidly as my father went to the toll.

He was an important man. I heard the attendant say, "But you shouldn't have waited, sir. We are honoured by your visit." He released the ratchet of the turnstile, and we filed through.

We entered the covered way of the bridge, a long dark tunnel of wood and metal, lit at intervals by dim incandescent lamps. I ran on ahead, feeling the familiar electric tingle over my body as I moved through the flux field.

"Mykle! Stay with us!" My father, calling from behind.

I slowed obediently and turned to wait. I saw the rest of the family coming towards me. The outlines of their bodies were strangely diffused, an effect of the field on all who entered it. As they reached me, and thus came into the zone I was in, their shapes became sharply focused once more.

I let them pass me, and followed behind. Salleen, walking beside me, kicked out at my ankles.

"Why did you do that?"

"Because you're a little pig!"

I ignored her. We could see the end of the covered way ahead. It had become dark soon after we started crossing the bridge – a presage of the evening of the day we were leaving – but now daylight shone again and I saw pale blue morning light, misty shapes of trees. I paused, seeing my parents and sisters silhouetted against the light. Therese, holding Mother's hand, took no notice of me, but Salleen, whom I secretly loved, strutted proudly behind Father, asserting her independence of me. Perhaps it was because of her, or perhaps it was that morning light shining down from the end of the tunnel, but I stayed still as the rest of the family went on.

I waved my hands, watching the fingertips blur as they moved across the flux field, and then I walked on slowly. Because of the blurring my family were now almost invisible. Suddenly I was a little frightened, alone in the flux field, and I hastened after them. I saw their ghostly shapes move into daylight and out of sight (Salleen glanced back towards me), and I walked faster.

By the time I had reached the end of the covered way, the day had matured and the light was that of mid-afternoon. Low clouds were scudding before a stiff wind. As a squall of rain swept by I sheltered in the bridge, and looked across the Park for the family. I saw them a short distance away, hurrying towards one of the pagoda-shaped shelters the Park authorities had built. Glancing at the sky I saw there was a large patch of blue not far away, and I knew the shower would be a short one. It was not cold and I did not mind getting wet, but I hesitated before going out into the open. Why I stood there I do not now recall, but I had always had a childish delight in the sensation of the flux field, and at the place where the covered way ends the bridge is still over a part of the Channel.

I stood by the edge of the bridge and looked down at the flux fluid. Seen from directly above it closely resembled water, because it seemed to be clear (although the bottom could not be seen), and did not have the same metallic sheen or quicksilver property it had when viewed from the side. There were bright highlights on the surface, glinting as the fluid stirred, as if there were a film of oil across it.

My parents had reached the pagoda – whose colourful tiles and paintwork looked odd in this dismal rain – and they were squeezing in with the two girls, as other people made room for them. I could see my father's tall black hat, bobbing behind the crowd.

Salleen was looking back at me, perhaps envying my solitary state, and so I stuck out my tongue at her. I was showing off. I went to the edge of the bridge, where there was no guard rail, and leaned precariously out above the fluid. The flux field prickled around me. I saw Salleen tugging at Mother's arm, and Father took a step forward into the rain. I poised myself and jumped towards the bank, flying above the few inches of the Channel between me and the ground. I heard a roaring in my ears, I was momentarily blinded, and the charge of the flux field enveloped me like an electric cocoon.

I landed feet-first on the muddy bank, and looked around me as if nothing untoward had happened.

iv

Although I did not realize it at first, in leaping from the bridge and moving up through a part of the flux field, I had travelled in time. It happened that I landed on a day in the future when the weather was as grey and blustery as on the day I had left, and so my first real awareness, when I looked up, was that the pagoda had suddenly emptied. I stared in horror across the parkland, not believing that my family could have vanished in the blink of an eye.

I started to run, stumbling and sliding on the slippery ground, and I felt a panicky terror and a dread of being abandoned. All the cockiness in me had gone. I sobbed as I ran, and when I reached the pagoda I was crying aloud, snivelling and wiping my nose and eyes on the sleeve of my jacket.

I went back to where I had landed, and saw the muddy impressions of my feet on the bank. From there I looked at the bridge, so tantalizingly close, and it was then that I realized what I had done, even though it was a dim understanding.

Something like my former mood returned then and a spirit of exploration came over me. After all, it was the first time I had ever been alone in the Park. I started to walk away from the bridge, following a tree-lined path that went along the Channel.

The day I had arrived in must have been a weekday in winter or early spring because the trees were bare and there were very few people about. From this side of the Channel I could see that the tollbooths were open, but the only other people in the Park were a long way away.

For all this, it was still an adventure and the awful thoughts about where I had arrived, or how I was to return, were put aside.

I walked a long way, enjoying the freedom of being able to explore this side without my family. When they were present it was as if I could only see what they pointed out, and walk where they chose. Now it was like being in the Park for the first time.

This small pleasure soon palled. It was a cold day and my light summer shoes began to feel sodden and heavy, chafing against my toes. The Park was not at all how I liked it to be. Part of the fun on a normal day was the atmosphere of shared daring, and mixing with people you knew had not all come from the same day, the same time. Once, my father, in a mood of exceptional capriciousness, had led us to and fro across the Today and Yesterday Bridges, showing us time-slipped images of himself which he had made on a visit to the Park the day before. Visitors to the Park often did such things. During the holidays, when the big factories were closed, the Park would be full of shouting, laughing voices as carefully prepared practical jokes of this sort were played.

None of this was going on as I tramped along under the leaden sky. The future was for me as commonplace as a field.

I began to worry, wondering how I was to get back. I could imagine the wrath of my father, the tears of my mother, the endless jibes I would get from Salleen and Therese. I turned around and walked quickly back towards the bridges, forming a half-hearted plan to cross the Channel repeatedly, using the Tomorrow and Yesterday Bridges in turn, until I was back where I started.

I was running again, in danger of sobbing, when I saw a young man walking along the bank towards me. I would have paid no attention to him, but for the fact that when we were a short distance apart he sidestepped so that he was in front of me.

I slowed, regarded him incuriously, and went to walk around him . . . but much to my surprise he called after me.

"Mykle! It is Mykle, isn't it?"

"How do you know my name?" I said, pausing and looking at him warily.

"I was looking for you. You've jumped forward in time, and don't know how to get back."

"Yes, but—"

"I'll show you how. It's easy."

We were facing each other now, and I was wondering who he was and how he knew me. There was something much too friendly about him. He was very tall and thin, and had the beginnings of a moustache darkening his lip. He seemed adult to me, but when he spoke it was with a hoarse, boyish falsetto.

I said, "It's all right, thank you, sir. I can find my own way."

"By running across the bridges?"

"How did you know?"

"You'll never manage it, Mykle. when you jumped from the bridge you went a long way into the future. About thirty-two years."

"This is . . .?" I looked around at the Park, disbelieving what he said. "But it feels like—"

"Just like Tomorrow. But it isn't. You've come a long way. Look over there." He pointed across the Channel, to the other side. "Do you see those houses? You've never seen those before, have you?"

There was an estate of new houses, built beyond the trees on the Park's perimeter. True, I hadn't noticed them before, but it proved nothing. I didn't find this very interesting, and I began to sidle away from him, wanting to get on with the business of working out how to get back.

"Thank you, sir. It was nice to meet you."

"Don't call me 'sir'," he said, laughing. "You've been taught to be polite to strangers, but you must know who *I* am."

"N-no . . ." Suddenly rather nervous of him I walked quickly away, but he ran over and caught me by the arm.

"There's something I must show you," he said. "This is very important. Then I'll get you back to the bridge."

"Leave me alone!" I said loudly, quite frightened of him.

He took no notice of my protests, but walked me along the path beside the Channel. He was looking over my head, across the Channel, and I could not help noticing that whenever we passed a tree or a bush which cut off the view he would pause and look past it before going on. This continued until we were near the time bridges again, when he came to a halt beside a huge sprawling rhododendron bush.

"Now," he said. "I want you to look. But don't let yourself be seen."

Crouching down with him, I peered around the edge of the bush. At first I could not imagine what it was I was supposed to be looking at, and thought it was more houses for my inspection. The estate did, in fact, continue all along the further edge of the Park, just visible beyond the trees.

"Do you see her?" He pointed, then ducked back. Following the direction, I saw a young woman sitting on a bench on the far side of the Channel.

"Who is she?" I said, although her small figure did not actually arouse much curiosity in me.

"The loveliest girl I have ever seen. She's always there, on that bench. She is waiting for her lover. She sits there every day, her heart filled with anguish and hope."

As he said this the young man's voice broke, as if with emotion, and I glanced up at him. His eyes were moist.

I peered again around the edge of the bush and looked at the girl, wondering what it was about her that produced this reaction. I could hardly see her, because she was huddled against the wind and had a shawl drawn over her hair. She was sitting to one side, facing towards the Tomorrow Bridge. To me, she was approximately as interesting as the houses, which is not to say very much, but she seemed important to the young man.

"Is she a friend of yours?" I said, turning back to him.

"No, not a friend, Mykle. A symbol. A token of the love that is in us all."

"What is her name?" I said, not following this interpretation.

"Estyll. The most beautiful name in the world."

Estyll: I had never heard the name before, and I repeated it softly.

"How do you know this?" I said. "You say you—"

"Wait, Mykle. She will turn in a moment. You will see her face."

His hand was clasping my shoulder, as if we were old friends, and although I was still shy of him it assured me of his good intent. He was sharing something with me, something so important that I was honoured to be included.

Together we leaned forward again and looked clandestinely at her. By my ear, I heard my friend say her name, so softly that it was almost a whisper. A few moments passed, then, as if the time vortex above the Channel had swept the word slowly across to her, she raised her head, shrugged back the shawl, and stood up. I was craning my neck to see her but she turned away. I watched her walk up the slope of the Park grounds, towards the houses beyond the trees.

"Isn't she a beauty, Mykle?"

I was too young to understand him fully, so I said nothing. At that age, my only awareness of the other sex was that my sisters were temperamentally and physically different from me. I had yet to discover more interesting matters. In any event, I had barely caught a glimpse of Estyll's face.

The young man was evidently enraptured by the girl, and as we watched her move through the distant trees my attention was half on her, half on him.

"I should like to be the man she loves," he said at last.

"Do you . . . love her, sir?"

"Love? What I feel is too noble to be contained in such a word." He looked down at me, and for an instant I was reminded of the haughty disdain that my father sometimes revealed when I did something stupid. "Love is for lovers, Mykle. *I* am a romantic, which is a far grander thing to be."

I was beginning to find my companion rather pompous and overbearing, trying to involve me in his passions. I was an argumentative child, though, and could not resist pointing out a contradiction.

"But you said she was waiting for her lover," I said.

"Just a supposition."

"I think you are her lover, and won't admit it."

I used the word disparagingly, but it made him look at me thoughtfully. The drizzle was coming down again, a dank veil across the countryside. The young man stepped away suddenly. I think he had grown as tired of my company as I had of his.

"I was going to show you how to get back," he said. "Come with me." He set off towards the bridge, and I went after him. "You'll have to go back the way you came. You jumped, didn't you?"

"That's right," I said, puffing a little. It was difficult keeping up with him.

As we reached the end of the bridge, the young man left the path and walked across the grass to the edge of the Channel. I held back, nervous of going too close again.

"Ah!" said the young man, peering down at the damp soil. "Look, Mykle . . . these must be your footprints. This was where you landed."

I went forward warily and stood just behind him.

"Put your feet in these marks and jump towards the bridge."

Although the metal edge of the bridge was only an arm's length away from where we were standing it seemed a formidable jump, especially as the bridge was higher than the bank. I pointed this out.

"I'll be behind you," the young man said. "You won't slip. Now . . . look on the bridge. There's a scratch on the floor. Do you see it? You have to aim at that. Try to land with one foot on either side, and you'll be back where you started."

It all seemed rather unlikely. The part of the bridge he was pointing out was wet with rain and looked slippery. If I landed badly I would fall; worse, I could slip backwards into the flux fluid. Although I sensed that my new friend was right – that I could only get back by the way I had come – it did not *feel* right.

"Mykle, I know what you're thinking. But I made that mark. I've done it myself. Trust me."

I was thinking of my father and his wrath, so at last I stepped forward and put my feet in the squelching impressions I had made as I landed. Rainwater was oozing down the muddy bank towards the flux fluid, but I noticed that as it dripped down to touch the fluid it suddenly leaped back, just like the droplets of whisky on the side of the glass my father drank in the evenings.

The young man took a grip on my belt, holding on so that I should not slip down into the Channel.

"I'll count to three, then you jump. I'll give you a shove. Are you ready?"

"I think so."

"You'll remember Estyll, won't you?"

I looked over my shoulder. His face was very close to mine.

"Yes, I'll remember her," I said, not meaning it.

"Right . . . brace yourself. It's quite a hop from here. One . . ."

I saw the fluid of the Channel below me and to the side. It was glistening eerily in the grey light.

". . . two . . . three . . ."

I jumped forward at the same instant as the young man gave me a hefty shove from behind. Instantly, I felt the electric crackle of the flux field, I heard again the loud roaring in my ears and there was a split-second of impenetrable blackness. My feet touched the edge of the time bridge and I tripped, sprawling forward on the floor. I slithered awkwardly against the legs of a man standing just there, and my face fetched up against a pair of shoes polished to a brilliant shine. I looked up.

There was my father, staring down at me in great surprise. All I can now remember of that frightful moment is his face glaring down at me, topped by his black, curly brimmed, stove-pipe hat. He seemed to be as tall as a mountain.

v

My father was not a man who saw the merit of short, sharp punishment, and I lived under the cloud of my misdeed for several weeks.

I felt that I had done what I had done in all innocence, and that the price I had to pay for it was too high. In our house, however, there was only one kind of justice and that was Father's.

Although I had been in the future for only about an hour of my subjective time, five or six hours had passed for my family and it was twilight when I returned. This prolonged absence was the main reason for my father's anger, although if I had jumped thirty-two years, as my companion had informed me, an error of a few hours on the return journey was as nothing.

I was never called upon to explain myself. My father detested excuses.

Salleen and Therese were the only ones who asked what had happened, and I gave them a shortened account: I said that after I jumped into the future, and realized what I had done, I explored the Park on my own and then jumped back. This was enough for them. I said nothing of the youth with the lofty sentiments, nor of the young lady who sat on the bench. (Salleen and Therese were thrilled enough that I had catapulted myself into the distant future, although my safe return did make the end of the story rather dull.) Internally, I had mixed feelings about my adventure. I spent a lot of time on my own – part of my punishment was that I could only go into the playroom one evening a week, and had to study more diligently instead – and tried to work out the meaning of what I had seen.

The girl, Estyll, meant very little to me. She certainly had a place in my memory of that hour in the future, but because she was so fascinating to my companion I remembered her through him, and she became of secondary interest.

I thought about the young man a great deal. He had gone to such pains to make a friend of me, and to include me in his private thoughts, and yet I remembered him as an intrusive and unwelcome presence. I often thought of his husky voice intoning those grand opinions, and even from the disadvantage of my junior years, his callow figure – all gangly limbs, slicked-back hair and downy moustache – was a comical one. For a long time I wondered who he could be. Although the answer seems obvious in retrospect it was some years before I realized it and whenever I was out in the town I would keep my eyes open in case we happened to meet.

My penance came to an end about three months after the picnic. This parole was never formally stated but understood by all concerned. The occasion was a party our parents allowed us to have for some visiting cousins and after that my misbehaviour was never again directly mentioned.

The following summer, when the time came around for another picnic in Flux Channel Park, my father interrupted our excited outpourings to deliver a short speech, reminding us that we must all stay together. This was said to us all, although Father gave me a sharp and meaningful look. It was a small, passing cloud, and it threw no shadow on the day. I was obedient and sensible throughout the picnic . . . but as we walked through the Park in the gentle heat of the day, I did not forget to look out for my helpful friend, nor for his adored Estyll. I looked, and kept looking, but neither of them was there that day.

vi

When I was eleven I was sent to school for the first time. I had spent my formative years in a household where wealth and influence were taken for granted, and where the governor had taken a lenient view of my education. Thrown suddenly into the company of boys from all walks of life, I retreated behind a manner of arrogance and condescension. It took two years to be scorned and beaten out of this, but well before then I had developed a wholehearted loathing for education and all that went with it. I became, in short, a student who did not study, and a pupil whose dislike for his fellows was heartily reciprocated.

I became an accomplished malingerer, and with the occasional connivance of one of the servants I could readily feign a convincing though unaccountable stomach ailment, or develop infectious-looking rashes. Sometimes I would simply stay at home. More frequently I would set off into the countryside on my bicycle and spend the day in pleasant musings.

On days like this I pursued my own form of education by reading, although this was by choice and not by compulsion. I eagerly read whatever novels and poetry I could lay my hands on: my preference in fiction was for adventure, and in poetry I soon discovered the romantics of the early nineteenth century, and the then much despised desolationists of two hundred years later. The stirring combinations of valour and unrequited love, of moral virtue and nostalgic wistfulness, struck deep into my soul and made more pointed my dislike of the routines of school.

It was at this time, when my reading was arousing passions that my humdrum existence could not satisfy, that my thoughts turned to the girl called Estyll.

I needed an object for the stirrings within me. I envied the romantic poets their soulful yearnings, for they, it seemed to me, had at least had the emotional experience with which to focus their desires. The despairing desolationists, lamenting the waste around them, at least had known life. Perhaps I did not rationalize this need quite so neatly at the time, but whenever I was aroused by my reading it was the image of Estyll that came most readily to mind.

Remembering what my companion had told me, and with my own sight of that small, huddled figure, I saw her as a lonely, heartbroken waif, squandering her life in a hopeless vigil. That she was unspeakably beautiful, and utterly faithful, went without saying.

As I grew older, my restlessness advanced. I felt increasingly isolated, not only from the other boys at school, but also from my family. My father's work was making more demands on him than ever before and he was unapproachable. My sisters were going their own separate ways: Therese had developed an interest in ponies, Salleen in young men.

Nobody had time for me; no one tried to understand.

One autumn, some three or four years after I started school, I surrendered at last to the stirrings of soul and flesh, and attempted to allay them.

vii

I selected the day with care, one when there were several lessons at school where my absence would not be too obvious. I left home at the usual time in the morning, but instead of heading for school I rode to the city, bought a return ticket to the Park at the railway station, and settled down on the train.

During the summer there had been the usual family outing to the Park, but it had meant little to me. I had outgrown the immediate future. Tomorrow no longer concerned me.

I was vested with purpose. When I arrived at the Park on that stolen day I went directly to the Tomorrow Bridge, paid the toll, and set off through the covered way towards the other side. There were more people about than I had expected, but it was quiet enough for what I wanted to do. I waited until I was the only one on the bridge, then went to the end of the covered way and stood by the spot from which I had first jumped. I took a flint from my pocket and scratched a thin but deep line in the metal surface of the bridge.

I slipped the flint back in my pocket then looked appraisingly at the bank below. I had no way of knowing how far to jump, only an instinct and a vague memory of how I had done it before. The temptation was to jump as far as possible, but I managed to suppress it.

I placed my feet astride the line, took a deep breath . . . and launched myself towards the bank.

A dizzying surge of electric tingling, momentary darkness, and I sprawled across the bank.

Before I took stock of my surroundings I marked the place where I had landed. First I scraped a deep line in the soil and grass with the flint, pointing back towards the mark on the bridge (which was still visible, though less bright), then I tore away several tufts of grass around my feet to make a second mark. Thirdly, I stared intently at the precise place, fixing it in memory, so there would be no possibility of not finding it again.

When satisfied, I stood up and looked around at this future.

viii

It was a holiday. The Park was crowded with people, all gay in summer clothes. The sun shone down from a cloudless sky, a breeze rippled the ladies' dresses, and from a distant pagoda a band played stirring marches. It was all so familiar that my first instinct was that my parents and sisters must be somewhere about and my illicit visit would be discovered. I ducked down against the bank of the Channel, but then I laughed at myself and relaxed; in my painstaking anticipation of this exploit I had considered the possibility of meeting people I knew, and had decided that the chance was too slender to be taken seriously. Anyway, when I looked again at the people passing – who were paying me no attention – I realized that there were subtle differences in their clothes and hair-styles, reminding me that for all the superficial similarities I had indeed travelled to the future.

I scrambled up to the tree-lined pathway and mingled with the throng, quickly catching the spirit of the day. I must have looked like any other schoolboy, but I felt very special indeed. After all, I had now leaped into the future twice.

This euphoria aside, I was there with a purpose, and I did not forget it. I looked across to the other bank, searching for a sight of Estyll. She was not by the bench, and I felt a crushing and illogical disappointment, as if she had deliberately betrayed me by not being there. All the frustration of the past months welled up in me, and I could have shouted with the agony of it. But then, miraculously it seemed, I saw her some distance away from the bench, wandering to and fro on the path on her side, glancing occasionally towards the Tomorrow Bridge. I recognized her at once, although I am not sure how; during that other day in the future I had barely seen her, and since then my imagination had run with a free rein, yet the moment I saw her I knew it was she.

Gone was the shawl, and the arms that had been wrapped for warmth about her body were now folded casually across her chest. She was wearing a light summer frock, coloured in a number of pastel shades, and to my eager eyes it seemed that no lovelier clothes could have been worn by any woman in the world. Her short hair fell prettily about her face, and the way she held her head, and the way she stood, seemed delicate beyond words.

I watched her for several minutes, transfixed by the sight of her. People continued to mill past me, but for all I was aware of them they might not have been there.

At last I remembered my purpose, even though just seeing her was an experience whose joys I could not have anticipated. I walked back down the path, past the Tomorrow Bridge and beyond to the Today Bridge. I hastened across and let myself through the exit turnstile on the other side. Still in the same day, I went up the path towards where I had seen Estyll.

There were fewer people on this side of the Channel, of course, and the path was less crowded. I looked around as I walked, noticing that custom had not changed and that many people were sitting in the shade of the trees with the remains of picnic meals spread out around them. I did not look too closely at these groups – it was still at the back of my mind that I might see my own family here.

I passed the line of people waiting at the Tomorrow tollbooth and saw the path continuing beyond. A short distance away, walking slowly to and fro, was Estyll.

At the sight of her, now so near to me, I paused.

I walked on, less confidently than before. She glanced in my direction once, but she looked at me in the same uninterested way as she looked at everybody. I was only a few yards from her, and my heart was pounding and I was trembling. I realized that the little speech I had prepared – the one in which I introduced myself, then revealed myself as witty and mature, then proposed that she take a walk with me – had gone from my mind. She looked so grown-up, so sure of herself.

Unaware of my concentrated attention on her, she turned away when I was within touching distance of her. I walked on a few more paces, desperately unsure of myself. I turned and faced her.

For the first time in my life I felt the pangs of uncontrollable love. Until then the word had had no meaning for me but as I stood before her I felt for her a love so shocking that I could only flinch away from it. How I must have appeared to her I cannot say. I must have been shaking; I must have been bright with embarrassment. She looked at me with calm grey eyes and an enquiring expression, as if she detected that I had something of immense importance to say. She was so beautiful! I felt so clumsy!

Then she smiled, unexpectedly, and I had my cue to say something. Instead, I stared at her, not even thinking of what I could say, but simply immobilized by the unexpected struggle with my emotions. I had thought love was so simple.

Moments passed and I could cope with the turbulence no more. I took a step back and then another. Estyll had continued to smile at me during those long seconds of my wordless stare, and as I moved away her smile broadened and she parted her lips as if to say something. It was too much for me. I turned away, burning with embarrassment, and started to run. After a few steps, I halted and looked back at her. She was still looking at me, still smiling.

I shouted, "*I love you!*"

It seemed to me that everyone in the Park had heard me. I did not wait to see Estyll's reaction. I ran away. I hurried along the path, then ran up a grassy bank and into the shelter of some trees. I ran and ran, crossing the concourse of the open-air restaurant, crossing a broad lawn, diving into the cover of more trees beyond.

It was as if the physical effort of running would stop me thinking, because the moment I rested the enormity of what I had done flooded in on me. It seemed that I had done nothing right and everything wrong. I had had a chance to meet her and I had let it slip through my fingers. Worst of all, I had shouted my love at her, revealing it to the world. To my adolescent mind it seemed there could have been no grosser mistake.

I stood under the trees, leaning my forehead against the trunk of an old oak, banging my fist in frustration and fury.

I was terrified that Estyll would find me and I never wanted to see her again. At the same time I wanted her and loved her with a renewed passion . . . and hoped, but hoped secretly, that she would be searching for me in the Park, and would come to me by my tree and put her arms around me.

A long time passed and gradually my turbulent and contradictory emotions subsided.

I still did not want to see Estyll, so when I walked down to the path I looked carefully ahead to be sure I would not meet her. When I stepped down to the path itself – where people still walked in casual enjoyment, unaware of the drama – I looked along it towards the bridges, but saw no sign of her. I could not be sure she had left so I hung around, torn between wincing shyness of her and profound devotion.

At last I decided to risk it and hurried along the path to the tollbooths. I did not look for her and I did not see her. I paid the toll at the Today Bridge and returned to the other side. I located the marks I had made on the bank beside the Tomorrow Bridge, aimed myself at the scratch on the bridge floor, and leaped across towards it.

I emerged in the day I had left. Once again, my rough-and-ready way of travelling through time did not return me to a moment precisely true to elapsed time, but it was close enough. When I checked my watch against the clock in the toll-booth, I discovered I had been gone for less than a quarter of an hour. Meanwhile, I had been in the future for more than three hours.

I caught an earlier train home and idled away the rest of the day on my bicycle in the countryside, reflecting on the passions of man, the glories of young womanhood, and the accursed weaknesses of the will.

ix

I should have learned from experience, and never tried to see Estyll again, but there was no quieting the love I felt for her. Thoughts of her dominated every waking moment. It was the memory of her smile that was central. She had been encouraging me, inviting me to say the very things I had wanted to say, and I missed the chance. So, with the obsession renewed and intensified, I returned to the Park and did so many times.

Whenever I could safely absent myself from school and could lay my hands on the necessary cash I went to the Tomorrow

Bridge and leapt across to the future. I was soon able to judge that dangerous leap with a marvellous instinctive skill. Naturally, there were mistakes. Once, terrifyingly, I landed in the night, and after that experience I always took a small pocket flashlight with me. On two or three occasions my return jump was inaccurate, and I had to use the timebridges to find the day I should have been in.

After a few more of my leaps into the future I felt sufficiently at home to approach a stranger in the Park and ask him the date. By telling me the year he confirmed that I was exactly twenty-seven years into the future . . . or, as it had been when I was ten, thirty-two years ahead. The stranger I spoke to was apparently a local man and by his appearance a man of some substance, and I took him sufficiently into my confidence to point out Estyll to him. I asked him if he knew her, which he said he did, but could only confirm her given name. It was enough for me, because by then it suited my purpose not to know too much about her.

I made no more attempts to speak to Estyll. Barred from approaching her by my painful shyness I fell back on fantasies, which were much more in keeping with my timid soul. As I grew older, and became more influenced by my favourite poets, it seemed not only more sad and splendid to glorify her from a distance, but appropriate that my role in her life should be passive.

To compensate for my nervousness about trying to meet her again, I constructed a fiction about her.

She was passionately in love with a disreputable young man, who had tempted her with elaborate promises and wicked lies. At the very moment she had declared her love for him, he had deserted her by crossing the Tomorrow Bridge into a future from which he had never returned. In spite of his shameful behaviour her love held true and every day she waited in vain by the Tomorrow Bridge, knowing that one day he would return. I would watch her covertly from the other side of the Channel, knowing that her patience was that of the lovelorn. Too proud for tears, too faithful for doubt, she was at ease with the knowledge that her long wait would be its own reward.

In the present, in my real life, I sometimes dallied with another fiction: that *I* was her lover, that it was for me she was waiting.

This thought excited me, arousing responses of a physical kind that I did not fully understand.

I went to the Park repeatedly, gladly suffering the punishments at school for my frequent, and badly excused, truancies. So often did I leap across to that future that I soon grew accustomed to seeing other versions of myself, and realized that I had sometimes seen other young men before, who looked suspiciously like me, and who skulked near the trees and bushes beside the Channel and gazed across as wistfully as I. There was one day in particular – a lovely, sunny day, at the height of the holiday season – that I often lighted on, and here there were more than a dozen versions of myself, dispersed among the crowd.

One day, not long before my sixteenth birthday, I took one of my now customary leaps into the future and found a cold and windy day, almost deserted. As I walked along the path I saw a child, a small boy, plodding along with his head down against the wind and scuffing at the turf with the toes of his shoes. The sight of him, with his muddy legs and tear-streaked face, reminded me of that very first time I had jumped accidentally to the future. I stared at him as we approached each other. He looked back at me and for an instant a shock of recognition went through me like a bolt of electricity. He turned his eyes aside at once and stumped on by, heading towards the bridges behind me. I stared at him, recalling in vivid detail how I had felt that day, and how I had been fomenting a desperate plan to return to the day I had left, and as I did so I realized – at long last – the identity of the friend I had made that day.

My head whirling with the recognition I called after him, hardly believing what was happening.

"Mykle!" I said, the sound of my own name tasting strange in my mouth. The boy turned to look at me and I said a little uncertainly, "It is Mykle, isn't it?"

"How do you know my name?" His stance was truculent and he seemed unwilling to be spoken to.

"I . . . was looking for you," I said, inventing a reason for why I should have recognized him. "You've jumped forward in time, and don't know how to get back."

"Yes, but—"

"I'll show you how. It's easy."

As we were speaking a distracting thought came to me: so far I had, quite accidentally, duplicated the conversation of that day. But what if I were to change it consciously? Suppose I said something that my "friend" had not; suppose young Mykle were not to respond in the way I had? The consequences seemed enormous and I could imagine this boy's life – my own life – going in a direction entirely different. I saw the dangers of that and I knew I had to make an effort to repeat the dialogue, and my actions, precisely.

But just as it had when I tried to speak to Estyll, my mind went blank.

"It's all right, thank you, sir," the boy was saying. "I can find my own way."

"By running across the bridges?" I wasn't sure if that was what had been said to me before, but I knew that had been my intention.

"How did you know?"

I found I could not depend on that distant memory, and so, trusting to the inevitable sweep of destiny, I stopped trying to remember. I said whatever came to mind.

It was appalling to see myself through my own eyes. I had not imagined that I had been quite such a pathetic-looking child. I had every appearance of being a sullen and difficult boy. There was a stubbornness and a belligerence that I both recognized and disliked. And I knew there was a deeper weakness too. I could remember how I had seen myself, my older self, that is. I recalled my "friend" from this day as callow and immature, and mannered with a loftiness that did not suit his years. That I (as child) had seen myself (as young man) in this light was condemnation of my then lack of percipience. I had learned a lot about myself since going to school and I was more adult in my outlook than the other boys at school. What is more, since falling in love with Estyll I had taken great care over my appearance and clothes and whenever I made one of these trips to the future I looked my best.

However, in spite of the shortcomings I saw in myself-as-boy, I felt sorry for young Mykle and there was certainly a feeling of great spirit between us. I showed him what I had noticed of the changes in the Park and then we walked together towards the Tomorrow Bridge. Estyll was there on the other side of the Channel. I told him what I knew of her. I could not convey what was in my heart, but knowing how important she was to become to him, I wanted him to see her and love her.

After she had left, I showed him the mark I had made in the surface of the bridge. After I had persuaded him to make the leap – with several sympathetic thoughts about his imminent reception – I wandered alone in the blustery evening, wondering if Estyll would return. There was no sign of her.

I waited almost until nightfall, resolving that the years of admiring her from afar had been long enough. Something that young Mykle said had deeply affected me.

Allowing him a glimpse of my fiction, I had told him, "She is waiting for her lover." My younger self had replied, "I think you are her lover, and won't admit it."

I had forgotten saying that. I would not admit it, for it was not strictly true, but I would admit to the wish that it were so.

Staring across the darkening Channel, I wondered if there were a way of making it come true. The Park was an eerie place in that light, and the temporal stresses of the flux field seemed to take on a tangible presence. Who knew what tricks could be played by Time? I had already met myself – once, twice, and seen myself many times over – and who was to say that Estyll's lover could *not* be me?

In my younger self I had seen something about my older self that I could not see on my own. Mykle had said it, and I wanted it to be true. I would make myself Estyll's lover, and I would do it on my next visit to the Park.

x

There were larger forces at work than those of romantic destiny, because soon after I made this resolution my life was shaken out of its pleasant intrigues by the sudden death of my father.

I was shocked by this more profoundly than I could ever have imagined. In the last two or three years I had seen very little of him and thought about him even less. And yet, from the moment the maid ran into the drawing-room, shrilling that my father had collapsed across the desk in his study, I was stricken with the most awful guilt. It was I who had caused the death! I had been obsessed with myself, with Estyll . . . if only I had thought more of him he would not be dead!

In those sad days before the funeral my reaction seemed less than wholly illogical. My father knew as much about the workings of the flux field as any man alive, and after my childhood adventure he must have had some inkling that I had not left matters there. The school must have advised him of my frequent absences and yet he said nothing. It was almost as if he had been deliberately standing by, hoping something might come of it all.

In the days following his death, a period of emotional transition, it seemed to me that Estyll was inextricably bound up with the tragedy. However much it flew in the face of reason, I could not help feeling that if I had spoken to Estyll, if I had acted rather than hidden, then my father would still be alive.

I did not have long to dwell on this. When the first shock and grief had barely passed, it became clear that nothing would ever be quite the same again for me. My father had made a will, in which he bequeathed me the responsibility for his family, his work and his fortune.

I was still legally a child and one of my uncles took over the administration of the affairs until I reached my majority. This uncle, deeply resentful that none of the fortune had passed to him, made the most of his temporary control over our lives. I was removed from school and made to start in my father's work. The family house was sold, the governor and the other servants were discharged, and my mother was moved to a smaller household in the country. Salleen was quickly married off, and Therese was sent to boarding school. It was made plain that I should take a wife as soon as possible.

My love for Estyll – my deepest secret – was thrust away from me by forces I could not resist.

Until the day my father died I did not have much conception of what his work involved, except to know that he was one of the most powerful and influential men in the Neuropean Union. This was because he controlled the power stations which tapped energy from the temporal stresses of the flux field. On the day I inherited his position I assumed this meant he was fabulously wealthy, but I was soon relieved of this misapprehension. The power stations were state controlled and the so-called fortune comprised a large number of debentures in the enterprise. In real terms these could not be cashed, thus explaining many of the extreme decisions taken by my uncle. Death duties were considerable, and in fact I was in debt because of them for many years afterwards.

The work was entirely foreign to me and I was psychologically and academically unready for it, but because the family was now my responsibility, I applied myself as best I could. For a long time, shaken and confused by the abrupt change in our fortunes, I could do nothing but cope.

My adolescent adventures in Flux Channel Park became memories as elusive as dreams. It was as if I had become another person.

(But I had lived with the image of Estyll for so long that nothing could make me forget her. The flame of romanticism that had lighted my youth faded away, but it was never entirely extinguished. In time I lost my obsessive love for Estyll, but I could never forget her wan beauty, her tireless waiting.)

By the time I was twenty-two I was in command of myself. I had mastered my father's job. Although the position was hereditary, as most employment was hereditary, I discharged my duties well and conscientiously. The electricity generated by the flux field provided roughly nine-tenths of all the energy consumed in the Neuropean Union, and much of my time was spent in dealing with the multitude of political demands for it. I travelled widely, to every state in Federal Neurop, and further abroad.

Of the family: my mother was settling into her long years of widowhood and the social esteem that naturally followed. Both my sisters were married. Of course I too married in the end, succumbing to the social pressures that every man of standing has to endure. When I was twenty-one I was introduced to Dorynne, a cousin of Salleen's husband, and within a few months we were wed. Dorynne, an intelligent and attractive young woman, proved to be a good wife, and I loved her. When I was twenty-five, she bore our first child: a girl. I needed an heir, for that was the custom of my country, but we rejoiced at her birth.

We named her . . . well, we named her Therese, after my sister, but Dorynne had wanted to call her Estyll, a girl's name then very popular, and I had to argue against her. I never explained why.

Two years later my son Carl was born, and my position in society was secure.

xi

The years passed, and the glow of adolescent longing for Estyll dimmed still further. Because I was happy with my growing family, and fulfilled by the demands of my work, those strange experiences in Flux Channel Park seemed to be a minor aberration from a life that was solid, conventional and unadventurous. I was no longer romantic in outlook. I saw those noble sentiments as the product of immaturity and inexperience. Such was the change in me that Dorynne sometimes complained I was unimaginative.

But if the romance of Estyll faded with time, a certain residual curiosity about her did not. I wanted to know: what had become of her? Who was she? Was she as beautiful as I remembered her?

Setting out these questions has lent them an urgency they did not possess. They were the questions of idle moments, or when something happened to remind me of her. Sometimes, for instance, my work took me along the Flux Channel, and then I would think briefly of her. For a time a young woman worked in my office, and she had the same name. As I grew older, a year or more would sometimes pass without a thought of Estyll.

I should probably have gone for the rest of my life with these questions unanswered if it had not been for an event of major world importance. When the news of it became known it seemed for a time to be the most exciting event of the century, as in some ways it was. The starship that had been launched a hundred years before was returning.

This news affected every aspect of my work. At once I was involved in strategic and political planning at the highest level.

What it meant was this: the starship could only return to Earth by the same means as it had left. The Flux Channel would have to be reconverted, if only temporarily, to its original use.

The houses in its vicinity would have to be evacuated, the power stations would have to be disconnected, and the Park and its time bridges would have to be destroyed.

For me, the disconnection of the power stations – with the inevitable result of depriving the Neuropean Union of most of its electricity – created immense problems. Permission had to be sought from other countries to generate electricity from fossil deposits for the months the flux stations were inoperable, and permission of that sort could only be obtained after intricate political negotiation and bargaining. We had less than a year in which to achieve this.

But the coming destruction of the Park struck a deeper note in me, as it did in many people. The Park was a much loved playground, familiar to everyone, and, for many people, ineradicably linked with memories of childhood. For me, it was strongly associated with the idealism of my youth and with a girl I had loved for a time. If the Park and its bridges were closed, I knew that my questions about Estyll would never be answered.

I had leapt into a future where the Park was still a playground, where the houses beyond the trees were still occupied. Through all my life I had thought of that future as an imaginary or ideal world, one unattainable except by a dangerous leap from a bridge. But that future was no longer imaginary. I was now forty-two years old. It was thirty-two years since I, as a ten-year-old boy, had leapt thirty-two years into the future.

Today and Tomorrow co-existed once more in Flux Channel Park.

If I did not act in the next few weeks, before the Park was closed, I should never see Estyll again. The memory of her flared into flame again, and I felt a deep sense of frustration. I was much too busy to go in search of a boyhood dream.

I delegated. I relieved two subordinates from work in which they would have been better employed, and told them what I wanted them to discover on my behalf. They were to locate a young woman or girl who lived, possibly alone, possibly not, in one of the houses that bordered the Park.

The estate consisted of some two hundred houses. In time, my subordinates gave me a list of over a hundred and fifty possible names, and I scanned it anxiously. There were twenty-seven women living on the estate who were called Estyll. It was a popular name.

I returned one employee to his proper work, but retained the other, a woman named Robyn. I took her partially into my confidence. I said that the girl was a distant relative and that I was anxious to locate her, but for family reasons I had to be discreet. I believed she was frequently to be found in the Park. Within a few days, Robyn confirmed that there was one such girl. She and her mother lived together in one of the houses. The mother was confined to the house by the conventions of mourning (her husband had died within the last two years), and the daughter, Estyll, spent almost every day alone in the Park. Robyn said she was unable to discover why she went there.

The date had been fixed when Flux Channel Park would be closed to the public, and it was some eight and a half months ahead. I knew that I would soon be signing the order that would authorize the closure. One day between now and then, if for no other reason, Estyll's patient waiting would have to end.

I took Robyn further into my confidence. I instructed her to go to the Park and, by repeated use of the Tomorrow Bridge, go into the future. All she was to report back to me was the date on which Estyll's vigil ended. Whether Robyn wondered at the glimpses of my obsession she was seeing, I cannot say, but she went without demur and did my work for me. When she returned, she had the date: it was just over six weeks away.

That interview with Robyn was fraught with undertones that neither side understood. I did not want to know too much, because with the return of my interest in Estyll had come something of that sense of romantic mystery. Robyn, for her part, clearly had seen something that intrigued her. I found it all most unsettling.

I rewarded Robyn with a handsome cash bonus and returned her to her duties. I marked the date in my private diary, then gave my full attention to the demands of my proper work.

xii

As the date approached I knew I could not be at the Park. On that day there was to be an energy conference in Geneva and there was no possibility of my missing it. I made a futile attempt to change the date, but who was I against fifty heads of state? Once more I was tempted to let the great preoccupation of my youth stay forever unresolved, but again I succumbed to it. I could not miss this one last chance.

I made my travel arrangements to Geneva with care and instructed my secretarial staff to reserve me a compartment on the one overnight train which would get me there in time.

It meant that I should have to visit the Park on the day before the vigil was to end, but by using the Tomorrow Bridge I could still be there to see it.

At last the day came. I had no one to answer to but myself. Shortly after midday I left my office and had my driver take me to the Park. I left him and the carriage in the yard beyond the gate, and with one glance towards the estate of houses I went into the Park.

I had not been in the Park itself since my last visit just before my father died. Knowing that one's childhood haunts often seem greatly changed when revisited years later I had been expecting to find the place smaller, less grand than I remembered it. But as I walked slowly down the gently sloping sward towards the tollbooths, it seemed that the magnificent trees, and the herbaceous borders, the fountains, the pathways, and all the various kinds of landscaping in the Park gardens were just as I recalled them.

But the smells! In my adolescent longing I had not responded to those. The sweet bark, the sweeping leaves, the clustered flowers. A man with a mowing machine clattered past, throwing up a moist green smell, and the shorn grass humped in the mower's hood like a sleeping furry animal. I watched the man as he reached the edge of the lawn he was cutting, turned the machine, then bent low over it to start it up the incline for his return. I had never pushed a mower, and as if this last day in the Park had restored my childhood I felt an urge to dash across to him and ask him if I might try my hand.

I smiled to myself as I walked on: I was a well-known public figure, and in my drape suit and tall silk hat I should certainly have cut a comic sight.

Then there were the sounds. I heard, as if for the first time (and yet also with a faint and distracting nostalgia), the metallic click of the turnstile ratchets, the sound of the breeze in the pines that surrounded the Park, and the almost continuous soprano of children's voices. Somewhere, a band was playing marches.

I saw a family at picnic beneath one of the weeping willows. The servants stood to one side, and the paterfamilias was carving a huge joint of cold beef. I watched them surreptitiously for a moment. It might have been my own family, a generation before; people's delights did not change.

So taken was I by all this that I had nearly reached the tollbooths before I remembered Estyll. Another private smile: my younger self would not have been able to understand this lapse. I was feeling more relaxed, welcoming the tranquil surroundings of the Park and remembering the past, but I had grown out of the obsessive associations the place had once had for me.

I had come to the Park to see Estyll, though, so I went on past the tollbooths until I was on the path that ran beside the Channel. I walked a short way, looking ahead. Soon I saw her, and she was sitting on the bench, staring towards the Tomorrow Bridge.

It was as if a quarter of a century had been obliterated. All the calm and restful mood went from me as if it had never existed, to be replaced by a ferment of emotions that was the more shocking for being so unexpected.

I came to a halt, turned away, thinking that if I looked at her any more she would surely notice me.

The adolescent, the immature, the romantic child ... I was still all of these, and the sight of Estyll awakened them as if from a short nap. I felt large and clumsy and ridiculous in my overformal clothes, as if I were a child wearing a grandparent's wedding outfit. Her composure, her youthful beauty, the vital force of her vigil ... they were enough to renew all those inadequacies I had felt as a teenager.

But at the same time there was a second image of her, one which lay above the other like an elusive ghost. I was seeing her as an adult sees a child.

She was so much younger than I remembered her! She was smaller. She was pretty, yes ... but I had seen prettier women. She was dignified, but it was a precocious poise, as if she had been trained in it by a socially conscious parent. And she was young, so very young! My own daughter, Therese, would be the same age now, perhaps slightly older.

Thus torn, thus acutely conscious of my divided way of seeing her, I stood in confusion and distraction on the pathway, while the families and couples walked gaily past.

I backed away from her at last, unable to look at her any more. She was wearing clothes I remembered too well from the past: a narrow white skirt tight around her legs, a shiny black belt, and a dark-blue blouse embroidered with flowers across the bodice.

(I remembered – I remembered so much, too much. I wished she had not been there.)

She frightened me because of the power she had, the power to awaken and arouse my emotions. I did not know what it was. Everyone has adolescent passions, but how many people have the chance to revisit those passions in maturity?

It elated me, but also made me deeply melancholic. Inside I was dancing with love and joy, but she terrified me. She was so innocently, glowingly young, and I was now so old.

xiii

I decided to leave the Park at once . . . but changed my mind an instant later. I went towards her, then turned yet again and walked away.

I was thinking of Dorynne, but trying to put her out of my mind. I was thinking of Estyll, obsessed again.

I walked until I was out of sight of her, then took off my hat and wiped my brow. It was a warm day but I knew that the perspiration was not caused by the weather. I needed to calm myself, wanted somewhere to sit down and think about it . . . but the Park was for pleasure, and when I went towards the open air restaurant to buy a glass of beer, the sight of all the heedless merriment was intrusive and unwelcome.

I stood on the uncut grass, watching the man with the mower, trying to control myself. I had come to the Park to satisfy an old curiosity, not to fall again into the traps of childhood infatuation. It was unthinkable that I should let a young girl of sixteen distract me from my stable life. It had been a mistake, a stupid mistake, to return to the Park.

But inevitably there was a deeper sense of destiny beneath my attempts to be sensible. I knew, without being able to say why, that Estyll was waiting there at her bench for me, and that we were destined at last to meet.

Her vigil was due to end tomorrow and that was just a short distance away. It lay on the far side of the Tomorrow Bridge.

xiv

I tried to pay at the tollbooth but the attendant recognized me at once. He released the ratchet of the turnstile with such a sharp jab of his foot that I thought he might break his ankle. I nodded to him and passed through into the covered way.

I walked across briskly, trying to think no more about what I was doing or why. The flux field prickled about my body.

I emerged into bright sunlight. The day I had left was warm and sunny, but here in the next day it was several degrees hotter. I felt stiff and overdressed in my formal clothes, not at all in keeping with the reawakened, desperate hope that was in my breast. Still trying to deny that hope I retreated into my daytime demeanour, opening the front of my coat and thrusting my thumbs into the slit-pockets of my waistcoat, as I sometimes did when addressing subordinates.

I walked along the path beside the Channel, looking across for a sight of Estyll on the other side.

Someone tugged at my arm from behind and I turned in surprise.

There was a young man standing there. He was nearly as tall as me but his jacket was too tight across his shoulders and his trousers were a fraction too short, revealing that he was still growing up. He had an obsessive look to him but when he spoke it was obvious he was from a good family.

"Sir, may I trouble you with a question?" he said, and at once I realized who he was.

The shock of recognition was profound. Had I not been so preoccupied with Estyll I am sure meeting him would have made me speechless. It was so many years since my time jumping that I had forgotten the jolting sense of recognition and sympathy.

I controlled myself with great difficulty. Trying not to reveal my knowledge of him, I said, "What do you wish to know?"

"Would you tell me the date, sir?" I started to smile, and glanced away from him for a moment, to straighten my face. His earnest eyes, his protuberant ears, his pallid face and quiffed-up hair!

"Do you mean today's date, or do you mean the year?"

"Well . . . both actually, sir."

I gave him the answer at once, although as soon as I had spoken I realized I had given him today's date, whereas I had stepped forward one day beyond that. No matter, though: what he, I, was interested in was the year.

He thanked me politely and made to step away. Then he paused, looked at me with a guileless stare (which I remembered had been an attempt to take the measure of this forbidding-looking stranger in a frock coat), and said, "Sir, do you happen to live in these parts?"

"I do," I said, knowing what was coming. I had raised a hand to cover my mouth, and was stroking my upper lip.

"I wonder if you would happen to know the identity of a certain person, often to be seen in this Park?"

"Who—?"

I could not finish the sentence. His eager, pinkening earnestness was extremely comical. I spluttered an explosive laugh. At once I turned it into a simulated sneeze, and while I made a play with my handkerchief I muttered something about hay fever. Forcing myself to be serious I returned my handkerchief to my pocket and straightened my hat. "Who do you mean?"

"A young lady, of about my own age." Unaware of my amusement he moved past me and went down the bank to where there was a thick cluster of rosebushes. From behind their cover he looked across at the other side. He made sure I was looking too, then pointed.

I could not see Estyll at first, because of the crowds, but then saw that she was standing quite near to the queue for the Tomorrow Bridge. She was wearing her dress of pastel colours – the clothes she had been wearing when I first loved her.

"Do you see her, sir?" His question was like a discordant note in a piece of music.

I had become perfectly serious again. Just seeing her made me want to fall into reflective silence. The way she held her head, the innocent composure.

He was waiting for a reply, so I said, "Yes . . . yes, a local girl."

"Do you know her name, sir?"

"I believe she is called Estyll."

An expression of surprised pleasure came over his face and his flush deepened. "Thank you, sir. Thank you."

He backed away from me, but I said, "Wait!" I had a sudden instinct to help him, to cut short those months of agony. "You must go and talk to her, you know. She wants to meet you. You mustn't be shy of her."

He stared at me in horror, then turned and ran into the crowd. Within a few seconds I could see him no more.

The enormity of what I had done struck me forcibly. Not only had I touched him on his most vulnerable place, forcing him to confront the one matter he had to work out for himself in his own time, but impetuously I had interfered with the smooth progression of events. In *my* memory of the meeting, the stranger in the silk hat had not given unsolicited advice!

A few minutes later, as I walked slowly along the path, pondering on this, I saw my younger self again. He saw me and I nodded to him, as an introduction, perhaps, to telling him to ignore what I had said, but he glanced away uninterestedly as if he had never seen me before.

There was something odd about him: he had changed his clothes, and the new ones fitted better.

I mused over this for a while until I realized what must have happened. He was not the same Mykle I had spoken to – he was still myself, but here, on this day, from another day in the past!

A little later I saw myself again. This time I – he – was wearing the same clothes as before. Was it the youth I had spoken to? Or was it myself from yet another day?

I was quite distracted by all this but never so much that I forgot the object of it all. Estyll was there on the other side of the Channel and while I paced along the pathway I made certain she was never out of my sight. She had waited beside the toll-booth queue for several minutes, but now she had walked back to the main path and was standing on the grassy bank, staring, as I had seen her do so many times before, towards the Tomorrow Bridge. I could see her much better there: her slight figure, her young beauty.

I was feeling calmer at last. I no longer saw a double image of her. Meeting myself as a youth, and seeing other versions of myself, had reminded me that Estyll and I, apparently divided by the flux field, were actually united by it. My presence here was inevitable.

Today was the last day of her vigil, although she might not know it, and I was here because I was supposed to be here. She was waiting, and I was waiting. I could resolve it; I could resolve it now!

She was looking directly across the Channel, and seemed to be staring deliberately at me, as if the inspiration had struck her in the same instant. Without thinking, I waved my arm at her. Excitement ran through me. I turned quickly, and set off down the path towards the bridges. If I crossed the Today Bridge I should be with her in a matter of a few seconds! It was what I had to do!

When I reached the place where the Tomorrow Bridge opened on to this side I looked back across the Channel to make sure of where she was standing.

But she was no longer waiting! She too was hurrying across the grass, rushing towards the bridges. As she ran she was looking across the Channel, looking at me!

She reached the crowd of people waiting by the tollbooth and I saw her pushing past them. I lost sight of her as she went into the booth.

I stood at my end of the bridge, looking down the ill-lit covered way. Daylight was a bright square two hundred feet away.

A small figure in a long dress hurried up the steps at the far end and ran into the wooden tunnel. Estyll came towards me, raising the front of her skirt as she ran. I glimpsed trailing ribbons, white stockings.

With each step, Estyll moved further into the flux field. With each frantic, eager step towards me, her figure became less substantial. She was less than a third of the way across before she had blurred and dissolved into nothing.

I saw her mistake! She was crossing the wrong bridge! When she reached this side – when she stood where I stood now – she would be twenty-four hours too late.

I stared helplessly down the gloomy covered way, watching as two children slowly materialized before me. They pushed and squabbled, each trying to be the first to emerge into the new day.

xv

I acted without further delay. I left the Tomorrow Bridge and ran back up the slope to the path. The Today Bridge was about fifty yards away, and, clapping a hand on the top of my hat, I ran as fast as I could towards it. I thought only of the extreme urgency of catching Estyll before I lost her. If she realized her mistake and began to search for me, we might be forever crossing and recrossing the Channel on one bridge after another – forever in the same place, but forever separated in time.

I scrambled on to the end of the Today Bridge, and hurried across. I had to moderate my pace, as the bridge was narrow and several other people were crossing. This bridge, of the three, was the only one with windows to the outside. As I passed each one I paused to look anxiously towards each end of the Tomorrow Bridge, hoping for a glimpse of her.

At the end of the bridge I pushed quickly through the exit turnstile, leaving it rattling and clattering on its ratchet.

I set off at once towards the Tomorrow Bridge, reaching for the money to pay the toll. In my haste I bumped into someone. It was a woman and I murmured an apology as I passed, affording her only a momentary glance. We recognized each other in the same instant. It was Robyn, the woman I had sent to the Park. But why was she here now?

As I reached the tollbooth I looked back at her again. She was staring at me with an expression of intense curiosity but as soon as she saw me looking she turned away. Was this the conclusion of the vigil she had reported to me on? Is this what she had seen?

I could not delay. I pushed rudely past the people at the head of the queue and threw some coins on to the worn brass plate where the tickets were ejected mechanically towards the buyer.

The attendant looked up at me, recognized me as I recognized him.

"Compliments of the Park again, sir," he said, and slid the coins back to me.

I had seen him only a few minutes before – yesterday in his life. I scooped up the coins and returned them to my pocket. The turnstile clicked as I pushed through. I went up the steps and entered the covered way.

Far ahead: the glare of daylight of the day I was in. The bare interior of the covered way, with lights at intervals. No people.

I started to walk and when I had gone a few paces across the flux field, the daylight squared in the far end of the tunnel became night. It felt much colder.

Ahead of me: two small figures, solidifying, or so it seemed, out of the electrical haze of the field. They were standing together under one of the lights, partly blocking the way.

I went nearer and saw that one of them was Estyll. The figure with her had his head turned away from me. I paused.

I had halted where no light fell on me, and although I was only a few feet away from them I would have seemed as they seemed to me – a ghostly, half-visible apparition. But they were occupied with each other and did not look towards me.

I heard him say, "Do you live around here?"

"In one of the houses by the Park. What about you?"

"No . . . I have to come here by train." The hands held nervously by his side, the fingers curling and uncurling.

"I've often seen you here," she said. "You stare a lot."

"I wondered who you were."

There was a silence then, while the youth looked shyly at the floor, apparently thinking of more to say. Estyll glanced beyond him to where I was standing, and for a moment we looked directly into each other's eyes.

She said to the young man, "It's cold here. Shall we go back?"

"We could go for a walk. Or I could buy you a glass of orange."

"I'd rather go for a walk."

They turned and walked towards me. She glanced at me again, with a frank stare of hostility. I had been listening in and she well knew it. The young man was barely aware of my presence. As they passed me he was looking first at her, then nervously at his hands. I saw his too-tight clothes, his quiff of hair combed up, his pink ears and neck, his downy moustache. He walked clumsily as if he were about to trip over his own feet, and he did not know where to put his hands.

I loved him; I had loved her.

I followed them a little way, until light shone in again at the tollbooth end. I saw him stand aside to let her through the turnstile first. Out in the sunshine she danced across the grass, letting the colours of her dress shine out, and then she reached over and took his hand. They walked away together, across the newly cut lawns towards the trees.

xvi

I waited until Estyll and I had gone and then I too went out into the day. I crossed to the other side of the Channel on the Yesterday Bridge, and returned on the Today Bridge.

It was the day I had arrived in the Park, the day before I was due in Geneva, the day before Estyll and I were finally to meet. Outside in the yard, my driver would be waiting with the carriage.

Before I left I went for one more walk along the path on this side of the Channel and headed for the bench where I knew Estyll would be waiting.

I saw her through the crowd: she was sitting quietly and watching the people, dressed neatly in her white skirt and dark blue blouse.

I looked across the Channel. The sunshine was bright and hazy and there was a light breeze. I saw the promenading holidaymakers on the other side: the bright clothes, the festive hats, the balloons and the children. But not everyone blended with the crowd.

There was a rhododendron bush beside the Channel. Behind it I could just see the figure of a youth. He was staring across at Estyll. Behind him, walking along deep in thought, was another Mykle. Further along the bank, well away from the bridges, another Mykle sat in long grass overlooking the Channel. I waited, and before long another Mykle appeared. A few minutes later yet another Mykle appeared, and took up position behind one of the trees over there. I did not doubt that there were many more, each unaware of all the others, each preoccupied with the girl who sat on the bench a few feet from me.

I wondered which one it was I had spoken to. None of them, perhaps, or all of them?

I turned towards Estyll at last and approached her. I went to stand directly in front of her and removed my hat.

"Good afternoon, miss," I said. "Pardon me for speaking to you like this."

She looked up at me in sharp surprise. I had interrupted her reverie. She shook her head, but turned on a polite smile for me.

"Do you happen to know who I am?" I said.

"Of course, sir. You're very famous." She bit her lower lip, as if wishing she had not answered so promptly. "What I meant was—"

"Yes," I said. "Do you trust my word?" She frowned then, and it was a consciously pretty gesture – a child borrowing a mannerism from an adult. "It will happen tomorrow," I said.

"Sir?"

"Tomorrow," I said again, trying to find some subtler way of putting it. "What you're waiting for . . . it will happen then."

"How do you—?"

"Never mind that," I said. I stood erect, running my fingers across the brim of my hat. In spite of everything she had the uncanny facility of making me nervous and awkward. "I'll be across there tomorrow," I said, pointing to the other side of the Channel. "Look out for me. I'll be wearing these clothes, this hat. You'll see me wave to you. That's when it will be."

She said nothing to this, but looked steadily at me. I was standing against the light, and she could not have been able to see me properly. But I could see her with the sun on her face, and with light dancing in her hair and her eyes.

She was so young, so pretty. It was like pain to be near her.

"Wear your prettiest dress," I said. "Do you understand?"

She still did not answer, but I saw her eyes flicker towards the far side of the Channel. There was a pinkness in her cheeks and I knew I had said too much. I wished I had not spoken to her at all.

I made a courtly little bow and replaced my hat.

"Good-day to you, miss," I said.

"Good-day, sir."

I nodded to her again, then walked past her and turned on to the lawn behind the bench. I went a short way up the slope, and moved over to the side until I was hidden from Estyll by the trunk of a huge tree.

I could see that on the far side of the Channel one of the Mykles I spotted earlier had moved out from his hiding place. He stood on the bank in clear view. He had apparently been watching me as I spoke to Estyll, for now I could see him looking across at me, shading his eyes with his hand.

I was certain that it was him I had spoken to.

I could help him no more. If he now crossed the Channel twice, moving forward two days, he could be on the Tomorrow Bridge to meet Estyll as she answered my signal.

He stared across at me and I stared back. Then I heard a whoop of joy. He started running.

He hurried along the bank and went straight to the Today Bridge. I could almost hear the hollow clumping of his shoes as he ran through the narrow way, and moments later he emerged on this side. He walked, more sedately now, to the queue for the Tomorrow Bridge.

As he stood in line, he was looking at Estyll. She, staring thoughtfully at the ground, did not notice.

Mykle reached the tollbooth. As he went to the paydesk, he looked back at me and waved. I took off my hat and waved it. He grinned happily.

In a few seconds he had disappeared into the covered way, and I knew I would not see him again. I had seen happen what was to happen next.

I replaced my hat and walked away from the Channel, up through the stately trees of the Park, past where the gardener was still pushing his heavy mower against the grass, past where many families were sitting beneath the trees at their picnic luncheons.

I saw a place beneath a wide old cedar where I and my parents and sisters had often eaten our meals. A cloth was spread out across the grass, with several dishes set in readiness for the meal.

An elderly couple was sitting here, well under the shade of the branches. The lady was sitting stiffly in a folding canvas chair, watching patiently as her husband prepared the meat. He was carving a ham joint, taking slices from beneath the notch with meticulous strokes. Two servants stood in the background, with white linen cloths draped over their forearms.

Like me, the gentleman was in formal wear. His frockcoat was stiff and perfectly ironed, and his shoes shone as if they had been polished for weeks. On the ground beside him, his silken stove-pipe hat had been laid on a scarf.

He noticed my uninvited regard and looked up at me. For a moment our gaze met and we nodded to each other like the gentlemen we were. I touched the brim of my hat, wished him and the lady good-afternoon. Then I hurried towards the yard outside. I wanted to see Dorynne before I caught the train to Geneva.

RED LETTER DAY

Kristine Kathryn Rusch

This story, which deals with how our future selves might seek to influence their younger selves, seemed to me to be the ideal way to close this anthology, as you will discover when you reach the end.

Kristine Kathryn Rusch is a prolific American writer and editor who has produced award-winning stories and books in the fields of science fiction, mystery and romantic fiction under her own and various pen names. Her time-travel story The Gallery of His Dreams *(1991), set at the time of the American Civil War, won the Locus Award as that year's best novella. It is included amongst a selection of her other shorter works in* Stories for an Enchanted Afternoon *(2001). With her husband, Dean Wesley Smith, she ran Pulphouse Publishing from 1987 to 1991 and she edited the prestigious* Magazine of Fantasy & Science Fiction *from 1991 to 1997. The following story was voted the most popular story of the year by readers of* Analog, *in which it was published.*

Graduation rehearsal – middle of the afternoon on the final Monday of the final week of school. The graduating seniors at Barack Obama High School gather in the gymnasium, get the wrapped packages with their robes (ordered long ago), their mortarboards, and their blue and white tassels. The tassels attract the most attention – everyone wants to know which side of the mortarboard to wear it on, and which side to move it to.

The future hovers, less than a week away, filled with possibilities.

Possibilities about to be limited, because it's also Red Letter Day.

I stand on the platform, near the steps, not too far from the exit. I'm wearing my best business casual skirt today and a blouse that I no longer care about. I learned to wear something I didn't like years ago; too many kids will cry on me by the end of the day, covering the blouse with slobber and makeup and aftershave.

My heart pounds. I'm a slender woman, although I'm told I'm formidable. Coaches need to be formidable. And while I still coach the basketball teams, I no longer teach gym classes because the folks in charge decided I'd be a better counselor than gym teacher. They made that decision on my first Red Letter Day at BOHS, more than twenty years ago.

I'm the only adult in this school who truly understands how horrible Red Letter Day can be. I think it's cruel that Red Letter Day happens at all, but I think the cruelty gets compounded by the fact that it's held in school.

Red Letter Day should be a holiday, so that kids are at home with their parents when the letters arrive.

Or don't arrive, as the case may be.

And the problem is that we can't even properly prepare for Red Letter Day. We can't read the letters ahead of time: privacy laws prevent it.

So do the strict time-travel rules. One contact – only one – through an emissary, who arrives shortly before rehearsal, stashes the envelopes in the practice binders, and then disappears again. The emissary carries actual letters from the future. The letters themselves are the old-fashioned paper kind, the kind people wrote 150 years ago, but write rarely now. Only the real letters, handwritten, on special paper get through. Real letters, so that the signatures can be verified, the paper guaranteed, the envelopes certified.

Apparently, even in the future, no one wants to make a mistake.

The binders have names written across them so the letter doesn't go to the wrong person. And the letters are supposed to be deliberately vague.

I don't deal with the kids who get letters. Others are here for that, some professional bullshitters – at least in my opinion. For a small fee, they'll examine the writing, the signature, and try to clear up the letter's deliberate vagueness, make a guess at the socio-economic status of the writer, the writer's health, or mood.

I think that part of Red Letter Day makes it all a scam. But the schools go along with it, because the counselors (read: me) are busy with the kids who get no letter at all.

And we can't predict whose letter won't arrive. We don't know until the kid stops mid-stride, opens the binder, and looks up with complete and utter shock.

Either there's a red envelope inside or there's nothing.

And we don't even have time to check which binder is which.

I had my Red Letter Day thirty-two years ago, in the chapel of Sister Mary of Mercy High School in Shaker Heights, Ohio. Sister Mary of Mercy was a small co-ed Catholic High School, closed now, but very influential in its day. The best private school in Ohio, according to some polls – controversial only because of its conservative politics and its willingness to indoctrinate its students.

I never noticed the indoctrination. I played basketball so well that I already had three full-ride scholarship offers from UCLA, UNLV, and Ohio State (home of the Buckeyes!). A pro scout promised I'd be a fifth round draft choice if only I went pro straight out of high school, but I wanted an education.

"You can get an education later," he told me. "Any good school will let you in after you've made your money and had your fame."

But I was brainy. I had studied athletes who went to the Bigs straight out of high school. Often they got injured, lost their contracts and their money, and never played again. Usually they had to take some crap job to pay for their college education – if, indeed, they went to college at all, which most of them never did.

Those who survived lost most of their earnings to managers, agents, and other hangers on. I knew what I didn't know. I knew I was an ignorant kid with some great ball-handling ability. I knew that I was trusting and naïve and undereducated. And I knew that life extended well beyond thirty-five, when even the most gifted female athletes lost some of their edge.

I thought a lot about my future. I wondered about life past thirty-five. My future self, I knew, would write me a letter fifteen years after thirty-five. My future self, I believed, would tell me which path to follow, what decision to make.

I thought it all boiled down to college or the pros.

I had no idea there would be – there could be – anything else.

You see, anyone who wants to – anyone who feels so inclined – can write one single letter to their former self. The letter gets delivered just before high school graduation, when most teenagers are (theoretically) adults, but still under the protection of a school.

The recommendations on writing are that the letter should be inspiring. Or it should warn that former self away from a single person, a single event, or a one single choice.

Just one.

The statistics say that most folks don't warn. They like their lives as lived. The folks motivated to write the letters wouldn't change much, if anything.

It's only those who've made a tragic mistake – one drunken night that led to a catastrophic accident, one bad decision that cost a best friend a life, one horrible sexual encounter that led to a lifetime of heartache – who write the explicit letter.

And the explicit letter leads to alternate universes. Lives veer off in all kinds of different paths. The adult who sends the letter hopes their former self will take their advice. If the former self does take the advice, then the kid receives the letter from an adult they will never be. The kid, if smart, will become a different adult, the adult who somehow avoided that drunken night. That new adult will write a different letter to their former self, warning about another possibility or committing bland, vague prose about a glorious future.

There're all kinds of scientific studies about this, all manner of debate about the consequences. All types of mandates, all sorts of rules.

And all of them lead back to that moment, that heartstopping moment that I experienced in the chapel of Sister Mary of Mercy High School, all those years ago.

We weren't practicing graduation like the kids at Barack Obama High School. I don't recall when we practiced graduation, although I'm sure we had a practice later in the week.

At Sister Mary of Mercy High School, we spent our Red Letter Day in prayer. All the students started their school days with Mass. But on Red Letter Day, the graduating seniors had to stay for a special service, marked by requests for God's forgiveness and exhortations about the unnaturalness of what the law required Sister Mary of Mercy to do.

Sister Mary of Mercy High School loathed Red Letter Day. In fact, Sister Mary of Mercy High School, as an offshoot of the Catholic Church, opposed time travel altogether. Back in the dark ages (in other words, decades before I was born), the Catholic Church declared time travel an abomination, antithetical to God's will.

You know the arguments: If God had wanted us to travel through time, the devout claim, he would have given us the ability to do so. If God had wanted us to travel through time, the scientists say, he would have given us the ability to understand time travel – and oh! Look! He's done that.

Even now, the arguments devolve from there.

But time travel has become a fact of life for the rich and the powerful and the well-connected. The creation of alternate universes scares them less than the rest of us, I guess. Or maybe the rich really don't care – they being different from you and I, as renown (but little read) twentieth-century American author F. Scott Fitzgerald so famously said.

The rest of us – the nondifferent ones – realized nearly a century ago that time travel for all was a dicey proposition but, this being America, we couldn't deny people the *opportunity* of time travel.

Eventually time travel for everyone became a rallying cry. The liberals wanted government to fund it, and the conservatives felt only those who could afford it would be allowed to have it.

Then something bad happened – something not quite expunged from the history books, but something not taught in schools either (or at least the schools I went to), and the federal government came up with a compromise.

Everyone would get one free opportunity for time travel – not that they could actually go back and see the crucifixion or the Battle of Gettysburg – but that they could travel back in their own lives.

The possibility for massive change was so great, however, that the time travel had to be strictly controlled. All the regulations in the world wouldn't stop someone who stood in Freedom Hall in July of 1776 from telling the Founding Fathers what they had wrought.

So the compromise got narrower and narrower (with the subtext being that the masses couldn't be trusted with something as powerful as the ability to travel through time), and it finally became Red Letter Day, with all its rules and regulations. You'd have the ability to touch your own life without ever really leaving it. You'd reach back into your own past and reassure yourself, or put something right.

Which still seemed unnatural to the Catholics, the Southern Baptists, the Libertarians, and the Stuck in Time League (always my favorite, because they never did seem to understand the irony of their own name). For years after the law passed, places like Sister Mary of Mercy High School tried not to comply with it. They protested. They sued. They got sued.

Eventually, when the dust settled, they still had to comply.

But they didn't have to like it.

So they tortured all of us, the poor hopeful graduating seniors, awaiting our future, awaiting our letters, awaiting our fate.

I remember the prayers. I remember kneeling for what seemed like hours. I remember the humidity of that late spring day, and the growing heat, because the chapel (a historical building) wasn't allowed to have anything as unnatural as air conditioning.

Martha Sue Groening passed out, followed by Warren Iverson, the star quarterback. I spent much of that morning with my forehead braced against the pew in front of me, my stomach in knots.

My whole life, I had waited for this moment.

And then, finally, it came. We went alphabetically, which stuck me in the middle, like usual. I hated being in the middle. I was tall, geeky, uncoordinated, except on the basketball court, and not very developed – important in high school. And I wasn't formidable yet.

That came later.

Nope. Just a tall awkward girl, walking behind boys shorter than I was. Trying to be inconspicuous.

I got to the aisle, watching as my friends stepped in front of the altar, below the stairs where we knelt when we went up for the sacrament of communion.

Father Broussard handed out the binders. He was tall but not as tall as me. He was tending to fat, with most of it around his middle. He held the binders by the corner, as if the binders themselves were cursed, and he said a blessing over each and every one of us as we reached out for our futures.

We weren't supposed to say anything, but a few of the boys muttered, "Sweet!", and some of the girls clutched their binders to their chests as if they'd received a love letter.

I got mine – cool and plastic against my fingers – and held it tightly. I didn't open it, not near the stairs, because I knew the kids who hadn't gotten theirs yet would watch me.

So I walked all the way to the doors, stepped into the hallway, and leaned against the wall.

Then I opened my binder.

And saw nothing.

My breath caught.

I peered back into the chapel. The rest of the kids were still in line, getting their binders. No red envelopes had landed on the carpet. No binders were tossed aside.

Nothing. I stopped three of the kids, asking them if they saw me drop anything or if they'd gotten mine.

Then Sister Mary Catherine caught my arm, and dragged me away from the steps. Her fingers pinched into the nerve above my elbow, sending a shooting pain down to my hand.

"You're not to interrupt the others," she said.

"But I must have dropped my letter."

She peered at me, then let go of my arm. A look of satisfaction crossed her fat face, then she patted my cheek.

The pat was surprisingly tender.

"Then you are blessed," she said.

I didn't feel blessed. I was about to tell her that, when she motioned Father Broussard over.

"She received no letter," Sister Mary Catherine said.

"God has smiled on you, my child," he said warmly. He hadn't noticed me before, but this time, he put his hand on my shoulder. "You must come with me to discuss your future."

I let him lead me to his office. The other nuns – the ones without a class that hour – gathered with him. They talked to me about how God wanted me to make my own choices, how He had blessed me by giving me back my future, how He saw me as without sin.

I was shaking. I had looked forward to this day all my life – at least the life I could remember – and then this. Nothing. No future. No answers.

Nothing.

I wanted to cry, but not in front of Father Broussard. He had already segued into a discussion of the meaning of the blessing. I could serve the church. Anyone who failed to get a letter got free admission into a variety of colleges and universities, all Catholic, some well known. If I wanted to become a nun, he was certain the church could accommodate me.

"I want to play basketball, Father," I said.

He nodded. "You can do that at any of these schools."

"Professional basketball," I said.

And he looked at me as if I were the spawn of Satan.

"But, my child," he said with a less reasonable tone than before, "you have received a sign from God. He thinks you Blessed. He wants you in his service."

"I don't think so," I said, my voice thick with unshed tears. "I think you made a mistake."

Then I flounced out of his office, and off school grounds.

My mother made me go back for the last four days of class. She made me graduate. She said I would regret it if I didn't.

I remember that much.

But the rest of the summer was a blur. I mourned my known future, worried I would make the wrong choices, and actually considered the Catholic colleges. My mother rousted me enough to get me to choose before the draft. And I did.

The University of Nevada in Las Vegas, as far from the Catholic Church as I could get.

I took my full ride, and destroyed my knee in my very first game. God's punishment, Father Broussard said when I came home for Thanksgiving.

And God forgive me, I actually believed him.

But I didn't transfer – and I didn't become Job, either. I didn't fight with God or curse God. I abandoned Him because, as I saw it, He had abandoned me.

Thirty-two years later, I watch the faces. Some flush. Some look terrified. Some burst into tears.

But some just look blank, as if they've received a great shock. Those students are mine.

I make them stand beside me, even before I ask them what they got in their binder. I haven't made a mistake yet, not even last year, when I didn't pull anyone aside.

Last year, everyone got a letter. That happens every five years or so. All the students get Red Letters, and I don't have to deal with anything.

This year, I have three. Not the most ever. The most ever was thirty, and within five years it became clear why. A stupid little war in a stupid little country no one had ever heard of. Twenty-nine of my students died within the decade. Twenty-nine.

The thirtieth was like me, someone who has not a clue why her future self failed to write her a letter.

I think about that, as I always do on Red Letter Day.

I'm the kind of person who *would* write a letter. I have always been that person. I believe in communication, even vague communication. I know how important it is to open that binder and see that bright red envelope.

I would never abandon my past self.

I've already composed drafts of my letter. In two weeks – on my fiftieth birthday – some government employee will show up at my house to set up an appointment to watch me write the letter.

I won't be able to touch the paper, the red envelope or the special pen until I agree to be watched. When I finish, the employee will fold the letter, tuck it in the envelope and earmark it for Sister Mary of Mercy High School in Shaker Heights, Ohio, thirty-two years ago.

I have plans. I know what I'll say.

But I still wonder why I didn't say it to my previous self. What went wrong? What prevented me? Am I in an alternate universe already and I just don't know it?

Of course, I'll never be able to find out.

But I set that thought aside. The fact that I did not receive a letter means nothing. It doesn't mean that I'm blessed by God any more than it means I'll fail to live to fifty.

It is a trick, a legal sleight of hand, so that people like me can't travel to the historical bright spots or even visit the highlights of their own past life.

I continue to watch faces, all the way to the bitter end. But I get no more than three. Two boys and a girl.

Carla Nelson. A tall, thin, white-haired blonde who ran cross-country and stayed away from basketball, no matter how much I begged her to join the team. We needed height and we needed athletic ability.

She has both, but, she told me, she isn't a team player. She wanted to run and run alone. She hated relying on anyone else.

Not that I blame her.

But from the devastation on her angular face, I can see that she relied on her future self. She believed she wouldn't let herself down.

Not ever.

Over the years, I've watched other counselors use platitudes. *I'm sure it's nothing. Perhaps your future self felt that you're on the right track. I'm sure you'll be fine.*

I was bitter the first time I watched the high school kids go through this ritual. I never said a word, which was probably a smart decision on my part, because I silently twisted my colleagues' platitudes into something negative, something awful, inside my own head.

It's something. We all know it's something. Your future self hates you or maybe – probably – you're dead.

I have thought all those things over the years, depending on my life. Through a checkered college career, an education degree, a marriage, two children, a divorce, one brand new grandchild. I have believed all kinds of different things.

At thirty-five, when my hopeful young self thought I'd be retiring from pro ball, I stopped being a gym teacher and became a full time counselor. A full time counselor and occasional coach.

I told myself I didn't mind.

I even wondered what would I write if I had the chance to play in the Bigs? *Stay the course*? That seems to be the most common letter in those red envelopes. It might be longer than that, but it always boils down to those three words.

Stay the course.

Only I hated the course. I wonder: would I have blown my knee out in the Bigs? Would I have made the Bigs? Would I have received the kind of expensive nanosurgery that would have kept my career alive? Or would I have washed out worse than I ever had?

Dreams are tricky things.

Tricky and delicate and easily destroyed.

And now I faced three shattered dreamers, standing beside me on the edge of the podium.

"To my office," I say to the three of them.

They're so shell-shocked that they comply.

I try to remember what I know about the boys. Esteban Rellier and J.J. Feniman. J.J. stands for . . . Jason Jacob. I remembered only because the names were so very old-fashioned, and J.J. was the epitome of modern cool.

If you had to choose which students would succeed based on personality and charm, not on Red Letters and opportunity, you would choose J.J.

You would choose Esteban with a caveat. He would have to apply himself.

If you had to pick anyone in class who wouldn't write a letter to herself, you would pick Carla. Too much of a loner. Too prickly. Too difficult. I shouldn't have been surprised that she's coming with me.

But I am.

Because it's never the ones you suspect who fail to get a letter.

It's always the ones you believe in, the ones you have hopes for.

And somehow – now – it's my job to keep those hopes alive.

I am prepared for this moment. I'm not a fan of interactive technology – feeds scrolling across the eye, scans on the palm of the hand – but I use it on Red Letter Day more than any other time during the year.

As we walk down the wide hallway to the administrative offices, I learn everything the school knows about all three students which, honestly, isn't much.

Psych evaluations – including modified IQ tests – from grade school on. Addresses. Parental income and employment. Extracurriculars. Grades. Troubles (if any reported). Detentions. Citations. Awards.

I already know a lot about J.J. Homecoming king, quarterback, would've been class president if he hadn't turned the role down. So handsome he even has his own stalker, a girl named Lizbet Cholene, whom I've had to discipline twice before sending to a special psych unit for evaluation.

I have to check on Esteban. He's above average, but only in the subjects that interest him. His IQ tested high on both the old exam and the new. He has unrealized potential, and has never really been challenged, partly because he doesn't seem to be the academic type.

It's Carla who is still the enigma. IQ higher than either boy's. Grades lower. No detentions, citations, or academic awards. Only the postings in cross country – continual wins, all state three years in a row, potential offers from colleges, if she brought her grades up, which she never did. Nothing on the parents. Address in a middle-class neighborhood, smack in the center of town.

I cannot figure her out in a three-minute walk, even though I try.

I usher them into my office. It's large and comfortable. Big desk, upholstered chairs, real plants, and a view of the track – which probably isn't the best thing right now, at least for Carla.

I have a speech that I give. I try not to make it sound canned.

"Your binders were empty, weren't they?" I say.

To my surprise, Carla's lower lip quivers. I thought she'd tough it out, but the tears are close to the surface. Esteban's nose turns red and he bows his head. Carla's distress makes it hard for him to control his.

J.J. leans against the wall, arms folded. His handsome face is a mask. I realize then how often I'd seen that look on his face. Not quite blank – a little pleasant – but detached, far away. He braces one foot on the wall, which is going to leave a mark, but I don't call him on that. I just let him lean.

"On my Red Letter Day," I say, "I didn't get a letter either."

They look at me in surprise. Adults aren't supposed to discuss their letters with kids. Or their lack of letters. Even if I had been able to discuss it, I wouldn't have.

I've learned over the years that this moment is the crucial one, the moment when they realize that you will survive the lack of a letter.

"Do you know why?" Carla asks, her voice raspy.

I shake my head. "Believe me, I've wondered. I've made up every scenario in my head – maybe I died before it was time to write the letter—"

"But you're older than that now, right?" J.J. asks, with something of an angry edge. "You wrote the letter this time, right?"

"I'm eligible to write the letter in two weeks," I say. "I plan to do it."

His cheeks redden, and for the first time, I see how vulnerable he is beneath the surface. He's as devastated – maybe more devastated – than Carla and Esteban. Like me, J.J. believed he would get the letter he deserved – something that told him about his wonderful, successful, very rich life.

"So you could still die before you write it," he said, and this time, I'm certain he meant the comment to hurt.

It did. But I don't let that emotion show on my face. "I could," I say. "But I've lived for thirty-two years without a letter. Thirty-two years without a clue about what my future holds. Like people used to live before time travel. Before Red Letter Day."

I have their attention now.

"I think we're the lucky ones," I say, and because I've established that I'm part of their group, I don't sound patronizing. I've given this speech for nearly two decades, and previous students have told me that this part of the speech is the most important part.

Carla's gaze meets mine, sad, frightened and hopeful. Esteban keeps his head down. J.J.'s eyes have narrowed. I can feel his anger now, as if it's my fault that he didn't get a letter.

"Lucky?" he asks in the same tone that he used when he reminded me I could still die.

"Lucky," I say. "We're not locked into a future."

Esteban looks up now, a frown creasing his forehead.

"Out in the gym," I say, "some of the counselors are dealing with students who're getting two different kinds of tough letters. The first tough one is the one that warns you not to do something on such and so date or you'll screw up your life forever."

"People actually get those?" Esteban asks, breathlessly.

"Every year," I say.

"What's the other tough letter?" Carla's voice trembles. She speaks so softly I had to strain to hear her.

"The one that says *You can do better than I did*, but won't – can't really – explain exactly what went wrong. We're limited to one event, and if what went wrong was a cascading series of bad choices, we can't explain that. We just have to hope that our past selves – you guys, in other words – will make the right choices, with a warning."

J.J.'s frowning too. "What do you mean?"

"Imagine," I say, "instead of getting no letter, you get a letter that tells you that none of your dreams come true. The letter tells you simply that you'll have to accept what's coming because there's no changing it."

"I wouldn't believe it," he says.

And I agree: he wouldn't believe it. Not at first. But those wormy little bits of doubt would burrow in and affect every single thing he does from this moment on.

"Really?" I say. "Are you the kind of person who would lie to yourself in an attempt to destroy who you are now? Trying to destroy every bit of hope that you possess?"

His flush grows deeper. Of course he isn't. He lies to himself – we all do – but he lies to himself about how great he is, how few flaws he has. When Lizbet started following him around, I brought him into my office and asked him not to pay attention to her.

It leads her on, I say.

I don't think it does, he says. *She knows I'm not interested.*

He knew he wasn't interested. Poor Lizbet had no idea at all.

I can see her outside now, hovering in the hallway, waiting for him, wanting to know what his letter said. She's holding her red envelope in one hand, the other lost in the pocket of her baggy skirt. She looks prettier than usual, as if she's dressed up for this day, maybe for the inevitable party.

Every year, some idiot plans a Red Letter Day party even though the school – the culture – recommends against it. Every year, the kids who get good letters go. And the other kids beg off, or go for a short time, and lie about what they received.

Lizbet probably wants to know if he's going to go.

I wonder what he'll say to her.

"Maybe you wouldn't send a letter if the truth hurt too much," Esteban says.

And so it begins, the doubts, the fears.

"Or," I say, "if your successes are beyond your wild imaginings. Why let yourself expect that? Everything you do might freeze you, might lead you to wonder if you're going to screw that up."

They're all looking at me again.

"Believe me," I say. "I've thought of every single possibility, and they're all wrong."

The door to my office opens and I curse silently. I want them to concentrate on what I just said, not on someone barging in on us.

I turn.

Lizbet has come in. She looks like she's on edge, but then she's always on edge around J.J.

"I want to talk to you, J.J." Her voice shakes.

"Not now," he says. "In a minute."

"*Now,*" she says. I've never heard this tone from her. Strong and scary at the same time.

"Lizbet," J.J. says, and it's clear he's tired, he's overwhelmed, he's had enough of this day, this event, this girl, this school – he's not built to cope with something he considers a failure. "I'm busy."

"You're not going to marry me," she says.

"Of course not," he snaps – and that's when I know it. Why all four of us don't get letters, why I didn't get a letter, even though I'm two weeks shy from my fiftieth birthday and fully intend to send something to my poor past self.

Lizbet holds her envelope in one hand, and a small plastic automatic in the other. An illegal gun, one that no one should be able to get – not a student, not an adult. No one.

"Get down!" I shout as I launch myself toward Lizbet.

She's already firing, but not at me. At J.J. who hasn't gotten down.

But Esteban deliberately drops and Carla – Carla's half a step behind me, launching herself as well.

Together we tackle Lizbet, and I pry the pistol from her hands. Carla and I hold her as people come running from all directions, some adults, some kids holding letters.

Everyone gathers. We have no handcuffs, but someone finds rope. Someone else has contacted emergency services, using the emergency link that we all have, that we all should have used, that I should have used, that I probably had used in another life, in another universe, one in which I didn't write a letter. I probably contacted emergency services and said something placating to Lizbet, and she probably shot all four of us, instead of poor J.J.

J.J., who is motionless on the floor, his blood slowly pooling around him. The football coach is trying to stop the bleeding and someone I don't recognize is helping and there's nothing I can do, not at the moment, they're doing it all while we wait for emergency services.

The security guard ties up Lizbet and sets the gun on the desk and we all stare at it, and Annie Sanderson, the English teacher, says to the guard, "You're supposed to check everyone, today of all days. That's why we hired you."

And the principal admonishes her, tiredly, and she shuts up. Because we know that sometimes Red Letter Day causes this, that's why it's held in school, to stop family annihilations and shootings of best friends and employers. Schools, we're told, can control weaponry and violence, even though they can't, and someone, somewhere, will use this as a reason to repeal Red Letter Day, but all those people who got good letters or letters warning them about their horrible drunken mistake will prevent any change, and everyone – the pundits, the politicians, the parents – will say that's good.

Except J.J.'s parents, who have no idea their son had no future. When did he lose it? The day he met Lizbet? The day he didn't listen to me about how crazy she was? A few moments ago, when he didn't dive for the floor?

I will never know.

But I do something I would never normally do. I grab Lizbet's envelope, and I open it.

The handwriting is spidery, shaky.

Give it up. J.J. doesn't love you. He'll never love you. Just walk away and pretend that he doesn't exist. Live a better life than I have. Throw the gun away.

Throw the gun away.

She did this before, just like I thought.

And I wonder: was the letter different this time? And if it was, how different? *Throw the gun away.* Is that line new or old? Has she ignored this sentence before?

My brain hurts. My head hurts.

My heart hurts.

I was angry at J.J. just a few moments ago, and now he's dead. He's dead and I'm not.

Carla isn't either.

Neither is Esteban.

I touch them both and motion them close. Carla seems calmer, but Esteban is blank – shock, I think. A spray of blood covers the left side of his face and shirt.

I show them the letter, even though I'm not supposed to.

"Maybe this is why we never got our letters," I say. "Maybe today is different than it was before. We survived, after all."

I don't know if they understand. I'm not sure I care if they understand.

I'm not even sure if I understand.

I sit in my office and watch the emergency services people flow in, declare J.J. dead, take Lizbet away, set the rest of us aside for interrogation. I hand someone – one of the police officers – Lizbet's red envelope, but I don't tell him we looked.

I have a hunch he knows we did.

The events wash past me, and I think that maybe this is my last Red Letter Day at Barack Obama High School, even if I survive the next two weeks and turn fifty.

And I find myself wondering, as I sit on my desk waiting to make my statement, whether I'll write my own red letter after all.

What can I say that I'll listen to? Words are so very easy to misunderstand. Or misread.

I suspect Lizbet only read the first few lines. Her brain shut off long before she got to *Walk away* and *Throw the gun away*.

Maybe she didn't write that the first time. Or maybe she's been writing it, hopelessly, to herself in a continual loop, lifetime after lifetime after lifetime.

I don't know.

I'll never know.

None of us will know.

That's what makes Red Letter Day such a joke. Is it the letter that keeps us on the straight and narrow? Or the lack of a letter that gives us our edge?

Do I write a letter, warning myself to make sure Lizbet gets help when I meet her? Or do I tell myself to go to the draft no matter what? Will that prevent this afternoon?

I don't know.

I'll never know.

Maybe Father Broussard was right; maybe God designed us to be ignorant of the future. Maybe He wants us to move forward in time, unaware of what's ahead, so that we follow our instincts, make our first, best – and only – choice.

Maybe.

Or maybe the letters mean nothing at all. Maybe all this focus on a single day and a single note from a future self is as meaningless as this year's celebration of the Fourth of July. Just a day like any other, only we add a ceremony and call it important.

I don't know.

I'll never know.

Not if I live two more weeks or two more years.

Either way, J.J. will still be dead and Lizbet will be alive, and my future – whatever it is – will be the mystery it always was.

The mystery it should be.

The mystery it will always be.

ACKNOWLEDGEMENTS

All of the stories in this anthology are in copyright and have been printed with the permission of the authors or their representatives, as detailed below.

CAVEAT TIME TRAVELER © 2009 by Gregory Benford. First published in *Nature*, April 2009. Reprinted by permission of the author.

CENTURY TO STARBOARD © 2004 by Liz Williams. First published in *Strange Horizons*, 2 February 2004. Reprinted by permission of the author.

WALK TO THE FULL MOON © 2002 by Sean McMullen. First published in *The Magazine of Fantasy & Science Fiction*, December 2002. Reprinted by permission of the author.

THE TRUTH ABOUT WEENA © 1998 by David J. Lake. First published in *Dreaming Down Under*, edited by Jack Dann and Janeen Webb, Voyager, 1998. Reprinted by permission of the author.

THE WIND OVER THE WORLD © 1996 by Steven Utley. First published in *Asimov's Science Fiction*, October/November 1996. Reprinted by permission of the author.

SCREAM QUIETLY © 2005 by Sheila Crosby. First published in *Farthing*, July 2005. Reprinted by permission of the author.

DARWIN'S SUITCASE © 2007 by Elisabeth Malartre. First published in *Jim Baen's Universe*, December 2007. Reprinted by permission of the author.

TRY AND CHANGE THE PAST © 1958 by Fritz Leiber. First published in *Astounding Science Fiction*, March 1958. Reprinted by permission of Richard Curtis Associates, Inc., agent for the author's estate.

NEEDLE IN A TIMESTACK by Robert Silverberg © 1983 by Agberg, Ltd. First published in *Playboy*, June 1983. Reprinted by permission of the author.

DEAR TOMORROW © 2013 by Simon Clark. New story, original to this anthology. Printed by permission of the author and the author's agent Pollinger, Limited.

TIME GYPSY © 1998 by Ellen Klages. First published in *Bending the Landscape: Science Fiction*, edited by Stephen Pagel and Nicola Griffith, The Overlook Press, 1998. Reprinted by permission of the author.

THE CATCH © 2004 by Kage Baker. First published in *Asimov's Science Fiction*, October/November 2004. Reprinted by permission of Linn Prentis Literary, agent for the author's estate.

REAL TIME © 1988 by Lawrence Watt Evans. First published in *Isaac Asimov's Science Fiction Magazine*, January 1989. Reprinted by permission of the author.

THE CHRONOLOGY PROTECTION CASE © 1995 by Paul Levinson. First published in *Analog Science Fiction*, September 1995. Reprinted by permission of the author.

WOMEN ON THE BRINK OF A CATACLYSM © 1994 by Molly Brown. First published in *Interzone*, January 1994. Reprinted by permission of the author.

LEGIONS IN TIME © 2003 by Michael Swanwick. First published in *Asimov's Science Fiction*, April 2003. Reprinted by permission of the author.

COMING BACK © 1982 by Damien Broderick. First published in *The Magazine of Fantasy & Science Fiction*, December 1982. Reprinted by permission of the author.